TUPPENNY TIMES

Beryl Kingston

CENTURY · LONDON

Reprinted by Century in 2003

1 3 5 7 9 10 8 6 4 2

First published in the United Kingdom by Macdonald & Co (Publishers) Ltd 1988

Century
The Random House Group Limited
20 Vauxhall Bridge Road, London, SW1V 2SA

Random House Australia (Pty) Limited
20 Alfred Street, Milsons Point, Sydney, New South Wales 2061, Australia

Random House New Zealand Limited
18 Poland Road, Glenfield
Auckland 10, New Zealand

ISBN 0 7126 7883 2

To Larry

Sir Joseph Easter = Lady Cecilia
1719 - 1794   1717 - 1796

Joseph = Elizabeth
1741-1790

Sir Osmond = Molly (1)   Jane (2)   *Died*   *Died*   Sarah = Henry
1774 - 1826   1792-1811   1801   1777   Bullen

Sir Joseph
1811

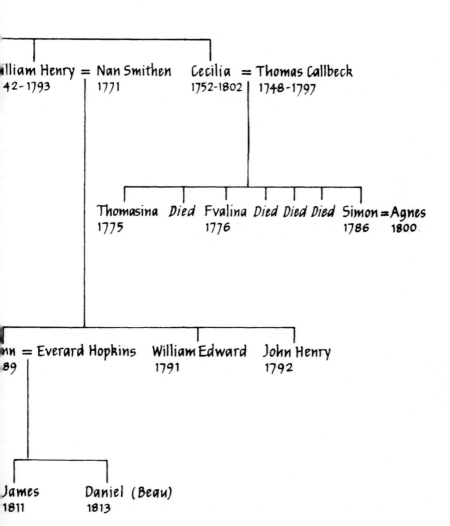

THE EASTER FAMILY TREE

William Henry = Nan Smithen   Cecilia = Thomas Callbeck
…42-1793   1771   1752-1802 | 1748-1797

Thomasina Died Fvalina Died Died Died Simon = Agnes
1775   1776   1786   1800

…nn = Everard Hopkins   William Edward   John Henry
…89   1791   1792

James   Daniel (Beau)
1811   1813

Chapter One

'Are we to be governed by cannibals?' Mr Howkins demanded, glaring at his wife. 'Is that what you want?' He was hot with anger, sweat beading from under his brown bag-wig and his forehead gleaming in the firelight.

Mrs Howkins remained deliberately calm, because she was accustomed to such outbursts, and because she knew tranquillity would annoy him. She smoothed out a crease from the skirt of her embroidered gown, settled her slippered feet more firmly upon the fender and inclined her head delicately towards him. 'I can hardly be persuaded,' she said, 'that sailors of His Majesty's Royal Navy have been reduced to such a parlous condition by a mere three years of peace that they are now devouring one another. Piracy I will allow, but cannibalism . . .' She raised her pale eyes to the ceiling of their little blue parlour, as though words failed her.

'Pirates, drunkards and savages, the whole pack of 'em,' her husband insisted, whacking a sea-coal with the poker as if he fully expected a pirate to be lurking underneath it. 'Well, they needn't think to deter *us*! No indeed! We shall stand up to 'em! Defy 'em, what!'

'The message could be sent in the morning, my love,' Mrs Howkins said mildly. 'A few hours' delay would be of little consequence.'

'The message will *not* be sent in the morning. Dammit woman, are we so downtrodden that we must allow a pack of unruly ruffians to control our comings and goings? I never heard the like! She shall go tonight, I tell 'ee!'

The she in question stood quietly before them, her hands clasped over her apron, her dark eyes downcast and her expression as blank as she could make it. Little Nan Smithen, fourteen years old, five feet tall and as thin as a lathe in a town full of portly men and overflowing women.

Such a turbulent face she had, so full of life and passion that every-thing about it seemed to be on the move, even when she was deliberately holding it still, dark hair springing from under her yellow mob cap in thick unruly curls, black eyebrows curved like wings in flight, brown eyes glinting with suppressed emotion, cheekbones taut, red mouth full and moist and ready to speak, strong chin jutting with determination. A storm of a face. And very different from the bovine countenance of her employer.

That's all very well for him to say, '*Our* comings an' goings,' she was thinking furiously. He don't have to do nothing about it. That's me has to come and go. An' if these ol' sailors start hitting anyone, that'll be me, an' all. But she kept her thoughts to herself because she didn't want to lose her job and all the regular meals that went with it. It had taken her five whole years and months of study with the seamstress and the hairdresser to reach the comfortable status of lady's maid to Mrs Howkins, and she had no intention of going back to scouring greasy dishes, not if she could help it.

Nevertheless, she was in a tricky situation and she knew it. Dusk was already edging its shadows into the narrow alley outside the window, and the longer he shouted the more likely it was that she would have to run this errand in the dark. Even at the best and quietest of times that was a task she would much rather avoid, and these were not the best and quietest of times.

Three years ago, in 1783, the war against some rebel upstarts in the American colony had suddenly come to a shameful end. It was all the fault of that young Mr Pitt, so people said. Although Mr Howkins swore it was 'Lord North, 'Od rot him!' But whoever it was, he'd given in to the rebels, withdrawn the Army and called the Navy home, away from the easy pickings of their licensed piracy to a most uncertain future in a nation suddenly committed to peace. Naturally enough, they didn't approve. It was more than any true-born Englishman could stand. They grumbled all the way back to England and when they finally disembarked in their nearest home port, they set off at once on an orgy of rioting and drunkenness to let their sentiments be known.

Three more ships of the line had come squalling into Yarmouth harbour that very afternoon with purple storm clouds rolling behind them, and now the east wind was tormenting the town and the inns were full of sailors drinking themselves into a fury. Young Billy Butter-field from next door had the black eye to prove it. It wasn't the night to be out of doors, but you couldn't expect the master to understand that.

'Either send somebody with her,' the mistress said, 'or leave the message until morning. That is my advice.'

'If I want your advice ma'am, I shall ask for it,' Mr Howkins shouted. 'In the meantime you would do well to hold your peace. The message will not wait, and there is nobody in the house to send with her, as you so foolishly suggest.'

True enough, Nan thought ruefully. Cook had gone visiting, the clerk had gone home, the housekeeper was sick and Jane and Abby, the two other live-in servants, were younger than she was.

'You ain't a coward, are you gel?' the master asked, mopping the sweat from his brow with his kerchief. The sight of her face annoyed him, as it always did. A servant had no call to look so determined. Nor so pretty. It was downright unsettling. Dammit, she must be cut down to size. It was imperative. 'Ain't a coward?'

Even if I was, I wouldn't let you know, Nan thought, and she looked up at him boldly. 'No sir, I am not!' she said firmly.

'Off with 'ee, then,' he ordered. 'No time to lose, eh!' The sealed message was thrust into her hands before her mistress could gather breath to protest again, and she was propelled into the darkness.

Plum Row was no better and no worse than all the other narrow lanes that ran in close parallel lines between the town wall and the quay. Like all the others it was little more than two feet wide and hemmed in by tall houses that loomed towards each other from either side. It was clean enough, for the cobbles were swept and the night soil removed, nearly every day, and in any case the southwest winds usually blew away most of the evil smells that accumulated there, but at night it was impenetrably dark. Now, in the dusk of this particularly dangerous night, with only the faintest glimmer of an occasional candlelit window to light the way, it was a menacing place and seemed to be full of jumping shadows and echoing shouts and screams.

She stood on the doorstep for a few seconds until her eyes had adjusted to the darkness, but the pause allowed her fear to grow too. Hasten you up, gel, she scolded herself. That's no way to get work done. Then she gathered her cloak about her, for it was early in March and miserably cold, and set off, walking as quickly as she could. Sooner there, sooner back home.

The only strong source of light in the alley that evening streamed from the inn half way down, but that was no comfort at all, for even from a distance she could see that the place was full of sailors, roaring and arguing, their distinctive black hats silhouetted against the yellow windows. What if one of them was to jump out and attack her? The very thought made her go cold. They carried knives in their belts, so Billy said. How were you supposed to protect yourself against a drunken sailor with a knife?

She began to run, trotting as quickly as she could, but with a little strength held in reserve just in case she really had to make a bolt for it. And to her great relief, she managed to sleek past the inn without being noticed and presently emerged into the wide walk of South Quay, where sufficient moonlight was reflected from the fast-running waters of the River Yare to allow her to see where she was going. But there were still too many shadows shifting beneath the lime trees and lurking under the upturned troll-carts, and the wind was making such a dreadful howling noise she was sure it would muffle every other sound. Why, a gang of sailors could be creeping up behind her even now and she wouldn't know. Oh, if only that weren't so dark!

She sped along South Quay pretending not to run, and occasionally daring to glance into the blackness behind her, but it seemed an interminable time before she reached the open space of Hall Quay and felt a little safer.

The Star Inn was almost entirely dark with only a single room half-lit by dull candles and containing the usual familiar group of local fishermen, six heads gossiping and grinning over their pewter pots. No harm there, praise the Lord. But next door, the Cromwell Inn was blazing with light, and although she couldn't see what was going on inside, it sounded far too fierce and raucous to be harmless. Never you mind, she comforted herself, nearly there. She could see the curved frontage of Mr Maypole's white house shining in the dusk on the other side of the green, and there was Mr Maypole himself standing in the open doorway, saying goodbye to his guests, fancy green waistcoat, yellow breeches and all. There were three converted troll-carts and quite a crowd of people standing before the door.

That's a bit of luck, she thought, and she skimmed across the green, much relieved that there were people around to receive her and that her errand would soon be over. The guests were still swirling from the house, the ladies shivering in their silk gowns and the gentlemen booming to Mr Maypole as they went, so she waited quietly on the edge of the crowd and watched. Twelve to dinner, she thought, counting them. That'll make work for his kitchen maids, poor souls. Then another troll-cart drew up and she had to step aside to make way for it, and one of the gentlemen, a little short chap in a brown beaver hat, climbed aboard and settled himself into the bucket seat.

And then, at last, leave-taking seemed to be over and she could walk forward and deliver her message. It was received politely but without much interest, 'Tell your master I'm obliged.' And that was that.

Now for home, she thought.

With the lights of Mr Maypole's fine house behind her, it suddenly seemed extremely dark on the open green, and the east wind was bitingly cold and wailing more wildly than ever. She could just about make out the shape of one of the troll-carts rocking ahead of her towards South Quay, but she couldn't hear it at all. Just across this old green, she encouraged herself, along South Quay. That en't far. But then what? That was a problem. Perhaps she ought to try going up the next row along. At least that would avoid that old inn . . .

She smelled the sailors before she saw them, a pungent mixture of beer, sweat, tar, damp cloth, gunpowder and musk that alarmed her even before she had time to understand what it was. She was on tiptoe at once, ready to run, turning her head fearfully, but they were already all round her, huge and terrifying, breathing like steam engines in the cold air, and grabbing at her with their rough, dark hands. 'How much ter fit ends, darlin'?' 'Paws off, Johnno, I seen 'er first.' 'Show us yer titties, gel.'

The sudden terror of their attack was like a vicious blow to the pit of her stomach. For a few seconds she was paralysed, as brutal fingers tore at her bodice and fumbled at her breasts. Then strength and anger flooded her system and she fought back, wriggling away from them, twisting and kicking, struggling to protect her body with her cloak and screaming at the top of her voice. But the wind whipped the edges of the cloak from her grasp and there were bodies everywhere, striped shirts inches from her eyes, rough canvas under her hands, bad breath and sharp teeth, eyes shining with lust. Oh, she knew it was lust, even though she'd never seen it before. And she fought on frantically, with her own high-pitched, terrible screams echoing in her ears, on and on and on, higher and louder than the wind, as they tossed her about from one to the other, slapping and pinching and fumbling. She was on her back, spread-eagled, with a huge sailor rolling about on top of her, his hand over her mouth, and she bit him and screamed again, heaving her body away from him, writhing and scrambling, her shoes slipping on the damp grass.

There was a rattle of wheels somewhere behind her left shoulder and in a detached way she realized that one of the troll-carts had drawn up beside her, the long curved shafts brushing her skirts, and she was vaguely aware that the horse was bucking and sweating and that the coachman was cursing and that there was a gentleman perched in the little bucket seat above the wheels looking down at her, pale-faced with concern. Then friendly hands reached down towards her from the side of the carriage, and she grabbed at them and was pulled to safety. The gentleman was flailing at the sailors with a horsewhip and shouting at them to be off and about their business. The horse was turning, tipping the carriage sideways. They were leaving the sailors behind. Some of them were already on the run.

She jumped to her feet, grabbing the side of the carriage so as to keep her balance. 'Varmints!' she yelled. 'Low-grade, smelly, cowardly varmints! I hope you rot in Hell for this! May you all be drowned dead. An' hung, drawed and quartered! Every last one on you. Lousy varmints!' She was beside herself with fury, hair streaming in the wind, bodice gaping open, torn cloak flapping behind her. How dare they treat her like that!

'You would be better seated, perhaps, my dear,' the gentleman suggested mildly.

'I hate 'em all,' she shouted. 'Every last one!'

'Understandably,' he agreed. 'But you might be better advised to hate them from a sitting posture. I would not wish you to be thrown from my carriage.'

What a kind man, she thought, and the thought calmed her, so that she sat down and stopped shouting. Then she realized that she'd lost her bonnet and was virtually naked from the neck to the waist and she pulled her cloak around her and set to work to try to re-lace the torn edges of her bodice and make herself respectable again. 'I ought to thank 'ee, sir,' she said, head down and fingers busy.

'No need,' he said kindly, and from the corner of her eye she noticed that he had taken a kerchief from his pocket and was mopping his forehead. 'I am happy to have been of service. You came to no real harm, I trust. We were in time, I think. You are not – um – hurt?'

'No, sir,' she said with some pride, 'I en't hurt, just hopping mad,

14

that's all. Low-grade, smelly varmints, I hope they gets hung, every last one on 'em.'

They had reached South Quay and were trotting along the cobbled roadway between the avenue of lime trees and a fine terrace of merchants' houses. The gentleman leaned forward and tapped the coachman behind the knee.

'Sir?' the coachman called without looking back.

'Stop, I pray you,' the gentleman said faintly. 'I must rest . . . a moment, that is all . . . you shall be taken home, I promise, child . . . oh, do pray stop.' And with that he turned up his eyes so that Nan could see the whites of them quite plainly, gave a peculiar groan and slumped sideways into the corner of the seat.

'My heart alive!' she said. 'He's took a fit.'

The coachman reined in the horse and turned round to see. He was unmoved by his master's predicament. 'That's nothin',' he said phlegmatically. 'He's always a-doing' that. Falls into a faint for the least little thing does Mr Easter! Hold the hoss.' And he handed her the reins and climbed down from his perch. 'Right alongside the door,' he said. 'That's a bit of luck. Soon have help, gel.'

'Aagh!' the gentleman groaned, making swimming movements with his gloved hands. 'You shall be escorted home . . . give 'ee me word.'

She put her hand on his forehead and was alarmed to feel how clammy it was. Why, the poor man's ill, she thought, and was annoyed by the coachman's callous lack of concern. But there wasn't time to say anything when the fellow came back, because he brought another liveried servant with him and the two of them immediately began to haul their master's groaning body out of the carriage, man-handling him like a sack of sea-coal.

'Have a care, do,' she urged, but her advice was lost in the wind. A groom appeared beside the horse's head and shouted something at her as he took the reins, but she couldn't hear him either, and now it was beginning to spit with rain. I en't sitting here to be drenched through an' through, she thought. But she wasn't going to walk home by herself either. She climbed out of the carriage and followed her rescuers into the house.

They had already dragged the gentleman through the front door and a housemaid in a pink gown and a huge floppy cap had come out to join them, candlestick in hand. Now they were half lifting, half carrying him along a narrow entrance hall towards the archway that led to the

15

main hall of the house, where she could see yellow light gleaming on a fine stone-tiled floor. By this time he was swooning in earnest and they were carrying him so clumsily he was in grave danger of being dropped onto the tiles. In fact his right hand was already brushing the ground so that his nice kid glove was smeared with dirt. 'Have a care,' she said again.

'That's no earthly good you sayin' have a care. He weigh a ton, so he do,' the second servant complained. 'Hold that light up, Jenny. You're a-droppin' wax all over his head.'

Nan put out a hand to steady herself against the wall and found she was holding an unobtrusive doorknob. 'What's in here?' she asked.

'The office,' Jenny said. 'That's the office, en't it Matt?'

Matt, who appeared to be the second of the two clumsy servants, grunted at her as though he didn't care what it was. He was supporting his master's back with one knee while he tried to manoeuvre the trailing arm back onto the poor man's chest, but for all his efforts he was only making matters worse. Now the top half of the merchant's body was crumpling towards the floor, and there was a scale of grey wax congealing on his forehead.

I don't care what it is, Nan thought. If I don't do something soon, they'll drop the poor old gentleman on his head. And she couldn't have that. Not after he'd rescued her so kindly. She opened the door quickly, before they could tell her not to, and there was just enough light from the candle for her to see a day-bed and a footstool just inside the room. 'Bring him in here,' she ordered. 'Put him down. Easy does it.'

They obeyed her as well as they could, and the maid with the candle endeavoured not to shed any more wax on her master, but once they'd arranged him on the day-bed none of them seemed to have any idea what to do next. He was such a proper-looking gentleman too, in his buckskin breeches and his cut-away waistcoat and his fine velvet jacket. 'Well then,' Nan said, looking at the three blank faces around her, 'what you generally do when he faints away?'

'We get the housekeeper,' the coachman said.

'Get her then, great fool! Hasten you up!'

'That's not my job. Matthew has to do that.'

She snorted her impatience at their foolishness. The poor gentleman's neckcloth was wound far too tightly around his throat. No wonder he looked so green. She knelt beside him and began to unwind it quickly to give him air. 'Run and get her, Matthew,' she ordered. 'And you,' glancing at the maid, 'put down the candlestick, there on the table, and get me a blanket and a linen cloth and a bottle of brandy.' The gentleman's fingers were bloodless and chill to the touch. His feet and hands should be chafed with brandy as quickly as possible or he'd take a chill, poor soul. 'I suppose you can take his boots off,' she said sarcastically to the coachman, 'or do Matthew have to do that an' all?'

The boots were removed. Sheepishly. And the poor man's feet were as cold as his fingers. But fortunately Jenny was soon back with two linen cloths and a decanter half full of brandy, followed by Matthew bearing a blanket, so the three of them set to work to rub and chafe, and presently the gentleman opened his eyes and said he was much obliged. So they wrapped him up in the blanket and made him comfortable, and he said he was sorry to cause them so much trouble.

'That's no trouble,' Nan told him briskly, to reassure him.

'I thought to rescue you, child, and now you rescue me,' he said ruefully. 'Matthew, you must escort her home. It is beyond my power now, I fear. All the way to her door, mind.'

She was touched by his concern and thought what a very pleasant smile he had. It quite altered the shape of his face, rounding his long pallid cheeks, lifting the corners of his eyes and even curving his lips, which until then had been so thin as to be little more than a pale line in the bland oval of his countenance. That's a nice old gentleman, she thought, and smiled back at him.

But then the housekeeper arrived in a blaze of candles, with two more men-servants carrying a wide chair. She took over the minute she stepped into the office, giving rapid orders to everybody in the room, except her master, and, after one brief disparaging glance, ignoring Nan completely. 'Your bed is warmed and ready, Mr Easter, sir,' she said. 'If you could just sit in this chair . . .'

'Stay there,' he said to Nan as he was borne away. 'Matthew will return for you presently.'

But Matthew took a very long time. And now that all the excitement was over, she began to realize that her face was stinging and that her arms ached and that she had a dull pain in her ribs. Never a one to waste time in self-pity, she took off her cloak and examined it carefully, promising herself that she would start repairs the very next morning. It was very badly torn, and the lining looked frayed. She picked up the candle and set it on the top of the desk in order to get a better light, and the change of position illuminated the ceiling. There were four

17

thick oak beams quartering the space above her head, and she was intrigued to see that they were decorated by elaborate writing, tall letters picked out in red and gold. That's a rhyme of some sort, she thought, and she lifted the candle above her head to read it.

> The poor that live in needie rate
> by learning do great riches gayne
> The rich that live in wealthy state
> by learning do their wealth mainteyne

There's truth in that, she thought. For hadn't Mistress Howkins taken her on as lady's maid because she could read and write a fair hand? And the rich grew richer no matter what. But then again, Mr Howkin's clerk was the most learned man she knew, and he was as poor as a church mouse in his old patched coat and his broken shoes. If I could be certain sure to gain great riches just by learning, she thought, I'd learn everythin' and anythin', so I would. Needie rate was a miserable life. But, young as she was, she already knew there'd be a great deal more to it than that.

There was a crunch of boots at the door and Matthew came blundering back.

'Master says I'm to take 'ee home,' he said, and to her annoyance, she saw that he was looking at her torn bodice. She swathed herself in the cloak immediately and carried the candle out into the inner hall, determined to be brisk and discouraging. She'd had quite enough to cope with for one evening.

But she needn't have worried, for he escorted her stolidly, saying little except that the master was safe a-bed, and that he hoped she would sleep sound after all her troubles.

It was a relief to be back in Plum Row again, in the warmth of the familiar kitchen. Cook had returned and she and the two kitchen-maids were hard at work kneading tomorrow's bread and grating hartshorn for tomorrow's jelly, but they stopped what they were doing the minute they saw the state she was in.

'Lawk's a mercy!' Cook said, throwing up her floury hands. 'What've they done to 'ee, gel?'

She was busy telling them the tale when the bedroom bell rang. 'That's the missus for you. Bound to be,' Abby said, grating hartshorn again at once, just in case the lady were to follow the bell. 'She been on an' on. Was you home? Was you home?'

'Best tell her quick and get it over with,' Cook advised.

But that was easier said than done, for when Nan had climbed the back stairs to Mrs Howkins' bed chamber, the sight of her bruises sent her mistress into hysterics, and the hysterics soon had Mr Howkins crashing up the stairs to see what was wrong.

'What's this? What's this? Control yourself, woman! Have you no pride?'

'Attacked by sailors!' his wife screamed. 'I knew it! I knew it! We shall all be murdered in our beds!'

'What! What! What!' the master roared, as if he were firing off shotguns. 'Did she take the message, what!'

' 'Course!' Nan said, coolly, looking him straight in the eye.

He nodded brusquely. 'Dammit!' he said, as Mrs Howkins' screams subsided into sobs. 'It ain't safe to walk the streets. You should never have sent her in the first place, ma'am. I told you so, you remember, but you would have your own way. Well, on your own head be it! You have no one to blame but yourselves, the pair of you. Good night to 'ee, ma'am.' And he marched across the landing to his own room, well satisfied with himself, leaving Nan furious and his wife annoyed out of her tears.

'Men,' Mrs Howkins said, sniffing, 'are the most detestable deceivers. How I endure this life I truly do not know. The human frame was not made to withstand such incessant perfidy. I wonder my heart did not stop beating when I saw you, Nan. I declare I thought it had. What a state of perturbation to be forced to endure. It is very hard, is it not? How shall I sleep in such a state?'

'We will try a hot possett,' Nan said, keeping calm as well as she could. It was extremely difficult because her bruises were becoming more painful and her mistress more irritating by the minute.

'I shan't sleep a wink,' Mrs Howkins promised. But when the possett had been made and drunk and the warming pan removed and the lady was finally brought to bed, she was snoring before the bed curtains were drawn.

It was another hour before Nan could get to bed herself. There were still her mistress's gloves to clean with fuller's earth, and her skirt-hem to be brushed, and her clean chemise to be ironed and set before the dying fire to air. By the time she took her candle and climbed the spiral stair from the kitchen corner to the attic room where all the women servants slept, she was aching all over.

19

'I shan't need no possett to lull me to sleep,' she said.

But she was wrong. For the first time in her life she slept badly, kept wakeful by sore ribs and tender arms and terrifying dreams.

Chapter Two

When Matthew came blundering into his master's bedroom at seven o'clock the next morning, the squall had blown itself out. The River Yare was peacefully green, rippling easily seawards, and the sky above the bare lime trees was as blue as a duck's egg.

'That's a fine mornin', Mr Easter, sir,' he observed, trying to fold the shutters without crashing them. And failing.

'It is, Matthew,' Mr Easter said, wincing at the clumsiness and the sudden dazzle of sunlight. His skull felt as fragile as an egg shell this morning. 'Is my hot chocolate . . .?'

'All ready, sir. On the table.'

'Ah!', closing his eyes and adjusting his night-cap. 'What day is it, Matthew?'

'Thursday, sir, as ever is. Due to meet that there Mr Pullinger eleven o'clock, sir.'

'Ah!' Mr Easter said again, his eyes still shut. 'Then I shall rise in – um – ten minutes. Kindly require Mrs Mather to send warm water if you please, Matthew.'

There was no need for them to look at each other, for their conversation was always the same. There was something very comforting about their early-morning ritual, this necessary pause between dream and reality. It made no demands on Matthew's sluggish understanding and it allowed his master a few private moments to digest the events of the last twenty-four hours and to ease himself into a good humour for the day ahead.

Matthew relinquished his noisy struggle with the shutter and crashed from the room, banging the door behind him, and Mr Easter sighed and sat up. Gradually, of course, and very gently so as to preserve the egg shells. Then he leant across the counterpane to test the heat of his chocolate with a tentative forefinger. It was always exactly the right temperature, but he was congenitally cautious.

Left to his own devices he would have preferred to stay in bed till midday. He wasn't at all sure whether he'd recovered from his fainting fit, and wondered, briefly, whether he ought to send for Mr Murdoch, his local physician. But as Mr Murdoch would be likely to prescribe leeches and prolonged rest, he decided against it. Being bled was beneficial. There was no doubt about that. But it always made him feel so wretched afterwards. And besides, he'd promised to meet Mr Pullinger, and a gentleman's word was his bond. That was something he was quite sure about.

Caught in the middle of an important family, between his older brother Joseph who was an exact copy of his father and his little sister Cecilia who was just like her mother, only more charming, William Henry Easter had always been an oddity, never really certain about anything and perpetually anxious, a creature apart, with no discernible character of his own and very little idea of how to acquire one. He had grown up privately, hiding away as much as he could, enduring his schooldays stoically, going to Oxford because it was expected of him, and avoiding his parents whenever possible.

When he was twenty-one his mother decided that the time had come to settle him in life. She saw no necessity for consulting him on the matter, in fact she only mentioned it to his father once. He was given an annual allowance and consigned to the merchant's life, which he had followed ever since. Now he lived in one of the family houses in Yarmouth, where he pretended to trade in herring, and had another of his own in Chelsea, where he dabbled, equally unsuccessfully, in the importation of tea and sugar. He accepted his lot without query and although he could hardly be said to be making a living, at least he gave the appearance of being busy. He enjoyed travelling, providing it was undertaken between ten in the morning and four in the afternoon, when he was well enough, and his wandering lifestyle enabled him to restrict his visits to the family seat at Ippark to two uncomfortable weeks at the end of every year.

Nevertheless his anxiety grew with the strength and persistence of an oak. By the time he was thirteen it had crystallized into a daily consideration of the state of his health; by the time he was thirty he had become a complete hypochondriac. Now at the settled age of forty-four he employed three physicians, Mr Murdoch in Yarmouth and two

22

others in Chelsea, and his personal medicine chest was carried with him wherever he went. It was the first reassuring thing he saw when he opened his eyes in the morning.

But this morning he'd barely given it a glance. He was too busy remembering the extraordinary events of the previous evening. Had he really horse-whipped a gang of ruffians? And rescued that little maid? Who could have imagined such a thing?

Sipping his chocolate, he wondered how she was. It would be cruel if she had taken any harm. Not that such a thing was likely. She'd fought back with such force, fine eyes blazing, standing up in the carriage, screaming abuse. What amazing strength! And he remembered how firmly she'd unbuttoned his chemise and sent poor Matthew about his business. A fine, healthy child.

'I have it in mind, Matthew,' he said, as his servant returned with the hot water, 'to send some little dainty or other to the little maid. To enquire after her health, you know. A custard cup or some such restorative. She did give us good service last night, did she not? 'Twould ill behove us to ignore it.'

'Yes, sir,' Matthew said, trying to look as though he understood.

'A betwitching child,' his master said, caressing his empty cup with his fingertips. 'She puts me in mind of the Angel Gabriel in the painting at Ippark.'

'Calves'-foot jelly,' Matthew observed, laying out his master's clean chemise.

'For an angel, Matthew?'

'That's a restorative, that ol' calves'-foot jelly,' Matthew explained. 'Do her a power of good.'

'A fitting choice,' Mr Easter approved. And smiled. 'How it will please her!'

It didn't. In fact it didn't please anybody. Cook was very annoyed. 'Don't he think we feed you gel, or what?' she said angrily. 'That's a downright insult, that's what. If that weren't a rich man, I should give un a piece of my mind.'

'That ol' sarvant feller was makin' sheep's eyes at our Nan,' Abby said, grinning at Nan. 'I seen him.'

Nan was sitting at the kitchen table bathing her bruises. The left side of her face was covered with purple blotches and her feelings were as tender as her flesh. 'I wouldn't take him even if he offered,' she said. 'Not if he was the last man in Christendom, great dumb ox!'

'He got it bad for you, I reckon,' Abby persisted. 'All that standin' round the door gawping.'

'More fool he,' Nan said, holding the cloth against her cheek and glaring at Abby across the top of it. 'Now you change your tune, do. I en't in the humour for that sort a' squit.'

In the sharp light of early morning she could see how disfiguring her bruises were and what a lot of damage those foul sailors had done to her one and only good set of clothes. It was going to take hours and hours to repair her cloak and her bodice was downright unsightly, cobbled together with an old ribbon and the rapid tacking that was all she'd had time for when she got up.

'Well,' Cook sniffed, 'seein' he's been so *gracious* as to send it, I suppose you'd better eat his precious jelly. There's your spoon.'

But there wasn't time for Nan to eat or answer, for the parlour bell was clanging. 'That'll be missus,' she said, putting down her cloth. '*Pamela* till breakfast, I'll lay any money,' Mrs Howkins always required 'a restorative reading' from her favourite novel whenever the master had upset her. Personally Nan thought it was a foolish tale and had no patience with the heroine who professed to love the hero and yet spent the entire novel keeping him at arm's length. It seemed an uncommon silly thing to do when she could have stayed where she was and enjoyed his love, and in all probability persuaded him to marry her into the bargain.

'Are we to keep un for 'ee, then?' Cook asked, looking down her nose at the jelly as though it were a dish full of cockroaches.

'Give un to the cat,' Nan said lightly as she reached the door.

'That's wicked waste, you ask me,' Abby said, looking longingly from the spoon to the dish.

'You have un then,' Nan said. 'That's all one to me. I don't mind. Put some flesh on your poor ol' bones!' Abby was already plump for her thirteen years and bid fair to be a hefty woman when she was grown. 'You have un. I got other things to attend to.'

The first volume of the expected novel was already on the side-table.

'A little reading,' Mrs Howkins explained. 'By way of a restorative, my dear. To lift our spirits, which you cannot deny we both stand sorely in need of.'

'Whereabouts shall I begin?' Nan asked, knowing very well.

'The seduction, my dear,' Mrs Howkins said, as if it had just occurred to her. 'The supreme moment when virtue is triumphant and the barbarous deceiver is forced to desist. Such a comfort to us, don't you think?'

The book fell open at exactly the right page, as well it might, since that was where it was always opened, and Nan settled herself on a stool at her mistress's feet and began to read.

'My good Pamela, be virtuous, and keep the men at a distance. So I was, I hope, and so I did; and yet, though I say it, they all loved me, and respected me, and would do any thing for me, as if I was a gentlewoman. But then, what comes next? Why, it pleases God to take my good lady; and then comes my master: and what says he? Why, in effect it is: "Be not virtuous, Pamela." '

Keep the men at a distance, she thought, as Mrs Howkins made purring noises of agreement and pleasurable anticipation. I done that last night and no mistake. And a sight more effective than that silly Pamela.

'I must renounce all the good, all the whole sixteen years' innocence, which, next to God's grace, I owed chiefly to my parents, and my lady's good lessons and examples, and choose the evil; so, in a moment's time, become the vilest of creatures! All this for what, I pray? Why truly, for a pair of diamond ear-rings, a necklace and a diamond ring for my finger.'

'Ah!' Mrs Howkins sighed again, twisting the pearl on her own finger.

If a rich man was to offer *me* jewels, Nan thought, I know what *I'd* do right enough. I'd take un. 'T would be a wicked waste otherwise. Except I'd get un to marry me first. If he loved me enough to offer me jewels, I reckon he could love me enough to put a wedding ring on my finger.

'Read on, my dear,' Mrs Howkins said, closing her eyes and turning her best ear towards her servant. So Nan read and her mistress was soothed as Pamela struggled yet again to preserve her well-tried virginity.

'Now,' Mrs Howkins said when the tale was done. 'You shall tell me all about last night's adventure. Every last detail. I feel well enough to withstand it this morning.'

She withstood it with great enjoyment, squeaking at the sailors' violence, sighing at Mr Easter's gallantry, snorting at her husband's hypoc-risy.

'You shall have a new bodice, my dear,' she promised, 'and a new cap with cherry ribbons and a fresh lining to your cloak. And I will write to Mr Easter this very afternoon to let him know how grateful we all are. A fine man, Mr Easter, from a fine family. They own a deal of property hereabouts. A very fine family.'

So the letter was written and sent around by Mr Howkins' clerk, who returned with a billet from Mr Easter to say he was charmed to have been of service, and that he hoped the little maid had taken no harm from her experiences and that the calves'-foot jelly he had sent had been received and enjoyed.

'Oh yes ma'am,' Nan assured her mistress when she was questioned about it. 'Very enjoyable that were.' Abby had said as much. Several times.

'You must be sure to thank the gentleman properly the very next time we see him,' Mrs Howkins ordered.

They saw him on Sunday when they were promenading in Market Square after morning service in St Nicholas' church. He was strolling towards them, deep in thought, with his hands clasped behind his back under his coat tails. They were almost toe-to-toe before he looked up, but then he greeted them most courteously, raising his brown beaver hat and smiling shyly. There was such a gentleness about him, Nan thought, and his face was every bit as kind as she remembered it, a nice, round, honest face with a firm chin and cheeks as pink as a baby's and a funny little button-nose, and really quite handsome blue eyes. He must have been quite presentable when he was young.

She bobbed him a curtsey and thanked him politely for the jelly she hadn't eaten, and Mrs Howkins talked to him at length about the unruly nature of the seafaring profession and declared herself 'wild with relief' that those three awful ships had gathered together the remnants of their awful crews and sailed away to torment someone else.

The next morning Matthew arrived in Plum Row with a box full of sugared almonds, 'for the little maid'.

'You've took someone's eye an' no mistake,' Cook said, 'but whether 'tis the master's or the man's that en't for me to say!'

'Load a' squit!' Nan said, handing round the sweetmeats and trying to keep her head down because she could feel a blush warming her cheeks. But she was beginning to wonder.

'She's turnin' red!' Abby said, delighted. 'Our Nan's a-turnin' red!'

'Have an almond,' Nan said. 'Take a big un.' Least she couldn't say nothing with her mouth full.

William Henry Easter was wondering at himself. It was most unlike him to take such an active interest in anybody, yet he had to admit that this child fascinated him. It wasn't that she was particularly pretty. Her face was too narrow for beauty, and her mouth too wide, and her eyebrows too thick, more like a boy's, if the truth be told. But she had such an abundance of energy, and such a straight determined walk, and such splendid dark eyes. A bewitching child.

Sunday slowly became the favourite day of his week. He would dress for his promenade with extra care, hoping to be greeted by a gush of gossip from Mrs Howkins and rewarded by the chance to tease little Nan. Occasionally, when Mr Howkins decided to accompany his wife, the outing was a disappointment, for then the little maid stood to one side and said nothing. But on most Sundays he managed to exchange pleasantries, and sometimes he provoked her to a witty rejoinder. A bewitching child.

At the end of April he found it necessary to visit London for a week or two and attend to his business there. When he came back the child had evidently taken a chill. He sent Matthew round at once with a little dish of candied fruits. And to his delight and astonishment, the little minx rebuked him, sending him a note by return.

'I beg you Mr Easter,' she wrote in her childish hand, 'that you will be so good as not to mention your gift of candied fruits, for which I thank you kindly, should we meet when I am walking with Mrs How-kins. She would not approve I think, you being a master and me a maid. I trust you will not think ill of me for writing thus. I am your obedient servant, Nan Smithen. P.S. They was delicious.'

He sent her an answer immediately, chuckling as he wrote. 'It shall be our secret. I am very glad you enjoyed them. William Henry Easter. P.S. It was a wise decision to let me know your mind upon this matter. I am very glad you did so, for I value honesty above all other qualities. Without it all our affairs must surely go awry. Yet I fear this opinion would not be shared by all mankind. Ah me, Nan, there are so many rogues in the world. God keep you and protect you, my child. W.H.E.'

Two days later he sent her a marzipan hoop and a sugar wafer. Then some comfits, then red gingerbread. They were all very palatable, but her initial worry remained. It really wasn't fitting for a master to send gifts to a servant, not even for a master as harmless as this one and a servant as deserving. What if he were to ask her for a favour? That was what masters did, as she knew from her readings of *Pamela*, and she could hardly say 'No' when he'd been so generous. Not that she had very much idea what sort of things favours were, except that they were dangerous and had to be refused. But she needn't have worried, for in the event the favour he asked was perfectly proper and perfectly possible.

At the end of May one of his London friends, a publisher called Joseph Johnson, wrote to tell him that Mr Chaplin's new mail coach company was opening up an express service between Norwich and London, which was expected to cover the distance in a single day. 'Wonders will never cease, my friend!' Since he was due to be in Norfolk at the time, he had taken the liberty of booking two seats on the very first run, which was scheduled for the second Monday in June. 'I should be honoured to have the pleasure of your company on this historic event.'

William Henry accepted the invitation, because of course, it *was* an historic event, and it was thoughtful of Mr Johnson to ask him. But he realized that he would have to leave Yarmouth very early in the morning, just at the very time when he would be most certain to feel out of sorts. The most careful and elaborate plans would have to be made to ensure that he would be well cared for on the first fragile stage of his travels. He would take Matthew to carry the medicine cabinet, which would be fully stocked with all the most efficacious remedies, and Mrs Mather should come too, to act as sick nurse and attendant.

And then, just when everything was arranged, Mrs Mather's daughter took it into her head to fall ill of the fever.

'If 't were anyone else,' Mrs Mather explained, 'I should say "No" straight out. You may depend upon it. But my own daughter, Mr Easter sir. My own daughter. You couldn't never expect a mother to leave her own daughter unattended.'

It was most upsetting. He could hardly order Mrs Mather to stick to their original plan, not that she would take any notice of him if he did. And besides, it would be unchristian to suggest it. The woman had a fever, and a fever needed most careful nursing, as he knew very well.

28

Who better? But it left him in a parlous position. Committed to a trip he couldn't avoid, for he'd given his word to Mr Johnson, and now he had nobody to care for him on the journey. He could be taken ill in the carriage with only Matthew to attend him, and although Matthew was a loyal soul and always obedient, he was too slow-witted to know what to do in an emergency. I could die on the road, he thought, panic rising.

But as fear flushed his throat, he suddenly remembered Nan Smithen. And was comforted at once. Little Nan, he thought, my healthy Nan. Why hadn't he thought of her before? She would know exactly how to nurse him. He would be safe in her dependable little hands, no matter how ill he might become. I will ask my little Nan to look after me. He sat down at once to write to Mrs Howkins entreating that she would do him the very great favour of allowing her little maid to accompany him, and his servant Matthew, to Norwich, at five of the clock, next Monday morning.

Mr Howkins said he thought it was all exceedingly unnecessary. 'Ain't the feller got servants of his own, dammit?' But his wife was charmed. 'Such a fine gentleman, my love. The family have property all over Yarmouth. We are honoured. He has offered to pay her a handsome wage. And besides, it will relieve us of the necessity of feeding her on Monday, which you cannot deny will improve our economy for the week.' So Nan was appointed temporary nursemaid, and sent to South Quay in her new bonnet and her newly lined cloak as soon as day broke on Monday morning.

The sky was still pearly with dawn and the river was asleep, calm as a pond and burnished pewter and white. It was going to be a lovely day. As she stood beside Mr Easter's kitchen door, waiting to be admitted, the sunlight was already quite warm on the nape of her neck.

Matthew was even more sleepy than the river. 'Tha's a fine ol' time to be up an' about!' he grumbled as he opened the door to her. 'Can't see what he got to go gallivantin' about the country for this time a' the mornin'. We're to go up to the drawin' room, so he say, just so soon as you've arrived. Which bein' as you have arrived, I suppose we'd better go up. This way.'

He led her through the kitchen, out into the hall and up the grand staircase, and she followed him, agog to see all the other rooms in this splendid house. It was very impressive. Much better than the Howkins' house, which looked quite poky by comparison, and nearly as fine as

29

the White Hart Inn at Schole where she'd first started work, and *that* was like a palace. At the turn of the stairs there was an arched window set with saints and shields in azure and gold, and the gentle rise of the treads was so easy to her feet she hardly knew she was climbing. It *was* a grand house and no mistake.

At the top of the stairs a galleried landing led them to the drawing-room, where Matthew shuffled his feet and knocked loudly on the oak door with knuckles like drumsticks. Mr Easter's voice called them in, faintly and politely, and they entered, avoiding one another's eyes and both feeling rather ill at ease because it wasn't usual for servants to be required in the drawing-room unless they were cleaning it.

The room made Nan feel worse. It was such a splendid place. Very old-fashioned of course, but that was to be expected with an owner like Mr Easter. It was panelled from the wainscot to the ceiling and every fourth panel was topped by the carved head of a cherub smiling as idiotically as she was. There were at least a dozen candelabra, each one standing on its own wooden plinth against the wall, a ceiling smothered in carvings and embossed mouldings, and, at the far end of the room, a fireplace that stretched from the floor to the ceiling. That was carved too in an intricacy of fruit and flowers and wooden figures that were human to the waist and lizard thereafter, every curl and swirl reflecting the red light from the first glow of the fire in the iron grate. A room for the gentry and no mistake. Fancy being the mistress of a room like that!

Mr Easter was slumped in a carved chair beside the fire. 'Is the carriage ready, Matthew?' he asked. And when he was told that it was, he sighed heavily and said he supposed they should make a start. But he didn't move from his seat. 'Travel is such a trial to the constitution,' he said to Nan.

'Is it, sir?' she said, and she couldn't help sounding surprised. She'd always found it fun.

'It is indeed,' he said, sighing again as he stood up and allowed Matthew to help him into his travelling cloak. 'Ah well . . .'

They eased him down the stairs as though he were tottering to his sick-bed, and the cook met them in the hall with a little covered basket which she gave into Nan's care. 'Be sure he takes it with un on the mail coach,' she instructed. 'He do tend to be forgetful. Give it to un, right onto his lap.'

And then they were out in the brightening sunshine of South Quay and their adventure was beginning. By now the tide was on the turn and several small boats were on their way down-river and the quay was busy with fishermen and their tackle.

They trotted past a muddle of boatyards and rope walks, riggers' lofts, forges and caulkers' yards, over mounds of chippings, and past a veritable tower of baskets, and so on over the swing bridge and out into the great flat plain where the carriage bounced and swayed on the uneven roadway.

It wasn't long before Mr Easter began to look decidedly green. 'Ah me!' he sighed. ' 'T is too early in the morning, little Nan.'

'You feeling bad, Mr Easter, sir?' she asked. 'Would you like some aqua-vitae, perhaps?'

But he only sighed.

He needs something to interest him, she thought. Something to take his mind off things. But there was nothing to interest him in the long flat landscape all around them, nothing but endless fields and windmills diminished by distance into frantic pepperpots, sails spinning. Yarmouth was just a pattern of bronze tiles and yellow brickwork on the eastern horizon with St Nicholas' tower and spire sticking out of it at one end and the cupola of St George's at the other.

The carriage threw them about and Mr Easter groaned and sighed and closed his eyes. If he goes any paler, she thought, he'll be sick as sure as God made little apples. There was nothing for it but to find some story to keep him occupied.

'First time I travelled by coach,' she said, 'I was a-hanging on underneath un.'

His eyes were instantly as round as pennies. 'My dear child!' he said. 'Had you fallen out?' The worry of it even brought a little colour back into his cheeks.

That's better, she thought, and grinned at him. 'No,' she said, 'I hadn't fell out, 'cause I never got in. Shouldn't 'a been anywhere near that ol' coach, if the truth be told. Never had no ticket you see.'

'A stowaway!' he said, delighted. 'Minx! You were a stowaway. And I thought you so well behaved. Dear me! But whatever prevailed upon you to run such risks? You could have been killed.'

' 'T was either that or go to work on the worst farm for miles. Didn't have much choice, really.'

'Dear me!' he said again. 'Could you not have stayed at home?'

31

She laughed out loud at his naïvety. 'Didn't have no home,' she said. 'Flattened, that was. Just a heap of straw and plaster.'

'But what happened? Was it a landslide? Surely your landlord would have built it up again.'

'Landlord!' she said, scathingly. 'Not him! He were the one what had un pulled down in the first place. Land enclosure or some such, so he say. Me dad was a cotter, had grazing rights on the common, just along by Fornham All Saints, little cottage, two rooms, chickens, a pig. And then one day everything changed. Can't remember much about un, if the truth be told. Gang of men with hooks pulling the thatch, some ol' mawther crying and carrying on. And then we was off to the hiring, me and me dad and me mam and me brother and sister, looking for work and a roof over our heads.'

William Henry clicked his teeth with pity. Matthew was fast asleep in the corner of the seat.

'Then along come this ol' mawther, and she say, "You'll do for Coppice Farm," she say. And I thinks to mesself, no I won't, you'll 'ave to get someone else. And I looks round and there's this great coach the other side a' the street, all ready for the off. They was taking the chocks away, kicking up a dust. So I goes hossing off, that very minute, and I slides underneath between the wheels, and I hangs on to the tailboard for dear life, and off they goes.'

'What happened then?' he said, too interested to feel sick.

'Went to Schole, so it did. There's a big coaching inn there, the White Hart.'

'I know it.'

'Got took on as a scullery maid. Hard work, that were, I can tell you, but a sight better'n Coppice Farm.'

What determination, he was thinking, looking at her fierce little face. And what courage! 'How old were you child?' he asked.

'Don't know,' she said, trying to work it out. 'Must 'a been about nine, or thereabouts.'

'And how old are you now?'

'Fifteen,' she said. 'Fifteen, Oak Apple day,'

'So young,' he said, 'to have done so much. And then, pray, what happened next?'

So she entertained him with stories, telling him how she persuaded Mrs Howkins to take her on as a housemaid, and how she begged to be allowed off in the afternoons to learn how to sew and how to dress hair so that she could be a lady's maid, and how she learned to read from the great Bible in the Howkins' parlour. And when she'd told him as much about her own short life as she thought fit, she kept him amused with gossip about her employers.

And so the journey passed without sickness and presently Mr Easter realized somewhat to his surprise that they were trundling in to Norwich.

'You had best waken Matthew, my dear,' he said. They were rocking across a wooden bridge over the river and she could see the clustered houses of a great city on the farther bank. Now they were out in the world and no mistake. She gave Matthew a quick jab in the ribs to wake him. At which he closed his mouth and opened his eyes and declared he hadn't been asleep, not he, not for a minute.

Soon they were grinding over cobbles in a dark street narrowed by traffic and teeming with people, farm carts and fine carriages, porters bent double by impossible burdens, even a huge-bellied coach wedged against a haywain whose driver was straining and sweating to dislodge his awkward load. It was a city, she thought, and full of happenings, blaring noise, strong smells, incessant activity. She was thrilled by it.

'What a place, Mr Easter, sir!'

'It has some consequence,' he agreed. 'Yes indeed. A fine castle, don't you think?'

The horses were blowing as they toiled uphill beside a grassy knoll. It was topped by a square castle like some gigantic fossilized honeycomb, and while she was still gawping up at it, the horses recovered their breath and went bowling along a wide avenue full of stylish carriages. And there, looming ahead of them at the junction of four haphazard roads, was the tall frontage of the Bell Hotel.

The new mail coach was already drawn up outside with its four greys snortingly impatient and most of its historic passengers aboard.

'Dear me!' Mr Easter said, lifting his fob watch out of his waistcoat pocket and studying it earnestly. 'I trust we are not late, Matthew.'

'Never you fear, Mr Easter, sir,' Matthew said. 'If that ol' coach en't goin', which it en't, you en't late. Stands to reason.'

But his master was already scrambling out of the carriage, hands a-flutter with anxiety. 'Dear me! Dear me! What if I have kept them waiting? What must they be thinking?'

There was a gentleman hurrying towards them through the crowds, arms outstretched. 'Mr Easter, my dear friend. I trust I see you well.'

33

'Passable, Mr Johnson,' William Henry said, sprinting forward to seize his friend by the hand. 'And how are you?'

'Recovered, as you see. I suffer less when the weather is dry.'

No wonder they're friends, Nan thought, watching them as they walked off arm in arm towards the coach, talking about their health. They're as alike as two peas in a pod.

And so they were. Two dapper gentlemen, short in stature, courteous in manner, both of them stooped and old-fashioned; two mild, unobtrusive gentlemen, the sort who would be lost in a crowd because there was nothing remarkable about either of them.

And at that thought, she remembered the hamper and Cook's solemn instructions. 'Take hold a' that,' she said to Matthew, thrusting the little basket into his blunt hands. 'Follow me!' It would be a poor thing if she lost sight of them before she'd completed her errand. She elbowed her way energetically through the crowds with Matthew lumbering behind her.

When she arrived at the Bell, Mr Easter and his friend had climbed into their seats behind the coachman and were busily fussing two travelling rugs around their legs.

'Your hamper, Mr Easter, sir,' she said, nodding at Matthew to show him that he was to lift it up to his master.

'How very kind!' Mr Easter said, receiving the hamper onto his padded lap and explaining to his friend, 'A few dainties to sustain us on the journey.' But then his smile faded and a look of intense anxiety creased his forehead and lined his cheeks. 'I have forgotten the letters,' he said. 'Oh dear! I have made no arrangements about my letters.'

'What letters are these, my friend?' Mr Johnson asked. 'May I be of service?'

'No, no, thank 'ee kindly,' Mr Easter said vaguely. 'Mrs Mather, my housekeeper you know, always sends me news of my affairs in Yarmouth whenever I travel.'

'And will doubtless continue to do so.'

'No, no,' Mr Easter said again. 'She is away from home, nursing a sick daughter.'

'Then your servant will oblige,' Mr Johnson said, looking at Matthew.

Matthew's bland face registered instant panic. 'No earthly use you lookin' at me, sir,' he said, forehead puckered. 'Can't read nor write. Never could.'

'The maid then,' Mr Johnson said.

34

'Nan, my dear,' Mr Easter said, looking imploringly at her. 'Would you be so kind?'

The coach was ready to depart. Chocks were being scraped away from the wheels and there was a bustle of leave-taking all around her. 'Yes, sir,' she promised, as the coachman gathered the reins together and began talking his four greys into concerted action. 'What should I write about?'

But the great vehicle was beginning to roll, its wheels crunching against the cobbles, and the watching crowd set up a cheer. She could see his lips moving but she couldn't hear a word he was saying. How was she supposed to know what to write about? Why hadn't he thought of this before and given her proper instructions? He was still mouthing words at her but it was all quite useless. Nevertheless she nodded brightly as though she understood, because there was no point in making a fuss now that she'd said 'Yes', and it would have been unkind to send him on his way still looking so worried.

And he smiled and waved and was quite cheerful again as the coach turned him out of her sight. What a funny man he was!

Chapter Three

Mr Easter's clerk had never approved of a housekeeper as a second source of information for his absent employer, as he was quick to complain to Nan when she came knocking at the office door next morning.

'I send him the most precise accounts,' he said haughtily, 'every Friday evening and every Wednesday morning, without fail. I see no reason why he should not be content with that. No reason at all. I am positive no clerk alive could do more, no matter how many years he may have been in the business. And, I might add, *I* have been twenty-six years in the business. Twenty-six years. Oh, there's no justice in it!'

'What sort of things am I s'posed to write about?' Nan asked, disregarding his intensity.

' 'Tis my opinion,' he said darkly, 'that some people are not above using spies. I say no more than that you understand. Not a word more than that.'

But he gave her ink and paper and promised to send her letters to the Mail along with his own.

' 'Twill be all gossip he'll get from me,' she said, because he was ruffling like a turkey-cock. 'I en't got the head for business.'

But she was wrong. As she was to discover during the next few days.

Her first letter was short and rambling. 'Mrs Mather is not returned. Matthew he caught his thumb in a drawer which is all swole up. Mr Maypole gave a dinner on Monday night, sea bream, a stuffed capon, and two rabbits so the kitchen maid say when I see her at market. Your obedient servant Nan.'

He sent his answer by return of post, thanking her most courteously for her letter, but following his thanks by two pages of closely written advice. She was to go down to the quay as soon as she could after the tide had brought in the latest cargoes and note what was arrived, what price was asked for it, what price was paid for it and by whom. 'Merchants have to keep a weather eye for such matters, I do assure you, my child. I am much obliged to you for all your kind endeavours, William Henry Easter.'

She went down to the quay the very next morning, as soon as Mrs Howkins was dressed and the shopping was done, and she was very much surprised by what she saw. 'A quantity of Dutch tiles, blue and white, very pretty come from Flushing,' she wrote in her next letter. 'The Dutchman he say sixpence each for them and then Mr Maybury he say they en't worth more than thruppence, and they argue and argue more than twenty minutes by the church clock and strikes a bargain at fourpence ha'penny. Then the Dutchman he bring out another chest of the same and another merchant, what I do not know the name of, he come up and the Dutchman he say sixpence and the merchant he say thruppence and they strike a bargain at thruppence ha'penny. And there weren't a pennorth of difference, for the tiles was all the same. I seen un. Which do seem funny to me.'

'You have witnessed your first business transaction,' he wrote back, 'and described it fully and fairly, for which service you have my warmest thanks. It is striking the bargain which is the most important part of any transaction, little Nan. That is the true art of the merchantman. One which I must confess, my dear Nan, I do not possess as yet. I am invariably the loser in any transaction which I undertake. That must be admitted, although it saddens me to do so. I make a poor bargain even when my endeavours are most serious and well-considered.'

She read the letter three times before she understood it, and then she was surprised to realize that she was feeling sorry for him. He en't artful like that Mr Maybury, she thought. That's why he's the loser. He's too kind and gentle to hold out for a good price. And she made up her mind that her next letter would be packed with information so as to help him.

But when she took it round to South Quay the following morning Mrs Mather had come back from nursing her daughter. And Mrs Mather was annoyed. 'There en't no call for the two of us to be writing to master,' she said tetchily. 'I can carry on now.'

'Weren't no call for the two of *us* to be writing neither,' the clerk said sourly. But she ignored him.

'Mr Easter must be judge of that,' Nan said, determined not to be put down by a housekeeper, no matter how fierce, and she took a pen and added a postscript across the back of the wrapper. 'Mrs Mather is returned. Do you wish me to continue writing? Nan.'

Oh, he did. Most certainly he did. For he found her artless letters perfectly charming and a great deal more informative than his clerk's or his housekeeper's. 'Pray do continue,' he wrote back. 'I am thirsty for news and need as much as you can gather.' Then he wrote a courteous note to his clerk, commenting at length upon all the facts and figures listed in his latest epistle and another to Mrs Mather assuring her that her correspondence was always needed and valued. But it was Nan's letter he opened first when the mail was delivered four days later.

Their intermittent dialogue continued all through July and well into August, and he spent more and more time remembering her and thinking about her, surprising himself by the strength of his feelings towards her.

I must take her a little present to reward her for all her efforts, he thought. A copy of Mr Cowper's comic poem, 'John Gilpin', perhaps. He could take it with him when he went back to Norwich. It would give him an excuse to spend some time in her bewitching company, the dear child. If only he could find some excuse to make the journey.

The trouble was that his affairs in London were in very bad shape and needed his constant attention if they were not to get any worse. His brokers had made so many bad bargains lately he was beginning to wonder whether he ought to sell off the tea business altogether. And to add to his difficulties, the weather in the City grew steadily more humid and uncomfortable. Men and horses were much plagued by flies and fleas and the summer sickness. And he suffered more than most, of course, despite the constant and expensive attendance of his two physicians.

'A few days on the East coast in the bracing air,' he suggested on their third visit, but tentatively because it was not his business to prescribe treatment.

They were dubious at first, considering this solemnly and then expressing the view that it might possibly prove efficacious, but might on the other hand aggravate all his symptoms, which would be cured in any case by the rigorous course of kaolin they were currently administering.

'It might be possible,' he suggested mildly, 'that I would thrive as well upon your excellent medicines in Yarmouth as I would do here in

Chelsea. With the added benefit of the sea air, of course. It is just a thought of mine, you appreciate.'

They deliberated upon this thought too and eventually decided to allow him to think it. Providing he bought a large quantity of their kaolin mixture to take with him on his journey.

It was exceedingly pleasant to be back in South Quay again, looking down at the tangled yellow curls of those familiar lime trees and all the polished masts and black hulls behind them, and the blue river running so easily under a blue sky. As soon as he had washed and taken a dish of tea and felt himself entirely at home again, he sent Matthew round to Plum Row with Mr Cowper's book.

He was back in less than ten minutes with the book still in his hands. Mrs Howkins had gone to visit her sister and she'd taken Nan Smithen with her.

'Are they like to be away long?' his master asked, covering his disappointment with a calm countenance.

'Ten more days, so that ol' clerk do say.'

It was too long. Much too long. For he'd given his word to be in St Paul's churchyard at four of the clock in six days' time. And a gentleman's word was his bond.

'You will – um – deliver the book, Matthew, as soon as they return. I will leave it here beside my bed, where you will see it when you sweep the room. You will be sure not to forget, will you not?'

'Certain sure!' Matthew promised. 'Leave un to me, Mr Easter sir.'

She wrote him such a pretty letter thanking him for his gift. 'That do make me laugh.' And she gave him a lively account of Mrs Howkins' visit and the daily catty exchanges that had passed between the two unloving sisters. And that made him laugh. But it wasn't the same as seeing her, and his disappointment was as sharp as his indigestion.

September came and then October and the herring fleets put out to sea. Now she wrote to him daily to keep him informed of the catch. He was impressed by how shrewd she was becoming. 'I seen your captain,' she wrote, 'and he say the catch is middlin, but John Butterworth, he say that old sea fairly leaping with herring. Tis my opinion the Captain speaks cool on account of a small catch do keep prices up, but if it were up to me, I know who I should believe. Captain speak cautious I reckon,

John Butterworth he speak from the heart. Your obedient servant, Nan.'

'I hope you are correct in your estimation of this year's herring,' he wrote back to her, 'for I have sold my interest in the business of tea importation, and I fear that sugar may soon follow, so your leaping fish might turn out to be my only means of livelihood.'

She paid no attention to his pessimism. Her next letter was full of excitement, for the Dutch Fair was approaching. 'Perhaps you will be back here in time to see it,' she wrote.

'I would not miss the fair for all the tea in China,' he answered, adding wryly, 'even if it were offered to me to make a profit on.'

The Dutch Fair was the biggest event of the Yarmouth year. In the olden days it had lasted from Michaelmas to Martinmas, with plays and parties and junketings of one kind and another on virtually every single day. Even now, shrunk to a mere fortnight of its former glory, it was an exhilarating festival and crowds came flocking to it from all over the country.

This year it began in a week of strong easterly winds, which brought a thick sea mist to shroud the town in the early morning and cleared it by afternoon to allow the sun to shine through like summer. The fishing boats sailing across from Zeebrugge and Flushing and Rotterdam made excellent time with such a driving force behind them. Within twenty-four hours of the appointed start, the long sandy beach beyond the Dene was crowded with shipping. And by the time William Henry came strolling across the field to join the festivities in the late afternoon of their second day, there were at least twenty Dutch fishing boats already drawn up on the sands, their hulls twice as tall as the tallest man, and their red sails dropped carelessly across the decks.

The burghers of Yarmouth were all abroad that afternoon and in holiday mood, some in greatcoats and fine beaver hats, with their ladies beside them dressed in all their finery, others in their sombre working clothes because they'd come to drive bargains. He was greeted cheer-fully by his friends who were glad to see their honest neighbour again, and guardedly by his competitors, so it didn't take him long to discover that the catch was every bit as good as Nan had predicted. And as he stood quietly listening to his clerk's account of the good prices the Easter fleet was commanding, he was wondering whether the little maid was anywhere about, and whether he would be able to see her in such a crowd.

There were fishermen everywhere, balancing baskets the size of carriage wheels on their heads with their wives plodding beside them in their long pin-tucked aprons and straw hats as broad as sunshades, sky-blue and tar-black and yellow as wheat. Everything you could imagine was being offered for sale, clogs, herrings, bloaters, wooden toys, fruits and sweetmeats, cane chairs and corn-dollies, and there were tables set up beside every ship between the muddle of dogs and horses and scampering children and the untidy mounds of barrels. The horses were working particularly hard that afternoon, kicking up plumes of sand as they trudged from sea to shore and back again with full panniers slung on either flank.

One was standing hock deep in the sea, patiently waiting to haul a boat ashore, while the local fishermen in their red caps and worn blue jackets unloaded the latest catch in their great cradle-shaped baskets, spilling silver fish like water drops with every swinging movement.

There were three young servant girls paddling in the sea beside them, catching the spilt fish into their aprons, giggling and teasing. They had looped up their skirts to keep them dry, and their bare legs gleamed white against the green water. They made a pretty picture, he thought, watching them idly as they skipped across the tumbling waves, scooping silver fish from the water, their loosened hair fluttering about their shoulders and the sea frothing at their feet. The younger fishermen were admiring them too, cat-calling after them and being ridiculously careless with the catch. Quite understandable, he thought, for they were attractive young women.

When he was young he had been moved by every pretty face too, and had done his best to flirt and pay court to the most eligible. But as the women behind those pretty faces invariably turned out to be far too like his mother, his ardour soon faded. And for the last decade he'd had as little to do with eligible women as possible. It was safer that way, and less demoralizing. Better to admire from a distance, as he was doing now.

But while he was quietly enjoying these private thoughts, he realized with a frisson of heightened pleasure that the young woman he was looking at was little Nan Smithen. Good heavens! His little Nan, no longer the child he had been remembering and imagining, but a woman,

41

a bewitching little woman with gleaming legs and little round breasts . . .

' 'Lo Mr Easter, sir,' she called looking up the beach towards him. 'did you have a good journey?' And her voice was exactly the same. She might have grown into a little woman during the last three months, but she was still his dear Nan, young and strong and independent and individual. But no threat. Oh no, indeed, no threat to anyone.

'Passable, my dear,' he said, walking towards her. 'One of the horses cast a shoe at Ipswich but we made good time notwithstanding. I trust I see you well.'

'Passable, sir,' she teased him, brown eyes laughing.

'We must talk of your remuneration,' he said, struggling to be businesslike because she was attracting him so strongly. 'Would you care to take a walk along the sands?'

She emptied her apronful of fish into the apron of the girl standing beside her, pouring them like water, wriggling and spinning, and her brown hands were deft, and her dark hair burnished by sunlight. Everything about her is so full of life, he thought, admiring her more than ever, as she paddled out of the sea, and straightened her skirt and picked up her clogs. A bewitching child.

But when they had walked right away from the fair and discussed remuneration and were finally on their own among the sand dunes, his pleasure evaporated into melancholy. As it so often did.

She sat with her back against a spiky tussock of marram grass and dried her sandy feet on the edge of her skirt. 'That's better,' she said.

'Ah, my Nan,' he said mournfully, thinking how very young she was. 'I am forty-five years old. How swiftly the years do follow one upon the other. Life's but a walking shadow, my dear!'

Talking in riddles again, she thought, slipping her feet into her clogs. That's his schooling, I dare swear, poor soul. And she looked brightly at his sombre face, hoping to cheer him.

'A poor fool that struts and threats his hour upon the stage and then is heard no more,' he said, more mournfully than ever. 'It is all vanity, Nan. Although heaven knows we have little enough cause for vanity. We are like the sands of the shore. Dull, numerous and of little account I fear.' He scooped up a handful of sand and held it thoughtfully. 'Here and alive today,' he said looking at the flaxen heap in his palm. The wind was already blowing the grains away, and he turned his hand slowly as he spoke and let the rest of it plume towards his feet. 'Gone and forgotten tomorrow.'

That's a load 'a squit, Nan thought and she rushed to disprove him. 'That don't have to be like that, Mr Easter,' she said, her brown eyes serious. 'S'pose life was like the sea instead 'a the sand. What then? Never the same two days running. One minute rushing on you so strong it knock the breath out your body, next minute calm as a mill pond. Now that's exciting.'

'With the breath knocked out of your body?' he said, smiling at her despite his depression.

'That's exciting,' she insisted. 'So what if that old sea do knock you about? He don't rage forever. Wind don't blow forever. You pick yourself up again, don't you? You fight on. The more he blow you down the more you get up again. Right?'

'Do you never feel afraid?' he asked.

'No,' she said, briskly, without even thinking about it. 'En't got time for that. I got too much else to do.'

He smiled again. 'Like running away and hanging between the wheels of the nearest coach?'

'Better than that ol' Coppice Farm,' she agreed.

'But do you never feel that the ways of the world are too strong for you, too – um – powerful?'

'No. There's always ways an' means, en't there?'

'What faith and energy you have, my Nan!' he said, and he suddenly leant forward and picked up her stubby hand and kissed it. He couldn't help himself. 'Ah!' he sighed. 'With you as my helpmate, how very different my life could be.'

Well, she thought, noticing the flush mottling his pallid cheeks, perhaps Cook with right after all. 'You caught the eye a' the master, my gel,' she'd said when that book arrived. 'You play your cards right, you could catch yerself a rich lover.' But Nan hadn't been interested in a rich lover then and she wasn't interested in one now. As far as she could tell from her limited observation of life and her extensive reading of *Pamela*, lovers were nothing but trouble, fickle and capricious and demanding, and giving quite as much pain as pleasure. But a rich employer would be a very different thing, and this kind man would make a very good employer.

'What sort of helpmate did you have in mind, sir?' she asked, withdrawing her hand, but gradually so as not to offend him.

He had no idea, because for once in his cautious life, he'd spoken without thought. 'You have such strength,' he said earnestly. 'Just the sort of strength I have always lacked. If I had your strength to help me . . . Ah!' And then his attention and his voice drifted away from her.

'You have only to tell me what way I'm to help 'ee, sir,' she prompted. 'I'm certain sure it could be arranged.'

'I thought of you day and night,' he said, surprising them both by the confession. 'All the while I was in Chelsea, with my business concerns in such a parlous state, dear Nan. I do believe it was your strength I missed during those difficult days. You can have no idea how greatly I was cheered by your letters.'

There was a breathy, urgent quality about his voice that alerted her. He was beginning to sound like a man declaring his love. Oh, surely not! Surely he didn't love her. 'T was not within the bounds of possibility. He was too old, for one thing, and she was too poor. But the suspicion kept her silent. She stared at him solemnly, busy with her thoughts, and in the silence words began to tumble from him again, almost of their own volition.

'I have come to value your good sense, Nan. You write so well and with such good sense. I looked forward to your letters with such . . . How can I convey this to you? You were my helpmate and my comforter all summer long. I have never said such things to any woman alive, but I say them now to you. What a blessing it would be to know that you were in my house, near to me whenever I needed you. Nan, my dear Nan . . .'

'As a servant do you mean?' Oh, let it be a servant, for I don't know how I should answer if he talked of love.

'No, no. I value you more highly than that. Oh, dear me, yes. Much more highly.'

Herring gulls were wheeling and mewing in the bright sky behind his head. She decided to speak to him frankly, for if he was thinking of asking her to be his mistress, the sooner he was disabused of the idea the better. 'I don't intend to take on lovers, sir, I should warn 'ee of that,' she said.

He was appalled at the thought of what he might have seemed to be implying. 'No, no,' he said at once. 'Nor that neither, I do assure you. I would not offer such an insult to any woman. And certainly not to you, Nan.'

She was relieved to hear it, but ashamed to have thought so ill of him, good kind gentleman that he was, with his honest face so distraught and his blue eyes so strained. 'Then tell me what you wish, sir,' she said, gently, because he was upsetting himself so much.

The moment was so full of emotion it was making him breathless. 'I believe I am asking you to marry me,' he said. And then he was appalled at his daring, and excited and afraid. To have such a pretty, passionate, headstrong creature for his very own seemed to him in that trembling moment to be the greatest happiness he could ever achieve. 'Yes indeed. I am asking you to marry me.'

Marriage! she thought, her mind baulking at the word and the idea. She had always assumed she would marry one day, and somewhere in the back of her mind was a vague impression of the sort of man he would be, young, of course, and handsome and ardent and full of admiration for her. Now she looked at Mr Easter, and wondered. 'To be your lady?' she asked. Lady of that fine house, with servants to do all the work, and plenty to eat. What a life that would be! Just like *Pamela*, when the master married the maid. Only better, because Mr Easter was a real gentleman.

'To be my lady and my wife,' he assured her, panting as though he'd been preparing to ask her for months and was desperate for her answer. 'How say you, Nan? You know my wealth and my family. You know my age and the state of my health. How say you?'

What a chance! She would never get another as good. He was old and dull and ordinary and not a bit like the handsome young man of her dreams, but he was undeniably rich and he was kind and gentle and good-tempered, and he meant what he said. She would be a fool not to accept such an offer. 'Yes,' she said firmly, 'I say yes.'

It rather upset her that his response was to burst into tears. 'Come now,' she said, 'don't 'ee cry. If you mean us to wed, we'd best see a priest. There's banns to be called and arrangements to be made. I've only an hour off work and then I'm due back at Plum Row with the fish.'

He dried his eyes and gave her his wry smile. 'And time, tide and fish wait for no man,' he said.

When he sat down to dinner that evening in his quiet dining-room at South Quay, William Henry Easter was signed and sealed and irrevocably committed. In three weeks he would move from the settled state of bachelordom which he'd enjoyed and endured all these years into the unknown hazards of matrimony. It made him dizzy to think of it. How could it have happened?

And yet it had. He remembered every minute of it, the rector of St George's smiling, the date agreed upon, Nan looking so young, standing on the church steps, his own fatuous voice saying how suitable it all was and knowing that he'd chosen St George's because it wasn't the parish church and a wedding there could pass relatively unnoticed. Anxiety was already descending upon him then, a lead weight on his presumptuous neck.

Before he parted from his new intended, he pledged them both to secrecy until the wedding. But he knew he was only buying time and a very short time at that, a mere three weeks. Then, Heaven help him, he would have to tell his formidable family. His flesh quailed and shook at the very idea. He knew very well that for an Easter to marry a servant was so absolutely unheard of as to be virtually impossible. And yet . . . it was high time he chose a wife . . . and he had as much right to a loving companion as any other man. Oh dear me! he thought, toying with his roast mutton, how would this end? He had no appetite at all. That had receded with his confidence.

Over in the kitchen in Plum Row, Nan wasn't worried in the least, because despite her extraordinary decision her life hadn't changed in the least. For the next two weeks she went about her work exactly as usual. The banns were called and she sat in the back pew in St George's at evening service and listened to them, although the names she heard, William Henry Easter and Ann Smithen of this parish, sounded foreign somehow and nothing to do with her. She met Mr Easter every morning when she went to market, and they smiled and talked politely, about the weather and the price of food and the progress of the Dutch Fair, and now and then Mrs Howkins allowed her to go down to the beach to visit the stalls, and now and then he would join her there and they would walk along the sands together and he would tell her about his literary friends in Chelsea and how very much he had missed her while he was there.

When her wedding day was a week away she gave in her notice to Mrs Howkins. It wasn't easy, having to keep everything secret the way she'd promised, but after a deal of thought, she found words that were guarded enough without sounding awkward. 'I been offered a new position, Mrs Howkins, ma'am.'

'Have you indeed?' the lady said, looking at her roguishly. 'It wouldn't be with Mr Easter of South Quay by any chance?'

'Yes, ma'am. 'Tis.'

'Just as I thought,' Mrs Howkins said triumphantly. 'Well you are a good gel, in all conscience. You work well. Your appetite is not excessive. I daresay you deserve it. When does he require you to start?'

'In a week, ma'am.'

'Fair notice,' the lady approved. 'I shall have to find a new maid, drat the man!' But she was looking pleased, nodding her artificial curls and smiling affably.

Whatever would she say if she knew I was going to marry him? Nan wondered, as she went back down the spiral staircase to the kitchen.

But she kept her counsel, and went about her work as usual, and in no time at all it was her wedding day and she was standing before the attic window in Plum Row, dressed in her old pink skirt and a braided bodice, with her cloak over her arm and a straw hat over her cap, checking her cracked reflection in the looking-glass that hung on the beam. Nan Smithen, lady's maid, about to become Mistress Easter and the lady of the house. And she still hadn't stopped to think whether she was doing the right thing or not.

He was waiting for her on the quay, offering his arm in that quaint old-fashioned way of his and covering his lips with a cautious forefinger as though they were conspirators. They strolled easily up the gentle slope of Barnaby Row towards St George's church, and there in a brown dusk beneath the blue and gilt of the high altar she gave her solemn promise that she would love and obey the stranger standing patiently beside her, and the priest proclaimed them man and wife.

After that the day acquired the drifting inconsequence of a dream. She had a vague recollection that they were both required to sign their names in a book and that the curate and his wife signed too, and said they were honoured. Then she and Mr Easter were out in the pale October sunshine, walking sedately back to South Quay, where Matthew was waiting beside the front door to greet them, and all the servants were lined up in rank order in the inner hall ready to be introduced to their new mistress.

The expressions on the faces gazing towards her gave her an unex-

47

pected sense of triumph. They were all so obviously surprised, and some of them were cross and trying to hide it, and some looked envious. She drew herself up, straightening her spine and trying to make the most of her five short feet and their envy, playing up her pride to have achieved so much, so young. *You* couldn't 'a done it, she thought, looking boldly back at them. But she knew she was putting on her bold face because she was feeling so vulnerable, and it could never have done to have shown them *that*, not now she was the lady of the house.

Then Mrs Mather came gliding forward from the head of the line, as befitted the senior servant of the household, to name all the others one after the other, her face frozen with disapproval.

'If,' as she said to the clerk later that evening, 'the master has so far took leave of his senses as to marry a common little maid, 't would ill behove us to complain.'

'Or comment,' the clerk said with the most aggrieved expression.

'*We* know how to behave,' Mrs Mather agreed.

'More than may be said for that bit of a girl,' the clerk grumbled. 'Did you see the haughty look she gave me? Insupportable! I cannot imagine what she thinks she is doing here.'

The bit of a girl, standing in the master's panelled bedroom with a new maid called Lizzie to wait on her, being dressed in the new yellow gown she'd found waiting for her on the bed, and a new lace cap that billowed above her hair like a cloud, and new embroidered slippers that pinched her toes, wasn't at all sure what she was doing there either. She walked down the grand staircase, carefully for fear of disturbing her finery, and sat in state in the panelled dining room, and ate the dinner that Matthew served to her, without tasting a mouthful, and made conversation with this man who was now her husband, without knowing what it was she said.

Then they sat beside the fire in his splendid drawing-room, while the servants bustled about in the bedroom next door, warming the bed and emptying the closet and sweetening the air and doing all the things she'd always done for Mrs Howkins, and he tried to teach her to play backgammon. But she was too inattentive to be a good pupil and he was too amorous. And presently Mrs Mather put her stony face round the door and begged to inform him, '*Mr* Easter sir,' that his room was prepared. She didn't look at Nan, and after a first curious glance, Nan didn't look at her.

'We will prepare for bed, my dear,' he said, and he sounded so courteous about it. 'Is Lizzie ready to assist my wife, Mrs Mather?'

It appeared that Lizzie was. The silk gown was folded and laid in the linen press, stays unhooked, cap unfastened, curls unpinned, slippers brushed, stockings and underlinen taken away to be washed, warming-pan swung away from between the sheets, and the new lady of the house, stripped to her chemise, snuggled down into a warm bed for the first time in her life.

'Leave the curtains!' she ordered, when Lizzie offered to enclose the bed in its draperies. She wanted to watch while her servant made up the fire and swept the grate, because a fire was such a pleasant thing when all you had to do was enjoy its warmth, and because tonight she felt unaccountably cold.

The fresh coals were just beginning to glow when the door to the dressing-room opened and Mr Easter emerged into the firelight. He looked odd without his neat wig and his gentleman's clothes. His hair was mouse-brown, shaved to within a quarter of an inch of his skull and swathed by an old-fashioned red flannel nightcap. The ankles rising bonily from the velvet of his slippers were white as paper, and mounding underneath an ill-fitting nightshirt was a belly as round as a barrel. He cut a poor figure, and for a moment, sitting up in his bed, with her back against his comfortable pillows and the warmth of his blankets all around her, she felt quite sorry for him, but then her mind was filled with the image of that other, handsome, young man she might have married, and for a few hesitant seconds she knew she was regretting her decision. But it was too late for regret. She had made her choice and given her word. Now she must go through with it, no matter what.

'We will say a prayer together, my dear,' he said, kneeling beside the bed and indicating by a slight inclination of his head that she was to join him there.

What a waste of all this lovely warmth, she thought, as her feet touched the chill floor. I hope he don't go on too long.

It was a hope that was echoed some twenty minutes later, when his lengthy orisons were completed and they had climbed back into a bed now appreciably colder and he had begun to initiate her into what he called 'the rites of matrimony'. As she had very little idea what to expect, she did as she was told, obediently lifting her chemise and opening her legs and keeping 'quite still', but the extraordinary bounc-

49

ing exercise that followed was not at all to her taste, especially as it hurt her and there didn't seem to be any end to it. 'No wonder they call un a prick,' she thought, as he pushed her into the mattress. And she was very relieved when he gasped to a halt.

Chapter Four

Nan was still feeling extremely sore when she woke up next morning.

Matthew was tip-toeing noisily around the room, opening the shutters and drawing back the curtains on his master's side of the bed. He was very careful not to look at Nan, as she was glad to notice. William Henry didn't open his eyes, but the two men spoke to one another in a disjointed murmuring way.

'Is the hot chocolate ready?'

'On the table, Mr Easter sir.'

'Two cups?'

'Yes, sir.'

'What day is it, Matthew?'

'Friday sir, as ever is.'

'Ah! Um – I shall get up in ten minutes, Matthew. Pray tell Mrs Mather – warm water.' Then he drifted off to sleep again.

I do believe he's forgotten all about me, Nan thought, sitting up beside him in the great bed as Matthew crashed from the room. I'll wager he don't even remember we was married. And she suddenly felt unaccountably irritable. 'Good morning!' she said loudly. To remind him.

The eye nearest to her opened at once and looked at her sleepily.

'My little wife,' William Henry said. 'I have ordered hot chocolate for you. I trust 'twill please you.'

But it didn't. She said it was too hot and frowned all the time she was drinking it.

Oh dear! he thought. Oh dear me! He seemed to have angered her, when that was the very last thing he intended. After the extraordinary pleasures of the previous night they should both have been so happy. He couldn't understand it. He drank his chocolate slowly, trying to

51

think of something to say to her. What sort of conversations did a man have with his wife first thing in the morning?

'We will breakfast at nine, my dear,' he said eventually, as he went off to his dressing-room to wash and prepare for the day, 'if that is agreeable. I have some small business to attend to, with Mr Mulvaney in the boat yard. I have given him my word, so I must keep it.'

'Of course,' she said, setting down her empty cup.

'My pretty Nan,' he said, standing in the doorway of his dressing-room to admire her, because even though she was cross, she looked perfectly charming sitting up like that in the middle of his great bed. 'What a fortunate man I am. Yes indeed. A most fortunate man. I declare I feel quite well this morning.' It was quite surprising how well he felt, and he'd slept like a dormouse, which was most unusual. 'I must dress now, my dear. You have everything you need, I trust?'

'No,' she said. 'What am I to wear?'

'Well now, as to that,' he said, smiling his wry smile, 'I do believe if you were to open the wardrobe you might well find something there that might suit.'

She scrambled from the bed and ran to the wardrobe, her ill humour instantly dispersed. And the great oak cupboard was full of pretty clothes, woollen gowns for the day and silk ones for the evening, embroidered aprons and lace caps and fichus, drawers full of underwear and fine silk stockings. There was even a tailor-made redingote made of scarlet wool with an elegant double cape, better than anything she'd ever seen on any lady, and just the thing for church a' Sundays.

It was undreamed-of abundance, and the sight of it spun her off into such pleasure she clapped her hands together like a child.

'Is it all for me?' she said.

'Indeed yes,' he beamed, 'for I cannot imagine that any of these garments would fit me!'

She ran light-footed across the room to fling her arms abut his neck and kiss him. 'Oh, they're beautiful! Beautiful! How can I thank 'ee?'

'You will need to turn the hem, or so the seamstress told us,' he said, smiling at her pleasure. 'They are left for your attention. And then we will go to the cobbler's and he shall take your size and we will have new boots and shoes all made to match. How will that be?'

'You are the dearest man,' she said, and meant it.

Later that morning when the first hem had been turned and she was sitting at breakfast in her new day-gown with her new husband, she felt she ought to apologize for being so ill humoured when she woke. 'I didn't mean to be so cross-grained, Mr Easter,' she said. 'I don't know what come over me, and that's a fact.'

'I daresay 'tis because you are new to this life,' he said, leaning towards her to pat her shoulder. 'New situations take a deal of getting used to, even for settled old gentlemen like me. How shall you pass your time while I am at business?'

'I shall see to dinner and go to market and then Lizzie and I will turn the hems on all my other new clothes,' she said happily.

'Perhaps you would like to visit your family for a day or two when your wardrobe is in order,' he suggested. 'See old friends, eh? How would that be?'

'I don't know where they are,' she said without much interest. 'They could be anywhere.'

'Do you not write to them, my dear?'

'There is no point,' she said, spearing a kidney happily. 'Not a one on 'em can read.'

'My poor child,' he said full of sympathy for her. 'How sad to have lost touch with all your kith and kin.'

But that was no sadness to her. 'I don't mind,' she said. 'We all end up out in the world on our own, don't we?'

You might have done, he thought wryly, but as to me . . . and he winced as he thought of his own fierce parents and felt guilty because he hadn't written to them either and he ought to have done. Especially now with Christmas and his annual visit so near. But he couldn't go to Ippark this Christmas, indeed he could not. He would write to them in a day or two and tell them he was too ill to travel. 'After Christmas, when the weather is improved, we will go to Chelsea,' he promised. 'It is livelier in London. Yarmouth is a trifle dull in winter-time I fear.' It always seemed empty and ordinary when the Dutch Fair was over, and it probably seemed even worse to her, being so young and never having known anything else of the world.

'Yes,' she said. 'I should like that. I could wear my new clothes then, could I not? You are very good to me, Mr Easter.'

Her new boots were ready in time for church on Sunday. The cobbler's boy brought them round at breakfast time and she was so excited she had to try them on there and then at the breakfast table, so that Mr

Easter could admire them. Then it seemed an age before it was time to don all her new finery and set out for church.

She stood in their fine bedroom with Mr Easter behind her and admired her new reflection in her best day-gown and her fine red coat and her red beaver hat and her black kid boots and her yellow kid gloves. Oh, she was a lady now and no mistake about it. A lady, with servants of her own to wait upon her and a doting husband to spoil her. What could be better? No more fetching and carrying, no more scouring greasy dishes or emptying foul smelling chamber pots or fighting off drunken sailors. Just a twice-weekly uncomfortable exercise, and that was soon over. A lady. Mistress Easter, lady of the house. I must remember to behave with dignity, she reminded herself, as Mr Easter gave her his arm to walk her downstairs.

She paid very little attention to the service that day. Church services were always boring, and the vicar of St Nicholas' went on and on and on. But she knew that all the women in the congregation were straining their necks to get a look at her, and that filled her with mischievous delight. Go on then, she thought, look all you like. Get your eye full. It don't worry me. But all the same she was nervous about the way they might treat her when she and Mr Easter began their after-service promenade.

They walked twice around the market square, and were greeted politely by people she couldn't remember ever having seen before. But as they returned to Priory Plain for the second time and were passing beside the low almshouses of the fishermen's hospital, where the old men slept like cats in the courtyard, they were met by Mr and Mrs Howkins.

Now we shall see, Nan thought to herself, looking her former mistress boldly in the eye.

The Howkins were more than equal to the challenge. Mrs Howkins had the situation assessed in one quick glance at her former servant's clothes. So the rumours were right after all. The little minx! 'My dear Mistress Easter!' she said nodding her tall bonnet. 'I trust I see you well.'

'Never better, Mrs Howkins,' she said, grinning despite her vow to be dignified, 'never better. How do you find yourself?'

'I have a new maid,' Mrs Howkins said, pursing up her mouth with disapproval. 'She does well enough, I daresay, but she can hardly be said to be up to the standard of her predecessor.'

'That I can believe, ma'am,' Mr Easter said, with his slow smile.

'Price of tea up again,' Mr Howkins boomed, bored by these interminable pleasantries. 'Scandalous! Don't know what the government thinks it's doin', dammit.'

'With the possible exception of this year's herring, trade is poor all round,' Mr Easter agreed diplomatically.

' 'Tis all the fault of those damn Frenchies, if you ask me. They want puttin' down, so they do. Puttin' down once and for all, every man jack of 'em.'

' 'Twould make a parlous gap in the market,' Mr Easter observed drily.

There were two old tabbies on the other side of the square craning their necks to get a better view. There you are, Nan thought, turning her body slightly so as to oblige them, and smiling straight at them as charmingly as she could. And they smiled back, nodding and bridling. She was having quite a little triumph. Oh, it was fun being Mr Easter's wife.

But it didn't last long. Three weeks later the letter arrived.

It was late afternoon and already quite dark. The candles had been lit and the fires stoked and she and Mr Easter were sitting in the drawing-room on the first floor, waiting for dinner, he smoking his pipe, she busy with her sewing, comfortable and at ease like an old married couple.

When Matthew arrived clutching a salver with the letter balanced precariously upon it, Nan thought he'd come to tell them dinner was served. But William Henry recognized the seal on the little roll of parchment, and paled visibly. There was no safety after all, not even in his own house.

It was from Ippark, as he feared, and in his mother's trenchant hand. Disquieting rumours had been heard. He was therefore to oblige them with a visit and an explanation, at his earliest possible convenience. They would expect him on Friday. 'You may bring one servant, as usual,' she wrote. '*No one else.*'

He put the letter in his pocket, hands trembling. 'I am afraid, my dear, I must leave you for a few days,' he said. 'I have some pressing business to attend to.' But he didn't tell her what it was.

The journey to London was cold and uncomfortable, for the roads had

55

been reduced to a quagmire by six days of torrential rain and then frozen into sharp ridges by two days of sudden frost. The Norwich coach was stuck in the mud three times, tipped into a ditch twice, and arrived late at Ipswich and later still at the Swan with Two Necks. He stayed at Chelsea overnight, but the house was cold and the pump frozen and even though his housekeeper did her best to warm him and feed him, a combination of raw conscience and damp blankets allowed him little rest.

The road south from London to Petersfield was in no better condition, and by now snow was threatening. They drove between fields white with hoar frost under a sky the colour of slate, and when they had to walk uphill to assist the horses, the mud underfoot was so thick and squashy they were soon caked to the knees with the stuff. There were only two other passengers inside the coach and they were red-nosed and snuffly, shedding gobbets of mud at every jolt, and shivering as flurries of sleet rattled against the windows. I am being punished, he thought miserably as the poor springing stabbed his spine. I shall catch the ague for certain. I do not see how it may be prevented. But 'tis no more nor less than I deserve. I daresay we shall be attacked by highwaymen too. 'Tis just the weather for it.

But the highwaymen desisted and presently they arrived in Petersfield, where the family gig was waiting for him. And there was old Dibkins standing beside the horse's head, with his fists under his armpits for warmth and so many ancient mufflers mounded round his neck and shoulders he looked like Humpty Dumpty. The sight of his old servant cheered him a little, but he wished they'd sent the curricle.

Dibkins rushed to welcome them. 'Very glad to see you, Mr William,' he said, offering an arm to assist his master into the carriage. 'Rotten old weather we're havin', eh? Be snow afore nightfall I shouldn't wonder. You'll be glad to get home. Now jest let's get you all wrapped up in this old rug. Shan't be a jiffy.'

'Where d'you want the luggage?' Matthew asked, drooping up beside him with the valise.

'Why, bless the lad!' Dibkins said. 'Don't 'ee know nothin'? In the boot. Where else? What a time he do take, Mr William! I never *seen* a boy so long-winded. Give it here, do, lad, or we shall be all night.'

There was such a cheerful energy about old Dibkins, settling the master, scolding the boy, urging the horse to move. But it didn't cheer William Henry. Foreboding crushed his chest with every creak of the gig, and by the time the little cart began to slither down the long icy drive towards Ippark House, he was biting his lips with anxiety.

There was something so uncompromising about the place, and it looked worse against that darkening sky, set four square in its cow-patted meadow, with dairies and stables subserviently beside it and a grey winter sky behind it, its redbrick frontage so perfectly balanced, nine windows looking north and south, seven east and west, stone faced, secure and certain of itself, staring across the rolling downs at the distant glimmer of the sea, dominating the landscape. A fine, elegant house. Like his fine, elegant mother. His heart sank at the sight of it.

'Here we are then, Mr William, sir,' Dibkins said, as the gig scraped to a halt outside the east door. 'Home and dry, eh?'

Oh, if only he were!

There was a good fire warming the hall and he was welcomed by his old nurse, who was exactly the same as she'd always been, so perhaps he was worrying unnecessarily.

'Everybody's here,' she said happily, taking his hat and helping him out of his damp coat. 'Mr Joseph and Miss Cecilia and all the dear children. We've put you in your old room, Mr William dear. Now you just trot upstairs and get out of those nasty, muddy clothes. We don't want you catching cold, now do we? They're all in the red drawing-room, when you're ready.'

He was obedient by force of habit, although it riled him that she was still treating him as a child, especially now that he was a married man. But that was his own fault, he thought, as he walked slowly upstairs. He'd allowed her to go on thinking of him as a child, that was the truth of it, and for far too long what was more, but how was he to stop her now, without upsetting her? Perhaps if his mother were to accept Nan and he was known as a married man . . . But that was most unlikely. Oh, dear me! Most unlikely.

The red drawing-room was full of children, just as it always was at Christmas time. There seemed to be more of them every year, shrieking and shouting and darting from place to place without warning. Four little boys in sailor suits playing leap-frog to the common danger, two infants in petticoats beating one another about the ears with drum sticks, a superior young lady with ringlets reading, (was that Thoma-sina?) and a superior young man in a velvet suit watching her, (that would be Osmond) and a bundled baby, whose red hair protruded from under a well padded pudding-cap, sitting in the middle of the carpet exercising his lungs. It made his head spin. But while it was spinning he realized, with a mixture of apprehension and pleasure, that this marriage of his might well result in children of his own. He wasn't at all sure in his present vertiginous state whether he would welcome children or not, but he comforted himself that at least they would be a great deal better behaved than this howling mob. Nan would see to that.

His parents were sitting on either side of the fire, ignoring the chaos around them as they always did, she bolt upright in the fierce stays of her youth, with her old-fashioned gown burdened with elaborate bows and her old-fashioned white wig immaculate above her raddled face, he slumped into his wing chair like a sagging pillow in a suit. As the years passed they were steadily growing into caricatures of their original selves, she whiter and more dry from the daily application of ever increasing quantities of powder, he redder and more choleric from the daily consumption of ever increasing quantities of claret. But even now when they were both over seventy, he found them so daunting that his mouth dried as soon as he saw them. He kissed them dutifully and hoped they were well.

'Ain't nothing the matter with me, son,' his mother said tartly. 'Which is a deal more than may be said about some other people.'

'Ah!' he said, feeling the blush descend from under his wig, but powerless to defend himself with the servants all about the room and listening.

'What?' his father bellowed. 'What's that you say?'

'*Pas devant*,' Lady Easter said firmly, leaning towards him and rapping him across the knuckles with her fan. 'Don't your sister look fine, eh?'

He agreed that she looked pretty, for she was wearing a splendid gown in the very latest style, but as she was reclining on the chaise-longue in her usual state of languid disability it probably wouldn't have been politic to describe her as fine.

'I do as well as I may,' she said when he enquired after her health. 'I declare my constitution grows weaker by the day. How I should manage without my dear Mr Callbeck to sustain me, I really do not know. That man is an angel, William, a positive angel.'

The angel was sitting on the other side of the room bouncing the red-headed infant on a far from angelic knee. He looked what he was,

58

the tough, uncompromising captain of one of His Majesty's men of war, with a rough red face and rough red hands and a voice as loud and incessant as a fog horn. 'Good journey?' he said, without looking up from his infant.

'Well – um – a trifle muddy, I should say.'

'Spot of mud here an' there never hurt anybody, did it my brave boys?'

'No, no, indeed,' William Henry hastened to agree, because it was just a little too easy for this bluff man to imply that he was a milk-sop. 'A fine child, sir,' he said, hopefully changing the subject.

'Our Simon?' his father said proudly. 'He's a little corker, ain'tcher, my beauty?' And he tossed the baby into the air.

Brother Joseph was looking out of the window at the frozen downs, with his wife sitting meekly beside him, half hidden by the swathe of the curtains. He had grown even more portly since last year.

'How's the tea trade, little brother, what?' he said, booming in exactly the same way as his father.

William Henry's head was beginning to pound, but he did his best to discuss the tea trade, and was quick to agree with his brother that the only proper place in which to invest extra capital was land. And one of the little boys leap-frogged into his legs and was applauded by his sea-faring father, and one of the babies was sick on the carpet, missing her uncle William's clean stockings by the merest splash, and causing her prostrated mother to emit shrieks of anguish. But at last nursemaids were rung for and the children were sorted out and despatched to their various nurseries to be fed, with the exception of Thomasina and Osmond, who being thirteen were allowed to dine in politer company.

By now, what with the children's noise and his own suffocating anxiety, William Henry was feeling sick.

It was an indigestible meal, five full courses, all well cooked, most lukewarm, and each more decorative than the last. The centrepiece was a lake made of green jelly on which a procession of sugar swans curved their wire-thin necks, and the last course was a dish of pippins with caraway comfits. In any other house he could have enjoyed it quite a lot. Now he was too sick with apprehension to do more than pick at it. For all the time his brother Joseph was discussing tenants with his father and his sister Cecilia was protesting that she was too delicate to eat another mouthful, truly, and her angelic husband was using his divine

59

powers to coax her into consuming another six, he was secretly preparing himself for the awful moment when the meal would finally come to an end and his mother would say . . .

'William Henry, you will be so good as to accompany your father and I into the blue drawing-room. Perkins, set the tables for cards. The children may play two hands before they retire. Well, come, come, do. Why do you tarry?'

Oh, he would have tarried a lifetime, if only he'd dared. But by now he was in such a state that only abject obedience was possible.

'Very well!' his mother said, when the three of them were settled around the fire and the servants had all gone away. 'Rumour has it that you've gone and married a serving gel. What is the truth of it, pray?'

If only she were not so blunt, William Henry sighed. A more tentative approach might have given him the chance to explain in an acceptable way.

'I am married, yes, Mother.'

'A servant?'

'Yes.'

'Speak up, boy, do. I cannot hear you. *Is* she a servant?'

'Yes, Mother, she is. But an exceptional girl, I do assure you. Uncommon talented . . .'

'Lord, boy, have you taken leave of your senses?' his mother said, glaring at him. 'You had no call to marry the detestable creature. Girls like that know what's expected of 'em and it ain't matrimony. Take my word for it. You could have kept her for a month or two, surely. There was no call to marry. What were you thinkin' of?'

'Half-witted,' his father opined. 'Ain't I always said so?'

'Frequently,' his wife said tartly, 'but to little purpose it would appear. Ah well, boy, we must give consideration as to the best method of removal. That is all that need be said about the matter. She ain't a Papist by any chance? 'Twould be uncommon good fortune if she were.'

'I have married her, Mother,' William Henry said stiffly. 'I wish to remain married to her.'

'Out of the question,' his father said, growing red in the face. ' 'S'blood, Cessie, what's the matter with the boy? Where's your sense of family, boy?'

'Can't imagine how I ever came to breed such a nincompoop,' Lady Cecilia said. 'Must have been that wet-nurse. Never did like the look of her. Cross-eyed, ye see. Said so at the time, you remember. Knew she weren't to be trusted, dammit. Something in the milk, I daresay, addled his brain.'

'Joseph's a good lad,' his father said, staring at the fire. 'Hunts well, ye know. Good seat.'

'We will get that lawyer fellow to see what may be done,' his mother said. 'A divorce or a separation of some kind. But I warn you, William, this is the very last time we shall redeem you from your ridiculous folly. We do not intend to make a habit of it.'

It was monstrously unfair. She was talking as though he were an utter fool, as though this marriage were prohibited. He gathered his courage as though it were a great shield he was pulling towards him for protection, for he knew that the moment had come when he would have to use it.

'Cecilia's a good gel, too,' his father went on. 'Married well. Obedient sort of gel, I always think. Pretty. No, no, Cessie, this one's the wrongun. You always get one wrongun in the pack. Law of nature, dammit. Most of 'em die young, of course.'

'Luckily, my love,' his mother said, 'he has a family to ensure that this folly will go no further. We will set the lawyers onto it in the morning. And in the meantime, William Henry, you will stay here out of harm's way and try to disport yourself in a proper manner.'

She speaks as though I were still a child, William thought. She doesn't care what I think or feel about it. The injustice of it was making his stomach churn, his sense of inferiority was making him sweat, and fear of the wrath he was about to provoke was inhibiting his very breath. But he spoke up, nevertheless.

'You do not understand me, Mother,' he said, deliberately calm. 'I do not have the slightest intention of divorcing my wife. We were married before the priest and according to law, and that is how I wish the matter to stand. You may see as many lawyers as you please, that is your affair, but I warn you, none of them may meddle in my marriage.'

There was a long, terrifying pause.

'Enlighten me, my dear,' his mother said eventually, in tones so acid it was a wonder they didn't burn holes in her tongue. 'Am I to understand that you refuse my offer of help?'

'I do.'

'That you intend to remain married to this – um – creature?'

'She is my own dear wife.'

61

His mother considered this in ominous silence. Then she gave judgement. 'If that is truly the case, and truly what you wish, you must understand that it would be impossible for you to remain a member of this family.'

'That is understood.' He had feared it, had known he might provoke it, but it was still terrible to hear it said.

'Your allowance would cease, as from this moment. You appreciate that? You would have no property rights, no rents, and no income, as far as I can see. The herring business would revert to your father. You would move from your present residence in South Quay. You would not be welcome here, ever again. Now, think carefully before you make reply. Is that what you wish?'

It was the moment of renunciation and they both knew it. 'Yes,' he said, and the word dropped like a stone into the elegant silence in the room.

'Very well, then,' his mother said, but she showed no emotion apart from a tightening of the lips. 'If that is your choice, so be it.' And she pulled the bell.

They waited in total silence until the butler came to answer her. Then her instructions were delivered with perfect sang-froid.

'Mr William has to return to London,' she said. 'Kindly inform Dibkins that the gig is to be ready by the east door in twenty minutes.'

'Goin' back, is he?' his father said. 'Ah well! Can't say I'm surprised. Joseph's a good chap, you know.'

Chapter Five

Back in Yarmouth it was trying to snow. Half-formed fragile flakes meandered vaguely past the drawing-room windows and a dusting of white powder was drifting along the quay. Mrs Mather declared it was no weather to be walking in, and certainly most people were keeping well indoors.

Nan was surprised to discover that even though she had plenty to occupy her, with meals to order and coals to buy and clothes to sew and a trip to the market every day no matter what the weather, she still found time to miss William Henry. She'd grown so used to his presence, to his dry, wry humour and his amazing patience and his quiet conversation of an evening, that now the house seemed dull and empty without him. She wondered how long he would be away. It must have been very important business, she thought, to have made him leave home so quickly, and just before Christmas too. She'd half a mind to go and read his letter and see what is was. She knew exactly where he kept them now, for she'd seen several stored neatly away after he'd answered them, and it would be pleasant to be in his study, where she'd seen him so often writing up his accounts. It was idle curiosity, no more, and it didn't occur to her that unexpected knowledge could be hurtful. Not that she'd have acted any differently if it had.

The key was where he always left it, suspended under the first shelf of the bureau, and the letters she unlocked were where she expected them to be too, in a neat pile, one on top of the next, with a paperweight to hold them in position. She picked up the top one and began to read, still idle and still merely curious.

'My dear son . . .' Why, 'twas from his family. How could that be business? 'Your ever loving mother.' Fancy! Was his mother a merchant too? She supposed it possible and read on, her curiosity stronger than ever, although she was well aware that she really shouldn't have been looking at his private correspondence. Now perhaps she would know what his family thought of their marriage. But the words she read made her heart contract with unhappiness. 'Rumours have reached us . . . so far descended into folly as to marry beneath you . . . you will oblige us with a visit . . . earliest possible convenience . . . bring one servant . . . *no one else.*'

She was terribly upset. She'd known all along that Mr Easter's family wouldn't approve of her, but she hadn't expected their rejection to be so very hurtful. It en't my fault I was a servant, she thought, folding the letter carefully and putting it back under the paperweight. And if *he* loves me they ought at least to see me afore they speak so spiteful.

Feeling miserable and young and inadequate, she wandered back into the hall. And just at that moment, by a piece of peculiar ill fortune, Mrs Clackett, the cook, began to outline her shopping plans for the day. Her voice echoed out of the kitchen, clear and bold and unavoidable, 'We will have two shoulders of lamb, I think. I know *she* said rabbit, hoity-toity crittur, but there en't no need to pay her no mind, I can tell 'ee that. She's only a jumped-up bit of a servant when all's said and done.'

The jumped-up bit of a servant recognized a challenge that would have to be answered no matter how down she might be feeling at the moment. If she was to be accepted as Mr Easter's lawful wife either in this house or in that place called Ippark, then sooner or later she would have to make a stand. Squaring her shoulders, she walked into the kitchen and stood before her adversary. 'I ordered rabbit pie, I do believe, Mrs Clackett,' she said as calmly as she could. 'I'm sure that is what you will buy, is it not? There is no call for lamb when the master is away.'

The cook was bending over the stove stirring the stock. She gave the ladle two sharp raps against the side of the pot and turned to face her unwanted mistress, gripping the great spoon before her like a bludgeon. 'An' if I don't agree,' she said insolently, 'what then?'

'Why, Mr Easter would have something to say,' Nan told her, standing her ground and horribly aware that the cook was a full head and shoulders taller than she was and twice as heavy.

'Mr Easter is away,' the cook said looking her mistress boldly in the eye, 'which I daresay you've a-noticed, bein' you sleeps with the man.'

The scullery maids were sniggering behind their hands. And Nan was so stung by the insult she couldn't think of anything to say.

'So it's lamb is it?' Mrs Clackett said, sensing victory.

It was an effort to fight on, but it had to be done. 'No, Mrs Clackett, it is rabbit pie.'

'Then you may cook it yourself,' Mrs Clackett said throwing the ladle down on the kitchen table so violently that all the moulds lined up in the middle of it leaped into the air, 'for I don't intend to take orders from a chit of a girl. That I don't.'

'You forget who I am,' Nan said. It was hard to keep control of herself because her heart was beating so painfully.

'Ho no I don't missie! I know who you are right enough. You're ol' Ma Howkins' lady's maid. Tha's who you are. Fine clothes don't make fine lady.'

'I might ha' been a lady's maid, one time, Mrs Clackett,' Nan said with dignity. 'That I'll allow. Howsomever, *now* I am Mrs Easter, and mistress of this house.'

The cook snorted and looked scornful.

'And if you means to stay on in this household, Mrs Clackett, in Mr Easter's employ,' Nan pressed on, 'you'd do best to remember it. I give 'ee my word when I gives an order 'tis to be obeyed, so 'tis. We need not run to the extravagance of lamb when the master is away. Rabbit, if you please.'

'Tha's the finish!' Mrs Clackett said. 'I en't stayin' in this house to be insulted by a lady's maid. Tha's that, *Mrs* Easter. I'm off. You may feed this precious household yourself, an' see if you can do it any more economical, which I very much doubt.'

Nan felt the colour draining from her face. This wasn't what she'd expected to happen at all. For a few seconds she was stilled by surprise and an uncomfortable emotion that felt far too much like fear. My heart alive, what've I done, she thought. I've lost the cook. And a good cook too, what's more. For whatever else might be said about Mrs Clackett, she was certainly a very good cook, and good cooks were hard to come by. What'll Mr Easter say? He'll be so cross. How was she going to explain it to him? And she was horribly aware of how young and powerless she really was.

The scullery maids watched as Mrs Clackett stomped across to the cloakroom cupboard and snatched her coat and bonnet from the peg. The kitchen was very quiet. Everything in it seemed to be waiting for what would happen next. Nan could hear the coals shifting in the stove and the faint 'plop plop' of the boiling stock. Then her determination returned and she began to fight back.

'You can't just walk out,' she said, chin up and face hard. 'You got to give in notice.'

'Watch me!' the cook instructed, jamming on her bonnet with both hands and some fury. 'Mr Easter'll understand. He'll see us right, bein' he's a man of honour and a gentleman. Which is a deal more than may be said for some others I could name.'

She means it, Nan thought, she's certainly going. But she had recovered her balance and now she spoke coolly. 'Very well. If that is what you wish, you may leave us now. We will hire another cook.'

Mrs Clackett was pulling on her mittens. She looked at the scullery maids, huddled together beside the sink. 'Well, hasten you up,' she said to them. 'You're a-comin' too.'

'You don't have to do what she say,' Nan told them. 'You got minds of your own, en't you?'

But they were already ducking past her towards the cupboard, snatching their cloaks, scuttling through the back door, escaping. It had taken her a mere ten minutes to lose every servant in the kitchen. Everything had got out of hand so quickly, like a floodgate breaking.

The slam of the back door was still reverberating in the empty room when Mrs Mather walked down the step from the hall, with two laundry maids struggling behind her with a heavy laundry basket. 'Tha's a deal of noise for a Monday mornin',' she said, sharp eyes rapidly understanding the state of the room.

'Cook's left,' Nan told her, speaking as calmly as she could. There was no point trying to hide it. 'You will have to hire another one.'

'Well now, Mrs Easter,' the housekeeper said, 'it's like this here. We got the copper a-boilin', and the laundry maids hired for the day, an' everythin' on the go, so to speak. Do you want for me to postpone the wash? I'm sure you understand that's what it'll mean if I'm to go traipsing off on the hunt for servants. Takes a deal of time to hire the right kind, I can tell you.' She spoke with perfect politeness, but her eyes were signalling a challenge that was quite as marked as Cook's had been. The two laundry maids, sensing a pause in their endeavours, put down their heavy basket and sat on it.

This time Nan understood the meaning underneath the words. Washday was a laborious and unsettling event, even in a household like this, where it was done regularly every month. It would be a callous

66

mistress who would ever do anything to disrupt it. 'No, no,' she said. 'Of course the wash must continue. Tomorrow will be time enough to hire new servants. There is cold meat a-plenty to see us through today. I'm sure someone could be found to bake the bread and make pickles and such, and a little dish of potatoes.'

This challenge was polite but strong. 'If I could spare *anyone*, Mrs Easter, I would do it. You may depend upon it. But then I could not be answerable for the completion of the wash. I'm sure you see my difficulty.'

Nan was quite cool now. She looked directly at her latest adversary, eye to eye. 'Well, as to that, Mrs Mather,' she said. 'if the worst comes to the worst, I will cook the meal myself.'

Which, since this particular worst seemed inescapable, she did.

It was very hard work, for she was cooking for a much bigger household than the one at Plum Row, and with no one to help her. And to make matters worse, the kitchen was clogged with the smell of dirty linen and clouded with steam from the little adjoining laundry room, and there was a constant grinding from the great stones in the mangle, and an equally constant procession of weary servants in and out of the place, folding wet sheets, preparing bowls of blue, mixing starch, hauling yet another tangle of dirty clothes from the basket, slopping buckets of used soapy water out of the back door. By four o'clock, when the meal was prepared, they were all working by candlelight and she was limp with steam and exhaustion.

'Make up the fire in the parlour, will 'ee,' she said to Lizzie, who had just come trailing damply into the kitchen to sit down for a few minutes.

'Now, mistress?' Lizzie sighed, wiping her forehead with the back of her hand.

'Now,' Nan said briskly. 'I made your meal, you make my fire. That's only fair.' She had no time left for sympathy.

She barely had time to digest her meal either, which was a great disappointment, because she'd got herself so comfortable, with her chair drawn up close to the fire, and her feet on the fender, and her stomach full of the choicest cuts of meat and plenty of sharp pickle, and the little parlour so snug and peaceful away from the kitchen. I shall sit here till I'm good an' rested, she was thinking, when the inner door was flung ajar and Lizzie rushed into the silence, mouth open and eyes bolting.

'Do 'ee come quick, mistress,' she said. 'The master's back an' in a mortal bad way.'

Nan put down her platter at once, wiped her hands on her napkin and ran down into the hall, with Lizzie twittering behind her. If he really was in a mortal bad way, the sooner she attended to him the better.

He certainly looked ill enough, drooping with fatigue and depression, and very very dirty. He stood in the middle of the hall, using the banisters like a supporting crutch, his face as pale as cheese, his eyes closed, and his boots and breeches so caked with mud they looked like a single garment.

'We come on horseback from Norwich,' Matthew was explaining. 'He been ill all the way. I never had such a time with him. Never in me life. He been ill all . . .'

'Fill the bed-warmer,' Nan said, cutting him short. This illness looked just a little too much like the real thing. 'Let's have you to bed, my dear,' she said, ducking underneath her husband's outstretched arm so that she could support him on her shoulders.

He opened his eyes briefly as she began to edge him towards the stairs. 'Ah Nan, my love,' he said, 'I am so unworthy,'

'You'll feel a deal better when you're in warm clean clothes,' she said.

'I shall never be better again,' he groaned. His depression was so intense it was pressing him into the ground. To have made so many terrible mistakes and unintentionally too. To have been cast off by his family. To have been rendered such a worthless husband, penniless, homeless, without prospects. How could he even begin to tell her? 'I am unworthy.'

'No you en't,' she told him firmly, hauling him to the top of the stairs. 'You just worn out, that's all 'tis.'

'Send for Mr Murdoch,' he begged. 'I fear I have taken a fever.'

Mr Murdoch, who arrived twenty minutes later, diagnosed a tertian fever and said he feared his patient's brain might be affected if action were not taken immediately. He prescribed six expensive pills of such impossible dimensions that it made poor William gag merely to have one in his mouth. And no sooner had he struggled the thing down his throat than he was violently sick. 'Excellent,' the physician said, when his patient finally lay back exhausted among the pillows. 'Soon have you in a better humour, Mr Easter. A good emetic is a sovereign remedy. Feed him a light diet, Mrs Easter and see that he takes one pill every four hours.'

Nan waited until the good doctor was out of the room. Then she threw the rest of the pills in the fire. 'You been sick enough for six pills already,' she said, when she saw how anxious her poor husband was looking. 'That's no tertian fever. That 'on't come back every third day, I promise you. That'll go away this very minute.'

Then she put a clean pillow under his panting head and set about nursing him back to health, sponging his forehead every hour on the hour, spoon-feeding him light broth and coddled egg, surrounding him with warmth and attention, and finally soothing him to sleep.

'What they been doin' to him down that Ippark place?' she asked when Matthew came crunching into the room much later that evening with another scuttleful of coal.

'Most peculiar, you ask me, Mrs Easter,' Matthew said. 'Only there five minutes we was, an' then that ol' coach was sent for an' we was on our way back. Had to stop at that ol' inn in Petersfield, first night, an' was those ol' beds damp! Fair runnin' with water they was.'

'No wonder he's ill, poor man,' she said, looking down at the pallor of his sleeping face. 'They've been unkind to him because he married me, that's what 'tis.'

'You got all you need, mistress?' It was very late and he was so tired his bones ached.

'Yes,' she said, recognizing his fatigue. 'Get you to bed, Matthew. All need our rest, don't us.'

'You can say what you like about Mrs Easter,' the housekeeper said next morning. 'She may be young, she may have sharp tongue in her head, she may be too choleric in temper, that I will allow, but she work as hard as any on us, and you got to admit she know the proper way to treat the master.'

'She been up half the night attendin' to un,' Lizzie said. 'She look like a ghost this mornin' so she do.'

'Do 'ee reckon he'll die?' Matthew said, finishing the last of his ale.

'Eat up your breakfast, do,' Mrs Mather said, to discourage such thoughts. 'We got a cook to hire.'

'Last dead man I see, was drowned,' Matthew said cheerfully. 'All swole up like a black pudden.'

'An' Christmas a-comin' too,' Lizzie said, lugubriously. 'Fancy a death at Christmas!'

'I likes a good funeral,' Matthew said, cutting himself another slice of bread.

William Henry was equally pessimistic. The days passed and the fever gradually subsided and certainly didn't recur on the third day, but his spirits remained obstinately low. Even on the fourth morning when he should have been feeling much relieved, he said he was still too weak to sit up.

'I am sorry to be such a trial to you, my dear,' he said, when she came back into the bedroom to tempt him to some breakfast. 'What would become of you were the fever to prove mortal?'

'Load a' squit,' she said trenchantly, helping him into a sitting position and tying a napkin round his neck. 'You en't nowhere near so hot today. You gettin' better by the minute.'

But he only smiled feebly. 'We all have to face death some time or another,' he sighed.

'You may face death when you please,' she told him sternly, 'but you en't a-facing it now. I never heard such squit. Sit you up and drink down this nice broth. Uncommon sustaining, broth is.'

He did his best to swallow a mouthful but he looked more doleful than ever.

She felt so sorry for him. 'This is all on account of that visit,' she said, holding the next spoonful under his chin. 'What they been a-doing to you? You tell me that.'

He closed his eyes and shuddered. But said nothing. How could he?

'I s'pose they was cross on account of you marrying a servant. That's about the size of it, en't it? Try another spoonful, just to please your Nan.'

'More than cross, my dear,' he said, turning his head away from the spoon and her uncompromising gaze. 'I had no idea they had such a very poor opinion of me. But they have seen to it that I cannot remain in ignorance. Oh yes indeed, they have seen to that. My father said I was a wrong un, the worst of the bunch.' The words still rankled. 'All of which is true, my dear. I cannot deny it. I am nothing more nor less than a wretch. Oh, dear me, yes. A poor wretch.'

She put the spoon back in the bowl and took hold of both his hands. 'You en't to talk such squit,' she said, 'you hear me. You're the best man ever trod shoe leather. A good, kind, patient ol' dear, so you are.

70

Them as says different is the wretches, you ask me. Don't you bother your ol' head with 'em. They en't worth it.'

What a comfort she was with her fierce little face. He managed a weak smile and sufficient courage to tell her how bad the situation really was. 'I fear I must tell you, my love, my family have cast me out, cut off my allowance,' he began.

She went on holding his hands, listening without a word until the tale was done, and the last dramatic words, 'we have no money, no home, no prospects,' had been sighed to a halt. Then she began to question.

'What about that house in Chelsea? That was yours, you said.'

He admitted it was. But rented.

'Can we afford the rent? You must have some money.'

Some, yes. But very little. A mere five hundred pounds, and his allowance had come to more than that, every year. His foolishness had reduced them to penury.

She ignored his self-pity. Five hundred pounds was plenty. 'Where d'you keep it?' she asked, severely business-like.

'In Mr Tewson's bank, in the City.'

'Well then,' she said, 'we en't destitute. We got a roof over our heads. We got money for rent and vittles. We shall do well enough. Can we afford servants, do you think?'

'Two,' he said. 'No more.'

'Then we will take Matthew and Lizzie.'

'I already have two servants in Chelsea,' he told her. 'Good servants.'

She accepted that at once. 'I'm glad on it,' she said. 'That Matthew's uncommon clumsy, and I don't reckon much to Lizzie neither. We shall do very well in Chelsea with your good servants, you'll see.'

'My dearest Nan,' he said, gazing at her with abject relief. 'What would I do without you?'

She had a pretty good idea, but she didn't enlighten him. 'We will stay here, till you're quite well again and the weather has improved,' she said, 'and then we'll go to Chelsea, and the rest of your precious family can all go hang. You're well rid of 'em. From now on, we shall do as we please. Now eat up your broth.'

He did his best to swallow another spoonful. ' 'Tis a mortal poor flavour, Nan,' he said, making a face. 'Not at all to Mrs Clackett's usual standard.'

'It en't Mrs Clackett's,' she admitted. 'I had a bit of an argument with Mrs Clackett. She was rude to me and I told her a few home truths. She walked out.' Now I'm for it, she thought, tensing herself for his displeasure.

But he laughed. For the first time since his miserable return, he laughed. 'I don't doubt it,' he said. 'Your home truths are uncommon strong, my dear. Tell me all about it.'

So she did. And he didn't seem to mind at all. 'One thing is for certain,' he said. 'This present cook is no good at all. We will hire another on Tuesday.'

'And go to Chelsea in the spring?'

'That too, my helpmate.'

But the Easter family had one more power to use, which brought all their plans abruptly forward. That very afternoon, a letter arrived with the curt instruction that William Henry was to be out of the house before noon on January 17, when Mr Ignatius Callbeck would be taking up residence and control of the fishing fleet.

So the cook had a reprieve and Mrs Mather had a headache and Matthew didn't get his funeral after all, only a new master.

And Nan and William went to Chelsea on one of the coldest days in the year, with the snow thick on the ground.

Chapter Six

Nan enjoyed the journey to London. It was exciting to be crunching over the snow, between white fields and brown hedges, under such a clear, pale sky, with steam rising from the horses' flanks and the coach-man singing at the top of his voice. It brought her sense of adventure into the sharpest focus. We'll show them Easters a thing or two, she thought. Calling her poor Mr Easter a wrong un! Spiteful creatures! Just you wait till we get to London. He'll be the best of the bunch then. Even an uncomfortable bed at Ipswich and the most unappetizing food at Colchester didn't dampen her enthusiasm.

On the last leg of the journey she begged to be allowed to sit outside on the gammon board behind the coachman, and although William Henry argued that she would be sure to catch her death of cold, or that the vehicle would overturn and injure her, she got her own way. And was rewarded by a view of the distant city that she never ever forgot.

Just before three o'clock they had reached the last uphill climb of their journey, just outside a little village called Chigwell. The passengers had got down, as usual, and trudged up the hill, slithering on the icy track, and at the summit they had paused to catch their breath, and drink a little brandy to sustain them, while the drag was being attached ready for the descent. William Henry had been too busy being miser-able, and Nan too busy drinking and chatting to pay much attention to the scene around them, but once she was back on her high perch, she realized that she was looking down on a truly magnificent prospect.

To her right, the land sloped down towards the valley of a narrow river, steel grey in the light of that January afternoon, and beyond the valley the hills were dark with trees: beeches, oaks and hornbeams in an immense brooding forest. The village with its church and a rambling street of old-fashioned timber and plaster houses lay immediately below her, looking ordinary and unremarkable. Buy beyond it was a vast landscape of undulating whiteness, like some great frozen sea, criss-crossed by the black lines of trodden pathways, and dotted with little villages and lone farmhouses trailing smoke. And beyond that, a mere twelve miles away from where she sat, was the great, sprawling City of London.

She was astounded by the size of it, for it was ten times bigger than any city she could ever have imagined and it looked magnificent, with the spires of so many churches spiking out of the grey mass of all those houses, and an abundance of white parks and squares smudged with trees, and the sharp black masts of an ocean of ships foresting the river. Smoke rose visibly from all those countless chimneys to gather in a brown-grey haze in the air above the town, and the sight of it made her aware of how rich and warm the place would be. And right at the centre, swelling above the rooftops, was a magical dome, glinting snow white and ice blue in the light of the sun which hung suspended in the sky immediately above it, glowing as red as a brass penny in the smoke cloud.

'That's beautiful!' she said, enraptured. 'I never see such a place. Never in all my born days.' It made her blood race just to look at it. 'I tell you, Mr Easter, that's just the place for us to make our fortune.'

William Henry, standing below her on the trodden snow, was rather less sanguine, having seen it all before. 'Perhaps that is easier said than done, my love,' he said mildly. 'A city is invariably full of fortune hunters.'

'They en't hunting like us, though,' she said. 'That's the difference. You'll see! Just you wait till we gets there!'

By the time they entered the city, the sun was almost down. They had passed several splendid houses on the Cambridge road, but it was almost too dark to see them, and when they inched between the black stones of a narrow gate into the City itself, it was like driving into the night. Then they were in a narrow street enclosed by six-storied houses and so full of people and horses and carts and carriages all milling about in the torch-lit dusk that it was impossible for anything to move at more than a walking pace. It was most exciting, and so was the Swan with Two Necks, which turned out to be a bustling inn with an inner court-yard big enough to hold a dozen coaches.

William Henry creaked out of the carriage, complaining that his feet were frozen beyond feeling and that he would be sure to get chilblains, and entreating the nearest groom to make haste and find him a flyer that would take him down to Chelsea before he fell ill of an ague. 'The sooner we are home, my love,' he said to Nan, 'the better 'twill be.'

She would have been quite happy to stand in the yard and watch the comings and goings, and listen to the sharp talk of the grooms and the coachmen. The cobbles were swept clear of snow, and despite the chill air it was really quite pleasant there in the crush of so many bodies and the exciting glimmer of the torchlight.

But a flyer was found and they were tucked inside it under the waterproof apron, and rattled away along the narrow lanes towards their new home. She had a confused impression of rows of lamp-lit shops, of windows heaped with merchandise – shoes and stockings, hats and bonnets, and fat rolls of cloth piled one upon the other. Then they were in a wide road that curved around some big church or other and travelling west.

'Is it far to Chelsea?' she asked.

'We will soon be there, little one,' he promised. 'What a wearisome business travel is, to be sure. I declare I ache in every single bone in my body.'

The little two-seater trotted on for another twenty minutes through wide streets and narrow alleys until they were finally out of the city and traversing a dark country lane, where the hedges were quite black for lack of light and the heaped snow made ghostly shadows on either side of them.

And then they were suddenly trotting along a cobbled street again. 'We are here,' Mr Easter said. 'Number 10, driver, if you please.'

Number 10 Cheyne Row was a tall narrow house in a tall narrow terrace, a fine modern house with long windows and a dependable air about it.

There was a lantern hanging above the front door and its beams spread just far enough to show her that there were three steps leading up to the door and that peering out of the nearest tall window was a grotesque little face, a clown's face with a mauve nose and an assortment of misshapen chins and two small dark eyes behind steel-rimmed glasses. It was wearing a large frilled cap so it was presumably female, and when it saw William Henry easing himself out of the flyer, it began to pull its mouth into rubbery shapes and wink its right eye. The movement caught his attention and he looked up and waved to it, at which it went off into a paroxysm of winks and contortions, and then disappeared.

'Who,' Nan said, staring with disbelief, 'was that?'

'Why Mrs Dibkins, to be sure,' her husband answered. 'My house-keeper, dear old Dolly Dibkins.'

He can't mean it, Nan thought. A creature like that couldn't possibly be a housekeeper. But there wasn't time to say anything more, because the door had opened and a second figure had appeared on the steps. And this one was even more peculiar. She couldn't even tell what sex it was.

It was exactly the same shape as a beer barrel, and much the same height, and it came lurching down the steps towards them as though it was being rolled from a dray. It was wearing a long dark apron which swathed it to the knees and a collection of shawls criss-crossed bulkily about its chest. Its hair stood up above its forehead in a matted crest like a well-worn scrubbing brush, and below the apron one leg sported a woollen stocking and a stout, black boot, while the other was encased in a cocoon of bandages and ended not in a foot but in a wooden wash-dolly. It rolled to a halt beside the flyer and beamed at Mr Easter.

'We got all ready for 'ee, Mr William, sir,' it said. 'An' this is your dear wife, I'm sure. I'll take the luggage, sir. Did you have a good journey?'

'Passable, Dibkins, passable.'

'Soon be inside in the warm, sir. Bed's all aired, sir, dinner's ready, we got a glass a' your London particular.'

Two servants, Nan thought, as she followed them into the house. Two good servants, he'd said, and they were little better than freaks. Well, I hope they can cook, that's all.

They couldn't. Dinner consisted of a roast fowl so tough it was virtually impossible to chew, roast potatoes burnt to cinders and a dish of greens that were liberally, and she hoped accidentally, embellished with boiled earwigs. The only palatable thing on the dinner table was the London particular, which turned out to be an excellent Madeira wine. It was going to be a very different sort of life in this house.

But at least the bed was warm, and after two day's hard travelling it was blissful to lie down to sleep in peace. There's a lot to be done, she thought, as she began to drift. 'We must talk about servants in the morning, Mr Easter,' she said.

'Must we, my love?' he murmured. 'I would have thought there was very little to say on that subject. We can only afford two with our affairs at their present – um – low ebb, as I know you appreciate, but fortunately that is the number we employ.'

Sleep was washing her away. 'In the morning,' she promised.

The next morning Mrs Dibkins came hobbling into the dining-room with a dish of sausages which she dropped on to the carpet at their feet. Nan was cross and didn't bother to hide it.

'Oh, Mr William-dear,' the old woman said, all her chins shaking with distress.

'It is of no consequence,' he comforted her. 'I had little appetite this morning. Get a little bowl, eh, and we will clean it up before it stains the carpet.'

'Why don't you scold her?' Nan said when Mrs Dibkins was out of earshot.

'She does her best, poor soul,' he said, kneeling on the carpet to gather up the sausages, which had rolled off across the carpet in every direction.

'Oh how foolish!' she said, jumping to her feet. '*She* does her best, so *we're* to starve, is that it? *She* can't see, so *your're* to clean up.'

'She is old, my love,' he said gently, still busy with the sausages. 'We must make allowances.'

'I don't see why,' she said. 'She can't cook because she can't see. She en't no earthly use, an' that's the truth of it. An' no more's her husband, great clumsy thing, clomp clomp clomp all the time. You should send 'em both packing, so you should, and get two young uns with a bit of life in 'em.'

He stood up and took her by the arm and led her down the room away from the sausages, patting her hand as they went. 'No, little wife,' he said, 'that would be a most unchristian action. They are old and enfeebled and need our care. You spoke hastily, my dear, and in anger. I know you would not truly wish me to send such faithful servants to beg in the streets.'

'Why not?' she said.

He turned his face towards her and the expression on it was suddenly cold. 'You are young,' he said shortly. 'You have yet to learn how to treat servants correctly. I do not forget Mrs Clackett, who was a good cook, in all conscience.'

The rebuke stung her. 'Then let us hire a housemaid to help them,' she said. 'Or a cook if we can afford one.'

77

'No,' he said again, smiling that infuriating bland smile of his. 'You know our fortunes, Nan, my love. Two we can afford and two we have.'

'But why *that* two?'

'For the very best of reasons I do assure you.'

There was no arguing with him, especially as Mrs Dibkins came bustling back into the room with a bowl full of slopping water and a mouth full of tearful apologies.

Very well, Nan thought, I shall set to and cook the meals myself, for I really can't abide any more of this sort of fare.

Which she did, and found to her great surprise that her presence was welcomed in the kitchen.

' 'Tis uncommon kind of 'ee, so 'tis, Mrs William-dear,' Mrs Dibkins said, when her young mistress announced that she'd come down to cook the dinner. 'I can't see as well as I did you see, Mrs William-dear. 'Tis mortal worrittin', so 'tis, for I do like to give good service to the master.'

'I shall go to market,' Nan told her, touched by the old lady's humility, 'and buy a brace of pigeons and we'll make a fine pigeon pie, with orange flummery to follow, which is one of his favourite dishes. Do we have any basil?'

'It died, poor thing,' Mr Dibkins said in sepulchral tones, as though the plant had been an old friend. 'We done all we could, Mrs William-dear, but it just give up the ghost.'

'I will buy another,' Nan said briskly. 'It won't die on *me*, that I'll warrant.'

It was meant as a rebuke to them for their carelessness, but they took it as a promise and applauded it. 'No indeed, Mrs William-dear,' the old lady said. 'What a blessing you've come for to share the master's life, me dear.'

Despite her initial annoyance with them, Nan couldn't help warming to the Dibkins, and she liked them more and more the longer they went on working together. They were both so fond of Mr Easter. Mrs Dibkins treated him like a child, clucking a napkin about his neck before he began to eat, patting hot bricks into the bed to warm his feet at night, urging him to take a nap in the afternoons, and calling him 'Mr William-dear' with the affectionate approval of a doting mother. And Mr Dibkins smiled and nodded, and didn't seem to notice that he was leaving trails of coaldust up and down the stairs. And although they were slow and short-sighted they did their very best to keep the house clean and comfortable.

The ground floor consisted of one very large room with windows at both ends, two looking out into the street, and one with a view of the little back garden. There were two fireplaces and two tables in the room too, so that whatever time of the day they happened to be eating a meal they could sit in the warmth of fire or sunshine, which was very pleasant now that their meals were well cooked. Breakfast was served at 'the garden table' and dinner taken overlooking the street, with the afternoon sun shining palely onto the carpet beside them.

In fact despite the hard work, life in Chelsea was very enjoyable. It was such an eccentric place, set haphazardly among the fields at a discreet distance from the wide curve of the Thames, and not a bit like any village she'd ever seen, being part market garden, part landing stage, half rural, and half urban. The old village consisted of a muddle of topsy-turvy buildings clustered around a square-towered church and a crumbling palace which the locals were proud to inform her had once belonged to Sir Thomas More, whoever he was. But to the north, seven new roads had been built, straight, proper roads, facing south into the sun or east towards the river, their terraced houses well proportioned, their paved streets lantern lit, like a slice of the city set down among the fields. And Cheyne Row was one of them. It pleased her to think that she lived at the better end of town.

And of course, London was a most exciting place. She soon discovered that winter here was called 'the season' and that King George and Queen Charlotte and all the ladies and gentlemen of their court, who were called 'the ton', were in town to enjoy it. She and William Henry went out with the rest of the London population to watch them; to Buckingham House to see the King pass plumply by in his gilded carriage; to St James' Park where the ton rode horseback or took the air in phaetons as clean and well-polished as they were themselves; and every day there was something or somebody new to see.

Sometimes, she and William Henry donned their heavy travelling cloaks and were rowed down the icy Thames from Chelsea steps to the City in one of the London river boats, and Nan was intrigued by the watermen who wore white sailor suits and black tar hats and spat their chewed tobacco into the river. And sometimes they went to the theatre and saw plays which were occasionally amusing, and the ton who were amusing all the time and positively dazzling, sitting in their boxes, shimmering with diamonds, the gentlemen in coats of figured satin or velvet or cloth of gold, the ladies in watered silks and embroidered damasks with ostrich feathers in their elaborate coiffures.

'With folk as rich as they,' she observed, watching them, 'there's fortunes to be made!'

'That, little one,' he said, 'is as may be. What think you of the play?'

He takes everything so placidly, she thought, watching him. He'll never make a fortune if he don't work at it. But he hardly seemed disposed to work at all. With breakfast at nine and dinner at three and an afternoon nap, and Sundays given over to church and the evenings to entertainment or to his club, business was curtailed to a mere three hours a day, spent dealing in sugar and treacle and such things, or checking the latest sugar prices. And that didn't seem anywhere near enough to Nan, not if he was going to make a fortune. I shall speak to him about it, she promised herself. At the very first opportunity, so I will.

But opportunities were hard to come by. There was always so much cooking and marketing to do, or he was trying to rest, or they were dining and couldn't talk too seriously for fear of causing him indigestion.

But eventually it was spring and their herb garden put out fresh leaves and bluebells grew beneath the quince tree like a patch of fallen sky. And when she walked down her little country street to the parade of shops that fronted the river, blackbirds were fighting one another on the green, clashing breast to breast and shrill with passion, their flexed wings like fierce black darts. The sight of them filled her with energy. Oh, there was so much to be done. They must improve their fortunes somehow and show those old Easters.

That afternoon he suggested that it might be a pleasant thing to take a short stroll beside the river. 'Not too protracted a promenade, my love, of course. We must take care not to overtire ourselves. But a turn in the sunshine, eh? To the Physic garden and back, perhaps. How say you?'

It was the opportunity she'd been waiting for. They talked weather and health until they had rounded the curve of the river and were out of sight of the village. The river was as blue as the sky and on the opposite bank the Surrey fields were green in the new spring sun. 'Everything coming back to life,' she said.

'Indeed yes.'

'Time for new ventures,' she said firmly. She had meant the words to be a suggestion but they sounded like a command.

'For those with the wit and the energy.'

'Both of which you got in abundance, Mr Easter.'

He smiled weakly. 'I fear not, my love,' he said. 'I have been sorely tried by this inclement season.'

'New ventures,' she said, her chin square with determination. 'You want to show your father he were mistook, that I do know.'

He took her hand and fitted it into the crook of his arm. ' 'Tis all long past,' he said, 'and quite forgotten. We do well enough little Nan. We have a good home and good food – Mrs Dibkins cooks a deal better these days, you will allow – and we have hardly touched our capital.'

'If Mrs Dibkins cooks a deal better that's because I go to the door to buy from the traders and spend half my day in that ol' kitchen, besides,' she said. 'You don't never imagine she could 'a made that hasty pudden last night, do you?'

He beamed at her. 'Exactly so, my dear,' he said. 'Which all goes to show what a wise judgement I made in choosing you as my wife.'

It was a pretty compliment and she accepted it prettily, but then just as she was gathering her breath and her wits to steer the conversation back in the direction she wanted, a dark figure walked out from the entrance to the Physic garden, and turning towards them, lifted his face in recognition. It was that funny old publisher fellow, Mr Johnson. Drat the man, she thought. What he got to go and put in an appearance for?

'Why, Mr Johnson, dear friend,' William Henry said, lengthening his stride. 'I trust I see you well.'

'Such a winter we have had,' the publisher said, shaking his old friend warmly by the hand. ' 'Tis little short of a wonder we are all survived to speak of it.'

'Allow me to present my wife,' William Henry said proudly.

Mr Johnson bowed courteously. 'I congratulate you madam,' he said. 'My felicitations to you both. Well, well, well, there must be something in the air this year. Mr Fuseli is returned to London a married man this very week. If this continues I shall soon be the only bachelor above seven and forty in the capital.'

'Fuseli, the painter?' William Henry smiled. He seemed uncommon pleased by the news. 'Who would have thought it? Do we know the lady?'

'Sophie Rawlins,' Mr Johnson said. 'One of his models, according to Mr Blake. A pretty creature, by all accounts. We shall see a' Thursday, for he comes to dine with me and Mr Paine.'

'Henry Fuseli!' William said again. 'Who would have thought it? And Mr Paine in London again, you say.'

'Perhaps,' Mr Johnson said, giving Nan his distant smile, 'I may prevail upon you to dine with us too.'

'We should be delighted,' William said. And Nan smiled, as that seemed to be expected of her.

There was no hope of coaxing the conversation back onto its original track now. Mr Easter could talk of nothing else but this Mr Paine and Mr Fuseli and Mr Blake and all his artistic friends, and what a pleasure it would be to see them all again. 'Such fine men, my love,' he said, as they walked together through the scented herb beds of the Physic garden. 'To hear them talk is an edification. Oh, I have spent some of the happiest hours of my life in their excellent company, I do assure you. And now you will join me there. What happiness!'

Privately Nan thought such talk would all be very boring. But at least they were going to dine out, which was exciting, and there was just a chance that she might find somebody at the dinner who would agree with her that he ought to do something to improve his fortunes.

Chapter Seven

It was an odd day, that day when they first went to dine with Mr Johnson. For a start the weather was most peculiar, with bright sunshine and sudden stinging showers and a strong south-west wind that blew them along the streets, their coats flapping before them like flags. Looking back on it afterwards Nan felt she should have known she was going to meet some extraordinary people, for she felt excited all the way there.

They took a river boat to the City, and walked up St Benet's Hill to St Paul's Churchyard. Thames Street was so crowded it took them the best part of five minutes to get across it. The pavements jostled with people, buyers and browsers, pimps and pickpockets, streetsellers, all sharp elbows and tin trays and grasping fingers, errand boys on the run regardless of other people's feet, and a raggle-taggle army of stinking beggars thrusting their sores and deformities at every nose. And as if that wasn't enough, the roadway was choked with carriages, for there was a banquet at the Mansion House and the ton were on their way to be wined and dined, their fine silks rippling like fire in the sunlight, their diamonds flashing, their pale painted faces gazing vacuously before them like masks. What excitement!

William Henry didn't notice any of it. 'Oh dear,' he panted, as they struggled across the road. 'We should have made allowances, Nan. We should have made allowances for so much traffic. Now we shall be late, I fear, and I do so abhor tardiness.'

'Never you mind,' she said, steering him past a butcher's tacky apron. 'We got time enough, you'll see.'

But only just. St Paul's was striking the hour when they knocked on Mr Johnson's unobtrusive door, and by the time they'd been ushered in and had climbed the darkening stairs to his first-floor dining-room, the meal was about to begin and conversation was well under way. The table was laid for twelve and ten of the seats were already occupied, two of them, as Nan was quite glad to see, by women.

What a dark room, she thought, peering into the gloom at all those shadowy figures swaying head to head, a dark secret sort of place, and green as a bottle with its heavy flock wallpaper and its looped curtains and that mottled green cloth on the table. But even as the thought was in her mind, a bright light came burning through the second door at the far end of the room and advanced towards her and the table. It was a servant with a tray full of oil lamps and his arrival brought a startling change.

As he set the first lamp in the centre of the table, the green setting receded into insignificance and it was the faces she noticed, intense, passionate faces leaning towards the light, foreheads burnished olive and amber, luminous eyes reflecting the bright flames beneath them, dark mouths all talking at once and in very loud voices.

The man who was speaking as Nan and William Henry came into the room had a heavy German accent. 'Aye! Zat is ze nub of ze argument,' he was saying gruffly. It was a surprise to Nan to hear such a deep guttural voice coming from such a small odd-looking man. He had a face like a cat, a triangular face, all forehead and little mouth, with yellow slant eyes and a long straight leonine nose and a mane of white hair silky as fur. 'Vhat are ve to say of mankind?'

Mr Johnson was sitting quietly at the head of the table, presiding. He had an expression on his face that she hadn't seen before, a proprietorial pride like the keeper of the menagerie when his beasts are being wondered at. Now, as a lamp was set on the wall beside him, he looked up and saw William Henry waiting to be noticed.

'Here are Mr and Mrs Easter come to join us,' he said. 'How say you, Mr Easter? Are we humans all the same? Pray do sit here. We have kept two places for you.'

William Henry was embarrassed at being the last to arrive. 'I am grieved to be tardy . . .' he began.

But Mr Johnson waved his apology aside. He was in a most expansive mood. 'But are we all the same?' he insisted, smiling his wry superior smile. 'How think you?'

' 'Twould make for a pretty dull sort of life if that were the case,' William Henry said, as he and Nan took their places at the table. 'Allow me to present my wife, Nan.'

'Pleased to make your acquaintance,' Nan said, smiling at them all as they smiled and nodded towards her, and feeling honoured to be one in such a company, but a little overawed too, it had to be admitted.

'Und my wife, Sophie,' the cat-like man said, narrowing his yellow eyes and turning his head towards the woman sitting beside him.

So he must be Mr Fuseli the artist, Nan thought, and she's the model he's married. Can't say I'd fancy him for a husband. He looks a rum un. But she looked at Sophie with admiration, for she was young and extremely pretty, with a well-rounded bosom and a fine white neck and huge, dark-blue eyes dramatic in the fragile heart-shape of her face. Her hair shone a rich brown in the candle-light and was plainly naturally curly, for it massed about her face in splendid disorder as though she had just that moment risen from her bed. But it was the expression on her face that made Nan warm to her most strongly. For, despite her beauty, she looked vulnerable, like a child lost in adult company. She's shy, I'll wager, Nan thought, and she smiled at her new acquaintance with fellow feeling, for truly the men at this dinner party were an overpowering lot.

The servant returned with a tureen of soup which he served discreetly as the conversation continued. The rum un growled into speech again. 'Ve must give ze most serious consideration to this matter,' he said, his yellow eyes teasing. 'Either ve are greated equal or ve are not. Und if ve are not, then our cousins in America a gross error have made.'

What is he talking about? Nan thought. What cousins in America?

And Sophie Fuseli looked across the table at her and winked. It was such a roguish expression it completely altered her face. The vulnerable air was gone in an instant, as though she'd suddenly woken up. Now she looked positively mischievous. Nan was intrigued, and winking back, she decided she liked her more than ever. But they didn't get a chance to talk to one another, for the conversation was dominated by the men, and *they* talked so fast and so passionately the three women couldn't get a word in edgeways.

They questioned everything, almost as if they were deliberately going out of their way to stand the world on its head, and although they all talked at once, it didn't take Nan long to realize that the leader of the group was the guest of honour, Mr Paine.

He sat in the middle of the table, in the middle of the room and all attention radiated towards him. A rugged man and certainly not handsome, Nan thought, for his nose was too prominent and his eyes too deep-set, the brows slanting quizzically towards each other as though he was perpetually on the verge of mocking laughter. But a tough man, she decided, watching as those sharp eyes assessed the company, and uncompromising. Not a gentle creature like her Mr Easter. He wore his own grey hair, simply cut, and had the confident air and weather-beaten skin of a soldier or a traveller, brown as leather against the pale London faces all around him. A leader without a doubt.

Sitting beside him was another man with equally strong opinions. They called him Mr Blake and were almost as ready to defer to him as they were to Mr Paine, which was odd considering how shabby he was and how often he trailed his sleeves in his food. But he certainly looked extraordinary, like a man ablaze. She watched him, fascinated, as he talked and talked, round cheeks fiery red and bulging eyes lustrous with emotion. The candles looked quite pale beside him. But he was making a terrible mess of his sleeves. And she would rather have talked to Sophie.

But the meal and the conversation went on and on, and although the food was excellent, the talk was baffling. Fancy saying that men were created equal when it was obvious that there were rich and poor and always would be. But no, according to them, it was the world that was wrong and the world that would have to be changed. There had already been a revolution in America, and soon, so they said, there would be another in France. They spoke of freedom and 'man's liberty to attain perfectability', which sounded most peculiar and couldn't be right either, could it? Surely all human beings were imperfect, born that way. But no, they disagreed with that too. Original sin was wrong. In fact Mr Blake declared he saw no evidence for it 'save the prejudice of priests' and they all applauded him and weren't shocked at all. Although she was, terribly.

But that night's topic was undoubtedly the inequality of wealth and how wrong it was and how it should be changed, for that was the topic they returned to again and again.

'Ideally,' Mr Fuseli said in his gutteral voice, 'ze aristocracy should see to it, zat zeir great wealth is distributed viz greater justice. Und if they vill not do this for themselves, from zeir great love for humanity, then humanity, from its great love for ze aristocracy, must do it for zem. No?'

And at that they all laughed as if the idea were some great joke.

'Society is ripe for revolution,' Mr Paine said, calmly. 'Change must surely come and so must the re-distribution of wealth. For I tell you the clergy and the aristocracy cannot hold back the populace for ever.'

She knew she was staring at them in amazement, but she couldn't help it. What an extraordinary idea it was. If they weren't rich, the aristocrats would be just like everybody else. The Easters would be just like everybody else. And wouldn't it just serve them right! Cutting her poor William Henry like that.

'I have just come back from Paris,' Mr Paine said, 'and I tell you, patience there is running very thin. Last week the price of bread was so high, the Parisians were deliberately overturning the bread wagons and auctioning the loaves at a price they could afford. Authority is being questioned, now, on every street of the city.'

'The aristocracy would do well to remember that the people are many and that they are few,' Mr Blake said fiercely. 'Howsomever, Tyranny is invariably blind as well as cruel.'

'Liberty has been tried and tested in the American colony,' Mr Johnson said. 'Now, if I mistake not, we shall soon discover whether it will transplant and take root in the old world of Europe. I must confess, I have my doubts. Europe is not America.'

'We have unleashed an idea,' Mr Blake said mopping his plate with a chunk of bread, 'and thought has the most powerful emanation.'

Oh dear, Nan thought, I can't understand a word of this. I wish they'd get to the brandy and let the ladies retire. And at that moment, as if she'd actually given him the order, the servant came into the room with the decanter.

She and Sophie were on their feet at once, and although they waited politely for Mrs Wotherspoon to precede them through the door, which was only right and proper because she was an older woman, once they were all safely on the landing, and the door shut behind them, they lifted their skirts and went running up the stairs, giggling like schoolboys let out of school.

'Quick! Quick!' Sophie said, 'where's the closet for pity's sake? I burst for want of it.'

'Me too!' Nan said, close on her heels. ' 'Tis all that wine.'

' 'Tis the door at the turn of the stairs,' Mrs Wotherspoon called as she came puffing up behind them.

'That's a mercy!' Sophie said, leaping towards it.

And it certainly was. Much relieved, the two girls continued their climb to the little room on the third floor that the servant was indicating.

There was a good fire in the grate and a kettle boiling on the hob and a tray set with tea things on a little side-table, but the room itself could hardly be said to be comfortable. It obviously did duty as library and withdrawing-room and repository for ancient manuscripts and old boots and a good deal else besides. There were cobwebs festooned from every corner and the dust lay silver-thick on the piles of browning paper.

The two girls grimaced at one another to show their disapproval of it, but Mrs Wotherspoon settled herself into the most comfortable of the three ricketty chairs drawn up beside the fire and commenced to make the tea. 'Female company is rare in this house, my dears,' she explained, 'but he keeps a fine tea, I assure you.'

'Do you dine here often?' Nan asked.

'No indeed,' Mrs Wotherspoon said, stirring the pot. 'I only came tonight to keep you company. When my dear Mr Wotherspoon informed me that there were to be two new brides at Mr Johnson's tonight, I knew 'twas my duty and acted accordingly.'

You were quizzy, Nan thought. You wanted to see what we were like. And the same thought had obviously occurred to Sophie, for while their eager chaperone was pouring the tea, she gave Nan another of her winks.

'What do 'ee think of London, my dear?' Mrs Wotherspoon said, handing the first cup to Nan.

' 'Tis an uncommon fine place, ma'am.'

'Have you been to the theatre? There is a fine play at Drury Lane, they tell me.'

'We saw it a' Thursday,' Sophie said, tossing her thick curls. 'Heinrich didn't like it.'

'Do you call your husband by his Christian name?' Nan asked in wonder. The casual use of such an intimate address had given her quite a shock.

'Why yes, indeed,' Sophie laughed. ' 'Twas his suggestion, my dear. 'Tis the new fashion.'

' 'Tis not a fashion to which I could accustom myself,' Mrs Wotherspoon said disapprovingly. 'Nor Mr Wotherspoon neither.'

'Heinrich is an artist d'ye see,' Sophie said proudly, 'and 'tis the purpose of art to set fashions. Or so he says. You should try it, my dear,' she said to Nan. 'It makes for such ease in conversation.'

Nan didn't want to disagree with her new friend, so she said she might and agreed that she and Sophie would call one another by their Christian names from then on, but privately she knew it would never do for her husband. Mr Easter was too old-fashioned for such things. It would shock him, just as it had shocked her, and he was much too nice and much too kind to be shocked unnecessarily.

' 'Tis the opening night of the Ranelagh season on April 15th,' Sophie went on. 'There are to be fireworks and music by Mr Handel and Mr Geminiani. 'Twill be uncommon fine. Shall you be there, Mrs Wotherspoon?'

'Indeed yes,' Mrs Wotherspoon said. 'I would not miss it for the world.'

'And you, Nan?'

Nan had to confess that she didn't know. 'We do not go abroad much,' she said, adding, 'as yet,' in case they thought Mr Easter mean.

'You must make one with our party,' Sophie said at once. 'I insist upon it. I could do with some young company, in all conscience. Heinrich's friends are all so old.'

'Is there dancing?' Nan asked.

'Indeed there is. 'Tis the principal attraction. Why, what's the matter? Do you not dance?'

'I know the country dances, of course,' Nan said, feeling most inadequate, 'but I fear the new ones would be . . .'

Sophie put down her cup and sprang to her feet at once. 'Why then we will teach you, will we not, Mrs Wotherspoon? They are easy enough in all conscience, once you have mastered the steps. Come, push the chairs away.'

So a space was cleared in the middle of the untidy room and the dancing lesson began, with Sophie humming the tunes and Mrs Wotherspoon clapping the rhythm, and the three of them jumping and leaping their way through reels and mazurkas, pavanes and gavottes and gallops until the steps were mastered and they were all so cheerfully hot that Mrs Wotherspoon said there was nothing for it, they would have to ring for the servant and have more tea sent up.

So the tea was brought and the fire made up, and after refreshing themselves the two girls returned to their lesson, Mrs Wotherspoon declaring she was too fatigued to stir. ' 'Tis a deal too much for my old bones,' she said, adjusting the fire-screen. 'Would I were as young as you, my dears.'

'Are you so young?' Sophie asked as she and Nan took up their positions in the middle of the carpet.

'I shall be sixteen Oak Apple day,' Nan told her.

'I am older by more than a twelvemonth,' her new friend said, 'for I was seventeen the day before I married Heinrich.'

'Ah!' Mrs Wotherspoon sighed, because she was five and thirty although she would never have confessed to it. 'Mere babies!'

'No we en't,' Nan said. 'There's many a one married a deal younger than we are, and all legal and above board.' Which was perfectly true.

It was nearly midnight when the dinner party came to an end and well past one o'clock before Nan and William Henry got back to Chelsea. All the street lamps had already been snuffed out, but there was a full white moon so they and their horse had enough light to see by. The moonlit village looked cool and peaceful after the heat and clamour of Mr Johnson's crowded rooms, even though the river smelt most pungently of tar and hemp, wet wood and rotting vegetation. As they clopped along Cheyne Walk, between the crescent of sleeping houses and the avenue of newly fledged lime trees, with the church tower casting a black oblong against the dark blue of the sky ahead of them, Nan was humming one of the new dance tunes.

' 'Twas a pleasant evening, was it not?' William Henry said.

'Oh, indeed sir, it was, it was.'

'And what were you ladies doing above our heads when you retired, pray?' he quizzed her. ' 'Twas an uncommon active retirement.'

'Sophie was teaching me to dance,' she said, beaming at him. 'She says she means to invite us to join her party for the Ranelagh Gardens opening.'

'Does she indeed,' he said as the carriage drew up in Cheyne Row. The news put him into something of a quandary, for if they accepted he would have to offer a return party of his own and that would be a greater expense than he could really afford. But her eager face was attracting him so strongly, he could not bear to deny her. 'Then we must not disappoint her I think,' he said, making his decision firmly. He could dip into his capital. Just this once.

It was a most successful evening, for Nan found the Ranelagh Gardens very much to her taste and the Fuselis were excellent hosts. They dined on roast beef and stuffed quails in one of the little oriental supper houses in the grounds, and then they took the air along the avenues and arbours, as an aid to digestion, while Mr Handel's music was played in the grandstand and the fountain played in the pond, and finally they all repaired to the Rotunda, which stood in the centre of the grounds like a great circular palace, drawing in dark crowds through all three of its gilded doors.

Nan thought it was the most exciting place she'd ever been in. It was so full of grand people, and the women were beautiful, dancing with attentive partners, their elegant gowns swaying like bells, or sitting in the side-boxes, fans a-flutter, absorbed in animated conversation. Many of them, so Sophie said, were members of the ton and yet they danced among the crowd for all the world like ordinary mortals. And Nan and Sophie danced with the best, for after their first turn upon the floor with their husbands, neither of them were short of partners, Sophie being much sought after because she was so pretty and Nan attracting attention because she was so lively and enjoying herself so much. By the end of the evening she had worn a hole in one of her dancing pumps, and earned invitations to three more Ranelagh evenings.

'You are launched upon zociety my dear,' Mr Fuseli said when they parted. And Sophie kissed her saying, 'I shall call upon you tomorrow.'

'London,' Nan told her husband when they'd finally said their prayers that night, 'is the best place in the whole world.'

'If you are in London, my love,' William Henry said, smiling at her bright face, 'then I must confess I am inclined to agree with you.'

It was a most entertaining summer. They went to suppers and to parties and to spectacular firework displays, and they took regular trips to Vauxhall and Ranelagh Gardens and the Theatre at Drury Lane, and Sophie Fuseli came to visit at least twice a week to tell Nan about the latest fashions or pass on the latest gossip.

And what gossip it was! The ton might look like gods and goddesses in their splendid clothes, but as Nan soon discovered their deity was undoubtedly of the Greek variety, for they all seemed to be having passionate love affairs and most were conducted quite openly as though they were proud of them. 'Look 'ee there!' Sophie would say. 'There goes Lord Alvanley in his carriage with his latest light o' love. And there's Lord Ponsonby, I do declare. That man, my dear Nan, is the greatest rake in London. Seduced three ladies in one evening, so they say, and I can well believe it for he's uncommon handsome. And there's

Miss Battersby a-riding with Lord Raffles, and a fine diamond in her hair, d'ye mark. 'Twill be his gift I warrant.'

'Do all the world take lovers?' Nan wondered. She and Sophie were walking in the sunshine in St James' park, watching the ton drive by.

'I daresay they do,' Sophie said lightly. 'Tis the fashion.'

'There was a time,' Nan confessed, 'when I was of the opinion that lovers were a deal of trouble.' Now she was beginning to wonder.

'Well as to that, my dear, it depends on how you take 'em,' Sophie said, and she chuckled, showing her neat white teeth.

'Do you take lovers, Sophie?' Nan asked, greatly daring.

Sophie looked at her for several seconds before replying. 'I will tell 'ee, my dear,' she said, 'if you give your solemn oath not to breath a word of it to Heinrich.'

The solemn oath was given, breathlessly.

'I have been an artists' model since I was twelve years old,' Sophie said. 'An agreeable occupation, if a trifle chilly. Sometimes, before I married Heinrich you understand, when the painter was attentive, one thing led to another, and then, if I had a mind to, I let 'em pleasure me.'

'Did they pleasure you?' How extraordinary to hear pleasure spoken of so lightly and easily.

'Indeed they did, or I would not have allowed it.'

What an admirable cast of mind, Nan thought, and her face showed her admiration.

'And you, my dear,' Sophie asked, giving her friend a sly look, 'have you never felt the power of passion?'

'Well . . .,' Nan hesitated, annoyed to feel a blush creeping into her cheeks.

'Never trembled with desire, nor thrilled to a kiss, nor gazed into his eyes and seen them burn with longing, nor yearned to be held in his dear, strong arms?'

'Well, no,' it had to be admitted. She could hardly imagine Mr Easter's eyes burning with longing. Even at those times. In fact, now she came to think of it, she realized that he always kept them closed at those times.

'Then you have missed a great deal, my dear, and I trust you will remedy it as soon as you may.'

'Take a lover, you mean?'

'Why not?'

It was a tempting idea. She'd danced with enough handsome partners by now to know how pleasant it was to be held in a young man's arms, and now and then when they quizzed her and paid her compliments and told her she was 'uncommon handsome' she had wondered with a vague but decidedly pleasurable longing how it would feel to be held and kissed by them. But as to whether there would really be no harm in it, as Sophie seemed to imply, she couldn't be sure. Finally, after pondering upon it for nearly fourteen whole days and nights, she decided to test out her husband's opinion upon the matter. If he thought it permissible, why then she might do as all the others did. When all was said and done, surely she had as much right to pleasure as anyone. If that awful Lord Raffles could be rewarded so, then why not Nan Easter?

She chose her moment carefully, waiting until one warm moonlit evening when she had allowed him her favours, which was at least a comfortable exercise now that she had learned how to position her body properly, but totally without sensation, of course, as always. As they lay side by side in their companionable way and his breath was beginning to purr towards sleep, she turned her head to look at him and venture her important question.

'They say Lord Ponsonby has took another lover,' she observed. 'What think 'ee of that, Mr Easter?'

'As little as I am able, my love,' he said, amiably.

'I don't know of a single person hereabouts what en't in love,' she said.

'No, indeed.'

'Is it wrong to take lovers, think 'ee?'

He pulled himself back from sleep, alerted by the intensity of her voice. ' 'Tis a mortal folly, my little one,' he said, 'for the pleasure of it is sure to be short while the pain may be life-long.'

'Oh no, Mr Easter, surely that en't so. The ton take new lovers every other week, an' I'm certain sure I seen no sign of pain in any on 'em.'

He put an arm under her shoulders to cuddle her, for that fierce face of hers was uncommon serious. 'They would not wish the world to see their pain,' he explained, 'even if they were kind enough to feel it, which I sometimes doubt. Howsomever, you need not bother your head about such things, my love, for you have a greater happiness than any they may aspire to.'

'Have I sir?' That was a surprise.

93

'Indeed you have. You are young and beautiful and faithful, a pearl among women in this naughty world. I'll wager there are many must envy your purity. And although I am a deal older than you are, my dear, you must know that I love you now and will love you till I die, "forsaking all other and cleaving only unto thee." That is a great good fortune, little Nan, and not to be thrown lightly away.'

It was true, she thought, lying quietly beside him. And she knew she couldn't take a lover, after all, but it was a disappointment, for she would have enjoyed being pleasured. Oh, indeed she would. Sighing, she turned upon her side and settled to sleep.

The sigh rebuked him, for that and her conversation confirmed his suspicion that his love-making meant little to her, and the knowledge saddened him and made him feel inadequate. This is all on account of that empty-headed Mrs Fuseli, he thought. Her talk is all folly. Would that she was elsewhere. And he wondered whether Mr Fuseli would be taking his usual autumn tour back to his native Switzerland. 'Twould be as well for all of us if that were the case, he thought. In the meantime I will pet my Nan. Their frequent entertainments were eating into his capital, but what of that? She was the dearest creature and deserved to be happy.

Chapter Eight

True to his established habit, and to Mr Easter's considerable relief, Mr Fuseli set off for the continent in the first week of October, exactly the same as usual, except that this time he took an excited Sophie with him.

'What an adventure 'twill be,' she said to Nan when the two of them were taking tea in Cheyne Row for the last time before her departure. 'I shall not see you again until the spring, my dear, which is the greatest sorrow, but think of it. We travel through France. Right through France. So without doubt we shall stay in Paris for at least a day or two! Paris, my dear! The very seat of fashion. I cannot wait to be there, I tell 'ee.'

Nan didn't doubt it. 'How I do envy you Sophie,' she said. ' 'Twill be uncommon dull without you.'

And so it was, for she had grown used to Sophie's lively company and although there was plenty of work to occupy her time and Mr Easter was particularly loving and attentive, she missed their tête-à-têtes, and Sophie's endless gossip.

'I shall buy you a news-sheet every day,' William Henry promised. 'They sell them upon the streets nowadays, I notice, and Mr Johnson tells me there is a new one out called *The Times* which is passably well printed. Mr Fuseli is well known in Switzerland, so there may be news of him from time to time, which you would like to read, I daresay.'

She thought him very kind and thanked him prettily. But there was no news of the Fuselis, only the most dismal accounts of bread riots and murders and gloomy prognostications that revolution was about to break out in Paris at any moment.

'I hope they don't go starting that ol' revolution when Sophie's there,' Nan said.

But Mr Easter said he thought it most unlikely. ' 'Tis my opinion,' he said comfortingly, 'that the French are too civilized to descend to revolution. Nothing will come of this, my dear, you may depend upon it.'

And as the weeks passed and nothing did, she was reassured. By November she had decided that as the news-sheets contained nothing but gloom and were barely worth reading she would turn her attention to the matter of new winter clothes, for William Henry needed new shirts and Mr Dibkins' coat was worn shiny and Mrs Dibkins could do with a nice thick skirt to keep her warm. But William Henry had developed a taste for the news, and now he bought *The Times* at regular intervals, to see how the world was wagging.

At the turn of the year he was much concerned over what he and the newspapers called 'a grave constitutional crisis'.

King George III had grown so mad as to be virtually certifiable and rumour had it that his son would soon be acclaimed Prince Regent. 'And then what will become of us I cannot imagine,' William Henry said, shaking his head sadly.

'King or Regent, what's the odds?' Nan said, sewing the last button onto his new flannel chemise. ' 'Tis all one to me.'

He explained patiently that the King supported the Tories and the Prince was surrounded by Whigs. A change such as this would mean that that terrible man Fox would become the Prime Minister instead of Mr William Pitt. 'And that is a change which can hardly be contemplated with equanimity.'

'Perhaps 'twill prove all talk like that ol' French revolution,' she said sagely, biting off the thread.

'Let us pray so,' he said.

'This chemise is ready to be fitted,' she told him, holding up the heavy garment for his inspection.

He took off his jacket, smiling at her. 'And an uncommon handsome chemise it is,' he praised.

Despite everything, the King recovered and the speculations *did* prove to be all talk and Mr Pitt remained in office. But the next item of news to catch William Henry's eye was a great deal more serious. He had bought a copy of *The Times* in an idle moment from a news-seller down by the Physic Garden without knowing it contained the terrible news that his brother Joseph was dead. He had taken a fall while out hunting and broken his neck. 'The title which he would otherwise have inherited will now pass to his eldest son, Osmond, who is presently at the University of Cambridge' the paper said.

It was quite a shock. 'Poor Joseph,' he moaned. 'And Father always bragged that he had such a good seat on a horse. Oh dear, oh dear! They will be sure to want me to attend the funeral, of course my dear. A chance for reconciliation perhaps. We must hope so.'

She didn't argue with him, although she had very grave doubts about whether the family would actually invite him to the ceremony. Which in the event proved accurate, for they went on ignoring him. But by then it was the end of February and she had a piece of news of her own that she knew would comfort him.

On the day the funeral was reported in *The Times* he was much cast down. ' 'Twould appear that my parents meant what they said at our last meeting,' he grieved. 'The rift between us is final, I fear. 'Tis hard indeed that I could not pay my last respects to my own brother. I confess we were never close, but he *was* my brother, in all conscience.'

'Never you fret yourself, my dear,' Nan said, patting his hand. 'For there is another member of your family you may pay your respects to whenever you wish. And one who will love you dearly, I dare swear.' And when he looked at her, wonderingly, 'A child of your own, my dear. How say you to that?'

He was enraptured by the news, and called her his own dear Nan, and his sweetest wife, and urged her to take the greatest care of herself and not to get overtired, and to be sure to tell him of the least little thing she wanted, for he would be sure to procure it for her. 'Oh, how I shall care for you, my dear,' he said, 'for now you are doubly precious to me. You shall be wrapped in cotton wool until the child is here, I do declare.'

'Fie upon you, Mr Easter,' she laughed at him. 'There en't no call for that, I can tell 'ee. I'm as fit as a flea and like to stay so.'

To his great delight, the baby grew daily and visibly and Nan remained splendidly well. By the time Sophie and Mr Fuseli returned to London in April the pregnancy was extremely obvious. Sophie said she was delighted by her friend's good news and came back the next day with an armful of flowers to congratulate her, and so much gossip it took the better part of three hours to recount it all.

'What a joy to see you so well,' she said. 'Some women droop so when they carry, but you fairly bloom, I assure you.'

And it was true. Pregnancy suited Nan Easter, and although she thought it undignified and ugly, waddling about with that great belly swollen out before her wherever she went, she kept her opinion to herself. Sometimes she woke in the morning yearning for the child to be born and for her own neat figure to be returned to her again. And sometimes she woke anxious at the thought that the child would soon be in the world and that she would have to care for it night and day even though she was sure she didn't have the faintest idea how to do it. And sometimes she woke with her head full of the most curious dreams, of visiting France, seeing the revolution, making a fortune, showing the Easters what was what.

But at last it was the middle of July and her time was up. She was relieved and surprised to find that giving birth felt so normal. It was hard work certainly, all that pushing and straining, but there was nothing frightening about it, and the baby was the prettiest little creature. A daughter, with pale blue eyes and her father's round bland face. Ann Easter, born on July 14th 1789, just six weeks after her mother's eighteenth birthday, on a day which the French were later to call 'the first day of the first year of liberty'.

But for Nan it was the first day of an unexpected enchantment.

Suckling the child was so pleasurable it made her want to purr like a cat. It was a sensual pleasure. There was no question of that, she knew it instinctively. But this time it was one she could share with her husband. To see the little creature rounding out day by day, learning to smile and coo and pat her bosom with its little fat hands was a continual and increasing joy to both of them.

'My daughter,' William Henry said with pride every time he saw them together, and when the news arrived that his daughter had been born on the very day that the long expected revolution had begun in France, he took it as a well deserved compliment.

'On the very day,' he said, pink in the face with excitement. 'I heard the news at Mr Johnson's. Mr Wotherspoon is just returned. He says the people of Paris have taken over the city. Imagine that! It appears they stormed the most terrible fortress, a dungeon called the Bastille. Muskets against cannon. What courage! And released the prisoners, who were all good men and wrongfully imprisoned, so Mr Wotherspoon assured me. And now they have declared a Republic in the great names of liberty, equality and fraternity. 'Tis a triumph. I never thought they would do such a thing, but they have, and all on the very day our dear Annie was born.'

'Well o' course' she said, easing her nipple from the baby's sleeping mouth. 'A special day for a special baby. What d'you expect?'

The special baby grew into a placid toddler, who sat in her own high chair at the dining-room table with her parents and babbled at them as they ate their meals, and was fed the choicest tit-bits by her doting father and allowed to cling to his cravat even with greasy fingers, because she was the 'prettiest baby alive'.

And when she was fifteen months old and heading towards the second Christmas of her life, her mother was happy to announce that she was expecting again. 'This time, Mr Easter, you shall have a son,' she promised.

And although William Henry protested that he would be perfectly happy with a family of girls if they were all as pretty as his dear little Annie, a boy it duly was. A fine fat boy, with the same blue eyes and pretty round face as his sister, born on March 28th. They christened him William Edward and called him Billy.

He was a happy little baby with a prodigious appetitie, and for the first nine months of his life he grew and thrived like his sister before him. Now William Henry had two babies to pet and play with and soon there were two high-chairs at the dining-room table and two eager red mouths to be tempted with tit-bits.

But when Annie was two and a half and little Billy a mere ten months, Nan grew suddenly and alarmingly ill. For three days she felt so sick she couldn't eat, and on the fourth day when she tried a little light arrowroot, she brought it all up again immediately, heaving and retching for such a long time that she felt quite weak afterwards.

William Henry was terribly alarmed. 'Should we send for a surgeon?' he asked, as Nan lay panting on the bed when the fit had passed.

Mrs Dibkins was sponging her mistress' forehead. 'A midwife, more like, sir,' she said, 'if you'll fergive me fer taking the liberty a' saying.'

'Oh!' Nan groaned. 'I can't be pregnant. I feel so ill.'

But pregnant she was, and this time it didn't please her. 'Am I to be sick like this all through?' she asked the midwife.

'No, no, Mrs Easter,' the midwife assured her. ' 'Twill pass by the third month, or the fourth at the most.'

But Nan was still being sick in March, when Billy was a year old and the new baby six months on its way.

'I can't abide much more of this,' she said to William Henry, after a particularly miserable day. 'There's never any end to it.'

Mr Dibkins had been hovering outside the bedroom door until she'd finished being sick. Now he came clomping into the bedroom. 'You jest let me take that ol' chamber, Mrs William dear, now you've a-finished with it,' he said tenderly. 'You'll feel a deal better with that out of the way.' And he covered it quickly with a thick napkin to deaden the smell.

'Thank 'ee kindly, Mr Dibkins,' Nan said wearily, and feeling she ought to apologize, 'I'm uncommon sorry to be such a nuisance.'

'You ain't a nuisance, Mrs William dear,' the old man said warmly and at once. 'Ho no! I won't 'ave that. 'Tis only nature when all's said an' done. Don't you go fretting your head.' He stopped at the door to look back at her with misshapen sympathy and she smiled at him, thinking how kind he was and what a lot of dreadful work she was making for him with all those awful chamberpots day after day. 'We'll 'ave 'er quite chirpy by an' by, won't us, Mr William?'

William Henry tried to comfort too. 'Think what a joy this child will be, when it arrives, my dear,' he said.

But she felt too sick to respond. 'I don't know how I'm to manage,' she said wearily. The difficulties this pregnancy brought seemed insurmountable to her. 'Annie's nearly two and a half and she still don't know how to use a chamberpot and Billy cries all the time. I'm sure my milk don't satisfy un.'

'Perhaps you should wean him.'

But she wouldn't hear of it. 'I fed young Annie fifteen months and Billy should have the same.'

'The sickness will pass,' he tried to assure her. 'When your strength returns, my dearest, you will feel quite differently.'

'It en't just a matter of strength,' she told him sadly. ''Tis a matter of time. I spend so much of the day puking, there en't the time for anything. If you want your clothes clean and mended, and your meals cooked, and the babies fed and sweet-smelling on top of all, I shall need forty-eight hours to the day, or a fresh pair of hands, and that's all there is to it.'

'Rest now,' he told her kissing her damp hair. 'There is no more needs to be done tonight.'

100

'Unless Billy wakes to be fed,' she said. But for once and mercifully he didn't.

I must get some help for her, William Henry thought, as he watched her sleeping later that evening. He could ill afford it, but there was still some capital that could be used.

William Henry was late back from the City the next afternoon and when he came tip-toeing into the bedroom where Nan was lying on the bed recovering from her latest bout of sickness, a small skinny girl crept quietly into the room behind him.

She looked about ten or eleven years old but it was difficult to tell because she was so scruffy. She had thin, pale brown hair under her thick, dark brown cap and her face was gaunt, with dark shadows under her eyes, a sharp peaked nose and dirt on her chin. She was wearing an ill-fitting dress of brown holland and an apron made of sacking. Her stockings were black and much darned and her boots broken down. Charity school or workhouse, Nan thought, assessing her, half-fed and ignorant, if I'm any judge. And certainly the child's skin had the dirty translucence of the very poor, and she stood subserviently, twisting the corner of that rough apron in very chapped hands.

'This is Bessie Taylor, my dear,' William Henry said, pushing her forward towards the bed. 'I have hired her to be nursemaid to our two babies and to help you in every way she can. She has promised me that she will do her very best endeavour, have you not Bessie?'

'Sir,' the child mumbled, looking at the carpet.

'She is to stay for ten days and then we will decide whether we wish to keep her or not.'

A girl to help me, Nan thought, shifting her body to get a good look at the child, but carefully so as not to provoke the sickness again. Why she's even smaller than I was at her age. They've kept her half-starved wherever she's been. She'll need some feeding up. Still, she could be stronger than she looks. 'Come here,' she ordered, and the girl walked meekly to the bed. 'How old are you?'

'Twelve, ma'am.'

'Where d'you come from?'

'The work'us, ma'am.' Twisting the corner of her apron.

'Which one?'

'Mr Coram's, ma'am,' looking up at her new mistress for the first

101

time with rather pretty blue eyes. A trusting face, Nan thought, for all its half-starved anxiety.

'She was a foundling,' William Henry said. 'Were you not, Bessie?'

'Yes sir.'

Nan sighed. A foundling didn't sound at all promising. 'So I don't suppose you know nothin' about lookin' after babies, do you?'

'Oh yes, ma'am. I looks after the littl'uns, most the time, ma'am.'

Nan looked at the child's anxious face and the bony arms sticking awkwardly out of that faded bodice. 'Well,' she sighed, 'we shall see, shan't we.'

Bessie Taylor's arrival in the Easter household was a blessing. Despite her reticence and her fragile appearance, she was actually as tough as a London sparrow and she knew a great deal about the way to handle and placate small babies. Within a day she had persuaded Nan to let her give baby William a titty-bottle, 'jest ter top 'im up like, an' get 'im ter sleep,' which worked like a charm, to everybody's relief, and within a week she had started to persuade Annie to do 'ca-ca's' in a chamber-pot instead of soiling her clout.

'You don't want all that nasty ol' cacky all over your bum, do yer pet,' she said, when she was dressing the little girl on her first morning. 'Not when you can be the cleverest gel alive.'

The child was enraptured by such attention and praise, and was soon following her new friend about the house, baby's pot in hand, declaiming that she was 'c'ever gel' and smiling like sunshine.

Even when she 'forgot', the new comer was kind to her. 'Ne'er mind,' she said. 'We all 'as our little mishaps now an' then, don' us. We won't tell no one, eh? That'll be our secret. Jest stand yerself still while I cleans yer bum down.'

Long before her ten days' probation were up, she was Ba-ba to little Annie, and 'that dear gel' to Mrs Dibkins, and an established member of the family. Whenever she wasn't looking after the two babies or washing their dirty clouts or fetching and carrying for her poor sick mistress, she was industriously sewing, sitting beside her truckle bed in the nursery washroom, long after everyone else was asleep, with the work held close to the candle. For Mrs Dibkins had been sent down to the haberdasher's on the very first morning to buy a length of pink cotton for dresses and heavy white linen for caps and aprons and even a quantity of cheap lawn for chemises and petticoats, and she couldn't

102

wait to get her new clothes sewn up and ready to wear. It took her more than a week, even with Mrs Dibkins to help her whenever she could, but the results were very pleasing. The master said so, when he passed her on the stairs on the eighth morning. 'Uncommon neat and serviceable. Quite so.'

But when ten days' probation were up, she was cast into a gloom. Her arms felt like lead and her back ached and her mouth seemed determined to fold itself down and cry. 'They won't keep me on,' she said to Mrs Dibkins when they sat down to their dinner after the Easters had dined. 'They'll send me back ter the work'us. I can feel it in me bones.'

'You eat hearty, gel,' Mr Dibkins advised, picking his teeth with the prong of his fork. 'The world looks a deal better on a full stomach.'

'Oh, lor,' Bessie said, lifting a portion of mashed potato into her mouth to show that she was obeying him, 'whatcher think they're sayin' up there?'

Up in the double dining-room Mr and Mrs Easter had already made up their minds.

'I wouldn't be without her now,' Nan said. 'Annie's like a new child. Well you've only to look at her to see that. And baby's settled down. Think how much he cried afore she came. And I do declare my sickness is better too. If you send her back you'll have me to reckon with.'

'Which is not an eventuality I could face with equilibrium, my love,' her husband said, smiling at her, 'so I suppose she must stay.' He took out his hunter and examined it closely. 'They should have finished their meal by now. Would you be so kind as to ring the bell?'

So the bell was rung and presently all three servants were standing before them, Bessie pale with anxiety and both Dibkins nodding and grimacing.

'The matter we have to decide between us,' William Henry told them, 'is whether Bessie is to become a permanent member of this household. How say you, Mr Dibkins?'

Mr Dibkins stamped his wash-dolly firmly onto the carpet and said he'd be jiggered if he could see any harm in it, savin' your reverence, Mr William, sir.

But when Mrs Dibkins was asked the same question, she seemed to have been struck with a kind of gibbering paralysis. She rolled her eyes and puckered her forehead and twisted her mouth and cheeks until her face looked more like a piece of newly wrung washing than flesh, but words were beyond her.

However, William Henry waited, smiling calmly, and after a final supreme struggle Mrs Dibkins gave her assent. 'She's a good gel, sir,' she croaked.

'That, Mrs Dibkins, is entirely our opinion,' her master said. 'My thanks to you both for your assistance. Bessie shall stay with us. And now my wife and I will take a little dish of tea, I think. Would you bring up the kettle for us, Bessie, now that you are part of the family?'

'Why did you ask their opinion?' Nan asked, when the kettle had been brought and all three servants had retired to the kitchen to scour the dirty dishes. The solemnity of the little ceremony had intrigued her.

'It is necessary for servants to know that they are important to the family they serve,' he said solemnly, watching as she unlocked the tea-caddy and measured out the tea, 'that their wishes are considered, even if they may not be paramount.'

'How of a wife?' she asked, feeling well enough to tease him. 'Are a wife's wishes to be considered?'

'Indeed yes,' he said, taking his cup. 'You have only to tell me what you want, my dear, and you shall have it.'

But what she wanted was not to be pregnant, and even Mr Easter, with all his love for her, couldn't grant her that.

Chapter Nine

Despite Bessie Taylor's help, the Dibkins' devoted nursing and William Henry's most tender concern, Nan's third pregnancy continued to be excessively uncomfortable. From very early on, the child had kicked with uncommon strength, banging its head against her bladder, pounding its feet against her ribs, wriggling and heaving almost as though it sensed how unwelcome its presence was and was struggling to get out. As the spring dragged on, it grew more and more tightly packed inside her ugly belly, but that only increased its endeavours. By May, its incessant squirming had irritated her beyond appetite and was preventing her from more than an hour's sleep at a time.

'I tell you, Bessie,' she said, when her little maid brought up her chocolate after one particularly sleepless night, 'even if I hadn't a' made my mind up to it already, this would most certainly be my last baby, if I knew how to bring such a thing about. I'm sick of it already and it en't even born.'

'Be better when it's 'ere mum,' Bessie said, trying to comfort. 'Be a lovely little baby when it's 'ere.'

But Nan had her doubts. Which in the event proved justified.

The child, a long skinny boy, was born at midnight on the first of July 1792 after a labour that lasted thirty-six hours and left his mother totally exhausted. Afterwards, she lay among the pillows, yellow with fatigue, while Bessie wrapped the awkward limbs of her new charge in soft linen and sponged the matted blood from his shock of black hair and crooned commiserations to his shrieks. ' 'E got a good strong pair a' lungs, ain'cher my pet,' she said. She didn't seem to notice what an ugly baby he was.

'Give un to me,' Nan said wearily. 'He'd best be fed or he'll waken the house.' But she didn't feel any emotion for him and she hadn't the slightest urge to feed him. It was as if her capacity for love had been drained with her energy. She begrudged him her milk as she begrudged him the agony and effort of his birth, her flesh recoiling from him, so that he fought her nipple and glared at her balefully even as he sucked.

If she hadn't been so exhausted she would have been upset by her lack of feeling for this child. She loved his brother and sister so dearly. They were so pretty and so affectionate, and so recognizably her children, with their fair hair and their little round faces and their snub noses and their babbling ways. But this child was foreign to her, like a gipsy, or a changeling. He had brown skin and little screwed-up eyes and a positive beak of a nose and a tangled mess of thick black hair that grew low on his forehead and extended into sideburns down his cheeks, like a grown man. A fuzz of it even grew down his back and along his arms. ' 'Tis the ugliest baby I ever did see, poor little mite,' she said. 'He look like a monkey, so he do.'

Bessie was shocked. 'Oh, don't say that, mum,' she begged. 'Poor little thing. Not when 'e's your own dear baba. 'E'll grow 'andsome, you'll see, when 'e's rounded out.'

But he didn't. Although the gypsy darkness of his skin lightened after a week or so, and the worst of his hair could be hidden under a cap, he remained scraggy and long-legged well into his second month, watching with the solemn face of a miniature adult while his brother and sister played piggy-back rides with their father and laughed and babbled beside him.

It worried William Henry that the baby didn't smile. ' 'Tis an odd child in all conscience, my dear,' he said. 'What does he enjoy, poor little man?'

She couldn't think of anything. He slept fitfully and woke screaming, and he fought at her breast every time he fed, stopping every few minutes to grizzle and protest, as if he liked her as little as she liked him. ' 'Tis an ill-humoured baby, I fear,' she said. She was gaunt with fatigue, and try as she might she still couldn't feel any emotion for the child. 'We must wait for him to grow out of it, I suppose. What else is there to do?'

'My poor John Henry,' his father said, patting the baby's bonnet, and full of aching pity.

But John Henry opened the black cavern of his mouth and screamed again, shrill piercing cries that Nan disliked more than anything else about him, for he screamed at her no matter what she tried to do to placate him, and the screams made her feel inadequate and guilty and,

106

it had to be admitted, more than a little afraid of him. 'Take him away, Bessie,' she begged, 'for pity's sake. I thought I should be better once he was born, but I declare it makes me worse just to look at him.'

The summer progressed and baby Billy learned to stand erect and stagger about from chair to chair, and three-year-old Annie took charge of him, because Bessie said Mama was a-weary and she was to be a good little duck and help all she could. When she wasn't acting as a nursemaid the child spent the rest of her day chattering to anybody who would listen, and during the long, hot days of July, William Henry taught her the alphabet. She learned quickly and easily, and he was inordinately proud of her. But little John Henry continued fractious, and the more he screamed, the more melancholy and lethargic Nan became, as if his excess of energy was draining hers away.

William Henry did everything he could to restore her, buying fruits and sweetmeats to tempt her appetite and escorting her to as many entertainments as he could afford, but all to no avail. After a single dance at the Rotunda she was too fatigued to stir from her chair, and even a spectacular firework display only served to weary her.

'We are invited to supper at Mr Johnson's,' he tried. 'A little lively company my dear, and who knows how you may feel.'

Unfortunately on the very morning of the supper party the London papers were loud with the news that the Paris mob had stormed the King's palace and butchered his Swiss guard, and that the entire royal family was now imprisoned in a place called the Temple.

' 'Tis exceedingly grave, my dear,' William Henry told Nan over breakfast. 'If the French people go so far as to kill their King, then there will be war between our two nations, I fear.'

But she had very little interest in the French or their affairs. 'If only baby wouldn't scream so,' she said, 'I do believe I could take to un.' It grieved her that she still had so little feeling for this child. And her sigh grieved him.

'What a blessing it is that we dine at Mr Johnson's tonight, my love,' he said. He always found his old friend's company so invigorating. It would be bound to cheer her.

It did nothing of the sort. It was very dull company indeed. Sophie wasn't there, Mrs Wotherspoon was asleep, and the only other lady at table was a scruffy looking creature called Mary Wollstonecraft, who was a writer and talked politics as loudly as any of the men in a rough dominant voice. Nan didn't take to her at all and couldn't understand half she said, for the talk was all of France and what the revolutionaries would or would not do. For although King Louis had been making speeches promising to support the Revolution ever since his nobles took fright and fled, it was now horribly plain that the French people did not trust him at all. Which Mr Johnson declared was hardly to be wondered at, since the gentleman was as wily as all the Bourbons and had long been secretly conniving at the overthrow of the revolution. The gentlemen around the supper table that evening were passionately interested in the constitutional problem this situation posed, and they spent hours happily discussing it. But Nan was profoundly and miserably bored.

By the time September began and baby John was three months old, she had sunk into such a gloom she barely stirred from the house. William Henry grew more and more alarmed by her lethargy, for she wouldn't allow him to send for a doctor and the change in her was becoming so noticeable he was fearful of some terrible disease. Finally he left Dibkins with a note for Sophie Fuseli when she next came to tea, urging her to do all she could to help her friend.

'Pray my dear,' he wrote, 'do see if you could prevail upon her at least to walk in the air. I do not mean to alarm you, howsomever I am most seriously concerned for her health, for I fear she may fall into a decline if she does not improve soon. Perhaps you could persuade her to take an expedition to Mr Rogers' in the Strand, where she may care to choose a shawl, or to Reeves Hosiery Warehouse. I leave it entirely to your discretion. Should you have any thoughts you might wish to communicate with me upon this matter, perhaps you would be so kind as to take coffee with me at Mr Galloway's coffee house, in the Strand, on Thursday morning.'

Sophie was rather surprised to receive such a request for she'd been visiting Nan nearly every week since the baby had been born, and although she was often listless, she did not think her melancholy, for she listened to the gossip and took tea and made no sad comment. Nevertheless she decided to do as he asked.

It was a balmy afternoon, the sky as blue as porcelain, only a handful of flies buzzing above the midden, and the fields beyond the garden bubbling with skylarks. 'Just the weather for an excursion,' she said.

'A promenade, will refresh us both. 'Tis is no weather to be pining indoors. I will tell you all the news as we go.'

' 'Tis all one to me,' Nan sighed, but she put on her bonnet, left baby Johnnie in Bessie's care, and allowed her friend to lead her from the house.

At Sophie's suggestion, they took a river boat to the City, past the Physic Gardens where the scented herbs were blooming in such sun-soaked profusion that the air was fragrant right down to the water's edge, and past the nursery gardens and apple orchards of Lambeth, where the fruit was red on the trees, and under Westminster Bridge where a group of city gentlemen were taking an argumentative stroll, and so on to the Arundel stairs. But Nan didn't seem to notice any of it, which was a bad sign. Perhaps Mr Easter was right.

As they docked at the Arundel Stairs, Sophie decided to open their conversation by a little gentle criticism of Mary Wollstonecraft since that lady was fair game among all the other female visitors to Mr John-son's. 'I cannot take her seriously, my dear,' she said. 'She might be a very clever woman, that I grant you, writing books the way she does and working on the review for Mr Johnson, but her stockings are so invariably wrinkled and I swear she hasn't taken a brush to that hair for weeks.'

But Nan wasn't interested. ' 'Tis an odd woman,' she said dully, and her tone didn't encourage Sophie to continue.

'I have read her book,' Sophie said trying hard. 'She has the poorest opinion of men, my dear. According to her, marriage is nothing but bondage and we would all do well to avoid it.'

'Indeed.'

'It seems to me,' Sophie said trying again, 'that she don't want to be attractive, like all the rest of womankind. She goes out of her way to be a frump. 'Tain't natural.' Surely Nan would rise to that.

But she didn't. In fact she had so little to say, that finally, when the two women had disembarked and were strolling up Arundel Street towards the Strand, Sophie decided that Mr Easter had cause for his concern, and that the time had come for a direct question.

'You have been melancholy too long, my dear,' she said. 'Pray tell me what ails you.'

'I do not know myself,' Nan confessed, walking slowly and sadly beside her. 'Would that I did.'

109

'Then tell me what it is that gives you the most pain to think upon,' Sophie suggested.

And the suggestion released a rather surprising confession. 'My life en't nothing but babies,' Nan mourned. 'Three in four years. Nothing but babies. And I tell you, Sophie, I can't stand no more on 'em. I'm fair wore out.'

'But Annie and Billy are such little ducks,' Sophie said. 'I thought you loved 'em to distraction.'

'Aye, so I do,' Nan said, but she looked more anxious than loving. ' 'Tis the other. A changeling, Sophie, I swear it. I cannot love un for the life of me.'

'You need a trip abroad to lift your spirits, that's how it is,' Sophie said taking her arm. 'Heinrich and I travel to Switzerland within the month and I declare I feel full of enthusiasm merely to contemplate it. You should visit Paris, my dear. I warrant your melancholy would be cured there, aye and in a trice too. You may depend on't.'

But Nan signed. 'Mr Easter wouldn't hear of it. We never travel abroad.'

'You may leave Mr Easter to me, my dear,' Sophie said. 'He has asked for my advice d'you see. We meet at Galloway's a' Thursday. And if that ain't more opportune, I should like to know what is. Should you like to see Paris, think 'ee?'

A trip to Paris would be uncommon pleasant, there was no denying it. 'Could it really be arranged?'

'With ease, my dear, I promise you.'

Even the idea of it was lifting Nan's spirits. 'Then I do believe I should,' she said.

' 'Tis done,' Sophie promised, smiling at her. 'Now as to this matter of babies. Babies can be prevented.'

Now this was the most extraordinary idea. A dream. Oh, if only she could be sure that she would never have another baby like Johnnie. What a relief that would be! 'Prevented? How?'

'By vinegar and sponge, my dear. You must read Mr Price's admirable pamphlet. There is no need nowadays for any woman to breed against her wishes. These are modern times.'

What miraculous news! It warmed Nan simply to hear it. 'If that's the case,' she said, 'then tell me what I must do.'

Which as they walked into the bustle of the Strand, arm in arm in their soft cotton gowns, with their embroidered kerchiefs draped artlessly about their fine white necks and their embroidered caps arranged artlessly above their fine thick curls, looking the very picture of genteel womanhood, Sophie Fuseli did.

'I shall buy a sponge this very afternoon,' Nan vowed, quite cheerfully. 'Where is the nearest apothecary?'

She bought her prophylactic sponge in St Martin's Lane, and that night she persuaded her embarrassed spouse that although it might look rather odd dangling from her waist on its long string, once it was in position he wouldn't know it was there. ''Twont do you no harm,' she said, 'and 'twill do me a power of good. You don't want scores of babies, now do you? Not when you got three good uns.'

By now, William Henry was beginning to wonder whether he had been wise to confide in such a sophisticated lady as Sophie Fuseli, but he gave in to his wife over this delicate matter because her melancholy did seem to be lifting at last and he would have been loathe to do anything to cast her down again. But he went to his meeting at Mr Galloway's in some trepidation.

And was agreeably surprised by Mrs Fuseli's good sense.

A change of scenery was the standard and obvious remedy for melancholy. Had I not been timid by my very nature, he rebuked himself wryly, I should have thought of it long before now. 'Where would you suggest that we travel?' he asked Mrs Fuseli.

'Why, to Paris, sir,' was her immediate answer. 'Where else?'

Paris sounded rather alarming given the volatile state of the French mob these days, but he thanked Mrs Fuseli kindly and said he would certainly consider it.

That night after sponge and vinegar had been put to the test for the very first time and he had found to his considerable relief that it was not as off-putting as he'd feared it would be, he broached the subject of a possible holiday abroad. Tentatively, of course, in case she did not approve.

'Mrs Fuseli is of the opinion, my love, that a trip to the continent is an uncommon good restorative.'

'That I can believe, sir,' she said, smiling to encourage him, for he was being very cautious about it.

'Would you care to travel abroad, little one?'

'Oh, indeed I would.'

'To Italy perhaps? Or France?'

'I should love to go to France. We could visit Paris. 'Tis the seat of fashion, so they do say, and a fair city.'

It occurred to him, watching her bright face, and glad to see her eager and excited again, that he had been much the same age as she was when he'd first seen the city of Paris, a stripling, just come of age, and now he was fifty-one and settled in his ways. I'm a pretty dull sort of fellow for a wife so young and passionate, he thought, I must grant her this, hazardous though it will most certainly be. But he was cautious to the last. 'The baby would have to be weaned,' he warned, 'for we could not take him with us.' He was remembering how adamant she'd been that Billy should be fed for fifteen months like his sister.

But she waved that difficulty aside. 'He shall have his first titty-bottle tomorrow, I promise.' Weaning young Johnnie would be no hardship, no hardship at all. After all, it wasn't as if he enjoyed her milk.

' 'Twould mean a sea crossing,' William Henry warned again. 'And in the winter time, too, we must not forget.'

A sea crossing! Even the words were so exciting they lifted her spirits. She could see herself sailing away like an explorer, in a dark cockleshell boat, further and further into the challenge of the sea, leaving all the petty miseries of home behind her. No yowling babies, no dirty clouts, just her and the wild sea and a foreign country where established order had been stood on its head and the nobility sent packing and the king himself arrested and imprisoned. 'I would love it,' she said, turning to look straight at him. ' 'Twould be an adventure!' And her face was fierce with the excitement of it.

'Then the matter is settled,' he decided. 'As soon as the baby is weaned and all arrangements made, we will travel to France. We could only stay for a week or so, you understand, for I have much business to attend to.'

'Oh, Mr Easter!' she said. 'Do you mean it? Do you really mean it?'

'Aye, little one. I do.' It would probably turn out to be a very grave mistake, but how could he deny her?

She flung her arms about his neck and rewarded him with rapturous kisses. 'That'll be the experience of a lifetime,' she promised.

He found her excitement quite touching. 'Now,' he said, smiling at her, 'we must build up your strength. I shall feel anxious on your account, my dear, until you are quite restored to your customary health and vigour. By Christmas you will be quite yourself again, I'm sure.'

So Johnnie was weaned and took to a titty-bottle full of Bessie's

112

special pap with remarkably good humour. And although it was a long and gradual process, by the middle of November, Nan was free of him and Bessie had pronounced him quite ready to be left.

And then, just as all their preparations had finally been made, news came from France that tossed poor William Henry into frantic indecision. King Louis XVI had tried to run away and had been recaptured at Varennes and brought back to Paris again under armed guard. And two weeks later, at the beginning of December, London learned that he had been arraigned to stand trial for his life before the Convention of the National Assembly.

The news caused an outcry in England, and Mr Johnson's supper table was loud with opinion about it. Some said that a king, being inviolable and sacred, could not be tried at all, others claimed that his attempted escape had constituted an abdication and so left him liable to the law, while others maintained that they heard there was evidence from papers found hidden in an iron chest that he was actually plotting the overthrow of the revolution and had spent more than thirty thousand francs to that end.

' 'Twill be the most important trial since 1649,' Mr Wotherspoon said with satisfaction. 'Would I could be there to see it. You travel to France in a week or two, do you not, Mr Easter? I must say I envy you.'

'I had intended so to do,' William Henry admitted. 'Howsomever, I do wonder whether it would be entirely wise, given the present situation.'

' 'Twould be as wise now as at any time since the revolution,' Mr Johnson said. 'At least this matter is being tried by law, which is a deal less bloodthirsty than war or revolution, you will allow.'

'A deal more civilized, certainly,' William Henry comforted himself. ' 'Tis true! 'Tis very true! But how if they decide on execution?'

'My dear friend!' Mr Johnson said. 'We should not impugn the French with such folly. They are a civilized race. They will choose exile, which is bad enough in all conscience, but the obvious alternative in the circumstances, since the mob must be placated.'

'Justice is adept at finding the least harmful solution,' Mr Wotherspoon put in happily, 'at least in the more serious cases with which it has to deal.' He spoke as though Justice were a personal friend and the expression on his face showed how confidently he expected a merciful outcome.

Sitting in the mellow shadows of Mr Johnson's green supper room,

William Henry allowed his fears to recede. The French would choose exile. Of course they would. He was sure of it.

And that was Nan's opinion too, when he asked her rather tentatively whether she would like him to postpone their trip for a month or two.

'Why no, sir,' she said. 'That ol' trial'll be an added spice, you'll see. Why we could get tickets and go and watch un. Think of that! 'Twill be more than Sophie Fuseli could do, for she's in Switzerland. I've a-trimmed my bonnet, do come and see un. Will it be grand enough for Paris think 'ee?' She was quite her old determined self again, leading him up the stairs to their bedroom, her face bright.

So despite his misgivings, their preparations continued, for he hadn't the heart to disappoint her now. Four weeks later they set off for Dover and the packet boat to France.

Chapter Ten

In France at last! It was almost too good to be true. Yet here they were. It had been an excitement to Nan just to see that brown coast growing on the horizon as the packet boat creaked towards Calais, and now, as she came tripping down the gang-plank behind her whey-faced husband, she was chirruping with pleasure.

Everything was new and different here, just as she'd known it would be, brown fields instead of green, louvred shutters across the windows, curved tiles on the roofs, quaintly dressed people speaking a foreign language. Why even the air smelt foreign, of spices and garlic and very strong onions, as well as the usual medley of horses and sweat and dirty clothes.

'En't you glad we come, Mr Easter?' she said.

But William Henry said he needed rest and a warm bed.

It was the first disappointment to her that they didn't get either. The hotel was a terrible place. They ate their supper in a room that was little more than a barn, with an earth floor and a blackened ceiling and draughts howling in through the cracks in every shutter, while the people round them shouted at one another in their nasal language and paid no attention to them at all. And although their bed was impressively tall and heavily curtained, the mattress was made of straw and they soon found they were sharing it with a colony of bugs. They woke bitten and exhausted to discover that there was only grey bread and coffee for breakfast.

William Henry was so cast down he could barely speak. To start the day without hot chocolate was insupportable. Indeed it was!

'Only one more journey,' Nan said, determined to be cheerful as they set off to meet the diligence that would take them to Paris. 'One more journey and then we shall be there. Think of that! They're bound to serve hot chocolate in Paris. Paris'll be different altogether.'

' 'Tis a mortal long journey!' he sighed.

'What's the French for brandy?' she asked, practical as ever.

She was making a very great effort to enjoy this holiday and to be as cheerful as she could, for he'd gone to a deal of trouble to arrange it for her, the dear man, and besides it took her mind away from the aching void she felt now that she was away from her children. She missed them all so much, even little Johnnie, which was rather a surprise. But it wouldn't have done to have said so. That would have looked like ingratitude.

The coach was a second disappointment to them. It was as uncomfortable as the hotel had been and ridiculously crowded. There were seven people seated inside where she would have expected four in England, and a rough, smelly lot they were too. The man on her left smelt of pigs and was far too fond of spitting, while the woman opposite, who had a wall-eye and a vacant expression spent the entire journey chewing lumps from a most repellent blood-coloured sausage. But she kept her opinions to herself, for it wouldn't do to let her husband know she didn't approve.

It was nightfall before the sausage was consumed and they had reached the outskirts of the city. And Paris was the biggest disappointment of all.

This time there was no distant sunlit view to whet her appetite and charm her senses. One minute they were driving past damp fields smelling of manure, and the next they were inside the city which was dark and oppressive and smelt like a cess-pit. It had begun to rain, a close-packed spitting precipitation that filled the air and obscured their vision. It was true the road they followed was lit after a fashion, but not in the way London was illuminated, with triple lamps set at regular intervals along the full length of a street. Here light was provided by a haphazard collection of ancient oil lamps and open torches, arranged without order or direction so that travellers passed from relative clarity to pools of ominous darkness. Cracked wagons and mud-smeared carriages racketted beside them and everywhere they looked dark foreign faces shouted and swore and scowled like gargoyles in the intermittent light.

'They're an ugly-looking lot,' she said cheerfully to Mr Easter.

Her outspokenness alarmed him. 'We would be better not to comment upon it,' he said, glancing fearfully at the other occupants of the coach.

'Them!' his wife said unabashed. 'I warrant they speak no more English than I do French. We may speak as we please in such company.'

'My dear!' he said, much alarmed by her temerity. 'There is a dangerous spirit abroad. I do not think we should provoke it.'

'They en't understood a word,' Nan said, flashing a bold smile at the sausage eater to prove her point, and being answered immediately by an affably toothless grin. 'See?'

'Who knows who may understand whom in these streets,' William Henry said, anxiously. 'There is an atmosphere to this place which I do not like at all. Oh, not at all. Do you not feel it?' He shuddered. 'Oh 'tis all as I feared 'twould be, my dear. Would we were not here.'

' 'Tis on account of it bein' night-time,' she said, determined not to allow him the chance to regret their journey. 'All the villains come out night-time. That's what 'tis. Be different by day, you'll see. We shall see all the heroes of the revolution by day.'

But next day when they set out to view the city, and buy presents for the children, and perhaps to see the King's trial, heroes were in very short supply, although the streets were crowded with citizens all dressed with self-conscious cockiness in the new, bold uniform of the Parisian proletariat, the men in long straight trousers, like the kind worn by watermen, only striped red and white or blue and white, the women in striped skirts and coloured aprons and neat plain bodices that showed no sign of stays being worn underneath, and both sexes sporting bright red triangular caps and red, white and blue cockades.

Nan stood on the hotel steps to watch their passing and thought they looked admirable. 'That's the new freedom,' she said with approval. 'I never did think much to those ol' stiff petticoats, nor breeches neither. This is a deal better, don't 'ee think?' And she made up her mind to discard her stays the very next morning. What a joy 'twould be never to be pinched by that hard ol' leather ever again!

The hotel was in a road called the Rue St Honoré, which since it ran from the eastern wharfs north-west across the city, was crowded with goods-carts and heavy wagons. But there were no carriages and no sign of any vehicle for hire, and the concierge, who sat in the entrance hall of the hotel knitting stockings at a dizzying speed, told them brusquely that if they wanted to get anywhere they would have to walk. Nan didn't think that was a hardship, even though the cobbles were so huge and rough it hurt her feet merely to stand upon them, but William Henry was put out, given the fragile state of his early morning constitution.

'Perhaps we would be better advised to wait until the traffic has cleared a little,' he tried.

But she was determined. 'I en't come all this way to sit indoors and wait,' she said, brown eyes fierce. 'I mean for to see the city and the trial. Ask her where 'tis.'

It appeared that it was being held in the Hall of the National Convention in the Tuileries, and that the public galleries were always crowded and that the concierge held out very little hope of her two foreign guests being able to obtain a seat. 'Tout le monde a envie d'être là,' she said, needles flashing. 'Mais citoyens, si vous achêtez une cocarde, peut être . . .'

There was a box full of red, white and blue cockades lying on the bench beside her. William Henry translated as well as he could, fumbling in his fob pocket for coins. 'She says it is very unlikely that we will manage a place at this trial, my dear. Howsomever, it seems we stand more chance of success if we wear a cockade. Deux, s'il vous plaît, madame.'

'*I'll* get us a seat. Just you watch!' Nan promised, pinning her cockade onto the side of her bonnet. 'Come you on, Mr Easter, you follow me.'

Which he did with exhausted meekness, as she pushed a way for them through the hubbub, past narrow alleys crowded with people and dogs and unkempt donkeys, and pungent with night soil that hadn't been collected for weeks, past tenements so ancient and badly built that they were flaking away and sagging sideways onto their neighbours, past the elaborate stone frontage of the splendidly upright Hôtel de Ville, with its fine clock and its two grand archways and its high sloping roofs shining grey-blue in the damp air, on and still on, until they reached the Place du Carrousel and the battered frontage of the Tuileries, where William Henry said he simply had to sit down and rest for a moment because his heart was palpitating and at his age palpitations were often the first signs of an impending seizure.

The square was full of people, all moving purposefully towards a dark entrance on the further side of the building.

'You shall sit down the minute we're inside,' Nan said cheerfully. 'I shan't let you take a seizure, never you fear.' But then she noticed that there were three other sources of attraction in the square and that people were flocking towards them too. 'We'll stop on our way across, and see what *that* is,' she said. 'Shall we?' And before he could reply, she trotted him off through the crowds towards the nearest gathering.

To find a young man, in the now familiar long striped trousers, straight-cut coat and red woolly cap of liberty, busily selling news-sheets, pulling them one after the other and very rapidly from a thick pile held under his left arm, and calling his wares in a harsh, hoarse voice. He had a leather purse slung on his right hip and there was a small tattered child standing close beside it feeding it coins as fast as their customers passed them into its hands. They were doing a roaring trade. In every sense of the words.

'I wager he makes more money in a day than we do in a week with those ol' Consuls of yours,' she said to William Henry as she dragged him off again towards the Tuileries. 'Perhaps we ought to try selling newspapers when we get back home. What you think?'

'I do believe the crowd has thinned out a trifle,' he said, looking across at the entrance and hoping to deflect her from planning his life.

'Come you on, then,' she said.

Whether it was on account of the cockades, or because of the ruthless way Nan pummelled through the crowds at the door, or simply because the Fates willed it so, they were sold two roughly printed tickets and allowed into the building. It was accomplished so quickly and so easily they could hardly believe it. William Henry was still mopping his fore-head and blinking with amazement when they were ushered into the public gallery of the renowned National Assembly and saw the king himself sitting below them.

The little theatre was as packed as the conciege had predicted, and marvellously warm after the chill of the streets outside, but Nan noticed with something of a shock that the men ranged on tiered seats all around the room were dressed entirely in the old style, from the powdered wigs on their old-fashioned heads to the neat breeches and woollen stockings encasing their legs. There were plenty of sans culottes around her in the gallery, but below, in the hall where justice was being administered, and in the two tiers of boxes where the gentry sat and watched, the old style prevailed. William Henry was considerably comforted.

'All is not lost, you see, my dear,' he said, squeezing himself onto the bench beside her. 'Reason will prevail here, I fancy, for these are sober men. You have only to look at them to see it. The world is not entirely wild.'

And certainly the king looked calm enough, slumped in an ordinary chair behind a low table covered in blue baize and apparently listening to a speech being made by a short man standing no more than a foot away from him. And the judges sitting above him at their round table on their round dais were listening too, their faces mild, like men passing the time of day after a good meal. But there was an air of extraordinary wildness among the two audiences, as if this event was some long exciting party. In the boxes the ladies and gentlemen were paying no attention to the speech at all but sipping liqueurs, and greeting their newly arrived friends with shrieks of delight and prolonged conversation, and in the gallery they were sucking ices and taking bets on the outcome of the trial. The air was sharp with the zest of hundreds of oranges which were being peeled and munched all over the hall. It was as if the trial and its spectators existed in two quite separate worlds.

'What's going on?' she asked William Henry.

' 'Tis hard to tell,' he said, straining his ears to catch the words of the speech. 'He seems to be speaking about taxation, my dear. La gabelle, yes, yes, that is the salt tax. I cannot imagine why the salt tax should concern the men who deliberate upon the life or death of a king. Poor man! He is very pale.'

But the next man who strode to the blue baize table and stood rigidly before it waiting for silence, showed them both exactly what was going on. He spoke one word, and one word only, but it was given with such dramatic finality there was no doubt what it meant. 'Mort!' he said, and the woman sitting next to Nan pricked a little hole in the red card she was carrying in her left hand and the sans culottes applauded.

'They're voting,' Nan said. 'And three ways if I'm any judge.' For the woman had three cards on her lap, one red, one white and one blue and there were pin holes in all three. 'Ask her, Mr Easter.'

'That would hardly be proper, my dear.'

'Well then, tell me the words and I'll ask.'

'Hush, my dear. There is another speaker at the table.'

This one made a short speech and nodded his head a great deal, before he cast his one-word vote. It was a different word this time, and recognizable. 'Emprisonnement!' Their neighbour pricked it on her white card, pursing her lips with displeasure.

'That's imprisonment, en't it?' Nan said to the woman.

'Oui citoyenne, emprisonnement. Oui,' the woman nodded.

'So what's "more"?'

'Death, I fear, my dear,' William Henry said.

'And that's the red card, "more", en't it?', touching it.

Cheerful agreement.

120

'So what's the blue?'

'Exil,' the woman said, and as if in answer to her, a man's voice voting below them came echoing up through the tangy air. 'Exil!'

'What excitement!' Nan said. 'To be here when they're counting the vote. Think of that!'

But after an hour of it, as the speeches dragged interminably on and the three cards still seemed to contain an equal number of pin pricks she grew tired of sitting still and waiting.

'They're taking a mortal long time,' she complained.

' 'Twill be dinner time presently,' William Henry agreed. 'I do not feel we should curtail our sustenance, even on a king's account.'

'Ask her how long they're like to be,' she suggested, and this time, since the woman appeared friendly, he did as she suggested, and was surprised to learn that the vote had been going on since eight o'clock the previous evening and that no final verdict was expected until equally late that night.

'Democracy would appear to be an uncommon slow process,' he said.

'Well, if that's the case,' his practical wife decided, 'I vote we go to dinner and see the sights, and buy some presents, and then come back here for the verdict.'

So they went to their dinner which was delicious, and they bought a wax doll for Annie and a box of toy soldiers for little Billy and a rattle on a stick for the baby, and afterwards they fell into conversation with two other English visitors, which passed the time most agreeably, and at seven o'clock they walked to the Tuileries for the second time that day. And were disappointed. For the entrance was blocked with arguing Parisians and there was no movement either in or out of the building. It appeared that the Convention hall was jammed to suffocation, and nobody, but nobody, was being admitted.

Nan was cross. 'We come all this way,' she said stamping her foot, 'and now we en't to see it. Damn fool Frenchies! Why didn't they try him in a bigger hall? They might ha' know'd there'd be a crush.'

The night air was bitterly cold, and William Henry had a red nose and numb hands, and was aware that she was attracting attention. 'We will return to our hotel, my love,' he said. 'There is no sense in courting an ague.'

'But then we shan't hear the verdict!' she wailed.

'We shall hear soon enough,' he said. 'We and all the world. For the news-sheets will print it tomorrow.'

And sure enough the paper-sellers were hawking the news when they woke the next morning. Nan had her clothes on in minutes and ran out to buy her copy, returning with the rough paper in her hand, demanding a translation.

William Henry was sitting up in bed sipping his coffee which had just been brought up to their room. He did his best to provide one. 'He is to be executed tomorrow morning, poor man,' he said. 'In the Place de la Révolution. By guillotine. Oh dear, oh dear!'

'I knew they'd execute him,' she said. 'A king executed! Imagine that! We must go and see it.'

He *was* imagining it and it was making him shudder. 'Surely, my dear, you do not wish to witness such a barbarous thing,' he said. 'It would be quite terrible. Oh no, I cannot believe such a desire in my own dear Nan.'

She poured coffee into her cup and set down the jug with a clatter. 'I en't come all this way to see history made and then go a-flinching away at the last moment,' she said. 'I knew they'd kill him. I always said so. You was the one what thought otherwise. So now I mean to see it done, make no mistake about it. I mean to see it done.'

And although he spent the day sighing and urging her to reconsider her decision, she was adamant. They went to the great cathedral of Notre Dame on a little green island in the middle of the river and ate a delectable meal in a gold-and-white restaurant near to an open air market called les Halles, and walked to the Bastille which was nothing more than a heap of rubble, and took a promenade along the grand parade that ran through the middle of the Elysian Fields, and she agreed with him that Paris was a civilized city and well worth exploring. But no matter what arguments he used, she still maintained that if the citizens of Paris intended to decapitate their king, she intended to see it.

She was awake at six the next morning, wide awake and trembling with energy, flinging the shutters back against the wall to see what was going on in the courtyard below them. It was still dark and the air was dank with mist which coiled into their bedchamber in long chilling swathes.

William Henry began to cough at once. 'Nan, my love,' he begged between spasms. '. . . I pray you . . . close the window . . . we shall both take a chill.' Even their morning jug of piping hot coffee did little to console him. Surely she didn't really want to see this dreadful thing! 'Would we not be better advised to stay within doors on such a day? Or at least until the mist has cleared. A fog is invariably pernicious, I fear, and we are uncommon close to the river.'

'That's almost cleared away now,' she said briskly, stepping into her petticoat. 'Time we was dressed. Street's full of people already. If we don't make haste, we shall miss it.'

So he had to make haste and although he made it as slowly as he could, shaving with meticulous care and hiding his spare cash and their two precious return tickets in a purse tucked under the mattress, eventually they were breakfasted and dressed and out on the cold cobbles, walking towards the appointed place along with half the population of Paris.

Such a crowd there was in the Place de la Révolution in the half-light of that early morning. The entire area was black with people, swirling for position in the swirling mist, their red caps everywhere, as thick as poppies in a field of corn. There were dark figures standing on the terraces of the Tuilerie gardens, and others perched high on the mounds of building materials that littered the courtyard, men remarkable in their striped trousers, women swathed in cloaks, young girls arm in arm, whole families, nurses, babies and all, eagerly waiting for the last act of the tragedy.

The guillotine stood in the midst of the people, on a high scaffold that had been erected between the central promenade of the Elysian Fields and the empty plinth that had once supported a statue of the king's grandfather. The executioner was ready and waiting and so were the national guard, who stood at ease in two close packed lines all round the scaffold, bulky in their heavy blue jackets and their black tricorne hats with their muskets bristling above their shoulders.

'There's space up that pile of stones,' Nan said taking his hand to lead him there. 'We shall get a better view aloft, you see if we don't.'

'We are well enough here, little Nan,' he protested mildly, for he really had no desire to see anything at all. But she was already pulling him towards the mound. She seemed even more energetic in this brutal city than she was at home. And of course it was a better view up on the stones. But bitingly cold, because they were exposed to the mist and away from the protection of the crowd. He fumbled his watch from his fob pocket and glanced at it to see how much longer they would have to wait. But he couldn't wish the time away, chill though it was, for that would mean hastening the king's end, and bringing closer the awful moment of execution.

The murky sky above the square gradually dissolved into a patchy greyness, the crowd grew denser by the minute, and the growl of their anticipation louder, and presently they heard the throb of distant drums and turned as one person towards the sound, faces alert with a terrible eagerness. 'Le roi! Il arrive!' Oh, poor man, William Henry thought, shivering in the damp air. What he must be suffering!

The people below him were parting to left and right to make way for a man on a fine white horse. He was followed by a troup of guardsmen marching four abreast and flanked by an equal army of sans culottes armed with pikes, and they, in their turn, were followed by a lumbering green coach. The king had arrived. The growl became a snarling roar so loud it even drowned the relentless beating of the drums.

William Henry realized that his heart was throbbing with fear, and glanced at Nan protectively. Being so young and slender and vulnerable, what must she be feeling, poor child? But she had caught the excitement of the crowds around them and was watching the coach as avidly as any.

It was several minutes before the clumsy vehicle could be inched through the throng and arrive at the scaffold, and then there was another delay before the awkward figure of the king blundered down to stand among the escorting guards. He was wearing a brown greatcoat and a three-cornered hat, which Nan thought rather dull for such an exalted person, but when three of the guards stepped forward and tried to remove them, he resisted quite strongly. There was a short argument, which annoyed the crowd, but eventually the king was led to the scaffold, stripped to his shirt and breeches and shorn for execution so that his fat bare neck could be seen quite clearly above his white waistcoat.

Then he walked to the edge of the scaffold and seemed to be signalling to the drummers to desist, which rather to William Henry's surprise, they did. Were they going to allow him to make a speech? The crowd fell silent too, and in the chill hush that followed, a voice spoke into the mist, 'Peuple, je meurs innocent.' Then the drums were rattling again and the people watched without sound as the figure above them was spreadeagled underneath the blade, his fat arms behind his back.

'This cannot be,' William Henry whispered.

But Nan said, 'Go on! Go on!'

And the blade came rattling down, gathering terrible speed as it went and hitting the king's neck with a crunch that could be heard all over the square. Blood spurted into the air, horrifyingly red, and the executioner stooped to pick up the severed head and display it to the crowd. But there was a further horror to gratify them. The king's neck had been so fat it had defeated the axe. His head was still attached to his body. So the guillotine was raised and dropped for a second time, and at that the crowd found tongue again and began to cheer, 'Vive la nation! Vive la république!' tossing their hats in the air and dancing with joy.

Nan dusted the palms of her hands against each other, ready to walk down to the scaffold and see the body, like everybody else seemed to be doing. There were scores of guardesmen on the platform now and they were cutting the greatcoat into little pieces and selling them off, and one of the guards was dancing and whirling the king's plait in the air, black ribbon and all. And just at that moment, William Henry turned up his eyes and fainted clean away.

Although she was secretly rather annoyed that he'd chosen such an inopportune moment to fall ill, she hauled his unconscious body into a sitting position against the largest block of stone and took off his gloves to chafe his hands. 'Come now, Mr Easter sir,' she urged, 'speak to your Nan, do.' She couldn't leave him in this state. He looked uncommon poorly.

His eyes fluttered open and gradually became aware of her. 'Nan, my dear,' he said. 'To make such a public exhibition . . . I am so sorry . . .'

'Hush now, my dear,' she said. 'There en't nothing to be sorry for. You just lie still awhile and get your ol' breath back.' But she glanced at the scaffold as she spoke and that one quick, faintly yearning glance told him more than she knew.

She is missing everything she wanted to see, he thought, looking at her little loving face, as waves of dizziness washed over him again. And she needs to see it too in all conscience, for how will she know the full horror of it if I keep her here? In his drifting state it seemed important to him that she should see it all and grow wiser from the view. 'Go you down, my dear,' he said faintly, 'for that is what you wish, is it not?'

Oh, it was, it was, as her face showed only too clearly. 'Are you well enough, Mr Easter?'

'Yes, yes indeed.'

125

'I'll not be long,' she promised. 'Now don't you go a-moving nowhere. I shall be right back.' And she was off at once, eagerly, oh, so eagerly.

'Twill be a mortal hard lesson for her to learn, he thought, closing his eyes again.

Chapter Eleven

There was such exhilaration in the square. Everywhere she looked people were dancing and shouting, kicking up heels and clapping hands, skirts twirling, clogs stamping, red caps hurled into the air, in a spontaneous outburst of manic rapture. Above the bobbing mass of all those chanting heads she could see the scramble around the guillotine, where people were busily dipping their handkerchiefs in the king's blood and the executioner was auctioning off the pieces of the king's coat, but the dance caught her up and whirled her along and as there wasn't the faintest chance of pushing her way through such a mêlée, she gave herself up to the passion all around her, and danced and shrieked with the best. Or the worst. It was marvellously exciting.

Presently, down by the guillotine, a raucous war-chant began, 'Ca ira, ca ira, ca ira,' and was quickly taken up by everybody in the square. The dancers caught hands and formed circles to stamp and shout, and Nan took the chance they offered and contrived to be tossed from circle to circle until she reached the crush at the foot of the scaffold.

The king's body still lay on the block, the severed neck dripping blood and looking to her fascinated eyes no more alarming than a newly butchered joint of meat. He was a fat ol' mawther, she thought, looking at the surplus flesh on his shoulders and the plump hands tied behind his back. She turned her head to look around her idly at all the eager faces pressing in upon the scaffold and the pressure of the crowd carried her on by several paces, so that when she turned back she found herself staring straight at the King's decapitated head. The executioner had set it down on the edge of the scaffold, as if it were of no consequence at all, a thick-set fleshy face with its glazed eyes open looking straight at her, and a gross pink tongue sticking out of its mouth. It gave her a shock that made her feel sick.

127

'Oh, my dear heart alive,' she said aloud. And then she was overcome with pity for it, and began to tremble.

Mr Easter was right, she thought, 'tis a terrible thing to kill a king. And she wished she hadn't come so close to the horror of it. I shall go straight back to that dear man right here and now she decided, and tell him he was right all along and I was wrong, and 'tis a terrible, horrible thing.

But the crowd carried her along despite herself, for there were far too many who wanted to gloat over their decapitated monarch. She realized that they were streaming towards the side of the scaffold and presently she was pushed aloft with all the others to stumble and jostle past the executioner himself. But at least she had a clear view of the square from that high platform, so as she was pushed along she glanced across at the pile of rubble where she'd left Mr Easter. And the pile was empty.

She was very alarmed, because he'd given his word to stay where he was, and she'd never known him break his word in all the time they'd been married. Something was wrong, she knew it. She must get back to him at once and find out what it was.

It took a long time to push through the throng because there were even more people in the square now and all in such a state of frantic excitement that it was impossible to see more than a few inches in front of her face. She struggled forward, being seized by rough hands and kissed on both cheeks and tossed and tumbled about, as the hot faces cheered and roared, 'Vive la république! Vive la nation!' It was like a huge street party, and made her feel worse than ever.

And then she heard the screams.

At first she thought they were simply yells of excitement, rising a little higher than the rest, but then the pitch became extreme and she knew they were screams of terror and was more afraid than ever. Oh, if only she were back with Mr Easter! What a fool she'd been to leave him. But it was impossible to push through the crowds, for they were all heading towards the screams, sure of a fight and eager to see it. There was a long knife flashing in the air a few feet ahead of her, blue steel bright against a line of red caps.

She wriggled frantically among the mass of bodies and suddenly the two broad backs immediately in front of her ducked to either side and were gone, and she found herself right on the edge of the fight. She had a quick terrifying glimpse of two furious men, one wielding a pike and the other that long blue knife, of several bulky women punching, of a child in petticoats trying to crawl away from them over the cobbles, one arm uplifted to protect its face, and in the middle of it all, lying spreadeagled on his back with his head in the lap of a boy in striped trousers, was William Henry.

What's he doing there? she thought stupidly. He couldn't be there. She'd left him on the rubble. Then she saw that his eyes were shut and that blood was oozing from his ears and his nostrils and trickling in a dark stream from the corner of his mouth, and fear squashed her heart most painfully and she pushed the fat women out of her way and ran to kneel on the cobbles beside him. 'What is it, Mr Easter dear? What is it?' He was so deeply unconscious he wasn't even groaning.

'You 'is missus?' the boy said in English, and when she nodded, chafing her husband's cold hands, ' 'E's in a mortal bad way. You oughter get 'im 'ome, you ask me. Where d'yer live?'

'Chelsea,' she said automatically. 'Mr Easter dear, speak to your Nan, do.' She was vaguely aware that people were restraining the two combatants and that someone had picked up the child and that a shrieking argument had begun somewhere behind her shoulder, but her eyes were focussed on that ominous blood dripping out of her husband's ears and her mind was going round and round asking the same question over and over again. What's happened? What's happened?

She must have spoken it aloud, for the boy answered. 'Took a fair ol' thump so 'e did. Back a' the 'ead. I seen it. Went down like ninepins.'

But the answer meant nothing to her. 'What's happened?' she said. None of this was real. He *couldn't* be lying here like this. She'd left him on the rubble. 'What's happened?'

The boy was speaking French across the top of her head. Giving orders by the sound of it, which seemed odd considering his age, for he couldn't have been more than thirteen. But presently four brawny arms descended into her line of vision and lifted William Henry by the knees and shoulders and went swinging away with him, one man calling as they went, 'Attention! Attention!' and the boy helped her to her feet and they followed after. But it wasn't real. It wasn't really happening

' 'E come out a' nowhere,' the boy said as they dodged through the crowd. 'They was punching seven bells out a' some gel an' her kid, an' up 'e steps, bold as brass, right smack in the middle of 'em. That gel got off out of it sharp as a razor, I can tell yer. 'E's got some spunk, your ol' man.'

129

That's a funny-looking boy, she thought, gazing at the earnest face talking beside her, all covered in pock-marks like that. No wonder I thought he was a Frenchie in that ol' red cap an' them stripy trousers. 'He'll come round presently,' she said, to comfort them both. 'You'll see.'

But when they'd carried him across the square and down a dark alley and into an even darker wine shop and dumped him on the counter like a sack of potatoes, he was still limp and silent, so limp in fact that when one hand fell from his chest it swung beside the counter in the most horribly lifeless way. A man called Jean-Claude was called for and came shuffling through the baize curtain behind the counter, preceded by the smoke from his pipe and grumbling.

He didn't seem the least surprised to find a man lying unconscious on his counter. 'Et puis alors,' he said, lifting William Henry's eyelids with a perfunctory thumb, 'il est mort.'

But more means dead, Nan thought. More, that's what they said in the Assembly. Oh he couldn't be dead. She wouldn't allow it. 'He en't more!' she shouted, grabbing at that dangling hand and holding it to her throat. 'He en't!'

The earnest boy was standing beside her, looking straight into her face with small earnest eyes. ' 'E is miss,' he said. 'I was tryin' ter find the way ter tell yer. 'E is. 'E ain't been a-breathin' this 'alf hour, to my certain knowledge. 'E is.'

'He en't,' she said, pushing him out of the way. 'He'll come round like I told you.' And she tried to look down at her husband to will him back to life, and found that she couldn't see properly. It was as if somebody had suddenly put a huge blindfold over her eyes so that she could only see through a shifting hole in the middle of total darkness, a shifting, badly focussed hole which gave her very little vision. There was his chest and the brass buttons on his coat and a blood stain by his lapel, but a long way away as though they were at the end of a tunnel, and beyond them, nothing, only that awful furry darkness. She put her hands over her eyes and knew they were trembling, but when she parted her fingers and made another attempt to focus, she could see so very little it made her belly shake too.

There was a lot of noise all round her, French voices going on and on and something thudding with a terrible rhythm that hurt her head, but she couldn't see. And he wasn't more. He wasn't. Oh she couldn't bear him to be more. It was the king that was more. Oh, dear God why couldn't she see? If she could see he wouldn't be more. But she knew with a deeper, inarticulate level of her mind that he was dead and that it was all her fault because she'd made him come to this awful city, and he hadn't wanted to. All her fault.

And then there was nothing except a terrible urge to run away, as far and as fast as she could. She must get away! Now! Now! There wasn't a minute to lose!

She ran blindly, staggering out of the shop and into the street, rushing towards the shifting path of that awful broken vision, blundering into walls, pushing at torsos she couldn't see, tears rolling down her cheeks, heart pounding, sobbing aloud, 'He en't more! He en't more!' over and over again.

When she finally gasped to a halt her legs were aching and her chest felt as though it was going to explode. She could just see the broken plaster of a rough wall somewhere to the left of her and she sank back upon it wearily and closed her eyes, too exhausted even to think. She had run because it was necessary and she had stopped running because that was necessary too.

Afterwards, she had no idea how long she stood there with her feet aching against the sharp stones of the street and her back pressed hard against that cold wall. It could have been minutes or hours, she neither knew nor cared, for by then she was beyond thought or feeling. But eventually an approaching roar brought her back to the world. There was such an unmistakable anger about the sound, like some great bull preparing to charge. She opened her eyes and looked around her, wondering where she was.

She was in a narrow street between two blocks of stinking, ramshackle tenements, six storeys tall and smeared by dirt and decay, plaster flaking from the walls, slates missing, doors rotting, windows grey with dust and either trailing broken shutters or strings of filthy rags that might have been the remains of old curtains or somebody's clothing hung out to dry. The street itself served as cesspit, farmyard, workshop and playground, and was full of rubbish of every kind, from the used straw and excrement piled against the walls, to the heap of broken wheels, split barrels, pot shards, and rusty metal where the local urchins climbed and scavenged. Two of them were standing in front of her gazing at her with sullen curiosity as she opened her eyes, but the noise had alerted them too, and before she could say anything they turned and ran off into the nearest doorway.

131

She just had time to notice the building immediately opposite, black stone oozing moisture, iron railings like spears, an iron gate and a courtyard where two ragged men waited like vultures. And then the street was suddenly full of angry people, men and women, red-faced and bare-armed in the heat of their rage, roaring as they marched, and carrying so many pikes and knives and muskets that the space above their heads bristled like a porcupine. They marched at such a rapid pace they were down the street and gathering before the iron gate before she could get out of their way.

She was so frightened she didn't know what to do. Instinct told her that they were exceedingly dangerous, but her mind had stopped functioning and she couldn't think where to run to get away from them. But as she dithered a warm hand seized hers and she was dragged into the partial protection of an open doorway. She was aware that there were smelly bodies all around her, watching but silent, and that someone beside her was whispering, 'Shush! Shush!'

It was the pock-marked boy. She could see his face quite clearly, even though it was dark in the doorway with the daylight fading, all that tousled black hair tumbling over his forehead from under his red cap and that flat nose and that wide mouth with the teeth inside it all higgledy-piggledy and sloping inwards. And he was frightened.

'Nick a' time, eh miss,' he said attempting bravado, but he didn't look at her. He was keeping his eyes on the mob.

'Where are we?' she asked, as the crowd pushed and roared. She was so frightened of them she was whispering.

'Faubourg Saint Antoine,' he said. 'One a' the worst places in Paris. An' that's the prison. You picked a fine place ter stop. We'll move on, first chance we get.'

But they didn't get a chance, because they were stuck. The pressure of bodies in front of them was so intense that there was no possibility of any movement at all except forwards into the prison, where, as Nan could see from the vantage point of her top step, the two ragged men were opening the gate.

'Who are all these people?' she whispered. 'What they doin'?'

'Sans culottes,' he whispered back. 'On the rampage. Someone's gonna catch it. That big feller's a choice spirit. 'E's got a cleaver.'

The big feller wore a butcher's bloody apron and was roaring drunk, like the two men who supported him on either side. She watched as the three of them staggered into the courtyard, and were greeted by a brutal cheer from the crowd already gathered there. A fierce-faced woman was sitting on the prison steps, sprinkling black powder into a brandy bottle. When she saw the butcher she stood up and thrust the bottle into his hands.

'Gunpowder,' the boy explained in answer to Nan's questioning look. 'Gunpowder an' brandy, gawd 'elp'us. I seen this afore. August. They done some terrible things in August. We oughter get out of 'ere, sharpish.' And he turned and spoke in urgent French to the woman standing behind them, his face strained with fear.

The butcher was drinking his terrible concoction, to raucous cheers, but there were other sounds now, rising above the general roar, high pitched wailing screams, howling entreaties, gabbled prayers, and she could see that three men were being dragged out of the prison door into the courtyard, and resisting every inch of the way, clinging to the door posts, squirming and kicking to free themselves from the hydra hands of the mob. Three thin, pale, ragged creatures, with shorn heads and haggard eyes, pitifully afraid of the howling anger all around them.

And then the butcher strode forward, pushing the rabble aside and spitting speckled foam, and he lifted his cleaver and brought it down with a crack against one of those shaven heads, and the wretch staggered backwards into the fierce woman, with the side of his face hanging off and blood pouring down his arm and the terrible scream he emitted gurgling and bubbling.

And Nan watched in horror, because there was no escape, and the mob surrounded the prisoners and beat them to the ground, so that the courtyard was full of flailing arms and punching fists, and long knives smoking with hot red blood, and faces distorted with hatred, and the terrible, tortured, endless screams of their victims. It was too dreadful to be believed. Too dreadful to watch. And there was no escape.

The boy was still hissing argument at the woman behind them, and somebody behind her was running into the house, dragging a dirty child after her and suddenly there was a space in the hallway big enough to squeeze through. 'Foller me!' she said, elbowing into it, because the fierce-faced woman was triumphing out of the courtyard, crowing like a cockerel and pinned to her blood-stained skirts were two human ears.

They pushed through the crush in the hallway, following the dirty child through the tenement and out into an inner yard that was so small and narrow and hemmed about with walls, it was more like a well than a courtyard. But there was a broken gate leading out of it between two dank walls, and below the gate was an ash path that ran along beside a row of overflowing privies and led them through the filth to another narrow alley.

'Where now?' she panted, not knowing which direction to take.

'This way,' he said, and he looked as though he knew where he was going, so she followed him.

They ran along alleys and through passageways as darkness gathered in the chasms between the tenements, and presently they emerged through a black archway and found themselves in a highway, a well ordered, civilized place, busy with carriages and cheerful with strolling citizens in their Sunday best. This day is just like a nightmare, Nan thought, walking into normality after all that unexpected horror. And like all the worst nightmares it had wrecked her memory. She had a vague sense that all was not well with William Henry, but try as she might she couldn't recall what it was.

'Where are we going?' she said to the boy, as they strode along.

And a carriage reined in just ahead of them, and Mary Wollstonecraft put her tousled head out of the window and called to her.

'Nan! Nan Easter!'

She ought to have been surprised, but she wasn't. Anything was possible now that they had gone beyond the bounds of what was normal and acceptable. Why shouldn't it be Mary Wollstonecraft?

'What are you doing in Paris?' Mary said, her rough face smiling. 'Can I give you a lift anywhere? Is Mr Easter with you?'

'We came to . . .' Nan began, and then she had to stop to get her thoughts into some sort of order. Why had they come? She couldn't remember. And where was Mr Easter? He hadn't been at all happy about this visit. She could remember that. He'd said the French were a violent race. Well that was true enough, in all conscience. But where was he?

The pock-marked boy had gone over to the carriage and was speaking to Mary Wollstonecraft in a low urgent voice, but she couldn't hear what he was saying and didn't particularly want to. The horse was impatient, tossing his head and chomping on the bit.

'Climb aboard,' Mary said. 'Your boy can ride postillion. We'll soon have you there.'

'I'm filthy dirty,' Nan apologized, looking down at her shoes and the hem of her red cloak.

134

' 'Twill clean,' Mary said, hauling her into the carriage. 'There's no harm in honest dirt. Continue, Jean-Paul. We shall soon be there, I assure you. What a blessing I chanced to see you.'

'Yes,' Nan agreed, as the carriage rocked forward. She would have liked to ask where they were going, but didn't like to, because she had a feeling she ought to have known. Oh, if only her memory would start functioning again.

Even when the carriage drew up in a dark alley in front of a wineshop she still wasn't sure. The place was familiar, certainly, and the proprietor seemed to recognize her, for he looked decidedly shifty when she and Mary strode into the shop. But . . .

'Où est le cadavre?' Mary Wollstonecraft was saying.

The man shrugged his shoulders. 'Le cadavre, citoyenne?'

'Oui, bien sûr, le cadavre.'

Memory, understanding and control returned to Nan in that instant. She knew so much and with such clarity, the kaleidoscopic muddle of fear and panic and revulsion suddenly shifting inside her head into logical acceptable patterns. She knew that she had run away in panic and that later she would be ashamed of herself, she knew that Mr Easter had been killed and that consequently she was now a widow and would have to care for her family all on her own, she knew that she was a foreigner in a lawless city and that she had been in very grave danger outside that prison and that Mary Wollstonecraft, the woman she had once mocked and derided, was going to help her now, even though she didn't deserve it, and she knew that the pock-marked boy was an ally too, and likely to remain one long after this moment was past. 'That man is called Jean-Claude,' she said. 'Mr Easter is dead. Last I seen of him he was lyin' on that counter.'

Jean-Claude assessed the change in their situation with equal rapidity. 'Par là, Madame,' he said courteously to Mary Wollstonecraft, and pulling back the baize curtain he led them all into the back parlour, which was small and dark and very cramped, being crammed with barrels and bottles, and containing an assortment of filthy children who were gathered round an upturned crate and seemed to be eating their supper, and two elderly females who were hard at work filling bottles. William Henry's body lay on a shelf just above their heads. He had been stripped of all his clothes except his shirt, and there was no hope of any doubt about his state now, for he was stiff and cold and his bare feet were quite grey.

135

But Nan was still quite calm. When Mary required her to identify the body, she agreed that he was her husband, Mr William Henry Easter, and pointed out that all his clothes were missing, and his signet ring, and his hunter watch, and his wig, adding that she would like to know where they were. And Mary translated all this to Jean-Claude, who shrugged his shoulders so violently it looked as though he was trying to sink his head into his neck, and then spoke long and volubly, addressing his words first to Mary, who argued back fiercely, and then to Nan, who remained impassive. For she knew, in this new chill state of hers, that Mr Easter's clothes had been stolen and that this man knew who had stolen them, and that nobody would be able to force him to return them.

'The fellow is a rogue,' Mary said furiously, when the argument had drifted to an inconclusive halt. 'We shall get no sense from him without recourse to law I fear.'

'It en't worth the effort,' Nan sighed. 'What's gone is gone. 'Tis a funeral I should be thinkin' of.'

'Do you wish to take the body back to England?' Mary asked.

The idea was abhorrent. 'No, no! I couldn't abide to travel with a corpse.'

'It shall be as you wish,' Mary reassured. 'I will arrange it for you should you so desire. I have lived in Paris these two months. 'T would be no hardship to me.'

'Yes. Yes. You are very kind.'

'Where do you stay?'

'In the Rue St Honoré. Would I were back in Chelsea!'

'You shall travel home so soon as all things may be arranged,' Mary promised. 'In the meantime, you shall stay with me. You and your servant both.'

'He en't my servant,' Nan said, looking at the pock-marked boy, but Mary wasn't listening. She had jammed her beaver hat firmly onto that tousled head and was speaking to Jean-Claude again, very sternly. 'You en't, are you?'

'Ah, but I would be, mum, given 'alf the chance,' he said at once. 'Paris ain't the sort a' city fer folks like us.'

'I got no money for servants,' she warned him.

'Don't need money, mum. Jest the ticket home. I'd look after yer, help with the – um – funeral an' all that, fetch an' carry, pack yer luggage, find yer seats, all sorts. Jest the ticket home, that's all.'

'You ready?' Mary said, returning to them.

'Well, why not?' Nan said. So many peculiar things had happened during this peculiar day, why not take on a new servant she couldn't afford? He could use Mr Easter's ticket. It would only go to waste otherwise. All this was little more than a dream anyway, and it would be better then travelling back to England all on her own.

And so, in the event, it was.

The next four days passed in the same dreamlike fashion. She walked from place to place concentrating on the movement of her feet, and signed forms, obediently, and met officials, and finally sat in Mary's carriage and was driven to a bleak cemetery where she stood, knowing herself conspicuous in her red cloak and watched while a dark coffin was lowered into dark earth. But she was quite numb and felt nothing beyond an untouchable calm.

Even when she and her new servant had travelled to Calais and were boarding the packet boat and the passengers all around her were bewailing the tempestuous state of the sea and the overcrowded state of the vessel, and the pock-marked boy was looking green, she was still as cool as though she were sewing in her parlour.

'In fer a bad crossin', mum,' the pock-marked boy said. 'Terrible weather, as Noah said to Japhet.'

'Yes,' she said. 'I don't doubt it.'

The storm was no concern of hers. Let that ol' sea rage, she thought. He don't rage for ever. Sooner or later he got to stop. The little ship tossed like a cockleshell and stank of vomit, but what of that? The pock-marked boy kept staggering up the companion way to be sick at the ship's rail and staggering back again, but what of that? And half way across the Channel the captain decided to haul in all canvas and ride out the storm, but what of that? She was going home to Chelsea, that was what she was doing. Going home. Wasn't she?

They rode out the storm for more than three hours. It was bitterly cold, even with her redingote *and* her cloak wrapped closely round her, and eventually she noticed how chill she was and saw that the pock-marked boy was horribly pale, and she pulled her mind back from its drifting stupor to talk to him.

'I don't know your name,' she said.

'Thiss, mum.'

'Thiss?'

'Well, me full name's Alexander Thistlethwaite. That's a bit of a mouthful, so ter speak, so they calls me Thiss.'

Her mind detached itself and drifted away again. She could hear him speaking, but the words were just a buzz below her and meant nothing. I can't go on like this, she thought and was aware that she felt vaguely guilty about the state she was in. She made another tremendous effort and heaved her attention back to listen to him.

'I worked fer M'sieu Santerre,' he was saying, 'him on the white hoss when the king come down fer the chop. I 'spect you saw 'im. Good bloke, M'sieu Santerre. Keeps a brewery. Good English ales, that sort a' thing. I was cooper's apprentice there.'

'What will you do in London?'

'Can't say, mum. Sommink'll turn up I 'spect. I been all sorts a' things in me time. You don't need a groom or nothing?'

'No,' she said. She had no idea what money she would have to live on now. 'I could be back to being a servant for all I know.'

'Not you, mum,' he said cheerfully. 'You got too much style. Still, we couldn't stay in Paris, could we? Not now we're at war.'

'Who's at war?' This was news, and stirred a flicker of curiosity.

'England and France, mum. Didn'tcher know?'

'No,' she said. 'I didn't.' But Mr Easter had known. Mr Easter had predicted it. If they chop off the king's head, he'd said, there will be war. The packet boat rose and lurched, and black black water pressed against the porthole. 'Oh no, I didn't know.'

Chapter Twelve

It was a dishevelled, sour-smelling company that crept ashore that February morning. A grudging dawn was just beginning to ooze through the murk of the eastern horizon, and Dover looked chill and unwelcoming, as if it had huddled in to the cliffs to avoid them and their storm. They had been aboard for a day and a night, and to most of them it felt like a lifetime.

Fortunately the royal George Hotel was awake and waiting for them, its yellow windows promising the stability of lamplight and hot food and blazing fires. The coffee room was familiar and reassuring, already warm despite the raw air of that early hour. The tables were laid ready for breakfast and a squad of waiters stood about like uniformed clothes-horses, hung with white linen napkins and surreptitiously rubbing the sleep from their eyes. Nan and her fellow travellers trooped in to be warmed and sustained, and soon the quiet room echoed with the chomp and clatter of feeding, and the air was clouded with the usual scents and smells of winter travel, the pleasantly tickling aroma of coffee and bacon and grilled kidneys and hot buttered toast, mingled with the stink of a score of dirty greatcoats visibly steaming dry.

Thiss' eyes bulged with hunger at the first smell of coffee, but Nan had no appetite at all. The peculiar medley of smells was triggering a memory of the last leisurely meal she and Mr Easter had taken in this very room, and that was more upsetting than she could bear. However, she bought a meal for Thiss with the remains of her money, because she was grateful to him for all his kindness. But she was too miserable for conversation.

The stage was late setting off that morning. They didn't get in to the Swan with Two Necks until after three o'clock, and it was nearly five before Thiss was carrying Nan's travelling bag up the steps of number 10 Cheyne Row. And having finally arrived, she remembered that Mr

Easter had always kept the key in the inner pocket of his greatcoat. It upset her to realize that she would have to knock to be let into her own house.

It was Bessie who opened the door, neat and trim in her pink dress with a clean white apron newly tied about her waist and a huge white cap flopping into her eyes. 'Why, Mrs Easter mum,' she said. 'Welcome home.' And then, seeing the expression on her employer's face, 'Whatever is it? Is it the master?'

And then the panelled hall was full of people, Mrs Dibkins, all working lips and wobbling chins and ready to cry, Annie and Billy squealing forward to greet their mother and cling to her damp skirts, Mr Dibkins clomping up the kitchen stairs with a tattered mop under his arm and his scrubbing-brush hair standing on end with surprise, Thiss bent sideways under the weight of the carpet bag, not sure whether to put it down and go, or to stay where he was. And all their emotions focussed on her, pressing upon her, waiting to be told, already half knowing the worst. As she led them into the double dining-room, she could feel the fatigue of their expectations dragging her down, so that her shoulders drooped and her spine ached.

'Sommink orful 'as 'appened,' Bessie said, tears welling from under that white cap, 'ain't it?'

'Mr Easter,' Nan told them, struggling for control, 'is dead. He en't . . .' And then there was a dull roar filling her ears and the carpet was rushing up towards her, and she put out her hands to protect her face as she fell.

They brought her round with sal volatile, and then Bessie whisked the children back into the nursery and Mr Dibkins took Thiss down to the kitchen 'to say what you got to say without no harm to no one, if you take my meaning', and Mrs Dibkins eased Nan out of her cloak and her greatcoat and her wet broken shoes and put her to bed like a child, with a hot brick under her feet and warm flannel over her head.

'You cry all you like, Mrs William-dear,' she said. 'What a dreadful thing! A dreadful thing. You cry all you like. You're home now, Mrs William-dear. You cry all you like.'

And as if the old woman had given her permission, Nan turned her head into the pillow and cried with abandon, because she had been a poor sort of wife in all conscience, and he had been a good man, and it had been because of her they'd gone to Paris and he hadn't really wanted to, and it was all her fault that he was dead.

140

She cried for the rest of the afternoon and most of the night, help-lessly and without feeling relieved, even though she could hear poor little Annie and Billy murmuring outside the door and she knew she was upsetting them and that she ought to try not to. Finally at two o'clock in the morning, when the ashes in the grate were barely glowing, she got up and lit a candle and opened Mr Easter's medicine cabinet and poured herself a dose of laudanum. 'You can't go on like this,' she rebuked her candle-lit reflection in the mirror. 'You got things to do.' And the most important of them was to earn a living. For there were children to feed and servants to pay and a house to run and without Mr Easter she was the only one who could do it.

She woke with the lurching sensation that she was falling through space. There was a metallic taste in her mouth and the swollen images of her nightmare were still clogging her mind. She'd been running down a filthy street in Paris, all alone, with the mob charging after her, bran-dishing cleavers. She knew that one ear had been hacked from her head. Or was it Mr Easter's? Mary Wollstonecraft was pulling her out of harm's way, but if she didn't run faster they would cut out her heart and squeeze it. She was still shuddering with the horror of it when she woke, and put her hand up to her ears, gingerly, just to make sure they were still there. Then she shook the nightmare out of her head and rang the bell. The sooner she stopped being silly and got on with the day the better 'twould be for all of them.

'The master,' Mrs Dibkins said, sidling into the room with both hands in the pocket under her apron, 'the master said I was to give this letter to 'ee, in the event – um – of anything should – um – happen to him. I'm that sorry, Mrs William-dear.'

'There are mourning clothes to sew,' Nan said, taking the letter but not looking at it. 'I will wear full black, and so will you and Mr Dibkins and Bessie, if you please, but half-mourning will be sufficient for the children. Lilac with black trim for Annie and Billy, white for John. We could manage that without too much expense. My red cloak will dye well enough, I fancy. We will start by removing the lining. I shall go down to the haberdasher's for a quantity of black serge and dyes and cottons and so forth just so soon as I'm dressed. My grey wool gown will serve well enough meanwhile.' And she was pleased with herself for being so cool and business-like.

The she looked down at the folded paper in her hand and recognized

William Henry's careful handwriting, and was momentarily afraid that her painfully gathered control would be lost all over again. Surely she'd cried enough. She broke the seal quickly and began to read.

'My dear wife,' William Henry had written. 'I write this to you, not, you must believe me, with the purpose of causing you distress, for that is a sin I would never willingly commit, but so that you may be informed of those things that are needful to be done, in any eventuality. For I must confess I am not at all sanguine about a happy outcome to this trip abroad. Mr Tewson, of Lothbury in the City of London, is both my banker and executor, who will, I feel sure, give you such help and advice as are needful. Would it did not behove me to consider such things.

'Howsomever, my dear little wife, I would earnestly entreat you to betake yourself with all speed to Ippark, which is my family seat, as you know, and there to cast yourself and our three dear children upon the mercy of my mother and my father, Sir Joseph and Lady Easter, who will, I am sure, be certain to sustain and support you. How could they do otherwise? I have given them great sorrow, I fear, and have been a most unworthy son, but they are good Christian souls and mindful of their family obligations.

'Dearest Nan, my dear little wife, I have loved you most dearly these six years, and I am most sensible of the benefits to me of your dear affection and your tender care of our three dear children. If you read this, I fear we shall only meet again in Heaven, which is a most profound sadness for me to contemplate. I can write no further. Hie you to Mr Tewson. He is a goodly man.

This with my fondest love, William Henry Easter.'

'Ho, Mrs William-dear, don't you go a-crying,' Mrs Dibkins said, gratified and distressed by her mistress's tightly closed eyes. 'He was a good man. We all got that to be thankful for.' But Nan wasn't crying. She had no more tears left to shed.

'He was, Mrs Dibkins. A very good man.' Oh how was it that she hadn't noticed his goodness? She'd been so careless, pushing him away and making him wait for the smallest favours. And now he called her his dearest wife, and sent her his fondest love. From the grave.

She rubbed her eyes with brick harsh fingers, wiping away her weakness. 'Come now, Mrs Dibkins,' she said, 'there's work to be done. He wouldn't want us to waste our time, howsomever we might be feeling, that I do know.'

142

'A dear, good man,' Mrs Dibkins said. 'I'll fill the copper, Mrs William-dear, shall I? A dear, good man.'

But not a very provident one, as Nan discovered after another week of nightmares, when her mourning clothes had been sewn and her cloak dyed, and suitably clad, she went to Lothbury to call on Mr Tewson.

Mr Tewson wore a blond wig which was so ridiculously artificial that it made her want to giggle, and beneath it, a professionally caring expression which was so condescendingly artificial that it made her want to provoke him, but he produced a file full of papers that had been left by Mr Easter and assured her that of course she would inherit, as next of kin and with children well under age. 'A straightforward case, my dear Mrs Easter,' he said unctuously. 'We must be thankful for such small mercies as the Good Lord sees fit in His wisdom to . . .'

'How much?' Nan said.

'A comfortable income I feel sure, dear lady.'

'How much?'

'Well as to that 'twould take a little while to ascertain, as I am sure you appreciate.'

'Then take a little while, Mr Tewson, pray do.'

He was disconcerted by such bluntness. 'I will write to you with all details in a day or two, ma'am.'

'No,' she said firmly. 'Now.'

So although he shook his head as if in vague remonstrance at such an unseemly request, another file was sent for and figures consulted and finally he steeled himself to divulge the total amount of her inheritance. It was two hundred and eighteen pounds, seven shillings and sevenpence farthing.

The sum didn't please her. 'Is that all? He had a deal more than that when we married.'

'Your husband sold his holding in the sugar company, as I daresay you know, ma'am, and he has – er – had been rather eating into his capital of late, Mrs Easter. But this is a fair inheritance, given all considerations. With careful management and sensible economy you should be able to live in modest comfort.'

She snorted. 'Time that money was put to work,' she said.

'It is doing very well in two per cent Consuls, ma'am, which are the most dependable shares upon the Stock Market, as I am sure you appreciate. In any case this is hardly the sort of sum to warrant other

143

investment,' he said, too smoothly, his eyes disparaging her presumption. 'If you will take my advice . . .'

'I shall give it thought,' she said. 'And now good afternoon to 'ee.'

He might have been a good man but he frittered that money away, she thought sadly as she walked down Gracechurch Street towards the Thames. Still, at least I knows what I got. That's something. And there's still them ol' Easters to visit. Not that she had any real hope of help from that quarter.

Nevertheless, she wrote a letter to her father-in-law that afternoon, informing him as politely as she could that his son was dead, and that she would like to come and see them, 'since that was your son's request, as revealed to me in a letter which I will show you should you wish.' And three days later a letter arrived from Ippark, written in a wavering hand, flamboyantly sealed and giving her permission 'to attend us on Monday, at three in the afternoon.'

'Nothing venture, nothing gain,' she said to Bessie, as the two of them washed the children and dressed them in their new mourning clothes ready for the journey.

'Where we going?' Annie said.

'To see your grandpa and your grandma, and ride on a coach. You'll like that, won't you?' Nan reassured her, for the child was looking doubtful. 'Now stand you still while I brush your hair. We all got to look our best.'

'Wish you luck, mum,' Bessie said. 'Here's the basket with baby's two titty-bottles. One thing, the milk won't go off in this cold. They might let yer warm it when you gets there. 'E don't like it cold. You 'ave ter take the chill off. Oh lor, I hope 'e ain't sick, mum. There's a nice thick cloth on the top in case. An' their night gowns. An' three sugar sticks. One each. An' a little bottle of laudanum, if the worst come ter the worst an' 'e won't settle. Oh lor, I hope it all goes off all-a-right.'

'Don't you go worrying, Bessie,' Nan said, 'He's much better behaved these days. 'He won't play tricks with me.'

He screamed and flung himself about all the way to Petersfield, refusing his bottle and finally being sick all down his sister's new black cape. At the Black Horse she booked a room for the night, and the landlady provided a dull meal for the children and warmed the baby's milk for her. By now she was so distraught she added two drops of laudanum to the mixture before she made another attempt to urge it

144

down his throat. After that the combination of drug and exhaustion finally silenced him. She wound him tightly in his shawl, bundled him in a blanket and packed him in the basket. Then she swung the basket across her shoulders, took her two apprehensive toddlers by the hand and set off to walk the three miles to Ippark.

It was farther than she thought and took longer than she'd planned, for Annie and Billy walked slowly over the uneven tracks. By the time they turned in at the lodge gates and there was a gravel path under their aching feet, they were all cold and tired and sorry for themselves.

The great square house was overpowering, such a military red against the meek pallor of the sky, such aggrandisement after the unassuming modesty of Cheyne Row; the home of people born to rule. She felt quite put down by it, but she put on a brave face and marched up the front steps chin in the air. 'This is where your papa lived,' she told the children. 'You got every right to be here.'

But they clung to her skirts in their nervousness, and gazed up open-mouthed at the imposing personage who had condescended to open the door. Which was hardly surprising seeing it was a butler in old-fashioned livery, curled wig and all.

'Yerse?' he said and the disdain and superiority he managed to convey in that one slurred syllable was truly remarkable.

But Nan was more than equal to him. 'Mrs William Easter and children,' she said coolly, 'come to visit her mother and father-in-law, Sir Joseph and Lady Easter.'

'Ah yes,' the apparition conceded. 'Follow me, if you please.' And he stood aside to allow them to enter the hall and then led them through an ornate door into a room so huge and so dazzlingly gold and white it felt as though it had been especially designed to overpower them. The sight of it annoyed Nan so much that she scowled despite herself, lifting that stubborn chin.

'If you would care to wait,' he said, giving the sick stains on her cloak one last disparaging glance.

She couldn't bring herself to answer him, and was annoyed that Annie and Billy were still gazing at him open-mouthed with awe. 'Shut your mouth up, Billy,' she warned her son as soon as the butler was out of earshot.

'Are we to sit down, Mama?' Annie wanted to know.

The chairs were upholstered in white damask. That'ud mark soon as

145

look at it, she thought. 'Better not,' she said. 'He won't be long, you'll see.'

He was more than a quarter of an hour, and the room got bigger and more impressive by the minute. There was so much light there and so many reflections, she didn't know where to look. She would have liked to ease that heavy basket from her shoulders and set it down on the carpet, but the carpet was the most delicate of tapestries, all pale blue and gold, and she was afraid she might make it dirty. She would have liked to sit beside the great fire blazing in the hearth at the far end of the room, but that would have meant trailing all across the carpet too and their feet were wet with walking. So she stood on the polished surround with her children beside her, where the butler had left them, and tried to avoid the reflection of their black unsuitability in the long pier glasses between the windows. Outside the central window, white stone steps lead down to a shaven lawn, and beyond the lawn the green fields spread and spread. Such limitless land, she thought, wondering whether it all belonged to the family, and knowing that that was what she was supposed to wonder. What a mercy Johnnie was still asleep.

But eventually the butler reappeared and led them through the room, being ostentatiously careful to keep them off the carpet. They passed through yet another door into yet more splendour.

Where the first room had been like sunshine, all gold and white lucidity, this one was heavy with all the colours of fire. The walls were covered with thick crimson paper patterned with leaves and flowers, two ornate pier glasses filled the space between the tall windows with reflected colour and convolutions of gilt, the ceiling was heavy with a bas-relief of golden vines dropping clusters of purple grapes, and dangling low from the central rose was a chandelier that was bigger than she was, containing more candles than she could count and dropping lustres like fat tears to catch the sunlight streaming in from the south-west window. And sitting beside the fire in red damask chairs padded with cushions were a very old gentleman and an even older lady, two of the oldest and oddest people she had ever seen.

They were both dressed in the old court style that must have gone out of date at least thirty years ago, the gentleman in a full-bottomed grey wig, and a long brown satin coat set with buttons from neck to hem, and damask breeches unbuttoned to release his belly and rib-boned at the knee, the lady with a high pink wig piled above her face and a wide gown of embroidered silk ruched on either side of her pink

146

petticoat, propped erect by her long stays and a rigid yellow stomacher. He was red in the face and fast asleep, she was powdered white as flour and very wide awake.

The butler smoothed himself out of the room, and the lady turned a nose as sharp as a quill and looked at her visitors. Her eyes were dark grey and piercingly shrewd in the white mask of her face. She had called this wretched servant gel to Ippark to put her in her place once and for all, and it pleased her to think how easily it could be done.

'Yes,' she said abruptly. 'What is it you want, eh?'

'If you please, ma'am,' Nan said, startled into servility by the old lady's attack, 'your son instructed that we was to visit you. Your son, Mr William Henry Easter.'

'Tomfoolery!' the old lady said. 'Why on earth should he imagine we would wish to see you? Always was a fool.'

'What's'at?' the old gentleman barked, waking with a jolt that shook all three folds of his belly.

'William Henry. Said he was a fool.'

'Qui' right,' her husband agreed. 'Good seat on a hoss though, damme.'

'That was Joseph.'

'Qui' right,' grunting back to sleep again.

'Died in France you said?' milady asked, gimletting back to her visitors. 'Don't surprise me. Always was a weakling. What did he die of?'

Nan straightened her spine in fury. 'He died in Paris,' she said with some pride, 'pertecting a young woman and her child. They was – were being attacked by the sans culottes.'

'Humph!' his mother said. 'An ungodly city. What was he thinking of to visit such a place?'

'He asked me to come here,' Nan said, firmly steering the conversation back to its original direction, 'to show you his children. Your grandchildren.' And she gave the two toddlers a push so that they had to step forward in front of her. 'This is Ann, the eldest, she's three and a half. Make your curtsey Annie. And this is William, who is nearly two. And this,' swinging the basket from her shoulders and setting it down before the fire, 'this is John Henry, who is but seven months old, and a mite young to be an orphan, I should say.'

Milady gave them a perfunctory stare. ' 'Tis all one to me,' she said.

'Your grandchildren,' Nan insisted, glaring at her. 'En't you got no care for your very own grandchildren?'

'La, child, I have thirteen grandchildren. What are three more, or less? Of no account I tell 'ee. There are grandsons a-plenty to further the line. Be off with 'ee. Beggars ain't welcome.' The quill-sharp nose turned towards the fire, and now Nan could see that in profile the long nose and upward tilting chin were little more than an inch apart, and she thought of Mr Punch throwing the baby downstairs and screeching, 'That's the way to do it!' and her anger rose against this callous ugly creature sitting before her and she stamped forward, to tell her what she thought of her, lady or no.

'The meanest ol' pole-cat look after her young, let me tell 'ee. There en't a crittur alive what 'ud turn their own young away. Not one crittur. You ought to be ashamed, so you ought. I don't wonder them ol' sans culottes went killing the gentry. Hard hearts make hard hands, or en't you never heard that?'

Milady was unmoved by the outburst. First she raised the white skin that would have been her eyebrows had they not all fallen out long ago. Then she pulled the bell rope.

'And don't you go thinkin' you've heard the last,' Nan roared on, 'because you en't. You ought to be ashamed, and so you will be one of these days, make sure on it. I never imagined for one minute that such as you would help such as us. No I never. Not for one minute. We shall help ourselves, that's what.' The butler had arrived and was walking across the room towards them. 'And one day, I shall come back to this place, and buy you all out, that's what. You just see if I don't.'

'This person,' milady said to the butler, 'is leaving.'

'Oh yes,' Nan said, swinging the basket onto her shoulders again and taking the two children firmly by the hand, 'I'm leaving. And I'll be back!'

'What's'at?' Sir Joseph said. 'Tea is it?'

Nan was still hot with fury when the front door slammed behind her. 'Come you on,' she said to her children. 'We'll show them dratted Easters a thing or two!'

'I's tired,' Billy complained as she hauled him down the steps.

'Are we going 'nother long walk?' Annie said, wearied just to think of it.

'It won't seem so far this time, you'll see,' their mother told them

148

briskly. 'Sooner we start, sooner we're there.' And she pulled them along the path towards the laurels.

And a face appeared from among the dark leaves and hissed at them. 'Psst! Psst! Mrs William! Round by this way if 'ee don't mind, ma'am.'

It looked a friendly face, if a little anxious, and there was something about it that seemed familiar, so they left the path and tip-toed round the laurel to see what it wanted.

'Name a' Dibkins, ma'am, brother to Mr William's man at Chelsea. I got the pony an' trap a-waitin' for 'ee, if you'll jest come this way. *They* don't know. I done it off me own back.'

'We're much obliged, Mr Dibkins.'

'Can't have our Mr William's little uns a-traipsin' all them rough roads this time a' day, with darkness comin' on an' all. Petersfield, was it, ma'am?'

The trap was waiting for them in the stable yard, with two thick blankets to tuck about their knees and waterproofs to cover their shoulders. It was a very welcome sight. 'Now jest let's get you all aboard,' Dibkins said. 'Nice an' comfy? Anythin' else you need ma'am? No? Then off we goes! Walk on, Jezebel. Easy does it.'

'You are very kind, Mr Dibkins,' Nan said when they'd left the lodge gates behind and were safely hidden by the woods on either side of the track to Petersfield.

'Think nothin' of it ma'am,' he said cheerily. 'Least I could do, when all's said and done, after all your late husban' done for my family. You heard a' that, o' course.'

'No, Mr Dibkins, I don't think I have.'

'Ah well, 'twas all a mortal long time ago,' he said soothing away her ignorance. 'Harvest time. Good year. Weather on the turn, so we was all hard put to it, you might say. Steady on, Jezebel! Easy now ol' gel, easy! I daresay that was how it come about. Being hard put to it, you see ma'am. Anyhow, the long an' the short of it was poor old 'Orrie he got his foot in the way of a scythe. Weren't no one's fault you understand, ma'am. Jest in the way like. 'Orrible deep cut, that was. Near enough took his foot clean off. Oh, they done their best, with dressin's an' white of egg an' all, but 'tweren't no use. Bein' so deep you see, ma'am. Had to come off come the finish. Poor old 'Orrie.'

The pony plodded on downhill, steaming gently, and Mr Dibkins regarded her ears and sighed. 'Poor old 'Orrie. Agony that was. Sheer mortal agony. An' then Sir Joseph he ups and says, "You was in the way

149

my man. You was culpable." Culpable, my eye. Savin' your reverence, ma'am. An' the long and the short of it was he give him the sack. Him an' Dolly both. An' Mr William, who was a good Christian soul an' mindful of his duties, God bless him, he took 'em both to Chelsea an' made servants of 'em, where they been ever since. A good man, Mr William. Like don' always breed like, I'm happy to say.'

All three children were asleep. For a few seconds, while Nan digested the story, there was no sound except for their soft breathing, the creak of the trap and the pony's padding hooves.

'We heard he was dead,' Mr Dibkins said sadly. 'An' then we seen you in your widder's weeds, so we knew, you see. A great loss, ma'am, if I don't presume to say so.'

'Yes,' she said equally sadly. 'It is.' How many more hidden kindnesses would she uncover now that he was dead and gone and past appreciation?

It was quite dark by the time they got to the Black Horse, and the children were still only half awake when Dibkins lifted them down from the trap and carried them one by one into the coffee room.

Nan offered him a threepenny bit for his pains, but he smiled it away. 'Sir Joseph paid for 'ee,' he said. 'Though he don't know nothin' of it, which I'm uncommon pleased to say.'

And then Johnnie woke up and began to grizzle, so that was the end of civilized conversation.

It took a long time and considerable effort to get all three children to bed. For a start there was no fire in their room and the air struck disagreeably chill. Then when hot coals had been brought in a shovel from the coffee room and a warming-pan ordered, and warm milk arrived for the baby who was screaming so much he was choking himself, Annie discovered that the chamberpot had a gaping crack in it and refused to use the thing for fear of 'cuttin' my botty'.

'I'll get another for you lovey,' Nan soothed. 'Don't 'ee fret.' And she rang the bell for the fourth time.

'You sure that's *all* ma'am?' the chambermaid said when she had brought them an undamaged chamberpot.

'Let's hope so,' Nan told her. 'I paid good money for this room and I means to sleep easy in it.'

'I only does the work in this place, that's all,' the chambermaid said.

It was past seven o'clock by the time the room was warm and all three children were finally asleep and Nan could think of dinner. As she went down the stairs dusting the palms of her hands against one another like triumphant cymbals, she realized that for the first time since William Henry had been killed she was actually hungry.

The fire in the coffee room was well established and giving out the most comforting heat. She sat on the wooden settle right in front of the fender, and ordered a hot meat pie and half a pint of porter. It seemed a very long time since she'd had the luxury of being on her own, warm and resting and about to be fed and, what was more important, with a chance to think. Now that she knew the full extent of her fortunes, or lack of them, she would have to decide what to do next.

There were three elderly gentlemen sitting on the other side of the fire, two soberly playing backgammon and the third, sitting rather apart and reading a news-sheet. As the waiter returned with her pie and porter, he looked up and smiled and said 'Good evening'.

A newspaper, she thought, looking at it as the first mouthful of pie dissolved on her tongue, that's the style, that's what I'll do. There's money in news, specially now with a war and a revolution all going on. Look how them young fellers was selling 'em during the trial. And she remembered how she'd urged Mr Easter.

The gentleman caught her thoughtful gaze and responded to it. He stood up, folded the paper, and carried it across to her. 'Would you care to read the news, ma'am?' he offered.

'Thank 'ee kindly,' she said. 'I would,'

'Reports from France are very grave,' he said.

'I don't doubt it.'

But it wasn't the news from France she wanted. That could stay hidden on the inner pages. She was interested in the advertisements, and by the time the pie was half eaten, she'd found what she was looking for.

'An established newswalk to be disposed of that brings in £1.12s a week clear profit; situated in the best part of London, and capable, with care and assiduity, of great improvement; such an opportunity seldom offers for an industrious person. Enquire tomorrow at No 16 Portugal Street, Lincoln's Inn Fields.'

That's it, she said to herself, I'll go there the minute I gets off that coach. I'll earn my living selling papers.

Chapter Thirteen

'Ba-ba,' little Annie Easter said, 'where is my Papa?'

Bessie was filling the copper ready to boil the baby's dirty clouts. For once she and Annie had the kitchen to themselves, for Mrs Easter had gone rushing out again the minute she'd got back, Mr Dibkins was 'attendin' to the fires, drat 'em', Mrs Dibkins was consequently sweeping coal dust from the stairs, and both the boys had been washed and fed and were now fast asleep in the nursery. 'Don't you go a-worritin' about your Papa,' she advised, frothing the hot water with a bundle of soapwort. 'Let's sing one of our songs, eh?'

But the child was too anxious to be deflected. 'No,' she said doggedly, 'but where is my Papa? Mama says he live in that house when we went to that house, but I didden' see him. Only that horrid old lady. I didden' like that horrid old lady, Ba-ba. Oh, where is Papa?'

Bessie removed the soapwort, dried her hands on her apron, and sitting on the kitchen stool, took the little girl on her knee. ''E's gone ter live with the angels, pet,' she said.

'When is he comin' back home?'

'Well, now,' Bessie said, frowning a little in her struggle to find the right words, 'when you go ter live with the angels, you don't come back 'ome. Not as a general rule.'

'Why not?'

'Well . . . I s'pose the angels don't want yer to.'

'I thought angels was good.'

'So they are lovey, ever so good.'

'They en't very good if they don't let Papa back.'

'Well, now,' Bessie said, holding the child's hands, 'I 'spect they won't let you back, because they gets so fond of you, once you're there a-livin' with 'em. They can't bear ter send you back ter this vale a' tears, that's what 'tis.'

152

'What's a vale a' tears, Bessie?'

'It's where you cry a lot.'

'Like Mama did when she come home from France?'

'Yes.'

That made some sort of sense, but provoked another worry. 'Is Mama gone to live with the angels?'

'No, pet. She's out. Gone a-marketin' I daresay. She's a rare lively one, your ma. She'll live with the angels one day though.'

'Why will she one day?'

'Well . . . we all goes ter live with the angels in the end.'

'You won't go ter live with the angels will you, Bessie?'

'Not jest yet awhile,' Bessie said cheerfully. 'I'm young yet.' And then, understanding the anxiety on the little girl's face, 'Your Bessie won't ever leave you, don't you fret.'

One of the bells dangling from the painted board above their heads gave a little leap and began to jangle.

'There's the door bell,' Bessie said, glancing at it, 'an' me with the clouts not washed an' you all any old how. Suppose it's yer ma, what'll she say?' She felt frightened just to think of it.

But it wasn't her ma, it was that funny boy Thiss, all dressed up like a groom and grinning on the doorstep.

'Come ter see the missus,' he said. 'She in?'

'No,' she said. 'I'm sorry.'

'Be long, will she?'

'Couldn't say.'

'How about lettin' me in,' he said grinning at her. 'I'm lettin' all the cold air in ter the 'ouse a-standin' here.'

'Well . . .' she dithered. 'I dunno. I ain't supposed to let people in when the missus is out.'

'I ain't people though,' he said. 'You can let me in. She wouldn't mind.'

'Oh dear,' she said still dithering but with an expression on her face that showed she was going to give in.

'Tell you what,' he said, 'I'll say I forced me way in. How'll that be?'

So she stood aside to let him in and not knowing what else to do, led the way down to the kitchen. 'Whatcher think a' me rig?' he asked, lifting his arms like a dancing master as he followed her. 'Smart as a carrot new-scraped, eh?'

'Very nice,' she admitted, returning to the washing. And then feeling she ought to make conversation. 'Stables is it?'

'Inn. One a' the coachin' variety. The Bolt in Tun in Fleet Street. 'Ard work I can tell yer. You get some cases in the City.'

'Can't say 'ow long she'll be, you know,' Bessie warned. 'She could be ages.'

'That's all right. I'll wait. I got an hour's leave.'

Then to her alarm she saw he was eyeing the remains of an apple pie that had been left on the sideboard after last night's supper.

'I s'pose there ain't a slice a' that there going begging?' he said, grinning that awful grin at her again.

'I can't give yer that,' she said horrified. 'What 'ud she say?'

But he was already reaching for the plate. 'She'd say "feed the poor lad afore he drops dead a' starvation", that's what she'd say.'

He was bewildering her. She didn't know whether to believe him or not. 'She wouldn't, would she?' But he was cutting himself a slice of pie, for all the world as if he owned it. Oh my lor!

'Do you know my Papa?' Annie asked, coming to stand beside their visitor as he devoured his impromptu meal.

'I've met 'im, Sunshine. A good man, your papa.'

'Gorn ter live with the angels, ain't 'e?' Bessie suggested quickly, before he could say something else he shouldn't.

'My! This is a pie an' a half!' he said. 'D'you want some?'

'She ain't s'posed to eat cold pie, on account of 'er stummick,' Bessie tried to point out.

But he ignored that. He ignored everything she said. It was most alarming. 'Goes down a treat,' he told the child. ' 'Ave a bite.'

They finished the pie between them, despite Bessie's warning grimaces, and then as the clouts were boiled he offered to turn the mangle, and empty the copper, and hang the little napkins on the clothes horse to dry. And they were just polishing the inside of the copper when the dining-room bell rang.

'That'll be the missus,' Bessie said, jumping with alarm. 'Must a' come back. I never 'eard the door. That's all the row you was makin'. Oh lor, what'll she say?'

'I'll go,' he offered. 'Give 'er a nice surprise.'

'She'll be cross,' Bessie said, 'as sure as eggs is eggs.'

Nan was still in her black cloak warming her hands before the fire.

'Well, well, well,' she said. 'Alexander Thistlethwaite or I'm a Dutch-man! How good to see you again. I see you got yourself a job,' she said.

'I'd still rather work fer you, ma'am. Inns is all very well, but it ain't like workin' fer a fam'ly.'

'Um,' she said thoughtfully, removing her bonnet. 'If that's the way the wind blows, you'd best hear what I got to say. Go you and tell the others I wants to see 'em.'

'Now,' she said, when he'd shepherded Bessie and little Annie and the two Dibkins into the room and she'd taken the child on her knee and they were all sitting uncomfortably on the dining-room chairs, because that was what she'd told them to do. 'I got something to tell 'ee. Mr Easter en't exactly left us with a fortune. I been to his family like he said, and they en't exactly left us a fortune neither. In fact they're a pack of ol' misers and they don't mean to part with a penny piece.'

'Which don't surprise me none, Mrs William-dear,' Dibkins said. 'Savin' your reverence.'

'So what I done is this. This afternoon I bought a newswalk, and a note in hand for seventy five pounds worth of news-sheets, and I means to make money selling papers. Now what you needs to consider is this. 'Twill take a while afore I see any sort of profit. One month, two, so long as six maybe. I've money for coals and money for food but little else. In time I shall earn plenty, make no mistake on it, but for the moment wages en't within the bounds of possibility. I can give you food and shelter and nothin' else. Now you'll need a bit of time to consider, that I do know. There's enough for a week's wages in hand if 'ee wants to leave me and try elsewhere. I shall give 'ee the best of references. That's what I had to say.' She was pleased by the way she'd told them. Even Mr Easter couldn't have done it better, although he would certainly have done it.

'Mrs William-dear, how could 'ee think it of us?' Dibkins said. 'When we come here along a' your dear husband, God rest his soul, we come for good, so we did. An' where's the good in us if we ups an' runs at the first sign a' trouble? That ain't the way of it at all. I say we stay, don't we Mother?'

Mrs Dibkins was in such an emotional state she couldn't say anything, but she screwed up her mouth and nodded her head in such a way as to indicate agreement.

' 'Twould mean no wages for a mortal long time,' Nan felt she had to warn again. 'I'd make it up to 'ee later. You wouldn't lose out, I give 'ee me word. But nothing now.'

'Board an' lodgin's all we ask, Mrs William-dear. You'll make a success, sure as eggs is eggs,' the old man said, squashing the top of his scrubbing-brush hair with the flat of his hand in his agitation.

'Bound to,' Mrs Dibkins managed after considerable nodding and winking.

'I'm obliged to 'ee,' Nan told them, and she meant it, for the house had to be run, and she would have precious little time for housework now. 'Bessie? What say you?'

The news had put Bessie into a panic. Did it mean she would have to look for a new position? Supposing she couldn't find one. Or they was cruel to her. Some places they was ever so cruel. No wages was a bad thing, she knew. How would she manage without? But then again she'd given Annie her word. This very morning as ever was. And the child looked towards her, squinting with anxiety, her forehead wrinkled.

'I couldn't leave the babies, mum,' Bessie said, smiling at her charge. 'I've give 'em me word. Besides this is the only 'ome I've ever 'ad. You're like family to me, as you might say. I'll stay if you'll have me.'

'Appreciated,' Nan said. 'I'd ha' been hard put to it to care for the children *and* go selling. So now it's only you, Thiss. What you got to say? I could give you work a-plenty, but I couldn't pay you for it.'

'Then I'll tell yer fair an' square, ma'am,' Thiss said, grinning at her, 'a bird in the 'and's worth two in the bush. I shall stay with the Bolt in Tun, rough trade an' all. I needs me drinkin' money.'

'Well that's a frank answer in all conscience,' Nan approved. 'I think none the worse of you for that.' There was an honesty about this boy that was very appealing despite his ugly face. 'Come back when I can afford you, eh? I should like to employ you after all you did for me in Paris.'

'Depend on it, missus,' he said, standing up. 'My respects, but I got ter be off now. I only begged an hour's leave, an' that's up long since.'

'Show him out then, Bessie,' Nan said, and she walked across the room to Mr Easter's writing desk and unlocked it. 'We've all got work to do, eh?'

So they dispersed to their various chores, and Nan took out her husband's account book, drew a neat line beneath his last entry, and began her own accounts. It was an undeniably pleasant moment.

She's a one, our Mrs William,' Dolly Dibkins said admiringly, when Nan set out with her new cart to collect the papers at five o'clock the next morning.

'You got to hand it to her,' Mr Dibkins agreed, walking downstairs with two full chamberpots to empty on the midden at the end of the garden. 'She don't give in, poor woman, which I daresay she'd like to. 'Tis a hard world fer a woman alone to make her way in, an' that's a fact.'

'You mind you don't slop them chambers, Horrie,' his wife warned. 'I got enough to do without that.'

Bessie was half way up the second flight of stairs on her way to the nursery. 'I think she's ever so brave,' she said. 'I wouldn't like to be her, I tell yer straight.'

Nan would have laughed out loud if she could have heard them. For their sympathy was entirely wasted. She had set out that morning warm with excitement, ready to conquer the world. For the first time in her life she was entirely in charge of her own affairs, with money to use as she pleased, and a new job to challenge her, and she was splendidly happy.

It was still quite dark and the air smelt of soot and excrement and sulphur and rotting vegetation, a dank emanation of river mist and congealed smoke and the palpable stench from the middens. But what of that? By the time the sun rose and the air cleared she would be in Mayfair selling the news. The river path was slippery underfoot but she paid little heed to that either, for her mind was busy estimating the number of papers she could expect to clear that day.

Yesterday afternoon when she'd bought the walk, she'd been too excited to make accurate estimates. She'd examined the map on the wall of the news office, and listened while the solicitor delineated the bounds with one fat, ink-stained finger, 'You have half the territory that now occupies the site of the old May Fair,' he said, 'from Bond Street in the west to Poland Street, Windmill Street and the Haymarket in the east, and from Pall Mall in the south to Oxford Street and the Tyburn Road in the north. A goodly walk, Mrs Easter, and well worth the expenditure, for as you see, you have one of the great squares, St James' Square, and Golden Square which is lesser, but contains a good clientele. I would defy anyone not to make a profit in such a milieu.'

He had advised her on the number of papers to buy too. 'For the usual day, two score of the *Morning Chronicle* and two score of the *Morning Post* for the gentry, who will be your most valued customers, of course. I daresay it would be politic to purchase an equal number of *Daily Advertisers* for cooks and coachmen and suchlike. It is a class of person that appears to wish to read these days, I cannot imagine why. You might also care to take a few copies of that new paper *The Times*. It purports to be a news-sheet and advertiser combined, although how that may be accomplished I cannot imagine.' There seemed to be rather a lot that was beyond the imagination of this legal gentleman. 'It is only 2d a copy, a trifling paper in all conscience, so even if it did not sell as you would wish, your loss would not be insupportable.'

She'd felt quite sorry for the tuppenny *Times*, listening to his disparagement. And now as she trudged up Whitehall past the rustling trees of the Privy Gardens and the sleeping bulk of the Admiralty towards Eleanor's lacy cross at Charing and the printing houses in the Strand and Fleet Street, she made up her mind to buy at least a dozen copies, just to show him.

Printing House Square was the last newspaper office on her route that morning and quite the most welcoming. The publishers of the *Chronicle* and the *Post* and the *Daily Advertiser* were merely names upon a door, and had long since delegated sales to their clerks, who were variously harrassed, preoccupied or half asleep, but Mr Walter, the printer and publisher of *The Times* came out to greet her in person. He was a most untidy man, and looked as though he had been sleeping in his clothes, with his hair uncombed, cravat rumpled, waistcoat unbuttoned and a quill pen sticking out of his back coat-pocket, but his friendliness and enthusiasm more than made up for his unorthodox appearance.

'You join a most select company, you know,' he told her cheerfully. 'I have eight newsmen and you will make nine. Allow me to bid you welcome. We dine together once a year, you know, on the first of January, for the pleasure of each other's company and to talk trade and suchlike affairs. I trust you will join us.'

She said she would be delighted.

'I'm glad on it,' he said, beaming a dishevelled smile at her from above the wreckage of his cravat. 'Now may I make so bold as to beg a favour?'

'Beg it,' she said, intrigued.

'My other newsmen are so kind as to take in advertisements for me, you know, and letters and essays and suchlike articles. They allow me to print their names and addresses on the paper to that end, you know. Would you consider such a service? For tuppence a week retainer?'

' 'Course,' she said, and was immediately shaken by the hand, with such a firm pumping action that her fingers were numb for several seconds afterwards.

And so she set off for her first day as a newsman.

It was very hard work and there was a lot to learn, but she worked with a will and learned quickly. At the end of that first chilly day, her back ached and her feet were sore, she had a raw throat from calling her wares so incessantly and what was worse, she'd only managed to sell half her stock of *Chronicles* and *Advertisers*, although all the tuppenny *Times* had gone bar one, and that at least was gratifying.

The next day it was drizzling with rain. First she adjusted her hat, then her order, taking fewer *Chronicles* and more *Times*, then her street cry. By the time she had covered half the walk, 'News! Newspapers!' had become 'Nu! Nu-pape-AH!' which was a deal easier to sing and seemed to be just as recognizable. This time she had fewer papers left over at the end of the day although her sales remained much the same.

'That en't good enough, gel,' she scolded herself as she sat at her desk back in Cheyne Row that afternoon, checking her takings. She'd made two shillings and fourpence, three farthings, which was barely enough to cover the cost of the family's meals, and left nothing over for rent or any other expenses. Something would have to be done to increase sales. She ate her dinner pondering it, and went to bed pondering it, and woke several times during the night pondering it, but she was no nearer a solution when she left the house at dawn the next morning.

By now she was beginning to recognize some of her regular customers, and to have the paper of their choice ready in her hand before they reached her. In St James' Square one of her gentlemen commented upon it. 'You're quick, ma'am.'

'Thank 'ee, sir.'

'Why bless me, if you were any quicker I should be readin' me paper at breakfast time, so I should, instead of carryin' it off to me club.'

'Well now, sir, should you care to read your paper at breakfast time, that en't outside the bounds of possibility.'

'Ain't it, though?' He was clearly interested.

'For an extra penny a week, I could deliver it through your door, sir, every morning, ready for breakfast, if that's what you require.'

'When should I pay you?'

'Of a Saturday morning?'

'Start tomorrow, pray do,' he said, and went off through the drizzle, whistling like a bird.

Nan made a note of their arrangement in the little notebook she kept hanging from her belt. An assured sale, she thought, that'll cut out a bit of guesswork, and she made up her mind that she would tout for such custom whenever she could. At first it was easier than she imagined it would be. By the end of the day, she had twenty more such regular deliveries. By the end of the week when Sophie came to take tea for the first time since her return from Switzerland, it was nearly a hundred.

Sophie was tearfully sorry to hear of Mr Easter's death and said how kind and patient he had always been and how entirely fitting it was that he should have died defending a woman. But she expressed herself 'quite amazed' by Mary Wollstonecraft's kindness. 'I do believe we misjudged her, my dear,' she said. 'There is a kind heart a-beating after all beneath those unbecoming clothes.'

'I am sure on it,' Nan said. 'She couldn't ha' been kinder had we been sisters born.'

'And now you are a business woman, I hear,' Sophie went on. 'Who'd ha' thought it? You must tell me how you fare.'

It was pleasant for Nan to be able to brag to her old friend that she was doing rather well.

However, her success nearly doubled her work, for now she had to walk the squares twice, once very early to deliver and again a little later to call and sell. Soon both pairs of her walking shoes were badly in need of mending. If only they'd *all* take deliveries, she thought, as she took the worst pair down to the cobblers. I shall have to do something to persuade 'em.

The next afternoon she left her handcart at Printing House Square and walked to St Paul's Churchyard to see Mr Johnson.

'How much would it cost to have a quantity of small cards printed for advertising purposes?' she asked, when they had exchanged commiserations and pleasantries.

He was intrigued. 'How big, pray, and for what purpose?'

'To slip through a letterbox and persuade them ol' mawthers down

St James' Square and such places that they ought to take their news with their breakfasts.'

'Prettily put,' he said. 'Eight by six inches would be ample. How many would you require?'

They settled for a gross, which he assured her would come out a deal cheaper than a smaller quantity, 'in the long run'. And because she was the widow of his dear friend, he would take a down payment of a shilling and postpone the remainder of the price until such times as she had earned it. 'A good man, your husband,' he said, sighing quite dolefully. And then returning to business, 'Now as to the wording.'

They were attractive cards, pointing out with Mr Johnson's careful tact that Mrs Nan Easter was now happily placed to offer a special delivery service to members of the gentry who resided in Mayfair.

It certainly sounded persuasive. So she was disappointed, when having delivered a card to every household in every street and square, the response was so sluggish. Only ten new orders in as many days. She delivered another set of cards, this time marking them 'For the attention of the master of the house'. But the orders still didn't materialize.

'What's the matter with 'em?' she said to Bessie when the girl was helping her dress for church that Sunday.

'Don't know, I'm sure, mum,' Bessie said pinning her mistress's dark hair into a neat chignon on the crown of her head.

'Wretched critturs,' Nan said, examining her reflection in the dressing table mirror. 'They en't men of sense an' that's a fact, or they'd ha' jumped at it. How am I supposed to pay the rent if they won't order more papers?'

'Perhaps you're being at bit too – well – impatient mum,' Bessie suggested timidly.

But Nan would have none of it. 'I'm the most patient soul alive,' she declared, stamping her foot. 'Oh, hasten you up, do. We shall be late for the service.'

But patient or no, there was nothing she could do to hurry her customers. A cold April passed into a showery May, and summer came suddenly blazing upon them in the middle of June, but whatever the weather, orders for deliveries increased at the rate of little more than a dozen a month and although she was gradually moving to the point when she would only need to walk the great squares once a day, she was moving at a snail's pace, and that didn't suit her temperament at all. She was full of impatient ambition. She wanted to employ a cook, and run a pony and trap to carry her rapidly from place to place for deliveries, and train up an assistant for the walk, that boy Thiss if he was still willing. But how could she do that if the blame fools wouldn't order more papers? She hadn't even got enough money to pay the annual rent, and the landlord was pressing.

The business preoccupied her to the exclusion of almost everything else. It was the first thing she thought about when she opened her eyes in the morning, checking on the weather and trying to estimate what effect it would have on sales, and the last thing she puzzled over before she drifted off to sleep at night, dredging her tired brain for new ways to increase trade.

Occasionally, when she found the time to consider it, she was upset that the children were growing out of their babyhood, and that she was missing it all because she was so busy. She grieved when little Annie had her fourth birthday and there was no money at all to buy her a present. She baked a special cake covered in sugar icing, and sewed a set of clothes from odd scraps of material for her French doll, and there was no doubt that the birthday party held in the little girl's honour was an uncommon happy occasion, but it wasn't enough. She was a dear, patient child and she deserved better than that.

However, by August Nan was making a steady enough profit to be able to pay three months' wages to all three of her equally patient servants. But that wasn't good enough either. There was still the annual rent to pay, and she knew she couldn't put it off for very much longer. In fact, at breakfast time the very next Monday she had a final demand from the landlord. The full amount of the rent, which he need hardly remind her had been 'outstanding these *four months*' was to be paid 'forthwith' or she would lose her tenancy.

'Now what's to be done, Bessie?' she said tossing the offending letter at the toast rack. 'I en't a-losing this tenancy and that's for certain. 'Tis my home so 'tis, Mr Easter's home, the children's, a family home where all's safe and secure, and everything ship-shape and orderly and how we likes it, so there's an end on it. But I can't for the life of me see how I'm to find the money. Oh, drat the man. 'Twouldn't hurt un to wait a while longer.'

Bessie was most concerned. For this was her home too, the only home she'd ever known, and she didn't want to lose it either. She cleared the breakfast things, thinking quietly, and presently, while her mistress was upstairs putting on her straw bonnet, she came creeping into the bedroom with an old leather purse in her hand and an anxious expression on her face.

'If you please, mum,' she said, dropping a curtsey, 'you can have my wages for a while longer if yer like. Not meaning no disrespect, mum. What I mean ter say is, 'tis my 'ome too, mum. I been uncommon 'appy 'ere, yer see. If 'twould help . . .'

But she didn't get any further because her mistress had darted across the room to hug her with furious affection, and call her a dear, kind girl and the best friend a woman ever had and thrust the purse back into her hands. 'You keep your wages, Bessie. You've earned 'em. We shall manage, never you fret.' For by now Bessie's tender emotions had brimmed into tears. 'We shall manage. I en't seen the landlord yet could get the better of Nan Easter.'

There were always ways of raising necessary cash, but it riled her to have to go cap in hand to Mr Tewson and beg a loan. He allowed it, but at an exorbitant rate of interest and only with the provision that it was repaid within six months. 'Perhaps you need to consider whether you are not living a little beyond your means,' he said, oozing a smile at her.

'You will allow me to be judge of that,' she said coolly, stopping him before he could deliver a homily. But it made her more determined than ever that somehow or other her business affairs must be improved.

Meantime a foggy autumn was already giving way to winter and soon there was a combination of cold weather and the concomitant falling sales to occupy her.

It was a very difficult season. Even without Mr Tewson's interest, she was hard put to it to pay her household bills without dipping into what little remained of her capital, with the price of sea-coal up, and good meat in short supply, and potatoes frozen black more often than not. February came and went and she'd been at work for a year but she was so busy she hardly noticed it. It would be Billy's third birthday in a day or two and she wasn't even sure she could afford an iced cake this time. Trade was improving, marginally, but she still hadn't saved any money towards next year's rent, and she still hadn't solved the problem of how to achieve the big sales increase she really wanted.

And then one afternoon late in March when she was plodding wearily home pushing her empty cart before her, she saw an elderly couple standing beside the blackened ramp that led down to the Horseferry

163

in Westminster. They had a newscart beside them, still containing far too many papers, and they stood meekly, she with her shoulders drooping and her face downcast, he leaning forward onto an ancient walking stick, and gazing dejectedly at the river.

The sight of them gave her a desperate idea.

Chapter Fourteen

Mr and Mrs Peabody had been selling newspapers from their self-selected post at the Horseferry for nearly eighteen months. It was not a comfortable trade nor a particularly lucrative one, expecially when north-east winds chilled them to the bone and sent their potential customers scurrying by. So on that blustery afternoon, when that strange young woman came striding purposefully into their lives, they were surprised and intrigued and Mrs Peabody was secretly just a little relieved.

'How's trade?' the young woman said, looking at the news-sheets that still lay unsold under their tarpaulin cover.

'Fair to middlin',' Mr Peabody answered, guardedly. It was too direct an approach and it made him feel threatened. He looked at the fine, red coat and the man's beaver hat that the young woman was wearing with such style and knew instinctively that if she were an adversary, she would be a formidable one.

''Tis an uncertain trade,' the young woman said and she sounded sympathetic. 'Yesterday I had more than a dozen over, today I could have sold twice that number.'

'Where do you walk?' Mr Peabody asked, relieved by the thought that she was only a fellow worker after all.

'Mayfair.'

'You've a good clientele thereabouts, I daresay.'

'Fickle. There's no dependin' on 'em.'

'Aye,' Mrs Peabody sighed, 'fickle's the word. We can't keep pace with 'em neither. Never the same mind two days together to my way of thinkin'. Is it any wonder we make a loss? Sometimes, I mean,' for she had caught her husband's warning frown.

'Well now, as to that,' Nan said, ignoring the frown and directing the information towards the greater eagerness of the weaker vessel, 'I have a plan in mind that would reduce risk and cut losses in this trade of ours. How say you to that?'

Mrs Peabody was enticed before her husband could intervene to warn her. 'If 'twere a goodly plan, what a blessing 'twould be.'

'Come to Galloway's coffee house at two of the clock a' Thursday and you shall hear more, I promise you.'

Then and a little late, Mrs Peabody thought to defer to her husband. 'What think you, Mr Peabody?'

Being slightly more worldly-wise and considerably more timid than his wife, that gentleman was now alarmed. 'Many's the plan I've seen an' heard,' he said, 'which, when it all come down to it, was nought but a matter of buying an' selling. I should warn 'ee I ain't exactly thinking a' selling.'

'I en't exactly thinking a' buying,' the young woman said, smiling at him. 'Come to Galloway's a' Thursday and I'll tell 'ee what I have in mind.'

When she'd gone swinging away towards the Five Fields, her bright redingote flapping behind her in the breeze, Mrs Peabody tried to make timid amends. 'There could be scant harm in hearing what she got to say?' she suggested. 'You must admit, Mr Peabody, trade is mortal bad these days, what with the war an' all. Listenin' don't commit us, do it?'

'I will decide a' Thursday,' he said, trying to exert what little marital authority remained to him after a lifetime struggling to make ends meet. 'How if 'twere a Smithfield bargain?'

'She looked honest enough to me,' Mrs Peabody said. 'That coat cost a pretty penny, I can tell you.'

'A' Thursday,' her husband said, endeavouring to sound firm about it.

Mrs Peabody sighed and tied her shawl more firmly about her waist to keep out the worst of the chill. Thursday was three days away. It seemed a long time to wait to hear what the young woman had in mind.

But it was a very short time for all the preparatory work that Nan had set herself to do. She intended to make the Peabodys an offer they couldn't refuse, so she needed to know a very great deal about their trade before they met.

Later that afternoon, she walked their territory, notebook in hand, estimating the wealth and class of their clientele. It was, as she was quick to realize, a small walk and not an impressive one, hemmed in by the River Thames, the market gardens around Tothill Fields, the gridwork of the Chelsea waterworks, the wilderness of the Five Fields, and the private gardens of the King's palace and St James' Park. There were a few fine houses along Whitehall and around the Abbey church-yard, but for the most part the streets were small and ancient, crammed with offices and humble with clerks. Just the sort of place for the tuppenny *Times*, which the Peabodys didn't appear to carry.

The next afternoon she went to Lincoln's Inn Fields. Mr Duncan, the solicitor in Portugal Street, was rather surprised to see her again so soon, and plainly thought she had come to report a failure, but she soon wiped the supercilious sneer from his face by her opening remark.

'I intend to buy the Whitehall walk,' she said.

He rustled through the latest list on his desk. 'Ah!' he said, 'I don't believe we have the details of that one.'

'No,' she agreed cheerfully, 'course you don't. It en't come on the market yet. I'm buying it tomorrow. What's a fair price, would you say?'

'Well now, as to that,' Mr Duncan stalled, 'I cannot be sure 'twould be in order to divulge such information. There being no transaction in hand, so to speak.'

'It en't a quarter the size of my Mayfair,' she said, ignoring his hesita-tion, 'and the clientele is middlin' to down at heel. Low sales, I should say, and poor prospects. Not an easy one to sell, even if it was to come your way.'

'I wonder you care to offer for it,' he said, supercilious again.

She strolled across the room to the map on the wall, and put her gloved finger on Westminster, looking at the size of it, in comparison with the great sprawl that was London. And her ambition erupted inside her brain, and flowed down her finger, warm as blood, pulsing onwards. She could almost see it, spreading in all directions right across the map like an unstoppable current. And she knew in that moment exactly what she wanted and intended to have, the sole and exclusive right to sell newspapers all over this great city. Two more newswalks would certainly cut her losses and increase her profits, but if she were to own them all, why then, there would be no more skimped meals and no more poor presents, and the rent would be a mere bagatelle.

''Tis a small corner, in all conscience,' she agreed, 'but I mean to buy every walk the length and breadth of London, so it en't wise to leave a corner begging, if you take my meaning.'

'Madam,' he said, horrified at such effrontery, 'have you any idea of the sort of sums such an enterprise would entail?'

'Thousands,' she said with splendid aplomb. 'That's nothin'!' Now that it was thought, it was possible, it was what she would do.

He was so taken aback, he not only gave her the estimate she wanted but also promised to draw up a deed of sale ready for Thursday and to keep her informed should any other walk come onto the market.

'Immediately, mind!' she instructed as she whisked her bright coat out of his office. 'I en't one to wait.'

So suitably informed, she went to Galloways on Thursday afternoon to meet the couple who, although they didn't know it yet, were to be the first employees in her projected empire.

They arrived timidly and a little before time, which pleased her, their greatcoats damp from the morning's drizzle. And when she had bought them coffee and settled them in a snug corner beside the fire, and allowed them to talk about the weather and clear the nervousness from their throats, she put down her cup and opened negotiations.

'I got a pretty fair idea of the worth of most things in this trade,' she said bluntly, 'so I don't intend beating about the bush. That's a fool's trick, and we en't fools.'

Mrs Peabody felt prevailed upon to agree.

'Very well, then, that being so, I shall tell 'ee what I have in mind straight out, and when I've done, I hope you won't feel no compunction answering me the same way. 'Tis to our mutual benefit. And profit I daresay.'

This time it was Mr Peabody's turn to nod his head, since she was looking him in the eye and seemed to expect an answer.

'The market value of your newswalk is £37, so I am reliably told. You might ask more were you to consider selling, that I'll allow, but you certainly wouldn't get it. Weekly profits, if I'm any judge, somewhere between ten and sixteen shillings. A fair living, Mrs Peabody, but it en't a good one. Leastways, not near so good as what I'm going to propose to 'ee.'

'We ain't sellin', Mrs Easter,' Mr Peabody warned, weakly and after an eruption of coughing.

'I know that, Mr Peabody,' she grinned at him. 'Leastways you en't selling enough, 'Tis a risky business. It en't dependable.'

Caught by the speed of her wit and her speech, he was forced to agree.

168

'Well then,' she said, grinning again, 'what I have to suggest to 'ee is this. Under certain conditions, I would be prepared to take over all the responsibility of ordering and collecting news-sheets and such like, *and* pay you fifteen shillings a week into the bargain simply for deliveries and selling. How say you to that?'

Mrs Peabody's eyes were round with the wonder of it. 'Could 'ee do it?' she asked, smiling at the proposition.

Mr Peabody's instincts knew there was a snag, but his brain still hadn't caught up with her first trick, so for the moment he had to say silent and perplexed, knitting his brows and coughing anxiously.

'Oh, I could do it, right enough,' Nan assured them. 'That en't the problem. The problem is whether you would want me to. That's the problem.'

'I don't see how 'tis to be done,' Mr Peabody ventured.

'By working in partnership,' she said smoothly. 'That's how 'twill be done. I takes the risks, and you does the walking, and I pays you for it. What could be fairer than that?'

Put that way it certainly sounded most attractive. 'A dependable income, Mr Peabody,' his wife said quite rapturously. 'Think of that!'

'Course I should have to buy the rights,' Nan said coolly. 'That's only fair and square, you'll agree, seeing as how I'm taking over all the risks.'

'Yes,' he said slowly. 'I see that.' But he was still so bemused he couldn't see anything clearly at all.

'When you've finished your coffee, we'll take a threesome over to Portugal Street and get it all signed and sealed,' Nan told them. 'No time like the present, I always say.'

And so, while Mr Peabody's wits were still limping uselessly along behind him, they did. It wasn't until he was walking quietly home again, with Mrs Peabody chattering happily beside him, that he realized that somehow or other he had done the very thing he'd sworn he wouldn't do. He had sold their newswalk.

'What luck!' Mrs Peabody chortled, nodding her bonnet at him. 'Fifteen shillin' a week, reg'lar. What luck!'

'She'll soon be out of pocket,' Mr Peabody said with lugubrious satisfaction.

'So she may,' his wife agreed, trotting along beside him through the jostle in the Strand, 'but that's her look-out.'

''Twill serve her right for bein' so quick.'

'She think she can change the walk, that's what 'tis.'

'She may try, but she won't change nothin', Mrs Peabody, you mark my words.'

Changes began at eight o'clock the very next morning, when Nan arrived at the Horseferry with her cart full of news-sheets. 'This is a new paper called *The Times*,' she informed them. 'It should sell well in this area, so I've bought you three dozen copies. Start by walking all the alleys between Petty France and Peter Street. Here's a map with the route all marked upon it, d'you see. Tuppence a copy.'

'But we never walk the alleys!' Mr Peabody protested.

'You do now,' she said firmly. 'Good luck to 'ee. I'm off to increase our trade in Whitehall and the Abbey Square. I shall be back here at ten to see how you've fared, so you'll need to look pretty sharp.'

And that was that.

They were very put out to be given their marching orders so brusquely, but they did as they were told and found to their surprise that the new tuppenny paper was really quite easy to sell. In fact many of the clerks already seemed to know it and like it, and professed themselves 'bucked no end' that it was being offered to them in their offices and so soon in the day. By the time ten o'clock sounded they had sold every copy bar one and Mr Peabody was beginning to wonder whether their new employer wasn't some kind of witch. A suspicion which grew even stronger when she came beaming down upon them at ten o'clock with the news that she had persuaded twenty of their established customers to take a newspaper every single day.

'How did 'ee do it?' Mrs Peabody asked in amazement.

'Trade secret!' Nan said, grinning. 'Now all you got to do is deliver 'em before seven o'clock, and collect payment on Fridays and Saturdays. 'Tis all wrote down for 'ee. There's the book.'

There was no arguing with her.

'It fair wears me out just to listen to her,' Mr Peabody complained. 'This'll mean two rounds. We never done two rounds before.'

Mrs Peabody had been considering the implications too. 'She'll have to pay us more for two rounds,' she said. 'That's only fair. We'll do it for a week an' then we'll mention it to her.'

But as they soon discovered, mentioning things to Nan Easter was a waste of breath.

'We agreed a fair wage,' she told them, gathering up the four lone

170

papers that remained from that day's sales. 'You signed your names to it, so you did.'

'But this is different,' Mr Peabody tried.

'No it en't,' she said, more sharp-tongued than usual because she was ashamed of herself for tricking them so cruelly. But it had to be done. That rent had to be paid. 'Our agreement was, what you may remember it being such a short while ago, that I was to do the ordering and take the risks, and you was to do the work and be paid fifteen shillings for doing it. Which *you* agreed was handsome. Where's the difference?' Her mittened hands were poised on the handles of the cart ready to push it away.

Put like that he couldn't think of any, however dissatisfied he might be feeling.

'At least we got our fifteen shillin's a week,' Mrs Peabody reassured, as their new mistress marched off. 'An' reg'lar.'

And so the work continued, and thanks to Nan's tirelessness, the orders for deliveries increased. By the end of April she had put aside sufficient money to cover the rent, and in addition to that she almost had enough cash in hand to consider buying another walk. And just at that moment, most opportunely, St George's Fields in Lambeth came onto the market.

Even though it meant spending another thirty pounds of poor William Henry's remaining capital, she didn't hesitate for a second. She knew now that the further her little empire extended, the bigger her profits became. With this walk she could afford to employ an assistant and hire a pony and trap.

When the papers were signed and St George's Fields was legally hers, she took another business walk to the Bolt in Tun in Fleet Street and asked for Alexander Thistlewaite.

She was momentarily surprised by the size of the young man who came lolloping into the foyer to find her. He was a good head taller than she was and had grown long in the arm and gangly limbed. His pock-marked forehead looked much the same, but the lower half of his face was now doubly scarred, nicked and blood-smeared by his first attempts at shaving. Why, he's a young man, she thought. But his expression was exactly as she remembered it, a bright-eyed perky friendliness, like a cock sparrow.

'Well 'ere's a turn-up!' he said, his pleasure obvious. 'Mrs Easter or I'm a Dutchman, which I ain't.'

171

'D'you still want to work for me and my family?' she asked him. 'I need a groom-cum-newsman. Twenty shillings a week and all found.'

'Live in?'

''Course.'

The answer was immediate. 'When do I start?'

Two days later they hired the pony and trap from Mr Butterworth's stables near the church in Chelsea, and Nan discovered that this fourteen year old Thiss had grown wise in the ways of horse-flesh during his stay at the Bolt in Tun. He took time over the choice of the pony, refusing one handsome bay on account of its 'wicked eye' and another passive creature because it was too badly spavined, and promising her that Pepperpot, the blue roan she finally chose, had 'a good eye and a easy disposition' despite his odd coloration, and would earn his keep, 'given good handlin'.

'That's up to you, Thiss,' she told him. 'You're the groom.'

'We shall get on like a house afire. Shan't we, Peps?' he said.

And so, for most of the time, they did. Although just occasionally when the wind was in the east or there was ice underfoot, the fire did get a little out of control.

But his master settled into the household at Cheyne Row as though he'd been living there all his life. While Mrs Dibkins grumbled away to make him up a bed in one of the attic rooms, Mr Dibkins took him on a tour of the establishment and told him what a fine thing it would be to have another man on the premises. 'I ain't as young as I was, to tell the truth of it.' And Thiss made cheerful conversation and agreed that you would need your strength 'with all them fires an' all,' and supposed it true that you 'have to keep a sharp look out for them tradesmen, artful beggars,' but actually it was Bessie he was looking out for.

He saw her at last as they were clomping down the attic stairs. She was just going into the nursery with two-year-old Johnnie grizzling in her arms.

'You got yer own way then?' she said, teasing him. 'Never mind boo-hoo, Johnnie!'

'Didn't I tell yer?'

'We shan't get a minute's peace now,' she warned Mr Dibkins.

For a moment the meaning of the words made Mr Dibkins feel he ought to defend their new workmate, but then he realized that the tone of her voice was giving her words the lie, and looked up to see that she was blushing, quite prettily, from behind the bushy screen of Johnnie's thick dark hair.

'Never seen that gel so uncommon animated,' he confessed to his wife, as the two of them were settling for the night in their narrow cell of a room beside the kitchen.

'Ho, but then you don't notice like I does,' Mrs Dibkins said cryptically.

'What ain't I noticed this time round?' he said, easing his wash dolly from the tender edge of his stump.

'Ho my dear,' his wife said, 'he been a-comin' to the area door every week, reg'lar as clockwork, week in week out, ever since the missus come back from France without the master – God rest his soul. You ready for them ol' bandages, my dear?'

'You ain't never tellin' me they're sweet on each other,' Mr Dibkins said, wincing as she unwound the bandages, 'because I won't believe it. Why, they're barely out their cradles the pair of 'em. No, no, 'tis a nonsense.'

Mrs Dibkins shook her chins at him and did her best to twist her rubbery features into a knowledgeable leer. 'Well, we shall see, shan't we,' she said. She was feeling rather aggrieved by the arrival of this unnecessary young man. There was no call to go hiring extra servants. Mr Easter would never have dreamed of doing such a thing. 'You can't depend on the young. Ho no! Always a-gallivantin'!'

But rather to her disappointment Thiss' gallivanting style was a positive advantage in his new career as a news-seller. There were scores of Bessies and Abigails slaving away in the basement kitchens of Lambeth, prepared to sigh for the quick wit and cocky walk of their new roundsman, ugly though he might be, and plenty of cooks prepared to bridle and giggle and pass the time of day with a young wag who always had something saucy to say for himself. Sales of the *Daily Advertiser* increased by the day, to Nan's considerable satisfaction. Soon she and Thiss were cheerfully dividing all new streets between them, she to the front door to seduce the master, he to the back to charm the maid.

It was a very busy summer, for there was plenty of news and most of it bad, so news-sheets were in great demand.

The stories from France were particularly blood-curdling. In June a new law had been passed by the National Assembly. Called the law of the Prairial, it established that it was the duty of ordinary but patriotic citizens to denounce their neighbours to the Tribunal, if they had reason to believe that they were traitors to the revolution. The tumbrels now made a daily procession through the muted streets of Paris, carrying convicted prisoners to the guillotine a dozen at a time. 'The citizens of Paris watch them go,' the *Morning Post* reported, 'but they say nothing, too sickened by the sight to cheer, too terrified by the power of the tribunal to protest. It is a blood-letting of a particularly vicious variety, and there appears to be no gainsaying it.'

Nan's regular customers were happily appalled. 'Mad dogs, these Frenchies. Can't think what the world is coming to,' one of her butlers said, as he paid the family account at the end of a particularly dire week. 'Always said we'd have trouble with them. Ever since that dark day when they killed poor King Louis.'

'I was in Paris at that time,' Nan told him, remembering. 'I saw the whole thing, trial, execution and all, so I did.'

He was most impressed and instantly sought her opinion concerning the barbarity of the French race. 'Liberty and equality!' he mocked. 'Damm lot a' nonsense. Don't 'ee think so?'

''Tis only a liberty to be beheaded these days,' she agreed. 'Can't see the sense in that. Never could.' She'd conveniently forgotten how exciting the king's execution had been and how much she'd enjoyed it, until she saw that dreadful head. Now it was enough that she could bear witness to the current horrors and increase her trade by her memories.

'A fine woman, Mrs Easter,' her regulars agreed whenever she was spoken of in the clubs and taverns where *Times* readers were beginning to gather. 'In France, you know. Saw the terror at first hand, by George. Plucky little woman, damme!'

In July, when the weather was fine and the streets especially crowded, she decided that the time had come for her two eldest children to assist her in her work. On several occasions she'd seen streetsellers with small children in tow, and noticed what an attraction a child could be, lisping its wares and offering dainties made especially tempting by the size of the hand that held them. It was no use taking Johnnie who was still far too prone to howl and throw himself about when thwarted, but Annie, who was now five, and three-year-old Billy were another matter. They looked so pretty, with their fair hair fluffed about their faces and white collars attached to their dresses to set off the porcelain pink of their skin, and they did as they were told, holding up papers to tempt the passers-by, and calling in their piping voices. And besides, it gave her a chance to see a little more of them.

When their first walk was completed she took them off to a coffee house in nearby Oxford Street for a dish of tea and a fruit tart or two.

'A treat for good children,' she said, as the little cups were placed before them.

Billy's eyes shone as the tarts were set in the middle of the table. 'Is them a treat for trildren too, Mama?' he asked, mouth watering.

'And well deserved,' his mother said. 'Take your pick, my lovey. You too, Annie.'

Their mid-morning treat soon became an established part of their working day, a welcome chance to rest and feed and talk to one another. And it wasn't long before their conversation had established a pattern too. For what the children wanted to talk about more than anything else was their father, who had died before either of them was old enough to remember and was therefore specially precious to them.

'He was a good man, wasn't he, Mama?' Annie would say happily. 'Bessie says.'

'A very good man,' Nan would reply. 'Kind and gentle and courteous.'

And Billy would ask, 'What's kert-chus, Mama?'

'He never said a bad thing to no one,' Nan explained, 'nor never did a bad thing neither. That's what courteous is, young Billy. Don't 'ee never forget it. A good man.' And then she would tell them stories, the same stories over and over again, it didn't seem to matter how many times, about how their father had bought clothes to please her when they were newly married, and how he'd taken Mr and Mrs Dibkins to his home in Chelsea when they'd been dismissed through no fault of their own, and how he'd hired Bessie to help when they were little, which they both considered immensely courteous, and finally and most frequently, how brave he'd been on the day he died.

The more often she spoke of him the easier and the more pleasurable it became, for although she still missed him, time and hard work were beginning to dull the sharp edges of her mourning into memory. And for the children the stories were unalloyed pleasure.

It was, she thought, watching them as they worked beside her in the sunshine, a sensible decision to bring them into the business.

Mrs Dibkins was of quite another opinion, which she expressed as loudly as she could whenever she knew Mrs Easter was in the dining-

175

room overhead to hear her. She hadn't been a servant at Ippark all those years for nothing.

'Poor little mites,' she shouted, 'traipsing about the streets all hours, when they ought to be learnin' their letters an' such. 'Tis a cryin' shame, so it is.'

'Now then mother,' Mr Dibkins whispered, giving the ceiling a meaningful glance. 'They don't come to no harm. 'Tis fine weather.'

'All in the dust an' dirt,' his wife grumbled on as loudly as ever. 'Ho, she don't think. Poor little mites. All work an' no play, you mark my words. 'Tain't good for flesh nor fowl. 'Tain't good for them an' 'tain't good for her.'

There was truth in that which he had to admit. 'Ain't for the likes of us to criticize, though, is it, mother?' he whispered. 'My leg's been givin' me some gyp, today.'

'She don't seem to see the need for play,' Mrs Dibkins shouted. 'You can't expect little children to work the way she do. 'Tain't nat'ral.'

But Nan took no notice of her criticism. She don't know nothing, silly old thing, she thought with happy superiority. The children were perfectly happy out on the streets, the work wasn't hard and the weather was fine. They could learn their letters later. While as to play, she really couldn't see the need for it. As she told Sophie Fuseli every time that lady came to take tea with her and suggested that she should come to some function or other.

'I've a deal too much to do, Sophie,' she would say.

And Sophie would pout and declare, 'You live like a hermit, my dear. A positive hermit. 'Tain't natural.'

But Nan was rewarded by her work. It sustained her and encouraged her and gave a zest to her life. And she truly believed that that was all she wanted and needed. Until the afternoon when she suddenly met up with Sophie Fuseli in the middle of the crowded Strand.

She and Thiss were in the pony cart, inching their way through the close-packed muddle of the traffic, when a chaise pulled up alongside them and a very fashionable head smiled out upon them. It was Sophie Fuseli, glowing with excitement and dressed in the very latest style, in a high-waisted cotton gown, exquisitely printed with blue, green and yellow flowers and bound under her bosom with pale blue ribbons, and a blue over-robe with tiny short sleeves. Her dark hair had been cut short and dressed in cunning curls to frame her face and fall in a froth from the blue folds of her elaborate turban. She looked delectable. Admiring her, Nan suddenly felt unfashionable and dowdy.

'Such good fortune,' Sophie said. 'I was on my way to Chelsea to see you, my dear. Pray do join me. Now we may travel together.'

So Thiss was sent ahead with the pony cart and Nan clambered aboard the chaise to join her friend.

'What think you of my gown?' Sophie asked when the vehicle was under way again. ''Tis the very latest style, my dear, and all in the new material.'

''Tis the prettiest I ever saw,' Nan said.

'Printed on a roller, my dear,' Sophie explained. 'Did you ever see anything so neat? And the shops fairly bursting with new designs and every one as fine. I had this made for me. What think 'ee?'

'I should like to look one half as well,' Nan said.

'Then so you shall, my dear,' Sophie said at once. 'We are but a stone's throw from Mr Roger's Emporium. We shall stop there on our way, so we shall. No time like the present, eh?'

It was simply too tempting to be resisted. 'You will lead me astray,' Nan laughed, agreeing.

'I sincerely hope so,' Sophie said. ''Tis high time you had some fun in your life. There is to be a masque at Ranelagh a' Saturday with dancing to follow. Heinrich has been in a foul mood these three days and says he will have none of it, but I see no reason why I should not attend. Say you will come with me, pray do. They say 'twill be a dazzling display.'

'A masque!' Nan said, catching her friend's excitement. 'I en't been to a masque since Mr Easter died.'

'All the more reason,' Sophie said at once. 'We will go together like two old widow women, and you shall wear your new gown. I won't take no for an answer, so consider it settled. You have hidden yourself away for far too long, you wretched creature.' And before Nan could put up any argument, she leant forward to tap her coachman on the shoulder. 'We are at Mr Roger's already. Stop here pray, John Joseph.'

As soon as she stepped inside the shop Nan could see that her old friend had not exaggerated. The shelves were stacked with the most beautifully printed fabrics she'd ever seen, the patterns clear-edged and repeated with quite miraculous precision, leaves and flowers in neat, straight, perfectly proportioned rows. They made the old handprinted cottons look amateurish and smudgy. She was charmed by them and chose a design of gold leaves and pink, white and blue rosebuds printed on a dark ground, which was expensive but well within her present means.

'Now you shall come to my new dressmaker and choose your pattern and be measured,' Sophie insisted. 'If the gown is to be ready by Saturday, there ain't a minute to lose. Come now, I'll not have argument.'

'I don't intend none,' Nan laughed. And it was true. The sight of all that delectable material and the thought of being dressed in such high style and appearing in society again almost as grand as one of the ton, had suddenly lifted her into a state of happy excitement such as she hadn't experienced since Mr Easter's death. It was as if she'd walked through a door into a different kind of world. 'You are quite right, Sophie. I been a hermit too long. T'en't natural.' The masque would be fun.

Now that she'd decided to dress in style it seemed an age before Sophie's obliging dress-maker could sew her new gown. But eventually it was finished, neatly lined, with its hem accurately turned, and its wrists buttoned, ready to be modelled. There was even enough material left over for a turban.

It occurred to Nan, on that Saturday evening, as she stood in her finery before the pier-glass in the upstairs drawing room, that she hadn't looked at herself in a long mirror since the day she'd dressed to go to France with Mr Easter. I've changed, she thought, and it en't just the new style. I en't as pretty as I was, but I reckon I'm improved just the same. The long straight skirt of her new gown made her look taller, but she was slimmer too and a good deal harder, her shoulders set so straight, her mouth narrowed, her eyes guarded, even against herself. I was twenty-one then, she thought, and there weren't nothing in my life 'cept babies. Now she was twenty-three and a business woman. And she was pleased to think that she looked it.

'We live in an age of change right enough,' she said to Bessie who was hovering beside her with the turban. 'And not all of it bad.'

'Don'tcher look a swell mum,' Bessie said. 'That 'at'll set it off a treat.'

The masque was very enjoyable. She had forgotten how delightful the Ranelagh Gardens could look on a fine summer evening, with coloured lanterns swaying among the foliage, and the ton strolling so elegantly beneath them along the avenues. The succulent aroma of roast pork and crackling drifted out upon them from the Chinese pavilions as soon as they arrived. Sophie declared herself 'wild with hunger' so they set off to find their supper table immediately and were soon happily consuming vast quantities of roast meat and potatoes, washed down with a goodly claret chosen by Mr Johnson.

It was pleasant to see him again, Nan thought, although he seemed a little subdued. The Wotherspoons were exactly the same as ever, loquacious and dowdy and dressed entirely in the old style, which she found very gratifying for it set off her own finery so well. But for all the dazzle of the place and the wit of the conversation, there were times during supper when she found her mind wandering back to the business of the day. Once she had sat among this very company and listened to every word. Now they could no longer hold her interest.

But they were friendly and amiable and as the comfits were served at the end of the meal, they were pleased to hear her news, congratulating her warmly upon doing so well in her chosen trade.

'Newspapers are all the ton, I hear,' Mrs Wotherspoon approved.

'You see them everywhere,' her husband said. 'I wonder they don't open libraries for them. A warm place out of the wind where one may sit and read, don't you know.'

'Or sell 'em in shops like so much cloth. Oh, I will take a yard a' *The Times* so I will!' Sophie laughed.

'They sell well,' Mr Johnson said, wheezing a little as he always did when Sophie began to tease. 'In our trade 'tis sales that are important, is it not, Mrs Easter?'

'If we don't finish soon you know,' Mrs Wotherspoon warned, 'we shall be late for the masque.'

So the conversation had to come to a halt, and just as it was getting interesting too. They drank down the last of the claret, scoffed the last of the comfits and set off for the Rotunda, which was already ablaze with candlelight and attracting crowds towards its three tall doors like dark bees to a hive.

The masque was topical and political and much enjoyed, for it depicted the death of Marat, who sat in a barrel in the middle of the Rotunda stage, rolling his eyes and marvellously white in the face, and was stabbed repeatedly and bloodlessly by a maniac Charlotte Corday. That lady was clothed in the latest style, turban, feathers and all, and the stabbing had a tendency to dislodge her head-dress, but she persevered, as befitted her heroic status, and when Marat had been spiked to her entire satisfaction she turned her attention to the audience, running amok amongst them declaring that her intention now was to catch 'that villain Robespierre and Maratize him'. The applause was rapturous.

But she was followed by a boy soprano who sang several shrill songs very badly and burst two buttons from his breeches and was horribly boring. Even before the first song had screeched to a close, Nan's mind was wandering again.

Newspapers sold in a shop, she thought. Sophie had meant it as a joke, but why not?

However, there was not time to think about it any further, for the boy soprano had finished and the bandstand had been rearranged behind him, and now the Master of Ceremonies had arrived and the hall was a-buzz with preparations for the opening minuet. In fact there was barely time for Nan to wonder whether there would be any old acquaintances in her party who would be prepared to partner her, when a group of excited young men bore down upon them, flashing their eyes at Sophie and begging to be introduced 'to the ladies'. So she and Sophie danced every single dance until they were both quite pink with pleasure and exertion.

'Did I not tell 'ee 'twould be a pleasant evening?' Sophie asked as they were being escorted back to their table after the fourth country dance.

'Where do they all come from?' Nan asked, glancing at the young men.

'Why, from the barracks, my dear. London fairly swarms with eligible bachelors.'

'And one in a fine red waistcoat more eligible than most, I think,' Nan teased, for she'd noticed how often that particular gentleman was on hand to dance with her friend.

'Well, as to that,' Sophie smiled, 'I will tell all when we meet tomorrow.'

'Should I visit you?'

'No, no, my dear. I will come to Chelsea. Heinrich is like a bear with a sore head, and besides, I like the privacy of your pretty garden.'

'I do not doubt it,' Nan said teasing again. But then another handsome young man was bowing before her, ready for the minuet. Oh what fun to be dancing again!

Chapter Fifteen

'You've took a lover,' Nan said, when Sophie was settled in the wicker chair out in the garden at Cheyne Row the following afternoon. Tea had been poured, Bessie had served macaroons and tea-cakes on a little side-table, and now the two friends could talk in private.

'Several,' Sophie said easily, 'and some uncommon handsome.'

'Red waistcoat?'

'Not of the best I'll allow, but entertaining for a week or so.'

Nan was grinning with admiration at her friend's aplomb. 'You make no secret of it,' she said. 'Does Heinrich know?'

'Well, as to that,' Sophie said, picking up the last fragment of her macaroon, 'Heinrich knows what he wants to know. He always has and he always will. Ah me! I thought him such a catch when we wed. Fuseli the artist. I know better now. He has a life of his own, my dear, and tastes I do not share.'

'A mistress?' Nan asked, fascinated. Who would fancy such an odd-looking man?

'Several,' Sophie said easily. 'Girls *and* boys, my dear.'

That was shocking but not unexpected.

'You do not suffer jealousy?'

'No, indeed. Why should I?'

'You will take another dish of tea?' Nan said, seeing that both their cups were empty. 'I do believe I should have been uncommon jealous if Mr Easter had been untrue.'

'Mr Easter was a rarity, my dear,' Sophie said. 'Heinrich is like the common run of mankind, only more talented. He travels abroad without me nowadays and shows me scant concern, save when he needs a model. Believe me, my dear, they are all selfish, almost to a man.'

'And yet you urge me to take a lover,' Nan laughed. 'There en't a deal of logic in that, my dear.'

'There's a deal of sense,' Sophie said, sipping her tea. 'Lovers give pleasure, Nan Easter, if you've the wit to handle 'em aright.'

'Selfish men?' Nan teased.

'Aye, selfish and fickle, and such as will use women ill if they ain't got the sense to prevent it.'

This conversation intrigued Nan because it seemed so likely to be true. Her gallant dancing partners of the night before had been attentive enough, in all conscience, but none had shown any signs of caring for her beyond the next reel. 'How is it done, pray? I would fain know the trick of it.'

'The trick,' Sophie said seriously, 'and you would be well to mark it, Nan, is to love 'em less than ever they love you. I find my next lover when the present one is most ardent, and I make it a point of honour to discard 'em all long before they tire of me.'

There was something so heartless about this philosophy that Nan winced. 'Can love be so controlled?' she asked. And she suddenly remembered Mr Easter saying, 'I shall love you till the day I die, forsaking all other.' 'No, Sophie,' she said. 'Surely not. If I were to love again, I couldn't treat un so, indeed I could not.'

A skylark uncoiled its burbling song in a leisurely spiral rising higher and higher into the blue air above their heads. In the field beyond the garden the ripe corn swooshed and rustled. And from the far distance they could hear the tiny, tinny jingle of cow-bells in the water meadows. It was a beautiful day.

'Then you would be a fool,' Sophie said sagely, 'and you would suffer for it.'

'Not all men are selfish,' Nan urged. 'Mr Easter was the kindest man alive. A courteous gentleman. Oh, most courteous. I tell 'ee, Sophie, if I ever do take a lover 'twill be just such another. And I shall love him truly, forsaking all other, as he will love me.'

'If I could make you such a man, my dear,' Sophie said affectionately, 'he would be yours this very day.' But her expression showed how little she thought it likely. 'In the meantime there is another ball at Vauxhall a' Thursday, where I can at least promise you partners a-plenty. How say you?'

'Why yes, of course, for there's a pleasure quite without pain.'

'Aye, true indeed,' Sophie said, tossing her curls. 'Always providing they are light on their feet!'

And it *was* a pleasure to be out in society again, going to the play or the fireworks, to dine upon a river boat or dance at the Rotunda, with young men a-plenty to squire her and compliment her, and pretty clothes to wear. But pain trailed in unbidden even on that easy scene. Once she was home again, in her quiet room in Cheyne Row, with the household asleep all around her, she found it impossible to sleep after such excitement, and knew with some sadness that for all her success as a business woman, she was lonely. And when she did sleep, her dreams were confused, mixing memories of her patient Mr Easter with fantasies of handsome young men who swore they would love her to distraction and then disappeared in a tumble of images that made no sense to her at all, waking or sleeping. In the morning she would be full of restless prowling energy, and would set off for work earlier than usual, sharp-eyed for faults.

On one such morning, as Thiss drove the pony cart briskly along the Strand towards the newspaper offices, the sight of a shop-keeper opening his doors reminded her of Sophie's joke about selling newspapers by the yard. 'I've a mind to open a newspaper shop,' she said to Thiss. 'We will call at Mr Duncan's after first delivery and see what may be done about it.'

'She's a one,' Thiss said to Bessie, when the two of them were having breakfast together with the children later that morning. 'I never know'd a woman with so many ideas.'

'Is it a *good* idea Thiss?' Annie asked, for sometimes her mother's sudden ideas were rather alarming.

But Thiss seemed quite sure nothing but good would come of it. 'A capital idea, Sunshine,' he said. 'You ever known yer ma 'ave an idea what didn't come up trumps?'

It took Nan nearly two months to find the shop she wanted, and much determined haggling before she could get it for the price she was prepared to pay, but it was well worth the effort and the wait. It stood on the corner of George Street and the Strand, not far away from the old Savoy Palace and the fine new frontage of Somerset House, so it was within strolling distance of all the newspaper printers, well placed for the carriage trade, and close enough to the vegetable market of Covent Garden to attract customers for the *Daily Advertiser*. A good position at a fair price.

It was a very dirty shop, having once belong to a cobbler, and it wasn't really as big as she would have liked it to be, although she was

183

happy to persuade herself that it probably looked smaller than it was because of the thick coating of dust on the windows and the mounds of debris the cobbler had left behind him. There was a fine drawing-room on the first floor which would make an excellent reading room, once it had been cleaned and furnished, and the room above it would provide adequate living accomodation and some storage. But its present state was of little consequence. She could already see exactly what it would be like as her first newspaper shop full of papers and customers. She set Thiss to work on it as soon as she had the key. With a good scrub through, clean windows, a lick of paint, a new counter and such like, it would be a model establishment. All it needed was Thistlethwaite elbow-grease and a good bold sign, which she would order from Mr Johnson that very afternoon.

Then different signs arrived at Mr Johnson's at the end of the week, each one saying 'A. Easter — Newsagent' within a variety of scrolls and lozenges, leaves and circles, and in an equal variety of colours. Following her husband's example, she took them home to Chelsea and involved her entire household in the choice. Even the two eldest children were allowed to stay up after dinner and give their opinion.

Mr Dibkins said he liked the two green and gold ones. 'Catches your eye sommink marvellous,' and Thiss said he thought a good bold lettering was best, 'seein' you wants ter be seen from the other side a' the street.'

'An' carriage winders,' Bessie volunteered.

Billy wanted to know why they didn't say, 'and sons' and was assured that they would the minute he and Johnnie were old enough.

And Mrs Dibkins screwed her mouth into contortions and winked and nodded as though her head were on a spring, and finally took herself off to the kitchen to boil a kettle for a pot of tea, because even after all that effort she couldn't bring herself to express any opinion at all.

But eventually and between them they chose the design Nan wanted, a plain oval shape outlined in gold on a dark green ground with the legend painted in large gold letters within it. Straightforward, clear and businesslike. Just like she was herself. And they had all been involved in the decision, just as Mr Easter would have wanted, which had pleased them and would please him, wherever he was. 'We will go to the Tower tomorrow afternoon,' she promised her children as she kissed them goodnight, 'and see the animals.' 'Twould be a fine way of celebrating her success. And on the way there she would put an advertisement in the *Advertiser* for a couple to run the shop.

She worded her advertisement with care. 'Reliable man or trustworthy married couple required to work in a new establishment between the City and Westminster. Pleasant accomodation over the shop is available for the right couple who should have energy, fortitude and honesty in abundance. Good references required. Apply in writing.'

'That should make them comprehend what manner of work 'twill be,' she said as she handed the paper to the clerk of the *Daily Advertiser*.

'Aye, it should,' he agreed. 'How many days?'

'Two.'

By the third day she'd had more than a dozen replies, and only three of them even faintly possible. But then the thirteenth arrived and the thirteenth was intriguing.

'Dear Mistress Easter,' it said, 'I have the honner for to supply to the advertissment what I seen in the *Daily Advertiser* me and my wife would care to supply being we worked for Mr Easter one time Great Yarmouth that were what you may remember I am yr obedient servant M Howlett.'

She had no idea who M Howlett was, but she wrote back to him at once instructing him to come and see her in the shop, adding 'bring your wife, I pray you.'

He attended promptly on the appointed hour, crossing the Strand with the darting nervousness of the countryman, eyes bolting. He was an awkward, bony-looking fellow in an ancient livery, his jacket patched at the elbows and his breeches shiny with wear, and to Nan, watching his approach from behind her clean shop-window, there was something very familiar about his gait, but as he walked watching his feet she couldn't see his face, so she couldn't be sure who he was. His wife trotted beside him, hanging onto his arm like a plump umbrella. There was something vaguely familiar about her too, but it wasn't until they entered the shop and said 'Good afternoon' that she recognized them both. The man was Matthew, Mr Easter's servant from South Quay, and his wife was Abby from Plum Row.

'My heart alive!' she said, beaming on them. 'What are you doin' in London?'

Matthew went ahead with his prepared speech, 'I wrote soon as I see the name,' he said solemnly. 'I say to Abby — diden' I, Abby? —

that'll be our Mrs Easter sure as eggs is eggs. Per'aps we shall suit bein' we're from Yarmouth an' all.'

But Abby answered the question. 'That ol' Mr Callbeck he was a rare ol' Tartar,' she said. 'We stuck him nigh on three year, then we ups an' packs an' comes to London. Never thinkin' there'd be the chance of a job with you. We didden' none of us know what had become of you, you see. Now after you an' Mr Easter went to London. Mr Callbeck never said nothin' about you, ever.'

'That don't surprise me,' Nan said, speaking coolly, because she was annoyed at this reminder of the way the Easters had cut her out of their family and because Abby's tone was just a little too familiar for her liking. 'Masters don't go discussing their affairs with servants as a general rule.'

'Mrs Howkins did,' Abby argued. 'Don't 'ee remember? She told us every last detail, so she did.'

Nan looked her new servant in the eye. 'If you mean to work for me, Abby,' she warned, 'there's one thing we'd better get straight right here and now. I en't a maid-servant no more. I own a business now. I run a shop. I'm the mistress.'

Abby understood before she'd finished speaking. 'Yes, mum,' she said, dropping her eyes in the approved fashion. 'No offence meant, I'm sure.'

'We should be honoured,' Matthew said, doggedly continuing with his speech, 'for to be took on. Bein' we held Mr Easter in such esteem so to speak. Bein' you wouldn't need no references, ma'am. Bein' you knows how strong I am. Bein' I'm willin'. I thinks I could say willin', ma'am. Bein' you knows the sort of service we could both — um —. Bein' . . .'

'When could you start?' she said, interrupting him quickly before he could think of any more reasons, and was rewarded by a smile of such relief and such affection it almost brought tears to her eyes.

So she hired them, because however glaring their faults, she knew she could trust them. And besides, it was such a pleasure to be eased by the gentle burr of their Norfolk dialect after years spent listening to the sharp, quick speech of the city.

Matthew was delighted with their good fortune. 'Tha's a stroke a' luck workin' for Mrs Easter,' he said to Abby. 'She's a rare one is Mrs Easter. Always was. I mind the time she first come to South Quay. She give orders to *everyone*. I never seen the like. Oh she's a rare one, right enough.'

'I know'd 'er longer'n you,' Abby said with great satisfaction. 'I know'd 'er when she was no more'n nine years old an' a scullery maid. She had a mind of her own even then.'

'An' now she's the missus,' Matthew said. 'Oh, she's a rare one, right enough. A. Easter — Newsagent eh?'

A. Easter — Newsagent opened her shop two days later and although she didn't admit it to anybody, not even to Thiss, it was rather an anxious time.

Her trade was nowhere near good enough. She haunted the shop at the end of every day, to check the figures and change the window display, and she was regularly disappointed to see that her sales were so small. It was true they picked up a little, after a week or two, but very, very slowly, and no matter how many or how few papers she put into the window, there didn't seem to be anything she could do to improve them.

But then, just as she was getting short-tempered with disappointment, the *Advertiser* was full of the exciting news that body snatchers had been seen at work in the City. 'At dead of night,' it reported, 'when decent citizens have retired to their well earned slumbers, evil men are abroad in the deserted churchyards of the city. They prowl in the darkness, disturbing the graves of the newly dead, desecrating the last resting places of our dear departed. Last night hooded figures were seen rapidly leaving the churchyard of All Saints in Pennyquick Lane. Where will they dig tonight?' It was splendidly lurid and it sold the paper like hot cakes on a cold day. And those who couldn't find a copy for sale on the streets came into the shop to buy.

Nan made a really healthy profit and ordered twice her usual number of *Advertisers* for the next three days, confident that if the story continued her sales would rise. It was a wise decision, for now there was such a demand for the paper that she couldn't meet it. And neither could the printers, who were very much aggrieved because they were only able to print at the rate of five hundred copies an hour and they could have sold double that number if only they could have got them out.

'Nothing sells so well as bad news,' Nan told her reflection at the

187

end of that first successful day. 'Long may it continue and the worse the better!'

In fact there was such a demand for 'all the latest details' that she decided to open the reading-room. It hadn't been decorated and there weren't enough chairs but there was sensation a-plenty and that was what mattered. Within a week she had thirty-two monthly subscribers and four who had paid up for a quarter.

'Who'd ha' thought it, Mrs Easter?' Matthew said, scratching his head with both hands as eager readers tramped up and down the stairs. 'I never could abide readin' mesself. Who'd ha' thought it?'

'Take up these extra copies while you're thinkin',' Nan instructed briskly, for Matthew's contemplation invariably inhibited action and the sooner it was stopped the better.

The body snatchers were speculated upon for more than a week, and sales remained high throughout. But then two cadavers were actually recovered from the hospital which had secretly purchased them and after a lengthy and public debate as to the rights and wrongs of the case, the body snatchers were brought to trial and the recovered corpses were re-buried. And the news was buried with them.

Sales fell, of course, but only slightly. 'There will be other events,' Nan said. 'Now they're used to coming to a shop for news they'll keep on coming, you'll see.'

But the next piece of news which was to occupy all the London papers was the weather, and that didn't please her at all. For the winter had begun and it was plain to everybody, from astrologers to artisans, that it was going to be a very hard one.

Chapter Sixteen

The first heavy snowfall of that winter obscured the sky all through the last day of November, with flakes as thick as goose feathers and a knife-edged cold. The first blizzard howled it into drifts within a week and from then on the cold was unrelenting. Snow fell with monotonous regularity, by day and by night, smothering all sound and most land-marks, and even though the main thoroughfares were usually trudged to a brown slush by mid-day, the rest of the world was a study in black and white.

Chelsea's ancient cottages were weighed down by an additional white thatch which dripped blackened straw and grew even blacker icicles. Frozen water hung in white suspension from black pumps. The church rose darkly among the white hummocks of its untidy yard. Black crows spread tessellated wings against a white sky. Only the chimney stacks displayed any colour, their red brick oddly naked, breathing out bold brown smoke into the grey air, the one sign of life and warmth in a cold deadened world.

Soon the streets were mounded with perpetual snow and the cobbles treacherous with impacted ice. Horses slithered and fell and were hauled to their feet by grooms made clumsy by cold and thoughtless cruelty. Beggars froze to death where they sat, their filthy rags as solid as rock, and were hauled ignominiously away in mud-ridged tumbrels to a pauper's grave. Funerals soon became a daily occurrence as the old, the young and the frail gradually succumbed to the season. And street traders of all kinds watched their custom dwindle, and grew poorer and hungrier by the day.

Supplies of food grew smaller too and more costly as the fields froze. By the end of the year root vegetables had disappeared from the market altogether and no matter how well they were cooked, potatoes remained obstinately hard and grey. Even the Season was affected, which didn't

189

please Sophie Fuseli at all. The theatres stayed open, but both the great pleasure gardens were closed and the only balls held that winter were private affairs in the great well-heated houses of the ton.

By the middle of December Nan's profits had been virtually halved. Her regulars still paid to have their papers delivered, cold or no cold, but there were far too few of them, and there were days when street sales were so small as to be scarcely worth the bother. However temptingly she offered her wares, her customers scurried past, heads down against the biting wind, swathed to the nose in shawls and mufflers and with their hats pulled over their ears, ignoring everything except their urgent need to get beside a fire again as quickly as they could.

In fact, if it hadn't been for the presence of her two winsome children, there were some days when she would have sold no papers at all. But a small child bundled about with shawls and scarves, hatted and hooded, and wrapped in a red cloak with a small chapped nose and rough cheeks to match, was still an attraction. Fortunately.

William was less help than his sister in cold weather, because he would keep running about or blowing on the unmittened ends of his fingers or stamping his feet in the slush and spattering them all with filth. But Annie was a good child, standing patiently and obediently in the trodden snow, and never complaining, no matter how cold she was. And she was often very cold indeed. There were days when her fingers were frozen into stiff little claws and when she got home it took Bessie quite a long time to chaff them into life again, unbending them one at a time, very gradually and painfully. But even then the child didn't complain. She was far too fond of her mother to do that. And far too worried about the roof.

Bessie had explained to her that Mama worked hard to 'keep a roof over their heads' and that she and Billy were to do everything they could to help her. Sometimes she would glance back fearfully at the roof as they left the house in the morning, just in case it had been taken away overnight. But the familiar grey slates were always there, so whatever it was that Mama was doing, she seemed to be doing it right. But it was a serious responsibility, even so.

Her two little brothers fought back all the time, shouting 'No!' and 'Shan't!' and running away or rolling about on the floor, and being smacked and shaken for their disobedience, but Annie would never have dared to offer such bad behaviour. Even when she was so cold that she felt sick, or so tired that she would have sat down in the snow, if that had been allowed, she said nothing, but stood stoically at her post, enduring, newspaper in frozen hand, aware of the burden of keeping that roof in place.

So on that miserable December day when she first felt ill, hot and dizzy and with no strength in her arms, she went on enduring. It was the only thing she could do, for she didn't want to upset Mama when she was working so hard. Besides it might make her cross, and that was something she couldn't even contemplate, leave alone provoke. For Annie was a gentle creature, like her father, and she shrank from any hint of unpleasantness, curling in upon herself, silently, like a rose folding for the night.

She told Bessie she didn't feel well, of course, when they were back home and Mama was safely out of earshot, and Bessie put her to bed and got a hot brick to warm her feet which were so cold she couldn't feel them, which was odd when the rest of her body was burning hot.

During the night she began to cough and her chest hurt her ever such a lot and Bessie got up and went bustling off downstairs and presently returned with a cup and gave her little sips of some syrupy stuff, which tasted quite nice but didn't stop the cough, even though Bessie had promised it would.

In the morning they were both tired out. When Billy came leaping on to the bed to wake her up, she didn't have the strength to tell him not to. But Bessie hauled him away and dressed him, and grumbled at Johnnie to look sharp, and after an age of loud voices that made her head throb, and kicking feet that jarred her aching arms, they all went away downstairs and left her to sleep again. As her mind began to drift away, she was glad she didn't have to get up and go to work.

'Where's Annie?' Nan asked, when Bessie ushered the two boys into the dining-room and settled them at the table. She was sitting before the tea caddy.

Bessie steeled herself for the struggle that would have to come. It was the first time in her life that she had ever dared to obstruct the will of an adult, and her heart was beating painfully just at the thought of it. 'If you please mum,' she said, timidly, 'she ain't very well this morning an' 'tis uncommon cold.'

'She can't stay in bed just because it's cold,' Nan said mildly. 'I don't always feel well, let me tell you, but I always turn out. We can't afford to spend our days rolling around in bed. That's not the way the world is. Go and get her.'

191

'No, mum,' Bessie said, blushing but steadfast. 'She ain't well, beggin' yer pardon.'

The blush alerted Nan. This might be serious. 'You two boys sit in those chairs and don't you dare move, not so much as an inch,' she said. Then she put the lid on the teapot and set off upstairs.

It surprised them both when Bessie, mild obedient Bessie, who wouldn't say boo to a goose, suddenly kicked up her heels and *ran* in front of her, charging up the stairs like a thing demented, to fling herself against the nursery door, legs astride and both hands clinging to the jambs, wild-eyed and scarlet in the face. 'No,' she shouted. 'Beggin' yer pardon mum, but you shan't take 'er out! No indeed you shan't! My poor lamb's ill, so she is. You shan't!'

'What is the matter with you?' Nan said, much surprised. 'Stand aside, pray do, and let us have a little less of this nonsense.'

But Bessie had completely misjudged her mistress's intentions, and went on defending her young. She burst into tears but she didn't stand aside. 'She's five years old, mum,' she said. 'Poor little mite. Five years old, that's all, an' she ain't a-goin' out in this weather with a fever, that she ain't, not if it was ever so.'

'If she's ill, the sooner I see her the better,' Nan said, wondering whether she would have to use force to pull Bessie aside.

But Bessie looked as though she'd been stuck to the door, and she was no longer the fragile child Mr Easter had hired when Johnnie was born. That red face had a womanly look to it, despite its present distortion, the short little body had put on weight and most of it was muscle, those outstretched arms were strong. Strong enough to over-power her mistress if it came to fisticuffs. Surely it wouldn't come to fisticuffs! Good heavens, what was the matter with the girl?

Fortunately, just at that moment, Thiss arrived. He'd finished his first delivery and had come home for breakfast. Bessie's squeals had him up the stairs in an instant.

Both women were really quite glad to see him. 'Ah, Thiss,' Nan said. 'She won't let me into the bedroom. Perhaps you can get her to see sense, for I'm sure I can't.'

'Annie's ill,' Bessie sobbed. 'She ain't in a fit state . . .'

'Now, don't be a goose, Bessie,' he said. 'Dry yer old eyes, there's a good gel, an' we'll all go in an' see what's what, eh?'

And to Nan's relief, that's what they did.

Annie was lying on the floor, with the sheets and blankets tumbled around her, tossing her head from side to side, muttering and groaning and completely delirious.

'Oh, my lovey!' Nan said, running to her side at once and lifting her damp head into her lap. 'Oh, what is it, Annie? My poor love!'

But the child was raving. 'I can't keep the roof up,' she groaned. 'Don't 'ee tell Mama. Ba! Ba! Where are you? Oh don't 'ee tell Mama, for pity's sake.'

'I'm 'ere, pet. Your Ba's 'ere.' Bessie said. 'Don't 'ee never think your Ba would ever leave yer. My poor lamb.'

'Best get 'er back ter bed,' Thiss said, and he lifted the child gently from Nan's lap and laid her back on the mattress.

'There's no roof!' Annie said wildly, grabbing at his jacket. 'No roof!'

'Thiss 'as got yer,' Bessie tried to explain. But the child groaned and couldn't understand.

'Leave 'er be,' Thiss ordered. 'She don't know who we are, neither one of us. Which ain't ter be wondered at, seein' the fever she got.'

But she knew who she wanted, fever or no fever. 'Ba!' she called. 'Ba! Ba!' And Bessie held her hand and smoothed the damp hair from her forehead while Thiss tucked the covers smoothly round her.

And Nan Easter, Nan the business-woman, Nan the empire-builder, Nan the mother, was superfluous. There was nothing she could do but stand to one side, her insides churning with fear, and wait until the fit subsided and the child was calm again. Then, of course, she took action.

'Run you to Mr Whiteman,' she said to Thiss. 'And you,' turning to Bessie, 'tell Mrs Dibkins to give the boys their breakfast and keep them downstairs no matter what. 'Tis a fever and they might go a-catchin' it. Then bring towels and a bowl of warm water and we'll sponge her down.' Then as they didn't spring to obey her orders immediately, and she was tense with anxiety, 'Hasten you up, do!'

Mr Whiteman was a modest physician with a gentle manner, which was why Nan had chosen him, even in the heat and worry of the moment.

He came to attend his little patient immediately, standing before her, grave and old-fashioned in his fustian breeches and his green cloth coat, saying nothing. His wig was unpowdered, a fact which Nan noted with approval, for it revealed that he put his patient before his appearance. But he took a long time to make any diagnosis, which annoyed her, especially as he did so many things that didn't seem at all necessary to her, and did them so slowly. First he had Bessie lift the

193

child's nightgown so that he could examine her back and chest and all four limbs, peering at them closely and saying nothing. Then he lifted her eyelids and looked at her unconscious eyes, and opened her mouth and fished out her tongue and looked down her throat, saying nothing. And finally he put his head right down onto her chest and appeared to be listening to that too.

'She has been ill for several days, I imagine?' he asked.

'Yes, sir,' Bessie said. 'She 'as, poor little mite. Two days to my certain knowledge.'

'Did she go out of doors during that time?'

'Yes,' Nan had to admit, and her heart lurched with anxiety and guilt. How was it that I didn't see she was ill?

'That would account for it, of course,' the doctor said and sighed heavily.

The sigh alarmed Nan and increased her guilt. 'Well,' she said sharply. 'What is it?'

'Your daughter has a congestion of the lungs,' he said sadly. 'That is the cause of her present fever. She is very gravely ill.'

Nan's heart contracted with such fear that it altered the sound of her voice. 'What is to be done?' she said, hoarsely.

'Very little, I fear,' he said truthfully. 'We could try bleeding. Or blistering, should you wish it. But I should tell you I have never known either practice to be efficacious in such cases. In fact it has to be admitted, there have been times when in my considered opinion such treatments have done more harm than good.'

'Then what will you do?'

'There is nothing any of us *can* do Mrs Easter,' he sighed. 'not for an illness of this kind. Nothing at all. I only wish there were. The fever must run its course, I fear. Keep a boiling kettle on the hob to moisten the air. That may ease her breathing, although it will not cure her, for there is no cure.'

'But she will recover?' It was only a question. There couldn't be any doubt about that, surely? It would be too cruel.

'The fever will run its course,' he repeated. 'It will get worse, I fear, but in a few days it will reach a crisis, and then one of two things will occur. Either she will turn the corner and get better. Or she will die.' And seeing the anguish on Nan's face, 'That is the truth of the matter, Mrs Easter. I cannot gloss it.'

Bessie was weeping, muffling her sobs with her apron. 'Hush up!'

her mistress told her, furious with fear. 'I got enough to worry about without you.'

'I will call again tomorrow,' Mr Whiteman said sadly. 'I do truly wish I could have given you other and better news.'

'Aye,' Nan said. 'So do I!'

But however much she might struggle against it, she was caged by the truth and couldn't escape from it, as the time passed slowly, day after delirious day, and Annie got worse and worse. She was ashamed by the careless way she'd treated her uncomplaining daughter, and was privately aware that it was far too much like the way she'd treated the child's father. Now she realized how very much her little girl meant to her, and knew how good and helpful and undemanding she'd been, and suspected with a palpable sinking of the heart that the child must have been afraid of her, because she'd been ill for several days and hadn't dared to tell her. 'You should have seen all this before,' she told her reflection angrily and every night. 'But not you. Oh no! You got to wait till they're dead or dying!' And she was anguished at the thought.

On Sunday, when the priest spoke to his Chelsea congregation about the evil of selfishness and the value of man's immortal soul, she listened for once, and took his words to heart. From then on, she said earnest prayers every morning and every night, promising God that if only the child could be spared she would do everything in her power to be unselfish, she would think of others, she would treat all her children with the most loving kindness. They would never work in the streets again, there would be more fun and pleasure in all their lives, anything, anything. But the moment of crisis had yet to be faced, and the nearer it got the more she dreaded it.

Bessie kept a constant vigil in the nursery and did her best not to cry when her mistress was in the room. And Thiss looked after the business. And the boys slept in Nan's room, confused and depressed by the air of gloom and anxiety that surrounded them. And Annie struggled for breath and burned with fever.

On Christmas Eve she was so very much worse, that Nan sent for Mr Whiteman again, even though he'd visited them in the morning, and she knew there was nothing he could do. Now every breath rattled in and out of Annie's constricted throat, and she writhed for air, choking and coughing until phlegm bubbled from her lips.

'It is the crisis,' Mr Whiteman said. But he was confirming what they already knew.

He and Nan and Bessie sat with their struggling patient all through the night, replenishing the kettle, relighting the candles, watching and praying but not daring to look beyond the moment. And towards dawn when a grey light began to filter through the darkness, and Annie had been sleeping rather less noisily for about an hour, she suddenly woke up and looked at them with intelligence. 'I's very thirsty Ba,' she said. 'Could I have a little water, pray?'

The cup was in her hand almost before she'd finished speaking, and she drank greedily, and asked for more.

'Is it . . .? Has she . . .?' Nan whispered. Tears were coursing down her cheeks and when she looked at Mr Whiteman she could see that his eyes were moist too.

'Yes, Mrs Easter,' he said. 'The crisis is passed. Praise be to God!'

After he'd gone, she and Bessie fetched bowls and towels and gave their poor little patient a gentle wash. She was pitifully thin, and she still coughed, but she was undeniably cooler and her breathing had eased. 'Soon 'ave you better now, eh my precious?' Bessie said. But Nan was so anguished she couldn't say anything.

Later that morning, when the child was asleep again, and Bessie had gone to get the boys up for breakfast, she remembered her prayers, and said genuine thanks to God for His infinite mercy. I will keep my word, she prayed, I vow it. Children are to be cared for, not used. I will never make such a mistake again. I couldn't have borne it if she'd died. I will keep my word.

The cold continued and street sales remained obstinately low, and early in the new year three more walks came onto the market because their owners could no longer afford to run them. All three were going cheap so Nan bought them at once, but this time true to her vow, she hired newsmen to run them. Then she and Thiss drew up a route map ready to tout for deliveries. Their new wealthy customers were delighted to have such a service offered. 'In weather so exceptionally inclement,' one titled lady said, 'tis a comfort to read of the misfortunes of others. We will take *The Times* and the *Morning Post*. 'Tis as well to keep abreast of affairs.'

To everybody's relief, Annie made a steady recovery, getting better as the weather got worse. By the time she was pronounced well enough to leave her bed and creep shakily downstairs to sit by the fire in the dining-room, the Serpentine was frozen solid, right the way across, and four of the seven streams in the Chelsea waterworks were too choked by ice to provide water for the populace.

'There is no end to this dratted winter,' Nan said, when Mrs Dibkins came hobbling into the dining-room one morning with half a kettleful of water and the news that the pump was dry.

'We can always boil snow, Mrs Easter-dear,' Mrs Dibkins said, chins a-quiver as she set the kettle on the hob. 'That's what we done last time. More than ten years ago, that were. Ho, what a time we had. They was skatin' on that ol' Serpentine then. Like a fair it was. Mr Dibkins'll tell you. They had roast chestnuts for sale, an' everyone on skates a-dancin'. Ho, my lor!'

'What's 'katin'?' Johnnie wanted to know. Now that he was two-and-a-half, and didn't roar quite so much, he'd been allowed out of his high chair and was sitting up to the table, but he was still so small that only his head and shoulders were visible above the cloth. 'What's 'katin', Ba?'

' 'Tis a way a' walkin' on ice,' Bessie said. 'A skate's like a sort a' wedge made a' bone. You ties it to yer shoes an' off you goes, a-whizzin' along. Quick as a bird.'

'Ho, what sport!' Mrs Dibkins said, watching the kettle spitting on the hob, so that she could lift it for Mrs Easter the minute it boiled. 'Quick as a bird! Oh my lor!'

Billy was thrilled by the idea. 'Could we go 'kating, Mama?' he asked, his eyes round with eagerness. Now that he was nearly four he was ready for any challenge.

Nan lowered her newspaper and looked at him sharply. 'No, you could not,' she said. 'The very idea! Do you all want congestion of the lungs? Is one not bad enough? We shall need some more bread, Mrs Dibkins.'

The boys thought her most unfair, but they didn't say so, of course. Not then. Not straight to her face. Young as they were they knew that you didn't argue with Mama. She was a deal too sharp for that. The most you could dare was a 'look' thrown venomously in her direction when she was busy reading the paper. You said what you thought later, to Thiss and Ba.

'It ain't fair, Thiss,' Billy said. 'We could go 'katin'. We wouldn't catch the digestion, would us, Ba?'

'I couldn't say, my lamb,' Bessie temporized. She was much too

197

much in awe of Nan to contradict her, even when she was well out of earshot.

'We could go a-Sunday,' Billy persisted.

'She wouldn't let *me*,' Annie said sadly. 'not when I been ill, she wouldn't.'

'Well not *you* per'aps,' Billy said cheerfully, 'but she could let *us*. It ain't fair, Thiss.'

'Tell yer what,' Thiss offered, 'you leave it ter me. Be'ave yerselves like good kids, an' I'll see what I can do.' There were ways round Mrs Easter's irascibility and the longer he lived in her household, the more of them he discovered. ' 'Er barks a sight worse'n 'er bite. I'll see what I can do.'

What he did was to drive her back to Chelsea by a different route the next morning after their first delivery in Marylebone. As she was quick to notice.

'I simply cannot imagine why you should want to drive through St James' Park, Thiss,' she said, looking across the snow-covered lawns to where small bundled shapes were already sliding and tumbling on the ice that had once been the Serpentine. 'You should be ashamed to be so artful, you rogue. That you should.'

' 'Tis a good healthy sport for young'uns,' he said, grinning back at her over his shoulder.

'Out in this cold all hours?'

'Warm as toast. On the move,' he urged. 'If you'll allow, mum, I'll prove it to yer.'

'Go on then. Prove it. If you can.'

So Pepperpot was reined in, and a gliding child enticed from the pond with the promise that he could 'earn hisself a farthin' if he done as he was told' and Nan was prevailed upon to lean down from the trap and feel how warm the urchin's hands were even inside extremely ragged mittens.

' 'E ain't wrapped up all that well neither,' Thiss said, standing beside the child and looking up at her hopefully. 'Warm as toast, ain'tcher?'

'Yes, mum,' the child said, 'D'yer want ter feel me face an' all?'

Nan declined the offer, his face being even dirtier than his grime-dark hands. But Thiss had made his point.

'Very well,' she said. 'You may hire skates for all of us and a sledge for Annie. Now let us ride home, or 'tis *my* lungs will be affected.'

'And you, mum?' Thiss asked, as he climbed aboard and clicked Pepperpot into motion.

'Me?'

'Shall I hire some skates for you an' all?'

' 'Course,' she said.

It was a great success. For the children it was a sudden and extraordinary adventure, and the sight of their mother gliding across the ice so elegantly was a revelation, for Nan was gratified to discover that she could still skate quite passably even though the last time she'd done such a thing had been back in the Yarmouth days when she was working as a lady's maid to Mrs Howkins. What a long time ago it seemed. And now here she was, the owner of six newswalks that between them covered nearly half the vast city of London. 'A. Easter, Newsagent.' She skated happily, turning out her toes to right and left in a steady satisfactory rhythm, avoiding the bodies hurtling towards her, keeping a careful eye on her convalescent daughter, in control of her feet and her life.

For Bessie and Thiss the fact that they were allowed out to play, in that tingling air, with no chores, for an entire afternoon, was a freedom they'd never known before. They spent the first half hour hauling the boys along between them, while Annie sat huddled in her rugs in the sledge and watched. And they were all astounded at how quickly the two children learned the entirely new art of sliding along on pieces of bone. Bessie declared that young Johnnie was soon skating better than he walked, which was true enough, for his walk was still something of a stagger. And Billy loved every minute of it, whether he was standing up, or gliding along, or rolling about on the ice, fat as a puppy in his padded clothes.

On that first afternoon Annie was content to sit warmly wrapped in her sledge and watch, but on the following day she ventured out onto the ice, and found to her great delight that skating was easier than it looked, and that the motion of it brought warmth to her cheeks and made her feel really well again. By the third day, all three children were really quite proficient, and could glide along with the best, following their mother or holding her hands and singing as they sped.

All of which delighted Thiss, for now he could skate at speed with Bessie, and that gave him the chance he'd been scheming for ever since the ice first froze, to put his arm round her nice, tempting waist and hold her cuddled up close to his side. Breath streamed from their open mouths and was parted by the speed of their movement to flow behind them on either side of their faces, like foam parted by the bows of a ship; their skates hissed; her cloak flicked and billowed like a sail; and he fancied he could feel the curve of her breast even through the layers of thick clothing she'd piled on against the cold. What sport!

And of course it wasn't very long before she slipped and fell and then they were able to roll over and over on the ice, thigh to thigh, giggling and squealing and very much aware of one another. And after that one or the other of them contrived to fall over every few minutes or so, and it took longer and longer to disentangle their limbs, and they needed more and more time to lie on top of one another and recover their breath. Or lose it.

And watching them Nan felt a pang of jealousy, for they were such an obvious pair and so happy in each other's company. The whole world goes two by two, she thought, and wondered whether she ought to take a lover, just for the sake of company.

On Sunday the itinerant street-sellers converged upon the park with hot potatoes and roast chestnuts and set up their stalls alongside the Serpentine to tempt the skaters and the hungry congregations that had come to take the chill air after Sunday service. The pond was crowded with skaters and tumblers so they did a good trade, particularly to Billy and Johnnie.

'My heart alive, this ol' skating do give 'ee appetite,' Nan said, tossing a chestnut from hand to hand to cool it. 'Just so soon as spring comes around and trade picks up again, I shall hire me a good cook, so I shall.' Old Mrs Dibkin's cooking was getting worse and worse.

But that day Mrs Dibkins produced an excellent dish of stewed mutton and followed it with apple dumplings and sugar syrup, so they were all well fed and well pleased.

'I hope the ice goes on an' on an' on,' Billy said. 'I like 'katin', Mama.'

'On an' on an' on an' on,' Johnnie echoed, trailing the syrup from his plate to his mouth in a long, sticky thread.

'Shall we go skatin' again tomorrow?' Annie asked.

'Like enough,' Nan said. ' 'Tis a healthy sport in all conscience. Eat properly, Johnnie.'

But the thaw came much quicker than any of them could have imagined. On Friday afternoon the Serpentine was frozen as hard as it had ever been and the sky was white with cold. Overnight the wind changed direction and there was a steady warming drizzle. By eight o'clock the next morning, the dawn sky was pale blue and the ice visibly cracking. Soon regular customers were blinking onto the streets again like bears after a long hibernation. 'Spring is on its way at last,' they said, and were happy to buy a paper, 'to see how the world wags after such a winter. What news of the war, eh?'

'I shall rent another shop,' Nan told her family, when profits had been high for the third week in succession.

But Annie looked worried. 'Will it be another roof Mama?' she asked.

'Another roof?'

'On the shop, Mama. For you to keep on.'

'Why bless the child, what's she talking about?' Nan said, looking at Bessie for elucidation.

'You know, Ba,' Annie appealed. 'What you said.'

By now Nan was remembering all those frantic ravings when the child had been delirious. They'd been about a roof too. 'Tell me what Ba said,' she urged, taking the child onto her knee.

'I'm to be a good girl an' help Mama,' Annie remembered, ' 'cause Mama works so hard to keep the roof on over our heads.' And she was startled when the adults began to laugh. But Mama was cuddling her so it was all right.

' 'Tis a way of talking,' Mama explained. 'A way of talking. That means I work hard to earn enough money for your food and this pretty gown you're wearing and new brooms for Mr Dibkins and hay for Pepperpot and such like. Did you think the roof would fall off, is that what 'twas?'

Tearful nodding.

'There's no fear of that, lovey,' Nan said, suddenly tugged with pity. How children suffer, she thought, and all so unnecessarily. That's a worry could have been stopped before it had a chance to begin, if only I'd known of it. And she hastened to reassure. 'I never known a stronger roof, nor a better house. And a new shop will bring us prettier clothes and even better food. So don't you go a-worrying your head about un.'

So the second shop was rented and while she was in the City Nan went to an agency and hired four new servants, a plain cook, a pastry cook, and two scullery maids. 'They start work on Monday,' she told the rest of her household when she returned well pleased with her morning's

201

work. 'The cooks live out, the maids live in. They can have the back attic. More hands, less work eh?' Then she went off to the drapers to order pink cotton for the scullery maids.

But if she expected her servants to be pleased with their new assistants she was very much mistaken. Mrs Dibkins was devastated. 'Ho my lor!' she said, when Nan had left. 'What she want to go an' do a thing like that for? I cooks well enough, Horrie. Ho, we shall never get on, you mark my words. Ho! Ho my lor!'

'Don't take on so, Mother,' Mr Dibkins said, patting her shoulder with clumsy affection. 'Don't let's cross our bridges, eh?'

'Ho, she's a tartar,' Mrs Dibkins wept, chins wobbling. 'To hire new servants. We shall be on the streets come nightfall Monday, you mark my words.'

And at that Bessie caught Mrs Dibkin's panic and wept until her nose was pinched like a beak and her cheeks were blotchy as measles. 'What she have ter go an' do a thing like that for?' she wailed to Thiss. 'We was all right as we was. Oh, why does everything have ter change? Why can't we all stay the same?'

The sight of that pinched nose roused a tender pity in young Thiss that he couldn't distinguish from love. 'Don't cry, goosie,' he said, taking his God-sent opportunity to cuddle her openly. 'Things've got ter change. That's the way a' the world. T'ain't all bad.'

'Oh Thiss, I'm sorry ter cry.'

'You cry as long as yer like,' he said, grinning at her, 'jest so long as you understands what's what. 'Cause the more you cries the more I shall 'ave ter kiss yer.'

'Will yer?' she said, thrilled by the idea.

'Won't I jest?' he said, suiting the action to the word.

For the rest of that week the atmosphere in Cheyne Row was taut as stretched wire as Mrs Dibkins went about her duties tight-lipped with disapproval and distress, and Nan felt guilty to have upset her so much and did her best to pretend to all of them that she hadn't noticed anything was wrong. It was galling to her to think she'd made such a bad mistake with the servants, particularly when she was treating her children so much better. Not for the first time she wished she could have been more like Mr Easter, who'd always known exactly the right way to treat everybody.

But when Monday arrived the cooks turned out to be quite amiable people after all. Mrs Jorris, the plain cook, told Mrs Dibkins her kitchen was a joy to work in. ' 'Tain't everyone can keep a place so lovely, Mrs Dibkins. I hopes you'll lend a hand now an' then when there's a rush on. I can see we shall get on like a house a-fire.'

And the food they cooked between them was mouth-watering. And nobody got the sack. And Annie, having had her private fear finally and comfortably dispersed, was quite well again. And Bessie got kissed every day, night and morning. So perhaps it was all for the best, after all.

Chapter Seventeen

The arrival of the year 1797 had no sooner been celebrated, with masques and suppers and all manner of pleasant occasions, when, to Nan's irritation, Mr Pitt's wretched government voted to increase the stamp duty on newspapers yet again.

'Oh I see how 'tis,' she said to Thiss and Matthew as they were sorting the papers in the shop ready to deliver them to the walks. ' 'Tis a mortal high duty meant to squeeze out the cheap press that he don't like.'

'They're a scurrilous lot, mum,' Thiss said, tying up the first completed bundle. 'You should see some a' the things they say about the Prince a' Wales and that there Mrs Fitzherbert. Enough to bring a blush to a seasoned trooper.'

'Tha's a fact, Mrs Easter,' Matthew said earnestly. 'A fact as ever is.' He hadn't read any of the penny papers, but he always supported Thiss in any opinion, being he was such a live wire and certain to be right.

'He don't consider honest traders,' Nan grumbled, counting out a score of *Advertisers*, flick flick flick. Now she would have to charge sixpence for the old tuppenny *Times*. It was an exhorbitant sum and would be sure to deter custom, but there was no way she could avoid it. And just as she'd got the new walk established too.

The firm of A. Easter, Newsagents was now selling newspapers, morning and evening, in every walk in London except two, and it took a great deal of time to get all her papers down to Somerset House to be stamped. 'Dratted man!' she said. 'There's the first two batches ready, Matthew. Off you go!'

Her life was certainly full these days, and for most of the time her newspaper business was doing well, sometimes exceptionally well. There was always plenty of entertainment in the busy capital and although she hadn't found the lover she dreamed of, she was never short of company. She now employed nearly fifty people in one capacity or another, and had a houseful of servants and a comfortable bank account.

From time to time she still worried about Annie, who was ill every winter with coughs and agues and rheums, and hardly seemed to be growing at all. She was seven years old and would be eight in July and yet she was half a head shorter than Billy, who wasn't yet six. But she was a good child and seemed happy enough, even when she was suffering from the rheum.

Billy had grown into a harum-scarum creature, it was true, but with a pleasant cheerfulness about him that was very endearing. But Johnnie! Ah me! It made her sigh just to think of Johnnie. At four-and-a-half he was still nothing more or less than a wretch, still given to hideous tantrums and massive sulks, a dark-haired, swarthy, unpredictable little monster, who brooded about the house, hunch-shouldered and secretive when he wasn't screaming the place down. She hadn't understood him or liked him when he was born and she didn't understand him or like him now, try as she might. No matter how furiously he was scolded or how fiercely he was whipped, he didn't improve. Sometimes she was at her wits' end with him and wondered how on earth she'd ever come to produce such a creature. And there were days when it was a relief to leave the house and get on with her work and forget him.

'There!' she said to Matthew as he returned with the first batch stamped and ready, 'that's the sorting done. What we need now is a good piece of news to bolster our profits.'

'We could do with a victory in this ol' war,' Thiss said. 'That 'ud bolster every one of us.'

England had been at war with France for four years now but nothing much seemed to have happened. The government had passed a law making it a crime to criticize the king, and another making it a crime for more than three working men to meet and talk together. The price of food had risen alarmingly, there were bread shortages and bread riots, and more soldiers to be seen strutting about in their bright uniforms, especially near the Chelsea barracks; but the war was a long way away, and being fought between Frenchmen and Dutchmen and Austrians and such. And even though the French were outflanked and outnumbered by an alliance of enemies, they seemed to be winning most of their battles, largely, so people said, because their armies were commanded by a brilliant young man called Napoleon Bonaparte, who seemed to have set out to conquer the world single-handed. He'd just defeated the Spanish and made them sign a treaty, which, so Mr Walter of the *Times* declared, would mean that England would have the Spanish fleet to contend with in addition to the French and could bring the possibility of invasion a deal closer.

So it came as quite a shock that spring when there was a mutiny among the men of the Channel Fleet who chose that moment to announce that they had put up with bad food and poor pay and appalling conditions below decks for just too long, and were refusing to leave Spithead and put out to sea until something was done about it. The dreaded penny press listed their demands and pronounced them reasonable, recalling the American War of Independence and the French Revolution, and writing in glowing terms of liberty, equality and fraternity. But the established press thundered against them as 'traitors in our hour of need', although the sixpenny *Times* maintained that they had much to be aggrieved about and urged conciliation. Which after several days and much debate was what the government decided upon as the most appropriate line of action. For at a time when invasion was more and more likely, it wouldn't have done to have no warships available to defend the southern coastline. So pay was increased and a Royal pardon issued and the fleet finally set to sea.

Three weeks later there was a second mutiny, this time among the men of the North Sea Fleet based at the Nore. But this one wasn't news, so it was savagely put down and the ringleader hanged. And it wasn't news because the papers were full of the marvellous tidings that England had won a victory and found a hero.

There had been a sea battle on St Valentine's day at a Cape called St Vincent somewhere off the south coast of Portugal. The Spanish fleet had been sent into the Mediterranean to support the French, just as Mr Walter had predicted, and Admiral Jervis had gone out to oppose them. During the battle the two divisions of the Spanish Fleet had drifted apart and for nearly half an hour, a British squadron, led by a young commodore called Horatio Nelson, had valiantly withstood the entire force of the Spanish van and so turned the battle in England's favour. What heroism! Then not content with simply saving the hour, Commodore Nelson had apparently boarded two Spanish men-o'-war and taken them as prizes. What daring! He was the darling of the hour. The papers were full of his exploits, with calls for an instant reward for such a hero. It was all splendidly exciting and sold marvellously.

Especially when he was awarded the cross of the Bath and promoted to rear-admiral.

Soon St Vincent parties were being held in great houses up and down the country and the Ranelagh gardens organized a 'grand firework display and spectacle'. The long pond in front of the Chinese pavilion was filled with two fleets of model warships lit from within like floating lanterns and lined up for the battle of St Vincent, which so the tickets proclaimed was due to commence at seven of the clock and would be 'the greatest wonder of the age' with real gunfire and 'all the sounds and smoke of battle properly simulated for the delectation of the audience'.

Nan took her entire household to see it, and although it didn't live up to its publicity it was certainly an unusual entertainment. The sounds of battle turned out to be half-a-dozen urchins screeching and cater-wauling from beneath a covered stage set in front of the pavilion, the cannon puffed a deal of white smoke into the audience, and three of the valiant warships caught fire, long before battle commenced. From then on, their charred skeletons impeded every formation and finally sank after the third volley of popping gunfire, dragging most of the English fleet down with them, which was hardly surprising since they were all linked together on long wires, but which made rather a non-sense of the great British victory.

However, the firework display was splendid. The centrepiece was a huge construction over ten feet tall which lit in a sudden blaze to reveal a white-hot *Agememnon*, gun decks glowing, as the trumpets brayed and squealed and the band played Mr Arne's splendidly martial hymn 'Rule Britannia'. The audience was entranced, and many a patriotic tear was shed before they all repaired to the supper tent for ale and porter and a cold collation.

The children enjoyed every minute of their unexpected outing, from the first fanfare of jubilation which began it, to the meat and cold pickles which brought it to a close. Annie liked the fireworks best and Billy preferred the food, but for Johnnie the highlight of the evening was the prize-fighting. It was something he had never seen before, nor ever imagined, and the sight of those two sweating men, naked to the waist, chests bruised, white breeches smeared with blood, torn fists thudding, was so exciting it constricted his throat and made his heart thunder in his ears. He stood before the canvas lost in admiration. Oh, if only he could be a man like that! Mama would be bound to love him then, if he were a man like that!

For although he had no words as yet in which to express his knowledge and certainly no desire as yet even to attempt such a thing, Johnnie Easter knew, in a vague, undeniable, instinctive way that nobody loved him. It was partly because of the bleakness that descended upon him every time he saw his mother, partly because of the way voices changed tone when they began to speak to him, and partly the combination of a variety of small unintentional slights that made him feel he was a creature apart, a child unwanted, a nuisance who should never have been born. He felt it most keenly when he yearned for Mama's affection, to be picked up and cuddled the way she cuddled his brother and sister. But although she washed him and dressed him and cut up his meat for him, she never kissed him and rarely gave him even so much as a hug. She would sit on the settle beside the fire, with Annie and Billy on either side of her, dividing her attention equally between them, while he had to sit on a stool at their feet.

Sometimes the anguish would be too intolerable to be contained any longer and it would break out from him like pus spurting from a boil, and he would roar and rage and scream until the extremity was past or he was too exhausted to go on. But that only made matters worse, for it infuriated Mama, and usually ended in a beating. And that meant he had to make supreme efforts not to do it again, so as to earn her approval. And he *did* try. He really did. Harder than anyone knew. But the awful thing was that the harder he tried the more impossible it became. Even when he was biting his lips to control himself, he knew that sooner or later the pressure would build up to such a degree that he would explode again and be punished again. From the knee-high vantage point of his five unhappy years there didn't appear to be any way out of it. Until he saw the prize-fighters. The admirable prize-fighters that everybody cheered and loved and admired.

As they all went trailing home to Cheyne Row in the lilac evening, he made up his mind that he would start practising to be a prize-fighter the very next day, as soon as he got up.

It was actually more difficult than he'd imagined. For as he realized as soon as he got out into the garden after breakfast, a prize-fighter needs a sparring partner, and although his brother seemed the obvious choice, his brother wasn't keen.

'Leave off,' he said lazily, as Johnnie pranced around him, fists squared. 'I got too much porridge in me belly for rough stuff.'

'Give us a fight,' Johnnie urged. 'Go on, Billoh. Put up yer mitts!' That was what they'd called out in the tent, and it sounded really war-like and brave. 'Put up yer mitts!'

'Mitts, my eye!' Billy mocked. 'Call those little things mitts?' His hands were nearly twice the width of his brother's, as he was happy to demonstrate. 'I wouldn't even call *my* hands mitts an' look at the size a' *them*.'

'Don't rag him Billy,' Annie warned from her perch in the apple tree where she was playing cat's cradle. 'You don't want his dander up.'

'Me dander ain't up,' Johnnie said earnestly. 'Honest! Just one, Billoh! I won't hurt, I promise.'

'No, you won't,' Billy said mildly, ' 'cause I ain't playin'.' And he went off to the other end of the garden with his toy soldiers, arranging them in neat rows on the grass, and humming to himself with satisfaction.

Johnnie tried whining. 'Oh, come on, Billoh! Come on! Why won't you! Come on! Just one. Come on!' circling the military formations, with his feet dangerously close to the soldiery.

'Don't keep all on,' Billy said, trying to ignore him. 'And mind your feet, do.'

'Just one,' Johnnie begged, and he started to jab out a fist at his brother's face as he circled, jab-jab, jab-jab, just like his heroes had done. It was a bad mistake, for one blow suddenly landed, jerking Billy's head to one side and marking his face with a red glow like a one-sided blush. For a second they were both very surprised.

'Right!' Billy said rising to his feet enraged. 'That's done it, Johnnie. You've asked for it now.' And he rushed at his brother, fists flailing in temper.

It wasn't quite what Johnnie had intended, but he set to with a will, trying to land blows like the prize-fighters, turning his body sideways away from the force of Billy's attack, moving his arms from the shoulder, elbows in the air. It made for a very unequal contest, for Billy was cross and attacking strongly and he was cool and dodging, even though he was afraid.

Annie dropped her cat's cradle and put the string in her apron pocket and climbed down out of the tree to go and get help. Neither of her brothers paid any attention to her, for by now the skirmish had got out of hand, several blows had hurt and they were fighting in earnest. By the time Bessie came puffing up from the kitchen, both of them had torn knuckles and Billy was spitting blood from a formidable punch in the mouth.

'What've you gone an' done ter my poor Billy, you horrid little monster?' she said, rounding on Johnnie.

The sight of the blood had sobered him at once. The sound of her voice terrified him.

'Now you're for it!' Annie said. And as he was trying to get some words into order inside his head ready to defend himself, the garden door was flung open and Nan came striding into the garden with Thiss behind her.

'Now what?' she said furiously. 'I declare I can't leave you children alone for five minutes without trouble.'

' 'E's knocked 'is teeth out!' Bessie wailed. 'Oh, you're a bad wicked varmint, so you are, Johnnie Easter. Look at 'is poor teeth, mum. 'Angin' be a shred.'

'Onny milk teeth,' Thiss said. 'Soon grow some more, son.' But his comfort fell on deaf ears because Billy was howling and Bessie was crooning commiserations and Nan was shouting in temper. 'Five minutes left and they're brawling like tinkers! Running wild. Growing up like savages. Well, this is the end of it. They must have a governess.'

That word stopped all other sound in the garden.

'A governess, mum?' Bessie said. And she looked so afraid that all three children were quite alarmed. They had no idea what a governess was, but they knew it would be painful.

'Yes,' their mother said firmly. 'High time their education was taken in hand. Take 'em indoors and clean 'em up. I will see to it at once.'

Now that she'd made her mind up to it, it had to be done quickly. That was the way she made decisions these days, at speed and without looking back. She sent in her advertisements that very afternoon and made her choice four days later when she had a bundle of applications and one that was quite outstanding.

It came from a lady signing herself Agnes Pennington (Mrs) and was accompanied by three excellent references, the first two praising her control and discipline, the third speaking warmly of her skill at 'dinning knowledge into dull heads.'

If that's the sort she is, Nan thought, she'll be a match for Johnnie no matter how he behaves.

The lady duly presented herself at Cheyne Row on the following afternoon and was interviewed in the drawing-room on the first floor, while Bessie and her three putative charges huddled together in Nan's bedroom next door and strained their ears to hear what was being said. Now that they knew that a governess was a person, they wanted to know what sort of a person it was.

'I don't like the sound of *her*,' Billy said. The lady's voice was loud and harsh and she laughed as though she was barking. 'Haw-haw-haw!'

'Hush!' Bessie implored. 'They'll hear yer.'

But they didn't, for Nan was too busy assessing the value of this new addition to her household and the governess was pre-occupied with giving a good impression.

Agnes Pennington was the daughter of an impoverished curate and a professional invalid. She had been born ugly and she grew uglier, with a face and figure that even her friends could only describe as eccentric. She was very flat-chested and made less of what little she had by walking with a stoop, her spine curved into a crescent. But it was her face that was her real misfortune, equine of nose and square of jaw with small brown eyes and a short narrow mouth that looked as though they had been added as an afterthought. She did her best to appear attractive, wearing the most fashionable of poke bonnets and arranging her brown hair in a row of smooth fat curls across her forehead, like a string of conkers, but they only served to make her face look more grotesque.

She called herself Mrs Pennington and wore a cheap wedding-ring and an air of irreproachable sanctity, but actually she wasn't entitled to either of them. But she had a quick wit, a sharp tongue and a thorough dislike of children, and with these three attributes she felt certain she could make her way in the world as a governess.

Now she was doing her best to persuade Mrs Easter than no child alive was beyond her control.

'I will make no bones about it, Mrs Pennington,' Nan was saying. 'My two eldest are reasonable children, always have been. You will get no trouble from them, I am sure on it. But you had best be told straight away my youngest is a wretch, a thoroughly nasty, disobedient child.'

'You may safely leave him to me, Mrs Easter, ma'am. I can assure you I have yet to meet the child who could better me.'

'I am glad on it,' Nan said, slightly relieved by the woman's firm tone, but saying an inward prayer that her Johnnie wouldn't prove to be the exception.

'How old is the child, ma'am, if I may presume to ask?'

'Just five.'

'An admirable age at which to be taken in hand,' Mrs Pennington said firmly. 'Old enough to be capable of reason and young enough to be malleable.'

'What's mall-able, Ba?' Annie whispered, staring at her brother. It sounded as though it could mean he was going to be whipped, and he was certainly looking very miserable and sucking his thumb. 'Take your thumb out your mouth Johnnie, do!'

'Hush!' Bessie ordered, afraid that her rebuke would make him yell and have them all discovered. 'You make so much as a peep an' we shall all 'ave ter go back ter the nursery.'

'Ten guineas a year, paid quarterly', their mother was saying. 'Will that suit?'

'You will not regret it, ma'am,' the rough voice said.

And three small hearts sank to hear it.

Mrs Pennington's arrival in the Easter household caused more of a stir than Mrs Jorris and Miss Trent the pastry cook and a whole procession of scullery maids had ever done. For a start she arrived with two large travelling trunks which Thiss and Mr Dibkins had to lug up six flights of stairs to the two rooms allotted to her on the third floor. There was some ribald speculation as to what they might contain, for Thiss swore they were heavier than lead coffins and it was a wonder he and old Dibkins hadn't bust a gut with the weight of them.

Then there was the matter of meals which the lady insisted should be served to her in her rooms since she was most certainly a cut above eating with servants and she did not have the proper rank and status to dine with the mistress, even a mistress whose origins were obviously far more common than her own. Mrs Pennington knew all about social proprieties and adhered to them religiously, even if other people didn't. It was a very great nuisance, and the scullery-maids who had to trail up and down stairs with her trays night and morning were much aggrieved.

'Her an' her airs and graces!' Mrs Dibkins growled to her great friend, Mrs Jorris.

'Neither flesh nor fowl, Mrs D, my dear,' Mrs Jorris observed darkly. 'That's how it is. Between you an' me, my dear, I never known a governess yet what didn't spell trouble.'

But whatever trouble she might cause in the kitchen, in the new domain of her classroom, Mrs Pennington's rule was absolute. On her first afternoon she had all her pupils chanting the alphabet, on her second they embarked on tables, and by the end of the first week a routine had been established which never varied. Once or twice the listening servants heard a childish voice, usually Billy's, raised in protest, and the sound of a slap, followed by muffled whimpering, but there were no tantrums and no roaring, and by the end of the day all three children were so exhausted that they crawled willingly to bed without fuss. It was a transformation.

At the end of the month Mrs Pennington made her first report to Mrs Easter. Annie and Billy were good children, she said, and learning fairly well, although slowly. But Johnnie was a delight to teach. A veritable delight. 'You have a clever son, Mrs Easter,' she said. 'So quick with figures. He has real talent.'

'Johnnie?' Nan asked, hardly able to believe her ears.

'Indeed yes, madam. He has taken to arithmetic as if he were born to it. A very clever little boy.'

'And does he behave himself?'

'Like an angel.'

It *was* a transformation. That afternoon at dinner she found herself observing him closely, almost as though she were seeing him for the first time. He was still an ugly little thing, with that sharp little face and that dark hair and those withdrawn, brooding eyes, but she fancied she could see a resemblance in him now. Not to Mr Easter, for there was nothing of that poor man's bland, fair countenance in this child. No, no, it was faint and fleeting but she fancied there was something of herself in this boy, after all.

But there was little time for fancies, for the very next afternoon the Holborn walk came onto the market. It was a most inopportune moment, just as she'd feared it would be, for she had so little spare capital available, that she had to arrange a loan with Mr Tewson in order to purchase it, and that took a great deal of time and effort and persuasion.

The deal wasn't completed until the middle of April and by then the walk had been neglected for several weeks and she knew she would have a difficult time to coax it into profitability. She and Thiss walked the area every day as soon as the papers were stamped, visiting and calling, showing a presence. But their trade grew slowly and more often than not they returned home to Chelsea tired and unsuccessful. The weather didn't help them either, being cold and wet and miserable.

So when Nan received an invitation from Mr Johnson with the news that he was giving a supper party 'in honour of Mr William Godwin and Mary Wollstonecraft, who is now returned to this country from Paris', she wrote back at once to accept. A party was just what she needed to lift her flagging spirits, and it would be pleasant to see Mary Wollstonecraft again, and besides, she was intrigued to find out why Mary's name was being linked with Mr Godwin's in this public way. They're lovers, I'll be bound, she thought. I wonder if Sophie knows anything about it.

Chapter Eighteen

It was a riotous party. She'd never known another quite like it. For a start there were so many people crammed together in Mr Johnson's green parlour that they had to eat their meal standing up, which was something she'd never seen done before, and very comical it looked, for very few people had solved the problem of how to cope with a full plate of food and a fork to eat it with *and* conversation and a glass full of wine. Sophie decided that it couldn't be done and left her plate upon a side-table, declaring, 'You need four hands and two tongues at the very least for *this* exercise.' But Nan thought it was fun, and did her best to eat and drink and talk all at once, as everybody else seemed to be doing.

And there were so many people there, writers and artists she hadn't seen since the old days when she came to dine with Mr Easter, Mr Cowper, the poet, her old friend Mr Wotherspoon, the book-binder, Mr Fuseli, of course, very loud and Germanic, and even Mr William Blake as untidy and enthusiastic as ever, talking and talking with his comfortable wife beside him. There was such a crush it was impossible to move more than two paces in any direction, but she knew that Mary Wollstonecraft was in the room somewhere, for she could hear her rough voice, and presently, by dint of gradual, dancing manoeuvres she contrived to edge through the crowd, plate, glass, fork and all, and stand beside her.

'My dear Nan,' Mary said, leaning down across her slopping wine glass to kiss her friend first on one cheek and then on the other in the French style. 'How well you look! And prosperous! The very picture of success.'

' 'Tis a change from the last time we met,' Nan agreed. And her eyes were acknowledging the changes in her old ally. For Mary was plainly and buxomly pregnant, her flowing bosom swathed in white muslin and the folds of her long blue gown voluminous, that untidy brown hair curling most prettily about her cheeks and her hazel eyes glowing.

'Yes,' she said. ' 'Twill be born in September. William hopes for a boy, but 'tis all one with me, providing 'tis strong and healthy. Now, do pray tell me how your business fares. Mr Johnson sent word of you from time to time, but I warrant he ain't got it right, nor told me all there was to tell.'

So although Nan was itching to ask her who the father was and whether she had changed her opinion of marriage, she had to postpone her questions, for Mary wanted to know exactly how she'd managed to succeed. 'You see how it is,' she said triumphantly when Nan had answered all her questions. 'A woman is as good as any man. All she needs is the chance to show her skills and not to be belittled and cast in an inferior mould. Men do us no service by pandering to our whims and assuming us to be witless.'

'You do not change your opinion?' Nan asked.

'Of the rights of women?' Mary said. 'Why no indeed. 'Tis plain common sense to treat both sexes in the same way. Nothing will alter that, for in truth there is little to chose between us in matters of wit and intelligence. Nor in strength or fortitude either.'

'Except that we breed.'

'Aye,' Mary said, laughing, 'so we do!'

And then Mr Blake and his wife appeared at her side to claim her attention, and their first conversation was over. But it was so good to see her again. As she pushed her way back to Sophie through the crush, Nan was warm with the thought that she had rediscovered an old and valuable friend.

Sophie was bubbling with gossip.

'She is pregnant, my dear. Due in September, so they do say.'

'I know it Sophie, and I wish her well.'

'Well, so do I my dear, of course,' Sophie said seriously. But then her eyes gleamed with mischief again. 'Do 'ee know who the father is?'

'I could hazard a guess 'twould be Mr Godwin.'

'Indeed it is. And they are *married*! Imagine that!'

That was news.

'At St Pancras' church, on March 29th, and uncommon quietly, so Mrs Wotherspoon says,' Sophie went on. 'I cannot imagine why she should want to marry such a man. He is feeble in the extreme, and a terrible scrounger, so Heinrich says.'

216

'I en't seen him,' Nan said, wanting to more than ever. 'Is he here?'

'Over by the window, talking to Mr Cowper,' Sophie said, turning her friend by the shoulder. 'Look. Middling-size, middling-aged, that's the man.'

A lifeless creature, Nan thought, gazing across the room at Mr Godwin's pale face and languid air. He may not be much of an artist but he certainly goes out of his way to look the part, and she noticed the badly tied cravat he was stroking with his long, pale fingers, and how his little round spectacles glinted in the candlelight, and how long and ugly his nose appeared above such a narrow, down-turned, pouting mouth. 'There en't a deal of spark in him,' she said, trenchantly. 'No match for Mary, in all conscience.'

'And that ain't all, my dear,' Sophie went on. 'They say she has another child and illegitimate by all accounts. A little girl, fathered by that wretched man, Mr Imlay. I met him once in this very room and an uncommon spoilt brat he was. Far too selfish to stay true to wife and child. What taste she has in men!'

'Did he desert them?'

'Aye, indeed he did, and in dire straits if all I've heard is true.'

'What became of the child?'

'Why as to that, I couldn't say,' Sophie admitted.

'I shall ask her,' Nan said. Now that she'd met her again, there was a great deal she wanted to ask Mary Wollstonecraft.

The party roared on and became steadily more dishevelled. By ten o'clock most of the guests were looking decidedly the worse for wear. There were far too many skirts and trousers stained with spilt food and far too many faces flushed purple with wine. In fact, so much wine had been consumed that most of the gentlemen were unsteady on their feet and several had sunk onto the few chairs that had been left standing against the walls. 'Time to go home, I think,' Nan said to Sophie. 'I shall make my adieus.' And she pushed off through the crowd to find her host.

And on her way she found Mary Wollstonecraft again. She and her new husband were sharing a chair, sitting back-to-back extremely uncomfortably, but still talking to the group of guests around them.

'You must come and visit us,' Mary said, as Nan kissed her goodbye. 'We live at number 29 at the Polygon in Somerstown. Say you will.'

'As soon as ever I may,' Nan promised.

'Tomorrow?'

'Tomorrow.'

'Bring your children,' Mary called as Nan struggled off again towards Mr Johnson. 'We will have a nursery tea-party.'

So the next afternoon, when her work was over for the day, Nan drove to Somerstown, taking her three children with her, all dressed in their Sunday best and a little apprehensive at being asked to 'visit' because it was the first time they'd ever done such a thing.

'Should we speak, Mama?' Annie asked, as they climbed out of the pony cart and looked up at the sixteen-sided block of houses that was the Polygon. It was a daunting building, and far too grand for comfort.

'If you are spoken to,' Nan said, taking Johnnie firmly by the hand before he could run off and disgrace her. Then they climbed the steps to number 29 and were admitted by an amiable maid in a grey gown and an embroidered apron, who told them 'Pray to follow me,' and led them upstairs to the drawing-room on the first floor.

It was a large room but exceedingly dingy and dirty, and crowded with dilapidated furniture. There were a sagging sofa piled with cushions, two footstools heaped with books and papers, three side-tables, two with broken legs, and all of them covered with objects of every kind, crumpled cloths, dog-eared sketch books, jars full of clogged paint-brushes and broken pencils, side-by-side with smeared cups and chipped saucers and a variety of dishes containing the remains of a variety of meals. Mr Godwin was reclining in an easy-chair by the window. He was dressed in a red velvet banyan and a purple smoking-cap, and he had a glass of claret in one hand and a bitten sponge-cake in the other.

'Upstairs, my dear,' he said vaguely. 'She expects you, I daresay. You see how it is with me. I must take my sustenance, my dear, or I shall be fit for nothing. Ain't breakfasted yet today. What a weariness life is, to be sure. And yet we must take what pleasure in it we may, savouring what is beautiful. I do not flatter myself when I say I am a good judge of what is beautiful. A good judge. Nay, the best. Take this cake for an example. I could not bring myself to eat it, I tell 'ee, if 'twere not made of the very *best* butter and the *freshest* of eggs. She is upstairs.'

Annie's eyes were as round as pennies, but true to her promise she didn't say a word. The maid ducked a curtsey at her languid master and led them up another flight of stairs to the nursery, which, as Nan was happy to see, was a considerable improvement on the squalor of the drawing-room. It was furnished simply with a deal table and six plain chairs, a truckle-bed with a white linen counterpane and a linen press in one corner, but the furniture was of little importance, for this was a room devoted to toys and children. There was a rocking-horse before the fire, and a circle of dolls on the bed, there was a top and a hoop and a skipping-rope and a Noah's Ark spilling wooden animals on the carpet; and a travelling trunk in one corner was simply bursting with soft toys of every kind. All three of Nan's children sucked in their breath in wonder. If this was 'visiting' it was going to be fun. But they stood where they were like good children and waited to be introduced.

Mary Wollstonecraft was sitting in one of the chairs with a small, fair child on her lap. Now she set the child on her feet and stood up clumsily to walk forward and greet them. 'This is Fanny,' she said, holding the little girl's hand and looking at Annie. 'My daughter. She's three years old, ain't you, Fanny? And you must be Nan's daughter. How old are you?'

Annie confessed to eight, but shyly, and Johnnie said he was five and 'pleased to meet you', but Billy was too busy staring at the table to say anything.

'We will take tea now,' Mary said, smiling at his rapt expression, 'and then there will be plenty of time to play, will there not?'

The table was set with all manner of tempting dishes, grapes and oranges, jellies and junkets, sponge cakes and comfits, and more iced cakes than they could count. But there wasn't any bread and butter, so none of Nan's children knew how to begin the meal. For you always started with bread and butter. That was the polite thing to do, even if you didn't want to. Now they sat up at the table while Mary made the tea, and they dithered, looking from the heaped dishes to their empty plates.

'Help yourself,' Mary urged them. 'Come now, don't be shy. Try a little jelly.'

'En't we to eat bread-an'-butter first, ma'am?' Billy ventured.

Mary laughed at him. 'Why, bless us, no,' she said. 'Why should there be rules for feeding? Tell me that. 'Tis Freedom Hall here. In this house you eat whatever you like whenever you fancy it.' And so they did. The boys were thrilled.

And when they were all stickily well-fed, they were allowed to play with all the toys, not one at a time, which would have been the rule at home, but all at once and any-old-how and not putting anything away when you'd finished with it. It was uncommon good sport.

Nan was surprised to see that her troublesome Johnnie was being most tender with Mary's fragile three-year-old, lifting her down from the rocking-horse, and patiently setting the wooden animals in line for her. She'd expected good behaviour from Annie, and she'd known that Billy would be boisterous if he wasn't corrected, but this new, gentle Johnnie was a revelation.

'You've uncommon handsome children,' Mary said, when her maid had cleared the table and the two of them were sitting watching the children play. 'Your little boy is quite striking.'

'Billy?'

'Why no, though he's handsome enough in all conscience. The younger, Johnnie. He favours you.'

It was really quite gratifying to hear such praise.

'I shall be glad when this child is born,' Mary said. ''Tis uncommon wearying to carry in the heat, and I've all June, July and August to get through.'

'I will visit as often as I may,' Nan promised. ' 'Twill help to pass the time.'

Which she did, and found that she was part of a large and lively company, for Mary had many friends and frequent visitors. And what talk there was during those long summer afternoons, of birth and death, of war and revolution, of lovers and husbands. And on all these matters Mary Wollstonecraft Godwin and her literary friends had fascinating things to say.

Annie and the boys were delighted with the arrangement too, for Freedom Hall was very much to their taste. It meant a whole afternoon away from Mrs Pennington and her schoolroom, and a chance to get out into the open countryside that stretched northwards beyond the Euston Road, where they walked and romped when the weather was fine and Mary Wollstonecraft felt fit enough for a promenade.

'I can see precious little difference between a lover and a husband,' she confessed to Nan one particularly warm afternoon, when the two of them were sitting with their backs against a haystack, watching their children at play. 'Both have it in them to be kind or cruel and a ceremony has no power to alter character.'

'And yet you married Mr Godwin.'

220

'Since he is father of my child,' Mary explained. 'A good man, in all conscience. He took my Fanny into his household without demur.'

'You did not marry Mr Imlay?'

'No. More's the pity. Which left him free to travel wherever he would without us, or take another mistress, or leave us when he thought fit. I cannot tell you the pain he caused me.'

'I am sorry to hear it,' Nan said with sympathy. And then she remembered Sophie's advice. 'Sophie Fuseli is of the opinion that the only way to handle a lover is to dismiss him first, and long before he tires of you.'

' 'Tis an excellent plan, in all conscience,' Mary agreed, 'but not one a woman in love could follow. There is too much warmth and urgency in love to allow for such cold-hearted treatment, sensible though it might be. We stay and we hope and we are grievously hurt, but there is no other way, for love binds us together for good or ill.'

'But there is pleasure in love too, is there not?'

'The highest,' Mary said, smiling, 'providing there is honesty too. That is the base of all good relationships, my dear. Without it there is no trust, no mutual help and comfort, and eventually, though it grieves me to say it, no love.'

'So you see no harm in an honest lover?'

'None,' Mary laughed. 'Have you one in mind?'

'No,' Nan admitted. 'There are many handsome creatures in the City but none I fancy for more than a day or two, if the truth be told.'

'And after a day or two you forget them, do you not?'

'Aye.'

'Then you do not love,' Mary said. 'If you did he would haunt your thoughts by night and day. Your boys are fighting, I fear.'

They would be, Nan thought, striding off to stop them, and just as the conversation was getting really interesting too.

'We will meet again next Wednesday,' she promised, when Thiss arrived with the pony cart at the end of that afternoon and her three sticky children were climbing happily aboard. ' 'Tis nearly the end of August, my dear. Your long wait will soon be done.'

'I will see you Wednesday,' Mary said, kissing her.

But although they didn't know it, that afternoon had been the last time they would ever see one another again.

When Nan arrived at the Polygon the following week, Mary was in labour. A very slow labour, according to her maid, but progressing satisfactorily, 'so the midwife says'. But the next day, when she made another brief visit, the news was very bad. The child had been born, a girl and very pretty, 'another Mary', but Mary Wollstonecraft was very ill indeed. The afterbirth hadn't come away, and although a surgeon had been sent for and had done his best to remove what he could of it, his patient was very weak and in a great deal of pain.

'Pray give her my love,' Nan said, 'and these flowers and tell her I will call again tomorrow and hope for better news.'

She called every afternoon for the next eleven days, and after the third day, Sophie came with her to keep her company, but the news from the sickroom got steadily worse and worse. On Saturday Mary suffered a shivering fit so violent it shook the bed frame, on Monday the doctors applied puppies to her breast to suck off some of her milk in the vain hope of helping her, but by Wednesday she was so weak her life was despaired of and little Fanny was sent away to stay with a friend. Thursday, Friday, and Saturday passed most painfully, but she clung on, fighting for her life, while her husband sat beside her offering her sips of wine to deaden the pain and growing more and more distraught. And finally on Monday morning, when Nan and Sophie arrived in the pony cart for the thirteenth time, anxious for news, the maid came down to tell them that her mistress was dead.

'At twenty to eight this morning,' she said, weeping freely, 'and how the master will make out, I do not know. The poor man is crazed with grief.'

'She was a fine, good, kind, suffering woman,' Nan said, pierced with sorrow. 'We shall never see her like again.'

'The good die young,' Sophie said, trying to comfort.

But that provoked more anger. 'Oh, Sophie! Why should they? 'Ten't fair! I only just found her again and she was a good friend to me.'

'We should like to attend the funeral,' Sophie said to the maid, ignoring Nan's passion for the moment, and speaking quickly because another carriage had arrived and she was sure it contained more friends of the Godwins anxious for news. 'Pray tell your master. 'Tis the last thing we may do for her, poor Mary.'

So they went to her funeral and watched as two weeping willows were planted on either side of her grave, and commiserated with Mr Johnson who was wheezing most terribly, and agreed publicly that it was no wonder Mr Godwin was too grieved to attend, and afterwards said privately to one another that he ought to have been ashamed of himself for staying away.

But as Thiss drove her back to the office in the September dusk, Nan's sense of loss was almost too acute for misery. To have found a friend and then lost her all within four short summer months was too cruel.

She grieved for more than a fortnight and she was still dispirited three weeks later when she came home from supervising the distribution of the evening papers, to find Mrs Dibkins hovering in the hall with a letter in her hand.

'That came the minute you left the house, Mrs William-dear,' the old lady said. 'Did we ought to have sent it round to the office? Ho lor! We been of two minds ever since it come.' As Nan could see because the wrapper was smudged with thumbprints.

'No, no, Mrs Dibkins,' she said, breaking the seal. 'Whatever it is, I dare say 'twill wait. Tell Mrs Jorris to serve whenever she is ready.' And she took the letter into the dining-room to read it by the fire.

It was from Sir Osmond Easter of Ippark in the County of Sussex, no less, and Sir Osmond Easter was aristocratically annoyed.

'It has been brought to our attention,' he wrote ('Our' Nan thought, scoffing at the word. Royalty, is he?) 'that you are engaged in common trade in the City of London and its purlieus, and moreover that to this end you have been making improper and illegal use of the family name. I have to inform you, madam, that the practice is to cease forthwith.' (Oh, is it? We shall see about that!) 'It is not the custom of this family to permit the use of our name in the pursuance of any trade whatsoever. You will oblige us. Given this day November 15th 1798 by the hand of Osmond Easter.'

She felt better at once, cheered by the most exhilarating fury. 'What sauce!' she said to the offending paper. 'I got something to say to 'ee, Sir Osmond Easter, this very minute, so I have!'

And she stamped across to the writing-desk at once to pen a furious reply.

'I have been trading under the name of Easter since *your* relation and *mine*, Mr William Henry Easter *died* and left me *destitute* with three young children to raise. Which your family showed *precious little concern* over, never having sent so much as a *penny* to us in all these years.

'Easter is *my* name. I came by it *honest* when I *married* Mr William Henry Easter which I have the papers to *prove*. I run an *honest* trade, much *respected* in this city which you should be *proud* to have your precious name associated with.

'Your kin by marriage, which you cannot deny, A. Easter.'

Then she made an excellent supper, rage having sharpened her appetite.

And that night she slept the sleep of the just. Or the justifiably angry.

Chapter Nineteen

Perhaps it was just as well that Nan Easter's fiery temper usually cooled overnight. When she woke the next morning her body was still warm with sleep and the residue of anger, but her head was clear and her business sense was reasserting itself. She had slept late because it was Thursday and that was the day when Thiss supervised the early delivery without her, so the morning had already begun. A pale September sun beamed two bright squares of colour onto the dinginess of her coverlet and the sky over the Chelsea fields was greeny-blue like a duck's egg. 'Tis a beautiful world, she thought, and she felt glad to be alive in it, even though Mary Wollstonecraft could no longer share it with her, and Sir Osmond, who could, was wasting her time by being objectionable. She got up and put on her bed-gown and slippers and went downstairs to the dining-room to read her letter again.

Now in the clarity of the morning, she could see that it might cause more problems that it would solve. And as she had no wish to be involved in litigation unless she was quite sure she could win, she decided to take Sir Osmond's letter to Portugal Street and seek advice from Mr Duncan.

'A wise move, if I may make so bold as to say so, madam,' he said. 'Devilish tricky, some of these old county families. If you will allow me to suggest a possible line of action?'

She would.

'It is my considered opinion that we should show these documents to our Mr Teshmaker. A young man, madam, but one with a sharp intellect. Yes, indeed. An uncommon sharp intellect.'

So the sharp intellect was sent for and presently came gliding into the room like a winter shadow. He looked extremely young to Nan, little more than a boy in all conscience, and slight into the bargain, for he was very thin and very pale and not a great deal taller than she was.

225

But there was something about the way he walked that intrigued her despite his insignificant appearance. He moved like a dancer, with a deliberate, sinuous grace that was at once attractive and unnatural. But it wasn't until their business had been concluded and he had retired to his cell again behind the wooden partition, that separated the inner office from the outer, that she realized what was giving him such a curious gait. The young man was lame. He wore an ordinary boot on his right foot but his left was battened within a leather tower with iron struts on either side of it and a six inch platform below it, which looked so horribly uncomfortable she had to avert her eyes.

He smiled back at her, patiently accepting his infirmity and her knowledge of it. For lame or no, he was clever and useful, and he knew it. And he also knew that she was one of the firm's most prestigious clients.

When Mr Duncan showed him the two letters, he read them gravely, saying with a smile that he could quite appreciate Mrs Easter's anger, which was entirely justified, but that perhaps a more moderate reply would be, shall we say, rather more judicial.

'Write one, then,' Nan told him. 'I en't sayin' I shall use it, mind.'

'That is perfectly understood,' he smoothed.

'Write it. Then we'll see.'

The letter was a model of barbed propriety.

'I have been instructed by my client, Mrs Nan Easter, of Cheyne Row, Chelsea, to reply to yr letter of the 15th inst. Whilst we appreciate yr concern apropos the correct and proper usage of yr family name, we would respectfully advise that there is no litigation whatsomever which would preclude the use of any name by such person or persons as have a legal entitlement to it, and that marriage invariably constitutes a legal entitlement. Furthermore, we would stress that the firm of A. Easter, Newsagents is a well known and respected firm in the City, which is rapidly becoming a byword for high standards and dependability, and as such, far from bringing disrepute upon the family name, would appear to us to complement the existing renown of that name. Yr Obedt servt, Cosmo Teshmaker, Duncan and Dukesbury, Portugal Street.'

'I doubt we shall have any further difficulties after that,' Mr Duncan said with great satisfaction when Nan had read the letter and agreed that it should be sent.

'I hope not,' Nan said. 'I've a deal too much to do to want to waste time on such as Sir Osmond Easter.'

That winter the news of the war was bad. And it grew worse in the New Year. As the first tentative buds of spring hesitated on the bare branches of the wintry elms and catkins shook like yellow lambs' tails in the late March winds, letters arrived from Ireland to say that Napoleon had tried to land troops there and had been defeated. There was considerable alarm.

'He means to invade us, one way or t'other,' Mr Walter said.

'He'll have a job while we got our Nelson to defend us,' Nan told him. 'A Norfolk man, our Nelson.' She was very proud of that. 'He'll see 'em off, you may depend on it.'

And sure enough news came through a few weeks later that Napoleon had taken his army off to Egypt, and that the invasion of England seemed to have been postponed.

London was quite light-headed and papers sold as soon as they were printed, thus proving that good news has quite as much pulling power as bad, given the right circumstances. And when October arrived and news came through that Nelson had followed the French and defeated them yet again, at a battle named after the Egyptian River Nile, the celebrations were riotous and rowdy. Nelson was raised to the peerage and given a pension of two thousand pounds a year by his adoring nation, and, rather gratuitously, the title of Duke of Bronte too, from a grateful King of Naples, and the *Times* was completely sold out for four days in a row.

But despite excellent sales Nan had a problem she couldn't solve. She had rented a new reading-room close to the law courts where coffee could be drunk and papers read for a quarterly subscription. Now she was beginning negotiations for a second and a third. Reading rooms were rapidly becoming as popular and well-frequented as the gentlemen's clubs they rather resembled, and she could see that they would soon be a most dependable source of income. But her third reading-room was proving extremely difficult to rent. Two others had fallen through at the last moment and without explanation and now the third was being delayed in the same infuriating way.

'Send 'em a letter,' she suggested to the useful Mr Teshmaker. 'See if you can't persuade 'em to put a spurt on.'

'Certainly, Mrs Easter,' he said. But then he waited, his little mousy face thoughtful and watchful, as though there were other things he wanted to say to her but didn't dare.

'Out with it,' she ordered. 'You've something on your mind, that I know.'

'It has occured to me,' he confessed, 'only occurred you understand – I have no proof as yet – but it has occurred to me to wonder whether these matters might not be – um – influenced in some way.'

'Influenced?' she said. 'By whom?' But she knew who he meant, even as she spoke, for the suspicion had occurred to her too, in her more spiteful moments.

'Well, as to that, ma'am,' he said smoothly, 'I could not, in all conscience, acquaint you with a mere supposition. Nor would you wish me to, I am sure. But I could make a few discreet inquiries, should you wish it. There could be no harm in that.'

'Do,' she said. 'I will pay you well for it. Privately, of course, for it en't part of your duty toward Mr Duncan.'

He shadowed away from her, face still thoughtful, eyes devious. And for the next few days he crept about the city, sleek and silent as the brown mouse he resembled, in and out of the dark taverns where city apprentices gathered to drink and gossip, listening and commiserating, quiet in his corner, picking up crumbs and scrapings, saying nothing. And at the end of the week he sent a letter to Nan Easter to tell her he had some information for her, which he felt sure she would wish to receive 'at her earliest convenience.'

She sent him a note by return. 'Come to Cheyne Row at six of the clock this evening.'

'Well, now,' she said, when he'd been settled by the fire in the drawing-room with a cup of coffee at his elbow like an honoured guest, 'what have you discovered?'

Now that they were face to face, he was almost afraid to tell her. He cleared his throat and bit his pale underlip, and studied the dancing flames, gathering his thoughts and his courage. 'I must tell you,' he confessed at last, 'it is as we feared. In all three cases, the rent agreement has been forestalled, and always, I am afraid to say, by the same firm, Messrs Taggart, Rosewort and Hagggerty, a reputable firm ma'am, who take commisions from time to time from . . .'

'Sir Osmond Easter, deuce take the man. I thought we'd dealt with him.'

'Sir Osmond Easter,' he agreed. 'Or Mr Thomas Callbeck, who is, as you doubtless know, his brother-in-law.'

'Devil take the pair of 'em,' Nan said, pink with fury at such underhand behavior. 'You must write to 'em forthwith, Mr Teshmaker. Tell 'em they en't to play such tricks, for they impede honest trade.'

'What they do, they *may* do,' Mr Teshmaker said apologetically. ' 'Tis nothing of which we may make complaint. It may be devious. In fact I would go so far as to declare that I myself believe it *could* be so described, but 'tis not against the law. We could write. We could complain. But it would do us no good.'

'Do you mean to tell me they may prevent me from renting as I wish, and I may do nothing about it?' she said, her anger growing visibly.

'That is the gist of it,' he said, paler than ever because she was so fierce.

'We'll see about that!' she said. 'I en't one to be put down by a gang of foxes, that I en't. They're to be stopped. You must see to it.'

'No orders are ever given in these matters,' he explained. 'No letters are written. Hints are dropped, that is all. There is consequently no evidence, and without evidence, there is no possibility of legal action.'

'That en't fair!'

'The law, Mrs Easter,' he explained again, 'is not meant to be fair.'

'Bah!' she said, quite forgetting her duties as a hostess. 'Don't talk to me, Mr Teshmaker. We must find a way round it.'

But there was no way round it, as Mr Duncan explained, and his colleague Mr Dukesbury confirmed the next day. 'If I may advise you Mrs Easter,' he said, 'I would suggest that you authorize all future transactions to be completed by this firm. It may not provide all the cover you require, for this City is a hot-bed for gossip, as I am sure you are aware, but it would be better than open negotiations in your own name.'

It infuriated her to be asked to stoop to subterfuge, but she agreed to it, because she really had no choice. If the business was to expand the reading-rooms had to be rented.

But she was still hot with anger when she got back to Cheyne Row that afternoon. 'Dratted Easters,' she told her children as Mrs Jorris served dinner. 'Now I got to go all hole-in-the-corner like some sneak thief, and all on account of that Sir Osmond, rot him. 'Ten't right.'

Billy and Annie murmured politely and didn't listen, but Johnnie was most attentive. Since his success as an arithmatician he had begun

229

to hope that his mother might just have a little love for him now and then. He wasn't sure, of course, for sometimes she spurned him as brusquely as ever, telling him to keep out of her way for she 'couldn't abide it', whatever 'it' was, but sometimes she smiled at him and seemed to be approving, so he watched her carefully.

Now he caught her rage and responded to it quickly. 'It ain't right, Mama,' he said hotly. 'I will put all right for 'ee, when I'm older, so I shall.'

She rewarded him with a smile. 'Aye, I believe you will, Johnnie. I believe you will. This is an excellent sauce, Mrs Jorris.'

What an odd child he is, she thought, looking at his serious face glowering at her across the table. Hardly like a six-year-old at all. But he means well, poor creature, and at least he don't scream nowadays. And she turned her mind to more important things.

If Sir Osmond and his gang of unprincipled ruffians were going to stop her from renting any more reading-rooms, she would have to find some other outlet for her papers, for the thirst for news sheets was growing by the day. The problem kept her wakeful all that night, but by daybreak she had thought of a solution. While Sir Osmond was impeding the renting of reading-rooms, she would supply papers to the gentlemen's clubs themselves. And she would start with the Reform Club in Pall Mall. Where else?

When the club secretary of the Reform Club appeared before her, looking puzzled, she came to the point immediately. 'I believe you have a reading-room in this club for the use of your gentlemen.'

He agreed that this was so, wondering why she should wish to speak of it.

'How if I were to tell you I could supply all the newspapers your gentlemen could ever require and all by seven of the clock, every morning, prompt?'

He was impressed. 'Could you do that, madam?'

'I am Nan Easter,' she said. 'I could.'

'It seems an excellent proposition,' he said. 'When could this arrangement begin?'

'Tomorrow,' she said.

And tomorrow it was.

It was almost too easy. Within a month she had acquired the concession to supply newspapers to every single club in the West End, bar one, and that, understandably, was the one which had the rather dubious honour of including Sir Osmond Easter among its members.

It was an excellent source of revenue and in an odd sort of way a marvellous private revenge. The triumph of it lasted all through the summer.

In May she celebrated her twenty-eighth birthday with a lavish party for all her friends. And in July when the weather was positively balmy, she bought extravagant presents for Johnnie's seventh birthday and Annie's tenth and took all three children to Vauxhall to see the fireworks. And in August they all spent the day in St James' Park watching the King review his volunteers.

It was an uncommon hot day and the volunteers fell into faints like nine-pins, which Billy thought was part of the entertainment. By four o'clock Sophie Fuseli declared she was so fatigued she wouldn't have enough strength left for the ball at the Rotunda that evening.

But Nan laughed her to scorn. 'You speak for yourself, Sophie Fuseli,' she said. 'I got strength enough to dance till dawn. Ready for anything, so I am.' The King's review ball was hardly an occasion to be missed and she'd bought a new gown for the occasion, and new gloves and a fine new feathered head-dress. 'You may stay at home if you like, but I'm a-going.'

'Heigh-ho!' Sophie said, feigning resignation. 'Then I'd best go with you, I suppose.'

The Ranelagh Gardens were extremely grand that evening, festooned with fairy-lights and with coloured water in all the fountains, and the Rotunda had been redecorated for the occasion. Now it was a dazzle of egg-shell blue and gold and lit by so many cascades of candles that the air was quite hot above their heads. The orchestra had been augmented too and was busily scraping away on its raised platform in the centre of the hall, providing gavottes and gallops and minuets to order, while the assembled company disported itself, pink in the face with exertion and candle-heat.

There was such a crush in the circular ballroom, it was almost impossible to find space in which to dance. Nan agreed to take a turn with several of the gentlemen from Sophie's party, but they trod on her feet and squashed her feathers and left sweaty handprints on her nice new gloves, so that she was quite relieved when the first interval was announced and it was time to walk to the tents for supper.

And as the hall began to clear, she saw the officers.

There were three of them lounging beside the bandstand, their blue jackets buttoned to the waist, displaying their handsome legs in long white doeskin trousers and black dancing pumps. They were all very tall and very slim, but the middle one was the tallest of the three, well over six foot and broad shouldered, with dark hair cut à la grecque and the most handsome face she had ever seen. But it was his legs she noticed first because they were so exquisitely long and they looked so elegant. Skilful tailoring had actually made them appear even longer than they were, for his trousers had been cut very high in the waist and were fitted so tight to his thighs that they looked like a second skin. He stood with the studied elegance of a heron, supporting his weight on one white leg while the other bent before it, toe to the ground.

'Who are they?' Nan asked, because it wouldn't have sounded correct to ask 'who is he?'

'Cavalry officers from the Duke of Clarence's, I believe,' Sophie said. 'They have a fine bearing.'

'Such long legs!' Nan said, mesmerized by them.

'An introduction I should arrange, ja?' Mr Fuseli teased, yellow cat-eyes flickering at her.

But she refused to be drawn. 'Yes,' she said, 'you should. One of them might be just the man to get me the concession to the barracks.'

He went off to find the master of ceremonies, roaring with saturnine laughter, and the party waited for him, watching as he and the Master approached the three young men and the preliminary talking began.

It surprised Nan to realize that she was feeling quite nervous at the prospect of being introduced to this young man, and that she wanted to know him and found him intensely attractive. And her senses began to prickle in the most exciting way. She turned her body deliberately aside to calm herself a little, and because it wouldn't have done to appear to be watching them. That was an old maid's trick.

So she missed their approach. They were standing beside her and around her, when the Master of Ceremonies stepped pompously forward to make his introductions. 'Mrs Fuseli, Mrs Easter, pray allow me to present Mr Fortescue, Mr Hanley-Brown, and Mr Leigh, Duke of Clarence's, up for the review, I believe you told me, gentlemen.'

The young man bowed gracefully, as though he were about to dance, and taking her gloved hand, raised it to his lips and kissed it. His skin was so tanned it seemed gilded in the candlelight, and his lips were as red as gules, and his eyes . . .! Oh his eyes were the colour of pale honey and so heavily lidded they made him look sleepy or arrogant or faintly predatory. In her present state of unexpected confusion, she couldn't decide which. He's like a leopard, she thought, all black and gold and handsome and smooth-skinned and full of power. 'Honoured to make your acquaintance,' he said.

Chapter Twenty

Calverley Leigh was a man with a double reputation, renowned among his fellow officers as a rattle and a Romeo. He was equally proud of both titles, although his friends and cronies would have been surprised had they ever heard him confess it. For the lethargic wit and insouciant charm that seemed so natural to him and made him such irresistible company for both male and female alike were not inborn accomplishments. They had been gradually and painstakingly acquired during his seven years with the Duke of Clarence's Light Dragoons.

As a child he had been skinny and awkward, with few talents and fewer prospects, the insignificant third son of an insignificant younger daughter of one of the lesser landed gentry. He'd had the ill fortune to be the final and belated offspring of that most rare of eighteenth-century accomplishments, a love match. So although he was the baby of the family he was a singularly neglected one, being separated from his sister and his two elder brothers by a gap of more than eight years, and from his parents by a chasm of style and attitude.

His father, whose proudest boast was that one of his distant cousins was racing manager to the Prince of Wales, ran a stud farm on the lower slopes of the Sussex Downs and bred horses for the cavalry. He was inordinately fond of his horses and took far more care over their breeding than he ever did over the upbringing of his children, maintaining that horses were a valuable source of income while children were nothing more nor less than than a noisome expense. He and his wife spent most of their time travelling abroad in search of pleasure and good breeding-stock. In fact they were away so often and for such long periods that there were times when young Calverley found it quite difficult to remember what they looked like.

However one consequence of this intermittent neglect was that he was allowed considerable freedom. When he was nine he was required to attend school, as both his brothers had done before him, and was sent on a daily trek down to the Grammar school in the nearby town of Steyning, but nobody paid any attention to him while he was there, so he was able to sit out his time in the low-ceilinged room, doing as little as he could, listening to the sound of passing hooves and day-dreaming.

For like his father before him, horses were Calverley's passion. He learnt to ride almost as soon as he could walk and from then on he spent every minute he could in the saddle. By the time he was ten, the grooms and ostlers declared with some pride that he could be trusted with any horse on the stud, even the youngest and most mettlesome. By the time he was fourteen and a long-legged, sharp-tongued gangly youth, he was so steeped in the art of handling horses that it was second nature to him. He knew when to coax and when to whip, when to encourage and when to reward, and the more he was able to control his mounts, the more he loved them. When he was fifteen his father gave him a fine cavalry horse of his own, which he called Jericho. Soon the rapport between them was so close they could have been one creature. In fact his school master, who said he never saw them apart, used to call them the Centaur, and even his mother, on one of the rare occasions when she actually noticed him, said he had 'a dammed good seat'.

It was almost the last thing she ever said to him, for two days later she took off on another one of her jaunts abroad, and never came back. His father returned without her, suddenly stooped and aged, his eyes red-rimmed and his breath foul with gin, to tell them all that she had taken ill of a fever, 'in county Sligo' and had died and been buried there. 'In county Sligo!' he said, over and over again, as if it were Sligo's fault. 'A malevolent county, boys, 'Od rot it! Why, oh why did we ever go to county Sligo?'

Calverley noticed her absence but he didn't miss her. Jericho was still alive and full of energy, galloping him out of the farm and away from sorrow. 'I love you better than any creature alive,' he told the animal, and Jericho flicked his ears and snorted and gave every indication that he understood entirely. 'Whilst you are living, nothing will ever go wrong for me.'

But his mother's death brought changes, as it was bound to. Within a year his sister had married a farmer and gone to live in Warwickshire, and both his brothers had taken the portion his father had set aside for each of them and gone too, the first to the abominable county Sligo to work with his uncle there, the second to Canada, which was a deal worse than Warwickshire, so his father said, 'being there ain't the least possibility of a visit there, neither one way nor t'other.'

And Calverley was suddenly alone on a stud farm that grew more and more dilapidated, with a father who sank further and further into drunkenness and melancholy. There was only one thing to be done about such a situation, and he did it. He begged his father to give him his portion early and as soon as he was eighteen, he bought himself a commission in the cavalry, casually letting it be known that he was related to Colonel Leigh, the Prince of Wales' racing manager, and choosing the Duke of Clarence's regiment because the blue and white uniform was so attractive and he thought he would look handsome in it.

It was the making of him. Good food and constant exercise put muscle on his scraggy bones, he grew taller and he acquired elegance. But best of all, within a year he had been sent to the Austrian Netherlands, where he discovered to his immense satisfaction that his superlative horsemanship brought him recognition and kept him out of danger on the battlefield, whether in the triumph of Neerwinder or the defeat at Hondeschoote. At the end of that campaign, the Clarence's were sent home to defend the south coast against Napoleon's threatened invasion, and now it was his mocking tongue that was valued and admired. 'Such a rattle!' his fellow officers would say, urging their society friends to include him at balls and dinners and supper parties, 'You *must* invite him, me dear. He'll have the table on a roar I guarantee.'

And so he did, with pithy comments about their absent friends and acquaintances, and mocking accounts of manoeuvres that didn't turn out as planned, and piercing vignettes of the folly of the overfed, the vain and the pompous. He was very popular. The court jester to the regiment. And his popularity soon made him much sought after by the ladies. Which led, in its turn to the acquisition of a second and even more enviable reputation.

He made his first tentative conquest two days after his nineteenth birthday and was proud of it although it gave him less pleasure than he expected, and despite the fact that the lady spurned him and called him a 'heartless wretch' and refused to see him 'ever again'. But as she'd also told him, during their more passionate moments, that he was 'devilish handsome' and that the sight of him quite made her swoon, he was encouraged to try again elsewhere and with more expertise. And it was true. He *was* handsome. The mirror of her face had told him that. Soon he had learned an entirely new vocabulary in which to flirt and cajole and tease and persuade, and it wasn't long before he realized that the techniques he'd been using all his life to handle horses could be used with equal and more rewarding effect to handle women.

By the time he was twenty-four and travelling to London to mount guard over the King's review of volunteers, he was convinced that there wasn't a woman in England he couldn't ride if he had a mind to. But better still, and far more comforting in the night hours when doubts still needled in to assail him, he had made up his mind to use his charms, while he still possessed them, to find himself a rich woman to marry. With the French war set fair to continue for years and little likelihood of a campaign to take him away from the country, he felt he was admirably placed for the pursuit, for there was just enough danger in the air to excite the ladies he courted but not enough to take him away from them. It was true that an invasion was always a possibility, at least during the months of spring and summer, and an invasion would certainly put him to the test at home, but he gave it little thought. For although he drilled and prepared for battles, he was in no hurry to embark on another real one. Life was perfectly satisfactory without such alarms.

As he stood before the bandstand that August evening with his two fellow officers lounging beside him, he was scanning the room for possible conquests, automatically dividing the ladies there into three categories, as though he were sifting them for market, the impossibles, the heiresses and the seducible.

'There's a deuced pretty creature,' he admired, looking at Sophie Fuseli as she pouted and preened and touched her thick curls.

'She ain't for you, Leigh,' Hanley-Brown said. 'Married to an artist, damme if she ain't. Little feller with white hair, d'you see?'

'German, I'll lay any money,' Calverley drawled. 'Looks like a gnome.'

'How much?' Hanley-Brown wanted to know, for like every officer in the regiment he was ready to gamble on everything and anything.

'A guinea?'

'You're on.'

'Ah, the perversity of beauty!' Lieutenant Fortescue sighed. 'To give her heart to such a creature and leave us languishin'.'

'That ain't the way of it, Forty,' Calverley said, observing her closely through those half-shut, sleepy-looking eyes. 'Mark how she moves. She don't move toward *him*, poor gnome, never the once. A lady whole of heart, you may gamble on it.'

'How much?' Hanley-Brown said again.

But Fortescue was looking at Nan. 'How of the little filly beside her?' he asked.

Calverley examined the little filly, knowledgeably. 'A trim figure, I'll grant you,' he said, 'but not to my taste.'

'They dress but poorly,' Hanley-Brown said. 'You'll not find your heiress here. Unless you fancy the dowager with the pearls.'

The dowager with the pearls was sixteen stone if she was an ounce. 'I need an heiress,' Calverley said, 'but not that desperately. No, no, my choice is made for this evening. An hour's dalliance with the delectable and heart-free wife to the artist.'

'No more?' Hanley-Brown teased.

'I could kiss had I a mind to.'

'Two guineas say you can't, damme.'

'Taken,' Calverley said at once. 'Take cover in the long walk when I give the sign, and you shall see 'twill be done before midnight, I'll warrant you. Request an introduction.'

But the Master of Ceremonies was already rolling across the room towards them with the German gnome in tow. And ten minutes later he was kissing the delectable lady's hand and gazing ardently into her beautiful blue eyes.

Sophie Fuseli was charmed by her new acquaintances and invited them all to join her party at the supper table. It was a lively meal for the soldiers were good company. Mr Leigh made them all laugh with his imitation of the troup sergeant subduing the newest recruits, and of course there were now three more partners for the dance. By the end of the meal, arrangements had been made and cards marked, and Calverley Leigh had begged the very next dance from the bewitching Sophie, and her husband, poor fool, had obligingly stepped down to allow him the honour.

As he led his new admirer onto the floor he looked back at Hanley-Brown and winked. And his eye was caught by the direct gaze and dark brows of the little filly, and for a fleeting second before the dance began he recognized passion, and wondered.

But then he was flirting with the beautiful Sophie, who knew all the right responses and gave them effortlessly. 'How if I were to tell you I consider you the most beautiful lady in the room?'

'Then, given the company, I would think you either blind, sir, or ungallant.'

'Love is blind, ma'am, is it not?'

'Aye, and strikes swiftly. So I am told.'

'An arrow to the heart, I do assure you.'

'Such pain, sir. I would be loath to give such pain to any man, especially were I to love him.'

'I see you have a tender heart, Mrs Fuseli, besides great beauty. Many must love you for it.'

'Aye, so they say,' she answered lightly. 'But women are weak, are they not, and men deceivers. How may we know when any of that sex speak true?'

'Maligned, dear lady,' he cried. 'Maligned, I vow it. Some of us would die ere we deceived.'

'I am glad on't,' she said, smiling her delicious smile and not believing a word.

Oh, she was just the companion he was seeking. Hanley's two guineas were virtually in his pocket. What a splendid choice he'd made!

Nan was dancing with old Mr Pomeroy, who was talking about the war. He always talked about the war, and he was always very boring. 'Indeed, yes, Mr Pomeroy,' she said, as the handsome lieutenant caught Sophie Fuseli about the waist. And she wondered how it would be when she was being held like that, and admired his long, long legs as they went tripping away along the dancing line. The dance after next, she thought, savouring her anticipation.

And the moment when she stood beside him on that floor was every bit as delightful as she'd fancied. He was so tall. The top of her head was barely on a level with his chin. So beautifully tall and he smelled so fresh, as if all his clothes were new or newly laundered, fresh and clean with just a trace of salty sweetness. And oh, so handsome, looking down upon her so tenderly with those beautiful eyes. What a pity he'd asked her for a set dance, for that meant they would be moving apart from one another on every turn, and he would only put his arm round her for the gallop.

'Do you live hereabouts, ma'am?' he asked politely, during the first figure.

'I live in Chelsea, just along the river.'

239

'But not born here, I think?' Turn and turn about.

'No,' she agreed, as they met up again at the end of the turn, and he swayed her body into his side ready for the gallop. What bliss to be held so! 'I was born in Suffolk, near Bury St. Edmunds,' she said as the gallop began.

'Place I know well,' he said, surprising her. 'Carried out manoeuvres there. Camped at a place called Fornham. The locals would have it a village. I can tell you 'twas no such thing.'

'A church, a farm, a smithy and a mill, and six low cottages, no more.'

'You know it well.'

'I should do sir, I was born there.' Turn and turn about.

'You were born dancing I believe,' he said, catching her into his side again. Oh, the delight of the easy intimate movement! 'You have the lightest foot of any lady in the hall.'

She took the compliment entirely seriously. ' 'Tis a pastime I enjoy, sir.'

'But only when you have a partner who is your equal for energy and speed, I rather think. The old gentleman who was so presumptuous as to offer the schottische was no match in all conscience. He went hobbling off defeated with the dance half done.'

'Old gentlemen do not have quite the same energy for dancing as young gentlemen,' she said. ' 'Tis true.'

'Nor young ladies either,' he answered, smiling sleepily at her with those beautiful eyes. Turn and turn about.

He considers me young, she thought, taking his second easy compliment as seriously as the first, and looking back brightly at him over her shoulder as she followed the figure. Until that moment it hadn't occured to her to think of herself in those terms at all. She had simply been a business-woman, neither young nor old. Now she knew that she wanted to be young, and she wanted it passionately. Young and beloved, like so many of the other women around her that evening. Or at least young and admired by this handsome officer.

'You should dance until you are too exhausted to set your foot to the ground,' he said, and the observation was made in tones so tender, he could have been talking of love.

'A gentleman may dance when he pleases,' she said, 'but a lady must wait for a partner, more's the pity of it.' And then she was quite alarmed at herself, because she had spoken carelessly and might have given him the idea that she was fishing for partners, which she didn't think she was doing because it wasn't her style at all.

But he answered her seriously and in the same tender tone. 'Then you must do me the honour for every single measure, ma'am, until the ball is over.'

'Only three are unmarked,' she said, admiring him more openly than she knew, and doubly happy because he'd asked her so warmly and because three dances were just the right number to have available. More and she would have appeared a wallflower and too eager, less and she would have had no time with him at all. Or no time worth mentioning.

'Then may I consider them mine?' Turn and turn about.

Oh yes, yes, yes, she thought, as she skipped away from him. You may indeed.

So they trod three more measures together and each more pleasurable than the last. But her next dance was with old Mr Pomeroy again, who huffed and puffed and smelled most vilely of stale sweat and musty jacket, and would insist on talking to her all the time, so that she couldn't look to see where the dashing Lieutenant was dancing. And with whom. Oh, if only there weren't such a crush!

And when her garrulous partner walked her back to their party, Sophie was missing too. 'Gone to promenade, I daresay,' her husband said, carelessly. It was a great nuisance, because Nan wanted to talk to her. 'She vill return for ze second interval.'

But she wasn't back until two dances after the interval, and then she and Mr Leigh came strolling across the dance floor together, very nearly arm in arm.

Nan's heart sank at the sight of them. Oh, surely he hadn't fallen for Sophie. That would be unbearable. And for the first time in their acquaintance she felt jealous of her friend and wished she wasn't quite so beautiful. 'You been away so long,' she said, 'we quite thought you were gone home.'

'We took a turn in the air,' Sophie said carelessly. 'Did we not Mr Leigh? Such a crush, my dear, I could scarcely breathe.'

'You must excuse me, ladies,' Mr Leigh said, smiling at them both. 'Dearly though I love your company, for this dance, and this dance alone, I am engaged elsewhere I fear.'

'You are fickle sir, fickle as all your sex,' Sophie admonished, waving her hand languidly at him as a sign that she would allow him to leave them. 'Pray do not forget that you are invited to supper at Whiteman's a' Thursday.'

He smiled at her lazily as he went off to collect his winnings.

'Do you invite me too?' Nan said as soon as he was out of earshot. And she made no attempt to mask her eagerness.

'Why yes indeed,' Sophie laughed, noticing the eagerness but deciding not to comment upon it. Yet. 'I would not dine without my Nan.'

It took Nan a long time and a lot of heart-searching to dress for that supper. Four dances with the attractive lieutenant had reduced her wardrobe to a heap of unfashionable rags. New material had to be bought at once and a new gown made in the very latest style, high, tight and uncomfortable under the bosom, with puffed sleeves and the lowest décolletage she had ever dared. She chose a red cotton print with flowers and sprays in ochre, black and green, partly because it suited her colouring but more because it was such an eye-catching design. This time he should notice her, whatever else he might do. For the truth was, the handsome lieutenant had taken possession of her every dream, waking or sleeping, and she thought about him so often during the day that it was hard for her to concentrate on her work.

A fact that was not lost on old Mrs Dibkins.

'Ho,' that lady said darkly, as she sat in the nursery with Bessie tacking hems, 'there's a man in it, you mark my words. I never see her give her titties such an airing before. Never ever.'

'D'you really think so?' Bessie said, all eyes at the thought. 'A new master! That'ud be a shock fer that ol' Pennington woman.' She and the governess were in perpetual conflict over the way the children should be treated. 'She'd 'ave ter mind 'er Ps an' Qs with a man about the house.'

'She got to catch 'im first,' Mrs Dibkins said, biting off her thread. 'She'll have to mind that sharp tongue of her'n if she want for to catch a man. Most men don't take too kindly to bossy women, an' that's a fact. Ho no! My lor, my side do pain me today!'

But they kept their opinion to the nursery. Not that Nan would have paid any attention to them, for she was in such a fever of excitement waiting for Thursday that she hardly heard anything except her dreams.

The desired day came round at last, and with a new thick shawl to protect her against the night air, should he wish to take a promenade after supper, and her hair dressed in side curls and a top-knot, that looked exceedingly elegant but felt as if it was scalping her, she set off for Whiteman's and the irresistible lieutenant. And was bitterly disappointed.

For a start Sophie had placed her right at the foot of the table, next to Mr Wotherspoon and about as far away from Mr Leigh as it was possible for her to be. And then they all went on to the card-rooms after supper to play Faro for an hour or so and she was separated from him again and lost a deal of money she could ill afford, particularly after the amount she'd spent on that useless dress. And then Mr Wotherspoon suggested that they should all go on to the play at Dury Lane, which most of them did. But that wasn't any good either for despite all her efforts she ended up sitting between Mr Fortescue and that awful Mr Pomeroy, while Sophie and Mr Leigh sat head-to-head, sharing a programme.

It wasn't until they were all squashed in the foyer afterwards waiting for carriages to take them home, that she managed to speak to him. But she made the most of her opportunity. 'I am giving a little supper party myself next Thursday. At Whiteman's, of course. At six of the clock.' Was Thursday time enough to have all prepared? No matter. Thursday it would have to be. 'I trust I may see you all there. I would be honoured by your company.'

They were delighted at the thought of another supper party so soon and said so happily, accepting her offer. And the handsome lieutenant smiled down at her from his beautiful height and agreed that he too would make one at her party.

It was a very little hope and a very small triumph. But it was enough, for this was *her* supper party and this time she could sit where she pleased. And where she pleased was next to Mr Leigh.

He was gallantly attentive and didn't look at Sophie once, although he spoke of her a deal too often, which was not a good sign. 'Mrs Fuseli tells me . . .' 'Mrs Fuseli is of the opinion . . .' 'Mrs Fuseli . . . Mrs Fuseli . . .' And it made her heart sink every time.

'Mrs Fuseli tells me you are a woman of business,' he said as the roast pork was borne in.

'True,' she said. 'I sell newspapers.'

'And deuced well, I hear.'

'Throughout London,' she said with some pride. 'In fact if 'twere not for the stubbornness of a certain Joshua Vernon, I could say I had the monopoly.'

'Then you are rich,' he said.

'In property and obligations,' she admitted, 'not in capital.'

'How so?'

He seemed genuinely interested, so she told him. It was better than talking about Sophie. 'If a business is to succeed,' she said, 'the more capital you plough back into it, the better. I set all my money to work, d'ye see. Every last penny of it.' And she went on to tell him how she planned to extend her empire.

Now that he had established that she wasn't an heiress, he found her business talk boring. 'You keep a good table, ma'am,' he said, scanning the rich food, and changing the subject.

'When I have guests,' she said honestly. 'At home I live simply.'

'If I were rich, ma'am,' he said. 'I should live well all the time. Oh, deuced well.'

She didn't doubt it. But then she noticed that there was no apple sauce on the table and she had to turn her attention to the waiters to make certain it was sent for. And by the time the food was provided to her satisfaction, he was entertaining again, giving a wicked account of the absent Mr Pomeroy trying to dance a schottische.

After supper they all went on to the Ranelagh Gardens where there were fireworks, and the Rotunda was open for dancing. And as she was their hostess, the gentlemen made sure that her card was marked for every dance. Which was polite and proper of them, but meant that there were fewer dances available for the lieutenant. But they managed five altogether and the fifth was a polonaise which put them in one another's arms for five dizzying minutes.

But then he ruined everything when the dancing was done and they were all bidding one another goodnight, by announcing, oh far too casually, that the regiment had been ordered on and that he would be leaving London in two days' time.

She was so upset she couldn't find anything to say. Of course, she'd known, in a vague, general sort of way, that the regiment would have to move on sooner or later, but she hadn't thought about it. She'd been too busy living from moment to moment, not thinking about anything at all except her need to be near him, her desire to see him again. And now he was going away. She was overwhelmed by the most exquisite sense of loss.

'You must write to us,' Sophie said easily, filling the silence.

244

'You may depend upon it,' he said. 'Good night, Mrs Easter. It has been a delightful evening.'

They were all saying the right things to one another, 'So kind.' 'Such a pleasure.' 'We shall meet again a' Saturday, if you mean to attend the play.' 'Indeed yes, I would not miss it for the world.' But he was walking away from her, those long legs gleaming white in the lamp-light. Walking away and she might never see him again. How could she endure it? Why hadn't he promised to write to *her*? She couldn't just let him walk away. It was too painful.

'Mr Leigh!' she called after him.

He stopped in his long stride and looked back at her. 'Mrs Easter, ma'am?'

And then she didn't know what to say, and was aware that her guests were looking at her with some astonishment. 'Pray do not forget,' she said, 'when the regiment returns I want a commission to supply you with newspapers.'

Laughter and interest and admiring comments, while he stood before her, smiling his languid smile.

'I shall see to it personally,' he said, bowed and was gone.

Chapter Twenty-one

Although she knew it was a foolish thing to do, and she could ill afford the time, Nan went down to the Chelsea barracks on Friday to watch the Light Dragoons ride out of town. It was a miserable morning, chill and dank and trailing white mist, but she walked up from Cheyne Row glowing with an absurd hope, sustained by the fantasy that he would see her as he passed, that he would realize how much he was going to miss her, that he would lean down from his horse to promise to write to her and pledge that he would see her again as soon as the regiment returned. She'd even put a visiting card in her pocket, ready to give it to him, when he asked for her address, as he surely must. It had been an almost constant day-dream for the last forty-eight hours. And like all fantasies it was soon dissolved by reality.

The moment the first troop clattered out through the barrack gates, it was plain, even to her, that the regiment was there to be looked at, and not to look. They rode in splendid order, heads held artificially high, gazing down their noses at the space between their horses' ears, knowing themselves admired, their breeches dramatically white against brown horseflesh and sheepskin saddle, black boots gleaming, white-sashed and red-belted, their red and blue mirleton caps topped by high red and white plumes, their gold frogging bold as sunshine against those fine blue jackets.

The handsome Mr Leigh's was the third troop out of the gate. And there he was, on a great chestnut horse, riding magnificently, but looking straight ahead, deliberately impervious to stares and admiration. The sight of him lifted her into a state of such heightened sensation it was as if someone had switched on the sun a few inches away from her eyes. She was acutely and painfully aware of everything around her, the chill of the air and the warmth of the troop, the ammoniac smell of horse flesh, the meaty reek of warm leather, the rattle and clank of accoutrements and the scrape of hooves on cobbles, people in the crowd chewing and spitting and coughing, his breath streaming from those aristocratic nostrils like white smoke, his gloved hands holding the reins, lightly, oh so lightly, those long muscular legs gripping the chestnut flanks, his face so dear and near and far away. And she knew she was yearning for him, her innards lifting as though they were being pulled upwards by invisible strings.

And then the troop had passed and she couldn't see him anymore. And the strings dropped and sagged and the daylight was cold and the town deserted, and the cobbles were sharp and dank and piled with horse-dung, because he hadn't seen her, and he didn't care for her, and he'd promised to write to Sophie Fuseli.

Come now, she scolded herself, that en't the way to go on, mooning about like some love-sick girl, and you a business-woman with a great firm to run and a daughter old enough to be at work. For Annie was ten now. You should be ashamed of yourself, so you should. The lieutenant is gone, so you'd best get on with your work and be sensible and forget un. Even if he was the most handsome man she'd ever seen and quite the most desirable.

She drove all her employees extremely hard that day, but when the evening came she was still full of restless energy, so she decided to take her children to the theatre, choosing a farcical comedy called *Pierre's Retreat*, because she thought it would do them all good to laugh. It was the first time they'd ever been allowed such a treat and all three were thrilled by it, although, as their mother observed, each in a different way.

Billy laughed uproariously at every joke and every chase and every stage-fall, and when the villain got his long nose stuck in the knot-hole of the hero's front door he jumped to his feet and clapped with pure delight along with half the others in the audience. But Johnnie sat quietly throughout. He smiled at the jokes and nodded agreement when evil got its come-uppance and clapped with enthusiasm at the end, but his enjoyment was private, as though he were imbibing this pleasure secretly and digesting it within himself. Watching him, Nan was surprised yet again by how different he was from his brother and sister.

Annie was excited just to be in a theatre and spent the overture looking about her at all the other members of the audience and admiring the fine clothes of the ton who were eating their supper in the boxes, but when Pierre took his first tumble, backwards out of an apple tree, she jumped visibly and then clenched her fists before her mouth with concern.

' 'Tis make-believe,' Nan whispered, patting her arm. 'He en't hurt.'

'It looks uncommon real, Mama,' Annie whispered back, but she was already recovering and relaxing.

What a tenderheart she is, Nan thought affectionately. And how like her father. And she felt more fond of her than ever.

It was an uncommon pleasant evening and she prolonged it for as long as she could after they'd driven home, sitting in the drawing-room with her three excited children, drinking hot possetts and re-living the play. But eventually Billy began to yawn and it was plainly high time they were all in bed.

Now she thought, as she kissed them goodnight, we shall all sleep sound.

But she was wrong. Once she was alone in her wide bed in her quiet bedroom, her mind sprang open to memory, no matter how hard she tried to prevent it. The handsome lieutenant held her about the waist, smiling that slow smile, and she danced and danced, longing to be kissed, breathing in the lovely clean smell of his skin, gazing into those beautiful honey-coloured eyes, knowing that she had fallen in love with him. Waking thought merged into erotic dream, and now she was kissed and kissed again, and held so close as she danced she could barely catch her breath, and turned to be tumbled on mattress and straw, and climbed Pierre's cardboard apple tree to fall and fall into the lieutenant's arms.

She woke bewildered and yearning as the sky above the Chelsea fields grew green with dawn. And she remembered Mary Woolstone-craft saying, 'If you love him he will haunt your thoughts by night and day,' and in that quiet, chill daybreak she began to suspect that her old friend had been right. But what could be done about it? It was true that he'd treated her courteously and had seemed to be interested in what she had to say. But in the sober light of early morning she realized that this was more like to be a passing interest than love and in any case she couldn't even hope that they would meet again. She didn't even know where the regiment had gone.

But Sophie Fuseli did.

That autumn, when Mr Fuseli had left for one of his trips, 'only a week or two, my dear, but 'tis enough', she came to take tea with

Nan, bubbling with the news that 'our three friends from the Duke of Clarence's' had come to visit her.

'Here to buy horses, I believe, or saddles or somesuch,' she said carelessly. 'We rode in Hyde Park, my dear. I must say, Mr Leigh has a fine way with horses.'

'Which you would expect in a cavalry officer, surely,' Nan said, endeavouring to speak calmly because she was shaken with jealousy.

' 'Tis a charming creature,' Sophie mused patting her curls, 'that cannot be denied.' But she had no idea when the charming creature would be in London again. 'They come and go,' she said vaguely.

'Did you not ask him? I'm sure I should have done.'

'Indeed I did not,' Sophie said, registering shock at the suggestion. 'A man such as he would be aggrieved to be asked for such particulars. And rightly so. 'Twould be most improper.'

'But you know where they are stationed, I daresay?' Nan asked, hoping she didn't sound too eager.

'In Dorset, my dear, and a most uncivilized place by all accounts. But they are to have a better posting in April.'

'How so?' Oh do tell me! Where is he going? I must at least have a hope of seeing him again.

'Well, as to that,' Sophie said, 'they are to mount guard upon the King when he visits Weymouth, as he does every summer, war or no war.'

'Aye, I know it. 'Tis reported in *The Times*.'

' 'Tis a great honour, so they tell me,' Sophie said. 'Personally I should find it an exceeding bore, but there is no accounting for the taste of the soldiery. Could I beg another dish of your excellent tea?'

Now that she knew where he would be in the spring, Nan was impatient for autumn and winter to pass. But this year the autumn days seemed longer than any she'd ever known even in the height of summer. It was a long time before the first of the winter gales brought an end to the threat of a French invasion for another year and it was nearly November before the King returned to the capital and the delights of the Season.

Nan did her best to enjoy the Season, taking her children to the play and organizing supper parties and joining Sophie in excursions to Vauxhall and the Ranelagh gardens, for this was a special season and there was much to celebrate. In a few weeks time the eighteenth century would be over, and such an historical event could hardly be allowed to pass without commemoration.

In December grand preparations began for the Ball of the New Century which was to be held at the Vauxhall Gardens preceded by 'fireworks and masques and all such delectable entertainments'.

'I shall buy tickets for us all,' Nan told Annie and the boys. 'We shall start the new century in style. How say 'ee to that?'

'Fireworks!' Billy said, thrilled at the idea. 'I can't think of a better way to start a century than fireworks.'

And very spectacular they were. Dramatic enough to tease Nan's mind away from thoughts of Mr Leigh for nearly thirty minutes. But when the last sparks fizzled away into the black sky, she missed him more than ever and remembered him more clearly. Oh, she thought, gazing at the white stars, I must see him again. I must.

'Now for the masque,' Billy said. 'Come on Annie, race you to the tent.'

In Europe, the brand-new nineteenth century began with fireworks of another kind, which were a considerable shock to the inhabitants of London. Napoleon Bonaparte, having contrived to be elected one of three consuls back in November had now, somehow or other, inched his two fellow consuls out of office, and been declared the one and only, undisputed leader of the French. It was very bad news indeed and very good for trade, but it cast a gloom over Mr Walter's customary New Year party.

' 'Tis a portent,' that gentleman said. 'He will do as he pleases now, Heaven help us all!'

'He has always done that, Father,' his son John said calmly, helping himself to the port.

'Howsomever that may be, now there is no power to prevent him,' Mr Thrale worried. He had been a brewer for so many years now that he could hardly remember the days when he had simply been a newsman, but he still came to Mr Walter's annual supper party, for old time's sake.

They were a very select company indeed these days, their numbers diminished to a paltry six, the two Walters, Nan, Mr Jasperson, the publisher, Mr Thrale and old Mr Vernon, whose tenacious hold on the Bedford Estate walk was all that stood between Nan and total control of all the newspaper sales in London.

250

'Ah,' Mr Vernon mourned, 'I had hoped that this new century would bring some changes for us. But no. Mr Bonaparte pursues his ambition without surcease. 'Tis a wicked world. You may take my word for it, mankind has more to fear from an ambitious man – or an ambitious woman – yes, indeed, or a woman – than it has from many an acknowledged sinner.'

'As to that, Mr Vernon,' Nan said, stung by his sly reference to ambitious women, ' 'tis folly to imagine that the calendar will change matters. If you want things to change, sir, you must change 'em yourself.'

'Amen to that,' John Walter said.

And as he spoke, Nan knew that she had solved her own problem. If she wanted to see the handsome lieutenant again she would have to do something about it herself. 'I intend to make changes,' she told the company. ' 'Tis high time I extended my trade to the provinces. There en't a deal more for me to do in London, you'll allow.'

'What shall you do?' Mr Walter asked, pleased that she was lifting them from their gloom.

'I shall open more reading-rooms.'

'Where do you have in mind?' John Walter said.

'Weymouth,' she said casually. 'With the King and his family in residence there all through the summer, there should be plenty of trade.'

' 'Twould be uncommon costly,' Mr Vernon said sourly. 'A risky undertaking, I should say.'

'Save your warning, Mr Vernon,' John Walter said. 'Mrs Easter thrives on risky undertakings.'

'I shall go there in May,' she said, 'and see what may be done.'

The week before her journey, she went to see Mr Tewson in Lothbury. 'I intend to travel to Weymouth,' she told him, 'to open a reading-room. There should be plenty of trade with the King and his family in residence.'

Mr Tewson thought it a capital idea and gave her the address of the nearest Tewson's banking-house, in Dorchester. 'You will pass through the town of your journey,' he said. ' 'Tis but a short ride from Weymouth and a busy town, I'm told. You might well find trade there too.'

'I might at that,' she said cheerfully. 'Oh there is no knowing what I might accomplish now I've started.'

She was glowing with excitement, as the banker observed. What an extraordinary woman, he thought, to be so carried away by the thought of extending her trade. The feminine temperament, indubitably. A man would take matters more calmly.

It was a very long journey and a very dirty one, for the roads were thick with dust so that they trundled along inside their own choking cloud, and neither of the inns at which they stayed overnight were more than indifferently cleaned. At Basingstoke the supper was cold and at Salisbury it was unappetizing, but, luckily for the cooks, Nan was too excited by now to do more than pick at her food.

On the afternoon of the third day, she arrived in Dorchester, where it was market day and the streets had been so well watered and so well trodden by bewildered sheep and cattle that they were squelchy with mud. But Weymouth was a mere seven miles away and the sun was shining. She hired a horse and cart, agreed a price after some determined haggling, and set off to find her love.

Because he *was* her love. She had to admit it. She dreamed of him every night, of lying in his arms, of being kissed, held, caressed – ah, such dreams! And she was jealous of Sophie, who had been her kindest friend for so many years. If I see him again, she thought, and 'tis plain he has no interest in me, then I must needs forget him. But if I see him again and he is glad of it, why then, who knows how things may fadge?

It was pleasant sitting out in the open air in the little, creaking cart as the dappled mare went ambling through the hilly countryside towards the sea. The afternoon sun was quite warm on her cheek and the air was wondrously fresh. She'd been working in the smoke of London for such a long time she'd forgotten how sweet-tasting fresh air could be. Oh, there was no doubt now that her life was changing, and changing for the better.

And how elegant and delightful Weymouth was. Her first view of it as they reached the top of the last hill was a charming revelation. There it lay below her, a small fishing town huddled about a low harbour wall in a muddle of tiled roofs, and crowded waterways, masts, spars and rigging, and a little to the left, a fine curved bay, an ancient crescent of blue sea and light brown sand, faced by a modern crescent of fine houses, and all contained by the green and lilac folds of the low hills, which curved round the bay like a protective arm and ended in a dramatic white headland well out to sea. The sight of it lifted her spirits even further. It was such a splendidly compact place. Oh, she would find him here, there was no doubt of it.

The carter set her down beside the harbour wall with the huddle of the old town behind her and the fine prospect of that crescent-shaped bay before her.

It was the most enticing prospect she'd ever seen and the mildest sea, blue as the sky above it, shimmering in the sunlight and so calm that its waves were no more than ruffles of foam dissolving at the water's edge. There were several elegant people taking a promenade on the pale sands, or strolling along the pebbled path beside the new houses, and quite a few horsemen, quietly ambling, although they were too far away for her to see their faces. Yet. But there was an ease and gentleness about the place. It was a marked contrast to the rush she was used to in London. A compact place, she thought, a calm place, an orderly place, a place where she could find whatever she wanted.

'Tha's the ol' king's house yonder,' the carter volunteered, pointing to a very ordinary red-brick villa which stood a little apart from the others in its own green gardens. 'A comes tonight, so they do say.'

'I could find lodgings in those terraces?' she asked.

'Bound to, ma'am,' he said. 'Bein' they'm all bran' new.'

It was a little more difficult than she'd imagined, for the terraces were already full of visitors, but eventually she found two rooms in a new lodging-house on the northern end of the promenade, not far away from a huge, rather forbidding building that her landlady said was the Burdon barracks. Then she set off to find the offices of the local paper, which the landlady also knew about. ' 'Tis called the *Sherbourne and Dorchester Gazette*. Printed in Dorchester, I do believe, ma'am,' she said. 'Mr Elsworthy is the agent hereabouts.'

Mr Elsworthy was very surprised by her visit, but he agreed that opening a reading-room would be a very good idea. 'I wonder they en't done such a thing before,' he said.

'Possibly because they didn't think of it,' she told him happily. 'And I did. Now, Mr Elsworthy, I shall need to advertise for an assistant to run this room.'

'My cousin . . .' he offered, tentatively.

The cousin, who was sent for immediately, turned out to be another rather younger Elsworthy with a weather-beaten face and hair exactly the same colour as the sand. She explained his duties to him, pointing out that all monies would be paid into Tewson's bank in Dorchester, and that his wage, which the bank would be empowered to pay him weekly, would rise and fall according to the number of subscribers he could obtain.

He considered this stolidly before agreeing to her terms, with an open smile that she found very encouraging. And then it was merely a matter of finding the right room for her trade.

'Well now, Mrs Easter, ma'am,' the younger Mr Elsworthy said, 'as to that, there's a fine chamber vacant this very minute in Charlotte Row just above Thomas's lending library.'

It was the easiest business she'd ever transacted. Within an hour, she was strolling back along the promenade towards her rooms and the only thing left for her to do was to inform the bank and write to Thiss to order the papers.

Down on the sands a string of amiable-looking horses was taking exercise. Or was it exercise? She stopped to watch as the first three plodded to a halt and their riders dismounted. Then as two young ladies came hesitantly forward to replace them, purse in hand, she realized that this was a seaside riding school, and the realization gave her an idea. For the first time in years she had time and money to spend entirely on herself. I shall learn to ride, she thought, why not? 'Tis just the time for it. And she went striding off across the shingle, straight-backed and determined.

The riding instructor chose a gentle gelding for her and helped her to mount and told her how to arrange her long legs within a side saddle that he swore was 'uncommon comfortable once you're accustomed' but which she found uncommon awkward. And then the string set off again, with a little breeze blowing off the sea to flick the ribbons of her bonnet into a tangle.

She was surprised by how far away the ground seemed, but the rocking rhythm of the gelding's steady amble was pleasant enough in all conscience and although her spine was rather stressed and her legs felt useless swung to one side like that, she was pleased to be keeping her balance. And then the gelding suddenly pricked up his ears and began to trot, which she wasn't expecting at all. The change of rhythm was so unexpected she couldn't adapt to it, but she was too proud to call for help. She clung to the reins, trying to pull the poor beast back, but he snorted disdainfully and seemed to be picking up more speed.

Then everything happened at once. She could hear the instructor thundering along the sand behind her, calling 'Hold on, ma'am!', and the gelding made an abrupt turn, took two steps backwards and broke into a gallop, and Nan lost her balance, clawed at the tumbling mane, struggled to disentangle her legs and finally slid from the saddle to land ignominiously on her back on the damp sand. The gelding jumped neatly across her body and headed for the sea.

She was very annoyed.

'Are you hurt, ma'am?' the instructor said anxiously, as she sat up and dusted the sand from her skirts with quick, cross hands.

'I tell you what,' she said scowling at him, 'that's an uncommon foolish way for anyone to ride, man or woman, with your legs a-going one way and your spine another. You fetch me a horse with a proper saddle and I warrant I shan't fall.'

'A gentleman's saddle do ye mean, ma'am?' he said, plainly shocked at the suggestion.

'Yes, yes,' she said briskly. 'Hasten you up, do. A proper saddle if you please.'

She was so firm about it, he did as he was told, although he grumbled about it all the time, saying it wasn't at all the style, especially with the King coming an' all, and he didn't know what the world was coming to, that he didn't.

But she took no notice of him. When she couldn't sit astride her new mount because her skirt impeded her, she simply lifted it up until it was above her knees. When her bonnet blocked her vision, she simply took it off and threw it on the sand. Then with her new horse held firmly between her thighs, she kicked him into motion with her heels the way Thiss always did, and off she went.

It was a marvellous improvement. This time she really felt she could control the animal, using her knees and her heels as well as her hands. This time she could share the rhythm of the ride. She was so happily engrossed, she didn't notice the other horseman until he was trotting beside her, and the movement of his body bowing towards her caught her attention. And she looked across, straight into the smile of the handsome lieutenant. Even though it was the very thing she'd come to Weymouth for, it was so sudden and unexpected it made her heart leap as though it was trying to jump into her throat.

'Why, Mistress Easter,' he said, 'what brings you to Weymouth?'

Surprise and excitement and gratification, all at once, shaking her, but she kept her balance and managed to answer him calmly enough. 'I have business here,' she said, rescued by pride and the need to concentrate. 'In three days there will be a reading-room in this place, and 'twill be all my doing.'

'Ah!' he said, smiling at her, 'I see how it is. London is grown too small to contain your energy.' He could have said ambition, but he thought better of it. 'I wish you well in your endeavours. And in the meantime, you ride I see.'

'I learn, sir.'

'And deuced well.'

Has he been watching me? she wondered. Did he see me fall? And she felt herself blushing at the thought and rushed to change the subject. 'You have a fine horse, sir.'

He noticed the blush as he'd noticed the fall, and her quick recovery and the spirited ride that followed. 'The best,' he said. 'Ain't you, Jericho?' And he leaned forward to address the words straight at the animal's head.

She was touched by the pride and affection in his voice. If this was the attention he gave his horse, how well he would treat a woman!

'Stay there!' he ordered abruptly. 'I will put him through his paces and you shall see how fine he is.' And he turned the horse's head and cantered off along the beach, scattering strollers to right and left.

She reined in her own horse and watched as Jericho turned and wheeled, side-stepping as deftly as any dancer, dropped to his knees without any warning, and finally galloped at full tilt towards her, coming to such an abrupt halt that he reared up on his hind legs pawing the air. It was a breath-taking display and she admired the horse almost as much as she admired the rider.

'Well, what think 'ee?' the lieutenant said. 'Ain't he the best?' His skin was glowing with exertion and he looked more handsome than ever.

'Magnificent,' Nan said, and found she had another question she could ask. 'Are you stationed nearby?'

'At the Burdon.'

Oh, what good fortune! Hadn't she hoped he would be there? Quick, quick, think of something witty to say that will keep him talking. But her mind was still spinning with the sheer joy of seeing him again, of being so close she could have put out her hand and touched him, just as she was touching the warm flesh of her horse's neck. The thought made her shiver and she gazed at Jericho's nose to calm herself again.

He was watching her, thoughtfully, and her instincts knew it and the knowledge encouraged her. She sat quite still, caressing that velvety neck, listening to the suction of hooves on sand and a seagull mewing above their heads, and for the first time in her life, she was waiting for somebody else to make the first move.

And he watched her. A mettlesome woman, he was thinking, and pretty enough. A good bosom and clean breath. She might be worth the conquest. That fire of hers could presage passion even if she wasn't an heiress. And who else was there in this benighted town? A few days dalliance with a new love was just what he needed, in all conscience. 'Do you have good lodgings?' he asked.

'I am assured so,' she said, smiling up at him. 'I have taken rooms in the new Royal Terrace. I cannot answer for the food, but the place is clean and the landlady seems obliging.'

'Which is more than may be said for most hereabouts,' he told her. 'An uncommon tricky breed, landladies, and prone to add extras if you so much as blink.' And he gave a mocking imitation. 'But my dear Lieutenant, you had a *plate* on which to eat your breakfast. Plates is *extra*, my dear Lieutenant.'

'I should break it over her head if she tried such tricks with me,' Nan said.

'Aye,' he laughed, 'I believe you would.' That fierce face was really quite attractive. Dammit, he thought, making up his mind. 'Twould be a game worth the candle. 'I have a pair of tickets for tonight's ball at the Assembly Rooms,' he offered. He hadn't, but he felt pretty sure he could get them. 'I should be honoured were you to agree to be my guest.'

'I call that uncommon civil,' she said, as the blood rushed into her throat, 'but if I accept your invitation, sir, you must agree to dine with me tomorrow.'

'An admirable arrangement, thank 'ee kindly,' he said, this time approving the blush. 'I will call for 'ee tonight at eight of the clock.'

'At eight 'tshall be.'

'I look forward to it,' he said as he rode away.

But not half as eagerly as she did. There were so many preparations to make, to say nothing of a supper to eat, as well as she could. What a blessing she'd brought that low-necked gown. 'Twas just the thing for a ball and it showed her bosom to advantage. But what should she wear with it, and how should she dress her hair? Oh, if only I were a beauty, she thought, studying her dark face in the honest glass of the dressing-table mirror.

But it was no use, she was dark of eye and heavy of feature, no matter how she arranged her curls. He will not love me, she thought. Not after Sophie Fuseli. I do not compare. And she was cast down by the sight of her inadequacies, and wished she'd had the sense to buy rouge and orris powder to enhance her colouring.

But it was too late, he was knocking at the door.

'Such beauty!' he said taking her gloved hand and kissing it. 'You will dazzle the company, ma'am. My life upon it.' And he sounded as though he meant it.

She arranged her shawl about her shoulders, touched the ostrich feathers in her hair, rather apprehensively, found her fan and picked up her reticule from the table where it lay ready packed with handker-chief and cachous and spare hairpins.

'Yes,' she said, taking his proferred arm and thinking, as ready as I shall ever be.

It was a marvellous evening, despite her misgivings. For a start there were so many people in the Assembly Rooms she knew, and most of them seemed pleased and not at all surprised to see her. London society had taken to the seaside en masse, bringing the latest dances with them, and a band that could play them properly. In fact the second dance that the lieutenant had marked on her card was one of the new shocking waltzes, the dance that required the men to hold their partners firmly round the waist all the time, and was causing such annoyance among the older members of society. What could be better?

She stepped out onto the floor in a dream and was soon in a delicious trance, with her feet spinning almost as wildly as her head, breathing in his lovely well-laundered scent, with his hand firm in the small of her back, and her body swaying against his at every turn. Bliss!

At the first interval they drank punch with three of her customers and made polite conversation and were rather circumspect, but at the second, when they had both danced until they were breathless, he suggested that they should take a turn in the air.

' 'Tis a warm night,' he said. ' 'Twill do no harm, I warrant you.'

She would have gone with him if an icy wind had been blowing. But he was right, it was a warm night and a magical one. The dark beach was full of cooling couples, strolling along the sands or ambling at the water's edge, silvered by moonlight. They could smell the sea although they couldn't see it, since it was as black as ebony except for its little white fringe of tumbling waves and a huge shimmering pathway that glittered across the darkness towards a full moon like a huge silver platter. The night sky was a velvety dark blue, pointed with bright white stars, which seemed to Nan more distant here beside the sea than they had ever been in London.

'True,' he said, when she commented upon it. ' 'Tis the quality of the air. Smoky air makes it difficult to judge distance, as any gunner would tell you.'

That was something she had never considered. 'A battle must be a fearsome thing,' she said, thinking how very brave soldiers must be to withstand it.

'No,' he said, and how noble he looked as he spoke. 'There is no time for fear once a battle begins. You are too hot and things happen too quickly. You act by instinct, which,' changing his tone and giving her the benefit of his most tender glance, 'to my way of thinking is the very best way to act.'

'At all times?' she asked, made eager by the sensuous tone of his voice. He spoke as though he was stroking her with words.

'Oh yes, my dearest. Instinct and love being kith and kin, the one will speak as true as the other, don't 'ee think so?'

He was holding her right hand in both his, and slowly unbuttoning her glove, stroking her wrist with his fingers.

'Does love never lie?' she asked tremulously, for he was easing the glove from her hand softly and gradually, gazing into her eyes all the time, and the combination of amorous look and gentle movement was making her shiver.

He lifted her hand and kissed her palm, lingeringly, his lips tantalizingly warm. 'Do your senses lie, my dearest one?' he said softly and now his mouth was within inches of hers, and they both knew how very much she wanted to be kissed.

'I think not,' she whispered, caught in the double spell of moonlight and strong sensation.

'And now?' he whispered, before he kissed her. Oh, such sensations, her breast lifting towards him, her body opening and aching as he kissed and kissed and kissed again.

'Now, now, now,' she said, hardly knowing what she was saying, but telling him everything he needed to know by the eager pressure of her lips.

259

He stopped kissing her, and lifted his head to look down at her, holding her about the waist, close and warm and exciting. 'Ah, if only . . .' he sighed.

'If only what?'

'If only I were not in barracks, my love. 'Tis a torment not to continue. You must know it. You tempt me beyond restraint, you beautiful, beautiful creature. If I only had rooms . . .'

'I have rooms,' she said.

'Do you mean it?'

'Yes, oh yes.'

'You do not fear scandal?'

'Oh, what of that?' she said tempestuously. 'I could dare any scandal to be loved so.'

'Should we return to the ball, think 'ee?' It was an unfair question because he was kissing her neck and stroking her thighs.

So they went back to the Royal Terrace, and although the landlady gave them a knowing leer, neither of them took any notice of her. There were other things to think of.

They didn't bother to light candles either, for the moon provided all the light they needed, and the place all the privacy. They were alone and unbridled and could kiss and caress as they pleased. Her shawl and ostrich feathers and his fine jacket were cast aside like rags, and somehow or other he had unlaced her gown while they were kissing. She had enough wit left to admire the skill of it even though her senses were swirling with the powerful sensations he was arousing. But when he lifted her clothes, gown and chemise and all, sliding his hands in a long caress up and up over her thighs and her belly and her breasts until the folds of cloth had been thrown away behind her head, she was lost to the moment, unable to think, abandoned to feelings so strong they were making her tremble. He held her face between his hands and kissed her deeply, and she answered him with a passion that surprised them both.

'Beautiful, beautiful, beautiful,' he crooned, stroking and kissing. 'My beautiful love, now I must love you. I must, must.'

'Yes, yes, yes,' she said as they tumbled into the covers. She had opened for him again. She wanted him, wanted him. 'Yes, yes, oh yes.'

And his member was an arrow piercing her with pleasure, strong and demanding and warm as fire, driving her up and up until the pleasure

260

exploded into ecstasy, sweeter and more overwhelming than anything she'd ever known.

She must have fallen asleep and slept for some little time, for she awoke with a start to the sound of church bells ringing riotously and for a few minutes as she swam luxuriously back to consciousness she thought they were ringing for her, and wondered who had told the ringers of her triumph. Then she realized what time it was and wondered why church bells were being rung in the middle of the night? And cannon being fired, too. Surely that low boom was a cannon.

The room was bright with moonlight and the lieutenant was standing beside the window looking out. He had put on his trousers and draped his jacket about his shoulders like a Hussar, but his chest and his right arm were still beautifully naked, the dark flesh edged with shimmering whiteness.

'What is it?' she said sleepily.

'They are going out to meet the King,' he said, still gazing down onto the promenade. And now she could hear footsteps on the pebbles below them and the murmur of greetings.

She got up and wrapped her nightgown about her, and went to stand beside him to see for herself. The sky was lightening with the approach of dawn.

'He was expected at three or thereabouts,' he said. 'He keeps good time.'

Lamps were being lit all along the promenade and the crowds below them increased by the minute. The night air struck cold on her heated flesh so that she gave an involuntary shiver. 'Take my jacket,' he said, wrapping the thick coat about her shoulders, and she was warmed by the cloth and his consideration.

'Will he be long, think 'ee?'

'They have sounded the cannon, so he must have passed the ridge.'

They stood side by side on the balcony, calm and beautiful with satisfied passion. 'I do not know your Christian name, Mr Leigh,' she said, feeling uncommon daring to be suggesting that he should tell her.

He seemed to approve of the new style for he smiled. 'Nor I yours.'

'I am called Nan.'

'And I am Calverley,' giving her a little bow, 'your most obedient . . .'

At the far end of the promenade people were cheering. 'There they

261

are,' he said, as four dusty, old leather coaches came trundling along the road, creaking and rattling. They passed directly underneath the balcony, and a white hand waved lethargically from the second one and then they were gone and the excitement was over. It was a decided anticlimax.

'I would have thought the King would be more grand,' she said as they walked back into the sitting-room.

'In Weymouth,' he said, putting on his shirt, 'he is old farmer George on holiday.' He was reaching for his stockings.

'You have to leave?' Even the thought of seeing him go was making her feel miserable.

'I fear so, sweetheart. I am on duty at six. I will return so soon as ever I may, depend upon it.' Over in the old town the church clocks were striking four.

He looked very handsome in his uniform. 'I love you so much,' she said.

'Then kiss me goodbye and sleep again,' he said, brisk and business-like, as if clothes had put formality between them.

'You will return?'

'I promise.'

'I could not bear to be cast aside,' she warned as they walked to the door. 'Not now.'

He kissed her again, lightly. 'Never fear,' he said. And was gone.

Chapter Twenty-two

For a moment when she woke the next morning Nan didn't know where she was. Then she remembered her children, and despite all the pleasure of the night before, or perhaps because of it, she felt guilty because she'd left them behind in Chelsea. She missed the sound of their voices and the thump and patter of their feet and she wished she could know how they were. And because she was missing them so much, she turned her thoughts quite deliberately to her business affairs and wondered whether Thiss had managed to get the papers stamped in time for the first delivery, and whether he would really have enough expertise to order the right number. And behind her thoughts, the sea hissed across the shingle and the gulls mewed and shrieked and something was rattling with an unfamiliar insistent rhythm.

It was somebody throwing pebbles at the window. She could hear the sharp patter of the little stones and then the long descending rattle of their fall. And singing. 'Nan, my Nan, sweet Nan arise, See the sun is in the skies, Trip my sweetheart, join your love, Nan sweet Nan.'

It was glorious, glorious morning and he had kept his promise and come back. She threw the covers aside and ran from the bedroom, bare-footed and hair streaming, to fling back the shutters and lift the window and lean out to greet him.

'Good morning to my love,' he called, bowing like a courtier.

She was ridiculously happy at the sight of him, looking up at her in that bright, beautiful uniform with the white sea shining like mother-of-pearl behind him. 'I thought you were on duty,' she said.

'I have sneaked an hour away, and all for love of you, "Nan sweet Nan!" '

'Hush up,' she said lovingly. 'You'll waken the house.'

'Dress,' he ordered. 'Make haste. I have a sight for you to see.'

'You are sight enough for me,' she said, leaning over the balcony towards him.

'I would sooner touch than see, sweetheart,' he said, smiling at her, 'so hasten down, I prithee.'

How could she refuse such an invitation? She was dressed in three minutes and down the stairs in two, to be caught in his arms and held against his lovely warm chest and kissed most satisfyingly, once, twice, three times, oh, more times than she could count, and regardless of the stares of the early morning promenaders. What bliss! And then they were off over the pebbles and along the beach, hand in hand and skipping like children, and she was giggling because she felt so happy.

They stopped beside the harbour wall, where she'd stood for her first view of the town yesterday afternoon. Was it really only yesterday afternoon? It hardly seemed credible, so much had happened. 'So where's this ol' sight you promised?' she teased. The promenade was full of genteel strollers, parasols already in use against the early morning sun, and there were poor folk and fisherfolk leaning against the harbour wall, and the king's modest house was surrounded by red-coated guards, standing four deep and more or less to attention, but there was no sign of anything that could be called a 'sight'.

'Patience,' he said. 'You shall see if you wait a little.'

But waiting was intolerable. She was far too excited to wait for anything. 'Tell me what 'tis,' she begged.

'There's a price,' he teased, catching her about the waist.

'Name it.'

But he didn't need to. They were kissing already. And while they were still rapturously mouth to mouth, the sight commenced.

There was a scuffle of kettledrums from the other end of the promenade and a wailing tune began, shrilled on fifes and fiddles, wavered a little, gave a shriek and several hiccups and became a march. At the sound of it the promenaders rushed to take up positions on either side of the royal guard and a group of very important-looking females went stomping down the beach towards the bathing machines, where they proceeded to remove their shoes and stockings and to loop up their skirts like fishwives.

'What are they doing?' she asked, intrigued and amused.

He put a finger across her lips, but it was more a caress than an admonition. 'Watch!' he said.

The fife band came to a halt alongside the guards, where after some arm waving which was, presumably, a discussion, it played a selection of sea shanties more or less in unison. And then the troop sergeant bawled and the guard sprang to rigid attention, and a short stout man wearing a red velvet banyan, and Turkish slippers and a turban, emerged from the side door of the king's house, followed by a creep of courtiers and several giggling ladies in silk day-gowns. He trotted across the promenade towards the beach, nodding at the crowds as he passed. King George III was going to take the waters.

'Long live King Jarge!' his subjects cheered, as he struggled up the steep steps into his bathing machine and the bathing women rolled up their sleeves and assumed grim expressions and Nan watched. Then to her great surprise, the fife band waded into the sea, polished boots, white breeches and all, still playing their shanties.

She began to giggle. 'Oh, what foolish critturs!' she said. 'To wade in cold water at this hour of the morning. That's downright ridiculous, so it is.'

'There is better to come, according to the seventh Hussars,' Calverley said, cuddling her. 'You wait and watch.'

So they waited while the band played as well as they could with the waves lapping their thighs, and presently their portly monarch emerged on the seaward side of his machine, now as naked as a baby and very pink, and wobbled his way down the steps towards the water, the folds of his belly swaying with the effort he was making. When his toes touched the water, he looked as though he was shivering, but the bathing ladies had no pity for him. They seized him roughly by the arms and dunked him like a doughnut. And at the exact moment when his head disappeared under the green water, the band struck up the first notes of 'God save the King'. Nan laughed until the tears ran down her cheeks.

'My heart alive!' she said. 'I never seen nothin' so ridiculous. Oh, poor old king! What he want to go and do a thing like that for?'

' 'Tis for his health,' the fisherman standing next to her explained. 'They calls it the sea cure. 'Tis uncommon popular hereabouts. All the physicians recommend it.'

'They would,' Nan said. 'Poor man!'

The poor man endured his immersion patiently, shaking the water out of his eyes like a dog as he emerged, and was then dunked for a second time, and a third, and a fourth, at which point his face was flushed quite purple and he seemed to be waving a royal hand at his tormentors as if he were begging them to desist.

But there is no one quite so determined as a woman who knows she is doing you good, particularly when the doing is painful, so his appeal fell on deaf, damp ears. While his subjects cheered and laughed and cat-called, and the leader of the pipe band sniggered, he was pushed under water twice more.

'Poor old Jarge,' the fisherman said. 'He do take his pleasures serious.'

By the time the royal spectacle was over and several other members of the court were emerging from their bathing machines in various states of nudity and trepidation, the crowds were beginning to disperse, and Nan was quite weak with laughter. 'Time for breakfast,' Calverley said, and they went off to a coffee-house to enjoy it together.

Oh, there was so much to enjoy together, even though he had to leave her from time to time to attend to his duties in the barracks. On the second evening they went to the theatre and agreed that the play was a foolish trifle, on the third to another ball in the Assembly Rooms where they were entertained by friends new and old and mocked every gouty dancer in the place. One afternoon they went to a cock fight, where they were both splashed with blood and Calverley lost a great deal of money through betting on the wrong birds, and every morning they rode along the wide beach in the sunshine, laughing and talking and happily energetic. And every night he escorted her back to her lodgings and up to her bed where they played and loved until their senses were sated and they were both quite satisfied. It was a joy to be alive. Particularly now that she had taken the precaution of buying a sponge and vinegar to protect herself against the possibility of any unwanted babies.

On the fourth day the first batch of papers arrived from Thiss in London, and with it a rather odd letter.

'My best respects to e Mistress Easter you shd know things aint what they shd be here abouts not meaning to corse alarum and not putting too fine a point on it Mistress Dibkins she aint what she was no more nothing to corse alarum. Mrs Easter we hope she aint on her way out we all felt you shd know of this. Other matters are not easy which may wait yr attention.

Yr obedt servt, Alexander Thistlethwaite.'

Oh dear, she thought. I've stayed away too long. I shall have to go back and see what's the matter. But she'd missed the bi-weekly coach to Dorchester and there wasn't another to London until the following morning.

'I'm uncommon glad to hear it,' Calverley said, when he arrived at her lodgings later that afternoon. 'You ain't thinking of leaving me, my charmer, surely. 'Twould break my heart, so it would. No, no, Nan, there's no cause for you to rush away. Come now, put on your bonnet. Your carriage awaits.'

'Carriage?' She didn't know whether to be pleased or not. It had been such a marvellous thing to see him that afternoon, standing on the pavement below her balcony, more handsome than ever and free for the hour or two he'd promised. But she ought to be travelling home and she knew it.

'Tomorrow's coach is a deal too soon for me,' he said, as though he'd read her thoughts. 'And now make haste, my love. We are off to the races.'

The officers of the Duke of Clarence's Light Dragoons had arranged a series of flat races up on the ridge that afternoon and the gentry had turned out in force to support them and place the odd bet or two. So the stakes were high and irresistible. Mr Hanley-Brown had a flutter on every race and swore he was 'coming out more or less even, me dear'. But Calverley did badly.

It didn't seem to worry him unduly. ' 'Tis all one,' he said lightly. 'Jericho will save us, you will see.' Jericho was running in the sixth race and his master was convinced that no other horse could 'hold a candle to him'.

Unfortunately their ability to hold candles was not being tested that afternoon. Jericho did his best, straining every nerve and muscle, but whether it was because of the strength of the opposition or because of the burden of carrying all their expectations in addition to Calverley's ten stone, he wasn't even placed. And they'd backed him so heavily. Calverley had gambled every last penny he possessed. And Nan, despite her wavering better judgement, had been persuaded to bet all the money she was currently carrying in her reticule. Now she had no cash left except the rent which she had prudently left behind in her rooms. ' 'Tis just as well I return to Chelsea tomorrow,' she said, as Calverley drove her back to Weymouth at the end of the meeting.

'How so, my charmer?' he asked, smiling at her. 'Do you wish to be rid of me, so soon?'

'No, oh no,' she said. 'it en't that. 'Tis because I got no money, and that's on account of your horse.'

He ignored her rebuke, smiling at her with the most melting tenderness. 'As to that,' he said, holding the reins with extra care because they were beginning the descent of the longest hill, ' 'tis the luck of the game. We shall win it all back at the next meeting, I promise you. Howsomever, if you must return to London, it would appear that you've picked a good time.'

'How so?' she asked, surprised and disappointed because he was accepting her departure now and she would have preferred him to go on objecting to it.

'According to Fortie, the King means to review his troops in ten days time, so 'twill be non-stop parades and drills with us. Clarence's will bear the brunt of it, you may be sure. All leave cancelled and that sort of thing.'

'Shall you miss me?' she asked, half teasing, half anxious.

'Desperately! How could you even ask it?' Those honey-coloured eyes so loving.

'Then you will write to me?'

'You may depend upon it, my love.'

But when the London coach pulled away from the town the following morning, she knew that she would miss him quite terribly. The yearning pain she felt as she watched him ride away was so acute it was as if her heart were being torn from her body. I will see what is wrong, she thought, and put it right and catch the very next coach back here again.

Back in Cheyne Row, Agnes Pennington was white with rage. 'It is not your place to question my decision,' she said furiously to Bessie Taylor. 'If I give orders that a disobedient child is to be deprived of her supper, I do not expect to come down to the kitchen and find her stuffing herself with roast meat and potatoes.'

She looked so horribly fierce that all three children had stopped eating, and poor Annie had almost stopped breathing, even though Bessie put a protective hand on her shoulder. Thiss was still out on his evening round and the scullery maids were hiding in the pantry, so there was no-one left to defend the children except Bessie and Mrs Jorris.

'I ain't starvin' my little Annie,' Bessie said, fearful but determined, 'not for you nor no-one. Not if it was ever so. Not if you was the Queen a' China.'

'Try not to be vulgar,' Mrs Pennington sneered, snorting down that long horsy nose of hers. She had narrowed her eyes until they were as small as pins, and her mouth was a tight, white line. 'Mrs Jorris, kindly remove that plate.'

'I got a job ter do, same as you *Mrs* Pennington,' the cook said, emphasizing the title with her customary sneer and interposing herself massively between the governess and poor, trembling Annie. 'It ain't no part a' my job ter take orders from no *governesses*.'

'I shall report you to Mrs Easter,' Mrs Pennington said, rigid with insult.

'Do!' the cook answered. ' 'Twon't butter no parsnips, I can tell yer. You eat up, girl,' she said to Annie. 'Don't pay 'er no mind.'

'I trust you realize that you are undermining my authority,' Mrs Pennington said and her voice was as pinched as her lips.

'Hoity-toity!' the cook answered. 'Eat yer nice pertater, Billy dear.'

But Billy wasn't at all sure that he ought to do any such thing because Mrs Pennington was snorting again and there were two dark lines of temper etched in her cheeks. She leant forward suddenly, bending from the waist, stiffly and awkwardly like a wooden puppet, and seized Annie's plate in both hands.

But Bessie was too quick for her. She had the other side of the plate in *her* hands before the governess could move it an inch. For a few fraught seconds the two women tussled for possession, while the children watched with horrified delight. Then the food skidded from the plate and spattered across the table to squelch onto the kitchen floor.

'Aaagh!' the cook shrieked. 'Look at the mess you're making on my nice clean flagstones.' It was an unnecessary order because they were all staring at it.

'I don't care!' Mrs Pennington said shrilly. 'It had to be done. I don't care. At least there can be no question of her eating anything now.'

'Oh, you wicked old woman!' Bessie shouted. 'You cruel, wicked old woman!' And she grabbed a bowl full of egg custard that was standing ready on the dresser and emptied it over Mrs Pennington's head.

There was a second's total silence while she and the governess glared at one another with hatred and disbelief, and all three children held

269

their breath, and Mrs Jorris continued to stare at the gobbets of meat congealing on her nice clean flagstones.

And it was just at that moment that Nan walked into the kitchen.

Annie turned pale, Johnnie bit his lips, Bessie burst into tears and Agnes Pennington took one look at her employer's furious face and threw herself backwards into the nearest chair in a fit of hysterics, screaming at the top of her voice and drumming her heels against the floor, while the egg custard dripped from the frills of her cap and rolled down her bodice.

'Stop that row,' Nan said, wading into the mêlée. 'Stop it at once, do you hear? I expect some peace in my own home, for pity's sake. This is worse than Bedlam. What's got into you all?'

But the governess was too far gone for control, and continued to scream and throw herself about so violently that she was in imminent danger of either breaking the chair or her back. 'Oh, very well then,' her mistress said, seeing there was no hope of persuading or commanding, 'if that's the way the wind blows, you may stay here and scream till you're blue in the face. 'Tis all one with me. Bessie, stop snivelling and bring the children up to the dining-room. They may finish their meal there. Mrs Jorris, I see there are more potatoes in the baking dish and the beef is warm. Kindly serve two more portions for me and Annie. Do we have no scullery maids?'

The latest pair had crept from the pantry and were standing anxiously beside the dresser. Now she turned and saw them. 'There's a deal to be cleaned up,' she said, calmly taking Annie by the hand, and swept from the room taking her children with her.

'Now then,' she said when they were settled at the table beside the garden window, 'what was all that about?'

Annie and Johnnie looked at one another anxiously. They didn't want to get poor Bessie into trouble and they weren't sure whether it was prudent to complain about the governess, because you never knew how Mama would take things. But Billy told the truth, straight out. 'Annie couldn't do her sums,' he said, 'so old Penny said she wasn't to have any supper an' Bessie said she was, an old Penny threw it on the floor, so Bessie threw the custard at her.'

'Mrs Pennington,' Nan corrected automatically.

'Mrs Pennington,' Billy agreed affably.

'Is this true, Annie?'

'Yes,' Annie whispered. 'I *do* try Mama. 'Tis uncommon hard sometimes and Mrs Pennington gets cross.'

'Aye,' Nan said easily. 'So I see. Well now, as to that, perhaps 'tis because you've learnt all you need to learn. You're a good age now. Too old for the schoolroom, I should say. I see no reason why you should be taught any longer.'

The relief on Annie's tear-stained face was quite touching. But Johnnie was looking alarmed.

'The boys must continue their lessons, of course,' Nan said quickly to reassure him, and she noticed that although Billy grimaced he didn't seem unduly worried. A cheerful soul, my Billy, she thought, and his next question didn't surprise her.

'Is there another custard, Mama?'

'I am glad you have a good appetite,' she said, ringing the bell for Mrs Jorris. Then she changed the subject because she could see from their hunched shoulders that Annie and Johnnie were still upset. 'I saw the King while I was away. He was bathing in the sea. What do you think of that?'

Thiss came back home while they were eating a gooseberry tart, there being no other custard. She was quite relieved to hear his cheerful voice, chattering up the stairs. There was somebody normal in the house at last. Now she could start sorting out all their problems and get back to Weymouth and her dear Calverley. I will send for Thiss as soon as this meal is over, she thought, for the sooner I start, the sooner I return.

But when the meal was done and she had gone upstairs to make a pot of tea in the drawing-room and a shame-faced Bessie had taken the children away to bed, it was Mrs Pennington who came knocking timidly at the drawing room door.

'Yes,' Nan said, coldly, 'you may come in, Mrs Pennington, and I hope you have something sensible to say to me.'

'I do apologize, Mrs Easter,' the governess said, her face blotchy but humble. 'I am truly, truly mortified to have behaved in such a way.' She had changed her dress and her cap and done her best to wash her hair, which now lay stuck to her forehead in flat damp clumps so that she looked more like a horse than ever.

'So I should think,' Nan said shortly, leaving her standing awkwardly beside the fire-screen. 'I en't at all certain whether I shall require your services any further after such a display.'

271

' 'Twill never occur again, I do assure you, madam.'

'It had better not.'

Encouraged because she wasn't being shouted at, the governess tried to justify her behavior. 'I was mortally provoked,' she said.

'Evidently.'

There was a pause while Nan drank her tea and Mrs Pennington bit her lip. ' 'Tis all on account of taking a moral stand,' the governess said, and now the self-righteous tone was returning to her voice. 'There are things you ought to know about your servant Bessie, Mrs Easter. Oh, yes indeed. Things that young woman would much rather were hidden. Not that they will remain hidden much longer if I am any good at arithmetic.'

'Oh yes,' Nan said very calmly. She was very interested but it wouldn't have done to show it.

'There have been goings-on in this house,' Mrs Pennington said darkly. 'Oh, not just while you've been away, ma'am, although heaven knows they've been bad enough then, in all conscience.'

Nan gave her a cool look across the top of her teacup. 'So?'

'That young man Thiss spends more time a' nights in the nursery with Bessie than he does in his own rooms. Oh, I've seen him sneaking in to her, don't you worry. I've kept an eye on 'em. I know the sort of things they do. They don't fool me. Carrying on, they are. And all under your roof and behind your back ma'am. 'Tis downright disgraceful, so it is.' Now that she'd told her scurrilous tale she was beginning to feel quite herself again. 'Downright disgraceful.' How proper and righteous the words sounded.

'You do not tell me anything I do not know already,' Nan said coolly. Poor Bessie to be spied upon by this dreadful woman. Are no pleasures ever to be secret? 'You do not know perhaps – indeed how could you? – they plan to marry. With my permission, of course. Indeed I might almost say with my connivance.'

The news struck Mrs Pennington quite dumb. It was very gratifying. 'Now as to this other matter,' Nan went on. 'I have spoken to Bessie and she has agreed that in matters of discipline and order within the classroom your word is law.'

The governess began to preen and pick up again. 'Most kind,' she murmured. 'I do appreciate . . .'

'Howsomever,' Nan continued, cheerfully and without remorse, 'your authority does not extend beyond the classroom. That must be clearly understood, or we shall part company immediately and without references. 'Tis not for you to say what the children may wear or eat or how they should behave themselves outside the classroom. That is a matter for Bessie to decide. I trust I have made myself clear.'

'Oh yes, ma'am. Indeed ma'am. I – um . . .'

'Good. In that case, you may continue to teach the boys, for the time being.' At least she was good with Johnnie and to have him content and well-behaved was a deal to be thankful for. 'Annie needs no further tuition. She will leave the classroom as from today. That is all, Mrs Pennington. Kindly tell Mr Thistlethwaite I would like to see him.'

Thiss and Bessie appeared together three minutes later. They stood as close to one another as they could get and it was plain from the expressions on their faces that they had been listening at the keyhole and knew what had been said, for Bessie was bolt-eyed with anxiety and Thiss was brazenly embarrassed.

'Sit down, the pair of you,' Nan said, grinning at them as they eased themselves onto the edge of two of her fine chairs. 'Thiss, you're an arrant rogue!'

'Couldn't resist, mum, as the fly said to the spider's web.'

'Ah well,' Nan said, trying to look cross and failing, 'you will have to marry, then. That's all there is to that.'

'She's only to say the word, mum. I'd 'ave 'er an' willin'.'

That made Nan laugh out loud. 'If the governess is to be believed, you've done that already, and many's the time.'

Poor Bessie was horribly embarrassed. 'We didn't mean no harm mum,' she pleaded. ' 'E don't take no fer an answer, that's the truth of it.'

'Never did, Bessie,' Nan assured her. 'So agree to wed and we'll have all settled. You will need two witnesses, Thiss. Family perhaps?'

Thiss grinned at her. 'I got bruvvers an' sisters all over the place,' he said. 'Don't ask me where. One a' me bruvvers went fer a soldier, 'nother was pressed, last I 'eard tell.'

'Parents then?'

'Dead an' gone the both of 'em. What was why I went ter France in the first place. Not 'avin' no family to speak of. No, no, Matthew Howlett will stand witness for me.'

Bessie was so surprised to hear it, she forgot herself and spoke out before Mrs Easter. 'How d'yer know?' she asked. ' 'Ave you arsked 'im?'

273

'Course,' Thiss said. 'Ain't erxacly a new idea this, yer know. Been on me mind fer some time, you might say.'

But Nan had been considering Bessie's matronly bosom rather than Thiss' mind. 'Not a minute too soon, if the child en't to be a bastard,' she said.

This time it was Thiss' turn to drop his jaw with surprise. 'You never said nothink,' he said to Bessie. And Bessie blushed and ducked her head and looked pleased with herself.

'There's a deal you need to say to each other to my way of thinking,' Nan told them. 'But first you must tell me of old Mrs Dibkins.'

The atmosphere in the room changed at once.

'She's mortal bad, Mrs Easter, mum,' Bessie said. 'She's got a great lump on her side the size of a duck's egg. Terrible great lump. I seen it.'

'She don't complain,' Thiss said. 'You ain't ter think that. She'd be mortal put out to be heard complainifying. She ain't said narry a word a' complaint. Not even when she took 'er tumble.'

'She fell?'

'All on a sudden, mum, an' couldn't get up again nohow, poor soul,' Bessie said.

It occurred to Nan that she hadn't seen either of the Dibkins since her return. 'Where is she?'

'Kep' to 'er bed these last three days,' Thiss said. 'Mr D's been a-carin' for her.'

'I will go and see her,' Nan said, and went at once.

The old lady was huddled in her truckle-bed in the corner of her claustrophobic room behind the kitchen. She had turned her face to the wall and appeared to be sleeping, but when Mr Dibkins stood up to greet his mistress in a harsh croaking voice, she opened her eyes and tried to turn onto her back. It was plainly beyond her powers. Mr Dibkins had to help her, hauling at her shoulders, while her hands clawed ineffectually at the blankets. But as her face was revealed by the light of the candle, Nan could see that she was very ill indeed and was ashamed because she hadn't noticed it before. Her odd distorted face had grown so thin she could see the bones under the taut skin that covered her cheeks, and the skin itself was a most unhealthy colour, a dirty greyish yellow.

'I am sorry to see you ill, Mrs Dibkins,' she said.

274

The old woman struggled to reassure her. ' 'Tis nothin', Mrs William – dear . . . Be up an' about . . . no time at all Mrs William – dear . . . that sorry to be a trouble . . .'

'Mrs Jorris has been that good to her you wouldn't believe, mum,' Mr Dibkins said. 'Little dainties, milk puddens, nothing too much trouble.'

'Can she eat them?' Nan asked, for it didn't look as though Mrs Dibkins had eaten a good meal for weeks.

'She does her best, mum,' Mr Dibkins whispered. ' 'Tis hard for her to keep things down if you take my meanin'.'

'Thiss shall go for a physician this very evening,' Nan promised. 'Rest all you can, Mrs Dibkins. I will be back presently.' The smell in the little enclosed room was making her retch, despite her sympathy.

'There you are, Mother,' Mr Dibkins said, much impressed by her generosity. 'You're to have a physician.' Servants were usually treated by an apothecary, so this was a great honour.

But honour or no, there was nothing this particular physician could do for his patient. 'She has an impostume beneath her right armpit,' he told Nan when he came up to the drawing-room after his examination much later that evening, 'and another on her neck, just below the nape. I have lanced them for her. They will take some little time to drain, for there is much puss, and the arm is angry. Howsomever, as to the other swelling – ah me – that is a malignancy which will not yield to treatment, I fear. She has suffered it for some years, I believe. Laudanum will relieve the pain, but I know of no cure for the swelling.' It was a remarkably honest diagnosis because it could easily lose him trade.

'She will not recover?' Nan said, and it was hardly a question, she was so sure of the answer.

'I fear not, ma'am.'

'Pray return tomorrow, Mr Crimshaw,' Nan said. 'She is a good servant. I would not have her suffer more than is needful.'

'Laudanum, ma'am,' Mr Crimshaw said and took his fee and his leave, shaking his head sadly. ' 'Tis the only thing.'

Poor old Mrs Dibkins, Nan thought, watching him from the drawing-room window as he climbed into his little black carriage and drove away. She don't deserve this, in all conscience. I must stay here for a week or two just to see how she goes along. I can hardly go rushing back to Weymouth when she's so very ill. And then I can keep an eye on Mrs Pennington, and find out what Annie would like to do now she

275

en't a scholar, and hear Thiss and Bessie have their banns called on Sunday. It was nearly midnight and she'd been back in the house for a little under four hours, but it felt as though she'd never been away. It seemed to her that her responsibilities had swarmed in upon her like angry bees the minute she got inside the door. During those few magical days in Weymouth she'd felt young and light-hearted, now she had returned to reality.

She was still looking out of the window, too tired to move on to the next moment. Cheyne Row was really quite well lit. She hadn't realized how good the street lighting was in Chelsea. Why, she could see every brick in the wall of the garden opposite. She wondered idly whether new lamps had been fixed while she was away. But when she glanced around her, she saw that the illumination was coming from the moon. And even the moon had changed. Now it was no longer the perfect silver orb that had glowed so romantically above the sea at Weymouth such a short time ago, but a dented, lop-sided circle, still valiantly reflecting light, but decidedly the worse for wear. I know how you feel, she said to it. Still, at least I got the worst matters in some sort of order.

But Matthew Howlett had another and equally pressing problem for her.

He was waiting for her in the shop in the Strand the next morning, busily sorting papers, but keeping one eye on the door ready for her entrance. He was so worried that he jumped visibly when she arrived and his eyes were bolting like a hare's.

'Good morning, Matthew,' she said, wondering what was the matter with him. 'I trust all is well.'

'Well, as to that mum,' he stammered. 'Most of the walks is passable.'

'And how is trade?'

'Fair to middlin', bein' it's summertime. Excep' for . . . What I means to say is, there is – um – What it en't my business for to . . .'

'Spit it out, Matthew. What's the matter? Stop blethering and tell me.'

'Well mum, bein' . . . What I means to say . . . I wouldn't want you for to think . . . Bein' I does me best, in all conscience . . . Bein' . . .'

She was too alert to waste any more time waiting for him to get to the point. She strode to the foot of the stairs and called for Abby. 'Abby! Come down here a minute, will you. You man's in such a moither I can't make head nor tail of un.'

276

So Abby descended with a baby in her arms and their two towsled toddlers creeping behind her, and admitted that there was trouble in one of the walks. 'We think he's cheatin' you, mum,' she said. 'He makes less an' less week by week. 'Ten't in the nature of things to lose so continual. Not with the rest on us a-picking' up.'

'Old Josh, is it?' Nan asked. She'd had her doubts about old Josh before she went away.

Bolt-eyed nodding from Matthew.

'Um,' she said, considering. 'Thank 'ee kindly, Matthew. 'Twas well done to tell me. I shall deal with this myself. It can't go on or we shall lose all trade north of the city. Are those his papers?'

Old Josh professed himself transported with delight to see her again, which aroused her suspicions even further, but he said he was 'quite agreeable' to sharing his walk with Thiss for a day or two.

'Watch him like a hawk,' she told Thiss. 'He's been cheating poor Matthew for weeks, if I'm any judge. Which is easy enough in all conscience, knowing what a booby Matthew is. So now let him think he may cheat you as easily.'

'Play dumb, eh?'

'Something a' that. If you do well you shall have the finest wedding-breakfast money can buy.'

'Leave it to me, mum,' Thiss said cheerfully.

But it was easier promised than done. Old Josh was more cunning than he looked, and although Thiss watched him most carefully for the next three days, when Sunday came he had made no progress.

So the watch had to be extended, and when Nan heard the banns called for the first time she was none the wiser. Later that evening she wrote a long letter to Calverley, explaining that she wouldn't be able to get back to Weymouth 'just yet' but assuring him that she dreamed of him and longed for him and loved him more than ever.

His answer arrived four days later. 'My love,' he wrote, 'I miss you to distraction. There is little to report. We parade, we drill. Went to the races a' Tuesday and did rather well. Jericho on form. Won back all our losses, so we have money a -plenty to spend when you return. A deuced good horse. I long to see you again. Your Calverley.'

She put the letter in her glove drawer, where she kept all her most precious possessions, and from time to time during her busy day she took it out again, to enjoy the sight of his handwriting, which was bold and black and flowing, and to re-read his words and remember him and miss him.

'I must go back to Weymouth soon,' she said to Thiss as they drove to the Strand on Monday morning. 'I mean to open a reading-room in Salisbury. 'Tis just the season for it. Keep your eyes open this time and your wits about you.'

But Old Josh was a sly old bird and by the time Thiss finally caught him actually putting cash into his own pocket, the banns had been called for the third time and the wedding was arranged and Nan had had to write three more letters to Calverley explaining her delay and was beginning to wonder whether she would ever see him again.

But business was business and a cheat was a cheat and she couldn't go rushing off to enjoy herself until both were settled to her satisfaction. Could she?

Chapter Twenty-three

It was the middle of July before old Josh was finally brought up before a magistrate and imprisoned, and by then Nan had a drawer full of letters from her lover, Annie had decided that she would stay at home and learn to keep house for her mother and Bessie and Mrs Jorris, Thiss and Bessie were man and wife, and Mrs Dibkins had recovered sufficiently to be carried out of her room to a place of honour at the wedding-breakfast, where she nibbled a little sugar icing to show willing and declared she was 'that happy she never did'.

''Twill not be long, my love,' Nan wrote to Calverley that evening, 'before I can be with you again. I miss you cruelly. Howsomever Mrs Dibkins improves a little and the wedding went well. I have hired a woman to replace that light-fingered Mr Joshua but she cannot start work for another ten days. Mr Teshmaker has drawn up a contract for all my future employees to sign which he says will indemnify the firm against all such losses in future. Would it were all settled. 'Tis weeks since I saw you last.

Your most loving Nan.'

And she sighed, because writing to him was pleasurable but it made her acutely aware of how very much she missed him.

On the morning after her wedding Bessie rose early, to help Mrs Jorris cook a special breakfast for her dear Thiss and her dear Mrs Easter, who'd been so kind and generous, what with the wedding and the wedding-breakfast and all. Mrs Jorris had decided on a dish of fresh scallops dredged in mace, beside the eggs and potted meats, and an old fashioned furmenty, that Mrs Easter particularly enjoyed. It took them rather longer than usual so they weren't quite ready to serve when Nan and Thiss got back from the stamping. So when someone came knocking at the door just at the very minute when they were ready to dish up, Mrs Jorris was not pleased.

279

'See who 'tis, Mrs Thistlethwaite my dear,' she said, 'an' send 'em packin'. We got enough to do without unwanted tradesmen.'

So Bessie trotted up to the door prepared for an unwanted tradesman and got the surprise of her life. Standing on the doorstep, 'fairly fillin' the frame' as she told Mrs Jorris afterwards, was one of the most handsome men she'd ever seen. He was wearing the full dress uniform of a cavalry officer and his arms were full of flowers, roses and honeysuckles and great white lilies.

'You must be Mrs Thistlethwaite,' he said. 'Is your mistress at home?'

'Why, yes, sir,' she said, amazed that he should know her. 'Who should I say is callin'?'

He put his finger on his lips like a conspirator. 'Don't say a word,' he begged. 'I've a mind to surprise her. Is she upstairs?'

'Yes, sir.'

'Then we will tip-toe up,' he said. 'You lead and I will follow, eh?'

It was beginning to be rather exciting and the flowers smelt like incense in the narrow hall. She led the way upstairs as quietly as she could.

Mrs Easter was sitting at her desk writing her accounts. 'Yes, Bessie,' she said vaguely. 'I shall be down directly.'

'If you please, mum,' Bessie said, grinning with excitement. 'You got a visitor, mum.'

And Mrs Easter looked up and saw the officer.

'Calverley!' she said. 'Oh, my dear love!'

And then the two of them were in each other's arms and the flowers were being crushed between them, and he was kissing her eyes and her cheeks and her mouth with such passion and urgency that Bessie decided to make herself scarce.

'Why didn't you tell me you were coming?' Nan said, when she'd got her breath back a little. 'I've just written you a letter.'

Actually he hadn't known himself until two minutes before he caught the coach. It was most unlike him to be travelling simply to spend time with a woman. But this woman, it had to be admitted, had a stronger influence upon him than any he'd ever pursued. She'd made all the others in Weymouth seem dull and ordinary, slow in their movements and their passions, barely attractive at all. Since her departure he'd done little but dream of her, remembering that dark face blazing with love, those strong legs gripping the horse, or running along the beach, or threshing and clinging beneath him in the throes of love. Oh, she

280

was a sterling creature, and just the sight of her now was making him amorous.

'I have ten days' leave,' he said, happily triumphant. 'Think of that, my charmer. Ten days and ten nights. How shall we spend the time?'

'I have to be out again in half an hour,' she said. 'But I will return so soon as ever I may, I promise you. Oh, Calverley, how good it is to see you. Have you breakfasted?'

'And waste time when I could be riding here to you?'

'Then I will feed you,' she said. 'Mrs Jorris has something special planned and now you can share it, my dear, dear love.'

It was a splendid meal and they enjoyed every mouthful, but all too soon she had to tell Thiss to fetch the pony cart.

'You must entertain my children whilst I am in the City,' she said as they were drinking their last cup of tea. 'They will be down presently to take their breakfast, so I will introduce them before I go.'

''Twill be a pleasure,' he said. But actually neither of them were quite sure about it.

Annie and the boys came down to breakfast a few minutes later, having been warned and tidied and made to wait by Bessie. They said 'how d'ee do' politely to their unexpected guest, and Annie was delighted and a little embarrassed when he bowed to her as though she were a lady.

'I had thought to meet a child,' he said, smiling his most charming smile at her and thinking what an unremarkable girl she was. Such an unremarkable face, cheeks rounded, small blue eyes, projecting forehead, mouse-brown hair. 'But you are already grown, I see, and grown uncommon pretty. No child, I'll wager.'

She admitted that she would be eleven in three days time.

'A woman, deuce take it,' he said. 'A beautiful little woman.' And was rewarded by quite a pretty confusion. Her brother William, who was proud to say that he was nine, was so very much like her in appearance and manner that he too was an easy conquest. Soon they were talking happily, 'man to man' about horses and uniforms and the manner in which a French invasion would have to be repelled if ever Napoleon managed to slip through the British blockade and cross the Channel.

'I see I en't required in this conversation,' Nan laughed. 'Entertain Mr Leigh till I return if you please, Annie. Boys, you are to be in the schoolroom in half an hour, don't forget.'

281

'Could they not beg leave of absence, just this once?' Calverley said, grinning at them to show he was an ally. And he was taken aback by the look of black fury that crossed the face of the younger boy. Deuce take it, he thought, surely he don't like learning. How unnatural!

'Tomorrow, perhaps,' Nan said, leaving the room. 'Bessie will bring you hot water should you need it.' And she beamed at him and was gone.

Annie proved to be a good hostess. She left the boys eating their breakfast and then arranged for warm water and hot towels to be provided for the lieutenant in the little washroom adjoining her mother's bedroom, and all as if it were the most natural thing in the world.

'You are uncommon kind,' he said to her, as she walked to the bedroom door to leave him.

She smiled at him with serious pleasure. 'I am happy to help you, sir,' she said.

Down in the kitchen Bessie was describing their visitor to all the other servants, including Mrs Dibkins who had hobbled out to her chair beside the window and was slowly drinking broth.

''Tis a lover,' she said rapturously. 'There ain't a shadder a' doubt. You should a' seen the way he kissed 'er.'

'What did I tell 'ee?' Mrs Dibkins said. 'I know'd there was a man in it, the minute she showed them titties.'

'Well, good luck to 'er,' Mrs Jorris said. 'She been a widow woman too long to my way a' thinkin'. Good luck to 'er.'

'How long's the gentleman a-goin' ter stay?' the youngest scullery maid asked. A guest meant a deal of extra work.

'Ten days,' Bessie said rapturously. 'Ten days a' love! What could be more romantic?'

Her opinion wasn't shared by every member of the household. Mrs Pennington didn't think well of their new visitor at all, nor of the new sleeping arrangements in the house. 'Downright disgusting,' she said hotly to Mrs Jorris, when she came into the kitchen next morning to collect her breakfast tray. 'I was coming down the stairs, minding my own business, and what do you think?'

Mrs Jorris had no idea what to think.

'This *strange* man walked out of Mrs Easter's bedroom, as bold as brass if you please. And with barely a stitch on. Barely a stitch! I

282

didn't know where to look. And then he had the effrontery to say good morning. I don't know what the world is coming to, upon my soul.'

'Same as it's always been coming to, I daresay,' the cook said phlegmatically. ''Tis her house, Mrs Pennington and I suppose she may do as she pleases in it.'

'I would expect her to show more decorum with children about,' Mrs Pennington said, her big nose purple with excitement. 'He didn't have a stitch on, you know. I'm sure I didn't know where to look.'

'So you say,' Mrs Jorris said with obvious disbelief.

'Those poor children,' the governess said piously.

She could have spared her sympathy, for Billy and Annie liked their mother's lover. He was handsome and he was fun and he talked to them as though they were grown up, which was very flattering. And when he and their mother came back from a shopping expedition on the third afternoon of his visit, with a set of splendid toy soldiers for Billy and a finely bound book for Johnnie and a positive maypole of ribbons for 'our pretty housekeeper' their approval was charmed into affection.

'If they marry 'twill be a fine thing,' Annie said stoutly. 'Look how happy Mama is.'

'D'you think he'd teach me to ride?' Billy wondered.

But Johnnie only scowled and said nothing. He thanked the lieutenant for his present, and he spoke when he was spoken to, but apart from that he kept his distance, sitting at the far end of the table at mealtimes, listening and watching, like a small dark conscience.

Calverley was puzzled by him. He would have liked to befriend the child, but it was impossible to do it, because he showed no interest in anything, neither horses, nor the war, nor soldiers, nor even Lord Nelson, who was plainly and rightly a very great hero to his brother and sister. He seemed impervious to any challenge and blind to every blandishment. Questions were parried with a chilly, 'I couldn't say.' Compliments were received with a polite, flat, 'Yes.' He looked so like Nan, too, with the same dark hair and dark brown eyes, but his mouth was held in a tight line and his nose was pinched and his face was so withdrawn as to be almost devoid of expression. He was Nan without animation, Nan without fire, a death-mask Nan. A most disconcerting child.

'I can't make head nor tail of your youngest,' he confessed to Nan as they were drinking mulled wine in the drawing-room after an evening at the theatre.

'Don't pay him no mind,' Nan advised. ''Tis a secret child. Always has been, always will be.'

'Does he talk to anybody?'

'I shouldn't imagine so. Mrs Pennington thinks well of him. She says he has a good head for figures. The governess, you know. A funny sort of woman. You will meet her tomorrow for we all dine together a' Thursdays.'

'I met her on the stairs,' he said, laughing to remember it. 'She don't approve of lovers, I can tell 'ee.'

'No more do I,' she teased, drinking the last of her wine and holding out her arms to him. ''Tis scandalous the way they go on.'

It was such a joy to be with him again, to love whenever they would, to ride together in Rotten Row, to be seen about the town as a pair. But that night she remembered that in two days time Sophie would be coming to visit her as she always did on a Friday, and she wasn't sure what her old friend would think of this affair, especially as Calverley had once paid court to her.

At breakfast on Friday morning she decided to tell him of the visit, for even though she couldn't bring herself to ask him whether he and Sophie had ever been lovers, just in case the answer was yes, she felt he ought to be warned.

He was splendidly tactful. 'If that is the case, my dear,' he said, 'I will visit my club this afternoon and return when the lady is gone. I am sure you don't need me around. And a good soldier always knows when to retreat, eh?'

Sophie had been travelling for the last six days and now she was bubbling with the latest gossip.

'My dear,' she said, 'I have been aching to tell you the news. What do you think? Mr Blake has left London! Gone off to live in Sussex, with Catherine and his sister and right beside the sea, if you ever heard of such folly. He writes to Heinrich to say it is Heaven on earth, but I cannot imagine how it could be any such thing, what with the damp air in such places and the French like to land at any time.'

Nan expressed suitable surprise and wondered what had brought about such a change.

''Tis Mr Hayley's doing, by all accounts,' Sophie said. 'A commission, I believe. But why he could not have stayed in London and waited for a better offer I cannot imagine. Heinrich says 'tis all for the best, but I would not wish to live in the very path of an invasion, I can tell 'ee.'

'Nor I, Sophie,' Nan said, sipping her tea and wondering how she was going to introduce the subject she really wanted to talk about. 'Nor I.'

'Heinrich has taken on a new pupil at the Royal Academy,' Sophie went on. 'An uncommon good painter, the whole world says so. His name is Mr Constable and he comes from Suffolk, so he tells me, which is your part of the world, is't not, my dear?'

Nan had very little interest in a new painter, uncommon good or not, but there was something about the breathless enthusiasm of her friend's voice that encouraged her. 'A lover, I'll warrant,' she said.

'Would it were so,' Sophie sighed. ''Twould be uncommon good fortune. But 'tis a steadfast creature I fear, and puritanical.'

'Then you must content yourself with a handsome lieutenant,' Nan said, delighted by her cunning.

'They're an odd lot in the barracks this season,' Sophie said. 'Not a one on 'em I fancy, I do assure you.'

'How of the gentlemen from the Duke of Clarence's?'

'La, I forgot them long ago.'

'Deuce take it, Sophie, I don't know how you can do it. I'm sure I couldn't.'

Sophie shot her a shrewd glance from under those long thick eyelashes. 'I take good care never to miss any man once he has moved elsewhere,' she said. ''Tis good advice, my dear, which you would do well to remember when your present lover finds a new love.'

Nan was so startled she blushed like a girl. 'How did you know?' she stammered. 'I have told no one of it, I swear.'

'Why, 'tis blazoned in every part of you,' Sophie said, smiling with delight at her friend's confusion. 'You bloom with it, my dear. You positively bloom. I wish you joy in him, whomsoever he is.'

''Tis Mr Leigh,' Nan said, quite unable to resist a full confession now that she'd gone so far. 'I met him at Weymouth.' Then she stopped, aware that she might have made a mistake, and looked up at her old friend, blushing and anxious but bold with love.

'I wish you joy in him,' Sophie repeated. And she seemed to mean it. ''Tis a handsome creature in all conscience, and good company.'

'Oh Sophie,' Nan said, so much relieved that she seized her friend's

285

hands and held them between her own, 'if you could only know how much I love him. 'Tis the dearest of men.'

'But a man merely,' Sophie warned, returning her grasp, 'and as such, fickle, my dear. They are all deceivers, every man jack of 'em. 'Tis as well not to grow too fond.'

'Mr Easter was not fickle, I think.'

'No, indeed. But Mr Easter was a rarity, as we've said many and many's the time. A one-woman man, your Mr Easter, whereas Calverley . . .'

'But men change, do they not?'

'Aye, when they are too old for love. Oh, Nan my dear, you surely do not hope to change that gentleman?'

Nan withdrew her hands from her friend's grasp and dusted them against each other in her old determined gesture, palm against palm. 'I love him,' she said, chin in the air. 'If he were to ask, I'd marry un.'

'La, Nan, he ain't the marrying kind. Be warned by one who knows.'

It was kind advice and well meant, but Nan was hurt by it. Sometimes Sophie's cynical view of mankind was very hard to take. 'Have you been to the play?' she asked, changing the subject.

'I have indeed, and uncommon foolish I found it.'

Later that night as she lay beside her lover in the easy intimacy of satisfaction, she realised that for all her cynicism Sophie had approved of this affair, just as Bessie and Thiss approved and Annie and Billy and Mrs Jorris.

'I am a fortunate woman,' she said, putting her head on his shoulder.

Although their ten days passed far too quickly, it was a blissful interlude and they were both saddened when he had to leave.

'I will return,' he promised, sitting astride his handsome chestnut, while she stood beside him on the pavement.

'And I will write.'

But when three weeks had passed and he hadn't been granted any more leave, and Mrs Dibkins was still well enough to sit in her chair for at least part of every day, she had another idea. 'I will travel to Weymouth without telling him,' she confided to Bessie, 'and surprise him just as he surprised me.'

'Oh mum,' Bessie said. 'What romance!'

But as it turned out, Weymouth was a surprise of the wrong kind.

Chapter Twenty-four

While Nan had been away, Weymouth had suffered a disconcerting sea-change. She had left a holiday resort basking in the sun of high summer and full of light-hearted people enjoying themselves; she returned to find a town shrouded in September mist, a town beseiged. There were hundreds of troops mounting guard along the chilly promenade and thousands more encamped on the damp hills behind the town. Her landlady had closed her boarding-house and fled, none of her remaining neighbours knew where, and although there were still plenty of visitors filling the new terraces, those who dared to take the air were sombre-faced with apprehension and spent most of their time glancing out to sea or examining the horizon with spy-glasses. It was rather alarming and not what she'd been looking forward to at all.

The Burdon barracks were bristling with activity, with a great deal of important coming and going, and an overpowering sense of closing ranks that made her feel foreign and unwelcome even at the gate. There were no encouraging smiles, only rows of tense withdrawn faces, troop sergeants barking orders, and no sign at all of Calverley. Finally she saw Mr Fortescue riding in through the gate and he told her, but brusquely and with one eye on the troop sergeants, that Mr Leigh was on guard duty in the look-out post at Upwey, and that if she'd take his advice she'd go straight back to London. 'Invasion could be any minute, ma'am,' he said, 'anywhere along this coast.'

If he thought to frighten her he was very much mistaken. 'Can't be done,' she said, cheerful now that she knew where her lover was. 'There en't another coach till morning, and that's the slow one through Dorchester, which I can't say I fancy.'

'Where do you stay?' he asked.

'I don't know,' she admitted. 'The White Hart, or the Golden Lion or the Crown and Sceptre I daresay.' For they were the three best coaching inns in the old town and there would surely be room in one of them.

The landlord of the Golden Lion had a room 'right enough' but he wasn't at all sure he ought to let her have it. 'Boney's back,' he explained lugubriously. 'Sittin' on the French coast a-watchin' us so the fisherfolk say, an' they'm the ones to know bein' they'm sailed across an' seen the beggar. Conquered Italy so he has, an' now he'm after us. He only need calm sea an' thick fog an' then the Lord have mercy, that's what I says. If I was you ma'am, I'd be off back 'ome on the very next coach, out of 'arm's way, so I would.'

'I got business in the town, Boney or no Boney,' Nan said. 'I can't stop living just because that dratted crittur's on the other side of the Channel.'

'Tha's the spirit, ma'am,' a fisherman called to her from the bar. 'Tha's what I says, Barnabas. Let ol' Boney go hang, I says. Drat the man, I says.'

' 'Twould be another song you'd be singin' if 'tweren't for all the ale you'm supped, John Mackleson,' the landlord said.

'I will take your room for six nights,' Nan told him before the two of them could begin an argument and delay her any further. 'If you will arrange for someone to show me up.'

' 'Twill be a guinea.'

'Aye, doubtless.'

So the potboy was called for and given her carpet bag to carry and the two of them negotiated the stairs which were as unsteady as John Mackleson and almost as noisy. Down below in the bar, where a deal of Dutch courage was being consumed, somebody was singing raucously.

'When lawyers strive to heal a breach,
And parsons practise what they preach,
Then Boney he'll come pouncing down
And march his men on London town!
Rollicum rorum, tol-lol-lorum
Rollicum rorum toll-lollay.'

The bravado of the words was vaguely encouraging. She gave the boy a ha'penny for his pains, bounced on the bed to test the mattress, and went to open the window.

There was hardly anybody in the street below her, except for two elderly women head to anxious head. The air was extremely chill and glancing up the street she saw that a white sea mist was swirling into the town from the direction of the harbour. Calm sea and thick fog, she thought. What if I've got here just in time for the invasion? It had been expected intermittently every spring and summer for the last three years, ever since Boney was given command of his Army of England, but until now she'd always been in London, which was concerned but distanced, never on the coast, and so she had never really understood how raw the fear of it was, here in the front line. Would it happen now, tonight? There was enough tension in the air in all conscience.

I shall have my dinner, she decided, and then I shall put on my pelisse and walk to Upwey and find him. There was nothing to be gained by sitting around waiting for him to come off duty, and she was full of nervous energy now that she was so close to seeing him again.

So that was what she did.

She and Calverley had walked the road to the ridge on two or three occasions during her last visit, because it was the natural extension of a stroll along the promenade, only more private. Now it was a ghostly place and full of ghostly people, odd dark shapes with limbs as thin as kindling-sticks and bodies deformed by bundles, silently trudging out of the town, shrouded to the knees by the dank white mist that was still swirling up from the sea, their hands bent and their faces obscured by the darkening clouds of a rapidly descending dusk. Some rode in donkey-carts, some pushed wheelbarrows piled with bundles, one group creaked along in an ancient hay-wain, but most were on foot and burdened with as many belongings as they and their beasts could carry. Their children stumbled behind them or were carried in shawls or rode piggy-back half asleep. It was an exodus and despite her high spirits, Nan found it disturbing.

Being unburdened, it didn't take her long to catch up with the nearest family, a man with a long saturnine face, and, walking a few meek paces behind him, his toothless wife and three dishevelled children.

'Where do you go?' she asked the woman.

'To Upwey,' the woman answered. 'I've a cousin there, a joiner same as my husband. He will give us room, praise be. 'Twill be safer there.'

'Is it far?' Nan asked, looking at the dragging heels of the smallest child, who couldn't have been more than four and was finding the going hard already.

'Three miles or thereabouts,' the woman said, and she whispered her explanation, 'Better a long walk and blisters than a bay-net in the belly.'

'You think the French are like to come tonight?'

'Like enough,' the joiner said. 'He en't come yet, 'tis true, but better safe than sorry to my way a' thinking. He got twenty thousand men on t'other side of the Channel, all a-massed an' ready for the off. 'Twould be plain folly to be stood in the way of such an army.'

They trudged on through the damp air while Nan digested all this.

'You travel light,' the woman said, looking shrewdly at Nan's empty hands.

'To the look-out post, no farther,' Nan explained. 'I have rooms in town for tonight and I mean to stay in 'em.'

'Then good luck to 'ee, ma'am,' the joiner said, 'for 'tis more than I'd do, in all conscience.'

By this time Nan was beginning to question the wisdom of it herself. But she walked on with them resolutely enough, until they reached the path that led off to Upwey and the look-out.

By now it was very dark indeed for the moon and the stars were hidden by cloud and the mist was beginning to thicken. She could only just make out the grey shape of the look-out station a few hundred yards to the left. It was a simple wooden building with a brick chimney and a brick-built galley set to one side, and an old ship's topmast standing rather forlornly before it, with a yard arm attached to it, and a flagstaff with truckle and sheaves ready to send the signal everyone dreaded.

She was cheered as she walked towards it, for the nearer she got to it the more sturdy and dependable it looked, with warm smoke rising from the chimney and lamplight in the window, and a midshipman on sentry go beside the flag staff. There was a single blue pennant drooping at the top of the mast, but no other signal, and that was heartening too, for it showed that the French hadn't landed yet.

She could hear voices coming from the far side of the hut and although the midshipman looked at her sharply, he didn't challenge her, so she walked boldly past him and knocked at the door.

It was opened by a dragoon in the familiar blue uniform of the Clarence's. He was surprised but respectful. 'Yes, marm?' he said.

'I have come to enquire what is known of the invasion,' she said firmly, and as she spoke, her eyes were taking in all the details of the little lamplit room, and scanning the faces of the men sitting around the table eating their supper. The third face she looked at was Calverley's.

He was surprised, just as she'd intended him to be, but to her disappointment she saw that his surprise was rapidly replaced by another expression that looked far too much like annoyance or even anger.

'No news yet, ma'am,' the naval lieutenant said politely. 'I would advise you to get within doors as soon as ever you can and to stay there till morning. 'Tis no night to be out walking.'

'The lady is a friend,' Calverley said, 'come to do business in the town. If she could stay with us until my duty is over, I will escort her back to Weymouth.'

The naval lieutenant was intrigued. 'You have a business in town, ma'am?' he asked.

'Indeed yes, and must be here for the next day or two to attend to it. I own the reading-room in Charlotte Row.'

He was impressed. 'Then you should certainly have an escort,' he said, looking from her to Calverley and back again, and guessing their relationship. 'Your relief is due in ten minutes, Mr Leigh. 'Tis quiet enough. You could cut off now should you wish it.'

Calverley had his jacket on before the lieutenant had finished speaking, but the hand he thrust beneath Nan's elbow was rough and angry, and he walked her back along the hill path in silence until they were safely out of earshot of the midshipman. Then he shouted at her.

'Nan! Nan! Have you no sense at all? Deuce take it, there could be an invasion at any hour. The weather's right for it, the tide's right for it, there are sixty thousand French troops in Boulogne waiting the signal. Deuce take it, how could you run such risks? We've been fighting mock battles up to our waists in sea-water for the past week. I wrote and told you. Why d'you not read my letters? Oh, whatever possessed you to come here now?'

'I thought you would be pleased to see me,' she said, shaken by the violence of his attack.

'I was pleased to see you. I am pleased to see you. I just don't want to see you dead, can't you understand? You must go home on the very next coach.'

'No man tells *me* what to do, Calverley Leigh,' she said, holding up her chin at him because he was frightening her. 'Now I'm arrived I mean to stay for at least a week.'

'A week!' he roared. 'One night is danger enough. Go home! Go home! D'you wish to be caught in a battle, you impossible woman, with your legs shot from under you, or your breast full of grapeshot, or your head blown off by a cannonball?' The dark path was full of distorted shadows and the town below them seemed to be holding its breath.

'Boney won't invade,' she said, brazen-faced with deliberate boldness. 'They been a-saying he'll invade for years and years and he en't landed yet.'

'He could land at any time,' he said with exasperated fury, 'and if he does, there will be a bloody battle right here on this beach, in this town. We will take as many people away from it as we can, but there will be killing. We're at war, Nan. Don't you understand? At war with the French, and the French are no respecters of persons, let me tell 'ee.'

'I seen the French in Paris in '93,' she said stung. 'Cutting off ears they were, drunk as lords. Hacked two men to death, right in front of my eyes. Killed my husband in cold blood. There en't a thing you can tell me about the French.'

He put his arm round her shoulders and held her tightly, and now he didn't shout. 'Then promise me you will go back to London on the very first coach. For I could not abide it if you were to come to harm.'

His sudden gentle affection was more moving than all his shouting had been. 'Do you love me so much?' she asked.

'Aye, my charmer, I do,' he admitted. 'So give me your promise, I beg 'ee.'

'If I go,' she said, softened to better sense, ' 'twill be because I have business to attend to in London. I en't a coward, I'll have you know.'

'You are brave and beautiful and utterly foolish,' he said, kissing her hair and adding quickly before her anger could erupt again, 'which is why I love you and why you must go.'

They walked arm in arm down the ghostly road, passing another straggle of fleeing shadows as they went, and now they could see the shape of the promenade below them, black as pitch and edged with a shifting tremor of sea foam. The sight of it made her shiver.

'Time you were warm within doors,' he said. 'Where do you stay?'

'The Red Lion,' she said. And then, feeling that they had recovered sufficiently for teasing, 'Where do you?'

'Well, as to that,' he said, and even in the darkness she could see that his eyes were tender, 'I have been detailed to stay with you all night I do believe. But only for your protection, of course.'

'Course,' she said, holding up her face so that he could kiss her.

That night, in her low-ceilinged room in the Red Lion they made love more tenderly than they had ever done. And afterwards, instead

292

of falling into his usual satisfied sleep, he told her how dearly he loved her and made her promise yet again that she would leave for London on the first coach out of Weymouth in the morning.

'If they invade,' she said, shivering at the thought, 'you will be in the thick of the fighting.'

'Like enough,' he said easily. ' 'tis what we are paid for.'

'Oh, my dearest,' she said, 'you must promise me to keep out of harm's way. For I couldn't abide it if you were to be hurt.' She couldn't even bring herself to suggest that he might be killed, but that thought was there too.

'Well now, as to that,' he told her gently, 'that ain't a thing I could either do or promise. It ain't a soldier's business to look out for his own skin.'

'But . . .'

He put his hand on her lips to silence her. 'I will give you a true promise, my charmer.'

'What is that?'

'I will come to Chelsea to visit you just so soon as ever I may.'

'I wish this war was over,' she said.

'If wishes were horses . . .' he said, stroking her bare shoulder. 'Come, let's have no more talk of war. I've to be on duty again at six.'

'Then we should sleep,' she suggested comfortably, knowing they would do no such thing.

'And miss what little time we have together?'

' 'Tis mortal quiet tonight.' There was no sound from the inn or the town, but they could hear the sea hissing on the beach below them.

'The tide has turned,' Calverley said. ' 'Tis on the ebb.'

'Then we are safe for an hour or two.'

'Safer,' he said. 'He could invade on an ebb tide if he'd a mind to, but 'twould give us the advantage, so it ain't likely.'

'Then how shall we spend the time?' she said, turning in his arms to kiss him. Oh, it was bliss to be with him again, even if there was an invasion threatened, even if they were to be parted so soon, even if he might have to fight the French. To be kissed by that soft, urgent, insistent mouth, to breathe in the lovely sweet-salt smell of his flesh, to be held breast to breast, thigh to thigh, warm and opening. 'Twas worth any risks.

Chapter Twenty-five

It was odd that such a fleeting, tempestuous visit should be so sustaining. But just as well, for Nan's return to Chelsea was a return to hard work and difficulties. She took a flyer to the Strand to see how her business was faring and found Thiss there supervising the distribution of the evening papers. He was surprised to see her but made no comment on her early return.

'Evening, Mrs Easter,' he said, tying the latest bundle firmly together with a length of string.

'There was an invasion scare at Weymouth,' she explained. 'There en't a soul left in the town. How is Mrs Dibkins?'

'Worse, mum, I'm sorry ter say. I reckon she's a-goin', if the truth be told. She's mortal bad.'

Nan looked out of the office window across the Strand to where one of her newsboys was standing beside one of her green and gold carts busily selling the evening papers to all the home-going crowds. I sell the news all over this great city, she thought, but I can't protect my lover from an invasion nor save my servant from a day's pain. 'Have you got the pony-cart?' she asked Thiss.

He had. 'Then straight home, if you please,' she said.

Bessie was looking out for her husband's return. She ran into the hall as soon as she saw Nan stepping down from the cart. 'I'm ever so glad you're home mum,' she said. 'Mrs Dibkins is ever so bad. I never seen 'er as bad as this.'

'Where are the children?' Nan asked, for the house seemed unnaturally quiet.

'Annie took the boys out fer a walk,' Bessie explained. 'I thought it 'ud do 'em good ter get out the 'ouse fer a bit, what with Mrs Dibkins so bad an' Mr Dibkins gone funny an' all.'

'Gone funny?' Nan asked. 'Mad, do you mean?'

'You'd best go down an' see, mum,' Thiss said, deftly rescuing his wife from possible impertinence.

So Nan gave her coat and bonnet to Bessie and she and Thiss went downstairs to the Dibkins' little cramped room beside the kitchen.

It was dark down there and evil-smelling with the cloying sickliness of approaching death. Old Mrs Dibkins lay on her back among her stained pillows. She was barely conscious and groaning in extreme pain. There was an empty feeding-cup on the table, beside a double-headed candlestick covered in wax droppings, and Mr Dibkins sat in the corner of the room clutching a laudanum bottle to his chest and glaring with anxiety and grief.

''E don't reckon she should 'ave no more,' Thiss whispered.

But the old man's hearing was as acute as his sorrow. ''Twould be the finish of her,' he said, fiercely, ''Twould kill her, the state she's in. How could I face *that*, Mrs William ma'am? I couldn't, could I? No, no, she's had more than enough in all conscience, these last twenty-four hours. Best leave well alone, that's what I says.'

'She's dying, Mr Dibkins,' Nan said as gently as she could. 'She's dying and she's in mortal pain. Give her the laudanum for pity's sake.'

'Shame on you, Mrs William, to say such a thing,' the old man said, tears oozing from the corners of his eyes. 'She ain't a-dyin', no she ain't. I shan't have it said. You'll pull through, won't you Mother?'

'She's in mortal bad pain, Dib,' Thiss said. 'Give 'er the laudanum, fer pity's sake. It ain't Christian ter let her suffer.'

'You are right, Mr Dibkins,' Nan said, changing direction, because she could see there was no point in trying to persuade the poor man. 'We cannot give her too much. But half a dose would do no harm.'

'Full dose 'ud kill her,' Mr Dibkins said stubbornly.

'Half a dose,' Nan said firmly. 'Half a dose would do no harm. Give me the bottle and I'll pour it for her.'

'No you won't,' Mr Dibkins said, still clutching the bottle to the brown fustian of his jacket. 'If 'tis to be done I shall do it myself, savin' your reverence, Mrs William ma'am.' And he eked a meagre teaspoon into the feeding-cup. But then he seemed to have forgotten what he'd done it for, and set the cup on the bedside table and looked at it curiously, like a man demented.

'She'll need a mouthful of sugar water, to take away the taste,' Nan said.

'Yes, yes, to be sure.'

'Shall I get it for her, or will you?'

'No, no, I'll get it.' But it was still several groaning seconds before he got up and shuffled off into the kitchen next door.

'Quick!' Nan said to Thiss, as soon as the old man was through the door. 'Double dose. Don't bother measuring, just pour it in.'

'Will it kill 'er, mum?' Thiss asked, pouring the drug into the feeding-cup.

'I shouldn't wonder,' Nan said re-corking the bottle. 'But what's the odds one way or t'other. She can't go on in pain like this.'

'That's true, mum,' Thiss said, lifting Mrs Dibkins with one arm under her shoulders. 'Come on Mother Dibkins ol' dear, soon 'ave you comfy, eh?'

They dribbled the drug into her mouth, but she was too far gone to know she was drinking, although she swallowed noisily.

'Tha's better ol' gel,' Thiss said, as Mr Dibkins returned with a little sugared water in a cup. 'Give it 'ere, Dib.'

'No, no,' the old man said. 'I must do it for her, Thiss. Thank 'ee kindly, I'm sure. She wouldn't want no one else, would you Mother?'

The laudanum took effect within ten minutes, but Nan stayed with her two suffering servants until she was quite sure that Mrs Dibkins was drugged beyond pain. Then she went upstairs to see if her children were back and to eat what dinner she could.

The old lady slept with her mouth open, snoring noisily, and as the evening progressed, the noise got steadily worse until by ten o'clock it was a prolonged and ghastly rattle.

Towards midnight it woke the children, who went creeping fearfully down the stairs to their mother's room to find out what was the matter.

''Tis Mrs Dibkins a-dying,' Nan told them, when they'd climbed into her bed and tucked their cold feet under the eiderdown. 'That's all 'tis.'

'Does everybody make that noise when they're a-dying?' John asked. Death was a very serious business to him now that he was eight and he wanted to glean as much information about it as he could.

'Some do, some don't,' Nan said, remembering the deaths she'd seen as a child in Fornham. 'Some dies easy, some dies hard.'

'Poor Dolly Dibkins,' Annie said, her pale face full of pity. 'She's been ill such a long time, Mama.'

'She has,' Nan said. 'But now 'tis nearly over. She en't conscious and she's more 'n half-way gone already.'

296

'Does she know she's making this row, Mama?' Billy wanted to know.

'No,' Nan said. ''Tis part of God's mercy that she don't hear nor see a thing. And now you must go back to your beds and try and get some sleep. 'Twill all be over by morning, you'll see.'

But it was nearly twenty-four hours before the snoring stopped and by then the sudden click into silence was even more dreadful than the death rattle had been.

Except to Mr Dibkins. 'There you are Mother,' he said with great satisfaction, 'a nice peaceful sleep'll make all the difference to 'ee. You sleep, me dear. Soon have you well again, eh?'

He was horribly determined that she hadn't died. When the undertakers arrived he refused to let them pass, standing at bay in the doorway with his stumpy arms akimbo and his scrubbing brush hair standing on end like a fighting cock's comb.

'Now what are we to do?' Nan said to Thiss, as the undertakers coughed and hesitated and looked to her for guidance.

'Leave this one ter me, mum,' Thiss said, to her relief, for she could hardly have hauled the poor old man out of the way. 'If you'll jest take the gentlemen upstairs an' tell Mrs Jorris ter keep the kitchen door shut fer a bit.'

'Now come along, Dad,' he said to Mr Dibkins when they were on their own. 'This won't do. We got ter let 'er rest poor soul. Ain't she suffered enough?'

'You ain't to put her in no coffin,' Mr Dibkins said furiously 'She ain't dead, Thiss. She'll be up an' about in no time, you'll see.'

'Quite right,' Thiss agreed easily. 'So I tell yer what, we ought ter set the room to rights, all nice an' clean for 'er. Shipshape an' orderly. She wouldn't like ter see it in a mess.'

That was undeniable and Mr Dibkins didn't deny it.

'If we lift 'er out the bed, gentle-like,' Thiss suggested. So they lifted her between them and very stiff and awkward she was. 'We'll jest put 'er in this box, jest fer the meantime, eh?'

'That ain't a coffin, Thiss?'

'No, no,' Thiss lied. 'That's a nice comfy old box. Jest the ticket. Now you nip off ter the linen cupboard, an' I'll get a bucket. We'll 'ave this done in next ter no time.'

Which was true enough. For even with Bessie sent to the linen cupboard to encourage and delay him, the undertakers had only just carried the coffin out of the house, when the old man returned. And then his

297

grief exploded into a rage that was quite terrible to hear. And Nan escaped, discreetly and thankfully, to the less arduous task of running a newsagents.

He wept and raged until the day of the funeral, but then to everybody's relief he came out of his room as meek as a mouse and allowed himself to be led to the church and sat through the service and the interment without saying a word.

'Thank heavens for that,' Nan said to Thiss as they stood beside the grave. But their relief was short-lived. The old man went home, still subdued, but then he walked straight down into the kitchen and locked himself in the broom-cupboard, announcing that he would stay there 'till Dolly comes home'.

'But he's seen her buried,' Nan said. 'He knows she en't coming home.'

''Tis grief, poor soul,' Bessie tried to explain. ''E ain't quite right in hisself jest yet a-while.'

'Then we must leave him there, I suppose,' Nan said resignedly. 'In the meantime we got a house to run and no housekeeper and no general man neither.'

'Except me,' Thiss said, 'an' I'm more partic'lar than gen'ral.'

It was the right moment to make an offer, Nan thought. She'd been considering what she would do ever since Mrs Dibkins took ill. 'How if you were to be my housekeeper, Bessie?' she said. 'Twenty pounds a year and all found.' It was great deal more than Mrs Dibkins had ever earned, but Bessie would be worth it.

Bessie's mouth fell open with surprise. 'Me, mum?'

'Could you do it, think 'ee?'

'Course she could,' Thiss answered for her. 'Couldn't yer, Goosie? Why you been doin' it al-a-ready, all these weeks.'

So it was agreed, although Bessie was still fearful enough to ask whether she would be expected to deal with Mr Dibkins.

'No,' Nan said. 'Leave him to me. He'll come to no harm in the broom-cupboard for a few days. Then if he don't recover, we shall see.'

But that night when she'd gone to bed, she heard his pathetic weeping in the cupboard below her, and she was torn with pity for him and decided to allow him to stay where he was for as long as he liked.

The next day she had a letter from Calverley. 'No invasion, you will be pleased to hear. Howsomever, the mild weather continues, more's the pity of it. We are all still on alert, although the fishermen report no movement on the other side of the Channel. Howsomever, there is no leave for anyone, no matter how strongly we urge it. I miss you to distraction. Pray for bad weather my love, and I will be with you within the day.

Your own Calverley.'

It was uncommon disappointing. Especially as the weather continued fair despite her prayers.

Fortunately there was a great deal of work to attend to, which in many ways was a relief to her, for it kept her out of the house and didn't give her time to think. A new street of houses was being built on the Lamb's Conduit Fields so there was a concession to be negotiated and trade to be canvassed, and Mr Teshmaker was of the opinion that the firm could withstand another newspaper shop in the city.

'You spend a deal of time on my business, Mr Teshmaker,' she said, on the day the concession was finally granted, 'which I appreciate.'

''Tis my pleasure, Mrs Easter.' Which was true, for he followed the affairs of A. Easter – Newsagent with particular attention.

'It occurs to me,' she said, 'that I might well appoint a solicitor to the firm. It grows so quickly, I declare there would be work a-plenty for such a man.' It was time for change and expansion. She had a new housekeeper now, and new servants, so why not hire a company solicitor?

He agreed that she had stated the case correctly.

'How if I were to offer such a post to you, Mr Teshmaker?'

He gave a swaying bow of acceptance and delight. 'I should consider myself honoured, ma'am.'

So honoured he duly was, and when he had worked out his notice with his old friend Mr Duncan, he moved into his own office above the shop in the Strand. It was, as he told his colleagues old and new, uncommon good fortune.

The mild weather continued even when the calendar declared that winter had begun. 'Most unseasonable,' people told one another, 'and all the better for that.' And in the middle of this 'summer in autumn' something else happened that could hardly have been expected either. Peace talks began in London.

Nobody thought they would lead to anything. After all, the war had been going on for more than eight years and despite any number of battles and campaigns nothing had been settled. Napoleon still ruled France and still seemed hell-bent on the conquest of Europe, and everybody knew that until he was defeated the war would have to go on.

''Tis talk, that's all,' old Mr Walter said to Nan. 'They could hardly patch up a peace now, in all conscience. Not with so many good lives lost.'

'I can't see our Nelson agreeing to *that*,' Nan said. But at least it was news and it sold papers, whether it was a serious attempt to bring the war to an end or no. And she'd seen so much talk come to nothing.

In the meantime, with the threat of invasion over for the winter, Calverley could at least get up to London to visit her. Which he did, three days later and uncommon pleasurable it was.

'I had almost forgotten what you looked like,' she teased as they were dressing to go to the theatre on their second night together.

'Then I must remind you,' he said, kissing her.

'Later,' she rebuked him, laughing, 'or we shall miss the play.'

'You lose your appetite for love, I see,' he teased.

'Indeed I do not,' she said pulling him towards her.

So they missed the play.

It was such a short leave. 'Four days!' Nan mourned as they parted, ''Tis barely time to say how d'ye do.'

'I shall be back within the month,' he promised. 'The regiment moves to Brighton in a week or two and Brighton is but a short ride from London.'

'I'd sooner they moved to Chelsea,' she said.

'Brighton is a fine town,' he said. 'Full of life. Belongs to the Prince of Wales. He's building a palace there, so they say. They have a race course and a theatre and assembly rooms. You must visit me there when the weather improves. You will love it.'

'I should love any place if you were in it,' she said, and then she sighed because she could see Thiss leading Jericho up the road, and their parting couldn't be delayed any longer.

'I will see you in ten days, if the weather holds,' he promised, kissing her goodbye.

And the weather did hold. Long enough for three more visits. But none of them long enough to satisfy either of them.

It wasn't until the end of January, when Bessie's baby was born, that the cold really began. And even then there was no snow and little frost and the sky was unseasonably blue.

The baby was a girl and a remarkably pretty one, given the undeniable plainness of her mother and the ugliness of her father. She was christened Penelope Ann, but Annie and Billy, who were much taken with her, rapidly re-named her Pollyanna. And Pollyanna she remained, a round-faced, well fed, placid baby who lay in her cradle and chortled while Bessie got on with her work.

Bessie took her new duties as housekeeper very seriously indeed, and for the most part did them well. Although even she couldn't persuade Dibkins out of his cupboard. He would stomp out in the early morning to light the fires and he would make occasional erratic sorties during the day to re-fill coal buckets and empty slops and ashes, but at night he retired to his bolt-hole with a bible and a two-headed candlestick and locked himself in.

'An' the Lord knows how he fares all night,' Bessie said, 'for he must sleep bolt upright all in among the brooms an' all. 'Taint as if he's got a chair ter sit in. I wish he'd let me fix him a bed.'

' 'Tis a man made obstinate by grief,' Nan said. 'We must let him get on with it, I fear. If he means to go without sleep 'tis his affair Bessie, that's my advice to 'ee. He'll come round sooner or later.'

But the spring came round before he did. And with the spring came the news that England and France had indeed signed a peace treaty, meeting at a place called Amiens to do it. After nine years and without victory or advantage, the war was ignominiously over. There was considerable outrage in all the newspapers, and a general opinion that had Pitt still been Prime Minister such a shameful thing would never have been allowed to happen.

But Nan was quick to see an advantage in it.

Chapter Twenty-six

Calverley Leigh was rather piqued when he received Nan's letter. For a start it wasn't the sort of loving missive he'd come to expect of her, being short and to the point and rather peremptory, 'Such good tidings this war being over. I shall be in Brighton on the morning stage Thursday. I have plans for the future, howsomever they will keep until I see you, Yrs in haste, yr own Nan.' Plans for the future sounded decidedly ominous. When an unattached female spoke of the future she invariably meant marriage. Surely she wasn't going to ruin their affair by making such an elementary mistake? Not his Nan.

He sighed as he set the letter aside. Which Hanley-Brown, who was stroking the side of his chin most delicately with a cut-throat razor, was quick to notice. 'A troublesome wench, I'll wager,' he said sympathetically, flicking a blob of soap and stubble into the dirty water in his washing bowl.

Calverley sighed again, easing on his trousers.

'Say farewell, my friend,' Hanley-Brown advised, tilting his head and lifting the razor for action. 'Game ain't worth the candle once sighin' sets in, I tell 'ee. Off with the old and on with the new, eh?'

'Right as ever, Tom,' he said cheerfully to his friend. And he tossed Nan's letter into the fire to give a public demonstration of how little he thought of it. If she tried to manoeuvre him into a proposal they would have to part company. It was high time for farewells. The affair had lasted far too long in all conscience. Nearly three years. It was a lifetime.

But when she came jumping down from the high step of the stagecoach, neat and trim in her green coat, with her feet so small in their laced boots and that wild face haloed by her bonnet and blazing affection at him, he forgot about farewells because he was so pleased to see her.

'Did you have a good journey?' he asked, returning her loving look because he just couldn't help himself.

'Vile,' she said, slipping her hand into the crook of his arm. 'I'm starving hungry and freezing cold and I've drunk all my brandy, every last drop.'

So he took her into the Ship Hotel at once to remedy all these deficiencies, and soon they were settled before the fire in the coffee room, side-by-side in two deep armchairs and an even deeper conversation, murmuring of that other appetite which they both shared so acutely now and which they knew they would satisfy as soon as their room was ready for them. And neither of them noticed that they were being watched with great interest by a gentleman in a dark blue coat who was sitting in the corner half-hidden by a copy of the local paper.

It was one of their happiest holidays, despite his suspicion, which now, bathed in the constant afterglow of satisfied desire, seemed petty and foolhardy. He would have been a fool to cast such a partner aside, and at night, lying within the charmed circle of her arms, he knew it.

They went riding in the rough, damp winds that blew off the Channel, and when she saw how tatty his saddle had become she insisted on buying him a new one. They walked on the beach until their faces were numb with cold and she couldn't feel her fingers, and then it was his turn to buy her a present, an embroidered muff lined with black fur. And they danced in the assembly rooms and went to the play and dined well and drank deep and loved whenever they would.

On Friday she bought a copy of the local paper and was highly entertained by the violent argument that was being conducted in its pages. The Prince of Wales had bought up three fine houses on land adjacent to his palace and had pulled them down to make room 'for stables' as the paper reported with furious indignation, 'the future king's horses being of greater importance to the gentleman than the future king's men.'

'And quite right too,' Calverley said, when he'd read the paper. 'Where would you find a nobler creature than a horse, dammit? Deserve the best, they do. I'd raze the whole town to make way for *my* stables, so I would, if *I* were Prince of Wales.'

But when they saw the gentleman himself, riding in his gilded coach with his current favourite, the corpulent Mrs Fitzherbert, squashed beside him, even Calverley had to admit that his future monarch was 'pretty gross' although adding sotto voce, 'It don't do to say it too loud, the laws bein' what they are.'

'A cat may look at a king,' Nan pointed out, looking at her king cattily.

'Aye, so she may, always providing she don't say a word to criticize him.'

'Why not?'

'Words are treason nowadays, my charmer. Did you not know it?'

No, she didn't, and she didn't much care either. 'Let's to the coffee house,' she suggested. 'All this fresh air gives me appetite.'

She's a passionate creature and no mistake, Calverley thought, watching her as she blew kisses at him across her steaming coffee-cup, and she hadn't said a word about marriage.

On the afternoon of the fourth day when a pale sun struggled through the clouds to make the wet sand shine, they took a promenade, along with most of the other idle cavalrymen in the town and the lone and interested traveller in the dark blue coat, and strolled down to Prinny's Royal Pavilion to see how work was progressing. And she still hadn't said a word about her plans, which was a miracle of self-control seeing that her head was crammed with them and time was running out.

The Pavilion was a great deal bigger than she had expected it to be, and the new stables were almost finished. They were very grand, built in the Hindu style like an Indian palace, as they could see quite easily for the workmen were hard at it inside the building, and the entrance was wide open. There were stalls for forty-four horses set round a huge circular court, and an elaborate fountain watering a pond in the middle of the court, and rising above their heads, in a quite extraordinary way with no visible means of support, a roof as round as an onion, sixty-five feet high, so Calverley said, with windows spraying downwards from the centre like long shining petals. It was amazing.

'That must have cost a pretty penny,' Nan said admiringly. 'How d'they get that roof to stay up?'

But that was an engineering feat he couldn't explain. 'Come round to the east front,' he suggested, 'and see what he's done there. 'Tis a fairytale building, no less.'

The wind blew straight upon them as they stood admiring the pavilion and its two oval-shaped wings. All the windows were topped by metal canopies, like curved green shells, and very elegant they looked in the pale sunlight.

' 'Twill be a marvel when 'tis done,' she said.

'There's a deal of building set in hand this year,' he told her, 'being it's peacetime and less demand for soldiery.'

It was the chance she needed, the opening she'd been waiting for all through these four happy days. She took it at once. 'There's a deal to be done everywhere now that we have peace to do it in,' she said. 'My own trade grows by the hour. I took on five new roundsmen only last week, and could use more.'

He heard her but without much interest. 'They say he has great plans for the garden,' he said.

'I have great plans too,' she said, and the eager edge to her voice alerted him at once.

'I ain't the marrying kind, Nan, I should warn 'ee,' he said, taking two steps back from her.

'Nor me neither,' she said easily, remembering Sophie's warning. 'No, no. 'Ten't marriage I'm thinking of. We are well enough as we are.' And she took his arm happily.

'I'm glad to hear it,' he said relaxing. 'Twas only business, after all, and business was entirely her affair.

'My plans are for the newsagency,' she said. 'Oh, Calverley my dear, you could be part of those plans.'

'Come now Nan,' he said, 'what earthly use would a cavalry man be to a newsagency?'

'The war is over,' she said urgently. 'There en't no need for cavalry now. Why not leave the army, and join me in the firm. You could have a partnership. I need a manager with so many new reading-rooms, and more to come, which I do not doubt. You've only to say the word.'

'My dear Nan,' he said stiffly, holding his body away from her in horror at what she was saying, 'no man worth his salt would ever permit himself to be kept be a woman. I could not consider it.'

'Squit!' she said trenchantly, removing her hand from his arm and facing him squarely. 'You wouldn't be kept. You'd earn your way so you would.' Why was he being so foolish?

'Have done!' he warned her, face frozen. 'I could not consider it.'

'The more fool you, then,' she said furiously. ' 'Tis a good offer. Many a man would jump at it.'

'Am I to be judged no better than the common run of mankind?' he said, drawing himself up to the full magnificence of his height, and haughty with stung pride.

305

Oh, he was splendidly handsome. 'We could be together whenever we wished,' she urged. 'No more partings, no more rushing back to camp, no more travelling. Think on it!' It was a most enticing prospect and her face showed it.

'You do not understand,' he said, looking down on her. 'My life is with the army. Always has been, always will be. I'm a cavalry man first, last and always. I thought you would have known that, after all this time. Why, in a month or so I shall buy myself a captaincy. And you ask me to throw all that away to be kept by a petticoat.' He was still appalled that she should even have thought such a thing.

'Ah, I see!' she shouted at him, exploding into sudden anger. 'That is how you view me, is it sir? As a petticoat! A petticoat! Well, pray allow me to tell 'ee, I run the biggest business in the biggest city in the world.'

'Howsomever,' he said, his anger freezing as hers flamed, 'you do not run me! Nor will you! I am my own master and I intend to remain so.'

'Oh!' she cried, stamping her foot. 'I never heard such squit. And the salary I'm offering better than anything you'd ever earn in your wretched army, captain or no. You're a blame fool, Calverley Leigh. A blame fool! That's what you are!' Her face was dark with fury.

'I will walk you back to the Ship,' he said, deliberately courteous because he was so angry. 'Then I have duties to perform.'

'Duties!' she mocked. 'What duties? The war is over so 'tis, or en't they told you?'

' 'Twill start up again just so soon as Napoleon is ready to invade us,' he said ominously as they walked away from the pavilion. 'This peace is a breathing-space, no more, no less. And one we would be foolish not to use to full advantage. There is more need of the cavalry now, I can tell 'ee, than there ever has been.'

She walked beside him scowling because he was saying all the wrong things and she couldn't think of an adequate answer.

' 'Tis a shameful peace,' he said, as they turned the corner and headed towards the inn, 'and I could not compound the shame by deserting the colours at this hour, even if I were to wish it, which I do not.'

The night-coach was drawn up outside the Ship, its four horses being backed carefully into the shafts. Nan made up her mind at once, at the sight of it. 'I shall go back to Chelsea,' she said crossly, 'there being nothing more to keep me here.'

'You will travel by night? Is that wise?'

It wasn't at all wise and they both knew it, for night travel was exceedingly hazardous, but she had made up her mind. 'I've a deal of work to do and no manager to help me do it,' she said tartly. 'Hold the coach!' she instructed the coachman. 'I've luggage to collect. I'll be with 'ee in two shakes.'

'Nan,' Calverley said. But she was already inside the inn and striding up the stairs and the sight of that determined spine made him equally determined not to plead. If she meant to run risks and make a fool of herself, so be it.

But he waited until she was settled inside the coach, angry though he was. 'I do not change my mind,' he said as the coachman gathered the reins and the horses snorted.

'Nor I,' she told him. And then her face was gone from the window and the coach was on its way.

He was so angry he had to go down onto the beach and hurl stones into the sea for nearly five whole miserable minutes, while the man in the dark blue coat watched him from one of the upper windows of the hotel. Deuce take it, whatever possessed her to make such a foolish suggestion? She might have known 'twould annoy. There'd been no need for it. And what if the coach were attacked or came to grief, as they so often did at night? Oh, there was no sense in her at all. And he knew that he missed her with a pain that was almost as acute as loss, and he was angry at himself for showing such weakness, and threw the next stone at a seagull who was bobbing on the water and had no business to look so self-satisfied.

'Damn the war! Damn the peace! And damn you!' he yelled. 'If she thinks I will write or visit after this, then she may think again.' And the seagull rose white-bellied from the water and flew calmly away from his wrath.

The next day he took a turn about the town with Hanley-Brown and Fortescue to hunt for another light o' love. And found a little Welsh girl who was called Myfanwy. She was passably pretty, with a fine full bosom, but she took a deuced long time to persuade, the worst part of a fortnight, and on the night he finally enjoyed her, if enjoyment was

307

the right word for a pleasure so fleeting, she ruined it all by telling him she would be returning to Wales the very next morning.

'I tell 'ee, Fortie,' he said gloomily to his friend when they were both back in barracks the following evening, 'the game ain't worth the candle.'

'Speak for yourself,' Fortescue said cheerfully. 'Mine is a wench of fire.'

But the only wench of fire that Calverley knew was Nan Easter, and he was too proud to go courting in that direction again. What a miserable thing it was that she should have insulted him so!

After another week, when he'd flirted with four more pretty creatures and decided against all of them, he began to wonder whether he might not write to his aggravating Mrs Easter after all. 'Twas a foolish quarrel in all conscience, and she would hardly be likely to repeat such a ridiculous mistake. And besides, he missed her cruelly.

But pride still held him back. It was degrading for a man to be in thrall to a woman, even a woman as spirited and passionate as his Nan. He waited another ten days before he put quill to paper, and then it was a most carefully composed letter.

'I have orders to visit London next Wednesday on a matter of some consequence to the regiment,' he wrote. It wouldn't hurt to give her some indication of his importance. 'Should you wish it I could call upon you in the afternoon.

Yr obedient servant, Calverley Leigh.'

Once the letter was on its way to Chelsea he regretted it and wished he could call it back. I have made a pretty fool of myself, he thought, and now she will mock me.

But it wasn't in Nan's nature to want to mock anybody and she was too busy to waste time in recriminations.

She'd still been in a furious temper when she got back to Chelsea, but a good meal and a good night's sleep put her back into a better humour. She woke the next morning aggrieved but energetic. If that blamed fool Calverley wouldn't join her as a business partner, then she'd strike out on her own, so she would. There were opportunities a-plenty in the City. 'Twas just a matter of choosing the best of them.

The shameful peace had been very good for her particular trade, despite Calverley's poor opinion of it. There was an unprecedented demand for daily papers, but unfortunately the printers couldn't meet it.

'I could sell twice the number,' she told young Mr Walter when she and Thiss arrived in Printing House Square to collect the first edition of *The Times* that morning, 'if only you could print 'em.'

'Would that I could,' John Walter said with feeling. Now that his father had stepped down and he'd taken over the ownership of *The Times* at long, long last, he was full of ideas for improving the paper, but he could still only print two hundred and fifty copies an hour. 'We are limited by the speed of our handpress,' he sighed. 'I've a mind to go to Germany, now that this war is over or at least in abeyance, for there are many say the peace cannot last. They have invented a new steam press there, so Meredew tells me, capable of printing a thousand sheets an hour. Think of that. 'Twould even satisfy the present demand, I'll wager. More than we could possibly sell.'

'If you could print 'em, John Walter, then I could sell 'em,' Nan promised, dusting the palms of her hands against each other, the way she always did when she was at her most determined. And she made up her mind there and then that if he bought this press she would ask for sole rights to sell all the papers he printed.

In the meantime there was money to be made from advertising. At the end of April she began to sell wall space in her shop in the Strand and in most of her reading-rooms, and it wasn't long before she realized that counter space could be made to earn its keep in this way too. But it wasn't enough. The returns were too small and there was no adventure in it.

Finally when six weeks had passed and she still hadn't heard from Calverley, she was so full of restless energy and so determined to expand her empire one way or another than she decided to consult a broker and see what he advised.

The man she chose was small and slight but he had big ideas.

'There are two means by which to make money today, Mrs Easter,' he said, looking at her shrewdly, 'providing you have the capital. One is to invest in commodities – tea, sugar, metals and so forth, the other is to buy shares in the African trade. The former is the lesser risk, the latter yields the greater profit.'

'African trade, eh?' she said, attracted by his enthusiasm. 'What sort of trade is that?'

'Why, between Africa and America to be sure, calling in to London or Bristol with tobacco on the return trip. The profits are very high, and eminently respectable. Several bankers of my acquaintance have grown rich upon it.'

It took her ten seconds to make up her mind. She would invest two hundred guineas in the cocoa trade and take half-shares in a new ship specially built for the African run.

I need no man to help *me*, she thought, as the pony trap rattled back to Chelsea. That blame fool can stay away as long as he likes, I shall see my profits grow whatever he does, or doesn't do.

Four days later, when there was still no letter from her lover, she went down to London Bridge to see 'her' ship and meet the master. The ship was called the *Esmeralda* and was a splendid vessel, capable of carrying an immense cargo. The master was a disappointment. His name was Jones and he was short and stocky with a brutal face and a bullying manner.

' 'Tis a fine trade, Mrs Easter,' he told her brusquely. 'Don't you go lettin' anyone persuade you otherwise.'

Her instincts rose against him at once. But with the broker's aid they came to an agreement remarkably swiftly and once it was signed and she was home again in Chelsea, she comforted herself that business was business no matter how ugly one of the participants might have been.

'I have branched out into a new line of business,' she told Cosmo Teshmaker at their weekly meeting.

He took the news with his usual calm. Until she told him what the business was. Then he was uncharacteristically critical. 'I feel I should warn you ma'am,' he said politely, 'the cocoa trade is not as dependable as it could be, just at present.'

' 'Twill improve,' she said. 'And in any case if it don't yield a big profit, the African trade will. Everybody says so.' She hadn't listened to the coffee-house talk for nothing.

'Indeed yes,' he agreed soothing her. 'Howsomever . . .'

'There en't no howsomever, Mr Teshmaker,' she said briskly. 'I shall make a fortune so I shall and then I shall start buying shops in the provinces. 'Tis is high time the firm expanded.'

But he still looked worried.

'You are too cautious by half,' she said, smiling at him.

He agreed with that too. 'Possibly so, ma'am. Possibly so.'

'Trust me,' she said.

Watching her walk out into the Strand, straight-backed and determined, he wondered whether he ought to have tried to tell her a little more about the African trade. She'd been in such a dominating mood, but perhaps he ought to have tried. For he knew, as she apparently did not, that the *Esmeralda* would be transporting slaves.

Calverley's letter was waiting for Nan when she got home late that afternoon. She read it with mischievous pleasure, delighted to think that he couldn't keep up the quarrel after all, and she wrote back by return of post. 'My dear Calverley, yes do call. I have a lot to tell 'ee, howsomever 'twill keep until we meet. I will prepare a supper for you, Yr loving Nan.'

Deuce take it if she ain't the most splendid woman, he said to himself, when her letter arrived, and the most sensible. And he sat down at once to write to her again, relieved to think that no real damage had been done by their quarrel.

And four days later he arrived in Cheyne Row with an armful of jonquils and a sheepish expression.

'Come you in,' she said, grinning at him. 'Mrs Jorris has made an almond hedgehog in your honour, and if we don't eat un direct 'twill lose all its quills.'

It was an excellent meal and he was gratified to see that Billy and Annie were pleased to see him again. After the meal he escorted the entire family to the play, and after the play they went on to the Rotunda to see the fireworks, and after the fireworks they made hot possets and drank them sitting around the embers of the drawing-room fire. It was past midnight before he and Nan were finally alone together and then she told him all about her new business ventures and how Mr Teshmaker didn't approve of them and what a success they were going to be. And for once he listened with apparent patience because he didn't want to annoy her again, even though he was creeping with desire for her.

And so love cured their quarrel. And the *Esmeralda* set off for Africa. And the uneasy peace continued.

Chapter Twenty-seven

That summer Nan opened a reading-room in Brighton. It was her thirty-third such property, and by October it was making a profit. It continued to pay its way all through the winter, despite the fact that the Regent and his followers were back in the capital, and that was very gratifying, because the profits from the cocoa trade were very small indeed, just as Cosmo Teshmaker had predicted, and there was no news at all from the master of the *Esmeralda*.

The spring of 1804 arrived late and it brought several surprises, none of them welcome to Nan Easter. At the beginning of May when small silky leaves were making a tentative appearance on the cold branches of the limes in Cheyne Walk, Mr Addington, the innocuous Prime Minister who had had the effrontery to succeed the great Mr Pitt when he resigned from office, suddenly found sufficient gall or moral strength or party support to re-open hostilities and declare war on the French. And to raise money for his endeavours he introduced a tax on property.

''Twill be a blow to this company,' Nan said to Cosmo on the morning *The Times* printed the news. 'Thirty-three shops and properties are a deal to pay tax on all of a sudden. You'd best estimate the total cost of the tax and the running costs of all our properties as soon as you can. If I get no news from Captain Jones, I may have to sell one or two of the weaker shops to make ends meet.'

It was rather worrying. And two days later, annoyance was added to anxiety, when Sir Osmond Easter re-opened hostilities between his branch of the family and Nan's, with a letter that had her roaring round to Cosmo Teshmaker for the second time that week and in the foullest of tempers.

'Look 'ee here,' she said, casting the offensive paper onto the counter. 'See what that pernicious varmint dares to write to me! Lord save us all, if he were here I should do un a mischief, so I should.'

Mr Teshmaker picked up the letter delicately and read it without altering his expression, having learnt by now that extreme calm was beneficial in all dealings with the volatile Mrs Easter.

'Madam,' Sir Osmond had written.

'It has been brought to my attention by a trustworthy member of my family that you have been seen in a public place in the company of a common soldier. May I remind you that as a member of my family you have a certain position to maintain, and that frequenting inns and consorting with common soldiers is hardly conducive to the maintenance of that position. I trust that I have made my opinion clear upon this matter and that you will amend your public behaviour forthwith.

'I write this as the head of the family to which you have the honour to belong. I would be failing in my duty were I not to warn you, and I trust you will accept this warning in the spirit in which it is being sent.

'Yr obedient servt,

Osmond Easter.'

'Write you and tell him I shall consort with whomsoever I please,' Nan instructed, 'and tell him 'tis no affair of his. I never heard such sauce! 'Tis more than human flesh and blood can stand.'

'Doubtless,' Mr Teshmaker said delicately, 'this has arisen because you have been seen at some social function or other in the – er – general company of – er – military gentlemen.'

'I have a lover who is an officer in the Duke of Clarence's regiment,' she said bluntly. 'He en't a common soldier, but even if he were I should consort with him whenever and wherever we pleased. 'Tis no concern of Sir Osmond's. Let him look to his own affairs. Write you and tell un that.'

'Leave it to me, ma'am,' Mr Teshmaker soothed. 'I will compose an answer this very afternoon. Meantime perhaps you would care to see the estimates for the new tax.'

They were even more alarming than she'd anticipated. 'Deuce take it,' she said, 'How am I supposed to buy newspapers if I've to pay such as this? 'Tis exorbitant.'

'I quite agree, ma'am,' Cosmo said. 'But exorbitant or not, it is the law, and the first demands for payment have already arrived.'

'I begin to regret the cocoa trade,' she said, 'and that's a fact. If it does no better within the month I shall sell. Meantime, the best thing to be done is to cut our losses on the two worst premises. 'Tis a poor thing that we have to sell shops to pay taxes. Do you have those figures too?'

She made her decision quickly because it annoyed her to be selling instead of buying and she didn't enjoy the uncomfortable feeling that her business affairs, far from improving and growing as she'd intended, were actually in decline. 'Islington,' she said. ''Twas a dark little shop, in all conscience. We're well rid of it. And Mr Cummings is more than ready to stop work, poor old thing. Young Jack can come back to the Strand. The third had better be the Lambeth shop. Deuce take it, what possessed that blame fool Addington to go declaring war? He might ha' known 'twould cost a fortune.'

So the shops were advertised for sale that afternoon, and then one of Mr Teshmaker's most careful letters was composed for the benefit of Sir Osmond Easter.

It was a most courteous epistle, thanking Sir Osmond for his 'concern for my client' which was, he felt sure, 'well meant if entirely unnecessary' and pointing out that in the course of her extensive business affairs Mrs Easter was compelled to 'meet and treat with all sorts and manner of persons', but stressing in his final paragraph that the said Mrs Easter was 'a lady singularly mindful of the obligations and responsibilities pertaining to her rank and quality.'

'It is my earnest hope that this letter will calm the gentleman,' he wrote to Nan, when he sent her a copy.

But Sir Osmond was not an easy man to calm. News of Nan Easter's financial troubles had reached Ippark, and the gentleman was delighted to think that his adversary had lost some of her strength. His next letter was even more aggressive. Business meetings he understood, he wrote. Had he not had experience a-plenty of such necessitous occasions? Howsomever, meeting with one soldier, or one officer, it was of little consequence which, in solitary inns apart from all other company was another matter and one which he had every right to be concerned about.

'I fear,' Mr Teshmaker said, when he went to dine with his old friend and mentor, Mr Duncan, 'this matter may not prove to have quite the ease of resolution that I had hoped.'

'An influential gentleman, Sir Osmond,' Mr Duncan agreed, mounding food onto his fork with careful precision. 'Able to bring pressure to bear. Pity she ain't more discreet.'

'Where would our business be if all women were discreet?' Mr Teshmaker murmured. A woman with Mrs Easter's admirable drive and passion could hardly be expected to live like a nun. I should value your advice on how this should be answered.'

'Try defamation of character,' Mr Duncan suggested. 'A hint that he may have gone too far in that first epistle of his. I doubt if he thought to take a copy. Just a hint, mind. There is no need to get embroiled.'

So the hint was insinuated into the middle of a suave paragraph full of placatory anodynes about the necessity for business meetings and the variety of persons and companies which might well be met on such occasions. 'My client is sure you would not wish to be interpreted as implying any such activity as would render you liable to prosecution for defamation of character.'

It was beginning to be quite an exciting battle of wits. 'Now we shall see what will be the outcome of *this*,' he said, with happy satisfaction as he dropped the firm's blue sealing wax in a neat circle across the folded paper. And he wondered wistfully, embossing the seal with his usual extreme neatness, what his passionate employer was doing in Brighton, with her much criticized lover.

She was telling him what a plaguey nuisance Sir Osmond was being.

'Let him write what he will,' Calverley said easily. ''Tis all one, my charmer. If he may take *us* to task for loving, he would have to do the same for most of his noble friends. 'Tis the fashion, so 'tis, and he should accept it.'

'I just hope Mr Teshmaker has put paid to un, that's all,' Nan said. 'Consorting indeed!'

'Captain Mauleverer will be major within the year, and his commission on offer,' he told her proudly. ''Twill not be long before you are consorting with a captain.'

'Meantime,' she said putting the wretched Sir Osmond out of her mind, 'how if my lieutenant were to escort me to supper. I'm starving hungry.'

When she got back to Chelsea three days later, she found a letter from Mr Teshmaker urging the immediate sale of her interest in the cocoa trade, 'which is now running at a loss, I fear,' and a note from Sophie Fuseli. 'Such bad news, my dear. I must see you at once. I will call every day until you return.'

It made Nan's heart sink. Now what? she thought. Have I not trouble enough as it is? What more could it be?

It was news of an old friend.

''Tis Mr Blake,' Sophie said, the minute she arrived the next afternoon. 'Mr Blake is arrested.'

It was astonishing news. 'Whatever for?' Nan said, leading the way into the dining-room.

'Sedition, my dear, if you ever heard of anything so foolish.'

'A mistake, surely. Mr Blake is a deal too wise to speak treason, no matter what he might think.'

'Oh no, my dear, 'tis no mistake. He is to stand trial, poor man. Apparently he turned a drunken soldier out of his garden and the fellow has sworn a deposition that Mr Blake uttered seditious words. There's a warrant taken out against him.'

'He'll never come to trial,' Nan said hotly.

'I fear he will,' Sophie said, 'and sedition is a hanging matter. I shall go to the trial and support him, as Heinrich dithers.'

'He will go with you, surely?'

'I doubt it, my dear. That is why I shall attend.'

'And travel alone?'

'Would you come with me, Nan?' Sophie asked. 'I would take it as the greatest kindness. We should not leave poor Mr Blake to face distress alone.'

That was very true, Nan thought. In times of trouble friends should support one another. Friendship was most valuable then, as she was beginning to appreciate as troubles pressed down upon her. 'Yes,' she said, making up her mind at once. 'I will travel with you, Sophie. You have my word on it. But they couldn't hang an artist, surely. The law would not allow it.'

'We live in dangerous times,' Sophie said. 'Even the law is no protection these days.'

It had better protect me, Nan thought, and she wondered what effect Cosmo's latest epistle was having on her cantankerous nephew.

'Calverley Leigh,' Sir Osmond Easter said, leaning back in his fine red chair in his fine red drawing-room at Ippark. 'You are sure of the name?'

'Oh indeed, Sir Osmond,' the gentleman in the dark blue coat replied. 'I was most particular to be told the exact name. Mr Calverley

316

Leigh, a lieutenant in the Duke of Clarence's Light Dragoons, and expecting to buy Captain Mauleverer's commission, so it was rumoured.'

'Indeed,' Sir Osmond said, hooking his silver snuff box out of the pocket in the hem of his long coat. 'Well now that *is* interestin', and no mistake. You've done well, cousin Jermyn. Will you take snuff, sir?'

'Happy to have been of service,' cousin Jermyn said, dipping the tips of his right thumb and forefinger into the snuffbox and then sprinkling the brown powder thoughtfully onto the forefinger of his left hand. 'Would you wish me to continue, sir?'

'Not for the moment,' Sir Osmond said happily, snorting his pinch of snuff first up one nostril and then the other, blowing like a horse. 'Deuced good stuff this. Best thing I know for clearin' the head, damme. A lieutenant, eh? And after a captaincy. Well well! I shall have to see about that.'

'You dine with General Mauleverer a' Thursday.' Sniff sniff.

'Aye, so I do.' Snort. 'There are more ways of killin' the cat, eh Jermyn?' A hint dropped here, a word spoken there. Oh 'twould be infinitely preferable to yet another letter from that dammed tricksy lawyer feller of hers. Damme, the feller was worse than a snake, always twistin'. You never knew what he'd be writin' about next. More than seven letters had passed between Sir Osmond Easter and Mr Teshmaker, and even though that wretched servant gel was plainly doing badly and losing trade, she was no nearer accepting his position as head of the family than she'd been at the beginning. Downright aggravation, so it was. No this manoeuvre had much more hope of a satisfactory outcome. If he couldn't thwart the servant, why then he'd spike the guns of the cavalry man, dammit.

He sneezed extravagantly, his slippered feet lifting from the carpet. 'Business meetin's, my eye!' he said.

It was a surprise to the entire regiment when Mr Leigh was passed over.

The winter storms had finally brought seas so rough that Napoleon's fleet would have to stay in Boulogne until the spring, and the regiment was exhausted with tension and inactivity.

'Can't understand it, damme,' Captain Fortescue said, trying to commiserate. 'At a time like this too. It don't make sense, Leigh, indeed it don't.'

It was a terrible blow to Calverley's pride. He'd been so sure of this commission and so had his friends and his troop. And now this. Judged wanting, not up to scratch. Perhaps, and this was the most painful thought of all, perhaps considered past his best.

I am twenty-seven years old, he thought, as he brooded on lonely sentry-go in the look-out post on Hollingbury Hill. I should be a captain at the very least, like Hanley-Brown and Fortescue. Or married to an heiress. That was a failure too, despite the rewards of his long affair with Nan Easter, for really he should have found a possible wife by this time. And to make matters worse, he wasn't even the acknowledged Romeo of the regiment any more. A confounded ensign had arrived that summer, among the rush of new recruits brought in to resume the war, and he had rapidly become a considerable rival. A fresh-faced, empty-headed youth with a shock of fair hair and no sense, a stripling, no more, with a boy's slender neck and a girl's tender skin. But he turned giddy heads, there was no denying it, and soon the cat-call went round the camp that 'Old Leigh's nose was out of joint!' *Old* Leigh! At twenty-seven! It was downright demoralizing.

Unfortunately for his self-esteem, there had been far too many lonely and wakeful hours spent in look-outs and on solitary vigils during that panicky summer. And to his frustrated disappointment, he'd had very little leave and Nan had had to stay in London for most of the season, for it really was too dangerous on the south coast. She wrote to him, warmly, if rather more occasionally than usual, but it was a bad time, and now his lack of success made it worse.

'I've a mind to leave the army and find some other employ,' he said to Hanley-Brown.

'You'd be a fool,' the new captain said, 'for you've a deal more reason to stay than to leave.'

But in the event, it was Jericho, Calverley's much loved chestnut gelding, who precipitated his master's departure from the Dragoons. Or to be more accurate a combination of Jericho, the new ensign, Captain Fortescue, too little success and too much port and pride. Matters had come to a head at a regimental dinner, when bellies were uncomfortably full and tongues dangerously loose and Captain Fortescue had reached that stage of manic drunkenness when any remark, however trite, is a reason for hilarity.

Down at Calverley's end of the table the junior officers were bragging about their horses.

'Time you turned that old nag o' yours over to the knackers,' the

318

ensign said, grinning stupidly at Calverley. 'He ain't the beast he was and that's a fac'.'

'Over to the knackers!' Captain Fortescue giggled. 'Oh my eye!'

'He could outrun your carthorse any day of the week,' Calverley said, stung.

'Carthorsh!' Fortescue giggled again, looking to see whether the port was being passed his way again. 'Oh my eye! Oh tha's rich! Carthorsh!'

'Stow it, Fortie!' Calverley warned, beginning to be irritated by his friend's stupidity.

'Ain't the way to shpeak t'shperior officher,' Fortiscue warned and he tried to point to the superior pips on his shoulder. And failed and found that very funny too.

'Tell you what,' the ensign went on, pressing his advantage, 'that nag o' yours is a danger to the troop. Too slow, damme. Could have had me down in the second turn.'

'A pity he didn't,' Calverley said.

'You'd ha' lost him if he had, damme. Face facts man, that crittur's past his prime. Too long in the tooth.'

'Like his owner!' Fortescue said. 'Oldesh lieutenant in the regiment, damme if he ain't. Oldesh lieutenant in the army!' And he fell into a paroxysm of giggles at his own wit.

It was suddenly all too much for Calverley, because it was true and it was being said publicly, even if they were all drunk. 'You impugn my honour,' he said rising stiffly to his feet, 'and the honour of my horse. You have my challenge, sir.'

'Who does, dammit?' Fortescue said, trying to focus his eyes. 'Who you a-challengin'?'

The table had grown ominously quiet, as heads turned and peered to see if the word challenge actually had been spoken. A duel, eh! What sport!

In the chill of the next misty morning, when Calverley and Captain Fortescue took loaded pistols and set out for the privacy of the Downs to keep their appointment, it didn't look like sport at all. It looked foolhardy and rather despicable, considering what a mortal long time the two of them had been comrades-in-arms. But they had to go through with it. It was a matter of honour now. And even though by great good fortune or the unsettling effects of formidable hangovers they both contrived to miss each other, the damage was done. For duelling was illegal and there were unavoidable consequences.

Captain Fortescue took his reprimand with a sore head but in good heart, apologized handsomely and was told that was the end of the affair. But Lieutenant Leigh was intransigent with hurt pride. He could not agree that apologies were in order, he maintained that he had been mortally offended and that any man worth his salt would have done the same, and finally, pushed to make a choice between apology and leaving the regiment, he offered his resignation which was instantly accepted, there being a buyer apparently waiting for it. He was a private citizen before he'd absorbed the two demoralizing facts that he'd fought a duel with his old friend and made a complete and public fool of himself.

'Downright sorry to see 'ee go, Leigh,' the General said. 'Give 'ee a word of advice, me boy. Mind the ladies. Been the downfall of many a good man, so they have. Ladies and gossip, don't ye know. Well, well. I wish 'ee good fortune.'

What a peculiar thing to say, Calverley thought as he saluted, for he'd never heard of an officer being refused a commission because of an affair. Quite the reverse in fact. And in any case, there were very few ladies in his life just at the moment. In fact he'd been more or less faithful to Nan ever since their row, and she was hardly the sort of woman to cause gossip.

But once he'd left the general's room, he put the puzzle from his mind, for there was another and greater problem for him to face. Now whether he would or no, he would have to find some new way to earn his living. He spent a hungover morning considering possibilities and had to admit that there weren't very many. He certainly couldn't work for Nan. That was quite out of the question. In truth, there were very few people he could work for, since the only two things he knew anything about were horses and military manoeuvres. Finally and in desperation he decided that the best thing he could do would be to write to his famous relation, the renowned Colonel Leigh, racing manager to the Prince of Wales, who was in Brighton at present supervising the local Derby.

It took a lot of thought and inordinate quantities of brandy. So much in fact that after it was written and dispatched he couldn't remember a word of it. But it must have been in order, for Colonel Leigh wrote back.

'I wld have liked to have met my relation,' he wrote, 'howsomever present commitments do not allow such a luxury. Shd Mr Leigh care to write to Mr Chaplin, who runs stage-coaches and may be contacted at the Cross-Keys in Wood St London, he might well find that the said Mr Chaplin wld have a use for him. I wish my relation well and have the honour to be,

Yr obednt servt J. Leigh (Colonel)'

It was at least a hope. So another brandy-enriched letter was composed and dispatched, and after an agonizing seven days, the answer came. If Mr Leigh would care to present himself at the Cross-Keys at seven of the clock on a Thursday morning, Mr Chaplin would be happy to meet him.

The next day was Wednesday. He packed a carpet-bag, said goodbye to his old companions, and caught the overnight coach so that he would have a day and a night with Nan before his appointment. 'At least my Nan will be glad of this,' he said to Fortie. 'For ain't she been urgin' me to come to London?'

'That's it,' Fortescue said. 'Look on the bright side.'

It was a very cold journey. He was as stiff as a corpse when he arrived at the Cross-Keys, and the early morning sun, which had risen as an apologetic white disc as they crossed the North Downs, was now completely obscured by dark blue storm-clouds which gloomed and lowered above the rooftops ominously full of rain. And as if to emphasize that he was in new territory now, and Nan Easter's territory at that, propped in a prominent position in the corner of the courtyard was a dapper green handcart with the legend 'A. Easter – Newsagent' painted in gold in its side. It was attended by a cheerful urchin whose green beaver hat was similarly labelled and who offered him a 'mornin' piper, Sir!' in the confident expectation that he would buy one. Which he did.

Then he took a flyer to Cheyne Row. By this time thunder was growling somewhere to the south of the river and the clouds overhead were as black as grapes. The air was oppressive and the streets awash with mud. He was quite glad when the flyer squelched to a halt beside Nan's door.

Bessie was very pleased to see him and ushered him in and took his carpet-bag and his wet cloak and hat and told him the missus was in the drawing-room.

He ran up the stairs two at a time in his eagerness to see her. She was sitting at her desk doing her accounts, wearing a wine-red day dress which looked exceedingly businesslike and with her hair drawn up into a tight knot on the top of her head, a no-nonsense knot.

'My heart alive, Calverley!' she said. 'What's brought you here today of all days? I'm just off to Chichester in four mintues. Thank 'ee, Bessie. Pray tell Thiss I'm nearly ready to leave.'

It wasn't very welcoming. 'Say you ain't pleased to see me!' he tried to tease her.

'Uncommon pleased,' she said, but she was busy with her accounts and didn't look at him.

He was cast down and showed it. 'Must you travel today?' he said. 'Delay until tomorrow. Or the day after. Business will wait, surely?'

'Today as ever is,' she insisted, and this time rather fiercely. 'I have promised to travel with Sophie Fuseli. A dear friend of ours stands trial for his life. 'Ten't a matter may be delayed.' Why, oh why did he have to turn up today of all days? What miserable bad timing!

'When do you return?'

''Twill depend upon the judge,' she said, cleaning her pen. 'Two days or three. Who can tell?'

He sighed heavily and the expression on his face was that of a discontented child. 'I've such news to tell 'ee,' he said, 'yet you mean to leave me the moment I arrive.'

'What is your news, you foolish crittur?' she said, putting down her pen. 'Tell me quickly.'

'I have left the army,' he said. 'I have come to London to seek employment with Mr Chaplin the coach-maker. There now, what think 'ee? We may live together as we please, with no more partings, just as you planned.'

He'd felt so sure the news would please her but she didn't even smile. She closed her account book, and went through the connecting door into her bedroom to collect her coat and bonnet and her carpet-bag without saying a word.

'How now, Nan,' he said trailing after her. 'I thought you would be glad of it.'

'My job wasn't good enough for 'ee, I notice' she said, putting on her coat. 'When *I* offered you said you would stay in the army for ever. How you change!'

'I have an appointment with Mr Chaplin tomorrow morning,' he said, trying to bluff it out. 'How if we went to the theatre tonight? There is a capital play at Drury Lane. This trial can wait, surely.'

She stood before the looking-glass to arrange her bonnet over that serious top-knot. 'I told you,' she said. 'I promised to go to Chichester with Sophie, and I'm late enough as it is. Now I must be off or I shall miss the stage. Shall I take you back to town or will you stay here 'til I return?'

The thought of being entertained in her house without her was suddenly demoralizing. 'I shall return to the Cross-Keys,' he said, still trying to make light of this, 'since you spurn me.'

They were back at the Cross-Keys so quickly he'd hardly had a chance to say more than four words to her. The storm was immediately overhead and a strong cold rain was buffetting into the chaise.

'You will have a bad journey,' he predicted, and although it shamed him to admit it, he was pleased to be able to say so.

'I do not doubt it,' she said, wincing as the rain stung her cheeks. She didn't want to go to this trial at all. There were far too many others things that needed her attention. She had sold her interest in the cocoa trade but cash was still parlously short and Mr Teshmaker had sent her a rather alarming note that very afternoon saying he 'felt they should meet as soon as possible to discuss a matter of some urgency, concerning your shares in the merchantman *Esmeralda*.' She hadn't even got time to attend to that and it sounded ominous. But she had given her word to Sophie, and she couldn't go back on her word, no matter what she might be feeling. Oh, if only he hadn't chosen this day to arrive! And he was right. It would be a bad journey.

It was actually worse than either of them could possibly have imagined.

Chapter Twenty-eight

Sophie Fuseli was waiting in the coffee room of the Swan with Two Necks. 'Oh my dear,' she said as Nan arrived late and breathless. 'I am so glad to see you. I could not have borne to travel alone. What kept you?'

'Calverley Leigh,' Nan said, as they walked from the coffee room into the courtyard. 'Took it into his head to leave the regiment, so he has, and come up to London, all on the gad, to beg Mr Chaplin to employ him. After all that ol' squit about staying a soldier for ever and ever, and turning down my good offer. What do 'ee think of that?'

''Tis a fickle creature,' Sophie said, as they took their seats inside the Chichester stage, 'like all his sex. Ain't I always said so?'

'To turn up now,' Nan grumbled, 'at such a moment.' She was still aggrieved at his bad timing.

The storm had increased its fury, with sheet lightning suddenly holding the sky transfixed in impossible brightness and thunder so menacing it hurt their eardrums and made the coach windows rattle. Their team of horses stood disconsolately between the shafts, while rain water dripped into their eyes and streamed from their sodden shanks. The coachman was declaring loudly that he was 'of two minds whether to take 'em out or no,' and the two outside passengers hadn't emerged from the inn.

It was dark and damp inside the coach and the padded walls smelt most disagreeably of trodden straw, damp boots, wet umbrellas and mildew. The two women were already wet and dirty, their travelling coats spattered with rain and their boots squelching mud, but at least they had the coach to themselves.

'You are a dear, kind friend,' Sophie said gratefully as the coach creaked away. 'I am uncommon glad I do not travel alone. 'Twill be a bad journey.'

''Tis a bad time,' Nan admitted, warmed by her friend's affection. And the warmth made her begin to feel that she had been rather uncharitable towards her lover. 'Poor Calverley! I gave him no kind of welcome at all.'

'Did he deserve any?' Sophie said, grimacing at the sight of her skirt.

'I have loved him a mortal long time, Sophie,' Nan said, 'and we have been so much apart. I could have been kinder, in all conscience.'

'He will forgive 'ee,' Sophie said easily. ''Tis a lover, not a husband.'

The cold was making Nan shiver, but the word 'husband' made her sigh too.

'What is it, my dear?' Sophie said fondly. 'Why do you sigh?'

Being enclosed in this little, private, travelling compartment made confidences possible. ''Tis a great sadness to me,' Nan said, 'that we never married.'

'He ain't the marrying kind, my dear. I told you that long since, as I well remember.'

'Aye, you did. And spoke true. 'Tis a sadness nevertheless. I liked being a wife, Sophie. There was honour in it. And safety.'

'Aye, my dear,' Sophie said sympathetically. 'I know it.'

'Had he asked me to wed when our affair began I'd have married him that very day,' Nan said sadly. ''Twas no joy to me to be known as a mistress. Not after being married to Mr Easter. It never felt entirely as it should be. But I kept such thoughts a secret, even from you, my dear.'

'And from Calverley I trust,' Sophie said shrewdly.

'Aye. From him too. There's a deal he doesn't know.'

'And is he like to now?'

'I think not.'

'Tell me, my dear,' Sophie said, 'were he to ask you to marry now, what would your answer be?'

'I do not know,' Nan said, and it made her feel sad to confess it. 'I truly do not know. He would be a poor husband, I fear. Not like my dear Mr Easter.' And she sighed again. 'Mr Easter was so kindly.'

'Aye he was.'

'There have been times since he died when I have been uncommon lonely.' It sounded a foolish thing to say, when she had a lover and children and servants and a business, but Sophie understood.

'It seems to me,' she said, 'that loneliness is the common lot of mankind, whether they are married or no. We have such a parlous need

325

for good company, my dear, especially in bad times, which is why I determined to attend this trial.'

'All is not well with Easters,' Nan said, confessing again. 'I have lost a deal of money in the cocoa trade.'

'Aye, so 'tis rumoured.'

'And now Mr Teshmaker writes to hint of trouble with my ship.'

'You have a ship, my dear?'

'I have half-shares in a merchantman.'

'What does she carry?'

'Tobacco, I believe. She plies the African trade.'

Sophie's face registered instant, round-eyed shock. 'Oh, surely not!' she said. 'Oh, my dear old friend, I did not think it of 'ee. Oh, not the African trade!'

The niggling doubt Nan had felt when she first met the master returned to fill the coach. 'Why not, Sophie?' she asked gently. 'Is there wrong in it?'

'It is the slave trade,' Sophie said bluntly. 'Did you not know it?'

'No!' Nan said, understanding perfectly now. Oh, how foul! How unutterably foul! Was that what Mr Teshmaker wanted to tell her? Oh, she would sell out the moment she got back to London. This was not to be endured. 'Oh, Sophie!'

But at that point the coach stopped and they had to get out in the rain and walk behind it with the two outside passengers as the horses struggled uphill, so their conversation had to wait.

The road was axle-deep in mud, so that the poor creatures slithered and were in danger of falling, and by the time they reached the top of the hill, Nan and Sophie were spattered with dark slime and horribly cold. And then to make matters worse they were joined by a farmer and his wife, who were both impossibly fat and took up far too much room inside the coach, *and* put paid to any more confidences.

They were also impossibly cheerful. 'This ol' weather'll perk up now we're aboard,' the farmer bragged. 'Always do, don't it, Mother?'

And Mother, who seemed to be imbecilic as well as overweight, nodded and chuckled as though they were all off on a picnic.

'This journey will never end,' Sophie whispered, turning up her pretty blue eyes to the roof, which was now oozing brown moisture.

'If she don't stop sniggering,' Nan whispered back, 'I shall do un a mischief, so I shall.'

The journey continued in bristling bad humour and incomprehensible jollity for several hours and many miles until the rain eased, spattered and finally stopped.

'Well, there's a mercy, say I,' the farmer declared. 'A mercy, don't 'ee think so, ladies?'

Nan and Sophie admitted that they were glad of it. But their gladness evaporated at once, when the gentleman creaked his bulk forwards and opened the window.

'Pray sir,' Sophie begged, 'do remember how injurious cold air . . .'

'Shut that window at once, sir,' Nan ordered.

But he paid no attention to either of them. 'Bless me if we ain't got an outrider,' he said peering through the gap he'd created. 'Look 'ee there, Mother. A deer, I do declare.'

But his wife said it looked more like a great dog. ''Tis too yellow for a deer.' And while they debated, the horses took fright and began to neigh, but in a terrible high-pitched panicky way, all on one note, which was horribly alarming. They could hear the coachman calling, 'Whoa there, my beauties! Prime your pistols Jack! Whoa there! Whoa!' And the coach gave a sudden lurch that threw them all violently about.

'Sit down, do,' Nan said to the farmer. 'You unbalance us all.'

And to Sophie's surprise, he obeyed meekly, his fat face puzzled.

Now they could all see through the window and sure enough there was an animal of some sort galloping along behind the black hedgerows, but it was moving too quickly and the light was too poor for them to catch more than an occasional glimpse. Of a tawny hide rippling with speed and shadow, of slim straw-coloured legs leaping at full stretch, of the twitch of a long tufted tail. A long tufted tail, Nan thought, staring at the place where it had been. No, surely not! A tuft of brambles perhaps, or old straw, but not a tail. For what sort of creature had a tail like that? And fear tightened her chest and made the sweat start from her forehead, for this was certainly no deer, this was a menacing, hunting animal.

'Where are we?' Sophie asked nervously.

'Coming into Midhurst, ma'am,' the farmer said. And a pistol exploded deafeningly above their heads, and the coach rocked as though it was about to overturn and the horses screamed again.

The farmer's wife began to wail. ''Tis a highwayman,' she cried. 'Hide your waluables! We shall all be killed! Put your purse inside your breeches, Mr Dean, I beg you. 'Tis the only place. Oh, oh, we shall all be killed!'

327

And the creature leapt through the hedge in one graceful bound to gallop sinuously alongside the coach. And it was a great tawny cat, yellow of eye and snarling. Nan had only ever seen such a creature in paintings but she knew what it was. A lioness pounding in for the kill.

For a second they were all too surprised to believe what they saw. Then the lioness sprang forward into the air as though she was flying and the coach tipped and there was a confusion of movement and sound, pistols firing, coachmen swearing, horses screaming, a drumming of hooves and wheels, as they slithered to right and left and were flung against the sides of the coach, grabbing at one another for support and finding none. And the coach went careering on at a terrifying speed, as Nan and Sophie screamed and the farmer's wife yelled that she wanted to get out and the farmer sat stunned and open-mouthed and dribbling.

And then, in the middle of their nightmare ride, they were in a town, rattling down a wide street, with people rushing out of their houses on either side, wide-eyed with horror at what they saw. One of the horses was groaning and they were beginning to lose speed, so that the crowd was able to keep up with them and run alongside, and now they could hear what was being said. 'Pull up, man!' 'The beast is done for.' 'Pull up!'

But they didn't pull up, they laboured on, swinging abruptly round a sharp corner, turning left, and struggling up a sudden gradient with excited people pressing upon them from every side, and the horse groaning more terribly than ever. Nan had a confused impression of dozens of hands reaching out towards them, and then they had stopped at last, and were climbing shakily out of their battered vehicle into the warmth of all those bodies crowded into the narrow roadway.

The leading horse, a fine bay gelding, was so badly injured he could hardly stand. His neck had been bitten in at least three places and now gaped open revealing raw red flesh oozing blood, and his shoulders were striped by long bleeding gashes where he had been clawed. He was foaming and showing the whites of his eyes in terror and the sweat stood on his flesh in oily globules. 'He's dying, poor crittur,' Nan said, and there were many others standing around her who were saying the same thing.

'What 'appened?' people were asking, as they went to hold the other three frightened horses, and assist the farmer's wife out of the coach.

'Attacked by a lion,' the coachman said. 'Come out a' nowhere.

Couldn't do a thing about it. Jack 'ere fired his pistol valiant. 'Tweren't a bit a' use.'

An old woman was leaning out of one of the dormer windows in a row of ancient cottages immediately in front of them. 'Lion, eh?' she said. 'That'll be Honeybun's menagerie.' And she shouted into the house, 'Run you to south meadow, Japhet, and tell un we got his crittur.'

A flurry of urchins erupted from the cottage door and tumbled together like excited puppies, down the flight of stone steps and into the street and through the crowd and were gone. But the gelding was leaning into his stablemates, dripping blood and breathing noisily, and he looked as though he was going to fall.

'Take un to smithy,' a labourer suggested.

'Use yer gun boy. Put un out of his misery,' the old lady said, sucking her cheeks. ''E don't look like to last the night.'

But Jack's much-fired pistols were empty and all the shot used up.

''Tis but a short walk to the Spread Eagle, ladies,' the coachman said to Nan and Sophie, 'if you would be so kind. We shall 'ave fresh horses at the Eagle. 'Tis but a step.'

'Are we your only passengers?' Sophie asked, bemused. There were no travellers outside the coach, and the farmer and his wife had disappeared.

But Nan was more concerned about the gelding. 'See to your animal,' she said. 'We may make shift for ourselves.'

'Take un out the shafts 'fore he brings all down,' the old lady advised from her seat in the attic window. And as this seemed sound advice it was acted upon, and the gelding was led limping away.

As they turned the second bend in the road, Nan and Sophie could see the Spread Eagle standing just below the brow of the hill and directly before them, striped with dark timbers, roofed with dark red tiles, puffing warm smoke from all its tall chimneys, its sign bold against the darkening sky. It was bitterly cold and they were both shivering. 'I shall be glad to be within doors,' Sophie said.

But when they got to the entrance, and Sophie was drooping with her hand on the latch, they could hear that there was a violent argument under way in the courtyard, and now that they'd seen so much Nan was determined to know what was going on. 'Go you in,' she said to her friend. 'I will follow later.' And she tucked her cold hands into her muff and marched into the courtyard.

The gelding was still standing, still groaning and still bleeding. His

329

three companions were being soothed and uncoupled, with Jack in anxious attendance. And the coachman was having a furious argument with a large belligerent man in a turkey-red coat. '. . . nearly killed my horse, look 'ee,' he was saying. 'A crittur like that should be locked up, not a-roamin' the countryside preyin' on the innocent.'

There was a red-and-white cart, labelled 'Honeybun's Menagerie', standing in the entrance to the yard, with a formidable man brooding in the driver's seat. He had a wall eye and a jutting chin covered with black stubble and he was presently engaged in spitting long brown streams of chewed tobacco between his pony's ears. There was a large dust-coloured net heaped in the cart and a cat o' nine tails and several iron bars, and squatting patiently and miserably among them, tied to the side of the cart by a rope, an elderly mastiff, grey-muzzled and red-eyed.

'Tell yer what I'll do,' turkey-red coat said. 'I'll take 'im orf yer 'ands. Give yer five pounds for 'im, that's what I'll do. Can't say fairer'n that, now can I?'

'I can't sell a company horse,' the coachman said. 'Sides, that ain't the point. You're responsible.'

The driver spat his last stream of tobacco all over his pony's head. 'Be we a-goin' to catch this 'ere beast a' yourn or bain't we?' he said. 'Be too dark to see if'n we don't git a-goin' soon.'

'Five pounds,' Mr Honeybun said. ''E's only fit fer the knacker's.'

Nan looked at the gelding, shivering and groaning with his blood dripping into a dark pool at his feet, and her pity erupted into fury.

'You're a cruel heartless man, so you are,' she yelled at Mr Honeybun. 'Have you no thought for what your wretched beast did to that poor creature? You may sell him to me,' she said to the coachman. 'I will give you five guineas for un and see to it he's kept alive what's more.'

'I'm orf if you bain't,' the driver said laconically, and he flicked his whip at his tobacco-stained pony and drove the cart out of the yard.

'Only fit for the knackers!' Mr Honeybun shouted, sprinting after him. And he leapt onto the cart and was gone.

The gelding looked as if he were going to fall. 'Make your mind up to it sharpish,' Nan said to the coachman.

'Well now, ma'am,' he dithered. 'Is your credit good, if I might make so bold as to ask?'

330

'I am Nan Easter, the newsagent,' she said with pride. 'If my credit en't good I don't know whose is. Come now, is it a bargain?'

So he shook hands on it and she gave him her note of hand. Then she set about getting some help for the animal. 'Run you to the nearest surgeon,' she said to a stable lad, who'd been watching the transaction open-mouthed, 'and beg him to come here with all speed. Tell him he has a deal of stitching to do. And I'll trouble you sir,' she said to the coachman, 'to bring a horse blanket or two. The poor crittur needs warmth.' Then she set off into the stables to arrange accommodation for her new possession.

The surgeon returned within ten minutes, happily ready to earn a good fee. He was a little put out when he discovered that his patient was a horse, but he recovered when he heard how much Mrs Easter intended to pay him. ''Twill take a while, ma'am,' he said, when he'd examined the gashes, 'and I cannot guarantee that he will ever do more than limp, even with my very best endeavours, for the muscles are torn. You will get no more work out of him, I fear.'

'Life is enough,' she told him briskly. 'Do what you can, sir and you shall be well paid for it, I promise you.' Then she dusted the palms of her hands against one another with satisfaction and stomped across the stableyard into the inn to find Sophie.

It was peaceful inside the Spread Eagle. There was a huge fire burning in a hearth bigger than a double bed, and the curtains had been drawn and the candles lit. One of the kitchen maids had made a pot of coffee and brought it to Sophie who was sitting in one of the three wooden settles that were drawn up beside the blaze. There were carpets on the floorboards and dark beams enclosing them protectively overhead. It was cosy and domestic and a long way away from the horror on the road.

They drank their coffee and warmed their feet on the hearth, and Nan told Sophie how she'd bought the gelding and Sophie said it was her opinion that it could take hours before they would be ready to proceed. And gradually the fire warmed their chilled limbs and released a numbing fatigue in both of them which was almost pleasant. They decided that now the horse was being cared for they didn't really mind the delay, and they were quite disappointed when Jack came humbly into the coffee room more than an hour later to tell them the coach was ready.

By now dusk was descending and the coachyard was lit with rushes.

331

To their relief, the coach had been dried and cleaned and fresh straw spread on the floor, and there was no sign of the bloodstains on the cobbles. But as they turned out of the yard, heading south towards the mill pond and the brooding, open countryside, they were passed by Mr Honeybun's red and white cart, now black and white in the rushlight, but still chillingly recognizable.

The sides of the cart had been raised, but from her high vantage point in the coach Nan could see right down inside it. And there was the lioness safely entangled in the net, her tawny fur pale and her wide paws holding down a joint of meat from which she was tearing huge bloody mouthfulls. It was a very big joint of meat, Nan thought. She could see two legs quite clearly and the remains of a muzzle. Why it was an entire animal, an animal about the size of a dog. And she realized that she was looking at the remains of the mastiff. Dear heavens! They'd used the mastiff as bait. Live bait!

'We live in a callous world, Sophie,' she said.

They drove south along a much-pitted road as the world grew dark as well as cruel all about them. Neither of them said very much until they reached a small village called Lavant and were passing a group of low rush-lit cottages and the high grey flanks of a singing church.

'We pray to a God of Love,' Nan observed sourly, 'and He lets great lions break loose.'

'And allows great poets to be put on trial,' Sophie agreed.

'And slave ships to trade.'

'Poor Mr Blake!' Sophie said. 'Why did he ever leave London? What hope does he have here? What hope do any of us have?'

'None we don't make for ourselves,' Nan said, grimly. 'An' that's a fact.'

And so they came to Chichester, which didn't look at all promising as a seat of justice, being a dark, muddy town set in the midst of a totally flat plain. It was an enclosed place, bounded by the square of a crumbling Roman wall just visible to them in the lamplight, and divided into quarters by its two main roads that ran north-south and east-west and were lantern-lit but so mud bestrewn that the coach wheels threw gobbets of the stuff against the windows like a thick putty-coloured rain. After Midhurst's instant involvement in their affairs the inhabitants of this town seemed sombre and withdrawn, going about their business stolidly in the flickering light and barely giving them a glance. They were mostly labourers and small-holders and their wives, Nan decided, peering at them through the gloom, for their horses were mud-caked to the saddle and they themselves were more like dung-smeared scarecrows than men. And her heart sank at the sight of them.

Even a roaring fire in the coffee room of the Dolphin Hotel and a plentiful supply of candles and warm water in their bedroom was quite unable to lift her spirits. Poor Mr Blake was doomed to suffer at the hands of these ignorant peasants, she thought, as she removed her filthy skirts and put on clean clothes and left her muddy shoes for the boot-boy. The lioness had been an omen. 'Twas a folly to come here, she thought. I wished I'd stayed in London with Calverley, and seen Mr Teshmaker and tried to get my business affairs in some sort of order.

Chapter Twenty-nine

The morning of William Blake's trial was very cold and miserably damp. Neither of the fires in the hotel dining-room had taken properly, so the room smelt of soot and struck very chill when Nan and Sophie came shivering down to see what was on offer for breakfast. They made a poor meal, for the kidneys were half done and the toast burnt, and they were still in an ill-humour when they set off in the spitting rain to find the Guildhall, which the landlord assured them was a mere step away from the hotel.

It was a small flint building standing all by itself in the middle of a windswept park, all that remained of an ancient friary, and easy enough to find, since everybody walking out of the hotel into the rain that morning seemed to be heading towards it.

Inside, under high oak beams, the court was assembling, rustics self-conscious in their Sunday best, artists in their London clothes, their neck-cloths dazzling white, the Duke of Richmond who sat in the judgement seat, formidable in red robes and a grey full-bottomed wig, six well-dressed magistrates and twelve uneasy jurymen ranged on two benches to the right of the judgement seat. Mr Blake was already in the court and sitting at a low table in the middle of the room, with his wife Catherine protectively on one side of him and his lawyer, who was a pale unhealthy-looking young man, on the other. None of them looked up as the little courtroom continued to fill. The lawyer was busy studying his papers, Catherine was busy studying her husband's face, and Blake himself, who was pale as wax but seemed composed, was staring fixedly at the table.

'Poor man,' Nan whispered, feeling sorry at the sight of him.

'Would we could help him,' Sophie said. 'He is in God's hands now, I fear.'

Mr Blake's lawyer, who was called Mr Rose, looked ill. From time to time he coughed into a large pocket handkerchief, and the strain of coughing brought tears to his eyes. I can't see him getting Mr Blake acquitted, Nan thought, as the great door was closed. But then the court was being gavilled to order, and the charge was being read. 'That William Blake, engraver of Felpham, had uttered seditious and treasonable expressions, to wit, Damn the King; damn all his subjects; damn his soldiery, they were all slaves; when Bonaparte comes it will be cut throat for cut throat and the weakest must go to the wall; I will help him.'

The words echoed into the high roof of the Guildhall and the jurymen shifted uncomfortably on their wooden benches and looked first at Mr Blake and then at the Duke of Richmond. And Mr Rose coughed into his pocket handkerchief and the Duke hauled his red robe about his shoulders and smiled with satisfaction.

'How do you plead?'

'*Not* guilty.' It was a loud, firm answer and given straight to the jury.

The Duke snorted in obvious disbelief. 'Mr Bowden,' he said.

Mr Bowden, the prosecuting counsel, proceeded to elaborate. He spoke through his nose in a superior sing-song, as though he were chanting in church, but the gist of what he said was far from Christian. Mr Blake, as he was sure the jury would agree, or at any rate might well find themselves thinking, was a known trouble-maker, and the companion of trouble-makers, a friend to known revolutionaries, men whose avowed aim was to establish a republic in this happy monarchy of ours. It did not surprise him in the least that such seditious words should have been spoken by such a man, one who would, he need hardly point out, take a member of His Majesty's dragoons by the arms, the very men who had so gallantly volunteered to save us all from the dastardly attentions of the French, and offer him violence . . .

At which point Mr Blake rose to his feet, eyes blazing and shouted, 'False!' in such a very loud voice that several of the jurymen jumped and the prosecuting counsel was quite put off his stride.

'I will have order in my court, sir!' the Duke said sternly, and he glared at Mr Blake and smiled at Mr Bowden, the difference between the two expressions being so marked it was impossible not to see which side he was on. 'Pray do continue, sir.'

So Mr Bowden continued with a great deal more in the same pompous strain. Nan's attention drifted away. The warmth of the great fire was making her drowsy, and it was hard to concentrate when all the speeches were delivered in such stilted English. She wondered how the gelding was and how she would manage when she sold her half-share of the slave ship and what Cosmo Teshmaker wanted to tell her and how Calverley was faring with the renowned Mr Chaplin. She would much rather be with her lover than sitting in a boring courtroom, and she wondered where he was and what he was doing.

He was in the stables at the Cross-Keys, selecting a team to draw the Ipswich coach that morning.

He and Mr Chaplin had taken to one another at once, for it was plain to both of them that they had a lot in common. They were both young and energetic for a start and they loved their horses.

Mr Chaplin glanced at Colonel Leigh's letter of introduction and then set it aside. 'Ain't who you know, but what you know, to my way a' thinking,' he said, and his grin was open friendliness. 'I need a man to buy fresh horses as and when the need arises, which it does, let me tell 'ee, at least once every week. I own three coaching inns, and ten stables and my business grows. Work for me, Mr Leigh, and I warrant you'll never have an idle moment.'

'Nor never want one,' Calverley said, impressed by the man's direct style.

'He says you're a good judge of horses,' Mr Chaplin said, nodding towards the letter. 'Are you?'

'I believe so.'

'Then pick me a team for the Ipswich stage.'

'On appearance, speed or staying power?'

'Staying power's the more important, but bear appearance in mind, eh.'

He chose four greys while Mr Chaplin watched him at work. 'These for the rear pair,' he explained. 'Good strong haunches to withstand descent, but docile and well matched. This gelding for the left lead. A good spirit, but he'll follow. And this,' indicating the largest of the four, 'this fine fellow to lead. 'Tis an independent spirit with a deal of courage, I should say. He'll need handling, but he's the one.' And he patted the white neck of his choice, while the animal tossed his mane and shuffled with impatience to be moving.

'You know your horses,' Mr Chaplin approved. 'Now, as to pay.'

In the Guildhall the first witness was being called by Mr Bowden,

'Private Scolfield please to step forward.' And Nan woke from her reverie to look at him, for this was the man who had accused Mr Blake of sedition.

He was a surly-looking creature and he gave his evidence as though he had learned it by heart. He had been in the painter's garden, he said, talking to the ostler, when the painter had come out of the house and thrown him bodily out of the garden, at which point the seditious words had been said. He agreed with Mr Bowden that there was no question but that they had been spoken, and spoken in the way he described.

When Mr Rose stood up to cross-examine there was an expectant hush in the little court.

'You were once a sergeant, were you not?'

Private Scolfield couldn't see what that had to do with it. But the counsellor persisted.

'You were, were you not?'

It was admitted grudgingly.

'Would you kindly tell the court the reason why you were degraded.'

The private was annoyed and looked it, but after a long pause he admitted that it was on account of having been a little the worse for wear on one occasion.

'Drunk, you mean?'

'Yes, sir.'

'Drunk and disorderly?'

' 'Twas said.'

'No further questions.'

Then Private Cock, the second witness was called.

Private Cock was nervous and confused. First he maintained that he had heard all the seditious words uttered. 'Yes sir, every single one.' Then under patient cross-examination from the frail Mr Rose, he admitted that he hadn't actually been anywhere near the garden where the fracas was said to have taken place, but had met up with his fellow soldier, beside the Fox Inn, where, so he said, he was certain he'd heard the painter say 'Damn the King!'

'When you began your evidence, you were certain you had heard the painter say all the other words on the charge, were you not?' the counsellor reminded him.

'Sir.'

'Your certainty would appear to be somewhat changeable,' Mr Rose

337

observed, coughing into his handkerchief. 'No further questions, your Grace.'

It appeared that there were no further witnesses for the prosecution either. But Mr Rose said he had several people he wished to call, Mr Grinder, the landlord of 'The Fox' and his wife, Mrs Grinder, Mr Cosen, the miller, Mrs Haynes, wife to the miller's servant and Mr Hosier, gardener to Mr Hayley, 'a gentleman well known to you, your Grace.'

The judge turned his head towards a gentleman sitting in the court and gave him a smile of such frozen courtesy that Nan knew at once that the two were adversaries. A rich man, she thought, looking at Mr Hayley's fine clothes, and used to getting his own way. He had a striking face, his dark eyes and black eyebrows contrasting strongly with soft grey hair, and he wore a plaster on his forehead, which, so Sophie whispered, was due to a fall from his horse. And it was clear from his expression that he disliked the Duke of Richmond as much as the Duke disliked him.

'Are *all* these witnesses really necessary?' the Duke said to Mr Rose, hoisting his robe about him again, and giving a dramatic sigh.

'If they were not, your Grace, I would not call them.'

'Oh, very well. Call them if you will.'

So they were called and gave their evidence, one after the other, hesitantly and in small voices made smaller by the dignity of the place, looking timorously at the great Duke as he glowered down upon them. But however much the Duke and Mr Bowden might bully, they were unshakable in their testimony. They had been as close to Mr Blake and the soldier as they were to the jury, and they hadn't heard one seditious word.

The questioning went on and the afternoon advanced and Nan grew drowsy again. Presently, while the first candles were being lit, the Duke came to a decision. ''Tis plain,' he said, 'that owing to the inordinate number of witnesses called in this case, we are unlikely to conclude today. That being so we will adjourn when the last witness has been heard, and final speeches and summing up will be held over until tomorrow.'

Mr Rose produced a second handkerchief and mopped the sweat from his brow.

'That's a very sick man,' Nan said watching him.

'But an uncommon clever one,' Sophie said. 'I do believe he might succeed.'

'How tiring this trial has been,' Nan said. 'I shall be glad of my dinner and a warm bed.'

But although she was fatigued, it was some time before she could sleep that night.

At first, while Sophie slumbered beside her, she lay wakeful, gazing through the window at the long shadowy shape of the cathedral on the other side of the road, and watching the play of cold moonlight on the green tiles of its roof, thinking of Calverley and the children and Thiss and Bessie and Calverley again. Then the tiles dissolved and became rippling water and floated away and she was in the coach and the lioness was leaping forward straight at her throat. And Mr Blake was sitting in a red and white cart with a rope round his neck and she knew he was going to be offered as live bait, and she cried out to warn him, but no sound came from her mouth, although she was straining every muscle. And the cart was being driven away as the guillotine came crashing down and blood spurted into the air like a fountain, an endless unstoppable fountain. And there was the lioness running alongside the coach and looking at her with its beautiful yellow eyes, and as she looked into its eyes she knew it was Calverley, riding his bay gelding, wheeling and turning and pulling up so sharply that the flailing hooves were right above her head and she was afraid, terribly afraid and yet she didn't know what she was afraid of. And she woke in a sweat with her heart thumping most uncomfortably.

The green tiles were still reassuringly moonlit. It was extremely cold and the hotel was silent all around her. Come now, she scolded herself, this en't the way to go on. And she got up, taking care not to disturb Sophie, and wrapping herself in a blanket like an Indian squaw. Then she raked out the fire and put fresh coals on the embers which were still glowing sufficiently to catch. And then as the coals began to burn and a little warmth reached her cold feet, she set herself to think of cheerful things, so as to put all the nonsense of nightmare out of her head.

You en't a baby, she scolded herself, you're a woman grown, thirty-two years old, and the owner of a company, even if it is running into difficulties at present, and besides that the mother of a daughter very nearly old enough to be married herself. And she turned her mind deliberately away from the memory of Cosmo's alarming letter and

339

thought about her daughter, knowing with comfortable assurance that she would be in bed and asleep.

Actually she was awake and for the last five hours she'd been assisting at a birth. Bessie had gone into labour that morning and a good deal earlier than they'd all expected. It had been a long, painful labour and Mrs Hopkins, the local midwife, had gone off home at ten o'clock that night saying she despaired of seeing the child until morning. So Annie had sat up with her dear Ba, giving her sips of raspberry tea to restore her spirits, rubbing her back which she said 'ached prodigious', stoking the fire and relighting the candles and generally making herself useful.

Neither of them could have guessed what overwhelming misery the birth would bring. They were looking forward to it, quizzing one another about what colour hair the baby would have and what sex it would be, counting the hours until they would be able to hold it in their arms.

It was born just after four in the morning, while Thiss was on his way round to Paradise Row to recall Mrs Hopkins, a boy, perfectly formed, but mauve with lack of oxygen and limp with lack of life. Annie was so frightened she didn't know what to do. She lifted the little slack body, trailing its long grey twisted cord and gave it a shake. 'Oh, breathe my little lovely,' she begged. 'Please breathe. Just give one little breath, that's all.'

'Give 'im ter me! Give 'im ter me!' Bessie begged. 'I'll see to 'im.' And she took the child and held him furiously against her breast, trying to force her nipple into his small, closed mouth. 'Once they feed,' she said, 'that brings the colour into their little cheeks sommink lovely. Oh, if he'd only open 'is eyes.'

But it didn't matter what either of them did, the child was dead, and presently, when Thiss returned with Mrs Hopkins, they all had to accept it.

Bessie wept until she was choking with tears. 'It ain't fair!' she cried over and over again. 'My own little boy, not even ter live fer a minute. Oh, it ain't fair!'

'Hush hush, goosie,' Thiss said, cuddling her and stroking her hair. 'We can have others.'

But that provoked a grief so extreme it frightened him. 'I don't want others. I want this one! This one! Oh, oh, oh, there's no justice in the world.'

340

'Oh Ba!' Annie grieved, standing forlornly at the end of the bed. 'If there was *anything* I could do . . .' But her love for her dear Ba was reduced to anguished impotence by this unexpected, miserable loss. Oh, there was no justice, no justice at all.

Calverley took an early breakfast that morning in the coffee-shop next door to Mr Chaplin's stables in Wood Street. He was feeling well pleased with the start he'd made and was anxious to meet his new employer again and be sent on his first assignment. He sat in front of the fire with his long legs stretched before him and his feet facing the flames and smiled happily to himself.

He was still smiling when an elderly man crossed the room towards him and eased himself into the chimney corner.

'Good day to 'ee, sir,' the man said. ''Tis mortal bad weather.'

''Tis, sir,' Calverley said affably noticing his companion's shabby coat and subservient stoop and assessing him as a servant of some kind to be greeted and ignored. He was very surprised by the man's next words.

'You are a friend to Mrs Easter, I believe.'

'Indeed,' he said smoothly despite his surprise.

'I am one of her minions,' the man said. 'One of her humble minions. 'Tis a great pity about her losses, sir. Oh, a very great pity.'

'Losses?,' Calverley asked, instantly alerted. 'What losses are these, sir?'

'Do you not know sir?' the man said, and his surprise was so marked it seemed feigned. 'She has taken a very great loss on the commodity market.' And he dropped his voice to a confidential whisper. ''Tis said she could not afford to pay her taxes and was forced to sell six shops in consequence.'

'Tush, man!' Calverley said, deciding to make light of it. ''Tis a bagatelle. Business is all a matter of profit and loss. Do you fear for your job, sir?'

'When the great stumble, the lesser fall,' the man said, nodding and assuming a wise expression. 'Howsomever, it may be as you say.' He drank from his pewter mug for a while and then looked up at Calverley again. His old face was malevolent. 'Ah well, sir,' he said. 'I mustn't keep 'ee. I just thought you should know of it sir, being you're a friend of hers.'

'Obliged to 'ee,' Calverley said automatically. His mind was still

341

digesting the news. If his Nan really had grown poor, he would have to find another lover to give him bed and lodging. What a cursed nuisance! I will find me another after my very first trip, he decided.

The old man had eased himself back onto his feet and was preparing to leave. 'My respects to Mrs Easter, sir,' he said. 'Tell her you spoke to me. She'll be glad on it, I'm certain sure.'

'What name?' Calverley asked.

'Mr Peabody,' the old man said, and now his malevolence was unmistakable. 'Mr Peabody of the Westminster Walk. She will remember.'

Back in Chichester the second day of the trial of Mr William Blake began late. Mr Rose looked more ill than ever and had arrived in the Guildhall nearly an hour later than the given time. But he seemed to be recovering as Mr Bowden made his final speech, reminding the jury that 'the nation is indebted to the military at this hour of national peril when invasion is expected hourly' and stressing that it 'would ill behove men of conscience and patriotism to allow a known trouble-maker to go free, if they knew him to be guilty of uttering the seditious words as charged.'

It was a persuasive speech and delivered straight at the jury, who quailed before it. Listening quite closely this morning, Nan wondered how Mr Rose could possibly counter it. But she need not have worried, for his final speech was masterly too, in its own quiet way.

'Here then gentlemen,' he began, 'is a charge attended with circumstances of the most extraordinary nature. A man comes out of his house for the purpose of addressing a malignant and unintelligible discourse to those who are most likely to injure him for it.' He smiled at the jury, knowingly, and some of them smiled back, as if to show that they could see how ridiculous it was. Then he simply went through the evidence, quietly and between bouts of coughing, reminding them of what had been said, and pointing up its significance. 'If,' he said, 'the words were spoken in the garden, the ostler must have heard them. If they were uttered before the public house Mrs Grinder must have heard them too. Yet you have heard them declare that neither of them heard any such words. In fact they totally overthrow the testimony of these soldiers . . .' There were two bright-red fever spots burning in his cheeks and he was unsteady on his feet, staggering back a pace or two and holding onto the table for support.

'A chair for Mr Rose,' the Duke ordered. And a chair was brought forward.

'I shall recover by and by,' Mr Rose said. Then he dropped his head onto the table in a faint.

There was a buzz of concern. Was the poor man too ill to continue? Nan wondered. What would happen now? Had he said enough to convince the jury? And they waited while Mr Blake stood beside his prostrate defender and the Duke consulted with his magistrates.

'It is the opinion of this court,' he announced, 'that it will be beneficial to all concerned if I proceed to the summing up. We see nothing to be gained by a further postponement.'

It was a rapid summary and while it was being given Mr Rose lifted his head and smiled weakly at Mr Blake and took a sip of brandy from somebody's hip flask. And at last, at last, the jurymen were being asked to give their verdict.

It was so quiet in the court as they waited for the foremen to announce their decision that the crackle of the logs on the fire was as loud as the breaking of glass. But it was a perfect decision and given clearly. 'We find the defendant not guilty, your Grace.'

The entire room erupted into cheers and applause and shrill whistles, and caps were tossed into the air, and Nan and Sophie hugged one another with excitement and Mr Hayley strode across the court, hand outstretched so that the Duke had no option but to take it and shake it, 'I congratulate your Grace!' he said with heavy, happy sarcasm, 'that you have at last had the gratification of seeing an honest man honourably delivered from an infamous prosecution.'

'Obliged to 'ee,' the Duke said sourly. And was roundly applauded for his sentiments. 'Clear the court!'

Nan and Sophie were still quite light-headed when they finally left the Guildhall. Relief had come so quickly after the interminable length of the trial, they'd hardly had time to adjust to it. They'd congratulated Mr Blake, of course, before he and Mr Rose went off with Mr Hayley, and they'd told one another how splendid it all was. And still laughing and talking, they'd walked down North Street towards the market cross, warm with excitement even in the cold air. And as they turned into East Street Nan couldn't help noticing what a cheerful, friendly town Chichester was, as people nodded and smiled in their direction.

Why, even the mud had dried. And when they got to the Dolphin, there was Mr Fuseli in a chaise, ready and waiting before the door.

'I came to hear the verdict,' he said, 'A good verdict? Ja. Now ve travel homvards.'

But Nan had no desire to share a long journey with Mr Fuseli. 'Thank 'ee, no,' she said. 'I need a good night's rest before I journey.'

So they set off without her, waving quite gaily from both windows. And she walked back into the hotel, glad to be alone.

And there was Calverley Leigh sitting in an armchair beside the fire with his long legs at full stretch and using up a deal of space.

'Nan, my charmer,' he said, standing up to greet her. 'Were you in at the kill?'

Her pleasure at the sight of him was chilled by the mockery in his tone. 'What kill, pray?' she said.

'Why, the mad poet's,' he said. ''Twas his trial you attended, was it not? When does he hang?'

His ignorance annoyed her, especially after the cruelty of Mr Honeybun and the tension of that trial. 'Fie on you, Calverley,' she growled at him. 'How could you say such a thing? He's a good man, so he is, who never did any harm to any living creature.'

'He was a spy, was he not?' Calverley said, but he didn't sound quite so sure of himself.

'That,' Nan said fixing him with a glare like a cat's sharp claws, 'is a load a' squit, which you know right well, and if you don't, the more shame to 'ee.'

'I only repeat what I've heard,' he said, even more crestfallen.

'A fool's trick!' she said. 'I wonder at you.' And she swept upstairs to change for dinner.

'Nan, my dear!' he said, following her, and taking the stairs two at a time. 'I take it all back. Every word.'

'Don't speak to me!' she shouted back at him, 'for I can't abide it! You should ha' stayed in London!'

'Don't 'ee dare to tell me what to do.'

'I shall do as I please!'

She had reached the door of her room, but he was too quick for her, and had interposed his long, handsome body between her and the door knob before her hand could touch it. 'No,' he said, bristling with anger and desire, 'you won't!'

344

'I will!' she shouted, bristling back, brown eyes glistening, dark hair bushing from under her green bonnet, wide mouth red with rage.

The sight of her, so wild and fierce, attracted him beyond anger. 'Nan,' he said, and the name was spoken so tenderly it was a love-call, an entreaty, almost an embrace. And desire rose in her too, suddenly and despite her anger and her fatigue, and she put out her hand, but whether to try to open the door or to plead with him or just because she wanted to touch him, she was too confused to know.

And he caught the hand and held it and drew her body towards his, bending his head to kiss her as they moved together. And the kiss was like a homecoming. 'My lovely Nan,' he said, between kisses. 'Oh, how I love you.'

After the third kiss she realized that he had opened the door and walked backwards into her room while they were kissing, and annoyance flickered in her again because he had enough self-control to play such tricks even when emotion was running so strongly in him. But then he was unbuttoning her gloves to kiss her wrists, and removing her coat to kiss her throat, and it was so delicious that now she couldn't remember what they'd been quarrelling about. 'We've both got too many clothes on,' she said.

''Tis a matter may soon be amended,' he told her amending it.

It was the most rewarding love-making and all the better for being unexpected.

Afterwards they lay among the blankets in a bed made warm by love and slept with contentment. The chambermaid arrived to ask if they required warm water to wash for dinner. She made up the fire, seeing how low it was, but they didn't stir. It wasn't until the afternoon had faded into darkness and she returned to light the candles and draw the curtains, that Nan opened her eyes and found enough energy to thank her.

'Shall I bring warm water for 'ee, ma'am?'

Calverley was still fast asleep. 'In half an hour,' Nan said.

But when the girl was gone she made no effort to get up. How ridiculous lovers' quarrels are, she thought, so quick and furious, and so easily made up. Oh, the world was a good place after all. Mr Blake had been acquitted, and her dear Calverley had not only come to London to live with her, but had followed her all the way down to this place too. There was no doubt how dearly he loved her.

'Um,' he said, stirring as he began to wake. And as he turned he

345

pulled the blanket to one side, revealing the full length of one side of his body, his chest tawny in the candlelight and muscular even in sleep, one golden-brown arm, one long white leg. Why, she thought, admiring him, he is only a leopard to the waist, below he is just a pale white man, the same as everybody else. And the thought was touching as well as surprising.

'You have white legs,' she said, stroking the one she could see.

'Um', he agreed, 'else I should not be able to stand.'

'But *white*.'

'Don't see the sun,' he explained. 'Trousers being required by army regulations.'

The mention of army regulations reminded her. 'Did Mr Chaplin give you a job?'

'He did. Start in a week.'

'I am glad on it.'

'Um.'

'I almost forget to tell 'ee,' she said. 'I have bought a horse.'

He was interested at once. 'Could you afford it?'

She was angered by the question. 'Why should I not, pray?'

Her anger revealed more than she knew. Perhaps Mr Peabody had been right. But this was not the time to press her about it, this was the time for charm and interest. 'What sort of horse?' he asked.

She told him all about it.

'If that's the case,' he said, touched by her concern for the animal, 'I daresay we had best return by way of the stables and see it.'

Chapter Thirty

Nan's gelding was still on his feet. His wounds were angry and he put no weight on his injured leg, but he was still standing.

'If he stands,' Calverley said, 'he'll do.' Privately he thought the poor beast should have been put out of its misery, but as Nan would certainly not agree with that, he kept his opinion to himself. However, he thought he ought to warn her that the animal's prospects were poor. 'He'll never walk more than a few paces,' he said, 'and then 'twill be a struggle. You will need to stable him here for the rest of his days, I fear.'

'Indeed you won't, sir,' the ostler said, aggrieved at the suggestion. 'This here stable's a-crowded out fit ter bust, sir. There hain't room fer the haminal perpetual, not if it was ever so, and there's a hend on it.'

Nan looked at him shrewdly, estimating whether she could bully him, and decided against it.

'If that's the size of it,' she said, 'we'll have a cart made for him, a good stout cart with padded sides to protect him on the road, and he can be drawn to London, so he can, poor crittur, just so soon as ever he's fit enough, and stay in my stables.'

There's no gainsaying this woman, Calverley thought, admiring her. And as she's prepared to spend money like this on an injured animal she can hardly have sustained any very great loss. Perhaps that wretched man was simply making mischief.

The ostler was so taken aback he could find no other objection. So it was agreed.

They returned to London in high spirits. And were met at the door by an anxious housemaid stammering the news of 'Mrs Thistlethwaite's poor baby, God rest his soul.' Nan went straight upstairs to commiserate, and Calverley straight to Covent Garden to buy a bunch of snow-drops.

Bessie was touched by his attention. ''Tis a good man, mum,' she said to Nan, as Annie arranged the little flowers in one of her mother's blue vases.

'He goes to Brighton tomorrow to fetch his horse, for he works in London now, with Mr Chaplin,' Nan told her. 'We shall see a deal more of him, I daresay.'

'And very welcome I'm sure mum,' Bessie said. But then she looked at the cradle which was still standing empty beside her bed and the tears welled into her eyes again. 'I'm so sorry mum. 'Tis jest I'm so low, that's all 'tis.'

'You shall have good nourishing food to build up your strength,' Nan told her, 'I shall see to it. Now rest, Bessie, my dear. Rest all you can.' And as soon as you're asleep, she thought, Thiss shall remove that cradle to the attic where it can't be a plague to 'ee.

'I shall be better when I'm up and about,' poor Bessie said, wiping her eyes. 'Work takes yer mind off, don't it mum.'

But although she agreed, Nan had other matters on her mind besides work. As soon as she was sure that Bessie had everything she could possibly need, she took the pony-cart and drove it to see Mr Teshmaker.

'Now,' she said when they were seated beside the fire in his little office. 'What is it you have to say?'

He was very uncomfortable and looked it. 'It is grave news, I fear, Mrs Easter.'

'Then out with it quick. Grave news grows worse with waiting.'

'Not to put too fine a point upon it,' he said. 'I fear you have been cheated. I went to the shipping office just before you left to enquire about the *Esmeralda*, which I have done daily, as you know, for some considerable time.'

'Yes, yes.' Impatiently.

He gathered breath and courage. 'There are no monies coming to you from that direction, I fear. None at all. The ship was lost on her second voyage and all trace of any transaction with you or anybody else went with her.'

A total loss! It was staggering news. 'Was she not underwritten?'

'No, madam. Slave ships rarely are.'

'I did not know of her cargo when I entered upon this business,'

Nan felt she should explain. 'I learnt of it but a few days since. Was she carrying slaves when she sank?'

'No one could tell me,' Cosmo said. 'For all I know she could be still afloat and trading. There are prodigious rogues in the business.'

''Tis a great loss,' Nan said, 'but I tell 'ee, Mr Teshmaker, I feel well rid of such trade.' But she was casting about in her mind to see how on earth she was going to sustain the loss.

'Shall you sell more properties?' Cosmo asked.

She considered it quietly. 'We run at a loss, I daresay.'

'In some weeks we earn a little.'

'But in most we lose, is't not so?'

He agreed that it was.

'We will not sell,' she decided. 'Sales cause gossip and gossip has an adverse effect on trade, and besides I have my shopkeepers to consider. When I started this business 'twas simply to earn enough money to feed my children and pay the rent, and in those days Mr Teshmaker, I thought no further. Now 'tis another matter altogether. Now I employ other people, more than a hundred other people, as you'll allow. 'Ten't a matter to be taken lightly, nor sold to pay taxes, nor allowed to fail. When great ones falter lesser ones fall. I will give my mind to it. There will be some other way, I'm sure on it.'

Mr Teshmaker said he agreed but he looked extremely dubious. 'We have four more months before we have to pay tax again,' he said.

Her energy was returning to her. Mr Blake had been acquitted, the gelding lived, there was always hope. 'There are still papers to sell,' she said, 'and news a-plenty. Someway or other we shall survive, you have my word on it.'

But it was horribly difficult, for it was winter and sales were always lower in bad weather. She cut back her expenditure in every way she could. Shops and reading-rooms stayed unpainted, gutters unrepaired, bills unpaid for as long as her creditors would allow. From time to time she borrowed what money she could from such bankers as she could persuade.

And Calverley watched and calculated and renewed his search for that long-dreamed-of heiress.

Matters began to improve a little when the spring arrived, for that season brought chill winds and sharp showers and a renewed threat of invasion, with British frigates prowling the Channel and spies returning with reports of huge troop movements in Boulogne.

''Tis all good for trade,' Nan said, reading the latest reports in *The Times*. But not good enough. What with the property tax and the rising cost of paper, her profits were still only marginal, and there were more debts to pay off than she could bear to think about. 'Would there were more papers for me to sell.'

And suddenly, one blustery March morning, there were.

She and Thiss arrived in Printing House Square to find the young Mr Walter tousled with excitement.

'My dear Mrs Easter,' he said, rushing to assist her from the pony-cart. 'Come in! Come in! The steam press is arrived. Oh, what a day this has been! I cannot tell you how thrilling.' His hair was standing on end and he was shaking with agitation. ''Tis the very latest, a Koenig and Bauer. 'Twill print two thousand sheets in an hour. Think of it! What a difference, eh? Two thousand, and yesterday we could only manage a mere two hundred and fifty. I could double the size of the paper. There is quite enough news to fill such an increase. I shall send out correspondents to all the major cities in the country. Oh, I cannot tell you what this will mean.'

Nan already knew exactly what it would mean, and exactly what she intended to do about it. Her trade could increase tenfold with such production. But with a little daring her profits could increase even further. Now at least there was a chance to change her fortunes. She followed Mr Walter into the print-room, gathering her wits and her energies.

The new machine was squatting in the middle of the room like some ungainly black beast, smelling of oil. It was enormous and uncompromising and modern, and it made the wooden hand-press look tatty and old-fashioned. Nan was very impressed by it. There was no question about the change and power it would bring. Two thousand papers in an hour were even more than she'd been calculating for. The mere thought of it excited her.

'When would you start to print with this machine?' she asked.

'Next Monday, Mrs Easter. Next Monday. Just think of it.' He plunged both hands into his hair and tugged at it, as though he were trying to lift himself off the ground in his rapture.

'How many copies do you intend to print?'

The question sobered him. 'Well now, as to that,' he said. 'I intend to double my numbers to five hundred at first, and see how they sell. Then I shall gradually increase, if there is demand.'

She had foreseen his caution. 'How if I were to offer to buy all two thousand copies every day starting on Monday?'

He was instantly interested. 'Could you withstand such a loss?'

She had no intention of making a loss. 'If you will grant me sole rights to buy your papers,' she said, 'and we can fix an adequate price for 'em, I will take two thousand copies every day, and more when there is news to warrant it.'

'You have the means to distribute?'

''Course,' she said, cheerfully, ignoring Thiss' surprise. 'Is't a bargain?'

'How of the price?'

'35 per cent of the cover price, which I would advise you to maintain,' she said at once, having considered that beforehand too.

Mr Walter took a notebook from the pocket of his jacket and a pencil from behind his ear, and did a few rapid calculations, using the side of his shining machine as an easel. 'Yes,' he said, nodding with satisfaction. 'I do believe we have a bargain.'

They had, and it turned out to be an extremely profitable one.

'Drive straight to the shop,' Nan instructed when they left Printing House Square. 'Matthew will need to bestir himself this morning and take this batch to be stamped. We have other matters to attend to.'

'You take the cake, mum,' Thiss said. 'Blessed if yer don't. Where we goin' ter store all that lot? Two thousand copies mum, 'tis a mortal pile a' paper.'

'Aha!' his mistress said, face ablaze with devilment, 'I know just the place. I've had my eye on un for weeks, so I have, just biding the moment. 'Tis at the other end of the Strand and just a few doors from Somerset House, which will be handy for stamping, you'll allow, and on top of that 'tis right bang opposite the Bull and Mouth. Just think of all the trade a-rolling in through those doors! And no mere shop neither! Hasten you up! We've work to do.'

Half an hour later, when they'd collected Mr Teshmaker and given poor Matthew his new instructions, they struggled back along the crowded Strand to their new premises, and Thiss could see what she meant by no mere shop. The ground floor of this building was more like four shops rolled into one, and above them four further storeys gave ample room for storage and offices and reading-rooms and a great deal more besides. He stared up at it in amazement at her daring.

'You'd need a fortune ter rent a place like that,' he said.

'A fortune,' she told him, jumping out of the cart, 'is what I intend to make, Mr Thistlethwaite. And to make a fortune, you spend one. I mean to have a shop in every main thoroughfare, where the world and his wife may come and buy. I tell you, Thiss, the old days are over. There will be no more wandering the streets hoping to sell the odd paper or two. Now we shall deliver to the door or sell over the counter and we shall sell thousands. Thousands, I tell you.' Her face was glowing with excitement, her wide mouth spread in a smile of triumph. 'I been a-waiting for this for a mighty long time. Now drive me to Mr Tewson's bank.'

Mr Tewson was horrified by her plans. 'But you have no capital, Mrs Easter,' he pointed out. 'This loan you require is preposterous.'

'This loan I require,' she said firmly, 'will earn you a prodigious return, Mr Tewson. I am willing to pay you over the odds.'

'How far over the odds, as you put it, if I may make so bold as to inquire?'

I have hooked my fish, Nan thought. She could almost see the calculations going on behind the banker's bland expression.

'Two per cent,' she said. It was a deal too much but she was so certain of success.

So the loan was granted.

Six new shops were rented in as many days, and twelve assistants hired to man them, and a fleet of carts acquired and painted in her green-and-gold livery ready to carry the papers from place to place. The new headquarters were furnished and decorated, with shelves in the storehouse and chairs in the reading-room, and the green-and-yellow sign painted boldly above all four doors.

And Mr Walter's first two thousand arrived from his new steam press, bailed and stamped and ready for sale on the day the famous spy L'Ami sent word that Napoleon had ordered his ships to break through the British blockade.

It was terrifying news, for it meant that the long-dreaded invasion could happen at any time. By patrolling the Channel and Spanish coast, Nelson and the British fleet had kept all French and Spanish men o' war pinned in harbour for the past two years, but as everybody knew there were many harbours and it took constant watchfulness. If the

French Admiral Ganteaume really had been ordered out of Brest with his twenty-one ships of the line and heaven only knows how many frigates, and Admiral Villeneuve were to break out of Toulon, with all his enormous fleet, they could be sailing up the Channel within days. And then Napoleon, who had been waiting malevolently at Boulogne for so long with his sixty thousand highly-trained troops and great guns and the flat-bottomed boats to carry them across, would most certainly invade, just as he'd been threatening for years. It was the most alarming news since the war began, and it sold Nan's entire purchase within half an hour of its delivery to her shops.

During the next few weeks the rumours intensified. In April news came through that Admiral Villeneuve had indeed broken out of Toulon and that a huge French fleet was now assembling in the West Indies. Fifty ships of the line, hundreds of frigates, more than even Nelson could withstand. The numbers increased with the panic. Soon the *Morning Chronicle* was reporting, 'Nobody in England can sleep in peace at night.' And all along the south coast the troops were on constant alert.

It was the most anxious summer anyone could remember, and as anxiety is always frantic for the latest information, Nan's newspaper shops were besieged, morning and evening. *The Times* was the most popular and frequently read of all the news-sheets in London, a fact which Mr Walter's competitors were not slow to appreciate. Soon his revolutionary presses were followed by others at the *Morning Chronicle*, the *Morning Post*, the *Observer* and even the *Daily Advertiser*. Other, lesser news-shops began to appear too, but they were never serious rivals to Nan, since she held the monopoly on *The Times* and very quickly bought up first options on all the other major newspapers too, so that her competitors had to come to her warehouse for supplies and pay her price, whatever it was. And it was often very high indeed.

Despite the panic all around her, Nan was too busy to be afraid. By the end of June she had fifteen more shops, by the end of July twenty-two, and her sales had increased by far more than the tenfold she had originally estimated. 'If Boney comes,' she said to Calverley when he got back from the Horncastle Fair, 'he will find me a rich woman, so he will.'

It was just like her, Calverley thought, to say 'if Boney comes' when everybody else was saying 'when'. 'There's a great demand for horses too, I can tell 'ee,' he said. 'Prices were up by more than a quarter at Horncastle Fair.'

'Did you get what you went for?'

'Aye. I did.'

'And extra pay to boot, I'll wager.'

'Aye. I did.'

It was a rich life, despite the panic.

But then a new rumour began that Lord Nelson had sailed after Villeneuve to the West Indies and that the Channel was undefended. So even when the Channel grew choppy with storms, the fear of invasion was still acute. People living along the exposed south coast felt vulnerable without the certainty that their hero was protecting them.

'If only them pesky Frenchies would stand and fight,' Thiss said, echoing the general sentiment. 'Lord Nelson 'ud soon show 'em what's what if it come to a battle.'

'Cowards,' Mrs Pennington said, narrowing her little eyes malevolently. 'Cowards to a man. They may be good at terrorizing women and children. That I don't doubt. That I will allow. But when it comes to blood and steel, that's quite another story.' And she gave such a derisive sniff that her long nose looked as though it was going to explode.

And then in August Nelson suddenly returned to England. 'Which,' as Mr Walter pointed out both privately to his friends and publicly in editorials, 'he would hardly have done had there been any immediate danger.' He spent a month at Merton with Lady Hamilton and their little daughter, and made frequent visits to London, where he was cheered wherever he went. And then equally suddenly he was gone again. London was full of rumours that the French fleet had gathered in Cadiz and that Nelson, who had sailed from Portsmouth in his flag ship *Victory*, was off to join the British fleet which was lying in wait for their enemies just off the Spanish shore.

And after that, as was the way once a fleet was at sea, there was no news at all. The armies defending the coast remained on alert. The famous spy L'Ami sent no reports. And there was only speculation to sell newspapers. But by then the mixture of excitement and fear was so intense, that the mere words 'Invasion' or 'Nelson' or 'British Fleet' in bold black print on a poster was enough to empty the shop of newssheets.

And finally on November 5th, news did come. And thrilling, heart-rending, marvellous, terrible news it was.

Nan could see that something important had happened the minute she set foot inside Printing House Square, for the place was in an uproar, with apprentices in tears and the printers, who were usually the most phlegmatic of men, actually running from place to place.

Mr Walter stood in the middle of the storm, looking more dishevelled than she'd ever seen him, with one pocket hanging from his jacket by a thread and ink stains spotting his cravat and his hair standing on end.

'There has been a battle, at last,' he said breathlessly. 'Off Cape Trafalgar, a glorious victory, the French and Spanish fleets quite overwhelmed, most of their ships captured, a glorious victory. But dearly bought, I fear, oh most dearly bought. Poor Lord Nelson is dead. The great, gallant Nelson. I had it post haste from the Admiralty at four o'clock this morning from dispatches brought by a lieutenant from the schooner *Pickle*. Arrived at the Admiralty at one in the morning so he did, and the First Lord in bed. They have sent to Windsor to tell the King. Oh, glorious, terrible news.'

Such longed-for success and such awful tragedy, all at one and the same time, was too much to endure. Nan was struck dumb by it. How could such a hero be dead? It was unthinkable.

'We are all safe from invasion now,' Mr Walter said in an attempt to comfort. 'Without a fleet Napoleon would never dare to cross the Channel.'

'Lord Nelson dead!' Nan grieved, trying to comprehend it. She stood beside Mr Walter's packing table and read his editorial idly, for want of something better to do, since a copy of that morning's paper lay open just underneath her fingers. 'We know not whether we should mourn or rejoice. The country has gained the most splendid and decisive victory that has ever graced the annals of England: but it has been dearly purchased. *The great and gallant Nelson is no more.*' And as she read the words, she realized how such news would sell. 'Print you treble the number this morning,' she instructed. 'I will take all of 'em.'

They sold so well that soon, to her great annoyance, pirate copies of *The Times* were being run off and sold on the streets. And the next day when all flags were flying at half mast and every window in the City of London was draped in purple and black, Mr Walter printed the full text of Admiral Collingwood's heart-broken dispatch, and the demand was even greater. For as the *Chronicle* said, 'If ever there was a hero who merited the honour of a public funeral, it is the pious, the noble and the gallant NELSON, the darling of the British Navy whose death has plunged a whole nation into the deepest grief.'

'Since the new printing machines came to London, there en't a single piece of news that en't made me rich,' Nan confided to her old friend Sophie. 'And the more terrible the news the greater the profit on it.'

''Tis the saddest world,' Sophie said mournfully. 'How we shall fare without Lord Nelson I cannot imagine.'

'His funeral procession will pass right underneath my windows in the Strand,' Nan said, practical as ever. 'Would you care to join me there, my dear? 'Twill be an uncommon fine spectacle.'

And so it was. The column of mourners was so long that the head of it had reached St Paul's before the end set out from Whitehall. There was the Prince of Wales in a fine, sober chariot and scores of noblemen looking suitably sad, and ministers and admirals and generals a-plenty, important as peacocks in their dazzling uniforms. And in the middle of it all a plain black funeral car escorted by two lines of ordinary sailors, in tarred hats and sailcloth trousers and stained striped shirts, walking with the swaggering roll of the sea-faring man, some scarred, some weeping and all immensely proud.

Nan took her entire household to the Strand to watch the procession, even poor, batty old Mr Dibkins, 'It being history, the like of which you en't never likely to see again', and Thiss held little Pollyanna up on the window sill to see it all, and Bessie wept tears of pride, clinging to Annie's arm, and Billy and Johnnie watched awestruck.

But Nan was thinking how extraordinary it was that this great victory and this great man's death had made her a rich woman. For she was. A very rich woman. And only a few months ago she'd been scrimping and saving. Her accounts had now become so complicated that she had handed them over in their entirety to Mr Teshmaker, but his weekly reports showed that her profits were increasing by the day. And this funeral would increase them even further. A rich woman. A very rich woman.

Standing beside her, Calverley Leigh was thinking much the same thing. He had noticed the expensive cloth of her new coat, and how many new gowns she'd had made that summer, and what a splendid necklace she wore about her throat, pearls and diamonds, no less. And it occurred to him that he might, he just might, be standing right beside the rich heiress he'd been hoping to find for so long. How if his dear

Nan turned out to be his rich wife too? 'Twas a tempting idea in all conscience.

She turned and smiled at him, and the diamonds at her throat were brighter than her eyes.

Chapter Thirty-one

Whether or not he had found his rich wife, there was no doubt that travelling the country as an agent for Mr Chaplin was very much to Calverley's liking. Although he missed the easy companionship of the regiment there were plenty of new friends among coachmen and horse traders. And on top of that there was the added pleasure of a return to the chase.

There were pretty girls a-plenty in every town he visited, and he was far enough from Nan and Chelsea to flirt without fear of discovery, to stay just long enough to achieve a conquest should he desire it, and still be able to escape the clinging that so often followed. So he rapidly established himself as a Romeo again. He might have lost the first, fresh charm of his youth but he was still deucedly handsome, damme if he wasn't, and a dog with the ladies, whether they were his delicious new light o' loves or his old passionate Nan.

He and his old passionate Nan had settled into an easy life as established lovers that suited them both rather well. His frequent travelling kept them apart just long enough to give their relationship an edge and prevent them from getting bored with each other, and her increasing wealth gave them the creature comforts they both enjoyed.

In that first winter, she bought him into one of the lesser gentlemen's clubs, Goosegogs in Jermyn Street, where he soon felt marvellously at home. It was one of the smaller and less prestigious establishments and not to be compared with White's or Watier's where the dandies and the gentlemen of quality foregathered, but the atmosphere was just right for him, raffish and mocking and light-hearted. A man could drink himself speechless if he wished or sit up all night at the gaming table or brag without fear of correction or tell risqué stories or give the eye to the young women in the street outside. And the port was excellent.

Annie and Billy were happy about this new arrangement, but Johnnie still didn't approve. No matter what his brother and sister found to say on Mr Leigh's behalf, he remained obdurately opposed to his presence in the house.

'It ain't proper,' he said, from the puritanical rectitude of his twelve-and-a-half-years. 'Mama had a good husband. Everybody says so. A fine man. 'Tis my opinion she lowers herself allowing that man to live with her.'

'Fie on you, Johnnie,' Annie said, gently, looking up from her sewing to rebuke him. 'There's no harm in Mr Leigh, and even if there were 'tain't our business to say so.'

'If he's such a fine man,' Johnnie insisted, his face sombre with disapproval, 'he would marry her. He takes advantage of her good nature.'

'Why should they marry?' Billy put in from his seat beside the fire. ' 'Tain't the style. Damme, half of London society take lovers.' He would be fourteen in March and took a detailed interest in the love affairs of the ton.

'Hush up!' Annie warned. 'He's coming upstairs.'

From time to time, when he was at home working with the horses in Mr Chaplin's London stables Calverley would take over one or two little jobs for Nan, collecting weekly takings, or banking them, or driving her to distant shops and reading-rooms. If she *was* going to be his wife, he might as well behave as though he were her husband. Occasionally, of course, no more than that, for there was no point in overdoing things.

There was still plenty of news and an ever-increasing demand for newspapers. After his defeat at Trafalgar, Bonaparte had withdrawn his Army of England from Boulogne at last, and having renamed it the Grand Army, marched it eastwards across Europe to attack the Austrians and the Russians. Just before Christmas news came through that he had taken Vienna and in the New Year reports arrived that there had been a battle at a place called Austerlitz and the Austrians and Russians had suffered a terrible defeat, but as it was all happening on the other side of Europe and no British troops had been involved, it could be read and enjoyed quite comfortably in England.

'That Boney's a wicked man,' Bessie said. 'Good job he's abroad tormenting the Russkies.'

It was an opinion shared by a good many others, including Nan.

And then, just when sales were booming, negotiations for three new shops south of the Thames were inexplicably held up. The rents had been settled and the agreements were ready for signature, but the solicitors procrastinated. Fortunately Calverley was at home and ready to be useful. 'I'll take a stroll in that direction,' he said to Nan. 'See what a little charm will do, eh?'

'Ask for the Lambeth Road property in the first instance,' she advised. 'I en't opened negotiations for that one, so 'twould be as well to secure it first.'

He was extremely put out, when his 'little charm' produced a letter from the company pulling out of the deal altogether, Lambeth Road property and all.

'I can't understand it,' he said to Nan. ' 'Tis all so without reason, damme.'

'Cosmo shall look into it,' she said, frowning with displeasure.

' 'Twas all arranged, believe me,' he tried to explain. 'There was no ill-will I promise you.'

'There is now,' she said, frowning more than ever. 'Oh, I've a fair idea what's a-going on. It en't you, Calverley. I'll lay odds 'tis that varmint Sir Osmond, blocking my business again, rot him.' And as he was perplexed, she told him all about her powerful nephew, and the way he'd been using his contacts to thwart her. ' 'Tis a venomous wretch, so it is. I thought to have seen the last of his spite, but this has all the makings.'

And so it proved to be. Cosmo brought the news to her in her office in the Strand four days later. The lawyers acting for the vendors in each case in question were also employed by Sir Osmond Easter. Pressure had plainly been brought to bear.

Nan was so cross she couldn't sit still. 'Unprincipled wretch!' she said, pacing about the office. 'Have we to start another round of useless letters? Rot him, why can't he leave us along?'

'What I cannot understand,' Calverley said, 'is why they withdrew their offer on the Lambeth Road property. I made no mention of your name during that particular transaction, so how did they know I was acting on your behalf?'

'Your association has been – um – known to Sir Osmond for some considerable time, sir,' Cosmo said. 'There was mention of it several years ago.'

'Is that true?' he asked Nan.

She had no time or taste for delving into the past. 'Yes, yes,' she said tetchily. 'What of it? It don't signify now.'

'It may have signified then,' he said. He was remembering the general's words when he left the regiment, 'Ladies and gossip,' he'd said. What if Sir Osmond Easter had passed on some gossip to influence the general. 'There was no real reason for Captain Mauleverer to refuse to sell me my commission, everybody said so, yet that is what he did. How if pressure were brought to bear then too?'

She stopped prowling and stood still to look at him. 'Very like!' she said. 'Such an action would be quite in character. Oh, I should like to get my hands on him. I'd show him a thing or two, so I would!'

It was really rather flattering to have her fling to his defence like that.

'Would you care for me to write to the gentleman?' Cosmo asked, cautious as ever.

She made a decision, chin in the air, face hard with fury. 'No,' she said, 'I would not. This has been a-going on quite long enough. 'Tis bad enough he's been interfering in my business affairs, but to block Mr Leigh's promotion is an act of sheer spite. Ugh! I en't a-tolerating that. I shall go down to Ippark myself, so I shall, and sort the varmint out once and for all.'

'Is that wise, Mrs Easter?' Cosmo demurred.

But wise or not there was no stopping her.

She made the most careful preparations for her second visit to Ippark. First she went to Messrs Harding and Howell's Grand Fashionable Magazine in Pall Mall, and bought herself a dress-length of the most expensive muslin in the shop, creamy in colour and embroidered with tiny flowers in pink and red and yellow. She ordered it to be made up for her in the very latest style, high in the waist and with a full straight skirt and long, ruched sleeves. Then she bought a pair of shoes made of red morocco leather and doeskin gloves and a little enamelled fob watch to hang upon her gown and a triple-crowned bonnet with a flattened brim that would reveal her face, for she had no intention of hiding from any adversary, however powerful. Finally she chose a length of fine red wollen cloth to make up into a long-sleeved spencer, that would button to the chin in case the day was chill but was cut away below the waist to reveal the full expense and glory of that muslin gown.

Then she made her very first major purchase as a person of rank and style, which was extremely satisfactory and gave her a pleasant sense of the power and influence that her new money had given her. She bought a new town chaise from Mr Chaplin and after knowledgeable advice from Thiss and Calverley, a pair of fine bay geldings at the London horse fair.

'An excellent pair!' Calverley said, approving her choice. 'They move well, damme if they don't, and they stand over a lot of ground. 'Tis my opinion you couldn't have bought better.'

And Thiss waxed quite eloquent over their wide brows and their big ears and their gentle eyes. 'They'll be a joy to drive, so they will, after ol' Pepperpot,' who it had to be admitted grew more and more cussed the older he got.

So the chaise was painted in her green-and-gold livery, sign and all, and Thiss was bedecked in a splendid new livery of his own, with a green topcoat and a coachman's hat and a flourish of fine linen at his throat, and the two of them set out to vanquish Sir Osmond.

Nan had written to her adversary with icy politeness offering him a choice of three dates on which she proposed to visit him, 'there being several matters which require our combined consideration,' and signing herself, 'Your aunt, Nan Easter.' And as he hadn't bothered to send an answer she chose the first date for him, a mild day at the end of May when the blackbirds and thrushes sang from every hedgerow and the sun was giving out quite a pleasant warmth. Three days before her thirty-fifth birthday.

'Now,' she said, dusting the palms of her hands against each other, 'we shall see.'

They made good time, reaching the wooded drive to Ippark on the afternoon of the second day, just as she'd intended. It was a great satisfaction to her that she was arriving in such style with all the marks of success clearly upon her, rich clothes, new chaise, smart groom, good horses. If anyone was watching from those imperious windows they couldn't help but be impressed.

The house was smaller than she remembered it and a good deal less grand, standing rather bleakly among cow-grazing meadows, its red brickwork subdued in the strong May sunlight and its stone dressings rather in need of repair. There was an empty dog-cart standing beside the garden wall and she was pleased to remark how shabby it was and how poorly it compared with her fine green chaise. And although the front door was opened by a footman of sorts he was in need of a shave and his livery was threadbare.

362

'Tell your master Mrs Easter has arrived,' she told him peremptorily, 'prompt on the hour, according to her promise.' And she lifted her little enamel fob watch so that he would notice it. 'It wants but a minute of three o'clock.'

It was chilly in that stone-flagged hall, for although there was a fire in the white marble fireplace, it gave out precious little heat. Things are not what they were, she told herself. I do believe their fortunes fade.

But then the footman reappeared to lead her into the red drawing-room, and there was Sir Osmond Easter, standing courteously to greet her. And Sir Osmond Easter was a surprise.

Over the years she had evolved an image of this man, as middle-aged, portly and overbearing. One of the old aristocratic heavyweights like his grandfather. But this was a young man, no older than she was herself, with a pale, bland face and rather watery blue eyes, wearing pale blue breeches and white silk stockings and lace at his sleeves like a dandy.

'Pray do be seated,' he said, and his voice was languid too, as if even the slightest effort would be too much.

What a precious crittur! she thought, seating herself in one of his red armchairs, and noticing that the red wallpaper was much faded since her last visit and that some of the paintings had gone, leaving tell-tale oblongs of darker paper to mark where they had been.

'I trust you made a good journey,' Sir Osmond drawled. 'You came by the stage, I daresay.'

'Oh, dear me no,' she said with splendid aplomb. 'I travel in my own town chaise.'

'Do ye now?' he said, and his drawl was so marked as to be almost an insult.

She knew that behind those half-closed eyes and that deliberately weary air he was assessing the expense of her clothes, and the knowledge gave her the extra nerve she needed to attack.

'I en't one to beat about the bush,' she said, 'so I'll tell 'ee straight. I don't meddle in your affairs, so I'll trouble you not to meddle in mine.'

He actually had the effrontery to laugh at her. 'My dear Mrs Easter,' he said. 'I have a deal too much to do runnin' the estate and so forth to have any time at all to interest myself in your small affairs, whatever they are.'

'You know right well what they are,' she said glaring at him. There was a two-day old copy of *The Times* lying on the table beside his chair. '*You* read *The Times*, I notice. *I* have the monopoly to sell it. And would sell more had I the shops to sell 'em in, which you been out of your way to deny me, sir. 'Tis an unkindness, so 'tis and unworthy of 'ee as a Christian gentleman.'

'La, ma'am!' he said, still smiling, 'you surely en't inferin' any wrong-doin' on my part?'

She was flustered by his calm. This wasn't the sort of reaction she expected from him. But she held her ground. 'I most certainly am.'

'That ain't wise, ma'am,' he said, smiling in the most smug infuriating way.

'Wise or not, 'tis the truth.'

'You would be hard put to it to prove such an accusation.'

She snorted with fury. 'Humph! 'Tis coincidence then that every single time I lose a shop 'tis a shop handled by some legal friend of yours?'

'My dear lady, a person of my rank would never do anythin' so unspeakably crass as to befriend a lawyer. A judge in chambers perhaps, but I presume you do not speak of a judge in chambers. No, I thought not. I have sundry acquaintances in the legal profession, but that is about as far as I would be prepared to go.'

'Friends, acquaintances. Judges, lawyers. What's the odds?' she said, confused by such a quibble. It was irritating that he took her attack so calmly. With right on her side *she* should be worrying *him*.

'Oh, very considerable,' he assured her blandly, 'as you would discover were you foolish enough to persist in this accusation.' The smile continued as if it were painted on his face, but this was a threat, and her senses prickled into alarm in recognition of it. Deuce take it, this interview was going badly.

'I see how 'tis,' she said, narrowing her eyes at him, 'you want me to believe 'tis all coincidence, that's how 'tis. Well, I en't such a fool.'

'Your losses, if such they are, could be due to a variety of causes, my dear Mrs Easter. London is a hotbed of gossip, as you are probably well aware. How any of us may determine the source of adverse comment in such a place is quite mystifyin', so 'tis.'

She picked up the copy of *The Times* and held it in her hand, waving it like a fan, to cool the heat of her rage. 'If something were to appear in this paper,' she said, 'as a result of gossip, you understand, and it were to imply that Sir Osmond Easter of Ippark in the County of Sussex was stooping so low as to interfere in the proper business affairs of a member of the newspaper fraternity, among whom I would go so far as to claim friends – oh many, many friends – then you could hardly complain of that either, could you?'

'Indeed I could ma'am,' he drawled, but there was just a flicker of concern on his bland face, and that encouraged her.

'Then so could I, sir,' she said rising. 'And that is my last word on the matter.' And she swept from the room, before she lost her temper irretrieveably and began to shout at him.

He waited until the door closed behind her. Then he rang the bell and sent for his secretary.

'We will proceed no further with the Nan Easter affair,' he said. 'The woman is venomous and has venomous friends. We will leave well alone, for the present.'

'Then she will buy the properties, sir,' the clerk pointed out. He'd been rather enjoying the battle and was disappointed to think it was petering out.

'No matter,' his master said coolly. 'She will come to grief in her own time, you may depend on it.'

Nan was still shaking with fury when she arrived in the hall. There was no sign of the footman and she was just stretching out her hand to the bell to summon him, when a door in the far corner of the hall was quietly opened and two faded ladies tip-toed out. They were as timid as rabbits, which they really rather resembled, for their brown eyes were limpid and anxious and they had long noses and very small mouths and their gowns, which were made of faded brown cotton, were as full-skirted as a rabbit's haunches and a similar texture and colour.

The taller of the two gave Nan a hesitant smile. 'We wondered,' she ventured, 'whether you would care to take tea?'

'Tea?' Nan said, cross and bemused. 'I've had enough of your brother, let me tell 'ee, without taking tea.' But she didn't ring the bell.

'He is not our brother, Mrs Easter,' the smaller one corrected with gentle sadness. 'We beg you not to think that.'

'The kettle is on the boil,' the taller one said, equally gently. 'We would consider it an honour, Mrs Easter.'

So slightly mollified and with some curiosity, she went to take tea.

At least it would give her a chance to recover a little before her journey home.

They led her from the hall into a small, pale green parlour, a modest, feminine room, delicately furnished, the pier glasses unobtrusive, the four chairs upholstered quietly in cream damask, the pictures maidenly, the tea table modest. There was a gentle fire in the wide grate where a kettle bubbled discreetly but forbore to blow steam, for that would have been altogether too vulgar and masculine. It was such a very different place from Sir Osmond's aggressive red drawing-room that Nan was charmed despite herself.

'Pray do sit down,' the taller said, and as Nan sat in the chair she'd indicated, 'we should have introduced ourselves before inviting you. It was most remiss. We are your nieces. This is my sister Evelina and I am Thomasina. 'Tis a curious name, is it not? My poor dear Papa so wanted a boy you see. I was such a disappointment to him.' She began to mix the tea in her little china mixing-bowl, working with great care and precision, her head stooped over the little rosewood box.

'Your husband was always so kind to us when we were girls,' Evelina confided. 'We were very fond of him, you know. He and Mama were brother and sister. It has always seemed such a pity to us that we lost touch.'

The tea was being brewed, its sharp aroma rising most appetizingly from the tea-pot. 'That was your grandmother's doing,' Nan said. 'She said she had thirteen grandchildren as I remember and that my three were of no consequence.'

'Indeed yes,' Evelina sighed. 'She was often most unkind, it has to be admitted. There *were* ten of us in those days and your three would have made thirteen. Now we are the only ones left at home. Our brother Simon is away at Oxford, and Osmond's sister Sarah is married and in the West Indies and all the others are dead, may their souls rest in peace. Oh, it would have been so pleasant to see our cousins.'

Thomasina handed Nan a little bowl of steaming tea. 'You must not allow cousin Osmond to upset you,' she said. 'His bark is a deal worse than his bite, you know. It is just that he takes his position as head of the family so seriously.'

'He was very good to us, when Papa died,' Evelina confided. 'He was killed at Cape St Vincent, you know. Mama was heart-broken. She only survived him for six months, may their souls rest in peace. And Osmond took us in.'

He took me in too, Nan thought bitterly, with all that talk. 'He has lawyers who refuse to allow me to rent the properties I need,' she told them bluntly, 'and when I charge him with it, he pretends to have no knowledge of it.'

'He is devious by nature, my dear,' Thomasina said. 'But I do assure you that he will modify his activity now. 'Tis always the way, believe me.'

'And nowadays,' Evelina said innocently, 'his influence does not extend beyond the city of London, whereas yours, I believe, does, does it not?'

'Indeed it does,' Nan said, sipping her tea. She was quite moved by their unexpected help and kindness. 'And what is more, I can assure you that in the very near future it will extend even further.'

'What a pleasure it gives us to hear that,' Evelina said. 'Does is not, sister?'

'Indeed it does,' Thomasina agreed. 'It does not do to let men have their own way all the time.'

'Especially,' Evelina said slyly, 'when it may be prevented.'

What splendid cousins they are, Nan thought, drinking their tea. And their cunning mollified her.

'I will write to you,' she said, when they parted. 'And you shall see how I prosper, Sir Osmond or no Sir Osmond.'

'Pray do, my dear,' Evelina said. 'And we will write to you. 'Tis as well for women to help one another when they may, do you not agree?'

Chapter Thirty-two

Back in Cheyne Row Calverley Leigh was organizing a party for the return of the conquering heroine.

'Something quite particular,' he told Mrs Jorris, 'for 'tis her birthday besides all else.'

It was the first time in his life that anyone had taken up the cudgels on his behalf and he was warm with pride at the compliment it paid him and easy in the satisfaction of knowing at last that his lack of promotion had been caused by somebody else's malevolence and not his own incompetence. Oh, she's a peerless creature, he thought, and when she returns she shall be petted and praised and fed with the choicest dishes.

'How of a pike?' Mrs Jorris suggested. 'Baked leisurely, stuffed with oysters and sweet marjoram and winter savory. She's mighty fond of fish.'

It sounded excellent.

'A cockatrice to follow, on a bed of green parsley. Made of capon and sucking-pig, of course, for 'tis not a dish to cheapen with boiling fowl and such like.'

'And new potatoes in butter sauce,' Billy hoped.

'And sorrel and spinach,' Annie said, for both these vegetables were sovereign remedies for unwanted spots on the face, and now that she was sixteen she was mindful of the need to keep her complexion clear.

So the menu was agreed upon, and the pastry-cook called in to provide a selection of sweet tarts, and the cooking began. It occupied the entire household with the exception of Billy and Johnnie who were still incarcerated in the schoolroom and Mr Dibkins who was having one of his turns and had incarcerated himself in the broom-cupboard with a box full of candles and a bible.

'Drat the man,' Mrs Jorris complained. 'I've been on an' on at him for the soft broom an' he won't so much as open the door. How we're to clear I cannot imagine.'

'Leave 'im be,' Bessie advised. 'I'll persuade him after dinner.'

But after dinner they were all so weary and well-fed, they decided to leave the clearing until next morning.

It was a splendid meal. The pike was delicious and the cockatrice was a great success, with its red leather cock's head and its gilded claws and its paper ruff tipped with saffron-yellow. During her journey home Nan had decided that her visit to Ippark had been a great success too. It was true that she hadn't achieved the abject apology she wanted and Sir Osmond could hardly be said to have admitted his guilt, nasty, slippery crittur that he was, but on consideration she felt that Thomasina and Evelina were probably right when they said he would mend his ways. I shall certainly keep my promise and write to them, she thought, for they were allies and they were kindly. In the meantime she would tell her family of a triumph, for that was what it very nearly was.

'I'll wager you sent that old Sir Osmond packing,' Johnnie said when they were all seated at table. He was most excited, his eyes blazing.

'Sir Osmond,' his mother told him, 'will not be meddling with our affairs again in a long time, I can tell 'ee.'

'Did you frighten him, Mama?' Johnnie asked. There was a peculiar intensity about his interest in this affair which Nan found slightly alarming. He looked as though he hated Sir Osmond, but that couldn't be the case, surely? Nevertheless her need to talk through the entire conversation with Sir Osmond and make sense of it so that it felt like the triumph she wanted it to be, was so intense she pressed on with her account despite misgivings.

'Oh, he was told right enough,' she said. 'I made no bones about it. He was told. "If you don't stop meddling in my affairs," I said, "then one of my friends in the newspapers shall print the full story of it." He didn't like that at all, I can tell 'ee.'

'I wish I could have been there to see it,' the boy said earnestly. 'Tell me all about it, Mama!'

So she did, word for very nearly remembered word, and it cheered them both immensely.

'Are we ready for the next course?' Calverley wanted to know when she finally paused for breath. He was exuberantly happy that the meal was such a success and like Johnnie he wanted to question her closely, not just about the visit but about what had been said of his blocked captaincy. But that, being rather more private, would have to wait until they retired.

It was a disappointment to him that she seemed to have lost interest in the subject when they finally got to bed. 'I've talked enough for one evening,' she said. 'Kiss me, do. I starve for kisses.'

'But did he admit . . .?' he tried.

She kissed him silent and for a few seconds he was most cruelly caught between rising desire and the need to hear her speak the words that would salve his self-esteem. Then desire overcame him and he resigned himself to love-making, vowing to renew the conversation when their senses were satisfied.

But when they'd reached that luxurious state, she found something else to talk about. 'I can smell that ol' honeysuckle right up here,' she said, sniffing the air appreciatively as she lay beside him against the pillows.

'What did Sir Osmond say of my commission?' he asked smiling lazily at her so as to encourage her.

'Oh, 'tis a heady perfume,' she said. 'You can smell it too, I'll wager.'

'What?'

'Why, the honeysuckle.'

'I can smell something burning,' he said.

She sniffed the air again, turning her head from side to side, nostrils dilated, like a rabbit. 'I do believe . . .' she said.

And a tongue of fire spurted from the floorboards in the corner of the room and licked along the wainscot, scorching as it went, and filling the room with the smell of burning paint.

Looking back on it afterwards, Nan was surprised at how calm they'd both been. Calverley got up and doused the flames with the contents of the water jug, moving quickly and easily as though he was throwing water across a stable yard. The flame hissed and disappeared leaving a sticky blackness bubbling on the floorboard. He tossed her nightgown towards her outstretched hand and put on his shirt and trousers.

'I will wake the house,' she said, and ran.

On the landing she could hear the fire crackling below her. Everything was happening with nightmare speed, but even so she wasn't afraid. Shielding the candle with the palm of her hand she ran up the stairs calling as she went, 'Wake up, all of you! Wake up!' so that the boys were already stirring by the time she arrived in their bedroom.

'Put on your clothes,' she said, 'quick as you can. A coal has jumped out of the stove. We must look sharp and put it out.'

Billy was obedient at once but Johnnie protested. 'Let the servants do it,' he said, turning on his side and pulling the covers over his shoulders. 'That is what servants are for, Mrs Pennington says so.'

'Lazy toad!' his mother roared, seizing the covers and hurling them on the floor. 'Get up! Get dressed! The house is a-fire!'

'What is it?' Annie said, appearing sleepily in the doorway in her nightcap and her long white nightgown.

'Put on a day-gown and your slippers and I'll tell 'ee as we go downstairs. You two get down to the kitchen so soon as you're ready. Take the jug and pail. Throw water on the flames.'

The noise she was making had alerted the servants. Thiss met her on the next flight of stairs, candle in hand, and was given his orders and went leaping off to the kitchen taking the stairs two at a time. Above him frightened faces peered down the stairwell, clowns' faces lit from beneath by a row of flickering candles, triangular eye sockets black as pitch, long black nostrils, distorted brows like fat yellow sausages. Despite fear and fire she couldn't help thinking how funny they all looked and was ashamed because she wanted to laugh.

'What is it, mum?' Bessie's voice said out of the darkness.

'Come down and bring Pollyanna,' Nan called. 'You must go next door out of harm's way the both of you.' For Bessie was pregnant again and needed protection. 'There is a fire. In the dining-room, we think. Bring your water-jugs and pails. No one is to stay upstairs.'

Mrs Pennington was standing at the top of the stairs, still fully dressed in her stern grey gown with a two-headed candlestick in her hand and those impossible curls still as tight as chestnuts under her cap. 'Surely you do not wish *me* to assist,' she said. 'After all I am hardly a servant.'

'You're a blame fool,' Nan said, already on her way to the kitchen, 'but this time you'll do as you're told, ma'am! Or burn and be dammed!' She was passing the dining-room door, herding the maids before her, and could see Calverley hacking at the floorboards with an axe. The carpets had been tossed aside and the floorboards were ablaze. 'Pass me all the water you can through the ceiling!' he was shouting. 'Hurry!'

Down in the kitchen Billy was already filling buckets and jugs at the pump and Thiss and Johnnie were throwing the water over the broom-cupboard, which was burning like a bonfire with red and yellow flames

371

leaping from its walls and roaring and crackling straight into the ceiling, and grey smoke billowing back into the kitchen in every direction.

'I'll pump,' she said to Billy. 'You throw.'

The pump creaked and groaned, jugs and buckets and basins passed from hand to hand, heavy and slopping, and back again light and dripping, the fire hissed as the water splashed upon it, and soon the smoke was so thick they could hardly see further than the smeared hands passing the next jug or receiving the next basin. And they worked frantically, pumping, passing, hurling, 'Quick! Quick!' Servants arrived from next-door to help them and the floor was awash with lukewarm water squelching under their feet, and the women's skirts grew so wet with it and so heavy they had to stop to tuck them up out of the way. The smell of burning wood and charred paint was so strong it made their eyes water, and mingled with it was another pungent smell that Nan recognized, but couldn't quite place, the smell of meat roasting. But what meat? Not beef, surely. Had they had beef for dinner? She couldn't remember. And still they worked, pumping, passing, hurling, 'Quick! Quick!' And there was no time, only heat and the smell of burning and smeared hands in the darkness and that terrifying crackling and the water hissing, hissing, hissing.

And at last the darkness changed and intensified, and Thiss was lighting candles, and glancing up from the pump Nan saw that the flames were gone and there was only a single column of smoke, black and oily, coiling upwards like some obscene, fat serpent from the wreckage that had once been the broom-cupboard and the welsh dresser. And she realized that she was cold and that her back ached horribly and that there were blisters on her hands.

Another pail was being thrust into the sink and she filled it automatically.

'Fire's out!' Calverley's voice said. He was standing just inside the kitchen door, as black as a sweep, his trousers torn and his fine shirt streaked with filth, but he was right, the fire *was* out.

Then there was such relief. Everybody talking at once, buckets clanging to the floor, Annie paddling to the kitchen table and sitting on it cross-legged and inelegant, her face drawn with fatigue, Thiss knocking the last steaming plank into the water round his feet, the smell of charred wood filling their nostrils, and still that odd unidentifiable whiff of roast meat.

'We kep' it restricted ter the cupboard,' Thiss said with some pride.

'Could 'a been a deal worse, mum, a deal worse. My ol' gel all right, is she?'

'She's in next door with Pollyanna,' Nan said, rubbing her face clean with the edge of her nightgown.

'More to the point,' Johnnie said, 'Where's Mr Dibkins?'

They'd all forgotten about Dibkins, Nan thought, and the fire had started in his broom-cupboard. His broom-cupboard where he hid away with his bible and his box of candles. 'My dear heart alive!' she said. 'Dibkin's candles!'

And Em, the maid of all work began to scream. 'Aagh! Aagh! Look there! Aagh! There he is! Look there!'

She was pointing at the charred pile of planks and ash and tumbled crockery that now filled the space where the broom cupboard had been, and the terror of her screams focussed all eyes upon it.

There was a figure lying in the debris, humped like some huge burnt cushion oozing black treacle. It had crimped black curls covering its skull, short and frizzy like a negro slave's but where its face should have been there was a terrible featureless blank, an oozing mask of stretched black leather with two holes for eyes. And Nan remembered the smell of roasting meat. Roasting meat! Dear God!

Then Mrs Pennington strode across the kitchen, boots swishing through the water and slapped poor Em across the face. The poor girl stopped screaming suddenly as though her breath had been cut off and for a few seconds there was a dreadful silence while they gazed at the blackened body and the water dripped mournfully from the walls and the timbers creaked and clicked.

Then Mrs Pennington's voice rose hysterically into the smoky darkness. 'Don't waste your sympathy!' she screamed, 'any of you. He was a crazy old man, and now he's burnt the house down and killed himself and it serves him right. Oh yes it does, it serves him right. It serves you all right. Don't think I don't know about you, because I do. I've watched the way you go on. I know all about you, godless creatures that you are!'

'Stop that!' Nan said, standing up with great weariness and greater dignity. 'You forget yourself.'

'I forget nothing,' Mrs Pennington shrieked. 'Nothing! All the immorality I've seen in this house. I do not wonder the good Lord saw fit to use that crazy man to burn it down. No, indeed. You brought it all upon yourself with your wicked, wicked ways. Oh I know. Don't you think I don't.'

'Leave my employ!' Nan said, angry despite her weariness. 'Do you hear me? Leave this house this instant! I will not have such as you teaching my children. My heart alive! To speak so at a time like this!'

'I will speak as I please,' Mrs Pennington raved, small eyes bolting, 'for you cannot stop me.'

'If we cannot stop you, we can leave you,' Nan said. 'There is nothing to be gained by staying down here in the dirt. We will go back to our rooms and clean ourselves up. I will take care of – all this in the morning.'

The servants from next-door began to leave and the sight of them made her remember her manners. 'I'm obliged to 'ee,' she said as they passed her. 'Tell Mr Cholmondley the house is safe. Say I'm uncommon grateful. You shall all have new clothes to make amends. I promise.' For they looked like a line of chimney-sweeps.

Mrs Pennington was snivelling, but nobody paid any attention to her. Not even Johnnie, who had been the first to creep from the kitchen, sickened by the sight of death and embarrassed by her terrible outburst. Now he sat in his bed shivering with emotion, willing himself not to cry.

Billy was crying openly. 'Poor old Dibkins! What a way to die!'

'People are so cruel,' Johnnie said. 'Even the best of them. There will be no more schooling for us now, I hope you realize.'

The thought dried Billy's tears. 'Good,' he said.

'What will Mama do with us, think 'ee?'

'We shall go to work, I daresay.'

'Shall you like that?'

'I shall like it well enough. It couldn't be worse than learnin', in all conscience.'

'I've brought you fresh water,' their sister said, appearing in the doorway with a jug in one hand and a candle in the other.

But what was the good of washing, Johnnie thought, when his one and only friend had been dismissed, and his schooling was over, and Mr Dibkins had died so horribly, and the house was wrecked?

Rest was quite out of the question for any of them. Back in their fire-smeared bedroom, Nan and Calverley washed as well as they could in their basin of cold water, and changed into clean linen. Then Nan made bandages from an old strip of sheeting and covered the burns that were bubbling into blisters on Calverley's hands and arms. And even though he thought it was namby-pamby, he let her do it, because he was too weary to protest. Then they sat beside the open window, looking down at the dark lawn and the pale petals of the magnolia and listening to the faint swish-swish of the green corn in the field beyond the garden, and they talked.

The smell of charred wood and dampness clogged the entire house. 'Shall we ever get away from this fire?' she said, sniffing the foul air. ' 'Tis on my hair, my skin, I know not what-all . . . We smell like gypsies. Oh, I never . . .'

'The worst of it is over,' he said, trying to put an arm around her to console her. It was a new experience for him to be comforting her. He'd wiped away a good many tears in his time, usually after seductions, and they'd all been easy enough. But he had always thought Nan too strong for tears, strong in will and mind and as determined as any man. So it was surprising and touching that she should be showing weakness now, and showing it in such a peculiar way, in quick nervous speech and jabbing darts of staccato irritability that was most unlike her usual forthright anger.

'Don't try consoling,' she said, shaking his hand from her arm. ' 'Ten't my style. We must decide what is to be done. There en't time for . . .'

'In the morning,' he said, 'while you attend to the stamping, I shall call in the undertakers and the builders and hire men to clean. You shan't know the place by breakfast time.' It really was the most extraordinary sensation to be taking charge of her like this.

'Mrs Pennington is to go,' she said, frowning at the garden.

'She will.'

'The boys can go to work. 'Tis high time. Idleness is bad for boys. Johnnie grows selfish with it. D'ye know what he said to me?'

'No, my love. What was it he said to you?'

But when she started to tell him, she found she had forgotten and no matter how hard she strained her mind to remember, it remained an obstinate blank. 'He said . . . He said . . . Ah! What was it we spoke of?'

' 'Tis no matter. You will remember in the morning.'

' 'Twas a waste of time talking to Sir Osmond,' she said abruptly. 'Like picking up jelly with your fingers, so 'twas.'

375

'What did he say of my commission?' It was a daring question to ask, but perhaps the moment was right for it now.

'We did not speak of it. He smiles. He denies knowledge. He speaks of nothing, I tell 'ee. Nothing.'

He was very disappointed, but he couldn't complain. Not now.

'I shall rent a new house,' she said, straightening her spine. 'First thing in the morning. That's what I'll do. A fine new house. We can't stay here in this filth.'

Chapter Thirty-three

Nan's smart tow-chaise cantered into Bury St Edmund's a few yards ahead of the London stage-coach. Thiss and Nan were cock a' hoop, for they'd been racing the larger vehicle for the last ten miles and two gentlemen riding outside had actually been laying bets against their success.

It had been an exhilarating journey, in marvellously fine weather and with frequent stops for refreshment, so it was only right and proper that they should end with a triumph. Cheyne Row and that evil-smelling house and Mrs Pennington's hysteria and Mr Dibkins' terrifying body were all left far behind. She had escaped.

The morning had started so badly, with the kitchen awash with water and Mr Dibkin's body still horrifyingly obvious even covered by a sheet and all the dirt and damage looking worse by daylight. Nan took her entire household to breakfast at Mr Quirk's coffee house beside the river, except Mrs Pennington of course, and while they were eating she told them her plans.

'I shall rent another house,' she said, 'while Number 10 is being repaired. We shall all move there so soon as 'tis arranged. Meantime I should be obliged if you would clean what you can. Mrs Pennington may leave when she wishes, for the boys will not be in the house,'

'Are we to assume that our schooling is now over, Mama?' Johnnie asked.

'Not a bit of it,' she said. 'Now you've to learn a trade. Arithmetic is all very well, my son, but it won't butter no parsnips, as you will very soon discover. So soon as you're breakfasted we shall go down to the Strand and I will introduce you to the manager there and you will start work. You'll begin with the stamping, which is a tedious business but you'd best know about it.'

He looked straight at her with that infuriatingly blank stare of his but he didn't complain or argue.

'Could I work in the warehouse, Mama?' Billy asked. Those vast stacks of paper in rooms full of shelves had fascinated him ever since she bought the shop, but he'd never been allowed to explore them.

'Stamping first, warehouse next,' she promised.

'I shall stay at Goosegogs for a day or two,' Calverley said. 'Make that my headquarters, eh. Somewhere dependable, whilst you're a-changing the world.'

So they all went their various ways. By nine o'clock she had rented a most prestigious house in Cheyne Walk, Mr Teshmaker was examining the agreement, the boys had finished their very first stamping, and she and Annie were being driven back to their damaged house. And quite suddenly, she knew that she didn't want to see the place again. Not that day. She couldn't abide it.

'We will go on a jaunt,' she said to her daughter, and even as she spoke she knew where she wanted to go. 'I've a mind to visit Bury St Edmunds and buy a shop there. I was born in a village close by and I en't seen the place in years. Are the horses fit for it, Thiss, what think 'ee?'

'We'll give 'em a run,' Thiss said cheerfully.

And here they were.

'St Edmund'sbury!' the coachman called to his passengers as he reined in his horses before the entrance to the Angel Inn. 'St Edmund's-bury. Centre of the universe, so the inhabitants would have us believe, and this 'ere is the centre of the town.'

This 'ere was the long slanting square she remembered from her childhood, built on the side of a hill just above the ruins of an old abbey and with a fine prospect of distant woods and fields, now mistily blue in the declining light of late afternoon. It was an elegant place, surrounded on three sides by fine houses, some newly built, others refaced in the new style, and it was full of elegant people taking an afternoon stroll and meeting and greeting each other with the slow, burring speech she remembered with sudden affection.

I shall do well in this place, she thought to herself. It had just the right sort of style. And how peaceful it was after the rush and scramble of the City. People and horses moved at a reasonable pace here, and there were no pushing crowds, even up by the Corn Exchange and Moyses Hall where the streets were many and narrow.

378

The inn immediately before her was five stories tall and very grand, with a balcony above the front door and a courtyard big enough to accommodate several stage-coaches all at once beside a number of smaller private carriages. Now the cobbled space was thronged with liveried servants struggling to unload bag and baggage, and ostlers uncoupling the sweating horses.

'We will settle into our rooms,' she told Annie,' and then we will take a short promenade before dinner. The sooner I start my search for a suitable shop the better.'

She found six possibilities before the end of that first walk around the town, and by the time they returned to the square she had seen and dismissed two of them and made appointments to view the others the very next morning.

'How wise we were to come here,' she said to Annie as the two of them set off down the steep slope of Abbeygate Street towards Angel Hill. 'I declare I feel quite myself again. I've worked up quite an appetite.'

Annie was just admitting that she too was ready for her dinner, when they emerged into the square again. Immediately opposite them was the high stone wall of the ancient abbey and an impressive gateway, its carved stone smudged and blackened but not displeasing in such a setting. She could see a public garden just inside its tall archway and the green of its lawns and the red and gold of its flowerbeds were a pleasing splash of colour in the brown square. ' 'Tis a romantic place, Mama,' she said. 'I could imagine just such a gateway in one of the new novels.' She was an avid reader of the new novels.

Her mother's taste was a good deal more practical. 'I prefer a nice comfortable hotel like the Angel. Or new assembly rooms, like those. Look there.'

The southern end of the square was dominated by a single building clearly labelled ATHENAEUM in bold block letters above its central pediment. Its balance was splendidly maintained despite the slope of the ground on which it stood, with six tall windows on either side of a columned porch and the raised balcony that stood above it, and an unobtrusive roof partly obscured by a stone parapet. 'Now there's an assembly room to be proud of, I'll warrant,' she said, 'and well placed what's more.'

She turned her head and glanced idly at the northern end of the square where a line of fine houses glowed in the evening sunlight. They were built of pale yellow brick with high sash-windows painted white and a doric arch around their imposing front doors. And she noticed that the largest of them was being offered for sale. 'Now *that's* the sort of building *I* like,' she said to her daughter. 'I've a mind to view it, so I have. What think 'ee?'

She viewed it next morning after she'd bought the shop in Abbeygate Street, and it was even better inside. 'The window frames are set back a good four inches,' the agent explained to her proudly, 'to prevent fire, you see, ma'am. A most wise precaution I have always thought. And I think you will agree that this is a most spacious room. A room with ton, is't not so?'

The room he was ushering them into was the drawing-room, which occupied the entire width of the first floor and had a fine view of the square. It was indeed a splendid room, decorated in duck-egg blue with elaborate mouldings on the ceiling picked out in gold, and two gold-and-white double doors with painted panels. But it was the little room at the top of the stairs that really caught her attention.

'A water closet,' the agent said. 'So convenient, don't you think, and the very latest thing. The water is pumped into the cistern so,' giving a rather energetic demonstration, 'and then you pull this handle up and down several times so, and down it all comes and the pan is flushed quite clean, do you see?' And so it was, with a stream of water positively swirling round the rim of that odd-shaped blue-patterned chamber pot on its awkward thick stem. But the wooden seat looked sturdy enough, stretching from one side of the little room to the other and there was a window for ventilation, which was a deal more than there'd ever been in the old-fashioned closets with their dreadful, smelly close-stools.

'My heart alive,' she said. 'That's an invention an' no mistake. Would we could have had such a thing when I was young. Annie, my dear, I've a mind to buy this house. Show me the rest of it, sir.'

So the bed-chambers were examined and the servants rooms in the attic and the housekeeper's parlour and the butler's pantry and the kitchen, which was behind the dining-room on the ground floor and had its own pump for fresh water and the latest iron range with two ovens for bread and pastries and another separate oven, all on its own, for roasting meat. 'Imagine that,' Nan said, much impressed. 'No more basting over that great hot spit, eh?' Oh, it was a very fine house.

' 'Tis just the sort of place for a lady like yourself, ma'am, if I may make so bold as to say so,' the agent said hopefully.

'It is,' she agreed, 'and if we can agree upon the price, I will buy it.'

Which, after some haggling during which the agent came off considerably worse than he'd expected, they could and she did.

'I have always envied the rich their country houses,' she confessed to Annie, after dinner that evening, 'and now I have one of my own, so I have. We will spend the summer here and winter in London. Bessie can keep house for us here and we'll hire a new housekeeper for Cheyne Walk. Think how healthy 'twill be for her little ones, and for you too, my dear. I have long thought the smoke of London a parlous bad thing for your weak chest. The boys can come down and join us too when they en't working. Oh, what a fine thing 'twas that we came here!' She was bristling with excitement. It was as if the fire had burned away the last of the old Nan, the old hard-working, penny-pinching Nan, and released a new woman, full of energy and enthusiasm, and with the money to indulge herself.

That night after Annie had retired, she wrote a long letter to Calverley.

'I have bought me a country seat here in Bury, for I tell you Calverley 'twas like homecoming to arrive in this place and the property to hand as if the Fates intended it. 'Tis a new house with all the latest devices for pleasant living. I propose to stay here for a day or two for there is much to do. Thiss and Annie will stay here with me. I know I may safely leave care of my London affairs with Billy and Johnnie. What good fortune to have two sons to run the business, with Mr Teshmaker to oversee them, of course. Let me know when Cheyne Walk is ready for occupation.

Your own most loving, Nan.'

Then she wrote to the boys.

Calverley was not pleased. Deuce take the woman, he thought, whatever possessed her to do such a thing? I don't want a house out in the sticks even if she does. But there was no doubt about her wealth now, and that at least was a comfort. To be able to rent a house in Cheyne Walk and buy another all on the same day was uncommon impressive. I do believe I shall marry her after all, he thought, infuriating though she is. And in the meantime he would live at the club and spend a few days of well-deserved leisure before his next trip to York for Mr

Chaplin. I shall have two bottles of port with my dinner tonight, he decided, for if he couldn't afford it, Nan certainly could.

Two bottles of the very best were being carried into the smoking-room as he strolled downstairs.

'Who's the lucky feller?' he asked the wine waiter.

'Colonel Leigh,' came the surprising answer. 'Come to talk horses with Mr Marshall.'

'Colonel Leigh?'

'Racing manager to the Prince of Wales,' the waiter said importantly. He was quite awe-struck at the honour of this unexpected visit.

But Calverley had shot off to find the club secretary and arrange an introduction. 'My cousin, sir,' he explained. 'We have corresponded from time to time, but never met. I should make myself known now the gentleman is in Goosegogs.'

So the introduction was made. 'Colonel Leigh sir, pray allow me to present Mr Leigh late of the Duke of Clarence's Light Dragoons, a relation of yours, I do believe. The only man I ever knew who fought a duel over the honour of his horse.'

'Meet at last, eh,' the Colonel said turning his florid face to acknowledge his relation. He was an impressive-looking man, being both tall and portly, as Calverley knew, for he'd seen him from a distance on several occasions. He was exquisitely dressed in a well-cut brown cloth coat, corduroy waistcoat, splendid leather boots and old-fashioned knee breeches, and he carried a gold-topped cane like so many of the carelessly wealthy did these days. 'I trust you won.'

'Indeed,' Calverley confessed modestly.

'Can't think of a better reason for a duel upon me soul,' the Colonel said. 'Horses being my line of country.'

'Pray allow me to presume upon our relationship and offer you dinner sir.'

'Obliged,' the Colonel agreed.

So they dined together and talked about horses and Mr Chaplin's coach fleet and the Prince of Wales' racing stable. And afterwards they drank wine together sitting in Goosegogs' highbacked chairs beside the bow window and talked about the war.

'Heard the news, have you sir?' the Colonel asked. 'Boney's a-bullyin' again, so he is. Now 'tis the Portuguese. They ain't to trade with us, so his lordship says. If you ever heard the like.'

'I trust they will resist him, sir,' Calverley said, gulping his port and admiring two pretty young women who were passing in their carriage.

'At their peril, I fear sir. He has an army ready to march through Spain and attack 'em.'

'They should send out the Clarence's to prevent him, damme.'

'Sir Arthur Wellesley is commissioned to lead just such an endeavour. I wonder you ain't heard.'

'Well, as to that,' Calverley said quickly sensing some criticism. 'Since I parted company with the Clarence's I've been kept too busy. Out of touch, I fear sir. Oh yes, I've been kept pretty busy. The Easter family needed my help d'ye see, to say nothing of all the work I do for Mr Chaplin. Big newsagent hereabouts, related to Sir Osmond Easter of Ippark.'

'Can't say I know the feller. Bit of a recluse, I daresay? Does he come up for the season?'

'On rare occasions I believe,' Calverley guessed. 'Ain't never seen the feller, although we correspond of course.' He was wading deeper and deeper into falsehood and the knowledge alarmed him and excited him.

But the colonel was losing interest. 'Thought the newsagent was run by a female,' he said helping himself to more port.

'Well as to that,' Calverley said with triumphant modesty, 'I think I may safely say that *I* am A. Easter – Newsagent, just at the moment, for the lady is away at her country seat.'

'Are ye now?' the Colonel said. 'Deuce take it, is that the time? I must be off, sir. I will see you at White's perhaps?'

'White's don't take kindly to those of us engaged in trade,' Calverley said. He'd never dared to think of White's, but this fortunate meeting was too good to waste.

'You need a sponsor,' the Colonel said, smiling at his distant cousin. 'I will see what I can do, considerin' you are a friend of the Easters.'

'Obliged to 'ee sir,' Calverley said rising to his feet as the illustrious gentleman began to walk away.

'Your servant, sir.'

'And yours sir,' Calverley replied, taut with excitement. White's! he was thinking. White's! Oh, he really had arrived.

The next morning reality returned and it all seemed very unlikely that the Prince's racing manager would concern himself with the affairs of such a distant and unimportant relation. But the gentleman was as good as his word. Two days later a letter arrived from White's with the request that Calverley Leigh Esq. would be so kind as to present himself for selection to membership of the club.

He spent the next few days in a frenzy of preparation. New clothes had to be ordered and made to his exact specification, for the cloth had to be the most expensive money could buy and the fit perfection. Nothing less would do for White's, whose members were renowned for their criticism of the smallest fault in matters of dress and style. He bought a gold-topped cane like the Colonel's to match his honey-coloured waistcoat, and a pair of exquisite riding boots to set off the fine fit of his new white breeches, and a brown beaver hat to tone with his elegant jacket, and with his neckcloth perfectly folded and his careless curls most artfully arranged, he and Jericho set off to join the Dandies.

It was a triumph. Although an uncommon costly one. He lost more money at the gaming tables on that first night than he could earn in a month. But he lost it with such careless grace that he soon established himself as a true member of the club, a hedonist whose caustic wit endeared him to all but the most elderly inhabitants, whose views were of little account in any case.

However the next morning the stack of unpaid bills he'd accumulated were worse than his hangover. Something would have to be done about them, and done quickly for he couldn't begin his career at White's with a reputation as a debtor. He stuffed the bills in his pocket and set off to the Strand to find Billy Easter.

He was in the warehouse supervising the morning dispatch, with a stout book before him and a pen in his hand, checking each batch as it passed him. 'Thirty-two *Advertisers*, that's right. Where's *The Times*?' He looked up briefly as Calverley approached and grinned happily.

'You do well, I see,' Calverley said.

' 'Tis a fair old job,' the boy said with some pride. 'Mama will be pleased, I think, when she returns.'

'Has she written to 'ee?'

'Home tomorrow,' Billy said happily. 'Then we can all move into Cheyne Walk, she says. Think a' that. Shan't we be swell? You're six *Chronicles* short, Mr Sampson.'

'Let's to Galloways,' Calverley said. 'I should like to buy you a pot of coffee, since you're such a hard-working gentleman.'

He could see that Billy was flattered, which was a good start. A good lad, young Billy, and like to prove amenable.

Over their second cup of coffee and after several choice compliments, he broached the matter of money. 'Little matter I'd like to sound your advice upon, damme, now you're a working man.'

'What is it, sir?'

' 'Tis a matter of money. Not a deal of money, I'll allow. A mere twenty-eight pounds. The truth of it is, William Easter, I'm short. Now what's to be done about it, think 'ee?'

Billy was flattered to be asked, but he had no idea what to answer.

Luckily Mr Leigh helped him out. 'Your mother usually gives me an advance on such occasions,' he said. 'Howsomever, now that she is away . . . You take my drift, William, I'm sure.'

So William was gradually drifted into the opinion that the best solution was for him to hand over the necessary twenty-eight sovereigns from that morning's petty cash.

'I will put it straight back,' Calverley promised smoothly. 'You may depend upon it. An uncommon civil arrangement, young Billy, for this way we don't need to bother your mother with it at all.'

Bemused by his apparent success, Billy agreed that he was right. It was rather pleasant to be doing business like this with Mr Leigh, standing in for his mother, an adult among adults.

'Between the two of us, eh?' Calverley said, winking at him. 'Could you drink a third cup?'

So when Nan and Annie returned the next afternoon, and they all sat down to dinner in their fine new dining-room overlooking the river, he kept his secret. Not that his mother gave him very much opportunity to tell her anything, for she was so excited about the house she'd bought in Bury.

'We shall spend every summer there,' she promised, 'and winter here. Think of that. Bessie will keep house for us. 'Twill be our country seat. Oh, I can't wait to get back there, boys. You will love it, I tell 'ee.'

She stayed in London for four weeks, just long enough to hire a housekeeper for Cheyne Walk, to supervise the repairs, and to satisfy herself that the business was running smoothly. Mr Teshmaker gave a glowing report of her two working sons. Billy he said was most dependable, but it was Johnnie who had the flair. 'Give him a year or two, ma'am,' he said, 'and he will order the papers for you as well as sorting them.'

'I am pleased to hear it,' Nan said. For if it was true, and Mr Teshmaker always spoke true, so there was no reason to doubt it, she could leave the business for a great deal longer next summer.

The next day, Calverley went to York and she and Annie returned to Bury. She had no idea when she would see him again, but for the first time in their relationship, it didn't concern her.

At the end of August the Clarence's returned to town and Calverley's old friends Captain Fortescue and Captain Hanley-Brown turned up at White's. They were delighted to see him.

'Damme if he ain't married his rich widow,' Fortescue said, eyeing Calverley's fine clothes.

'Not quite,' Calverley said. 'Soon will. 'Tis a matter of time, that's all.'

'And who is the lady, pray?' Hanley-Brown wanted to know.

'Nan Easter.'

'The prosperous Nan?' Fortescue giggled. 'Oh, you're a dog, Leigh. Always was, always will be.'

'When do you wed?' Hanley-Brown asked.

'Well, as to that, we ain't fixed a date. She's out of town for the summer. In her country seat.'

'Well, upon my soul!' Fortescue said. 'I can't imagine the dashing Nan stuck in the country. 'Tain't her style.'

' 'Tis a fancy merely,' Calverley said. ' 'Twill soon pass. I'd lay money on it.'

Perhaps it was just as well that neither of his friends took him up on such a wager, for he'd have lost his money if they had.

Nan spent most of her time in Bury that autumn. She was having a spendthrift holiday quite unlike any other she'd ever taken, and enjoying it immensely.

The lawyers made very heavy weather of the sale of the house but they increased speed once she'd spent an hour in their chambers. 'I en't got all the time in the world,' she said briskly, 'so I will tell 'ee what I propose. If I move into that house before the end of the month you shall have a bonus of ten per cent on top of the fee we've agreed. If I don't I shall deduct two per cent of the fee for every day's delay. How say you?'

They were so alarmed they agreed to her terms almost at once, telling each other afterwards that they'd never known such a client, never in all their born days, but excusing their frailty before her onslaught by declaring that a woman with such determination would be bound to bring them more custom if they kept on the right side of her.

So she moved into her fine house on her third visit to the town and furnished it at great expense and in the latest style, buying a fine oak table and a set of chairs made locally according to Mr Chippendale's book, and a chaise-longue and four matching armchairs, and new feather-beds for her entire household, and a red, green and gold carpet for the drawing-room to match the red curtains and the gold decorations on the plasterwork.

She was full of energy, choosing fabrics and wallpapers and bed linens, hiring servants, arguing with tradesmen, terrifying Mr Orton, the manager of her shop, and always determined to get her own way. In October she began to entertain, befriending the more prestigious of the local tradesmen and their wives, seeking out the Mayor and several members of his corporation, and making her position in this small society richly evident. And among all the others, she took her next-door neighbour under her flamboyant wing.

Miss Amelia Pettie was fifty-eight and looked seventy, a small, frail lady with powder-white, wrinkled skin, faded blue eyes and pale-yellow ringlets carefully arranged on either side of her shrunken cheeks. She had a considerable fortune and no self-confidence, so she lived alone, except for her servants in a house very nearly as big as Nan's but nowhere near so fine. She was always on the verge of apologizing for something and had the most annoying habit of fidgeting with her bonnet or her lace cap whenever she was worried or confused.

'Drat the woman,' Nan said to Bessie after the lady's first appearance at a tea party, 'Why don't she leave that cap of hers alone, always clawing at it. 'Tis a wonder she don't pull it off her head.'

' 'Tis her false hair, mum, that's what 'tis,' Bessie explained, watching to see that the parlour-maid was clearing the tea things properly. 'She's mortal afraid of it a-slippin'. Jane told me.'

It appeared that Jane was Miss Pettie's lady's maid and knew all her secrets. 'Her hair's gone thin, poor soul,' Bessie went on as the parlour maid left the room, giggling quietly. 'All them yeller ringlets is false,

387

hair pieces every last one of 'em, sewn to a band an' the band pinned under her cap, d'yer see mum? So they give her the fidgets on account of she can't never be certain they ain't a-slippin' out a' place. Poor soul!'

'Poor soul indeed,' Nan laughed, but she was thinking how sad it was that Miss Pettie couldn't keep such a sordid little secret to herself. But that was the way of the world. Servants always knew every last little detail about their masters' lives. And she wondered what would be said about her when Calverley eventually swallowed his pride and came to live in Bury with her. There's a price to pay for everything, she thought, and the price for wealth was gossip. But well worth paying when it had given her such a fine house to live in. Oh, well worth paying.

At the end of October, Bessie's baby was born. It was a fine, strong boy and they called him Tom, because, as his father explained, 'He's got enough ter contend with bein' called Thistlethwaite, poor little beggar, without another mouthful fer a Christian name an' all.'

And after that, the winter set it with frosts and chill winds and it was plainly time for Nan and Annie to return to Chelsea.

But even though Calverley continued to brag to his new friends at White's about his rich fiancée, the famous Mrs Nan Easter, somehow or other he didn't get around to proposing to her.

Chapter Thirty-four

In the spring of 1808, just before Nan's third summer in Bury, Colonel Leigh's predictions were fulfilled. Napoleon Bonaparte marched a French army through Spain to attack the Portuguese. And Sir Arthur Wellesley set sail for Lisbon with 20,000 British troops to oppose him.

There was considerable jubilation in London, for now at last the British army was to take the field again, which was exactly what everybody had been wanting them to do for years. And as every Englishman knew in his bones that the British fighting man was a match for anyone, there were high hopes that the French war would soon be over and done with. It had dragged on long enough in all conscience, with inflation getting worse and worse and high food prices and shortages and a waste of young lives that was now becoming noticeable.

'High time we showed old Boney what's what,' Thiss said as he and Nan set off to Printing House Square. ''E'll meet 'is match now, so 'e will.'

It sounded very likely, Nan said. But what was certain was that such good news brought an increase in the demand for newspapers. Her London shops were again beseiged by eager customers. It was quite like the old days when Nelson won his victories at Cape St Vincent and the Nile and Trafalgar, and it kept her so busy she was rarely in the house. As she wrote to Thomasina and Evelina Callbeck, 'There is so much work my present newsmen are exhausted. I take on new sellers by the day and still we cannot meet the demand. 'Tis a fine thing for trade, howsomever it do wear out shoe leather.'

In the May the Clarence's received their marching orders. Calverley went round to White's at once to see what more he could discover about it, and there he met Hanley-Brown and Fortescue in the foyer. They were glowing with excitement.

'Off to the wars, eh?' Hanley-Brown beamed. 'Just signin' off here, don'tcher know? What sport!'

'Bit of luck meeting you Leigh,' Fortescue said. 'Wouldn't need a racehorse by any chance, would you?'

'Fine filly,' Hanley-Brown said. 'Two-year-old, goes like the wind.'

Until that moment Calverley had never thought of owning a racehorse, but immediately the suggestion was made he could see that it was just the sort of stylish possession for a man in his position, and what was more it would be a palpable source of income. His interest was immediate and practical.

'How much do you ask?'

'Hundred guineas,' Fortescue said. 'We have half-shares, d'you see. Could you stand such a price?'

'Easily,' Calverley said. He couldn't, but he felt pretty sure he could persuade young Billy to cough up, and as luck would have it Nan was away in St Albans, renting a new shop. 'Where do you stable her?'

'Newmarket,' Hanley-Brown said eagerly. 'She's a deuced strong filly.'

'Who is your trainer?'

'Richard Prince. A good man. Trains for the Prince of Wales now and then, don'tcher know?'

Calverley didn't know but he assumed a knowledgeable expression. 'I will consult with my cousin,' he said with splendid aplomb. 'Colonel Leigh, you know, the Prince's racing manager. What is the name of the filly?'

'Pirouette,' Hanley-Brown said, impressed by the mention of Prinny's trainer. 'Did well over the Rowley Mile in April. Tell him that.'

'We are off in ten days,' Fortescue said. 'I should like the matter signed and settled before then. 'Twould be a sad thing to leave such a creature in unknown hands.' He was growing quite sentimental about the filly, now that she was up for sale, which was odd considering he'd only set eyes on her three times and had cursed her roundly on the last occasion because she'd come in fourth and lost him a deal of money.

'Give me two days to raise the money,' Calverley said. And he went straight off to the stockroom to see Billy.

'A hundred guineas,' Billy said, sucking the end of his quill pen. 'That's a powerful amount of money. Does Ma agree?'

'Never known her refuse yet,' Calverley said easily.

390

'Perhaps we should ask her,' Billy worried. 'She should be back the day after tomorrow.'

'If I wait half a day I shall lose the chance. Never get another filly like it, not at this price, devil take it.'

So Billy allowed himself to be persuaded, although very much against his better judgement, and the filly was bought. And Calverley went down to Newmarket, where, on the very afternoon that she passed into his ownership, and to her trainer's secret surprise, she came in third in the half mile and won him nearly a quarter of the price he'd paid for her. He was very well pleased and pronounced her 'a sterling creature'. But on her next outing, she reverted to form, and lost him thirty-five guineas, so that he came back to London considerably out of pocket. And as Nan was back, he couldn't touch young Billy for any more cash. It was deuced annoying.

I shall have to marry her, he thought. I never have enough money these days, and 'tis downright demeaning to have to go begging to young Billy, amenable though he always is.

Actually, had he known it, young Billy was beginning to suspect he was being used. He'd spent two sleepless nights worrying about it, for a hundred guineas was far too much to have gone missing from the takings without being noticed and Mr Leigh showed no sign of putting it back. Finally he decided to tell his brother.

'What do 'ee think?' he asked, when supper was over and the two of them had retired to their bedroom and the full tale had been told.

'I think he's dishonest,' Johnnie said. 'He don't ask me, you notice.'

There was an unpalatable truth in that. 'No,' Billy said shamefacedly. 'What should I do, Johnnie?'

'We will tell Mr Teshmaker,' Johnnie decided. 'He's a good man, *and* he knows about the law.'

Mr Teshmaker took the story with his customary calm, and had instant and practical advice to offer. 'We must hope that this matter may be resolved without loss,' he said. 'Howsomever, that is something you may safely leave to me. Might I suggest that in the event of any further requirements for loans of any kind, from whichever quarter they may come, you refer the matter to me. Inform the person concerned that you are no longer empowered to handle the firm's money. That would be quite in order.'

'Do you think he will tell Mama?' Billy asked when he and Johnnie were back at Cheyne Walk that evening.

391

'In his own time, I daresay,' Johnnie said. 'He's a wily old bird.'

But the wily old bird had already decided that if he could he would keep all knowledge of this affair from his mistress. She had too high an opinion of the extravagant Mr Leigh, and might not take kindly to those who baulked him, no matter how proper their motives. No, he would watch and wait. Sooner or later the gentleman would grow careless or too greedy. Then perhaps something might be done.

But Calverley was very cautious that summer and he stayed cautious for well over a twelvemonth. Although he ran up considerable debts during the year, he took care not to approach young Billy until Nan had gone down to Bury. Then the boy's well-rehearsed rebuff came as quite a shock.

'Uncommon sensible,' he said, covering at once. 'Quite agree. Got to keep these things regular, damme if you ain't.' But his heart was pounding quite painfully. Who'd ha' thought the young pup would go blabbing to that legal feller? Deuce take it, he thought, now what am I to do? I wish I hadn't bought that damn filly. She's nothing but expense. But he couldn't sell her because her form was too well known. Deuce take it, what am I to do?

Luckily the fortunes of war gave him an opportunity. In August news came through that there had been a great British victory at the place in Spain called Talevera and that Sir Arthur Wellesley was to be Viscount Wellington by way of reward. And Nan wrote to him from Bury to say that a grand ball was planned as a celebration. He made up his mind at once. He would beg four days leave of Mr Chaplin and go down to Bury and escort her to the ball. 'Twould be a romantic setting in which to ask her to marry him. For the sooner they were man and wife the better. What if Mr Teshmaker were to speak to her before he got the chance to propose? No, no, he'd delayed too long already. They would have to marry and marry soon. Matters were becoming too complicated.

Unfortunately he'd reckoned without Miss Amelia Pettie.

She was taking tea with Nan and Annie when he and Jericho arrived in Angel Square, and the sight of him put her into an immediate and voluble flutter.

'Now here's Mr Leigh,' she said, patting her ringlets. 'He will tell you, my dear, I'm sure on it. Won't you, Mr Leigh?'

He gave her his most charming smile. 'Indeed I will, Miss Pettie, if you tell me what 'tis.'

'Should Annie attend this ball, think 'ee?' Nan said, laughing at her neighbour's confusion.

It was plain that they'd all made up their minds about it, so he agreed at once. 'What could be better? Then I shall have three pretty ladies to escort.' At which Miss Pettie went quite pink and clutched at both sets of false curls at once, and Annie smiled and ducked her head in shyness.

But it was a confounded nuisance, for it meant that Nan spent the next three days supervising the making of her daughter's 'very first ball gown' and hardly had any time to speak to him at all, even in bed, for she sat up so late there was barely time to kiss her before she fell asleep. And Miss Pettie was in and out of the house every minute of the day chattering and giggling and gossiping and getting in the way. 'She will be the belle of the ball, will she not, Mr Leigh?' she asked, at least three times a day. 'And who knows, she might make a match.'

And he would agree and smile until his jaws ached, wishing she would go away. But at least the atmosphere was good and Nan was happy and that was a good omen.

And the ball was a great success. He bought flowers for all three women, daisies for the old lady, red roses for Nan, and forget-me-nots for Annie, 'to match your pretty eyes, my dear'. And even though part of his mind was busy and watchful waiting for the opportunity to propose to his elusive Nan, he was touched by Annie, who looked shy and pretty in her simple white gown and wore his blue flowers in her hair. There was such a wistful air about her, as if she were yearning for a partner who wasn't there. It made him feel positively paternal to watch her. He made sure that she was introduced to plenty of partners and took care to dance with her himself whenever her card was unmarked.

But Nan was impossible, being partnered by so many unnecessary gentlemen she hardly had a dance left on her card for him. 'Who are all these people?' he asked tetchily, when she returned to him after the supper interval. 'You surround yourself with strangers.'

'They en't strangers to me,' she said, laughing at him. 'They're my neighbours and my customers. All good for trade, my dear.'

But impossible for romance. However, he stayed cheerful and smiling and quick on his feet, handsome in his brown coat and his yellow waistcoat and his fine white breeches, encouraged because he knew he was being admired by several young ladies in the hall, even if

Nan wasn't paying him enough attention. When we are home in our bedroom alone, then, he thought . . .

But even then he was thwarted, although in the most appetizing way. For Nan was in splendidly amorous mood and had no intention of talking, and when they had loved to their mutual satisfaction she turned on her side and slept almost at once, pausing only to tell him sleepily that he'd had been 'uncommon kind to Annie'. And when he woke in the morning she was already up and dressed and gone. He couldn't believe such bad fortune. He'd been in the house for four days and he hadn't found one single suitable moment. If that wretched Miss Pettie comes round to talk about the ball, he thought, I swear I'll throttle her.

But she did and he didn't. Instead he smiled and made polite conversation and watched the clock steadily revolving towards the time when he would have to leave. And it was such a perfect day too. Angel Hill was golden brown in the sunshine.

Miss Pettie took her leave after Thiss had been sent to collect Jericho from the stables. I have fifteen minutes, Calverley thought. It was desperately little time.

'We will take a turn about the square while we wait,' Nan said, when she'd waved goodbye to her everlasting neighbour.

'Must we?' he said, heart sinking.

'Indeed we must. On a day like this 'twould be a waste to be within doors.'

So as he didn't dare to annoy her by argument, they stepped out of the house and took a brief walk about the square. After a few moments Annie joined them, demure in her straw bonnet and her long-fringed shawl, and walked with them as far as the Abbey gardens, where she spent most of her afternoons these days.

They watched her as she disappeared through the medieval gateway.

'I shall walk on to Mr Turnbull's shop once you are gone,' Nan said. 'I've a mind to build a summer-house in the garden. What do 'ee think of that?'

'I've a mind to make changes myself,' he said.

'Then you shall speak to Mr Turnbull too.'

The idea of proposing to the builder made him laugh out loud. 'Mr Turnbull ain't the one to be told the sort of changes I have in mind.

'Then who is, pray?' she asked, intrigued.

'Why you are, my charmer.'

394

She stood quite still with one gloved hand resting on his arm. 'That sounds uncommon serious. You'd best tell me.'

It wasn't the right moment and he knew it, but it was too opportune to miss. 'I will tell 'ee,' he said, 'I have been giving serious thought to my life. I begin to wonder if I ain't the marrying man, after all.'

She threw back her head and roared with laughter, showing her teeth. 'Oh, you foolish creature,' she said. 'If this don't beat cock-fighting. You en't the marrying kind. You said so many and many's the time.'

'Mayn't a man change?'

'Aye. With good reason.' But her eyes were mocking him.

This was all going wrong, setting off the wrong emotions, using the wrong words. He decided to try another track. 'I have loved you all these years,' he pleaded, 'and now I talk of marriage you laugh.'

'And so I should think,' she said dusting her gloved hands against each other, swish, swish, and gave him a grin. 'Here's Thiss with your horse.'

Damn Thiss, he thought. Couldn't he have taken a little longer? Oh, she's an infuriating woman! I'll wager she ain't paid the slightest attention to what I was trying to say. And he rode out of the square quite cast down with disappointment.

But he was wrong. The next morning when the sunshine was still balmy and Bury placid and peaceful beneath it, Nan was considering what he'd said. She had taken it as a joke, but perhaps he meant it. Had he spoken so to test her? To discover what she thought of the idea perhaps? And what did she think of the idea? She wasn't at all sure. If he'd asked me years ago, when we were first lovers I should have said yes, without another thought. Now . . .

She put on her bonnet and shawl and took a promenade through the town to consider the matter, and by the time she returned to Angel Hill she had come to a decision. The first thing she ought to do would be to broach the subject with her children. With subtlety, of course, and simply, so as to test their opinion. And as the boys were still in Chelsea she would have to start with Annie.

'We will take tea in the garden,' she said to Bessie that afternoon. Her back garden was shaded and private and would be a good place for such a conversation.

Even so they had both taken two dishes of tea and Annie had eaten one of the cook's famous wafer-cakes before Nan could pluck up courage to begin. Delicate conversations were always difficult and this one was almost impossible.

Eventually she began to talk about surprises, telling her daughter how very surprised she had been when she saw Miss Pettie at the ball in her new wig. 'Have you ever been surprised so?' she asked hopefully.

'No,' Annie said blandly, sipping her tea.

'Now, as to that,' her mother said, forcing the conversation on, 'would it surprise you to know that *I* wouldn't be a bit surprised if there wasn't a wedding in our family some day soon.'

Annie's response was immediate and extraordinary. She put down her cup and clapped her hands together. 'Why Mama, how did you know of it? Has he spoken to you?'

'Not in so many words,' Nan admitted, rather stunned. 'Things have been said, you understand, in passing, in a manner of some delicacy, as you'll appreciate. To tell the truth, I cannot say I am exactly hopeful of a proposal but on the other hand 'twould be no great surprise.'

'Oh, Mama!' Annie said, and her cheeks were quite pink. 'How should you answer were he to suggest it?'

'Well now, as to that,' Nan said, choosing her words with care, ''twould depend, in part, upon your opinion on the matter.'

'How can you doubt my opinion, my own dear, darling Mama?'

She knew that Annie liked Calverley but such extreme enthusiasm was really rather extraordinary. 'You would say yes to it?'

'Oh, indeed I would. Yes, yes, a thousand times! He is such a dear kind man.'

This seemed a little extravagant too but Nan agreed to it.

'He may not be handsome,' Annie bubbled on. 'That I'll agree, and he may stoop a little . . .'

'Stoop?' her mother said. 'The very idea! He does *not* stoop. And 'tis my opinion he is exceedingly handsome. Particularly on horseback.'

'I do not recall ever having seen him on horseback,' Annie faltered.

'Oh, come now,' Nan said. 'You've seen him many's the time, here and in London.'

'As far as I know, Mama, Mr Hopkins has never been to London.'

'Mr Hopkins?'

'That is who we talk of, is it not?' Annie said but she was beginning to look rather anxious about it.

396

'Mr Hopkins the curate?' She'd seen him several times in church on Sundays, and a pale, stooping, insignificant creature he was.

'Yes, Mama.'

There was a long, ominous pause while Nan stared at her daughter and Annie's bottom lip began to tremble.

'Have you been a-telling me you expect to marry a curate?' Nan said at last.

'Oh yes, indeed Mama.'

It was such a surprise Nan spoke without thought. 'Oh, what squit!' she said. 'I never heard such squit in all my life!' she shouted. 'You en't a-marrying no curate. You can do better than *that* in all conscience.' But the minute the words were out of her mouth she regretted them, for she could see from the expression on her daughter's face that this was a serious matter.

Annie stood her ground, pale-faced and trembling. 'I am sorry you should learn of it like this, Mama,' she said, 'but I tell 'ee true, I mean to marry Mr Hopkins, with or without your permission.' Then she burst into tears and ran into the house, missing Bessie by inches as she ran.

'Why, whatever is the matter, my lamb?' Bessie said, but the girl was gone. They could hear her running into the house and up the stairs, weeping loudly, and after a while her bedroom door was slammed and locked.

'What is it, mum?' Bessie asked.

'She wants to marry the curate,' Nan explained, running into the house.

'Now come, Annie,' she said, when she'd reached the bedroom door. 'This won't do. Come out and we will talk on it.' She was speaking in the most reasoning tone she could manage, but it was no good.

'Go away!' Annie sobbed. 'I won't talk to you. I won't. You have broken my heart. Go away!'

And there she stayed, refusing to come out, or to talk to anyone except Bessie, or to eat anything except bread and water. Quiet, sensible Annie, behaving like a girl bewitched.

Miss Pettie called to see if she could help, and crept up the stairs and spoke softly at the door. Her words had no effect at all but she came down to the drawing-room twittering with excitement.

''Tis just like a novel, Mrs Easter,' she said, patting her curls. 'A heroine dying of love. The romance of it, my dear! Poor Annie!'

397

Her mother was not impressed by such talk. 'Humph!' she snorted. 'That's as maybe. Howsomever, one thing is for certain. She can't go on living like a novel for ever. She'll come out by and by, like her brother does.'

But she went on for three more days, and still showed no signs of coming out of the room or into her senses. By then, Nan was beginning to worry.

'Can't *you* coax her?' she said to Bessie. 'Make her eat something at the very least.'

'She means to marry the gentleman or die, so she says,' Bessie worried.

'She can't go on like this,' Nan said. 'She will make herself ill.'

'Perhaps Mr Leigh could get 'er ter see sense,' Bessie said. 'She's quite beyond me, mum.'

So Nan wrote to Calverley, who would surely be back in Chelsea by this time. 'Annie has taken leave of her senses. She says she will marry a curate or die, if you ever heard such squit. I can do nothing with her. Come you home do, for we are all at our wits' end with her caterwauling.'

He arrived late the next morning.

'She is in her bedroom still and won't come out,' Nan said without preliminary.

To his credit he went upstairs at once, and Nan and Bessie, listening in the hall, heard him knock. ''Tis Mr Leigh, my dear,' and Annie's answer. 'Pray wait a little, sir, and I will let you in.'

'How now, my pretty?' he said when the lock had been drawn for him.

'Oh, Mr Leigh,' Annie sobbed. 'I mean to marry Mr Hopkins and Mama says I must not. How am I to live? I love him with all my heart.'

He sat her down upon the chaise-longue, and drew up a chair to sit before her.

'Tell me all about it,' he said.

398

Chapter Thirty-five

Everard Emmanuel Hopkins much prefered to be called James. He felt like a James, and on the rare occasions when he checked his appearance in the modest hall mirror of the modest lodging-house where he had two modest rooms, he was reassured to see that he looked like a James, a quiet, unobtrusive young man with mouse-brown hair, mouse-brown eyes, a snub nose and rather crooked teeth. He walked with a slight stoop and his head was usually slightly bowed, so that his vision was restricted to the solid ground beneath his feet and he had to look up to almost any person who spoke to him. A James without a doubt.

Everard Emmanuel had been his father's choice, and it hadn't surprised anybody. For his father was Bishop Hopkins, no less, and Bishop Hopkins had always known exactly where he was going in the world. So naturally he knew exactly what path his infant son would tread, and he knew it from the moment the child was born. Into the church, of course, and thence steadily upwards by easy preferment until he too reached a bishopric. So he named him accordingly.

It was a bitter disappointment to him that the boy grew up without any ambition at all. He went into the Church obediently enough, but having got there he discovered that what he really wanted was to serve the poor.

'I would be happy to be a curate all my life, Father,' he told his infuriated parent with disarming gentleness. 'Doing Christ's work, you know.'

'The boy is a fool,' the Bishop said to his wife over dinner that evening. 'Wants to waste his talents on the poor, if you ever heard of such a thing. However, if he wishes to be a curate all his life, he might as well go to St James in Bury. At least he will mix with a better class of parishioner.'

'He needs a good wife,' his mother said. 'Someone to make him see sense and keep him on line. We must pray for a good wife for him.'

So they prayed, directly to God of course, as befitted their high status.

And later that summer, Everard Emmanuel who preferred to be James met Annie Easter in the Abbey gardens in Bury St Edmunds.

It was a purely accidental meeting, of course, for neither of them would ever have dared to plan a rendezvouz with a member of the opposite sex. James had gone for a brief constitutional stroll before his modest dinner, partly because he hoped it would give him the appetite to do justice to his landlady's very dull food and partly because he felt it politic to keep out of her way while it was cooking, as the process always seemed to make her short-tempered.

He was walking quietly around the ornamental flowerbeds, watching the gravel in his usual quiet way, when a ball of white wool rolled into his line of vision. He stooped to retrieve it, thinking no further than that he would return it to its owner, but as he straightened, he found himself staring into the eyes of a charming girl. She had stooped to retrieve the wool too and now, seeing it already in the curate's hands, was moving away from the confusion of a collision. When they eyes met, their faces were little more than six inches apart.

'My dear lady!' James said breathlessly. 'I trust I did not alarm you. I had no idea you were there, upon my life I did not.' What pretty blue eyes she had, staring at him in alarm, and her forehead as round as a baby's.

'Pray do not apologize, sir,' she said politely, dropping her eyelids in the most delightfully modest way, and stepping backwards away from him towards the seat on which she'd been sitting until that foolish wool rolled away from her. 'It was entirely my fault for being so care-less.'

He was still holding the ball of wool and as she picked up the white stocking she had been knitting, the thread tightened between them, holding them together. The sight of it sent poor James into a tremble of alarm.

'Ah! Dear me! Yes!' he said. 'Allow me to return your wool. Yes!' And he thrust it at her so clumsily that it fell through her fingers and rolled off into the wallflowers as though it had a life of its own.

His embarrassment was increasing by the minute. 'I am so very sorry,' he stuttered, and this time he went down onto his black knees and crawled into the flowerbed to effect a proper retrieval. Which made matters worse than ever, for by the time the wool was found and carried back to the seat it was tangled and twisted and had acquired half a spider's web and rather a lot of leafmould.

'I have made matters worse, I fear,' he said abjectly. She was the nicest girl he'd ever seen, so it was really only to be expected that he would make a fool of himself before her. 'I cannot tell you how sorry I am.'

'Pray do not distress yourself,' she said. 'It is always happening.' She had already picked off the spider's web and was removing the leafmould with deft, patient fingers. What a kind young lady she was.

'Would it help if I held one end?' he offered. He had a vague recollection that he had seen two young women winding a ball of wool from a skein so he knew that it required two pairs of hands.

'It would be better if you held the stocking,' she said, 'Thank you kindly.'

So he held the stocking while she unravelled the knots, and they fell into conversation, which was a quite extraordinary thing, for he had never held a conversation with a young lady before. Not in all his twenty-one years.

She told him her name was Annie Easter and he confessed to James Hopkins and the curacy of St James' church, which did not surprise her, she said, for she attended the church every Sunday and had often seen him there.

'I live on Angel Hill,' she confided. 'Just across the way.' Then, since the tangles were all smoothed away, she took up her knitting again and told him that the stocking was for the housekeeper's daughter who was called Pollyanna and was an absolute duck.

And as she spoke a real live duck and a drake waddled towards them over the green, their plump breasts full as eggs and their heads swaying from side to side with the urgency of their walk.

'How trusting they are,' she said. 'They see no harm in us.'

'They expect us to feed them,' he told her. 'It is cupboard-love I fear, Miss Easter, not trust.' But the ducks certainly did look very trusting. There was something almost dog-like about them, looking up so brightly, their round eyes like amber beads.

'No sir, it is a natural trust,' she insisted, but gently, oh so very gently and in the most womanly manner he could ever have imagined, if he'd ever had the temerity to imagine any such thing. 'It is the natural

401

confidence that all living creatures should repose in mankind, if only we were worthy of it.'

'Oh how true!' he said, captivated. 'You have hit upon my sentiments exactly. We are so unworthy. We behave so badly.' And then he blushed, realizing that what he was saying sounded as though he was finding fault with her. 'Mankind, I mean, of course, mankind in general. I trust you do not think I was speaking in any way – er – personally.'

'But are we not of mankind also?' she said earnestly. 'We are all to blame, I fear.'

'Yes, yes, of course,' he agreed again, more confused than ever.

'Being members of one church.'

'Yes indeed, of one church.' What delicious blue eyes she had! And such an open, trusting expression.

'There is so much cruelty in the world,' she sighed. 'I don't have a crust for these poor birds, not a single crust.'

'I could go home and get some, should you wish it.'

The blue eyes approved. 'Could you? Could you really?'

Oh, indeed he could. He could indeed. Perhaps she would care to walk with him, if it wouldn't fatigue her. It was only a step away.

And so they fed the ducks, who pressed in upon them with beady-eyed ferocity until they were quite sure there wasn't a crumb left. And at that point the church clock struck the hour and James realized that he was going to be late for dinner. He was very alarmed.

'I must go, I fear, Miss Easter,' he said, his ears pink because he was afraid she might think him rude. 'I trust we shall meet again. I always take a promenade, before dinner, somewhere hereabouts, if the weather is fine.'

'If the weather is fine,' she said, looking straight into his eyes in such a charming way she made him quite breathless.

'We could feed the ducks,' he suggested. 'Tomorrow perhaps?'

'If the weather is fine,' she repeated, blushing.

And it was. It was. It was fine for the next four blessed days, which was long enough for the ducks to be fed to capacity and for James and Annie to establish a routine.

Soon they were meeting to walk and talk on every day except Sunday, innocently happy in the new May sunshine and chaperoned by the eyes of his congregation. And on Sunday, of course, they would see one another in church, and he could hold her hands in greeting when she arrived, and again when she left, and spend most of the intervening service smiling at her whenever she was looking his way and feasting his eyes upon her when her head was reverently and properly lowered to read her prayer-book.

It wasn't long before the rector became aware of what was going on. Or to be more accurate, the rector's wife, for he was an amiable and rather dreamy soul who might have missed the signs, but his wife missed nothing.

'You must write to the Bishop at once,' she told her spouse. 'The good man must be acquainted with all that is going on.'

So the Bishop was acquainted.

'Wonders will never cease!' he said to his wife when he read the letter over his breakfast. 'It appears that Everard Emmanuel has fallen in love.'

'With whom?' his wife said, lowering her eyes suspiciously. She had a very low opinion of falling in love. It could lead to all manner of ridiculous consequences and was not a trustworthy way to find a partner.

'She seems highly suitable, my dear,' the Bishop said, returning to his kedgeree. 'The only daughter of Mrs Easter, the London newsagent, and cousin of Sir Osmond Easter of Ippark. A goodly pedigree, you will allow, my dear.'

'A pedigree is one thing,' his wife said, only slightly mollifed. 'But will she be able to handle Everard Emmanuel? That is the matter we have to consider. He will need a wife of some character if he is not to remain a curate all his life. You must invite her to stay.'

The Bishop chewed over her suggestion with his kedgeree. 'We will give a dinner party,' he decided when his mouth was empty. 'For Harvest Home.'

'But Harvest Home is months away.'

'There is no need to rush such things, my dear. If it is a passing infatuation it will have passed by the autumn. If it is not then we may hope for better things. May I trouble you for another cup of your excellent tea?'

So in due course of time Annie was sent her invitation, and having contrived to be allowed to stay on in Bury for a week or two to nurse little Pollyanna who was recovering from the measles, she sent a polite acceptance in her very best handwriting. There was no need to say anything to her mother just yet. In fact she really didn't want to say anything to her mother at all, just in case she was cross, for she still found her sudden temper too awful to contemplate. The thought of the visit was worrying enough without being shouted at beforehand.

But although she and James were rigid with nerves, the visit was a success. The Bishop was quite taken with little Miss Easter, who was surprisingly well-read for a tradesman's daughter, with an excellent knowledge of Mr Wordsworth's poetry. And she gave a quite delightful answer when he asked her opinion as to whether a young curate should aim at a parish of his own.

'Oh yes, sir,' she said. 'I think he should. His own flock! What a challenge that would be.'

And James had to agree with her, his ears bright-pink with embarrassment, because a dinner party was not the place at which to conduct a discussion on the ethics of church preferment.

Later he tried to explain things to her. 'I wish to follow Christ in all His teachings,' he said earnestly. 'I cannot believe that He intended the shepherd to be wealthier than his flock.'

'You have the kindest heart,' she said, admiring him. 'I cannot believe that you will ever be wealthy, for you will give away all your worldly goods, will you not?'

If he'd had any worldly goods at that moment he would have given them away for the right to kiss that tempting little mouth. But it wasn't the right moment for either. Not yet. Not yet. Particularly as she was due to return to London in a day or two.

'You will write to me,' she asked unnecessarily when he came to see her off.

'Oh, depend upon it,' he said, loving her with his eyes. 'Every day. You have my solemn word.'

And so their gentle romance continued. And the Bishop and his wife waited for news. And Bessie was sworn to secrecy. And Nan remained in ignorance.

But when another year had passed the Bishop couldn't contain his soul in patience a moment longer and Everard Emmanuel was summoned to the presence.

'Now look 'ee here,' the Bishop said without preamble. 'Your mother and I need to know your intentions towards Miss Easter.'

'Entirely honourable Father, I do assure you,' James said earnestly.

'Tush boy. I know that. When do you intend to marry? That's what we want to know. We have arrangements to make, you know.'

404

James was so embarrassed his ears felt as though they were on fire. 'Well,' he said. 'As to that, father . . . As to that.'

'Bless me!' the Bishop said to his wife. 'I don't believe the foolish creature has asked her.'

'Well . . .' James said, shifting from foot to foot.

'Oh, bless me!' the Bishop said again. He needed rather a lot of assistance from his Maker that morning. 'Did you ever see such a noddle? My advice to 'ee boy is to go straight back to Bury and propose to the lady. That's what my advice is. Oh, bless me!'

But when poor James went trailing back to Bury and his various and difficult duties, he found his beloved sitting in the Abbey gardens in floods of tears.

'My own dear love,' he said, forgetting his caution at the sight of her distress. 'What is it?'

'Oh, Mr Hopkins!' she cried. 'My mother has found out about us. I have been kept to my room this last week. What are we to do?'

'You must tell me all about it,' he said, producing a handkerchief to dry her eyes.

So she did, between renewed tears on her part and more solicitous dabbing on his, and when her tale was done it was his turn to tell her about his unreasonable parent. 'He may be a Bishop,' he finished, 'but I do feel he lacks sensitivity. For truly I do feel I should be allowed to propose to you in my own good time and not his.'

'How true!' she agreed, smiling weakly at him for the first time since their meeting. 'But what are we to do? Mr Leigh says he will help us, but I don't see how he can.'

'Who is Mr Leigh, my love?'

'I blush to tell you Mr Hopkins. He is my mother's lover.'

'Dear me!' he sighed. ' 'Tis a godless generation, I fear. My poor dear love. But perhaps he may persuade her?'

'We must pray so,' his beloved said.

'Yes,' he said, thinking how pretty she looked when her eyes were swimming with tears. Most women grew blotchy when they cried, but she was charming. He dropped on one knee before her. 'My dear Miss Easter,' he said with sudden gallantry, 'I love you with all my heart. No matter what may happen, or what difficulties we may have to face, one day I will marry you, upon my word of honour, if you will have me. Oh, I will make you so, so happy.'

'Mr Hopkins,' she said seriously. 'You are a good man, and if you are proposing to me, my answer is yes.'

And at that and because there was nobody else in the gardens on that chilly day, he kissed her.

When Calverley had left his comforted Annie in the gardens, he walked briskly back to Angel Square where Jericho was waiting beside the pavement and Nan and Bessie were waiting in the hall.

'Well?' Nan said, without preamble.

'She is in love,' he explained. 'Quite wild with it. I fear you will have to let 'em marry, for she means to break her heart if you refuse.'

'She can marry whom she pleases,' Nan said trenchantly, 'and could have known it days ago if she'd had the sense to come out of her room and talk.'

'Humour her,' he said, walking to the door. 'Invite the young man to tea. I must go Nan, I fear. I've to be in Norwich by three o'clock and Jericho ain't as young as he was.'

She kissed him lovingly. ' 'Tis sound advice,' she said. 'God speed 'ee.'

So Everard Emmanuel received a second summons in as many weeks. In great trepidation and in his best clothes he duly presented himself at Angel Hill for her inspection.

The splendour of her drawing-room made him feel like a fly in a trifle. And the lady herself was formidable, sitting before the fire on her elegant chaise-longue with the tea things laid out neatly on a little table before her, her red gown so uncompromising, her brown eyes so direct.

'Sit down, sir,' she said, as though he were a dog.

He sat obediently.

'You will take tea,' she ordered, in the same brusque tones.

'Ma'am,' ears glowing.

It was uncommon difficult to take tea with Mrs Easter. She thrust the cup at you so roughly, and glared at you when your trembling made it rattle, and then just when you'd worked up sufficient courage to lift it to your lips and sip, she said,

'You wish to marry my daughter, I believe.'

His throat constricted so violently it was all he could do to swallow the tea. But he answered her bravely, 'Yes, ma'am, I do.'

406

'You have very poor prospects, young man,' she said sternly. 'What makes you consider yourself worthy of such a match?'

'It is true,' he said earnestly. 'My prospects are poor but your daughter loves me nevertheless, and I love her with all my heart.'

'Humph!' she snorted and continued the inquisition.

Afterwards he couldn't remember any of the questions she asked, although they went on interminably. She was so quick, stabbing a second query at him before he'd finished answering the first, but he held on grimly, staring at the red and green threads in the carpet under his feet, and re-iterating over and over again, as his final inescapable reason, 'I love her, Mrs Easter.'

'You young things are all the same,' she said when twenty minutes had passed and he was still saying the same thing. 'You think you may live on air.'

'God's blessed manna fell from the air upon the children of Israel,' he reminded them both, doggedly serious.

There was a faint scuffling sound outside the further door, smothered voices and a furtive scrabbling and somebody giggling. Nan jumped up at once, swept across the room, skirts swishing and flung the door aside. It was such a quick movement that the listeners were caught off balance and fell into the room in a giggling heap. Bessie and Annie and little Pollyanna.

'Oh, Mama!' Annie pleaded from where she crouched on her hands and knees. 'Pray do not be cross with Bessie, I beg you. 'Twas all my fault, although I could not help it, truly I could not.'

Pollyanna was sitting in her mother's tumbled lap, James had risen to his feet still clutching his teacup, and they were all looking at Nan, fearfully and hopefully.

'Blamed fools the lot of you!' she said. And to the curate's amazement she put back her head and roared with laughter, showing her teeth. 'Oh, oh!' she laughed. ' 'Tis worse than a comedy, so 'tis. Oh, very well Annie, if that's what you want you'd best marry the man, for I can get no sense out of him save that he loves you. And now get up do, for I can't abide the sight of you grovelling upon the floor.'

Then there was bedlam in the room as Annie ran into her lover's arms and Bessie burst into happy tears and Calverley came rushing in through the other door loud with congratulations.

So a second kettle was brought to the boil and a second tea taken by all of them, this time with pastries and much pleasure. And the wedding

407

was planned. It was agreed that Annie should stay in Bury for the winter and buy her trousseau and supervise the arrangements, since, as Nan remarked 'You can't abide to be parted,' and that the ceremony would be held on the first day of May the very next year, and that the Bishop would be asked to officiate.

And Annie asked Mr Leigh if he would 'be so very kind as to give me away', which pleased him so much that he lifted her clean off her feet and waltzed about the room with her, swinging her round and round until her skirts billowed like a bell.

'Love conquers all, you see my dearest,' the curate said when he parted from his beloved in a hall left tactfully empty for them. 'It was just a matter of keeping faith.'

'Now that we are engaged to be married,' Annie said, eyes shining, 'I suppose you may kiss me whenever you please.'

'It is the custom I believe,' he said, and proceeded to enjoy it.

Chapter Thirty-six

So Everard Emmanuel accepted the benefice of St Lawrence's Church at Rattlesden from his father the Bishop, because he would have a wife to support now, and Annie Easter married her curate in the church of St James in Bury St Edmunds and a very pretty picture she made standing before the altar in her blue watered silk with a modest poke-bonnet to hide her blushes. Calverley gave the bride away, looking exceedingly handsome, and the Bishop conducted the service looking extremely grand, and the wedding-breakfast, which was held in the Athenaeum, was the biggest and most lavish that the citizens of Bury had ever seen.

The Bishop was impressed. Whatever cobweb doubts he might still have had about the strength of his new daughter-in-law's character or the suitability of her family were swept away by the brisk broom of her mother's forceful personality. 'A capital family!' as he told his wife later that evening. 'Capital! A lady of charm and capacity without a doubt.'

He had been a trifle perturbed by her first letter to him, in which she had expressed her 'very great pleasure that our two important families are to be allied', for trade, however prosperous, could hardly be compared to the undeniable status of a bishopric. But the lady herself was a revelation, so slight and thin and yet with such force and speed, quick in her movements, her wits, her speech and her decisions. A woman of mercury, and uncommon well-dressed. The Bishop had an eye for such detail, and he missed none of it now, from the diamonds and pearls at the lady's throat to the exquisite and costly embroidery at the hem of her gown. He liked her shrewd eyes and the dark hair springing so forcefully from her temples and that wide, uncompromising mouth. Why, she had success written all over her. Not the sort of lady to endure a mere curate as a son-in-law, nor to allow him to remain a country parson for long.

'I knew this marriage would be the making of him, when our foolish boy brought dear Annie to dine for the very first time,' he told his wife as they walked to their places at the wedding breakfast, 'and I am rarely mistaken, as I think you will allow. Yes, indeed, an excellent match!'

Dear Annie was so happy in her excellent match she was virtually speechless with pleasure. The service had been so awesome and magical she still wore the charm of it like an aura, all those faces gilded by candlelight and beaming love at them both, and the hymns rolling upwards into the high blue and gold of the ceiling, echoing and calling, and circlets of gentle candles flickering yellow warmth, and the great gold cross pulsing like a beacon. And James, her own dear James, looking at her with such affection, and saying, oh so passionately it made her tremble, 'with my body I thee worship'. Now she sat beside him in her beautiful blue gown in the splendid blue and gold of the banqueting hall of the Athenaeum, breathing in the heady scent of spring flowers, light-headed with champagne, and it seemed to her that the whole world was blue and white and gold and beneficent, and that it would be springtime for ever and ever.

Nan was well pleased with the wedding too. It was a relief to see that Annie was quite herself again after her incomprehensible behaviour. And the wedding breakfast was so well organized it all went without a hitch. Or very nearly.

It was Johnnie who caused what little trouble there was, dratted boy. He'd seemed so pleased about his sister's marriage, wishing her well and offering to help her move into the rectory, so it was rather a surprise when he suddenly launched into a violent verbal attack on two of the guests. But then, as his mother knew only too well, nobody could ever be sure what was going on inside his swarthy head.

The meal was over and the dancing was about to begin and the bridal couple were circulating to talk to family and friends in the time-honoured way, when Nan became aware that voices were being raised at the other end of the room, and set off at once to see what was happening. What she found made her very angry.

On a kindly impulse she had invited Thomasina and Evelina from Ippark, and they had duly arrived, clutching carefully wrapped gifts and plainly delighted to have been asked to join the family celebration. Now they stood beside the stairs to the minstrels' gallery cowering together like frightened rabbits while Johnnie ranted at them, his face quite distorted with rage. 'How she could have done such a thing I

410

cannot imagine! After all the cruelty your family unleashed upon her when she was poor and widowed. She asked for bread and you gave her a stone. She asked for help and you kicked her from the door. Now you impel her into shameful action. I wonder at you. Have you no —'

He got no further because his mother seized him by the arm and dragged him painfully into the nearest anteroom, hissing as she went, 'Hold your peace, boy! D'you hear me? Hold your peace!' He was so surprised that he lost his breath, so her orders were quite unnecessary.

When they were in the little room and alone, she turned upon him with venom. 'How dare you speak to my guests like that?' she roared. 'Have you no sense of propriety at all?'

'They are Easters, Mama,' he said, his face still suffused with rage.

'*Easters!* How could you bring yourself to invite such people after all they've done to you? Members of that wicked family.'

'You are an Easter too, let me point out.'

'I am your son,' he said proudly. 'I do not count myself an Easter and I never will.'

'Deuce take it!' she swore. 'I never heard such a load of old squit. Of course you're an Easter. Who do you think your father was. Now you go right back in there and apologize. You frightened those two poor old creatures fair out of their wits. I'm downright ashamed of 'ee, so I am.'

'No,' he said, obdurately. 'I will not.'

'You will.'

'I will not.'

'Then you will go home and missing the dancing,' she said, glaring her annoyance at him. 'How dare you make such a scene at your sister's wedding?'

He turned on his heel without another word and left the room and the building. Infuriating boy!

Fortunately her two beleaguered relatives were very understanding. When she got back to the assembly room they were talking to Calverley, who was at his most charming and had managed to imply that the boy had taken rather too much to drink, and confused them with somebody else. 'Not used to it, you see Miss Thomasina. Pray do allow me to refill your glasses.'

'I do apologize,' Nan said, joining them as the waiter poured champagne. 'When you were so very kind as to come all that way.'

'Boys will be boys,' Evelina said mildly. 'We did not take him seriously, I do assure you.'

'When the wine is in,' Thomasina smiled, 'the wit is out.'

'I shall have something to say to him when the wedding is over,' Nan promised.

But in the event, Sophie Fuseli had something to say to her which put all thought of Johnnie's ill manners quite out of her head.

The newly weds had departed in a flutter of rose petals and a landau loaned by the Bishop; the guests had said tipsy farewells and were now being sped on their way by the charming Mr Leigh, in so many coaches and carriages that Angel Hill was quite muddled with them; Billy was cheerfully drunk and had been carried hiccoughing to his bedroom; and Nan's fine house was suddenly quiet, an empty beach deserted by the tide, for the only guest to remain was Sophie Fuseli, which was only right and proper considering she was her oldest and dearest friend.

The two women kicked off their shoes as soon as they'd climbed the stairs to Nan's fine drawing-room. Nan had ordered tea to refresh them, but Sophie threw herself down on the chaise-longue declaring that she was too tired for anything.

'Such a wedding, my dear!' she said. 'I vow I have never seen another as fine.'

'If Johnnie hadn't been such a pest 'twould have been perfection.'

'A wretch, I fear,' Sophie commiserated. 'Will he apologize, think 'ee?'

'Not he. A more determined crittur I never came upon. Oh no, he'll stay in his room till morning, and breakfast early to avoid us, and be out and away before we can see the going of him. Annie looked well, did she not?'

'A credit to you, my dear.'

'Calverley has been uncommon kind to her.'

'Aye,' Sophie said. 'I do not doubt it. She is young and pretty, and whatever else you may say about that gentleman, he always had a soft spot in his heart for youth and beauty.'

There was an edge to her voice that made Nan look up at her sharply. ' 'Tis a fatherly interest,' she rebuked, 'no more, I do assure you.'

'A proper interest, beyond question,' Sophie agreed, smoothing the already smooth muslin of her gown. 'In that direction at least, my dear, his interest is perfectly proper.'

412

That unnecessary gesture, combined with averted eyes, and a tone of voice overloaded with meaning, alerted Nan to prickling alarm, despite her fatigue. 'You'd best say what you have to say, Sophie,' she said. 'For a hint is a thing I cannot abide. Out with it, I prithee.'

Sophie looked her old friend straight in the eye. 'He has another mistress, my dear,' she said.

Nan had always known she would hear something of the sort, sooner or later, but to hear it spoken now, after he'd proposed to her, now when she was rich and secure, now on this special day, was so painful it was as if someone was squeezing her heart in a vice. But she spoke coolly, 'She is young of course.'

'About Annie's age, I fear.'

'And pretty?'

'A vacuous face,' Sophie temporized, 'with little character.'

'But pretty.'

'Some would say so.'

'What is her name?' It was necessary to know everything.

'Mistress Meg Purser,' Sophie said. 'Daughter of a groom at the Swan with Two Necks, so they say, and mistress to at least four others, to my certain knowledge, before she caught his eye. 'Tis a passing fancy, I would lay money on't. 'Twill pass. Howsomever, there has been talk, my dear, so I thought it best to tell you of it myself before others could gossip.'

'You are a good friend, Sophie. I'm beholden to you,' Nan said, when the extreme pressure of that inward vice had eased enough for her to speak again. 'And he is nothing more than a fickle wretch, which you have known all along.'

'Shall you tax him with it?' Sophie asked, leaning forward to pat Nan's listless hands.

'Aye, I daresay,' Nan said, doing her best to sound unconcerned, 'should occasion arise. I'm a deal too fatigued at present for any such caper.' And she was relieved to be rescued by the timid knock on the door that announced the arrival of the tea.

Nevertheless it was not knowledge she could deny or forget. It was hooked into her gut like a tapeworm, and even though she did her best, during what remained of the evening, to talk and laugh as though nothing were amiss, she was drawn and drained by it.

Calverley was in his element. After an afternoon and an evening when he'd been an admired host without the burden of responsibilities, he was in the most genial and expansive mood, complimenting Sophie on her style and beauty, Nan on her management of the wedding, teasing Bessie out of her tears, talking horses with Thiss, still the life and soul of the party, even though it was now limited to the five of them.

It wasn't until he and Nan were preparing for bed that he made the first serious mistake of his day. 'How now, my Nan,' he said, giving her his most dashing smile, 'with your daughter married and gone, what better time for us to marry, eh?'

The worm clenched its terrible jaws. 'You have another mistress, I'm told,' she said. 'She en't like to take too kindly to such a notion, I'm thinking.'

It took him aback that she knew about it, but he laughed aloud, trying to brazen it out. 'Come now, Nan,' he said. 'You know my style. I've had women a-plenty. What of that? You are the one I want to marry.'

'Seems to me,' she said, turning away from him to clean her face with rose-water, 'we heard some words today concerning this matter what ought to give 'ee pause for thought.'

He was actually thinking hard behind those sleepy eyes, casting about frantically for an excuse or a diversion, regretting his folly in courting the delectable Meg so openly, cursing Sophie for telling tales. But he said nothing.

'Forsaking all other, till death us do part,' she quoted, looking at him in the mirror. In the chill of her anger, she was noticing, almost for the first time, how much weight he'd put on recently. In a year or two that rounded belly would be a paunch, and that gilded chin would droop into jowls. You en't the charmer you was, my lad, she thought. 'Forsaking all other, eh?'

'Well, as to that,' he said carelessly. ''Tis an old fashioned notion. Of no account in these new times, I tell 'ee. I wager there ain't more than three men in the whole of London would abide by it.'

'More's the pity,' she said, unpinning her hair. 'To my way of thinking the world has come to a parlous state when loyalty en't worth the candle.'

'If 'twill content 'ee, I will see no more of the wench,' he said. 'You have my word on it.' But he'd made his offer too late to placate her, as the set of her jaw revealed only too clearly.

' 'Tis all one to me,' she said, climbing into bed. 'You're a faithless wretch, Calverley Leigh, and not one I'd wish to marry. So let us have no more on it.'

It was a set-back, he could see that, but not a defeat. She seemed more weary of him now than angry. 'Howsomever, one you might love from time to time, I daresay?' he suggested, smiling at her in his most amorous way.

Despite the worm, she was warmed by his affection. 'If I've a mind to,' she said, snuffing out the candle. 'Now I've a mind to sleep.'

But it was several days before he could court his way back into her arms and even though their love-making was intensely pleasurable there was still a distance between them, made worse by the fact that he had to leave for Exeter the very next day. And from then on they were both kept so busy, he buying horses and she buying shops, that they had no time to quarrel and barely time for conversation. He took care not to refer to marriage, and made a point of bringing her pretty presents whenever he returned from one of his trips. But even so it was more than three months before the worm was finally stilled and she was smiling at him and welcoming him almost in the old way. All of which was a considerable trial to him because his creditors were now so numerous and so insistent it was everything he could do to keep them away from litigation.

'I do assure you, gentlemen,' he said, over and over again that summer, ' 'tis a matter of time before I am possessed of a considerable fortune. You shall all be paid. You have my word on it.'

'I've had your word on it, these many years,' the ostler wrote from his London stables. 'Words don't buy hay, Mr Leigh, and 'tis seventy guineas outstanding as from this morning.'

And the secretary at White's took to dropping reminders beside his plate at every single dinner. It was uncommon irritating.

Finally he strolled down to the Strand and took Billy to the coffee house. But his answer was unnervingly familiar. 'I would like to oblige 'ee, Mr Leigh. You know that. Howsomever, all such matters have to be referred to Mr Teshmaker. 'Tis company policy. Why not ask Mama?'

So he had to agree that that was what he would do, and that it was of no consequence, no consequence at all.

Now there was only Johnnie between him and ruin. It was a slight hope, but his only one. That night he took the boy to dine at Goosegogs, 'to introduce you to me friends, eh,' and plied him with brandy and careful compliments. But it was as impossible as ever to carry on a conversation with this young man. He spoke so little and with such lack of expression.

'How old are ye now?' Calverley asked when their second brandy had been served.

'Eighteen, sir.'

'A young man, damme. I tell you what, Mr Johnnie Easter, you should be in charge of the shop by now. I've a mind to speak to your mother about it.'

Silence

'We shall see you married next.'

Silence. Not even the flicker of an eye.

'At your age I was all for going on the Grand Tour, damme if I wasn't. What think 'ee? Would 'ee like to travel?'

'Not particularly.'

'Would you care for another brandy?'

'No thank 'ee.'

'Some other beverage perhaps?'

'No thank 'ee.'

'Now look 'ee here,' Calverley said, driven to directness by the boy's infuriating lack of response. 'The fact of the matter is, I've run into one or two little debts. I'm – er – a bit short of cash, dammit. What d'you think should be done about it? I ask you as man to man.'

'I couldn't say.'

'Could you see your way to a loan?' He could hear the wheedling note in his own voice and was ashamed of it, but this had to be done. 'I would ask your mother if only she were here. But you see how it is . . .'

'No, sir.'

Was that no to the loan or no, he didn't see? 'Fifty guineas would see me clear. How about it?'

Johnnie looked up suddenly and spoke at some length. 'It ain't my money to give,' he said. 'Nor yours to take, I'm thinking.'

'Your mother would give it were she here.' It was irritating to be lectured by this surly young man. 'Why quibble?'

'Precisely because it belongs to my mother, sir, and not to you or to me.'

What shrewd, hard eyes the boy has, Calverley thought. Best to try

416

another tack. 'I will let you into a little secret,' he said confidentially. 'Your mother and I mean to marry. We do not noise it abroad but 'twill be a matter of months merely. That is all. Then of course all this money that we are both treating with such caution, – a proper caution, I don't deny it – all this money will be legally mine.'

'When it is, sir,' Johnnie said with icy politeness, 'then you may use it as you think fit, as you may use her, poor woman. But if you do marry, you will marry without my blessing, and until that time, let me tell 'ee sir, I shall do all in my power to prevent you.'

'Impudent puppy!' Calverley roared. 'Have I to be told who I may or may not marry by a youth of eighteen? I never heard the like!'

Johnnie put his empty brandy glass down on the table and rose to his feet with superb dignity. 'Thank 'ee for the dinner and the brandy, sir,' he said. 'Now pray allow me to wish you good evening.' And he staggered out of the club.

Deuce take it, Calverley thought, pouring brandy down his throat to ease his temper, the boy's a wretch. I should never have asked such a hard heart. I might have known 'twould fail. But deuce take it, what is to be done now? The street outside the window was crammed with carts and horses and for a moment he was irritated by the noise they were making. Then they gave him an idea. I shall go to Newmarket, damme if I don't, he thought, and try my luck with the horses.

Newmarket was better than the best physic. He'd forgotten the excitement of the place, the thunder of hooves, the familiar voices calling the odds, the heavy smell of trodden turf, leather and liniment and the pungent sour-sweet sweat of horses. It lifted his spirits at once. Pirouette seemed to be in good form, quite amazingly unproved according to Mr Price. So he booked in at the Rutland Arms until the end of the meeting and entered his filly for the Five Hundred Guineas, with the vague hope that she might be placed. Then he wrote to Nan, partly to show her that she was in his thoughts, and partly to spike Johnnie's guns before the wretch could talk to her and make mischief.

' 'Tis an uncommon good meeting,' he write, 'with plenty of entertainments and many friends hereabouts which I have not seen for years. Jericho cast a shoe on the way. Pirouette is in good shape. Johnnie and I had words before I left. We were both too far gone in drink to know what we were saying. Goosegogs serve a capital brandy. I trust he will not concern you with it, for 'twas all nonsense. Your own Calverley.'

417

The last day of the meeting was chill and misty but his friends, old and new, were in high good humour and came rollicking to the inn to collect him. 'Uncommon poor weather,' they told him cheerfully, but they were full of ideas for improving it and most of them could be carried in the hamper they'd so thoughtfully provided, pork pies, veal pies, chicken and ham pies, pressed tongue and potted meats, to say nothing of an assortment of spirited beverages to keep out the cold, like cherry brandy and sloe gin and British Hollands flavoured with essence of cloves. All of which he seemed to have consented to pay for, it being, as they were happy to point out, 'your day at the races today, me dear.'

It was a cheerful excursion and the cherry brandy proved to be an excellent antidote to damp even if it did make him feel rather fuddled by the middle of the afternoon. 'Nothin' like a nip,' he said happily, as he stood by the rail waiting for the three o'clock start.

And a familiar voice at his elbow said 'Could you spare a nip for an old soldier?'

He turned rather dizzily, ready to send the beggar packing, and found himself staring at his old friend Captain Hanley-Brown.

'My dear chap! What a pleasure to see you!' he said proffering the brandy bottle at once. 'Feel free, me dear chap, feel free.'

But as Hanley-Brown took a swig from the bottle, Calverley saw how terribly changed he was, his clothes old and soiled, his hair grey at the temples and his round face so lined it looked at though somebody had squashed it between two weights. But worse than any of these things, oh far, far worse, was the wooden stump where his left leg had been.

'Left it at Talevera,' Hanley-Brown explained, noticing the direction of Calverley's glance. 'Took clean off by a cannon ball, so 'twas.'

'My dear feller!'

'Can't be helped. Fortunes a' war, don't cher know. Have you married your rich widow yet?'

'No, no. But 'tis only a matter of time.'

'Still playing the field eh?' Hanley-Brown said admiringly. 'You always were a dog for the ladies. I wish I could say the same, damme. 'Tis all changed now, so 'tis. Women don't take kindly to wooden underpinnings, and that's a fact. I must pay for my pleasures now, or go without. You don't know what a lucky dog you are.'

'Pray take another nip of sustenance,' Calverley said so as to deflect him from his gloom. ' 'Tain't the weather to be standing about.'

418

'At least you've two legs to stand upon,' Hanley-Brown mourned. 'Which is more than may be said for me. I say, this is dammed fine brandy. Don't know when I've tasted better.'

So naturally one of Calverley's new friends had to be dispatched to replenish the bottle, and, equally naturally, the two old comrades in arms spent the rest of the afternoon re-living old campaigns, between frequent 'nips of sustenance'.

By the time the runners were being lined up for the Five Hundred Guineas, neither of them could stand without support. They clung to the rail trying to focus their eyes upon their hopes.

'I backed our filly, don'tcher know,' Hanley-Brown said. 'A hundred to one on.'

'D'you meanter shay, backed her to win?'

'Backed her to win. Five shillings. Hundred to one one.'

'I shall do the shame,' Calverley decided. 'Be sho good as to shupport me, sir.'

They staggered to the nearest bookie but he declared it was too late. 'They're off, sir. Look.'

'Deuce take it,' Calverley complained. 'How's a man to bet if the dammed horses run before he's ready. Must have a bet, damme.' And he pulled a handful of sovereigns from his pocket and shook them at the bookie. They were all that remained of his pay, but he held them with the air of a man to whom such riches were nothing. So the bet was placed even though the field had disappeared into the mist.

'Go to – winnin' posht,' Hanley-Brown suggested. 'Shee – finish.'

Then punters all around them were peering into the mist, and they could hear hooves drumming towards them. And presently the heads and shoulders of the runners appeared, disembodied between the blue vapour swathing their legs and the smoke clouding from their bodies. For a few seconds it wasn't even possible to make out the colours, but then they drew closer and Calverley suddenly realized with a shock that almost sobered him that Pirouette was lying third. Then he and Hanley-Brown were yelling 'Pirouette! Come on Pirouette! Come on!' and the noise and excitement reached a crescendo fit to burst their ears, and she was making ground, she was second and still coming on, she was straining every muscle. And the sweat-blackened bodies flashed past his view, and his filly had won by a short head.

He couldn't believe his luck. Five Hundred Guineas! 'Twas a fortune.

419

'Congratulations, sir!' Mr Prince said when his employer had collected his winnings. 'I told 'ee she'd run well. 'Tis a tidy old sum sir!'

'It *is*, Mr Prince.'

'You'll be thinking of settling your stable bills now sir, I daresay.'

He was in such a state of stunned euphoria he wasn't thinking at all. But why not? He could settle all his bills now, every single one.

So he paid Mr Prince and collected his winnings from the bookie and gave Hanley-Brown a fiver, 'for old times sake' and staggered back to the hotel where there was another account to be met for an incomprehensible quantity of food and drink. Then he put his winnings under the mattress and fell across the bed, stupid with cherry brandy and good fortune. Luck was on his side after all. One more stroke like that and how could she refuse to marry him? Blessed by fortune, he thought, and slept as though he'd been pole-axed.

Chapter Thirty-seven

'What is to be done about it?' Johnnie said, scowling across the table at his brother and Mr Teshmaker. 'If they marry he will fritter away our livelihood in less than a year. You may depend upon it.'

The three men had dined together in the City and now they were gathered in Mr Teshmaker's quiet office with cigars lit and brandy before them as an aid to digestion and thought, and Johnnie had passed on Mr Leigh's carelessly given information.

'Howsomever, Mr John, as I need hardly point out, they are not married yet,' Mr Teshmaker said, narrowing his eyes against the smoke from his cigar, 'and that being so, and with the constrictions we have placed upon him, there is no way in which the gentleman can obtain monies from the company other than from the hands of Mrs Easter herself.'

'Which he does often enough, in all conscience,' Johnnie said, 'and gambles it away or spends it on one of his whores.'

Billy was shocked, as his brother had intended. 'Oh, Johnnie! He don't, do he?'

'I fear so, Mr William,' Mr Teshmaker said smoothly. 'Meg Purser had some pretty trinkets last summer and was not slow to flaunt them. Howsomever, 'tis of very little consequence. The matter which should properly concern us now is the matter of this proposed marriage.'

'He shouldn't spend Mama's money on other women,' Billy complained. 'Why, that's the sort of low trick you'd expect of some low crimping-fellow, with no morals, damme if it ain't.' Rain was pattering against the window panes like an irritable accompaniment to his anger.

'What he spends upon his women is nothing to what he would spend if he got his hands on Mama's entire fortune,' Johnnie said. It was taking Billy a mortal long time to appreciate what a parlous position

421

they were all in. 'All our good work would go to waste, yours, mine, Mr Teshmaker's, Mama's.'

'I'll tell 'ee what's to be done,' Billy said, leaning forward towards them until his face was within inches of the candle flame. 'We will tell her how he presses us for money. That's what we'll do. See what she thinks of him then.'

If only I were twenty-five, Johnnie thought. I could run this firm so well, if I were old enough, and Mama would allow it. But he knew it could never happen. It wouldn't occur to her that her 'wretch' would like to inherit. The firm would go to Billy, if it wasn't fritted away by her feckless lover, and Billy, affable though he undoubtedly was, would make a poor leader. His affection was quick enough, but his wits were slow. Look what an unconscionable time he'd taken to understand what was going on now. And gullible too. If Mr Leigh made up to him, he'd forgive and forget, *and* watch him put his hands in the till again without misgivings. Oh, if only I were twenty-five. Eighteen was no age to be taken seriously.

Billy was still ranting his solution. '. . . tell her every last detail. That's what.'

'An admirable suggestion,' Cosmo said diplomatically, removing the candles to a safer position. 'And one we will most certainly act upon, should your mother accept the gentleman. Meantime, I feel it would be more politic to continue with caution. 'Twould be poor tactics to use our cannon before we have need of 'em. No no, 'tis my opinion we should save our fire.'

'And say nothing!' Billy said, throwing himself back in his amazement so that the candles on the sconces behind him guttered in the draught he was causing. 'Nothing!'

'Your mother is a woman of infinite good sense,' Cosmo said, 'which I need hardly tell 'ee. She may refuse the gentleman, in which case our warning would merely serve as an irritant, and an unnecessary one at that.'

'Or she may accept him,' Johnnie pointed out quietly.

'That is the other eventuality,' Cosmo agreed. 'And if she does, then we shall have at least three weeks in which to enlighten her. I will tell you now, gentlemen, that I have not been idle upon this matter over the years. There is an account book in the corner cupboard there, which contains a list of all the monies Mr Leigh has either borrowed, from you, Mr William *and* others, or attempted to borrow, from you, Mr

422

John and you, Mr William *and* others, and I can tell 'ee that both are formidable sums.'

The brothers were impressed, and a little surprised that their quiet servant should have been so devious. He smiled at them. ''Tis my living too,' he said.

'I have such plans for this company,' Johnnie confided, his tongue loosened by the brandy. 'We could extend so easily. Now that the roads are improved, Mr Chaplin will soon be running coaches to every town in the kingdom. We should follow him. There would be trade a-plenty, I'm sure on it.'

'Such a venture would take a deal of organization,' Cosmo said, but his expression was encouraging.

'Organization is nothing to our Johnnie,' Billy said proudly. 'You should see his room at home, Mr Teshmaker. Full of coach timetables, damme if it ain't. He can tell you what days all the stage-coaches run, to the very hour, what's more. And should you want to know how long 'twould take to get to any town you care to name, why Johnnie's the man. He's an absolute marvel at it.'

'All of which knowledge could be used to ensure the transportation of newspapers,' Cosmo said, understanding at once.

'Indeed,' Johnnie said with pride.

'Have you told your mother of this?'

'No.'

'Then, if you will allow me to advise you, I would suggest that you do. It would be necessary to wait until a suitable moment presents itself, of course, and it would need to be done tactfully. Howsomever, I feel certain you could engage her interest.'

'If it ain't all given over to Mr Leigh,' Johnnie sighed. It was against his nature to be optimistic.

'Rot him!' Billy said, helping himself to more brandy. 'Can't see what she sees in the feller.'

At that moment, she was seeing a very pretty gold cross set with amethysts, which her newly affluent lover had bought in Cambridge on his way back from Newmarket.

'Fie upon you, Calverley,' she teased him, when she took it from its little padded box. 'D'ye think to bribe me?' But it was a delightful present and she was filled with pleasure at the sight of it.

'Sweets to the sweet,' he said. 'Or ain't you in the humour to be courted?'

'You may court all you please, you foolish crittur,' she said, 'providing you don't ask me to wed. Have you heard the news? The poor old king's gone mad again. In a straitjacket so they do say. What will become of un, poor soul? I shall wear this cross with my purple silk at the New Year's Ball.'

By the New Year's Ball every newspaper reader in London knew what had become of poor old King George. He was now so completely and irretrievably mad that he was to be 'put away' and the Prince of Wales was to be appointed Regent. There was much speculation as to the sort of government he would form now that those two great antagonists Mr Pitt and Mr Fox were dead, and the speculation increased the sales of all Nan's newspapers.

But although she was pleased that her profits were improved, she was more interested in the entertainments that would be bound to follow. The Regency Bill was passed in February, and sure enough there were masques and pageants and military reviews and a sudden crop of patriotic plays. And three weeks later the Regent held his first levee in his new London residence. It was such a huge success he decided to hold another even bigger one in the summer.

'Now that will be an uncommon grand affair, I can tell 'ee,' Nan said to Calverley, 'if the first was anything to go by. Would I could be there to see it.'

'To mix with Prinny's set?' he mocked her.

'I can see no reason why not,' she told him. 'I'm as rich as many he makes one with. A sight richer if the truth be told. And a sight better too, in all conscience. 'Tis only snobbery that keeps out "trade".'

It was a passing conversation which she soon forgot, particularly as she received a letter from Annie in the very next post telling her that she was to be a grandmother in October. But because he knew he would see Colonel Leigh within the next week or so, Calverley acted upon it.

The invitation arrived at the end of March, and although it was addressed to them both he insisted that she open it. It was very impressive, being printed in gold leaf on vellum, no less, and it requested the presence of Calverley Leigh Esquire and Mrs Ann Easter at Carlton

House for 9.00 pm on June 19th 1811 to attend the levee of H.R.H. the Prince Regent.

'My heart alive!' she said, eyes shining. 'How did 'ee do it?'

'Trade secret,' he told her, warmed by her delight.

'My heart alive!' she said again. 'What shall I wear?'

She took particular care over her dress and appearance for this grand occasion, knowing how many important people would see her there. Calverley said he would wear his plain blue frock-coat and his blue beaver, which were the most stylish garments he possessed, with a white stock and white breeches to set them off in the Brummel-approved manner. But for Nan the choice wasn't quite so easy. She decided against the white muslin so beloved of all the young girls that season, choosing instead one of the heavy, dark figured satins that complimented her colouring and set off her diamonds and pearls and was more appropriate to her age. As Thiss drove them down the wide cobbled Mall towards the colonnaded facade of Carlton House, she was preening with excitement and satisfaction.

They were received in a hall entirely hung with blue embroidered silk, and drowsy with the scent of hundreds of pink and red roses. It seemed to Nan that half of London was already in the room, from elderly generals in full dress uniform to young nymphs in transparent gauze, and it surprised her that so few people were paying attention to the new arrivals even when their names were most pompously announced. She found them fascinating and watched them make their entrance, one after the other, like over-dressed actors posing for applause. And the seventh name to be announced after her own arrival was that of Sir Osmond Easter and his wife.

He seemed to have discovered enough cash to dress well for this occasion, for he was sporting a bottle-green tail coat with discreet gold buttons, an embroidered waistcoat, new pink trousers and the customary pair of gold fobs dangling at his waist. But it was his wife who interested Nan. A new wife, obviously, for she looked excessively nervous and awkward, and extremely young, barely out of the schoolroom. The poor creature was heavily pregnant, her belly rising from under the constraints of a high blue waistband and lifting the front hem of her empire gown a good four inches above the ground. Two Easters due this autumn, Nan thought, for Annie was about as far gone. Well, well, who would ha' thought it?

But then of course it was necessary to push her way through the crush and make sure that Sir Osmond knew she was there. It was a little triumph.

'Why, nephew!' she said, with artlessly feigned surprise. 'What a pleasure to see 'ee to be sure.'

He was very annoyed and for a second his face showed it. Then he recovered and they introduced their partners, which was another moment of most enjoyable spite. 'Mr Calverley Leigh, of whom you have heard, I daresay.'

'Your servant, sir.' Oh, if only he were! She'd make him jump so she would.

'I trust Miss Thomasina and Miss Evelina are well.'

'Oh yes indeed,' the new Lady Osmond said, smiling shyly.

'Pray give them my regards when you return. 'Tis pleasant to have such friends in one's family, is it not?'

But the crush shifted around them as she spoke and Sir Osmond took advantage of it to make his escape. She watched him retreat well pleased with her successful sarcasm, but then the wretched man contrived to have the last word. 'My dear,' he drawled, as he steered his wife through the crowd, 'the *people* one is forced to meet nowadays! Who would have imagined we would have to mix with *tradesmen* in such a place as this? Really the Regent has no *ton* at all.'

'Oh!' she roared, bristling towards his departing back. 'Let me get at un! I'll give un such a piece of my mind, so I will!'

But fortunately they were all rescued by the announcement of the arrival of the Prince Regent, and the astonishing sight of her new ruler put Sir Osmond's rudeness out of her mind. It really was a most theatrical appearance. He was decked out in the full dress uniform of a Field Marshall, embellished with heavy gold embroidery along every seam and set with jewels at every vantage point. He was fatter than ever and the wide cloak he wore for his entrance, which was made of heavy blue velvet lined with white silk, seemed designed to accentuate his girth. The shoulders were padded so as to extend for a full eighteen inches on either side of his collar and above the padding, they were hung with accoutrements, a triple silk bow, an embroidered coat of arms and a long, red velvet epaulette. Thus attired he rolled into the assembly, acknowledging bows and curtseys with a faint movement of one fat gloved hand.

'I never seen such a fat old mawther in all my life,' Nan whispered to Calverley. 'He's a deal worse than the last time we saw un.'

426

'Hush!' he whispered back. "'Tis a hanging matter to be heard a-saying such things, and I wouldn't have 'ee hung, my charmer, not for the world.'

'Now to the banquet,' she said, licking her lips.

The banquet was as expensive and sumptuous as the Regent, and equally vulgar. It was held in the gothic conservatory, an edifice of such overpowering extravagance that it quite took Nan's breath away, for it was really more like a cathedral than a greenhouse. Arched columns, heavily and exotically decorated, supported a ceiling where fan vaults erupted from fan vaults and chandeliers depended from chandeliers. The entrance to the garden was a high altar, the lanterns hanging from every archway were painted icons and beyond them the windows were all stained glass. The supper tables filled its entire length, all two hundred feet of it, and the tureens and dishes and plates were all of silver.

There were mulligatawny soup and turtle soup, salmon and trout and turbot surrounded by little silver smelts. There were barons of beef and saddles of mutton and vegetables of every kind piled upon silver dishes. There was iced champagne for everyone, and port and sherry, and even claret for the ladies. Peaches and grapes and pineapples were piled on silver platters before every sixth place, and the pièce de résistance was a fishpond full of live gold and silver fish set in the table before the Regent's elaborate chair. It fed a stream that flowed between banks heaped with flowers right along the full length of the tables and back, taking the fish wherever they cared to swim.

'They say this entertainment cost £150,000,' Nan's immediate neighbour informed her with some awe, watching as two gold fins pursued one another through the clear water.

Nan didn't doubt it. It was excessive, like the company. The way they all ate! Scoffing the meal as though they were never likely to get another. No wonder they're all such fat old mawthers, she thought.

By the time they got home she was so swollen with food she could barely breathe. 'I en't the shape for over-eating,' she complained, removing her tight gown. 'My heart alive, just look at that belly. That's gross, so 'tis.'

But he was admiring it and growing obviously amorous.

'Now don't 'ee start,' she warned. 'I got enough to do digesting all that food without you starting, and I've to travel back to Bury in the morning.'

'Could you not stay a day or two?' he asked. He was horribly short

427

of cash again, and he'd been hoping he could get her into the right mood to ask her for a loan.

She had put on a loose day-gown and flopped onto the bed with her feet on the pillows. 'No,' she said, 'I can't. I want to see how Annie's faring.' She'd spent the entire summer with her daughter, sewing the baby's layette and preparing its nursery, and uncommon pleasant it had been. 'I shall be back in September.'

'You care little for me, I see,' he teased, leaning over her to kiss her forehead. 'I declare I would fare better with you these days if I were six months old and in a cradle.'

'You give me indigestion with all that squit,' she said mildly. 'I'm too full of food to argify.'

The next day the papers were full of rapturous accounts of the Regent's glorious levee, and the *Chronicle* had some very complimentary things to say about 'Mrs Easter of A. Easter – Newsagents' and 'her handsome escort Mr Calverley Leigh', who were 'an example to the company for their stylish appearance and their learned conversation.' Nan read them on her way to Bury, wondering what she could have said to the editor of that paper to make him so obsequious.

Later that week she wrote to Thomasina and Evelina to tell them all about the levee, as she'd promised, and to rebuke them, gently, for not telling her about Sir Osmond's marriage. 'She looks a kindly creature,' she wrote. 'Do pray give her my warmest regards.'

'It was most remiss of us not to tell you of the wedding,' Evelina wrote back. 'Howsomever, we assumed you would read of it in the papers. 'Twas announced in *The Times*, you see my dear. Molly is a dear girl, which is plain to be seen, is it not, and uncommon fond of Osmond. At present she is not at all well, which is a great distress to us all, but we hope to see her improved when the child is born.'

But when the last week of September arrived and the child was born, Molly took a fever, and within three days she was dead. This time Nan *did* see the news, which was duly announced in *The Times* and arrived in Cheyne Walk on the same morning by private letter from Ippark.

'We are desolated,' Thomasina wrote, 'having grown so fond of her. ''Tis a strong baby, for which I suppose we must be thankful, a boy and to be called Joseph after his grandfather, which will not surprise you I think. We must pray for the safe delivery of your daughter's child. Such a pretty bride. We often speak of her.'

The news struck Nan with a sudden and irrational terror. 'I must go to Bury and see Annie,' she told her family, passing the letter to Billy. 'What if she were to need care, and me not there to give it?'

Calverley was travelling for Mr Chaplin, so there was nobody there to try to dissuade her. Both the boys thought it entirely sensible and sat down at once to write letters to their sister, while their mother was throwing clothes into her travelling bag. And Thiss was delighted. 'Won't the missus be pleased?' he said, as they set off through the fallen leaves that rustled along Cheyne Walk.

It might have been a rhetorical question, but it turned out to be a considerable understatement.

They arrived in Bury St Edmunds as the dusk was falling, and Bessie came out of her parlour at once at the sound of Nan's key in the front door. When she saw her mistress standing in the hall with her dear Thiss carrying the luggage over the doorstep behind her, her face underwent an extraordinary series of changes. First her neck turned red, then she put her hand into her mouth like a baby, and then she burst into tears.

Thiss flung the luggage on the floor and took her in his arms. 'Come on, Goosie!' he soothed. 'Don't take on. That ain't the way. I shall think you ain't pleased ter see me, you go on like that.'

'Pleased ter see yer!' she said, eyes brimming with tears. 'Pleased ter see yer! Why, Thiss, I'm that pleased ter see yer, I can't put words to it. 'Tis just it bein' unexpected-like. That's what done it, me dear. Bein' unexpected-like.' Then she realized that Nan was staring at her, and she turned to apologize. 'Oh, Mrs Easter, mum, what must you think? I'm so sorry, mum, an' you standin' here in the cold an' all, an' after such a long journey too. What must you think?'

'I will take tea in the drawing-room,' Nan said, brusquely, because she'd found all that unexpected emotion rather upsetting. 'And then I'm off to Rattlesden to see Annie.'

But Bessie explained that the drawing-room was cold.

'There's no fire there,' she apologized. 'We keeps it shut up winter-time, yer see, as a general rule. Not expecting you or nothink. I'll get one lit directly, but it'll take an hour or two to warm through. My parlour's nice an' cosy, mum. You're more than welcome there.'

So Thiss went off to attend to the horses, and the housemaid was rung for and told to light fires, and the parlour it was. Soon the two of them were sitting before the stove and the tea was brewed and young Tom was blowing the fire with the bellows and Bessie was telling her mistress the latest news about Annie.

'She'll be that glad you're to be here fer the birth after all,' she said. 'They took my Pollyanna on fer nursemaid. Went up three weeks ago.'

'I'm glad on it,' Nan said. 'She will be a great help.'

'Very well pleased with 'er they are, mum,' Bessie said, glowing with pride and hot tea. 'A good gel, though I says it as shouldn't.'

'And Annie is truly well?'

'Blooming, mum,' Bessie said. 'She was a bit cast-down when you left. Well that's onny natchrul.' Then she burst into tears again. 'Oh, don't mind me, mum,' she begged. ''Tis just it bein' unexpected-like. Thiss coming home.'

'Do you miss him so much, Bessie?' Nan asked. The strength of Bessie's feelings was surprising after all these years.

'Oh yes,' Bessie said. 'When he first goes away, I miss 'im all the time. Ain't a minute 'a the day I don't find mesself a-thinkin' of 'im. Well you know how it is, mum. 'Tis a mortal long time October ter May. But there,' drying her eyes for the second time that afternoon. 'Mussen' grumble. It gets better. You gets used to it. You can get used to anythink in time, can't yer mum?'

'Why didn't you tell me you missed him?' Nan insisted. And underneath the words was the uncomfortable thought that she ought to have known this without being told.

'That wasn't fer me ter go a-tellin' you things like that,' Bessie said. 'You got a business ter run.'

And then Thiss came into the room and asked if there was any beer, so beer had to be found for him, and Bessie went bustling off to find it.

'Your Bessie misses you in the wintertime,' Nan said.

'She does that.'

'And you miss her?'

'Sommink chronic.' But he didn't complain or say any more about it, and Nan found that even more distressing than Bessie's tears.

'Blamed fools the pair of you,' she said. 'You should ha' said, so you should. Fancy missing one another so much and saying nothing of it! Well I shall put an end to all, so I shall. I shall hire another coachman and you shall stay here and run my East Anglian affairs for me.' It was the obvious solution and came to her so easily. 'You could ha' done it

430

years ago, if we'd only thought. You en't to be parted in the winter never ever again.' She was as cross about it as if somebody else had parted them.

Thiss turned his head to look at her, and the beam on his ugly face spread from ear to ear. 'My eye!' he said rapturously. 'Just you wait till I tells the ol' gel. She'll be like a dog with two tails.' And he went hurtling out of the kitchen to find her.

How they do love each other, Nan thought, touched and shamed by their devotion. And she remembered Mr Easter and the way he'd spoken of love and marriage all those years ago. 'I shall love you till the day I die.' And he had, faithfully and truly, the dear good creature that he was. And the words of the marriage service echoed in her mind, 'and forsaking all other, cleave thee only unto her, so long as you both shall live.' Calverley might claim that fidelity was old-fashioned nowadays, and for all she knew he could be right, but it was still something to value for all that, and her instincts knew it. My Annie will never give her dear James a moment's doubt, and James will always be true to my Annie. It was how a marriage should be. And she smiled at little Tom, who was sitting in the chimney corner, building a little house with his wooden bricks.

And then Bessie and Thiss came running back into the kitchen to thank her, and Bessie cried all over again, and little Tom climbed into his mother's lap and cried too, although he didn't know why. And at that Nan decided it was high time they all turned their attention to more practical matters, so she despatched Bessie to the kitchen to see about some mutton chops for dinner and Thiss to the stables to get the pony-cart ready to take her to Rattlesden.

It was quite dark by the time the two of them set out again and even with a lantern swinging at either side of the trap, they had a hard time of it among the ridges and ditches of the narrow lanes that led from Bury to Woolpit and Drinkstone and the hidden valley of Rattlesden village. But the welcome Annie gave them made up for all their bruises and finally convinced her mother that she really was fit and well.

'Oh, how good you are Mama!' she said to Nan. 'To come all this way, and in the dark too. Shall you stay the night?'

'No, no,' Nan said, laughing and kissing her. 'Bessie is preparing dinner. But I shall be back here in the morning so I shall, for I mean to stay in Bury till this babe is born.' The memory of poor little Lady Easter was still too raw.

431

Fortunately Mrs Annie Hopkins was made of sterner stuff than poor little Lady Easter. Ten days later, she weathered the birth of *her* son with remarkable ease, and a fine, pretty baby he was. His father christened him James, of course, but within two weeks everybody was calling him Jimmy. Nan stayed in the vicarage until Annie was up and about again, and by then the newest member of her family had completely bewitched her.

She returned to Chelsea full of happy energy.

'Oh, what a deal we have to look forward to!' she said to Calverley, 'There's a new year a-coming and work to be done.'

'How if we were to marry in the new year, my charmer?' he tried.

But she was already on her way out of the house.

Chapter Thirty-eight

So many extraordinary and dreadful things happened in 1812 that looking back on it afterwards, people called it the star-crossed year. None of them worried Nan Easter, for the worse they were, the better they sold newspapers. And besides, she had a grandson to entertain her now.

The year began with the news that the Regent was ill in bed, delirious so it was said and 'raging with the irritation of his nerves.' He had been showing his daughter how to dance the Highland fling and had fallen and twisted his ankle, which was hardly a surprise considering how fat he was. It seemed rather extravagant behaviour for such a small injury, and the general opinion in London was that he bid fair to follow his father into madness. In fact his brother, the Duke of Cumberland said quite openly that he thought his brother's illness was '*higher* than the foot, and that a blister on the head might be more efficacious than a poultice on the ankle.'

However the royal invalid recovered in time for the first Ball of the year and the news that Napoleon was building up a great army to invade Russia.

This was looked upon as extravagant behaviour too, for the French army in Spain was doing badly. 'You'd ha' thought he'd've had enough on 'is plate a-fighting old Wellington,' Thiss said, when Nan went down to Bury on a flying visit. He was very proud of the Duke of Wellington, whose reported victories looked relentless, Ciudad Rodrigo in January, Badajos in April, taking the British army steadily across Spain towards Madrid and pushing the French farther and farther back towards the Pyrenees and their own frontier, 'which they ought never to've crossed in the first place.'

Good, bad or extraordinary, the news went on selling papers and making profits for the Easter empire. 'I don't care what 'tis,' Nan was fond of saying, 'providing we en't being invaded.' But even she was amazed by the item that was printed in *The Times* on May 12th. Mr Spencer Perceval, the Prime Minister, had been murdered in the lobby of the House of Commons. The man who shot him was a bankrupt called Bellingham who said he had gone to the house to kill 'that villain Leveson Gore', but as Leveson Gore wasn't available and the Prime Minister was, he'd shot the Prime Minister instead.

'What a wicked, wicked world we live in,' Sophie Fuseli said, when she and Nan had read the full account over tea that afternoon. 'There are times, my dear, when I simply cannot credit the wickedness of mankind.'

' 'Tis is a bad old year,' Nan agreed, but she didn't really believe it. Not with little Jimmy growing into such a fine, fat baby.

To Calverley Leigh, however, it was an uncommon bad year. He spent part of his winnings on a silver spoon for the christening of Annie's baby. But from that easy moment on, he ran further and further into debt, and the more he owed the more heavily he gambled, and the more heavily he gambled the more he owed. Soon he had frittered his fortune away and even a sizeable increase in his wages from Mr Chaplin did little more than stave off disaster for a month or two.

In the summer he persuaded Nan to pay off three of his most pressing creditors and to square his accounts at White's and Goosegogs before she went rushing off to Bury, but there never seemed to be any chance to talk to her about marriage and he was very seriously in debt. For most of the year he felt as though he were riding an unbroken colt, so unpredictable were the demands upon his purse and his emotions. The Meg Purser affair was over, as he'd promised, but there were others, and they all seemed to expect trinkets for their favours these days. Howsomever, at least Nan knew nothing about them, for he was now exceptionally discreet, and took care to restrict his courtships to towns that were a safe distance from home. But he owed money to so many creditors that he'd lost count of the number, his tailor, his wine-merchant, both his clubs, a ferocious money-lender, the list was endless. But he no longer let such matters concern him. Nan grew richer by the day and sooner or later her money would have to be at his disposal. The war would surely soon be over, everybody said so, and Napoleon defeated and then she would accept his proposal. All he needed was to keep his affairs secret and his creditors at bay until after their marriage, that was all.

He would have been annoyed had he known how closely all his activities were being followed by Nan's two sons, but as they were being advised by Mr Cosmo Teshmaker and grew more cautious as the year progressed, he remained in undisturbed ignorance.

'We have weathered a twelvemonth, you see, and no marriage,' Mr Teshmaker said, when they dined with him that autumn.

'The debts mount,' Johnnie observed. 'He had another three demands this very morning, and one from a money-lender.'

' 'Tis my opinion he's a-working himself up to ask her,' Billy said. 'That blue coat was bought for a purpose.' Now that he was turned twenty-one and had a dress allowance from his mother, he knew from experience that new clothes were one of the easiest ways to dazzle the ladies.

How much they have changed, Cosmo thought, remembering the skinny boys they'd been when they first started work five years ago. Now they were tall and handsome, each in his own particular way, Billy stocky and open-faced and sandy-haired, Johnnie slim and brooding and dark, and each had a new air about him these days, Billy's assured and ebullient, Johnnie's assured and mysterious. They had let their hair grow long and wore it in the new romantic style, with strands brushed forward to frame their foreheads, and they dressed well, like gentlemen of business.

'Have you spoken to your mother yet, Mr John, concerning your plan to extend our trade?'

'No,' Johnnie said, scowling slightly. ' 'Tain't a conversation to be rushed, Mr Teshmaker.' He wanted to be sure that he had every last detail carefully worked out before he committed himself.

'No indeed,' Cosmo hastened to agree. 'Christmas might be an appropriate time perhaps?'

'Perhaps, if *he* don't dominate her attentions.'

'Or propose to her in the meantime,' Billy said.

But the autumn passed without proposal, as far as they were aware. Which was hardly to be wondered at, for their mother was busier than ever and when she wasn't working she was visiting Rattlesden.

In September news came through that Napoleon had crossed the River Neiman on June 23rd with an army of 450,000 men and invaded Russia unopposed and just as he'd planned.

Johnnie read every word of all the reports, avidly and half in awe of

Napoleon's daring, but Billy and his army of friends paid very little attention to it. Having discovered the pulling power of good clothes, they were far too busy flirting with as many young ladies as they could. And when they weren't flirting, they were drinking themselves silly. In their opinion Wellington's victory at Salamanca which was reported a few weeks later was considerably more important. 'Pulverized the enemy, so he did, damme,' Billy said proudly. 'Can't beat the British infantry.'

But although the French had suffered heavy losses, there were deaths on the British side too and among them was Captain Fortescue of the Duke of Clarence's Light Dragoons.

Calverley was far more upset by the news than he admitted. To impress Billy and Johnnie he pretended to shrug it off. 'You have to expect losses in the army, damme if you don't. That's war, me dears.' But he grew heavy-eyed with the tears he hadn't shed and as soon as he could, he retired to Goosegogs for a week to recover, drinking himself insensible every night and running up another enormous bill he knew he couldn't pay.

Now barely a day passed without some news from Spain or Russia, and as it was very good news for the Allies and worse and worse for Napoleon it sold at speed. Nan was so busy she was out of the house by six every morning and rarely returned to it before eight at night. But Calverley comforted himself for her absence with the thought that all this activity was making her richer and richer, which would be bound to benefit him in the long run.

In November, they heard of a terrible battle at a place called Borodino, and read that the Emperor had marched his Grand Army into Moscow. But it turned out to be a hollow victory, for he found the city deserted, the population having left their homes and taken their food and disappeared into the countryside. On the night after his invasion, a handful of guerillas returned under cover of darkness and set fire to the place. By morning more than half the city was in flames.

'What courage!' Londoners said, looking at their own city with affection. 'To burn down your own homes rather than hand them to an enemy. What courage!'

By the end of that star-crossed year the Russian campaign was over. Of the 450,000 men who'd crossed the Nieman that summer a mere 20,000 came limping home, starving and frost-bitten and totally defeated, beaten by the ferocity of the Russian winter, for which they were neither clothed nor prepared, and the anger of the Russian people who would rather destroy their homeland and everything upon it than allow an enemy to occupy it.

London had very little sympathy for their suffering. 'Serve 'em right,' people said to one another. 'They should a' know'd better than ter go a-tangling with the Russkies.'

It was a cold winter in London too, even though it didn't snow, but just before Christmas news came through from Spain that the French had been defeated there too.

'We've a deal to celebrate, I'm thinking,' Calverley said to Nan as she snuggled down inside the warm bedclothes late one December evening. 'How if we were to . . .'

'I intend to celebrate Christmas in the new style this year,' she told him, 'like the Duchess of York. We will all go down to Bury so we shall, for we can't expect the baby to travel to London, and we'll give presents to one another on Christmas morning before we go to church, just like she does. 'Tis a capital idea, don't 'ee think so?'

'Yes,' he said, agreeing because he had to, although he was inwardly quailing at the thought of how much it would cost him. 'I can think of another capital idea, my charmer.'

'I don't doubt it,' she said, snuffing out the candle. 'What shall I give to little Jimmy?'

She enjoyed her preparations for this new-style Christmas. Buying presents had always been a pleasure to her, so the chance to give something to every single member of her household was a great excitement. And the boys were delighted at the thought that they were to have four whole days away from work in the company of their sister and her baby and dear old James.

They arrived in Angel Hill laden with parcels so early on Christmas morning that only Bessie was up and about to receive them. They couldn't wait to give their presents. Breakfast could be taken later, could it not, Billy said. First things first. And he was up the stairs two at a time to call his mother, who met them on the second landing, rubbing the sleep out of her eyes.

'Fie on you both,' she scolded them happily. 'Your sister en't arrived yet. Nor Mr Leigh. Nor Mr Hopkins neither, for he must conduct his Christmas service before he may ride over. So you must just bide your souls in patience, you bad boys!'

437

'We brought Annie a necklace of little coloured beads,' Johnnie said, kissing her, 'and a rag doll for baby Jimmy.'

'What do 'ee say we take the chaise and drive out to meet her?' Billy said.

'Now?' Nan said, amazed at their energy. 'At this hour?'

'Why not?' Johnnie said. 'We ain't seen our Annie for months and months, have we Billy?' And he called down the stairwell. 'Bring the chaise, Thiss.'

So the chaise was brought and the two of them donned their great-coats and hats again, and clambered aboard, laughing and talking.

'Back for breakfast!' Billy called as the roan began to trot. 'What've we got? I've a monstrous appetite!'

'Oh, what a blessing mum, to have our dear boys here for your new Christmas,' Bessie said, waving to them until they were out of sight.

And a splendid Christmas it was, the giving of gifts being an inno-vation they all enjoyed. Calverley produced a ring for Nan, set with turquoise and pearls, and gave it to her with an intensity it was hard for her to ignore. She put it on the middle finger of her right hand and thanked him with a kiss, but she was aware that both her sons were watching her closely, and she was glad that at least they had the good sense not to comment.

Rather to her surprise it was Johnnie who had brought the most imaginative presents. Besides the necklace and the rag doll, he pro-duced a fringed shawl from Sicily for Bessie, which made her look extremely fine, and a straw hat for Thiss, which made him look happily foolish, and two fine water-colours for his mother, which had to be hung in the place of honour immediately, once they'd decided where the place of honour was. And he spent most of Christmas day crawling about the drawing-room carpet with his nephew.

Watching him, Nan wondered if she had ever really known this son of hers. He had always been such a secretive, withdrawn child and now here he was romping with the baby as happily as any two-year-old. But she noticed that he was still withdrawn among adults. When Billy went racketting off with his friends, he stayed at home to read or work on his notes. But she even found his taciturnity endearing these days. It reminded her of William Henry whose quietness had been an outward sign of his dependability, although she hadn't understood it at the time.

From time to time during their four-day holiday they took tea alone together and talked about the firm as if they were business associates and not mother and son. She told him how aggravating it had been to have the rent or purchase of new shops blocked by 'that wretch Sir Osmond,' and remembered the times when they had walked through the streets of Mayfair together, selling *The Times* for tuppence. And on the fourth day he told her about his plans for expansion.

'We should open a newsagent's shop in every town that Mr Chaplin serves,' he said eagerly, 'with papers delivered daily on his coaches. It could easily be done, Mama. I have worked it all out.'

'Have you indeed,' she said, rather tartly, for she wasn't sure she approved of his interest, 'and have you negotiated for the new premises, too? They could run into hundreds, I hope you realize.

'Two hundred and forty-two, to be precise.'

She laughed out loud at this. 'What a fellow you are!' she said, and now there was admiration in her tone. 'And how long would it take to set up this mighty enterprise?'

This was a question he hadn't expected. 'I couldn't say for certain, Mama,' he admitted. 'A lot would depend upon the availability of properties and the speed of our lawyers. Mr Teshmaker would be most useful in this respect, I'm sure. I could work out an estimation for you, if you wished.'

'Aye,' she said, warmed by his honesty. 'Pray do so. 'Tis the sort of business I enjoy. When could you start?'

'This very afternoon,' he said eagerly.

She laughed at him again. 'Finish your holiday first,' she told him. 'And have another piece of shortbread.'

He began his estimation as soon as he got back to Chelsea, and by February he had worked out what he called 'a plan of campaign', breaking down the whole operation according to coach routes.

Nan read it with approval and close attention, and when she'd absorbed all the information in it, she made her decision. 'Begin with the Portsmouth route,' she said. 'We already have shops in Petersfield and Portsmouth. Now see if you can open them in Esher, Cobham, Guildford, Godalming, Liphook, and Portsea Island.'

'They will be trading before the summer,' he told her solemnly. 'You have my word on it.'

Actually it took him a great deal longer than he'd expected. The shops in Guildford and Godalming were open by the beginning of July, just in time to sell the news of the Great British victory at Victoria,

Esher was ready in October when Annie announced that she was expecting again, but negotiations for the Portsea Island shop took such a long time, they were only just completed in December when news of another and even greater victory arrived.

The British and Portuguese had fought a decisive battle against the French and their Spanish allies at a place called Nive. Sixty thousand troops took the field on either side and by the end of the day thirteen thousand of them were dead. But Wellington had been declared the victor. Now, so all the newspapers agreed, there was no doubt that the British would win the war. It was only a matter of time. 'Your second baby could well be born in peacetime,' Nan wrote to Annie, for the child was due at the end of January.

The entertainments arranged in London to celebrate the victory were truly sumptuous, with firework displays in Hyde Park and St James' Park, and balls and masques in which the costumes grew more costly and fantastic by the day. Not to be outdone, the theatres planned elaborate fantasies too.

The Theatre Royal in the Haymarket promised 'an evening of delectation the most wondrous to behold, with dazzling transformations and effects and all newly written for the occasion.' So naturally Calverley bought two tickets for one of the side-boxes in the dress circle so that he and Nan could join in the festivities. Or to be more accurate, he pledged that he would pay for the tickets when he came to collect them that evening, for he had no money in hand until Mr Chaplin paid his wages later that afternoon.

It turned out to be an extraordinary evening. But it began terrifyingly.

He had just collected his most-needed wages from Mr Chaplin at the Swan with Two Necks and was strolling through the crowds in Milk Street heading towards the river and home, when he was suddenly seized from behind and dragged backwards into an evil-smelling alley.

It was done so quickly and with such expertise he had no time to call out or fight back. One minute he was walking and whistling, swinging his gold-topped cane in his usual jaunty way, the next the cane was being twisted from his grasp and held hard across his throat, blocking his wind-pipe. A dark face grinned diabolically six inches in front of his eyes, '*Mr* Calverley Leigh, sir,' it mocked. 'If I ain't mistook. Friend a' Mr Ebenezer Weingarten, wot 'as the rare misfortune a' doin' business wiv 'ee, *Mr* Calverley Leigh, sir.'

Rough fingers were frisking his pockets and there was a strong smell

440

of stale urine emanating from the dank walls behind him. 'What do you want?' he said, speaking as haughtily as he could, and struggling to dislodge the cane from his throat. But he knew what the ruffian wanted, there was no need to ask.

'Little matter 'a six hundred smackers, guvnor,' another voice said behind him, and the cane was jerked most painfully against his throat.

'Tell your master he shall have it at the very first opportunity.'

'Oh my eye,' Dark Face mocked. 'We got a prime cove 'ere, boys. The very first oppertunity, eh, what? This 'ere's yer oppertunity *Mr* Calverley Leigh, sir. We're the ones wot makes oppertunities, *Mr* Calverley Leigh sir, out the kindness of our 'earts.'

Another face leered out of the darkness into Calverley's diminished line of vision. This one had lost most of its teeth except for two isolated, dark-brown stumps and had one eye covered by a triangular black patch. 'Give 'im a wherrit across the chops, eh Charlie?' it said hopefully, raising a huge fist.

'Not if he comes dahn wiv the derbies,' Dark Face said, 'which seein' he's a-got the oppertunity I'm a-certain 'e'll oblige. Wot's 'ee got there, Jerry?'

'Four sovereigns an' twenty crowns.'

'Well, that ain't a deal, considerin',' Dark Face said. 'You'll 'ave ter do better'n that won't yer, *Mr* Calverley Leigh sir, otherwise we shall 'ave ter visit you again, as I might say.'

A black hand was dangling his purse on the end of a knobbed stick. ' 'Tis for Mr Weingarten,' Calverley said coldly, 'so be certain I shall tell him to expect it.'

'Oh my eye,' Dark Face said, 'wot a suspicious cast a' mind we've got, *Mr* Calverley Leigh. Whap 'im one Jerry, fer bein' a suspicious cove.' And then a fist landed in his stomach like a sledge hammer, winding him and draining all the strength from his legs, so that he fell in a heap, gasping and retching. And the dangling purse was caught in a flying hand, and they were gone, taking purse and cane, in a flurry of heavy boots and stinking rags.

For a few seconds he lay where he had fallen, pulling air painfully into his lungs and struggling not to be sick. Deuce take it, he thought, as waves of nausea tugged upwards from his bruised stomach, I've come to a parlous state if I'm to be set upon by heavies. I shall have to pay old Weingarten off somehow or other. Or cut and run.

In the meantime there was a theatre to visit. And Nan to court.

Perhaps if he caught her in a happy moment she would settle some of his bills. Oh, there was always hope. Deuce take it, I do need a brandy.

It took him some time to find a landlord who would allow him to run up a bill for the liquor he needed, but eventually he found succour of a sort in a low tavern beside the Thames, where he washed his face and hands, and brushed his clothes and made himself presentable enough for the Haymarket, although how he would pay for the tickets he had no idea.

Fortunately the theatre was filled beyond capacity and Nan had already bought their tickets. There was such a crush in the foyer that it took him more than ten minutes to move from the entrance to the auditorium and stand beside her. She was surrounded by a horde of her friends and acquaintants all talking at once and saying how wonderful it was for Britain to have won such a victory. They were all dressed to the nines and sweating with excitement and heavily perfumed, so the smell in that small enclosed space was enough to bring tears to the eyes but the atmosphere was charged with emotion as well as perfume and a good deal of that emotion was already happily erotic. In the press of so many bodies, what was more natural and easy than to kiss and fondle? he thought, catching his amorous Nan to his side, relieved that she was too excited to notice any change in him.

Inside the theatre it was better and worse, for there the heat from so many bodies had already accumulated to such a stifling degree that necks and bosoms were turkey-red and fans were constantly a-flutter. But here in the intimacy of plushy darkness, kisses could linger and hands explore further, so excitement and enjoyment increased, and the terror and pain of that dark alley receded.

' 'Twill be a good evening, I fancy,' Calverley murmured into his beloved's neck. 'How if you were to crown all by agreeing to marry me?'

'How indeed?' she said, turning her head so that they were mouth to mouth. And the curtain opened as they kissed.

Despite the flamboyant claims of its publicity it turned out to be rather an indifferent show. Choirs sang patriotic songs at the tops of their voices, dancers dressed as men o' war drifted about the stage as well as they could given the weight of their costumes, and there were several pageants which looked spectacular but said little, and a soprano who said a very great deal and expected to be applauded at the end of every sentence whether or not the audience had actually been able to hear it, and then sang a very short song.

By the interval Nan was rather bored with it all, and was beginning to cast a critical eye on the state of Calveley's jacket, but the interval was lively and that rescued him from comment. Orange-sellers pushed through the crowd with their laden baskets as soon as the curtain fell, and were lifted up bodily by various men in the audience to be carried over the assembled heads to their next customers, a feat which was much enjoyed, especially by the lifters. Hampers were produced, Nan having brought one that was uncommon well-packed, and wine bottles opened and soon the entire place had become a cheerful picnic. By the time the curtains were raised on the second act most of the audience were so happily inebriated they were ready to applaud anything, and Calverley had relaxed back into his easy life.

The second act opener was actually well worth applauding. When the curtains parted, the audience saw to their delight that the stage had been filled with a huge wooden structure painted red and black, from which elaborate dragons belched flames and red imps hung by their toes, and which bore a six foot placard which proclaimed it. 'The Castle of Discord'.

After a dance in which French and Spanish men o' war strutted about the stage chanting hideously that the English were no match for them, 'hooray, hoorah!' a figure dressed to represent the dreaded Napoleon Bonaparte with cocked hat, tight belly, black boots and all, was lowered into position onto the topmost turret, where he delivered himself of a rousing speech and was booed to the echo. Whereupon cannons were fired from the wings and the stage was filled with grey and white smoke. This was supposed to cover the next act of the proceedings, when scores of stage hands, suitably dressed in black shirts and trousers, galloped upon the stage to effect the transformation. Unfortunately it cleared a great deal quicker than was expected and the removal men, finding themselves suddenly exposed to the applause and cat-calls of the audience, fell into a frenzy of panic and in their struggles to remove the Castle of Discord as quickly as possible, brought the whole thing tumbling down upon the stage, red imps, fire-breathing dragons, Napoleon and all.

The audience was enraptured by such a well deserved accident, but the manager was afraid that it would set fire to the curtains, and sent the removal men back onto the stage with buckets of water with which they doused everything in sight, including the front row of the stalls. Then the splashed curtains were closed, and he came out apologetically before them to explain that the stage would be cleared and the spectacle continued 'so soon as was humanly possible' and begged them all to be 'so very kind as to indulge the theatre with their patience' which he promised them would be 'for the shortest possible time.'

The shortest possible time went on for nearly ten minutes and by then the audience had stopped laughing and were growing decidedly restless. And Calverley took the opportunity to talk to his lovely Nan of marriage.

' 'Tis nearly peacetime, my charmer,' he urged, stroking her breast. 'Surely we should marry now. Oh, my lovely Nan. How *can* you refuse me, when I love 'ee to distraction? Say you'll be mine, my charmer. Say it, do.'

She was enjoying the caress so much she paid no attention to what he was saying. 'Um,' she said, drowsy with desire.

He stopped fondling her and looked at her closely in the half light. 'You agree?' he said. 'We shall wed?'

She gathered her wits. 'No,' she said sharply. 'I en't agreed. I don't know. You must wait till I do.'

'No, deuce take it,' he said, made bold by desperation and brandy. ' 'Tis a bona fide offer and I will wait no longer.' And before she realized what he was doing, he jumped up onto the ledge that rimmed the dress circle and both boxes and balanced there. 'I will run from this end to the other, so I will,' he shouted. 'I vow it, unless you promise to marry me.'

Heads below him tilted up to see what the noise was about, and soon he had gathered the attention of everybody in the stalls below and the circles above him. 'What is it?' people said. 'What's amiss?'

And he stood on the ridge, one foot in front of the other, balancing most precariously, arms outstretched, spine straight, head held high, white legs magnificently long, laughing at her. 'Say the word, my charmer, or I run.'

'Have done and come down,' she hissed at him. 'You make a spectacle of yourself.'

But that only spurred him on. He turned to his attentive audience and spoke to them, directly and very loudly. 'I am driven to extremes of love. Tortured beyond endurance, so I am. You see before you, ladies and gentlemen, a heartless hussy. I lay my heart at her feet. I beg

444

her to marry me. She says nothing. Nothing! Neither yes nor no. Now I can bear it no longer. If she will not speak I will run along this ledge. If I fall and die, my death is at her door. If I run and live surely she must accept me. How say you?'

They cheered him. 'Bravo!' 'Well said, that gallant man!' 'Here's to 'ee!' And they called advice to Nan. 'Accept him!' ' 'Tis a valiant man!' And one or two who knew them by name, called up to beg him to come down or her to give in.

'You bully me sir,' she said furiously. 'Very well then, run if you must.' And immediately the words were out of her mouth she regretted them, for he set off at a trot, those long legs loping forward, those dear arms stretched like wings, and she could see how easy it would be for him to fall, and she called out, 'have a care, do!' so that the audience rebuked her.

Half way along the ledge he paused and turned his body to look back at her, and the audience held its collective breath and waited. 'My life in your hands,' he called. 'Am I to return?'

But she wouldn't be bullied like this. 'Do as you will,' she said, her voice echoing in the hushed auditorium.

So he continued his run and this time two of the drummers played a dramatic drum-roll to accompany him. And the audience followed his every movement, gasping, 'Ooh! Ah! Phew!' as he stumbled, swayed, pretended to be about to fall, recovered and ran again. 'Accept him, for pity's sake!' they called to Nan. 'He will fall to his death, so he will.'

But he had reached the other side of the theatre and was standing with his hand on the curtain of the opposite box, whose occupants had already stretched out their hands to help him down.

'Say you will marry me!' he called to her.

'No!' It was intolerable to be bullied so. But undeniably romantic. Even in the midst of it all, torn and muddled by so many conflicting emotions, she was thrilled by how romantic it was.

'Say you will marry me or deuce take it, I shall jump into the stalls and end it all.'

There was uproar in the stalls, with people on their feet, struggling to get out of his way and others shrieking to Nan to change her mind and white faces turned towards them from every side.

He held up one hand for silence and at last it was given. 'Well?' he said.

The pressure from his daring and all those anxious faces pleading towards her was too much. 'Oh, very well,' she said into the silence. 'Yes. I will marry you.'

Then how the audience cheered and applauded and shouted approval. 'Come down,' she mouthed at him over the tumult, but his performance wasn't over. He bowed to the audience, still holding on to the curtain, and then instead of jumping down into the box as they expected, he suddenly turned and sprinted back along the ledge, light-footed as a cat, to leap into the box beside Nan and kiss her soundly. He was home and dry with his rich wife, his own dear, loving Nan, home and dry and he need never fear creditors again. The applause was deafening.

After that, the continuation of the advertised spectacle was a definite anticlimax.

'Now you will tell John and Billy, will you not?' he asked when they were home at last and had loved to their mutual satisfaction. The sooner this news was known, the better.

'Why should the whole world know of our affairs?' she said sleepily. ' 'Tis enough you have involved a theatre, surely.'

And as she spoke she remembered the theatre, the heat, desire, fear, and noise of it, in a swift close-packed muddle of sights, sounds and emotions and beneath them all, like an odd aftertaste following a fine meal, a lurking sense that there had been something contrived and dishonest about the whole affair. I would be a fool to marry this man, she thought, as sleep rocked into her mind, and she knew she didn't want her sons to know anything about it.

Chapter Thirty-nine

Calverley broke the news to his two future step-sons at breakfast the next morning.

'The Stamp Office must do without your mother today, boys,' he said cheerfully.

Billy was alarmed, his round face creased with concern. Was Mama ill? he thought glancing at her. But no, she seemed as lively as ever, eating with relish, that dark hair springing from her forehead as strong as wire and her brown eyes fairly gleaming with health. 'What is it?' he asked. 'What is the matter?'

Johnnie understood at once. The moment had come at last. His mother had been persuaded. He looked at her with protective pity, feeling remarkable cool now that battle had finally been joined.

'We have an appointment with a priest,' Calverley explained, looking horribly smug. 'To arrange for the banns to be called for our wedding. What think 'ee to that, eh my brave boys?'

Billy was so upset he couldn't answer, but Johnnie got up at once and walked round the table and kissed his mother dutifully. 'I wish you every happiness,' he said. 'We both do, ain't that right, Billy?'

'Oh yes, yes,' Billy said, blushing. 'Do indeed, Mama.' And he kissed her in his turn, and was rewarded with pats and smiles and kisses so that he blushed all over again.

Then there was an awkward pause as neither of them knew what to say next. Johnnie recovered first. 'As you are otherwise engaged, Mama, he said, 'Billy and I had best make haste and get down to the Strand.' And their mother laughed and agreed and the two of them made their escape.

Once they were in Cheyne Walk and out of earshot, Billy began to wail. 'Oh, Johnnoh, what are we to do? Who'd a' thought it? What are we to do?'

'We will tell Mr Teshmaker,' Johnnie said, thrusting his hands into the pockets of his greatcoat. 'That's what we'll do. And Mr Teshmaker will show her that account book. Come along, Billy, the banns only give us three weeks grace, so there ain't a minute to lose.'

Back in the house, Nan and her lover were dressing for the street too, and Calverley was rejoicing. 'There you are, ye see, my dear,' he said, putting on his beaver hat. 'They don't mind at all. Did I not tell 'ee?' When they'd woken up that morning she'd been quite worried about how her sons would take the news, so he was delighted to be able to prove her wrong.

'Aye,' she said, 'you did.' But she was thinking, that just shows how little you understand either one of them. For Billy had been blushing, which was always a sign of distress in him and Johnnie's voice had been far too guarded.

'They are fine boys,' he said easily, 'like their mother.' And the compliment warmed her. But then he spoiled it all by his very next words. 'Are you ready? I've to be in Edinburgh in three days time, so I must set off as soon as we've seen the priest.'

'Today?' she asked, and the cold winds of disappointment blew above her again. 'But that will mean that you will be away at Christmas time.' She had such plans for Christmas now.

'Not if I hurry, my charmer.'

'Christmas is a mere eight days away,' she said. 'You could never ride to Edinburgh and back and do business in eight days. 'Twould kill the horses. And besides, Annie will be here within the week. Why not wait upon her? Think how pleased she will be to hear our news.' She had no doubt at all about Annie's reaction.

'It cannot be done, my charmer.'

'Why the rush, pray?'

Actually it was to put a safe distance between his ribs and Mr Weingarten's heavies. His bruises had spread and deepened overnight and they hadn't been helped by his activities in the theatre and the lovemaking that had followed. Now he was extremely sore and tender. But it wouldn't do to tell her any of this. 'I am expected there in three days time,' he lied. 'Much though I love 'ee, stern duty calls! What shall I bring 'ee back from my travels?'

'Yourself,' she said, 'seeing we are betrothed.' Anything else she would have to pay for.

448

They strolled together arm-in-arm past the elegant houses of Cheyne Walk towards the church, and although Nan was still plagued by the thought that what they were doing was as contrived as a play, she couldn't help feeling happy too. I am walking to church at last, she thought, with my own dear love, to fix the date of our wedding. And why not? The limes were bare and the river bank muddy, but above them the clouds were small, drifting fleeces in a china-blue sky and below them, the river caught its rich colour in a shimmering looking-glass where the river boats skimmed like swallows between their own white wings of water. 'Oh!' she said. ' 'Tis a grand ol' world!'

He gave her his sleepy smile and made the most of the opportunity she was presenting him.

'While I am away,' he said, 'there is a little matter you might care to attend to on my behalf.' And he smiled again to show her that it was really of very little consequence.

'Tell me what 'tis,' she said easily.

'I have run up one or two debts,' he said, still smiling. 'Nothing serious. You know how it is. But my creditors press.'

Her happiness clouded. 'How much?' she asked. 'And to whom?'

'How much?' Billy said. He was so surprised and upset that his eye-brows had disappeared into his hair. 'How much?'

'Nearly two thousand pounds,' Cosmo Teshmaker repeated with patient satisfaction.

' 'Tis a fortune!' Billy said, plunging his fingers into his hair. 'A fortune! And all gone to waste, dammit. You must speak to her at once, Johnnoh. 'Tis unspeakable, so 'tis.'

'If you will allow me to advise you?' Cosmo suggested calmly.

'Pray do,' Johnnie told him with equal calm.

'I would suggest that you two gentlemen say nothing of this to your mother until after I have had an opportunity to acquaint her with the facts, and perhaps not even then. It is imperative that you do not annoy her in any way. Criticism of her accepted lover might well lead to unpleasantness, which in my opinion 'twould be politic to avoid. We need to ensure that Mrs Easter is kept fully aware of the helpfulness and support of her sons, the good work they do for her in the firm, their abiding concern for her. She should not see them as opponents.'

Billy scowled but his brother saw the sense of it. 'Think how she roared when I dared to criticize those awful Easter women at Annie's wedding,' he said. 'We will do as you say, Mr Teshmaker. Providing you show her this account book as soon as you can.'

'I will write this very morning,' Cosmo assured them, 'time being of the essence in this matter. There are business affairs which need her attention, so my letter need not alarm her.'

Billy was still so entrammelled by indignation he hardly heard what was being said, but Johnnie heard the meaning and its import. How tender-hearted he is, he thought, smiling agreement at Mr Teshmaker; he would like to do this without hurting Mama. And he knew that he didn't want his mother hurt either, not by anyone. 'We will work together,' he promised Cosmo. 'I am grateful for your advice, sir.'

It seemed appropriate to Nan that the weather should change as soon as Calverley had said goodbye. The bright sky faded as they kissed and the air grew suddenly chill.

'I shall be home in time for Christmas,' he promised as he mounted old Jericho, 'and if that ain't to be, why then, my charmer, I shall be at the altar rail on January 16th. You may depend upon't.'

She felt quite despondent waving goodbye, but then a messenger boy arrived with a letter from Mr Teshmaker to bring her back to the world, and she remembered that Sophie Fuseli would be coming to take tea tomorrow afternoon, and that Annie would be arriving in a day or two, and that there was Christmas to prepare for and a wedding-dress to make and a deal else besides, and she took the letter and walked back into the house, opening it as she went.

Sophie declared herself quite thrilled by the news and said she would be most happy to be a witness.

'Meg Purser is a thing of the past, is she not?' Nan asked, as they sat before the fire, drinking their tea. She was almost certain of the answer, but in her present state of fluctuating emotions, she needed reassurance.

'Gone and forgotten, my dear,' Sophie said easily. 'There are others, of course, as I'm sure you know, but none of any consequence.'

Cold winds blew again. 'You do not think me foolish to wed un, I trust?'

'You will do well enough,' Sophie said, 'for at least you know his faults. Howsomever, it must be said that in matters matrimonial there

450

is always one who gains and one who stands to lose, and it has been my observation, that most of the losers are wives.'

'Oh, come now, Sophie, not all. You married well, did you not?'

Sophie gave her old friend a long cool look. 'Those who suffer most, say least,' she said. 'Mr Fuseli may be a great artist, that I will allow, but as a husband, my dear, he is a most difficult man. There are things about his behaviour which are so obscene that I would not breathe a word about 'em to a living soul. But you may depend upon it, they are things which have made my life a shameful misery.'

'Sophie, my dear friend!' Nan said, shocked by the confession.

'I will tell 'ee this,' Sophie went on, 'since I have told so much. There is a room in our house which is kept locked, day and night, and I believe it is kept locked because it contains paintings which are simply too lewd and immoral to be seen. 'Tis a vicious man, despite his manifold talents.' And now there was no doubt about the pain she suffered, for her face was riven with it.

Whatever else, Nan thought, my Calverley en't vicious. Foolish perhaps and weak, but not vicious. 'Sophie my dear,' she said with sympathy. 'Would I could help 'ee.'

'Well, as to that,' Sophie said, reverting to her old light tone, 'you could cut me another slice of that excellent fruit cake if you had a mind.'

It was odd, and a little shaming, that Sophie's revelation should turn out to be a comfort to Nan, but a comfort it undoubtedly was. As she drove to the Strand later that afternoon to see Mr Teshmaker as he'd requested, she was remembering her lover with renewed affection. Foolish perhaps, but always loving. Not a man to hurt her with vice or unkindness of any sort. Oh yes, indeed, they would do well enough.

Mr Teshmaker was working quietly in his office, his neat head bowed over neat paper, the panels behind him smudged by the darkness of that winter afternoon. As soon as she entered, he rose in one swooping movement to glide to the fire and set a chair for her and make her welcome.

Accounts were examined and found accurate, takings were discussed and pronounced acceptable for the season. Then she opened her more important topic.

'I daresay you have heard my news, have you not, Mr Teshmaker?' she said.

451

'Madam?'

'Mr Leigh has asked me to marry him and I have accepted him. How say you to that?'

'I congratulate the gentleman to have achieved such a wife. 'Tis uncommon good fortune for him.'

'And for me too I trust, Mr Teshmaker.'

'Fortune,' he said carefully, 'devolves upon the husband. That is the legal position in this country at present. A wife has no legal rights at all, I fear, in the event of her marriage. She may not hold property. That passes to her husband, as does all her capital. In your case you would be signing over all your holdings in the company. Even the name, I fear, to which you would no longer be entitled. Of course Mr Leigh may wish to continue to trade under the name of Easter, since it is an established name and the one under which you are known. Howsomever, it is also possible that he may, at some future date, wish to sell the business.'

'Oh no!' she said horrified at the idea. 'That he would not. I am sure on it.'

'*You* would not ma'am,' Cosmo said sagely. 'That *I* am sure on, for 'tis your hard work which has made it what it is. But for a second party, it could well prove to be a different matter. Easy come, easy go, as the saying has it. Mr Leigh has a greater need of money than either you or your sons.'

'How so?' she said, for his words had been heavy with unspoken meaning.

'As you are aware,' he explained gently, 'it has been part of my brief, for some considerable time now, to keep accounts of the daily expenditure of this firm. That being so, I have had occasion to notice such sums as have been credited to Mr Leigh, either by you, ma'am, or your sons.'

'My sons?' she said, very surprised by his revelation. 'Why should my sons have given Mr Leigh monies?'

'That I couldn't say, ma'am. Howsomever, perhaps you would care to examine the records I have been keeping, facts being a deal more reliable than opinions, wouldn't you agree?' And he slid the account book across the desk and opened it for her perusal.

She read it in complete silence and he waited, sitting still and watchful before her.

'Well as to that,' she said, when she'd finished, ' 'tis nothing new to

452

me, Mr Teshmaker. I have known it for years. Mr Leigh is a spendthrift. What of it? I think no less of him for that.' To see his faults laid so clearly before her had made her feel an overpowering sympathy for Calverley. He was under attack, however subtle, and so she defended him.

'No indeed, ma'am,' Cosmo hastened to agree, masking his disappointment. 'I implied no criticism of the gentleman. The accounts were kept as a matter of course, as are all transactions for the company.'

'Perfectly correct, Mr Teshmaker,' she said. Then she dusted her hands against each other, swish, swish, by way of changing the subject, and Cosmo, discreet to the last, removed his offending evidence.

'*Now* what are we to do?' Billy said, when the lawyer had reported his lack of success. 'We must speak to her now, surely.'

'I will speak first,' Johnnie told them. 'There is another way to be tried. Wait until Annie is arrived. The wedding ain't till the middle of January. Mama told me yesterday. A lot may happen in a month.'

'Let us hope so,' Cosmo said.

Annie Hopkins arrived late in the afternoon next day, her advanced pregnancy wrapped so stoutly in greatcoat and travelling-rugs that she looked like a Christmas pudding, with James anxiously protective beside her, and Thiss and Bessie and Pollyanna and young Tom to carry her luggage. Jimmy had been a dear, good little boy all the way, sitting on Bessie's lap and playing with his toys, she said, and, yes, they were all well, and she was as fit as a flea.

The house in Cheyne Walk was suddenly full of activity, as servants ran to stoke fires and carry hot water to the bedrooms, and Thiss staggered in and out of the front door with carpet-bags and trunks and hampers, declaring cheerfully that it was 'like movin' a regiment'. But after an hour's happy chaos, Bessie took Tom and Pollyanna and little Jimmy away to the nursery for tea, and Thiss went off to see to the horses and Nan was alone with her daughter and her son-in-law at last.

She told them her news as casually as she could, for she was still tender after the shock of that account book, and felt she had to protect herself a little against the possibility of disapproval. But she needn't have worried, for Annie's reaction was immediate and unequivocal.

'My dear, darling Mama,' she said, throwing her arms round her mother's neck and hugging her as well as she could with the bulk of

453

the baby in between them. 'Oh, I am so happy for you! When is it to be?' And she was delighted to learn that Calverley and her mother had decided to delay their wedding until her baby was born. 'Oh, how very dear of you,' she said. 'January the sixteenth is a perfectly splendid date, for I shall be up and about by then.' The baby was to be born in Chelsea so that Nan could look after little Jimmy while his mother was in bed. 'What will you wear Mama? One of the new silks perhaps?'

Her enthusiasm was like a tonic. Soon the two women were discussing clothes and planning a trousseau, and Nan grew pink-cheeked with pleasure and very nearly certain that she had made the right decision after all.

'What a Christmas it will be,' Annie said rapturously, 'with a baby to look forward to and a wedding to plan. Oh, I love weddings Mama!'

And it was an excellent Christmas, even though the weather was miserably cold and Calverley didn't get home. He sent a letter which arrived on Christmas Eve, sending his 'fondest love' and his 'most abject apologies', but by then Nan was so caught up in the festivities she felt little more than a passing sadness at his absence. He would return in time for the wedding and that was what counted.

The Reverend James Hopkins caught the afternoon coach back to Bury so as to be in Rattlesden in time for midnight mass. 'I shall return immediately after Epiphany, my dearest,' he promised, kissing Annie goodbye. 'I leave you in the best of care, I know, but I shall be anxious until I see you again. You will be sure to eat well and keep warm and avoid chills, will you not?'

'You have my word,' Annie said.

'Oh, my love,' he said, gazing at her earnestly, 'what if the child were to come early?' For it was expected in the first week in January.

'The midwife will attend me whenever it is born, my dearest. All will be well.'

'I shall worry about you.'

'Go now, James, my dear,' she urged, pushing him towards the door, 'or you will miss the coach.'

'I shall return immediately after Epiphany,' he repeated.

But the weather was to make a nonsense of all their plans.

Christmas Day was dank and cold, but with blazing fires in every room and piping-hot food at every meal none of them noticed it. They walked

454

to church warm with excitement and returned on the trot warm with singing, and for the rest of the day they sat snug and enjoyed one another's company, eating their huge Christmas dinner, playing cards and charades all afternoon and finishing the day with carols and hot punch and mince pies. It wasn't until she got to bed very late that night that Nan realized that nobody had said a word about Calverley all day long, and what was worse she hadn't even given him a thought herself, but by then she was so tired and so happy she thought little of it.

The next morning they woke to a thick fog.

'What a mercy we've cold meats a-plenty to keep us going fer a day or two,' Bessie said. 'I shouldn't like to be out in that lot an' that's a fact.'

'Let's hope 'tis clear before any of us need to travel,' Nan said.

But it got steadily worse, and by the third day, when she and Johnnie had to leave the house to attend to the stamping, it was a real pea-souper. Coils of sulphur-coloured vapour heaved against the window panes like a nest of ghostly serpents, and the candles gave out such a reluctant yellow light that even indoors they could barely see what they were doing.

Outside, it clung and persisted and thickened. It was so bad on the fourth morning that Matthew had to walk beside the horses with a lantern, simply to get her from his shop to her headquarters.

'My heart alive, Mrs Easter, ma'am,' he said thickly through the mound of mufflers protecting his nose and mouth, 'tha's a fog an' a half, an' no mistake. You can't see hand in front of your face.' And he held his own hand out before him to prove his point.

Nan watched as his dirty glove disappeared into swirls of even dirtier yellow-grey vapour. 'I will make what haste I can Matthew,' she promised. ' 'Tis no weather to be out of doors.'

It was a sentiment shared by everybody in the city. Beasts were still driven in from the outlying farms for slaughter at Smithfield and vegetable-carts gloomed in through the murk towards Covent Garden hung about with lanterns like lurching will-o'-the-wisps, but those who had no need to stir abroad stayed in their darkened houses and huddled beside the fire.

And so the old year ended in gloom and the New Year of 1814 began. Epiphany came and was celebrated in Chelsea church even though the fog was so thick the congregation could barely see their priest through its vapours. But although Annie sat by the window all next day peering into the murky darkness, there was no sign of her dear James. 'If he don't hurry the baby will be here before he is,' Annie said.

'He will come as soon as ever he may,' Nan said. 'Coaches en't running yet awhile and he could hardly walk all the way. We must have patience, I fear.'

'I miss him so much,' Annie said. ' 'Tis the first time we've been parted for more than a half a day since the day we were married.'

'I miss Mr Leigh,' Nan said, but even as the words were in her mouth she realized that they weren't true. She'd hardly missed him at all, she'd been so happy surrounded by her family. 'This ol' fog can't last for ever. That's one consolation.'

Another, which she kept to herself, was that the weather had removed any necessity for her to make a decision. She felt that her future was being decided for her, by sulphur fumes and chill. If Calverley returned in time for the wedding, she would marry him, if he didn't perhaps she would think again. In the meantime there was nothing any of them could do except wait, Annie for her baby and the Reverend Hopkins, she for Calverley and her wedding, London for the long-expected peace and better weather. It was as if the fog had entered her mind, numbing rational thought.

John Henry's mind was as clear as daylight. The fog was a blessing in disguise, he explained to Billy, for with luck it would maroon the contemptible Mr Leigh in the wilds of Scotland where he couldn't marry their mother. But they should not grow complacent. No indeed, they should take advantage of the opportunity it offered.

Billy had chilblains and a cold in the nose and wasn't at all sanguine about their chances of success. 'He'll barry her, you'll see,' he said. 'I'd bet boney on it.'

'Not if we use our wits,' Johnnie said. 'I intend to speak to her after dinner tonight. Then it's your turn.'

It was an uninspiring dinner that evening, for the last of the Christmas meats had been eaten and boiled mutton seemed poor fare by comparison. When the dishes had been cleared and Annie had retired for her rest, Nan poured brandy for herself and her sons. ' 'Twill be warming,' she said, 'and 'twill settle some of that grease. Mutton fat lies uncommon heavy on a stomach. My heart alive this fog's gone on a mortal long time.'

Johnnie looked at his mother seriously over the rim of his glass.

'When it does lift Mama,' he said, 'Billy and I will have to start looking for a job.'

'A job!' she said. 'What sort of squit is this?'

'It ain't squit, Mama. We've a living to earn.'

'And the family firm en't good enough for 'ee. Is that it?'

'Oh no!' he said passionately. ' 'Tis the best firm in the City. I would work for it gladly, all my life. Howsomever . . .'

'Howsomever? There en't no howsomever so far as I can see.'

'While the firm belongs to the family,' he said speaking slowly because he was struggling to find just the right words to convince her, 'none of us need fear, or look for work elsewhere, for we work together, as a family firm, each of us doing our best for the good of the others, to increase trade, to grow richer, confident, d'you see, that we shall all benefit.'

'Oh, I see how it is,' she said. 'You fear that Mr Leigh will change things once we are married.'

'It is possible.'

'Well, 'tis all squit, let me tell 'ee. There'll be no changes while I'm head of the firm. Leastways, no changes we don't all want.'

'But you will not be the head of the firm, will you Mama? Not if you marry Mr Leigh.'

'Bah!' she said furiously. 'I never heard such foolish talk. If that's all you've got to say, I may part with your company, for Billy can talk to me for the rest of the evening. Good night to 'ee.'

'I bean the same thig, Mama,' Billy said.

'Then you can be off with your brother,' Nan said, waving her brandy glass at him. 'You make me mad, the pair of you.'

They put down their glasses and crept to the door, defeated.

'And let me tell 'ee,' she said. 'I will marry whom I please.'

'Then we must work elsewhere,' Johnnie said coldly, and left the room before she could berate him any further.

'Oh Johnnoh!' Billy said when they were both safely upstairs in his bedroom. 'She'll barry him as sure as fate.' And he blew his nose like a trumpet.

'The battle ain't lost till she's at the altar rail,' Johnnie said grimly. 'And at least the weather's on our side.'

Chapter Forty

The weather continued to be an ally to John and William Easter. There was still no sign of Calverley Leigh and no news from him either, and fog was to obscure the lower reaches of the Thames valley for another six days. And then, when it finally dispersed, dissolving as insidiously as it had gathered, it was replaced by a biting cold and a sky the colour of pewter and the first ominous flurries of snow.

The city was filthy. Brick walls oozed into a cold sweat, soot-black and oily, streets squelched with evil-smelling mud and well-trodden horse-dung, beggars were mud statues, caked in grime from matted hair to scabby feet, and the cesspits, which hadn't been cleared since the fog began, were so foul they could still be smelt more than half a mile away if the wind was in the wrong direction, and Bessie declared you couldn't get away from them no matter where you went.

Nan Easter made no attempt to get away from anything. She hired six more maids-of-all-work, rolled up her sleeves and began to set her house in order, starting in the bedrooms and working downwards. Annie's baby could be born any day now and she had no intention of allowing her second grandchild to arrive in a dirty house. Hard work kept her mind away from Calverley and her marriage and the worsening weather outside her windows, and besides, she couldn't abide filth. The dining-room floor was being sand-scrubbed on the afternoon that the Reverend Hopkins finally arrived at Cheyne Walk, mud-caked and bone-weary, visibly drooping with fatigue.

'The roads into London are well nigh impassable for snow,' he told Nan and Annie as they rushed to attend to him. 'There are drifts six feet high on the Norwich road. There isn't a coach can get through.'

He'd been on the road for nearly four days and had an uncommon hard time of it. 'On the second coach a blizzard blew up and we were stuck in a drift for hours,' he said. 'The men from the nearest village had to walk across the snow on planks in order to dig us out. I have never experienced such a journey in all my life.'

'Oh, you foolish creature,' Annie said, chafing his cold hands. 'You should have stayed at home in the warm until the weather improved.'

'I missed you too much, my love. You and little Jimmy. I thought of you every hour of the day, and most hours of the night too, I must admit, wondering how you were and if the baby were born. I cannot bear to be apart from you, and there's the truth of it.'

'You are the dearest of men,' Annie told him most lovingly, 'but now you must wash and change into warm, clean clothes or you will take a chill.'

So he went obediently to do as she said. And watching them, Nan was touched by their concern for each other. He came all that way, she thought, through blizzards and snowdrifts just to be with my Annie. And Calverley hadn't even sent a letter.

The next day heavy snow began to fall in London too, and it fell intermittently for the next week, a crisp, cold cover to newly-cleaned pavements and mud-ridged pathways, cesspits and vegetable gardens, roofs and window-sills. And on the tenth day, when it lay so thickly it reached the top of the Reverend Hopkins' boots when he trudged out to fetch the midwife, Annie's second baby was born.

It was another boy and a very pretty one, with large, dark eyes and the dearest little snub nose and a dusting of golden down on the crown of his nice, round head. His parents greeted him by his chosen name, which was Daniel, but his brother, who was allowed to tip-toe in to see him before he went to bed instantly called him Beau. And Beau he remained, the newest and prettiest member of the Easter family.

It wasn't until he was nearly one week old that Nan realized he had been born on the very day she had chosen as her wedding-day. And she still hadn't heard a word from Calverley. But perhaps I am being unfair to him, she rebuked herself. For very few letters were getting through to the City, and the weather in Scotland could easily be worse than the weather in England.

But not much worse. On the day after Annie completed her fort-night's lying-in, Matthew Howlett came running to the house, wild with excitement because the Thames was frozen.

'Solid all the way from London Bridge to Blackfriars,' he said, puffing with the exertion of his run. 'Notices up every which way you look. Safe to cross, it do say, Mrs Easter. I never seen the like. There's folk a-skating and a-walking all about right where the river was. I never seen the like.'

Nan put on her hat and coat at once. 'Come you on,' she said to her family. 'Here's a sight you don't see but once in a lifetime. Bessie, bring the children. Oh, what sport!'

So they left little Beau sleeping in the warm with a parlour-maid to watch over him, and bundled themselves into all the clothes they could find and swathed their heads in mufflers and packed their feet in woollen stockings and heavy boots, because it was several degrees below freezing outside and the wind was sharp as a cut-throat razor, and off they all went, along with half their neighbours.

And it really was an extraordinary sight, to see their great, wide, perpetually-moving Thames now held completely still, its waters frozen into a solid blackness, and yet, amazingly, still ridged by waves as though it had all been frozen in an instant. The coal barges and river boats were stuck fast, their timbers groaning under the pressure of the ice, and on every bank people were gathering, like a great flock of starlings, all a-babble and a-chatter, milling and moving beside the unaccustomed stillness. London Bridge was empty and looked forlorn, the City was deserted, and above it all the dome of St Paul's shone blue against a grey sky. It didn't seem real.

'Come you on!' Nan said. 'I en't never walked on the Thames before and now's the time to try.' And she lead Tom and Pollyanna out onto the frozen waves, her breath streaming before her. Two seconds later they were all tumbled on the ice in a shrieking heap, Nan flat on her back and giggling, Tom on his knees, crawling and slithering and Pollyanna sitting where she'd fallen, red-nosed and white-cheeked but laughing with excitement.

'You need skates, mum,' Thiss said, staggering up to rescue them.

'So we do,' Nan agreed, as he hauled her to her feet. 'We had some once, I remember, when the Serpentine froze.'

'They're in a box in the corner-cupboard in the kitchen,' Bessie said, dusting the snow from her son's greatcoat. 'Lawks-a-mercy, look at the state a' yer.'

'What sport!' Nan said. 'Hie you home this instant, Thiss, and fetch 'em.'

Johnnie and Billy had retreated to the bank too and were happily hurling snowballs at each other, but Annie and little Jimmy were several yards out and still on their feet, sliding cautiously along with James stooping beside them, stalking like an anxious heron. 'Look look!' the little boy called. 'Walky on de water!'

It became the family clarion call. 'Walky on de water!' they would say as they came shivering down to breakfast in the snow-white morning, 'Walky on de water!' swathing their heads and shoulders with thick shawls, 'Walky on de water!' hanging their bone skates over their shoulders. It was colder than any of them could remember, pumps were frozen and food in short supply, London was snow-bound and completely cut off from the rest of the world, but they were going to the Ice Fair.

By the time they all went home for dinner on that first day, the surface of the river had become a public thoroughfare called, with the cockney's cheerful humour, Freezeland Street. What else? On the second morning Nan bought a sledge padded with fur, and a thick fur rug, so that baby Beau could join them, snuggled into it, right down in the warm, where the icy air couldn't mar his tender lungs, and she and the children and Thiss and Bessie, and Johnnie and Billy, when they'd done what little work they could, spent the whole day on the ice on their skates and played for as long as there was daylight.

At around noon on that second day the peddlers and hawkers arrived with hot pies and brandy balls and gingerbread and chestnuts and oysters, and very welcome they were. By mid afternoon stalls were being set up on either side of the new thoroughfare, crowded close together for warmth and trade, butchers and pastry cooks, barbers and bakers, toyshops and skittle alleys, ballad-mongers and balloon-sellers, gin-sellers and beer-sellers, and furmety booths. And by the third day the printing presses followed them down. Nan opened her own tent half an hour later. It was green and gold, of course, and clearly labelled 'A. Easter – Newsagent' above a sign which proclaimed 'News hot from the press'.

She did a phenomenal trade. It was such a novelty to buy a paper at an ice fair, even if there wasn't much in it except news of the freeze. But that was exciting enough. On the fifth day the Lord Mayor organized an ice feast and roasted an ox, right in the middle of the river, and all work stopped in the capital so that everyone could enjoy the great event. Nan set up two more tents immediately and set Billy and Johnnie to man them, on their bone skates of course.

'The family firm on ice,' Billy said happily, as bulky skaters hissed up to buy. 'Ain't we a team, Ma?'

461

'To be proud of,' she agreed. And so they were. 'Tis a fine firm I've founded, she thought, and 'twould be folly to let anyone change it, no matter how much I might love 'em. The fog had cleared from her mind too and now, in this frozen air, she was seeing things with inescapable clarity.

The next afternoon Mrs Jorris and the kitchen-maids slipped home early to prepare a goose, and a fine, sweet bird it was and made very good eating. And when the meal was done, the entire family retired upstairs to the drawing-room to sit about the fire, as they usually did of an evening, drinking port and brandy and roasting chestnuts on the hob. They piled cushions by all the doors and windows to keep out the draughts, and they heaped the coals half-way up the chimney, and they set their chairs and sofas in a half-circle round the hearth. A charmed circle, Nan thought, as they relaxed into warmth and well-being after the biting air and physical effort of the day.

They sat at such ease in the golden light of fire and candle, their cheeks reddened and their faces glowing, their movements as slow and gentle as weed under water, and they talked in the intermittent drowsy way of the well-fed, fatigued and satisfied.

Billy was lying on the second chaise-longue, with one foot propped on his brother's knee and his head a mere inch away from Nan's shoulder. 'I hope the freeze goes on and on for months and months and months,' he said, tossing a hot chestnut from hand to hand to cool it.

'Mr Weatherstone would have a hard time of it if that were the case,' James said, mildly. Mr Weatherstone was his curate, who was currently doing all the work at Rattlesden, and just the thought of him made poor James feel guilty.

'Mr Weatherstone is a good man,' Annie comforted, leaning over the arm of her chair to pat him. 'He will understand that you cannot command the weather, my love. We could not travel home in this cold, not with Jimmy and little Beau.'

Jimmy was lying on the other chaise-longue beside his grandmother, half asleep with his head on her lap, and right in the middle of their circle. Nan stroked his fine hair lovingly. 'You may stay here as long as you please,' she said. ' 'Tis an uncommon fine thing to have my family all about me.'

'Amen to that,' Johnnie said, turning his head to smile at Annie, but keeping his body still, for baby Beau was lying on his chest, fast alseep.

462

'If we are to be marooned I can think of no better company.' And he kissed the baby's soft head.

'What if the war were over,' James said. 'It could be, for aught we know.'

'Then 'twould be over and we none the wiser,' Billy said cheerfully.

'What a blessing it would be, to be sure,' Annie said.

'I have such plans for the firm once the fighting's done,' Nan told them. 'We do so well in London, tis time we expanded. I've a mind to sell pens and paper in my shops, as well as the news.' The lack of any letters during the freeze had made her aware of their importance.

'Capital idea, Mama,' Billy said, nibbling.

'Will trade increase in peacetime, think 'ee?' Johnnie asked.

'If it don't,' Nan said, 'then *we* shall have to see to it.'

Smiles, ease, agreement, a sense that they would achieve their intentions, no matter what. We are a great firm, Nan thought, Billy is right, a great family firm. And it occurred to her, watching them as they sat within the barrier of their close half-circle, arm against arm and head to happy head, that they were a human barrier too, a barrier against all harm, all comers, all eventualities. She had spent two months in their company now and she'd enjoyed every moment of it. And she knew too that a part of that enjoyment was because she could always be honest with them. There had been no need to hide her feelings or prevaricate or refrain from comment as there so often was when she was with Calverley. With her family she could speak her mind without fear or favour. Even to Johnnie. We are cut off from the world and none of us care, she thought. And she looked from one to the other of them, loving them all.

And even though the snow lay thicker than ever next morning and there was still no letter from Calverley, she didn't care about that either.

By this time they were all so accustomed to skating about all day that it seemed the natural way to move. Which was just as well, for the extreme cold was to last for another six weeks. Snow fell every single day and fresh vegetables were in parlously short supply and all coach journeys were abandoned, but the high jinks continued unabated. It suited Nan Easter as though it had been arranged to please her. She could enjoy her family's rumbustious company without restraint, there was no need to think about her wedding, and the Ice Fair kept her happily and rewardingly busy.

She was quite disappointed when the weather improved and the now familiar ice began to crack. But then just as the stalls were being packed up and warning notices posted, the first mail coaches began to arrive, with a letter from Calverley dated January 6th, saying he might have to stay in Scotland 'for a little longer' and, what was more important and immediate, dispatches from Spain with the news that Wellington had won a great victory and that the British army was in France.

'I do believe we could travel home now, my love,' Annie said to her patient James.

'We could and we should,' he said. 'I have left Mr Weatherstone to bear the burden quite long enough.'

So they left two days later and the house seemed horribly empty without them. But Nan had little time to miss them, for the very next morning Mr Walter had a dispatch from his correspondent with the army, telling him that Russian and Polish troops had reached Paris and ridden through the Champs Elysées in triumph, and that the French Senate had declared the Empire at an end. Napoleon was to be handed over to the allies and the war concluded.

The relief was as extraordinary as the freeze had been. Church bells rang all morning and people ran out into the streets to hear the news and tell one another how wonderful it was. It was as if the capital had been besieged, by long war, long winter and long freeze, and now at last it was April and springtime, the snow had melted and the sun was shining.

'Go you at once,' she said to Billy and Johnnie that afternoon, 'and buy me threescore pens and three reams of writing paper from such as offer the best quality and a reasonable price. Start with Mr Ebros in the City Road. There'll be a deal of writing now to spread this news, so let us be ready to take the trade. I will visit all the shops in the City and tell 'em what we propose.'

She was so happily busy it was almost a surprise when she came home for dinner that afternoon to find Calverley waiting for her in the drawing-room, sitting in the big armchair before the fire. She kissed him warmly enough but her senses recoiled from him, for he smelled of horses and muddy roads, and he was travel-stained and strange almost as though he were a foreigner.

'My heart alive,' she said. 'Are the roads clear at last then?'

' 'Twas a parlous journey,' he said, smiling at her most amorously 'Say you ain't glad to see me!'

But she didn't say it, even though she could have done.

They had dinner together on their own, for the boys were still busy in the City, and they talked of travel and the weather and the new baby and the Ice Fair, and in the middle of the meal Bessie came in to Nan with a letter from Annie.

'There is to be a grand victory ball in the Athenaeum on Saturday,' she wrote. 'Pray do leave your work for a day or two, Mama, and come down and attend. We could have a victory party, could we not, and you could announce the new date of your wedding to all the world. Think how appropriate and romantic 'twould be.'

Nan smiled wryly at that. ' 'Tis from Annie,' she said and she told her lover about the victory ball. But she didn't say anything about a new date for their wedding. 'Should I attend, think 'ee?'

'You should,' he said. ' 'Twill be a grand occasion.'

'Shall you join us?'

'Oh, indeed I shall.'

So when the meal was done and the two of them had returned to the drawing-room, she wrote back to her daughter, accepting her invitation. 'We will all attend the Ball and I will throw a victory dinner for the family on the same evening. Mr Leigh is returned and sends his regards to you. I would consider it a great kindness if you would buy tickets for me and Mr Leigh and your brothers, and for Thiss and Bessie and Mr Teshmaker too, as well as yourself and James. Tell Bessie she is to order the best dinner possible, no matter what it might cost, and ask her if she and Thiss will be so kind as to join us at table. I trust you are all well, I will tell you all my news at our victory dinner. I have such plans for the firm now that the war is over.

Yr ever loving mother, Nan.'

'Now,' she said, when she'd sent the letter to the Post, 'how shall we spend our evening?' The boys were still out so they had the place and the time to themselves.

'I'm off to White's, my charmer,' he said. 'Catch up with the news, renew old acquaintance, that sort of thing.'

She ought to have been disappointed, or hurt, or aggrieved, but she wasn't even surprised.

'We will talk when I return,' he said.

'If you en't too late,' she answered.

'I will be back before midnight,' he promised.

And so he was. But only just. The boys were home and fed and asleep. To her great relief they had made no comment when they heard

465

of Calverley's return, for they had other matters to occupy them now, like the price of good quality writing-paper and whether or not they should stock writing-ink as well as quills, even though all three of them knew that a decision would have to be made. Now she waited for him and that decision, sitting cool and calm and alone beside the drawing-room fire, where she'd sat at ease within the charmed circle of her family just a few days ago.

He came up the stairs as light-footed as a cat, and strode across the room on those long, lithe legs to bend from his handsome height to kiss her. He still smelled like a foreigner to her and he was amorous with brandy. 'Ah what it is, to be with you again, my charmer,' he said. 'Now we must choose another date for our wedding, must we not?'

She gave him a long, cool look, as he left her side to pour himself a brandy from the decanter on the side-table. He was so confident. 'After all these years,' she said. 'I cannot see the need for it.'

He was put out by her lack of enthusiasm. 'You gave me your word, don't 'ee forget,' he said, still holding the decanter.

'Under duress,' she said, and she turned away from him and looked at the fire, her spine very straight.

'How now,' he said, teasing her because he was alarmed. 'What's this? Maidenly doubt? That ain't my Nan.'

'We en't neither of us young no more,' she said seriously, 'and you en't a-telling me there's a deal of passion left between us either.'

'I love 'ee to distraction,' he vowed, coming to sit before her in the other armchair. But the words sounded false, even to him.

She grinned at him. 'You do talk a load a' squit sometimes, Calverley. More than four months you've been away from me, I hope you realize. That don't look much like passion to me.'

' 'Twas the weather,' he said lamely.

'Mr Hopkins travelled to London in a blizzard to be with my Annie.'

'Well then, he was fortunate,' he said scowling.

'No, my dear. He was driven by love. That's how 'twas. They couldn't abide to be parted, neither one on 'em. Whereas you . . . You were happy enough in Scotland with a new light o' love.'

For a second he wondered whether to deny it, but her face was so stern he decided to brazen it out. 'Come now, Nan,' he said, smiling his most charming smile. 'You know my character. 'Tain't in my nature to live alone.'

'Nor would you, were we to marry,' she said shrewdly.

'I'm an old dog to learn new tricks,' he admitted. And then he felt shamed to have been pushed into such a confession. 'Come now. Why do we talk so foolishly, when we've a wedding to arrange?'

She ignored that, setting her feet on the fender and picking up the poker to rake out the fire. 'Mr Teshmaker tells me you could change the name of the firm were we to marry.'

'Perish the thought,' he said, teasing again but feeling that this was beginning to look like a battle of wills and that he ought to give all his attention to it. Surely she wasn't going to refuse him. Not after all his effort in that theatre.

'But you would have legal rights to all my money and all my property, would you not?'

'Aye, I daresay. What of it?' Trying to speak lightly.

'I will tell 'ee what of it,' she said looking straight at him, poker in hand. 'You could spend every penny, so you could, and me powerless to stop 'ee.'

'Nan, Nan,' he said, trying desperately to charm her, for he could see his hope of a rich marriage falling away like the spent ash dropping into the grate between them. 'How could 'ee think such a thing?'

'Very easily,' she said, returning the poker to its hook, 'having seen your accounts.' And as he looked puzzled, 'Mr Teshmaker has kept an account of all the monies you've begged and borrowed from my firm over the years. 'Tis a formidable sum.'

The sudden knowledge that she knew about his extravagances struck a chill into the centre of his brain, despite the warmth of the brandy. Would she scold?, he wondered, looking at her ruefully. She'd have every right to. But she didn't. She sat still and formidable watching him, like a commanding officer, or Mr Chaplin when he was about to dismiss a groom.

'A man must live,' he tried.

'So must a flea, they say. But not on me.'

'That's deuced hard, my charmer.'

'That's the truth.'

There was a long pause while he frowned at the fire, and she watched him, loving him still but almost unmoved by his distress.

Then he tried another gambit. 'You do not love me,' he said, looking pitiful.

It was a crushing disappointment that she laughed at him. 'Oh, I love 'ee well enough,' she said. 'That en't the point. I could love 'ee

467

well enough whether we married or no. The point is, what should I gain if we *were* to marry? You en't like to be faithful, you'll allow. You'd be gadding about the country half the time pursuing other women. You'd spend all my money. You'd run up debts for me to pay. What would change?'

It was necessary to make her some sort of promise or he would lose her. And how would he pay his debts then? 'I would change!' he said, holding up his head to look her full in the eye.

She put back her head and roared with laughter, teeth gleaming in the firelight. 'How of the old dog, eh?' she said. 'No, my dear, you wouldn't change. Nor would I wish it, for then you would be other than you are. You wouldn't change and neither would I. We en't the marrying kind, neither one of us. You have itchy feet, my dear, and I'm a woman of business.'

It was true, he thought, looking at her as she sat, straight-backed and determined, before the fire. She *was* a woman of business and a very fine one. As great in her own sphere as the redoubtable Mr Chaplin was in his, and now he came to think about it, a very similar creature. It was odd that he hadn't seen the similarity before. But until this moment he'd never thought of her as anything other than a mere woman, handsome, headstrong, passionate, to be loved when he would, left when he would, like all the rest of her kind. Had she been a man, he thought, I would have recognized her power a deal sooner than this. Nan Easter, woman of business. What a chance I've missed.

Thoughts and emotions shifted inside his head like a kaleidoscope muddled by brandy. He realised too that he was going to have to accept defeat from this woman, that somehow or other he had lost his advantage. He had stayed away too long and made too many mistakes. But at least the knowledge brought a return of grace and honesty. 'You will not marry me,' he said.

'No,' she said, and although she was rejecting him, and they both knew it, she spoke kindly, 'I will not. I have a fine family to lead and a great business to run and the truth of it is they're a deal more important to me than any affair, even one as pleasurable as ours has been.' And the truth of it was as clear as the cold light over the frozen Thames. It was her family that held her affections now, and the great firm she had founded that took her attention and roused her energy.

He stood up and looked down at her, his face extremely handsome in the firelight. 'If we do not marry,' he said, trying his last gambit, but

this time with dignity, 'then we must part. We cannot go on as we are.'
If she wouldn't marry him he would have to find some other woman
who would. In Ireland, perhaps, with his brother. But certainly not in
London where his debts were known. 'I shall go to Ireland. We shall
not see one another again.'

It did not pain her to accept it, even though until that moment she'd
had a vague hope that they might continue their affair in the old style.
But what was there to continue? It was over and best acknowledged
so. After all the passion of their long affair, they were both so calm at
its ending.

'You will tell your family,' he said.

'Before the victory ball at Bury on Saturday. They should all be told
at the same time, I think.'

'Yes,' he said. 'That is best. Should I be there too, think 'ee?'

'If you wish. Annie would take it kindly if you were, for I told her in
my letter that you would attend, don't forget.'

'Aye, so you did,' he said, numb with brandy and sadness. But it
seemed to him that her letter had been written years ago, in some other
life, before he lost her. Whatever other women he might find to love,
he thought, there would never be another like his incomparable Nan.

They looked at one another in the firelight for a long, bitter-sweet
moment.

'I shall return to my club for a day or so,' he said.

'Yes,' she said, smiling at him. 'That is best too.'

He saluted her, as though she were an officer. He couldn't have
explained why, but it seemed a fitting thing to do. Then he left her.

Chapter Forty-one

'There's something afoot, Mr Teshmaker,' Billy said happily when he and Johnnie met up with their old friend the next morning. 'He came back last night and then went straight off to Goosegogs. Wasn't in the house more than half an hour. That don't look much like a wedding to me. What do 'ee think?'

'The signs are certainly auspicious,' the lawyer agreed, showing them their mother's letter. 'I am invited to join you at a victory party at Bury this Saturday, and no mention of the marriage, as you see.'

'And yet she is so happy,' Johnnie said, remembering his mother's bustling exuberance at breakfast that morning. It didn't make sense.

'Wait, watch, say nothing,' Cosmo advised. 'We may learn more at Bury St Edmunds. When do you travel?'

'On the ten o'clock on Saturday morning,' Billy said. 'Shall you ride with us?'

Nan couldn't wait to get to Bury. She was teeming with energy, her brain filled with burgeoning plans for the future, her hands perpetually busy. She did all her work at twice her normal speed, walking so quickly that nobody could keep up with her. By midday on Friday she was packed and ready to travel.

The weather matched her mood exactly. It was one of those fine spring days when the world is suddenly full of colour and movement, the blue sky heaped with fat steam-clouds visibly scudding past, the grass on the river-bank green and shimmering, limes and planes uncurling new leaves, and all about her a babble of spring voices, thrushes tremulous, robins flute-clear, a flock of finches flying like darts, chi-chi-chi. Oh, it was a grand old world!

Her travelling companions were as excited as she was and, like her, had come prepared for a riotous journey, with claret and brandy and spiced hollands a-plenty. Even before they left London they were treating one another like old friends and by the time the coach came rocking in to Angel Hill they were singing patriotic songs in a cheerfully inebriated chorus.

'Good bye, Mrs Easter dear,' they called as she set off through the crowded square. 'Good luck to 'ee. May you prosper in all your endeavours.'

'No fear of that!' she called back. With the war over and trade bound to pick up and no spendthrift to hold her back, she could hardly fail.

Angel Hill was full of her old friends, out to take the air and see the sights, for Bury was in celebratory mood and a state of extreme excitement, every street crackling with bunting, the balcony of the Athenaeum draped with Union Jacks, balloon-sellers bouncing their wares at every corner and a military band playing at full and cheerful blast on the hustings in front of the Angel Hotel. Little Miss Pettie declared she couldn't hear a word anyone was saying, but wasn't it grand? And the Mayor declared it was 'Capital! Capital! Capital!' And Mr Cole who kept a bookshop in the Buttermarket and was usually the quietest of men, was in such an emotional state he couldn't answer her greeting for blowing his nose and coughing.

At the corner of Abbeygate Street she paused in her progress to look down the hill towards her house, and the sight of it reminded her of Annie and Beau and little Jimmy. I will buy him a balloon, she thought, and she turned back to the balloon-seller at once. 'A red one,' she said, pointing to her choice, which was bobbing like a live thing in the centre of the pack.

But the red balloon was even wilier than she was. The moment it had been disentangled from its restraining companion, it slipped its string, caught the next strong gust of air and went floating off uphill, above the roofs and chimneys of Abbeygate Street, lilting and dancing as it went, blood-bold against the blue sky.

The balloon-seller was most upset. 'I'm sorry ma'am,' he said, fumbling with the strings. 'An' the very one you was wantin'.' But Nan wasn't sorry at all. She was watching the balloon's escape with a marvellous sense of release and fellow-feeling. That's just like me, she was thinking, set free, cut loose, going up and up wherever the wind takes it. Oh, there's no stopping it. And she watched its erratic upward progress with delight.

''Tis downright vexation, so 'tis,' the balloon-seller said, watching his little profit disappear. 'Dratted thing!'

'That's a free spirit,' Nan told him laughing. 'That's progress, that is. Now find me a tame one for my little grandson. I've a busy day ahead of me.'

And so it was, marvellously, rewardingly busy, with meats to buy for her victory dinner, and rooms to prepare for all her visitors, to say nothing of a ball-gown to alter and two local shops to visit. And the next day she woke early to the sound of hammering and got up to find that the May Fair was being erected in the square outside her bedroom window.

'What sport!' she said to Bessie, who came into the room almost at once in answer to the bell. 'A Victory Ball, a family dinner and a fair on top of all. Jimmy will love it.'

'An' so will young Tom,' his mother said. 'I never know'd such a boy fer the swings.'

'Two sets this year,' Nan said with approval. 'And a coconut shy, look 'ee there.' And a merry-go-round and beer tents and gin tents, and stalls selling everything from brandy balls and oysters to bootlaces and horse brasses. 'What could be better?'

The rest of the day passed in a bustle of excited preparation, with meats to roast and puddings to boil and pies to bake and the whole house spiced with the aroma of cooking. Annie and her family arrived in the middle of the afternoon and of course little Jimmy had to be taken to the Fair at once. He was still on the swings with his grandmother and Pollyanna and young Tom, when the London coach came rattling into the square with Johnnie and Billy and Mr Teshmaker aboard. By now there was such a crowd and so much noise in the square that conversation was quite impossible.

'I will tell 'ee my news at dinner,' Nan called down to them from the swing. 'Look after Mr Teshmaker, boys.'

'Is Mr Leigh to join us?' Billy called back, but the swing had already taken her out of earshot.

Neither his brother-in-law nor his sister knew the answer either, although as Annie pointed out, the table had been set for eight, so it looked likely. And, sure enough, twenty minutes before the meal was due to be served, the gentleman galloped in to Angel Hill in fine style on a new bay mare. 'And who bought that for him, I

472

should like to know?' Johnnie said to his brother as they watched the arrival from their bedroom window.

''Twill be a wedding present, sure as fate,' Billy said gloomily. And he went down to dinner quite melancholy.

But it was such an excellent meal, with five full courses and elaborate sugar fancies between each and every one, and a plentiful supply of good wines, that he cheered up almost at once, especially as the talk was all of family and business, and he and Johnnie were petted and praised for their part in the new expansion. They dined well, enjoying one another's company, and Mr Leigh cracked jokes and filled glasses and kept the conversation flowing in his usual easy way. It was over two hours before the butler arrived with the port and brandy to finish the meal and still not a word had been said about the wedding. Annie and Bessie looked across at Nan for the signal to withdraw.

'No,' she said. 'We will all take brandy together today. 'Tis a special occasion and I've special things to say to 'ee.'

So the brandy was poured and the port passed and her family exchanged glances with one another and then looked at her and waited.

'I have asked you all to dine with me today for a purpose,' she said. 'It en't just a victory we've to celebrate, for I've things to say to 'ee that will concern 'ee, each and every one, being as we're a family firm. You've heard how I mean to expand to writing-paper and pens and ink. There's a demand for such articles already and one that's like to grow now that the war is over. I mean to make our business grow with the demand, so I do, and far beyond London what's more. That being so, I can tell 'ee 'twill not be long before 'tis too big for any one person to run. Too big even for me, and I've a deal more energy than most.'

They smiled and laughed in agreement at that, and she noticed that Annie looked at Calverley.

'So,' she went on, 'I been a-giving the matter the most careful thought and it do seem to me that changes will need to be made. There are some have urged me to marry and share the burden with a husband, and there was a time when I agreed to it, under duress, mark you. But I have to tell 'ee I en't the marrying kind and that's the truth of it. I been a widow too long and I like my independence. So what I propose to do is this. I propose to take my two sons into

473

the firm as managers, Billy to take charge of warehousing and distribution, Johnnie to be responsible for sales throughout the country, with salaries commensurate, as you would expect. That being so, the firm will henceforth be known as A. Easter and Sons. I have given orders for the London signs to be altered as from today.'

There was a stir about the table as people turned to congratulate Billy and Johnnie, and she paused in her speech to give them time to do it. Bessie had to kiss them both, of course, which was only to be expected, and Annie was saying, 'Well done, well done.' Calverley said, 'Bravo!' and she looked across at him and smiled, admiring his style.

'You won't regret it, Mama,' Billy said happily, grinning at her.

'I know that,' she said, smiling back.

Johnnie was looking extremely serious. 'In two years Mama,' he said solemnly, 'I will double your profits. I give you my word.'

And she smiled at him too, as various hands clapped in approval. And then the stir subsided and all eyes turned towards her again.

'In addition,' she said, continuing, 'I intend to organize sales on a regional basis, with one manager in charge of each region. 'Twill take some little time, I know. Howsomever, East Anglia is well established already. We got a capital manager for East Anglia in Mr Thistlethwaite and living right here in this very house. And I tell 'ee, I can think of no one better to handle the London trade than my old friend Mr Cosmo Teshmaker.'

Heads swivelled at once to look at Cosmo and to her great delight she saw that he was blushing with pleasure.

'You do me a great honour, Mrs Easter,' he said, smiling gravely at her.

'Squit!' she said cheerfully. 'I know a good man when I see one.' And sitting opposite him was another. Dear old Thiss. Dear old dependable Thiss, grinning and approving.

So the fortunes of the firm of 'A Easter and Sons' and the future of its founder were settled. And Nan looked at Calverley again, facing her at the other end of the table.

He was sitting very still, brooding and watchful and more like a leopard than she'd ever seen him, looking round the table, gathering their attention. She realized that he was going to make a speech too.

'Ladies and gentlemen,' he said, smiling lazily, 'may I beg a

474

moment of your attention?' And they gave it, in their various ways, Thiss guardedly, Annie sadly, Cosmo with just the merest hint of triumph on his quiet face, Bessie with sympathy.

'I too have reached a moment of change,' he said. 'My seven year contract with Mr Chaplin's firm ran out last year, as some of you may know, and since then I have been giving serious thought to the direction my life should take. Now that this long war is finally over and Boney safely escorted to Elba by our gallant men o' war, I feel the time has come for me to depart too. But to a more hospitable island, I promise you. It has long been my – ah – intention to leave this country and join my brother on his stud farm in Ireland – as Mrs Easter will confirm. That being so, I should tell 'ee that this will be my last night in this house, for I leave for Ireland at first light tomorrow. Eat, drink and be merry my friends, for tomorrow we part.'

'Good luck to 'ee sir,' Thiss said, raising his glass. 'I drink to your success, sir.'

'Well, as to that,' Calverley said smoothly, 'I feel we should all drink to the continuing success of the firm of "A. Easter and Sons." I give you, "The Firm", ladies and gentlemen. "The Firm".' It was admirably done, and watching him, Nan was suddenly torn with pity for him, because he was so handsome and he had such style and she'd loved him for so long and with such passion, and now she was rejecting him. But the future was calling to her, and much too powerfully to allow her to deny it for a spasm of pity.

And so the toast was drunk, and while their glasses were still being drained, the hall clock struck the hour. 'If we're to be at the Athenaeum for the opening quadrille,' Nan warned, 'we must make haste.' And she stood up to show them that the meal was over.

Billy went rushing off to prepare at once, and she noticed that Calverley walked out of the room with Annie and Mr Hopkins, and that Cosmo was escorting Bessie and Thiss. But Johnnie remained behind, standing beside the window, with his hand on the curtain, watching the torch-lit fair.

She snuffed all the candles except for the eight beside the mirrors and the room was suddenly cast into gentle shadow. Then she went to stand beside him. The square below them was full of little glittering lights, yellow as glow-worms in the gathering dusk, and the Athenaeum gleamed whitely against the mauve sky.

475

'Could you truly double our profits in two years?' she said.

'I believe so.'

The business-woman in her was intrigued, the mother impressed. This was the way forward. 'Tell me how,' she said.